THE WAY OF THE WIZARD

EDITED BY
JOHN JOSEPH ADAMS

PRIME BOOKS

Prime Books
www.prime-books.com

For more information, contact Prime Books:
prime@prime-books.com

ISBN: 978-1-60701-232-0

TABLE OF CONTENTS

Introduction

John Joseph Adams

In 2004, *Forbes Magazine* declared J.K. Rowling, author of the wizard-themed *Harry Potter* series, a billionaire. That was the year the film *Harry Potter and the Prisoner of Azkaban* was released, earning $795.6 million worldwide in the box office and grossing millions more in licensed merchandise. It can be hard to explain the appeal of the wizard in cinema and literature, but when reduced to the brute language of dollars and cents, it is clear that in the realm of the imagination, the wizard is king.

Stories of magic have tantalized readers and listeners since the dawn of language. Myths are dotted with enchanters and witch-doctors. The fairy tales of the Grimm brothers were stories rich with witches and sorceresses and magicians. Homer's ancient epic, *The Odyssey*, depicts one of the first magic-users in all of literature: the wicked sorceress Circe. Even Shakespeare featured wizards in his fiction, from the Weird Sisters of *Macbeth* to Prospero in *The Tempest*.

But wizard literature has exploded since World War II. In a time when technology has given humanity the ability to fly, to communicate instantaneously with people on the other side of the globe, to travel to the moon—even to shatter atoms themselves—wizards have become even more popular, despite the wonder and magic offered by modern-day technologies. Also, magic-users have moved from the sidelines and into the limelight; where once a wizard was a supporting character or perhaps a villain, now he is the protagonist. Merlin has effectively upstaged Arthur.

J.R.R. Tolkien deserves much of the credit for the popularization of fantasy literature; *The Lord of the Rings* rocked the foundations of the fantasy field, and its influence continues to be strongly felt more than fifty years after its initial publication. The creatures and archetypes that Tolkien described have become source material for fantasy enthusiasts of all kinds.

Gandalf, with his long white beard and otherworldly wisdom, forms our standard picture of a wizard—but he isn't the only kind of wizard out there. In the last five decades, innumerable varieties of wizards and other magic-users have been imagined, and magic itself has come a long way as well. It is no longer just the stuff of staff-carrying old men or witches with bubbling cauldrons; now there are just as many sorcerers making magic happen with their own force of will or spinning creations out of magical languages. Witches are as likely to use electromagnetics to pull magical energy out of ley lines as they are to sacrifice goats to devils.

As writers draw their inspiration from a wider net of folkloric resources, their witches and wizards get their own variety of ethnic flavors. This anthology features shamans working from their aboriginal tradition, witches pulling spells from the words of the Bible, and even necromancers tapping into ancient Egyptian wisdom to suit their own nefarious purposes. If the typical milieu for a fantasy adventure starts in a rustic inn, these extraordinary stories feel as if they begin in the spice market of an exotic bazaar; which is all to the good: magic comes in too many flavors to keep it bound up in the Western European tradition.

Writers might bring new influences to their treatment of magic and the characters who use it, but the importance of the wizard in literature has not changed. Wizards, being possessed (usually) of uncommon intelligence, typically know a great deal more than the other characters in stories; his wisdom might be rooted in evil or it might be rooted in kindness; the wizard might give helpful advice, or he might set the protagonist on a journey of hardship and privation. Whatever he chooses to do, the wizard's actions change the hero's life forever.

Today, as I mentioned above, we quite often see the wizard himself playing the hero's role. Perhaps this is because once the wizard stood for all the things people did not understand about the world, and now the wizard represents the weight of our knowledge. In a time where technology has given any ordinary person the kinds of abilities that were the stuff of fairy tales two hundred years ago, anyone can be a wizard. Everyone is extraordinarily powerful.

But power has a weight, an obligation. It must be carefully used. We read about wizards because the choices they make are our choices writ large. In many stories, a wizard's mistake can cause his own death—or even the destruction of the entire world. Our own choices can be just as fraught with danger. The automobile can whisk us to and from distant destinations, but a wrong move could mean a deadly accident. An X-ray can diagnose a broken bone, but too much exposure to radiation can cause cancer. A nuclear weapons system can deter a threat, but a misused nuke can set off global war and nuclear winter.

After centuries of dreaming and yearning for magic, we now have it, or at least a taste of it. We love wizards because, no matter how much power we attain, we can always dream of more.

To read about magic is to stir up ancient dreams that live on inside the human mind. They are dreams of wonder and adventure and curiosity. And in a time when it is easy to reduce the world to dreary facts and figures—when economists can put a dollar figure to every human creation and natural resource—it's vital that we have somewhere to go to recharge our dreams.

So read these stories, and in them, find a magical path to walk and a wondrous dream to dream. What you discover—no matter what the economists say—will be priceless.

GEORGE R.R. MARTIN is the best-selling author of the *Song of Ice and Fire* epic fantasy series, which is currently in the process of becoming a television series for HBO. Martin has also written a range of other novels including *Fevre Dream, The Armageddon Rag, Dying of the Light,* and *Hunter's Run* (with Daniel Abraham and Gardner Dozois). He is a prolific author of short stories, which have garnered numerous nominations and wins for the field's major awards, including the Hugo, Nebula, Stoker, and World Fantasy awards; most of these have been collected in the mammoth, two-volume *Dreamsongs.*

One of the oldest of human desires is to shed our clumsy human bodies and run wild and free with the animals—or to soar through the air with the birds. Legend is full of accounts of people who can transform into animals, such as werewolves, or of animals that can transform into humans, such as the *huli jing* (fox spirits) of Asian mythology. Frequently such transformations involve an animal skin, such as in the tales of the Navajo skinwalkers. There are also countless stories about selkies or swan maidens. Often in fairy tales these creatures will take off their animal skins and become human, and a young man will steal the skin, trapping the creature in human form, and force her to marry him. These stories seldom end happily. It seems that humans were meant to be humans and animals were meant to be animals, and no good ever comes of trying to defy the natural order of things.

Our next story is one of the darkest of all such tales. Of course we want to run with the animals, but this story reminds us of that old advice: be careful what you wish for.

In the Lost Lands
George R.R. Martin

You can buy anything you might desire from Gray Alys.

But it is better not to.

The Lady Melange did not come herself to Gray Alys. She was said to be a clever and a cautious young woman, as well as exceedingly fair, and she had heard the stories. Those who dealt with Gray Alys did so at their own peril, it was said. Gray Alys did not refuse any of those who came to her, and she always got them what they wanted. Yet somehow, when all was done, those who dealt with Gray Alys were never happy with the things that she brought them, the things that they had wanted. The Lady Melange knew all this, ruling as she did from the high keep built into the side of the mountain. Perhaps that was why she did not come herself.

Instead, it was Jerais who came calling on Gray Alys that day; Blue Jerais, the lady's champion, foremost of the paladins who secured her high keep and led her armies into battle, captain of her colorguard. Jerais wore an underlining of pale blue silk beneath the deep azure plate of his enameled armor. The sigil on his shield was a maelstrom done in a hundred subtle hues of blue, and a sapphire large as an eagle's eye was set in the hilt of his sword. When he entered Gray Alys' presence and removed his helmet, his eyes were a perfect match for the jewel in his sword, though his hair was a startling and inappropriate red.

Gray Alys received him in the small, ancient stone house she kept in the dim heart of the town beneath the mountain. She waited for him in a windowless room full of dust and the smell of mold, seated in an old high-backed chair that seemed to dwarf her small, thin body. In her lap was a gray rat the size of a small dog. She stroked it languidly as Jerais entered and took off his helmet and let his bright blue eyes adjust to the dimness.

"Yes?" Gray Alys said at last.

"You are the one they call Gray Alys," Jerais said.

"I am."

"I am Jerais. I come at the behest of the Lady Melange."

"The wise and beautiful Lady Melange," said Gray Alys. The rat's fur was soft as velvet beneath her long, pale fingers. "Why does the Lady send her champion to one as poor and plain as I?"

"Even in the keep, we hear tales of you," said Jerais.

"Yes."

"It is said, for a price, you will sell things strange and wonderful."

"Does the Lady Melange wish to buy?"

"It is said also that you have powers, Gray Alys. It is said that you are not always as you sit before me now, a slender woman of indeterminate age, clad all in gray. It is said that you become young and old as you wish. It is said that sometimes you are a man, or an old woman, or a child. It is said that you know the secrets of shapeshifting, that you go abroad as a great cat, a bear, a bird, and that you change your skin at will, not as a slave to the moon like the werefolk of the lost lands."

"All of these things are said," Gray Alys acknowledged.

Jerais removed a small leather bag from his belt and stepped closer to where Gray Alys sat. He loosened the drawstring that held the bag shut, and spilled out the contents on the table by her side. Gems. A dozen of them, in as many colors. Gray Alys lifted one and held it to her eye, watching the candle flame through it. When she placed it back among the others, she nodded at Jerais and said, "What would the Lady buy of me?"

"Your secret," Jerais said, smiling. "The Lady Melange wishes to shapeshift."

"She is said to be young and beautiful," Gray Alys replied. "Even here beyond the keep, we hear many tales of her. She has no mate but many lovers. All of her colorguard are said to love her, among them yourself. Why should she wish to change?"

"You misunderstand. The Lady Melange does not seek youth or beauty. No change could make her fairer than she is. She wants from you the power to become a beast. A wolf."

"Why?" asked Gray Alys.

"That is none of your concern. Will you sell her this gift?"

"I refuse no one," said Gray Alys. "Leave the gems here. Return in one month, and I shall give you what the Lady Melange desires." Jerais nodded. His face looked thoughtful. "You refuse no one?"

"No one."

He grinned crookedly, reached into his belt, and extended his hand to her. Within the soft blue crushed velvet of his gloved palm rested another jewel, a sapphire even larger than the one set in the hilt of his sword. "Accept this as payment, if you will. I wish to buy for myself."

Gray Alys took the sapphire from his palm, held it up between thumb and forefinger against the candle flame, nodded, and dropped it among the other jewels. "What would you have, Jerais?"

His grin spread wider. "I would have you fail," he said. "I do not want the Lady Melange to have this power she seeks."

Gray Alys regarded him evenly, her steady gray eyes fixed on his own cold blue ones. "You wear the wrong color, Jerais," she said at last. "Blue is the color of loyalty, yet you betray your mistress and the mission she entrusted to you."

"I am loyal," Jerais protested. "I know what is good for her, better than she knows herself. Melange is young and foolish. She thinks it can be kept secret, when she finds this power she seeks. She is wrong. And when the people know, they will destroy her. She cannot rule these folk by day, and tear out their throats by night."

Gray Alys considered that for a time in silence, stroking the great rat that lay across her lap. "You lie, Jerais," she said when she spoke again. "The reasons you give are not your true reasons."

Jerais frowned. His gloved hand, almost casually, came to rest on the hilt of his sword. His thumb stroked the great sapphire set there. "I will not argue with you," he said gruffly. "If you will not sell to me, give me back my gem and be damned with you!"

"I refuse no one," Gray Alys replied.

Jerais scowled in confusion. "I shall have what I ask?"

"You shall have what you want."

"Excellent," said Jerais, grinning again. "In a month, then!"

"A month," agreed Gray Alys.

And so Gray Alys sent the word out, in ways that only Gray Alys knew. The message passed from mouth to mouth through the shadows and alleys and the secret sewers of the town, and even to the tall houses of scarlet wood and colored glass where dwelled the noble and the rich. Soft gray rats with tiny human hands whispered it to sleeping children, and the children shared it with each other, and chanted a strange new chant when they skipped rope. The word drifted to all the army outposts to the east, and rode west with the great caravans into the heart of the old empire of which the town beneath the mountain was only the smallest part. Huge leathery birds with the cunning faces of monkeys flew the word south, over the forests and the rivers, to a dozen different kingdoms, where men and women as pale and terrible as Gray Alys herself heard it in the solitude of their towers. Even north, past the mountains, even into the lost lands, the word traveled.

It did not take long. In less than two weeks, he came to her. "I can lead you to what you seek," he told her. "I can find you a werewolf."

He was a young man, slender and beardless. He dressed in the worn leathers of the rangers who lived and hunted in the windswept desolation beyond the mountains. His skin had the deep tan of a man who spent all his life outdoors, though his hair was as white as mountain snow and fell about his shoulders, tangled and unkempt. He wore no armor and carried a long knife instead of a sword, and he moved with a wary grace. Beneath the pale strands of hair that fell across his face, his eyes were dark and sleepy. Though his smile was open and amiable, there was a curious indolence to him as well, and a dreamy, sensuous set to his lips when he thought no one was watching. He named himself Boyce.

Gray Alys watched him and listened to his words and finally said, "Where?"

"A week's journey north," Boyce replied. "In the lost lands."

"Do you dwell in the lost lands, Boyce?" Gray Alys asked of him.

"No. They are no fit place for dwelling. I have a home here in town. But I go beyond the mountains often, Gray Alys. I am a hunter. I know the lost lands well, and I know the things that live there. You seek a man who walks like a wolf. I can take you to him. But we must leave at once, if we are to arrive before the moon is full."

Gray Alys rose. "My wagon is loaded, my horses are fed and shod. Let us depart then."

Boyce brushed the fine white hair from his eyes, and smiled lazily.

The mountain pass was high and steep and rocky, and in places barely wide enough for Gray Alys' wagon to pass. The wagon was a cumbersome thing, long and heavy and entirely enclosed, once brightly painted but now faded so by time and weather that its wooden walls were all a dreary gray. It rode on six clattering iron wheels, and the two horses that pulled it were of necessity monsters half again the size of normal beasts. Even so, they kept a slow pace through the mountains. Boyce, who had no horse, walked ahead or alongside, and sometimes rode up next to Gray Alys. The wagon groaned and creaked. It took them three days to ascend to the highest point on the mountain road, where they looked through a cleft in the mountains out onto the wide barren plains of the lost lands. It took them three more days to descend.

"Now we will make better time," Boyce promised Gray Alys when they reached the lost lands themselves. "Here the land is flat and empty, and the going will be easy. A day now, perhaps two, and you shall have what you seek."

"Yes," said Gray Alys.

They filled the water barrels full before they left the mountains, and Boyce went hunting in the foothills and returned with three black rabbits and the carcass of a small deer, curiously deformed, and when Gray Alys asked him how he had brought them down with only a knife as a weapon, Boyce smiled and produced a sling and sent several small stones whistling through the air. Gray Alys nodded.

They made a small fire and cooked two of the rabbits, and salted the rest of the meat. The next morning, at dawn, they set off into the lost lands.

Here they moved quickly indeed. The lost lands were a cold and empty place, and the earth was packed as hard and firm as the roads that wound through the empire beyond the mountains. The wagon rolled along briskly, creaking and clattering, shaking a bit from side to side as it went. In the lost lands there were no thickets to cut through, no rivers to cross. Desolation lay before them on all sides, seemingly endless. From time to time they saw a grove of trees, gnarled and twisted all together, limbs heavy with swollen fruit with skin the color of indigo, shining. From time to time they clattered through a shallow, rocky stream, none deeper than ankle level. From time to time vast patches of white fungus blanketed the desolate gray earth. Yet all these things were rare. Mostly there was only the emptiness, the shuddering dead plains all around them, and the winds. The winds were terrible in the lost lands. They blew constantly, and they were cold and bitter, and sometimes they smelled of ash, and sometimes they seemed to howl and shriek like some poor doomed soul.

At last they had come far enough so Gray Alys could see the end of the lost lands: another line of mountains far, far north of them, a vague bluish-white line across the gray horizon. They could travel for weeks and not reach those distant peaks, Gray Alys knew, yet the lost lands were so flat and so empty that even now they could make them out, dimly.

At dusk Gray Alys and Boyce made their camp, just beyond a grove of the curious tortured trees they had glimpsed on their journey north. The trees gave them a partial respite from the fury of the wind, but even so they could hear it, keening and pulling at them, twisting their fire into wild suggestive shapes.

"These lands are lost indeed," Gray Alys said as they ate.

"They have their own beauty," Boyce replied. He impaled a chunk of meat on the end of his long knife, and turned it above the fire. "Tonight, if the clouds pass, you will see the lights rippling above the northern mountains, all purple and gray and maroon, twisting like curtains caught in this endless wind."

"I have seen those lights before," said Gray Alys.

"I have seen them many times," Boyce said. He bit off a piece of meat, pulling at it with his teeth, and a thin line of grease ran down from the corner of his mouth. He smiled.

"You come to the lost lands often," Gray Alys said.

Boyce shrugged. "I hunt."

"Does anything live here?" asked Gray Alys. "Live amidst all this desolation?"

"Oh yes," Boyce replied. "You must have eyes to find it, you must know the lost lands, but it is there. Strange twisted beasts never seen beyond the mountains, things out of legends and nightmares, enchanted things and accursed things, things whose flesh is impossibly rare and impossibly delicious. Humans, too, or things that are almost human. Werefolk and changelings and gray shapes that walk only by twilight, shuffling things half-living and half-dead." His smile was gentle and taunting. "But you are Gray Alys, and all this you must know. It is said you came out of the lost lands yourself once, long ago."

"It is said," Gray Alys answered.

"We are alike, you and I," Boyce replied. "I love the town, the people, song and laughter and gossip. I savor the comforts of my house, good food and good wine. I relish the players who come each fall to the high keep and perform for the Lady Melange. I like fine clothes and jewels and soft, pretty women. Yet part of me is only at home here, in the lost lands, listening to the wind, watching the shadows warily each dusk, dreaming things the townsfolk never dare." Full dark had fallen by then. Boyce lifted his knife and pointed north, to where dim lights had begun to glow faintly against the mountains. "See there, Gray Alys. See how the lights shimmer and shift. You can see shapes in them if you watch long enough. Men and women and things that are neither, moving against the darkness. Their voices are carried by the wind. Watch and listen. There are great dramas in those lights, plays grander and stranger than any ever performed on the Lady's stage. Do you hear? Do you see?"

Gray Alys sat on the hard-packed earth with her legs crossed and her gray eyes unreadable, watching in silence. Finally she spoke. "Yes," she said, and that was all.

Boyce sheathed his long knife and came around the campfire—it had died now to a handful of dim reddish embers—to sit beside her. "I knew you would see," he said. "We are alike, you and I. We wear the flesh of the city, but in our blood the cold wind of the lost lands is blowing always. I could see it in your eyes, Gray Alys."

She said nothing; she sat and watched the lights, feeling the warm presence of Boyce beside her. After a time he put an arm about her shoulders, and Gray Alys did not protest. Later, much later, when the fire had gone entirely dark and the night had grown cold, Boyce reached out and cupped her chin within his hand and turned her face to his. He kissed her, once, gently, full upon her thin lips.

And Gray Alys woke, as if from a dream, and pushed him back upon the ground and undressed him with sure, deft hands and took him then and there. Boyce let her do it all. He lay upon the chill hard ground with his hands clasped behind his head, his eyes dreamy and his lips curled up in a lazy, complacent smile, while Gray Alys rode him, slowly at first, then faster and faster, building to a shuddering climax. When she came her body went stiff and she threw her head back; her mouth opened, as if to cry out, but no sound came forth. There was only the wind, cold and wild, and the cry it made was not a cry of pleasure.

❧

The next day dawned chill and overcast. The sky was full of thin, twisted gray clouds that raced before them faster than clouds ought to race. What light filtered through seemed wan and colorless. Boyce walked beside the wagon while Gray Alys drove it forward at a leisurely pace. "We are close now," Boyce told her. "Very close."

"Yes."

Boyce smiled up at her. His smile had changed since they had become lovers. It was fond and mysterious, and more than a bit indulgent. It was a smile that presumed. "Tonight," he told her.

"The moon will be full tonight," Gray Alys said.

Boyce smiled and pushed the hair from his eyes and said nothing.

Well before dusk, they drew up amidst the ruins of some nameless town long forgotten even by those who dwelled in the lost lands. Little remained to disturb the sweeping emptiness, only a huddle of broken masonry, forlorn and pitiful. The vague outlines of town walls could still be discerned, and one or two chimneys remained standing, jagged and half-shattered, gnawing at the horizon like rotten black teeth. No shelter was to be found here, no life. When Gray Alys had fed her horses, she wandered through the ruins but found little. No pottery, no rusted blades, no books. Not even bones. Nothing at all to hint of the people who had once lived here, if people they had been.

The lost lands had sucked the life out of this place and blown away even the ghosts, so not a trace of memory remained. The shrunken sun was low on the horizon, obscured by scuttling clouds, and the scene spoke to her with the wind's voice, cried out in loneliness and despair. Gray Alys stood for a long time, alone, watching the sun sink while her thin tattered cloak billowed behind her and the cold wind bit through into her soul. Finally she turned away and went back to the wagon.

Boyce had built a fire, and he sat in front of it, mulling some wine in a copper pot, adding spices from time to time. He smiled his new smile for Gray Alys when she looked at him. "The wind is cold," he said. "I thought a hot drink would make our meal more pleasant."

Gray Alys glanced away toward the setting sun, then back at Boyce. "This is not the time or the place for pleasure, Boyce. Dusk is all but upon us, and soon the full moon shall rise."

"Yes," said Boyce. He ladled some of the hot wine into his cup, and tried a swallow. "No need to rush off hunting, though," he said, smiling lazily. "The wolf will come to us. Our scent will carry far in this wind, in this emptiness, and the smell of fresh meat will bring him running."

Gray Alys said nothing. She turned away from him and climbed the three wooden steps that led up to the interior of her wagon. Inside she lit a brazier carefully, and watched the light shift and flicker against the weathered gray wallboards and the pile of furs on which she slept. When the light had grown steady, Gray Alys slid back a wall panel, and stared at the long row of tattered garments that hung on pegs within the narrow closet. Cloaks and capes and billowing loose shirts, strangely cut gowns and suits that clung like a second skin from head to toe, leather and fur and feathers. She hesitated briefly, then reached in and chose a great cloak made of a thousand long silver feathers, each one tipped delicately with black. Removing her simple cloth cloak, Gray Alys fastened the flowing feathered garment at her neck. When she turned it billowed all about her, and the dead air inside the wagon stirred and briefly seemed alive before the feathers settled and stilled once again. Then Gray Alys bent and opened a huge oaken chest, bound in iron and leather. From within she drew out a small box. Ten rings rested against worn gray felt, each set with a long, curving silver claw instead of a stone. Gray Alys donned them methodically, one ring to each finger, and when she rose and clenched her fists, the claws shone dimly and menacingly in the light from the brazier.

Outside, it was twilight. Boyce had not prepared any food, Gray Alys noted as she took her seat across the fire from where the pale-haired ranger sat quaffing his hot wine.

"A beautiful cloak," Boyce observed amiably.

"Yes," said Gray Alys.

"No cloak will help you when *he* comes, though."

Gray Alys raised her hand, made a fist. The silver claws caught the firelight. Gleamed.

"Ah," said Boyce. "Silver."

"Silver," agreed Gray Alys, lowering her hand.

"Still," Boyce said. "Others have come against him, armed with silver. Silver swords, silver knives, arrows tipped with silver. They are dust now, all those silvered warriors. He gorged himself on their flesh."

Gray Alys shrugged.

Boyce stared at her speculatively for a time, then smiled and went back to his wine. Gray Alys drew her cloak more tightly about herself to keep out the cold wind. After a while, staring off into the far distance, she saw lights moving against the northern mountains. She remembered the stories that she had seen there, the tales that Boyce had conjured for her from that play of colored shadows. They were grim and terrible stories. In the lost lands, there was no other kind.

At last another light caught her eye. A spreading dimness in the east, wan and ominous. Moonrise.

Gray Alys stared calmly across the dying camp fire. Boyce had begun to change. She watched his body twist as bone and muscle changed within, watched his pale white hair grow longer and longer, watched his lazy smile turn into a wide red grin that split his face, saw the canines lengthen and the tongue come lolling out, watched the wine cup fall as his hands melted and writhed and became paws. He started to say something once, but no words came out, only a low, coarse snarl of laughter, half-human and half-animal. Then he threw back his head and howled, and he ripped at his clothing until it lay in tatters all about him and he was Boyce no longer. Across the fire from Gray Alys the wolf stood, a great shaggy white beast, half again the size of an ordinary wolf, with a savage red slash of a mouth and glowing scarlet eyes. Gray Alys stared into those eyes as she rose and shook the dust from her feathered cloak. They were knowing eyes, cunning, wise. Inside those eyes she saw a smile, a smile that presumed.

A smile that presumed too much.

The wolf howled once again, a long wild sound that melted into the wind. And then he leapt, straight across the embers of the fire he had built.

Gray Alys threw her arms out, her cloak bunched in her hands, and changed.

Her change was faster than his had been, over almost as soon as it began, but for Gray Alys it lasted an eternity. First there was the strange choking, clinging feeling as the cloak adhered to her skin, then dizziness and a curious liquid weakness as her muscles began to run and flow and reshape themselves. And finally exhilaration, as the power rushed into her and came coursing through her veins, a wine fiercer and hotter and wilder than the poor stuff Boyce had mulled above their fire.

She beat her vast silvery wings, each pinion tipped with black, and the dust stirred and swirled as she rose up into the moonlight, up to safety high above the white wolf's bound, up and up until the ruins shrunk to insignificance far beneath her. The wind took hold of her, caressed her with trembling icy hands, and she yielded herself to it and soared. Her great wings filled with the dread melody of the lost lands, carrying her higher and higher. Her cruel curving beak opened and closed and opened again, though no sound came forth. She wheeled across the sky, drunken with flight. Her eyes, sharper than any human eyes could be, saw far into the distance, spied out the secrets of every shadow, glimpsed all the dying and half-dead things that stirred and shambled across the barren face of the lost lands. The curtains of light to the north danced before her, a thousand times brighter and more gorgeous than they had been before, when she had only the dim eyes of the little thing called Gray Alys to perceive them with. She wanted to fly to them, to soar north and north and north, to cavort among those lights, shredding them into glowing strips with her talons.

She lifted her talons as if in challenge. Long and wickedly curved they were, and razor sharp, and the moonlight flashed along their length, pale upon the silver. And she remembered then, and she wheeled about in a great circle, reluctantly, and turned away from the beckoning lights of the northlands. Her wings beat and beat again, and she began to descend, shrieking down through the night air, plunging toward her prey.

She saw him far beneath her, a pale white shape hurtling away from the wagon, away from the fire, seeking safety in the shadows and the dark places. But there was no safety in the lost lands. He was strong and untiring, and his long powerful legs carried him forward in a steady swift lope that ate up the miles as if they were nothing. Already he had come a long way from their camp. But fast as he was, she was faster. He was only a wolf, after all, and she was the wind itself.

She descended in a dead silence, cutting through the wind like a knife, silver talons outstretched. But he must have spied her shadow streaking toward him, etched clear by the moonlight, for as she closed he spurted forward wildly, driven by fear. It was useless. He was running full out when she passed above him, raking him with her talons. They cut through fur and twisted flesh like ten bright silver swords, and he broke stride and staggered and went down.

She beat her wings and circled overhead for another pass, and as she did the wolf regained his feet and stared up at her terrible silhouette dark against the moon, his eyes brighter now than ever, turned feverish by fear. He threw back his head and howled a broken bloody howl that cried for mercy.

She had no mercy in her. Down she came, and down, talons drenched with blood, her beak open to rend and tear. The wolf waited for her, and leapt up to meet her dive, snarling, snapping. But he was no match for her.

She slashed at him in passing, evading him easily, opening five more long gashes that quickly welled with blood.

The next time she came around he was too weak to run, too weak to rise against her. But he watched her turn and descend, and his huge shaggy body trembled just before she struck.

Finally his eyes opened, blurred and weak. He groaned and moved feebly. It was daylight, and he was back in the camp, lying beside the fire. Gray Alys came to him when she heard him stir, knelt, and lifted his head. She held a cup of wine to his lips until he had drunk his fill.

When Boyce lay back again, she could see the wonder in his eyes, the surprise that he still lived. "You knew," he said hoarsely. "You knew . . . what I was."

"Yes," said Gray Alys. She was herself once more; a slender, small, somehow ageless woman with wide gray eyes, clad in faded cloth. The feathered cloak was hung away, the silver claws no longer adorned her fingers.

Boyce tried to sit up, winced at the pain, and settled back onto the blanket she had laid beneath him. "I thought . . . thought I was dead," he said.

"You were close to dead," Gray Alys replied.

"Silver," he said bitterly. "Silver cuts and burns so."

"Yes."

"But you saved me," he said, confused.

"I changed back to myself, and brought you back, and tended you."

Boyce smiled, though it was only a pale ghost of his old smile. "You change at will," he said wonderingly. "Ah, there is a gift I would kill for, Gray Alys!"

She said nothing.

"It was too open here," he said. "I should have taken you elsewhere. If there had been cover . . . buildings, a forest, anything . . . then you should not have had such an easy time with me."

"I have other skins," Gray Alys replied. "A bear, a cat. It would not have mattered."

"Ah," said Boyce. He closed his eyes. When he opened them again, he forced a twisted smile. "You were beautiful, Gray Alys. I watched you fly for a long time before I realized what it meant and began to run. It was hard to tear my eyes from you. I knew you were the doom of me, but still I could not look away. So beautiful. All smoke and silver, with fire in your eyes. The last time, as I watched you swoop toward me, I was almost glad. Better to perish at the hands of she who is so terrible and fine, I thought, than by some dirty little swordsman with his sharpened silver stick."

"I am sorry," said Gray Alys.

"No," Boyce said quickly. "It is better that you saved me. I will mend quickly, you will see. Even silver wounds bleed but briefly. Then we will be together."

"You are still weak," Gray Alys told him. "Sleep."

"Yes," said Boyce. He smiled at her, and closed his eyes.

Hours had passed when Boyce finally woke again. He was much stronger, his wounds all but mended. But when he tried to rise, he could not. He was bound in place, spread-eagled, hands and feet tied securely to stakes driven into the hard gray earth.

Gray Alys watched him make the discovery, heard him cry out in alarm. She came to him, held up his head, and gave him more wine.

When she moved back, his head twisted around wildly, staring at his bonds, and then at her. "What have you done?" he cried.

Gray Alys said nothing.

"Why?" he asked. "I do not understand, Gray Alys. *Why?* You saved me, tended me, and now I am bound."

"You would not like my answer, Boyce."

"The moon!" he said wildly. "You are afraid of what might happen tonight, when I change again." He smiled, pleased to have figured it out. "You are being foolish. I would not harm you, not now, after what has passed between us, after what I know. We belong together, Gray Alys. We are alike, you and I. We have watched the lights together, and I have seen you fly! We must have trust between us! Let me loose."

Gray Alys frowned and sighed and gave no other answer.

Boyce stared at her uncomprehending. "Why?" he asked again. "Untie me, Alys, let me prove the truth of my words. You need not fear me."

"I do not fear you, Boyce," she said sadly.

"Good," he said eagerly. "Then free me, and change with me. Become a great cat tonight, and run beside me, hunt with me. I can lead you to prey you never dreamed of. There is so much we can share. You have felt how it is to change, you know the truth of it, you have tasted the power, the freedom, seen the lights from a beast's eyes, smelled fresh blood, gloried in a kill. You know . . . the freedom . . . the intoxication of it . . . all the . . . you know . . . "

"I know," Gray Alys acknowledged.

"Then free me! We are meant for each another, you and I. We will live together, love together, hunt together."

Gray Alys shook her head.

"I do not understand," Boyce said. He strained upward wildly at his bonds, and swore, then sunk back again. "Am I hideous? Do you find me evil, unattractive?"

"No."

"Then what?" he said bitterly. "Other women have loved me, have found me handsome. Rich, beautiful ladies, the finest in the land. All of them have wanted me, even when they knew."

"But you have never returned that love, Boyce," she said.

"No," he admitted. "I have loved them after a fashion. I have never betrayed their trust, if that is what you think. I find my prey here, in the lost lands, not from among those who care for me." Boyce felt the weight of Gray Alys' eyes, and continued. "How could I love them more than I did?" he said passionately. "They could know only half of me, only the half that lived in town and loved wine and song and perfumed sheets. The rest of me lived out here, in the lost lands, and knew things that they could never know, poor soft things. I told them so, those who pressed me hard. To join with me wholly they must run and hunt beside me. Like you. Let me go, Gray Alys. Soar for me, watch me run. Hunt with me."

Gray Alys rose and sighed. "I am sorry, Boyce. I would spare you if I could, but what must happen must happen. Had you died last night, it would have been useless. Dead things have no power. Night and day, black and white, they are weak. All strength derives from the realm between, from twilight, from shadow, from the terrible place between life and death. From the gray, Boyce, from the gray."

He wrenched at his bonds again, savagely, and began to weep and curse and gnash his teeth. Gray Alys turned away from him and sought out the solitude of her wagon. There she remained for hours, sitting alone in the darkness and listening to Boyce swear and cry out to her with threats and pleadings and professions of love. Gray Alys stayed inside until well after moonrise. She did not want to watch him change, watch his humanity pass from him for the last time.

At last his cries had become howls, bestial and abandoned and full of pain. That was when Gray Alys finally reemerged. The full moon cast a wan pale light over the scene. Bound to the hard ground, the great white wolf writhed and howled and struggled and stared at her out of hungry scarlet eyes.

Gray Alys walked toward him calmly. In her hand was the long silver skinning knife, its blade engraved with fine and graceful runes.

When he finally stopped struggling, the work went more quickly, but still it was a long and bloody night. She killed him the instant she was done, before the dawn came and changed him and gave him back a human voice to cry his agony. Then Gray Alys hung up the pelt and brought out tools and dug a deep, deep grave in the packed cold earth. She piled stones and broken pieces of masonry on top of it, to protect him from the things that roamed the lost lands, the ghouls and the carrion crows and the other creatures that did not flinch at dead flesh. It took her most of the day to bury him, for the ground was very hard indeed, and even as she worked she knew it was a futile labor.

And when at last the work was done, and dusk had almost come again, she went once more into her wagon, and returned wearing the great cloak of a thousand silver feathers, tipped with black. Then she changed, and flew, and flew, a fierce and tireless flight, bathed in strange lights and wedded to the dark. All night she flew beneath a full and mocking moon, and just before dawn she cried out once, a shrill scream of despair and anguish that rang and keened on the sharp edge of the wind and changed its sound forever.

Perhaps Jerais was afraid of what she might give him, for he did not return to Gray Alys alone. He brought two other knights with him, a huge man all in white whose shield showed a skull carved out of ice, and another in crimson whose sigil was a burning man. They stood at the door, helmeted and silent, while Jerais approached Gray Alys warily. "Well?" he demanded.

Across her lap was a wolfskin, the pelt of some huge massive beast, all white as mountain snow. Gray Alys rose and offered the skin to Blue Jerais, draping it across his outstretched arm. "Tell the Lady Melange to cut herself, and drip her own blood onto the skin. Do this at moonrise when the moon is full, and then the power will be hers. She need only wear the skin as a cloak, and will the change thereafter. Day or night, full moon or no moon, it makes no matter."

Jerais looked at the heavy white pelt and smiled a hard smile. "A wolfskin, eh? I had not expected that. I thought perhaps a potion, a spell."

"No," said Gray Alys. "The skin of a werewolf."

"A werewolf?" Jerais' mouth twisted curiously, and there was a sparkle in his deep sapphire eyes. "Well, Gray Alys, you have done what the Lady Melange asked, but you have failed me. I did not pay you for success. Return my gem."

"No," said Gray Alys. "I have earned it, Jerais."

"I do not have what I asked for."

"You have what you wanted, and that is what I promised." Her gray eyes met his own without fear. "You thought my failure would help you get what you truly wanted, and that my success would doom you. You were wrong."

Jerais looked amused. "And what do I truly desire?"

"The Lady Melange," said Gray Alys. "You have been one lover among many, but you wanted more. You wanted all. You knew you stood second in her affections. I have changed that. Return to her now, and bring her the thing that she has bought."

That day there was bitter lamentation in the high keep on the mountain, when Blue Jerais knelt before the Lady Melange and offered her a white wolfskin. But when the screaming and the wailing and the mourning was done, she took the great pale cloak and bled upon it and learned the ways of change. It is not the union she desired, but it is a union nonetheless. So every night she prowls the battlements and the mountainside, and the townsfolk say her howling is wild with grief.

And Blue Jerais, who wed her a month after Gray Alys returned from the lost lands, sits beside a madwoman in the great hall by day, and locks his doors by night in terror of his wife's hot red eyes, and does not hunt anymore, or laugh, or lust.

You can buy anything you might desire from Gray Alys.

But it is better not to.

DAVID BARR KIRTLEY has been described as "one of the newest and freshest voices in sf." His work frequently appears in *Realms of Fantasy*, and he has also sold fiction to the magazines *Weird Tales* and *Intergalactic Medicine Show*, the podcasts *Escape Pod* and *Pseudopod*, and the anthologies *New Voices in Science Fiction*, *The Dragon Done It*, and *Fantasy: The Best of the Year*. I've previously published him in my *The Living Dead* and *The Living Dead 2* anthologies and in my online science fiction magazine *Lightspeed*. Kirtley is also the co-host (with me) of *The Geek's Guide to the Galaxy* podcast.

Everyone loves treehouses. Our distant ancestors lived in trees, of course, so maybe it all goes back to that. In fact, the Korowi people in Papua New Guinea still live in tree houses, as protection against a neighboring tribe. Some modern treehouses reach rather spectacular levels of scale and luxury, but nothing like what you'll see in our next story.

"I was visiting my grandmother," Kirtley says, "and she uses a computer program called *Family Tree Maker*. When I glanced at the box for that, it gave me this idea for a literal tree that the family lives in, where each branch of the tree corresponds to a branch of the family. (Good fantasy ideas often come from literalizing metaphors.) Then I got the idea that if a line of the family died out, their branch of the tree would wither and die as well, which immediately started suggesting possible conflicts. It's hard to come up with a fantasy idea that hasn't been done a million times already, and this was one I don't think I've ever seen before. It took me a long time to work out exactly how things would unfold. I spent a lot of time drawing tree diagrams."

FAMILY TREE
DAVID BARR KIRTLEY

Simon Archimagus rode his horse through a twilight forest. A rapier hung at his side, and as he moved he muttered a spell that would slay any insect who presumed to land upon him.

He turned onto the narrow dirt trail that led to his abode. A short time later he glanced back and noticed a horseman behind him. As Simon was the sole resident in these parts, he could only assume that he was being followed. He moved one hand to his sword, while with the other he sketched a diagram in the air, preparatory to unleashing battle magic.

The rider neared. He wore a loose white shirt and feathered cap. The dimness made it hard to judge his features, but he didn't seem hostile. Then Simon knew him. Bernard.

As the rider trotted up he called out, "Brother."

Of all Simon's male relatives, Bernard, his youngest sibling, was perhaps his favorite, though that wasn't saying a lot. Bernard seemed not to have changed much—same thick brown hair and ingenuous eyes. A bit pudgier, maybe. Simon said, "How'd you find me?"

"Magic." Bernard added with a touch of pride, "You're not the only wizard in the family, you know."

"No." Simon gave a half-smile. "Just the best."

Bernard chuckled. "No argument there." He glanced up the trail. "You live nearby?"

The game was up. Simon's family had located him, at last. So, "Yes," he said.

"Then grant me hospitality, brother. We need to talk."

Simon hesitated, then said, "All right." He gestured with his head. "This way."

They followed the trail, which wound its way up the hillside. The horses panted and snorted. After a time, Bernard said, "So are you going to tell me why you disappeared?"

"I doubt it," Simon said.

"We worried."

Simon stared off into the sky. "My branch is still there, isn't it? You knew I was all right."

"We knew you were *alive*," Bernard said. "You might've been sick, imprisoned—"

"I wasn't."

"I see that." Bernard sighed. "But yes, your branch is still there. Mother's kept everything just the way you left it. She misses you, Simon."

"I'll bet."

Bernard lapsed into silence. Then he asked, "What the hell have you been doing with yourself all these years anyway?"

Simon didn't answer. The two of them crested the hill and looked out over the moon-silvered grasses of the meadow below. Simon waited for Bernard to notice the tree.

Finally he did. He gasped. "Is that . . . ?"

"Yes." Simon couldn't help grinning. "It's mine."

The giant oak was indigo in the darkness, its trunk dotted with small round windows that glowed with warm light from the rooms within.

Bernard stared in wonder. "My god. You did it. You crazy bastard, you actually did it. I don't believe it."

"Believe it." Simon spurred his horse. "Come, I'll give you the tour. Come see what your clever older brother has wrought."

They approached the tree, then dismounted and led their horses toward an archway that passed through into its trunk. Above them to either side huge gnarled roots loomed darkly. Simon gestured, and a portcullis made of thick thorn branches lifted open. He and Bernard passed into the stable, where they left the horses feeding happily, and from there the two men climbed a broad staircase that was lit by wall-sconces blazing with faerie fire. All around was spell-forged woodwork that still lived, and grew. They made their way to the kitchen, where Bernard fixed himself a sandwich and stretched out on the windowsill. "It's a fine tree, brother," he said. "But still rather . . . modest, isn't it? Compared to our inheritance, your birthright."

Simon leaned against the doorframe and crossed his arms. "I could command it to grow larger, like the other. More branches, rooms."

"So why don't you?"

"It's sufficient to my needs." Simon had never shared his relatives' appetite for palatial suites nor for the endless squabbles over who should lay claim to the floorspace of which deceased ancestor.

Bernard glanced about. "And you live alone? Don't you miss the comforts of family?"

"Brother," Simon said wryly, "believe me, having lived sixteen years among the scions of Victor Archimagus, the comforts of family are something I'm happy to forego for a good long time to come."

Bernard chewed his sandwich and stared out the window. He said, "My wife, Elizabeth, has given me a child, at last. A son."

Simon felt obliged to say, "Congratulations."

"The presentation ceremony is next month," Bernard added. "I'd like you to be there."

Simon moved to the cupboard. "I have a prior engagement. But thanks."

"Simon, this is serious. Victor's ghost is displeased by your continued absence, and the branches he's grown for our brothers' boys have seemed less grand than they might be. I want my son to have only the best."

"Please." Simon poured two glasses of wine. "I doubt that even the spirit of Victor Archimagus would punish your infant child for my transgressions. In fact, this whole line of emotionally manipulative argumentation seems to me to have mother's fingerprints all over it. Did she put you up to this?"

"What, you think I can't act on my own?"

Simon passed him a glass. "I'll take that as a yes."

"All right," Bernard said, accepting the wine. "Yes. But she has her reasons, beyond the obvious." He took a sip. "We need you, Simon. Tensions with the descendants of Atherton have never been higher. If it comes to a fight—"

"It won't."

"You've been away," Bernard said. "You haven't seen how bad it's gotten. Malcolm provokes us constantly."

Simon shook his head. "The children of Franklin and the children of Atherton have been at each other's throats for years. It's never come to bloodshed, and it never will."

"What if you're wrong?" Bernard said. "Look, you're not overfond of your close kin, we know that, but are you really just going to sit back as we die in a feud?"

"I'm confident in your ability to look after yourselves."

Bernard grimaced. "Ordinarily, yes. But there's a complication."

"Oh?"

"Meredith."

At the name, Simon felt a jolt. He set down his wine glass. "What?"

"Yeah, I guess it didn't work out with Duke what's-his-name—"

"Wyland."

"Yeah, so she's back. And she scares me, Simon. Her magic has become very powerful." The fear in Bernard's eyes was real. "That's why we need you. To balance things. If you came back it might actually help keep the peace, because they'd think twice about messing with us."

Meredith, Simon thought. After a time, he said, "Maybe a short visit."

Bernard grinned, leapt to his feet, and patted Simon's shoulders. "That's it. Now you're talking."

Later, after Bernard had departed, Simon hiked up to the highest branch of the tree, opened a small door, and strode out onto the balcony. For a long time he sat there in the darkness, clutching his wineglass absently and staring at the mist-shrouded hills, thinking of Meredith.

A month later Simon stood and regarded the tree of Victor Archimagus.

It was gigantic, its trunk as wide around as a castle wall. A good way up, the trunk split into a great V—the two branches that had grown upon the births of Victor's sons, Franklin and Atherton. From there the branches continued to climb and divide—one for each legitimate male heir—and now over a hundred descendants of the late wizard resided within the tree's luxurious chambers. (Female children were married off and sent away—Victor had never been a terribly enlightened sort.) The tree was a virtuoso feat of spellcraft, the first of its kind, and upon its creation Victor had been so impressed with himself that he'd taken the surname Archimagus—master wizard. Simon was the only one to have successfully replicated the spell. Families that possessed the rare gift of magic seemed always to be afflicted with low fertility, but the fact that Victor's tree grew larger and grander depending upon the number of offspring had ensured a frenetic effort to proliferate his adopted surname, and had also—perhaps inevitably—led to a rivalry between the descendants of Franklin and the descendants of Atherton over who could produce the greatest number of male heirs. At the moment it happened that the two halves of the tree were in perfect balance. Today's presentation ceremony for Bernard's infant son would change that.

Crowds had come from all the surrounding towns, and other wizards had come from farther afield, and now several hundred people were gathered in the shadow of those soaring branches. The children of Franklin had spared no expense to ensure a spectacle. Wooden poles were set in the earth at intervals, with garlands of sweet-smelling flowers stretched between them, and tables were piled high with cooked quail and poached eggs. Simon made his way past dancers and jugglers and lute-players, and into the roped-off area that was reserved for members of the Archimagus family. Here all the men, and many of the women, wore swords.

Bernard appeared at Simon's side and took his arm. "Thank you for coming, Simon. Here, mother wants a word with you."

As Simon moved through the crowd, heads turned to watch him, and conversations halted abruptly, then resumed in murmurs. Meredith's brother Malcolm, glowering, red-haired, black-clad, turned to confer with his gang of goonish cousins.

Simon knew what everyone was thinking: The runaway returns, the descendant of Franklin who's most gifted in the ways of magic. This changes everything.

Simon spotted his mother, still lovely as ever, dressed in an ostentatious blue gown. She wore her prematurely silver hair in a single braid, and her face had a few new lines in it, which only made her look even more conniving. She was engaged in an animated conversation with Meredith's mother, a plump woman who had on too much makeup over a pallid complexion and whose wavy crimson hair was like a fiery halo.

When Simon's mother spotted him, she waved and called out, "Simon, there you are."

Meredith's mother tensed. She glanced back over her shoulder at him, her face apprehensive. Simon's mother wore an expression just a shade shy of smug. This scene was playing out, Simon felt sure, precisely as she had intended.

As Simon approached, his mother reached for him and said warmly, "Welcome home."

He allowed his cheeks to be kissed. "Just a visit, mother. My home is far away now."

"Yes, of course." She turned to Meredith's mother and said, "Have you heard? Simon lives in his own tree now. He managed to duplicate the very spell that produced our own arboreal estate."

Simon smiled modestly, uncomfortably.

"Oh, how wonderful," said Meredith's mother, with dubious sincerity. "Is that what you've been doing, Simon? Studying magic? How nice. Your mother has been terribly lax about keeping us up to date on you." She added, "You must be very dedicated, to have sequestered yourself away from your family all these years."

"Oh, he is," said Simon's mother, her tone incrementally chillier. "And the results speak for themselves, wouldn't you say?"

"Oh, indeed," said Meredith's mother. "You know, Simon, my daughter is around here somewhere. You two should chat. She's quite the sorceress herself these days."

"Yes," said Simon's mother, "we're all so delighted to have Meredith back with us. She's much too good for that silly duke."

Meredith's mother narrowed her eyes just a trace. Then she glanced over Simon's shoulder and said, "In fact, I think I see my daughter now. Meredith, dear! Come here a moment. Look who's back."

Simon steeled himself, and turned.

She was taller than he remembered, more confident, her features sharper. She wore a red blouse and a skirt with a swordbelt, and her chestnut hair was shorter than it had been, now just brushing her bare shoulders. But she was still Meredith. He'd imagined this meeting so many times, and now here she was, before him.

"Simon," she said, and moved to embrace him, somewhat stiffly, then backed away. She and her mother faced Simon and his like pieces on a chessboard.

Meredith's mother said, "Remember how the two of you always used to play together?"

"Yes," Simon said, watching Meredith, who stared back, her expression neutral.

"Yes," Simon's mother put in. "The two of you always were the most gifted wizards in the family."

"A bit competitive about it too, as I recall," said Meredith's mother. "Though I suspect, Simon, that these days Meredith may have you beat."

"Oh," said Simon's mother, "I don't know about that."

A moment of awkward silence.

Then Simon's mother added, "We must arrange a little contest some time, to settle the matter."

"Indeed," said Meredith's mother. "That would be most interesting."

The mothers fell silent. Simon and Meredith eyed each other. Simon felt that he should speak, but couldn't think what to say. Fortunately the trumpets sounded, signaling that the ceremony was about to begin.

Meredith nodded to Simon, then she and her mother strolled off, and were soon lost amid the crowds streaming toward the rows of benches. Simon and his mother found their seats, and for a time Simon exchanged a few words with various relatives.

Then Bernard made his way to the front of the audience, and behind him came Elizabeth, a slender, mousy girl, holding their infant son. The couple mounted a raised wooden platform and stood gazing up at the broad southern expanse of Victor's tree.

Bernard shouted, "Victor Archimagus! Honored ancestor! Hear me!"

A great oval section of the tree rippled, as if its bark were a stretch of calm water suddenly disturbed by the movement of a lurking monster. The undulations became more pronounced. There was churning, swirling . . .

Then a giant wooden face appeared, extruding from the trunk like a man emerging through a waterfall. The face was handsome, bearded, vain. The face of Victor Archimagus, its eyes empty, alien.

It boomed, "I am here."

Simon had always found the thing repugnant. It was just like Victor to leave behind this ghost, this ponderous, unfeeling simulacrum to ensure that his unhealthy domination of his family continued on down through the ages.

Bernard called, "I am Bernard Archimagus, and this is my lawful wife, Elizabeth. We wish to thank you, great wizard, for all you've done and continue to do for your family." Bernard continued in this vein, praising Victor's multifarious accomplishments and abiding generosity. Simon glanced across the aisle, to where the descendants of Atherton were seated, and sought Meredith's face, but she was blocked from view.

Finally Bernard took the infant from Elizabeth's arms, held him aloft, and cried, "I present to you, noble Victor, my firstborn son, Sebastian Archimagus. May he never fail to please you."

For a long moment Victor's face seemed to regard the child, though really it was impossible to say where those empty eyes were staring. Finally the face said, "I am well pleased."

Then the whole tree began to shudder. Leaves shaken loose fell across the crowd like rain. Victor's eyes glowed with an otherworldly light. The base of the tree bulged, as if a geyser were filling it from below, and this effect traveled up the trunk to the great V that marked the division between Franklin and Atherton, and from there followed the Franklin branch, causing it to enlarge. The magic flowed up branch after branch, tracing the ancestry of Sebastian, and everywhere it passed it was making the rooms within more spacious and extravagant, Simon knew. Finally the magic reached the branch that had grown on the day of Bernard's own presentation ceremony, and from that branch a new growth sprouted forth, lengthening and thickening and blooming with windows and balconies and bright green leaves, all in the space of a minute. The crowd oohed and aahed.

The children of Franklin burst into raucous cheers. The polite applause from the children of Atherton was noticeably more subdued.

The celebration went on well into evening, and when it was over Simon followed his relatives back to the tree. They shuffled through the main gates and into the great hall—a vast, cavernous space filled with tables and benches, the far wall of which was occupied by a shrine to Victor. From there the families divided, descendants of Franklin to the right, descendants of Atherton to the left, climbing two giant staircases that spiraled around each other and which led back to their respective branches. Simon made his way up to his own branch and his old chambers, which as Bernard had promised had been kept exactly as he'd left them.

Then Simon lay in bed, staring at the ceiling. After a time, he slept.

He was woken by a frantic pounding at his door. He rolled over and squinted at the window, and saw that it was morning. He crawled from bed and opened the door. In the hallway stood his sandy-haired young cousin, Garrett, who said, alarmed, "The baby. Sebastian. He's sick."

Garrett went scurrying off. Simon dressed and made his way down into the rooms of his late father, then up again into Bernard's section of the tree. A newly-created archway framed the stairs that led to Sebastian's branch.

Simon knocked on a door, which was then pulled aside, revealing Bernard's face, upon which hope and worry warred. "Simon," he said. "Come in."

Simon entered the chamber, where Elizabeth sat in a rocking chair, clutching her son.

"A fever," Bernard explained. "There were so many people around yesterday, all wanting to hold him. Uncle Reginald sneezed on him, I think. I'm sure it's nothing, but . . . "

Simon nodded. He greeted Elizabeth, then took a look at Sebastian, who seemed pale.

A short time later Garrett returned with Simon's mother in tow. When she saw the baby, she froze. She was silent a long time before saying, "It'll be all right. But he should have healing. Simon dear, I don't suppose your talents at the gentler side of magic have improved any these past years?"

"Sorry, no," he said.

Garrett piped up, "I'll get Clara."

"Wait," said Simon's mother. "No. Fetch us Meredith, please."

Bernard was shocked. "Mother," he grumbled, "we don't need any help from *her*."

Simon's mother said, "She's a powerful healer, far more so than Clara, and everyone knows it. She's here now. We must take advantage of this opportunity." She waved at Garrett and said, "Go."

He went, and returned an hour later with Meredith. All eyes were upon her as she entered, crossed the room to Elizabeth, and said, "I'm sorry to hear that Sebastian is unwell. I'll do what I can. Here." She held out her arms.

Reluctantly, Elizabeth handed over the child.

As soon as Meredith touched him he began to cry. She held him to her chest and closed her eyes, then stood like that for a minute, murmuring, as Sebastian wailed. Elizabeth shot a worried look at Bernard, who glared at Meredith.

Finally Meredith looked up. "There. All done." She returned the baby to Elizabeth.

"Thank you," Simon's mother said quietly.

Meredith departed, meeting Simon's gaze briefly as she closed the door behind her.

Two days passed, and Sebastian continued to sicken, but there was nothing more to be done, as any further healing magic would simply disrupt the operation of Meredith's more powerful spell. That evening Bernard came to Simon's chambers and said, "Simon, I need you. Elizabeth has taken Sebastian up into his branch, and she refuses to come out."

They made their way through the arch and into the newly-grown section of the tree. The halls were dim and deserted, and as they climbed Simon could hear wind rustling the leaves outside, as well as, more faintly, the sound of a woman sobbing. In an empty room they found Elizabeth sitting on the floor in the corner, holding Sebastian. Darkness hid her face.

Bernard knelt beside her. "Darling, please. Come downstairs."

"No," she said.

Bernard turned to Simon, who knelt beside her too and said, "Elizabeth, listen to me. We can't stay here. If he dies—"

"He won't!" she cried.

Simon said, "If the branch—"

She shook her head. "I don't care."

"Well, I do," Simon said. "Come on, give him here." He took hold of Sebastian and lifted him from her limp arms. She trembled.

Bernard helped her to her feet, then held her as he guided her down the stairs, and Simon walked beside them, carrying the baby.

When they crossed the threshhold into Bernard's section of the tree, Simon breathed easier. If a male line of the Archimagus family died out, the corresponding branches of Victor's tree withered as well, which could be dangerous for anyone inhabiting them. Thus branches that seemed imperiled were generally abandoned.

Simon sat on a sofa with the baby while Bernard put Elizabeth to bed. When Bernard emerged, he said, "It's strange, isn't it?"

"What?" Simon said.

"She's such a great healer, but she can't even help a sick child?"

"You think her talents are exaggerated?"

Bernard was grim. "Or she's not really exercising them on our behalf."

"No. I won't believe that, not of Meredith. I know her."

"You *knew* her," Bernard said. "People change."

Simon sighed. "Get some rest. You're exhausted." He nodded at the child in his arms. "I'll watch him. He'll be fine."

Bernard hesitated. Then: "All right. Goodnight." He walked over and kissed Sebastian's forehead.

"Goodnight," Simon said.

Two nights later, as Simon lay in bed reading, he heard a rustle from his desk. He glanced up and saw one of his pens jittering. Then the quill swept up into the air, stabbed itself into an inkpot, and began a wobbly dance across one of his parchments. Simon tossed aside his book and hurried over.

The quill lay itself down beside a few words of Meredith's flowery script: *I have to see you.*

Simon's heart leapt. He snatched up the pen and scrawled, *Meet me in the garden*, then set the pen down.

A moment later it came to life again, and wrote, *I will.*

So down into the trunk of the tree he went, and out the postern gate, and down the hillside, where the long grasses swayed, and across the bridge over the gurgling stream, to the garden where he and Meredith had played as children, and where they'd met in secret, later, on nights like this. The place was guarded by a high stone wall from which the ivy dangled, and the gates were all rusted partway open, and inside were cobbled walks that wound among the trees like the paths of drunken men, and shallow ponds ringed with lily pads, and hedge mazes into which a boy and girl could vanish together and not be found by anyone.

He waited for her, by the marble bench beside the statue of the sad old lion, who was missing one ear, and it made Simon think of that other night, years ago. This time she came though, her dark form slipping along the pathway like a ghost. Simon hurried to her, and took her in his arms. "I missed you," he whispered.

"I missed you too," she said, into his shoulder.

He held her like that for a long time, there beneath the moon.

Then he said, "Come away with me."

She drew back, staring. "What?"

"Did you ever love me?" he asked.

"Yes."

"Then come away with me. I was right, wasn't I? We belong together. Not with them. No good will come of staying here."

"Simon." She pulled away, and sat down on the bench. "No. It's impossible."

"Why?" he said.

"I told you—"

"Yes." He sat down beside her. "You told me. That you'd been promised to another. Well, no longer."

"And that Victor would not be pleased—"

"But I have my own tree now," he said, "so we wouldn't—"

"And our families," she said finally.

"We can live without them. I've shown that, haven't I? If you ever loved me—"

She looked away.

"Meredith," he pleaded. "Forget them. We'll start our own family, and they'll be the best damn wizards anyone's ever—"

"I'm sorry," she said. "Simon. I'm not like you. I can't just walk away and never look back."

He stood, and scowled into the shadows.

After a time, she said, "Simon, we need to talk. About these rumors."

"What rumors?" he said.

"That I'm only pretending to heal Sebastian." She was indignant. "Or even that I put a curse on him. It's absurd."

Simon glared. "This is why you wanted to see me?"

"It's one reason," she said. "Simon, this is important. Things are getting out of hand. Your family's trying to incite a—"

"*My* family?" he said. "Your brother—"

"Malcolm," she said cooly, "is a boor. A childish one. Ignore him. The only person he's a danger to is himself. It's your side that's the threat. That's another reason I can't just run away with you, even if I wanted to."

Simon chuckled. "So you're all that stands in the way of the mighty Franklin clan? You must think pretty highly of yourself."

"Well, maybe I do," she said.

"And yet Sebastian sickens every day."

"Which is sad," she said, "but no fault of mine. Sometimes people get better and sometimes they don't. You know that."

"Or maybe you're not as powerful as you let on."

She stood. "Keep pushing me, Simon, and we'll see how powerful I am."

He laughed again. "Is that a threat? You think *you* could beat *me*?"

"I know I could."

Simon said, "I'm the one who unraveled the greatest spell of Victor Archimagus."

"Which is impressive," Meredith said acidly. "Impressive that you'd waste so many years trying to match the egomania of a man you despise. But while you were busy with your precious tree, *I* was busy with all the other areas of study that I'm sure you neglected, including battle magic, so don't take me on, Simon. It'll be no contest."

He said loudly, "I made my 'precious' tree for you. For us. So that someday—"

"Well I never asked you to!"

They stood there in the darkness, angry.

Then she said, "I think this conversation is over." She added, more gently, "Rein them in, Simon. For both our sakes. If *you* ever loved *me*, rein them in."

She turned and strode off down the path, flanked by rows of poplars that stood like sentinels. And beyond her the garden wall, and beyond that the crest of the hill, over which loomed the long black limbs of Victor's tree.

When she was gone, Simon remembered that other night, long ago.

"You can't marry him," he'd told her. "It won't work out. You'll never be happy. Meredith, you don't have to go through with this, it's not too late. Come away with me, now."

And she'd told him all the reasons why not, and asked him where they'd go.

"I don't know," he'd said. "We'll figure something out." And when she'd refused again he'd said, "Well, I'm leaving. Tonight. No matter what. You can come with me or not. I'll pack some things and wait for you in the garden, in case you change your mind."

And he'd stood there, by the marble bench, watching her window, as the night grew chill. He'd watched her lights go out, and then, later, when he knew she hadn't changed her mind, he'd walked away, and never looked back.

And now he strode down gravel paths, thinking over her reasons—again. In the end only one of them really mattered. Family. As he slipped out the garden gate, he paused to glare up at Victor's tree.

Just then there came a great cracking sound that echoed across the violet sky, and one of those branches tore free and tumbled down, plummeting to the earth.

The following afternoon the Archimagus family gathered at their private cemetery on a hill overlooking Victor's tree. The sky was a solid gray slate, the air thick and oppressive. A few words were said. Elizabeth wept ceaselessly.

Simon avoided eye contact with Meredith, who was now the focus of near-unanimous suspicion from the children of Franklin. She kept her face devoid of expression. At one point during the service, from the back of the crowd there came a single soft guffaw, perhaps in response to some whispered remark. Bernard glanced back over his shoulder, in order to identify the offender. Simon didn't have to look, he knew the voice. Malcolm.

Bernard's eyes were full of a cold, dead rage, and for a moment Simon half thought—and in that instant half hoped—that Bernard would go tearing through the crowd and disembowel Malcolm. But after a few seconds Bernard hunched his shoulders and turned back toward the grave of his son.

The next week was stiflingly hot. Simon slept on a blanket on his balcony, and even so he awoke constantly, bathed in sweat. During the day most members of the Archimagus family congregated in the great hall, where the air was cooler, but even that expansive space began to feel cramped, as the children of Franklin and the children of Atherton vied for tables, jostled one another, and exchanged words.

One afternoon there came a hurried knocking at Simon's door. He opened it to find Garrett standing there, panting. The boy said, "It's Malcolm. You have to come. Now."

Simon strapped on his sword, and followed Garrett down the stairs.

When Simon arrived in the great hall, he saw Malcolm's gang lounging at their accustomed tables, which were covered with an assortment of potted plants.

Nearby stood a knot of young men from among the descendants of Franklin, including Bernard, who were glaring at Malcolm and his cousins and conferring angrily. The rest of the crowd, several dozen relatives, were evenly split between the children of Franklin and the children of Atherton, and the two sides eyed each other with open hostility. Simon hurried forward.

"Simon!" called Malcolm then, with false cheer. "There you are. Come take a look at this."

Simon approached, wary.

Malcolm nodded to the plant in his hand. "I've discovered the most delightful diversion, the perfect way to pass a hot summer's day. An acquaintance of mine delivered these last night. They're all the rage in certain foreign climes, I'm told."

Simon frowned at the plant, which was some sort of miniature tree with spindly limbs and dense, brushy foliage.

Malcolm held up a large knife. "Here's how it works. You shape these trees into the most elegant forms simply by removing branches you find undesirable. So, take this one here." He poised his blade below one of the tree's tiny branches. "I don't like it at all."

He flicked his wrist and the branch fluttered down, landing on the toe of his boot. He kicked the branch aside onto the floor.

Bernard began hurling curses. A few of his relatives herded him away, murmuring at him to just ignore Malcolm, who affected nonchalance as he leaned back against the table and remarked, "I guess he's not a fan." He returned his gaze to Simon and held up the knife again. "How about you, Simon? Want to give it a go?"

"No thanks," Simon said.

"Pity." Malcolm slipped the knife back into his belt sheath. "It's quite fun."

"Well, I think you've had enough fun for one day," Simon said. "So why don't you take your little tree, and your little friends here, and move along. Now."

Malcolm smiled. "No," he said airily, crossing one leg over the other, "I'm comfortable here."

"But here's the thing," Simon said, sketching a diagram in the air. "I can make you rather *un*comfortable." Pale blue smoke rose from his fingers. He was bluffing though. He had no intention of unleashing magic in a situation like this.

And Malcolm knew it. He laughed. "You think you're so scary. That's why your mother summoned you back here, to frighten us. But you and I both know that if you harm me, my sister will destroy you."

Everyone in the room was watching. Malcolm stood up, so that he was eye to eye with Simon, and hissed, "It's you who's afraid. Because she's good. The best wizard in the family. Too good for you."

That struck a nerve, more than Malcolm could know, and Simon felt a hot rush of fury.

Malcolm called to the assembled children of Atherton, "You're all afraid of him! Why? What's he going to do?" He shoved Simon in the chest, forcing him back a few steps. "Huh? What're you going to do?"

Simon glared, smoldering.

"Ha," Malcolm said, turning away. "You see—"

Simon launched himself at Malcolm, tackling him to the ground.

The room erupted with shouts, as Simon straddled Malcolm and belted him several times across the jaw. Malcolm clawed for Simon's face, but Simon swept those arms aside and punched him again.

Then Malcolm went for his knife.

He drew it from its sheath and waved the blade at Simon, who grabbed Malcolm's wrist and slammed it against the floor, once, twice, to jar the weapon loose.

Then Simon was flung aside, onto his back, by Bernard, who had a rapier in his hand. As Simon watched, Bernard drew back the sword, then skewered Malcolm where he lay.

No! Simon thought.

He rolled to his feet. Weapons were being drawn all around him.

"Wait!" he cried. "Stop!"

But it was too late. The children of Franklin and the children of Atherton came together in a clash of steel. Malcolm's gang rushed Bernard, who backed off, slashing at the air to keep them at bay. Simon drew his own sword and leapt to help. Malcolm, hacking up blood, was dragged away from the fighting by one of his cousins, Nathan—a stolid young man who for whatever reason had always been fiercely loyal to Malcolm.

Simon ducked and cut and parried. He didn't use magic—he might need all the magic he could muster to defend himself against Meredith, he knew—but some of his relatives let loose with spells, and there were occasional flashes of light and small explosions. The whole chamber convulsed with violence, generations' worth of rivalry and mistrust unleashed at last, there in front of the shrine to Victor Archimagus. Soon Simon's blade was slick with blood, his hand sticky with it. Faces appeared before him—angry faces, faces he remembered from childhood, faces he hadn't spoken to in years, and he thrust his sword at them.

Sometimes one of the descendants of Franklin fell—Simon saw Garrett cut down by one of Meredith's uncles—but more often the casualties were among the descendants of Atherton, and soon many of them lay strewn across the floor, trod on or tripped over by the remaining fighters. Then the children of Atherton broke and ran, retreating pell-mell up the great staircase that led to their branch.

Meredith, Simon thought. He had to find her, though whether to protect her from his family or to protect his family from her he couldn't say.

He followed along as the children of Franklin pursued the children of Atherton up into their branches, many of which had now withered and fallen, with no male heirs left to sustain them, and Simon saw one of Meredith's cousins cornered and slain while pounding at a solid wall that had been an archway just moments before. There was nowhere for the children of Atherton to go except higher into the tree, no way for them to escape except a doomed leap from a window or balcony.

As Simon hurried through the chambers of Meredith's grandfather, he heard a handful of men from among the children of Franklin shouting, "This way! They're up here," and the men went charging through an archway and up the stairs into the branch of Meredith's uncle Kenneth, Nathan's father. Simon followed.

He caught up with the men just as they burst into a large parlor, at the far end of which stood a group of people clustered around Meredith, who knelt over the prone form of Malcolm, her hands pressed to his gory chest as she attempted to heal him. Meredith's mother was there, and a few cousins by way of her uncle Fletcher, and a few other relatives, many of them holding swords. Nathan stood by a window, gazing out. "No!" he cried. "No! It's falling! It's . . . it's gone."

Meredith sagged. Malcolm's branch had withered. He was dead.

Nathan glanced toward Simon, then drew a sword and moved to Meredith's side. Simon eyed him. Nathan's brothers had been slain in the battle downstairs. And his father. Simon had seen the bodies.

Meredith stood then, turning to regard Simon. She was tall and grim and wrathful, her hair dancing on ethereal winds, arcs of lightning adorning her fingers, eyes full of a fiery hatred. Simon beheld those eyes and knew there could be no more pleading, no more chances. His dreams had died along with Malcolm.

The men beside Simon hesitated, reluctant to confront the family's most powerful sorceress, and Simon didn't blame them. "Get out of here," he told them. "Go. I'll handle her."

The men exchanged glances, then fled.

Meredith strode forward, deathly silent. *Don't take me on*, she'd told him. *It'll be no contest.* He was terribly afraid that she'd been right.

She halted in the center of the room, her arms outspread. "I warned you, Simon." Her voice trembled with rage. "You brought this on yourself—so help you. You think you can face me? Well, here I am. Take your best shot. You won't get another."

One shot at this, Simon thought.

He thrust his palm at her, hurling from it a double dozen points of magical light, which spread apart as they flew, growing larger and transforming into spinning daggers, so that she faced an incoming wall of lethal blades.

Meredith raised her hands, summoning a glowing ghostly shield. Daggers that struck it vaporized, and the rest sped past her. She regarded Simon almost with pity then.

He turned and bolted back down the stairs.

"Coward!" someone cried.

And Simon *was* afraid. But not of Meredith, not then, as he vaulted the steps three at a time.

For some of the daggers that had passed her by had impaled themselves in Nathan, including one that had caught him full in the throat. Meredith would see this, and would guess that he'd been the intended target after all, and would wonder after the fate of his father and brothers. And then she'd realize . . .

Simon ran. The branch around him shuddered, the wood fading, becoming dry, gray, pitted. Through the windows he saw leaves turn brown and blow away in great dark clouds.

He neared the archway. A rift appeared in the ceiling ahead, spilling down rays of sunlight between him and safety. As the floor gave way he leapt across the threshold.

A deafening crack. He turned and saw Meredith, back up the tunnel, dashing toward him, dragging her mother by the hand, other relatives running at her side, as the branch plunged from view.

Simon rushed forward, to see what had become of them. But even as he tried to peer out, the archway, now framing blue sky, was absorbed back into the tree, and wood grew to seal the breach, and the portal shrank and shrank, like an eye closing itself, forever.

A few days later the Archimagus family gathered at their private cemetery to hold a mass burial. The battle had been distinctly one-sided, and the children of Atherton were now a much smaller contingent. They stood in silence, looking weak and frightened. As per the terms of their surrender, they'd accepted full responsibility for the whole unpleasant affair, had handed over all their weapons and valuables, and would soon be exiled. Simon wondered where they'd go. They'd lived their whole lives in Victor's tree. Simon couldn't picture them anywhere else.

After the ceremony, as people drifted off, Simon lingered over the grave marker that read MEREDITH WYLAND.

His mother sidled up beside him and said, "I knew you could beat her."

He was silent.

She added, "We're safe now. Thanks to you."

He glanced back over his shoulder at Victor's tree, its two halves now absurdly unbalanced. The sun shone between its branches, making Simon squint.

His mother said, "I just hope now you'll be happy." She began to walk away.

He called after her, "What does *that* mean?"

She paused and looked at him, then at the grave marker. "You know, Simon, that dreadful girl always had a most unwholesome influence on you. That's all."

He said slowly, "Mother, I have a terrible intuition that much of what has transpired of late has done so according to some design of yours."

"Of mine, dear?" She laughed. "Oh Simon, you always were such a brooding, mistrustful child. I blame myself. Silly, I know."

She turned away again. He was about to say more when there came a horrendous creaking noise that filled the valley. As the Archimagus family watched, aghast, Victor's tree began to list to the right, from the weight of so many Franklin branches. Then the tree toppled, slamming to the ground, dashing those branches to pieces and raising up a massive plume of dust that could be seen for miles.

Simon Archimagus galloped his horse along a moonlit ridge. He'd been going on more and more of these solitary rides lately. He liked the calm, the peace. When his horse ran, its hoofbeats and the wind sometimes drowned out his thoughts, for a time.

Finally he rode back to his tree—the tree he'd thought to one day share with Meredith and the children they would have together. Sometimes, on nights like this, as his horse sprinted through the dark, reality seemed less certain, and he would imagine that it had all been a mistake, that she'd survived somehow, secretly, and would come to him. Or that their duel had been just a terrible nightmare, and that his dreams of a life with her were the true state of things.

He passed through the gate, beneath the portcullis of thorn branches, and into the stables.

He made his way up the staircase.

"Dad!" called a boy's voice. "Dad!"

Simon wandered into the kitchen. A blond boy poked his head through the door and said, "Oh, hi Simon. Have you seen my dad?"

"No," Simon said. "I just got back. Is something wrong?"

The boy scowled. "Jessica took my horse and she won't give it back."

"Your . . . horse?"

"My toy horse," the boy said. "Dad gave it to me, and I *told* her not to touch it, but she took it and now she won't give it back, even though it's mine."

Simon said, "Well, maybe you should just—"

"I should kill her," said the boy, without irony. "Like you killed that evil witch Meredith."

Simon stared. "Look, Brian—"

"I'm Marcus," the boy said.

"Marcus." Simon sighed. "Let's go find your dad, okay?"

The boy trailed Simon through halls and up stairs. Books and toys were scattered about. Sometimes children barrelled past, heedless.

Simon found the adults up at the top of the tree, lounging on the balcony. Bernard was there, and Elizabeth, and Simon's other brothers, and a few other relatives. *It's only temporary*, Bernard had promised, *just until we can find someplace else to live.* But they showed no signs of moving on, and had even begun hinting to Simon that he should command his tree to grow larger, to better accommodate the children.

Simon's mother stepped from the shadows, holding a glass of wine. She beamed at all her sons, together under one roof again, at last.

"Oh, Simon. There you are," she said brightly. "Welcome home."

SUSANNA CLARKE is the best-selling author of the novel *Jonathan Strange & Mr. Norrell*, which won the Hugo, Locus, Mythopoeic, and World Fantasy awards. She has also written several short stories, which have appeared in *The New York Times*, *The Magazine of Fantasy & Science Fiction*, and on the BBC's *7th Dimension* radio program, as well as in anthologies *Starlight* (Vols. 1-3); *The Year's Best Fantasy & Horror*; *Black Swan, White Raven*; *Black Heart, Ivory Bones*; and *Sandman: The Book of Dreams*. Most of these tales have been collected in *The Ladies of Grace Adieu and Other Stories*. Clarke currently resides in Cambridge with her partner, fellow writer Colin Greenland.

It's good to be the king. You've got it all—castles, servants, feasts, horses, clothes, jewels, and power. Power most of all. You command armies, your word is law, and everyone kneels and calls you "your majesty." It's wonderful.

Wizards have power too, and if you're the most powerful sorcerer in the land, someone who can transform a pig into fish with a wave of your hand, well, that's a pretty darned good place to be as well. So who's more powerful? The king or a wizard?

And what if the king of the nation and the most powerful wizard in the realm are one and the same person? Wow, now that's power. Nobody can stand against you, right?

Well, before you get too cocky it's always good to remember that no matter how lofty your position may seem, there are always greater powers out there. Even a wizard lord must bow before the hosts of heaven, and all the powers of a sorcerer king may prove futile against the power of pure pig-headed stubbornness. (And the humble hero of our next tale is very cantankerous and very, very stubborn.) Wizards of the world take warning.

John Uskglass and the Cumbrian Charcoal Burner
Susanna Clarke

This retelling of a popular Northern English folktale is taken from *A Child's History of the Raven King* by John Waterbury, Lord Portishead. It bears similarities to other old stories in which a great ruler is outwitted by one of his humblest subjects and, because of this, many scholars have argued that it has no historical basis.

Many summers ago in a clearing in a wood in Cumbria there lived a Charcoal Burner. He was a very poor man. His clothes were ragged and he was generally sooty and dirty. He had no wife or children, and his only companion was a small pig called Blakeman. Most of the time he stayed in the clearing which contained just two things: an earth-covered stack of smouldering charcoal and a but built of sticks and pieces of turf. But in spite of all this he was a cheerful soul—as before unless crossed in any way.

One bright summer's morning a stag ran into the clearing. After the stag came a large pack of hunting dogs, and after the dogs came a crowd of horsemen with bows and arrows. For some moments nothing could be seen but a great confusion of baying dogs, sounding horns and thundering hooves. Then, as quickly as they had come, the huntsmen disappeared among the trees at the far end of the clearing—all but one man.

The Charcoal Burner looked around. His grass was churned to mud; not a stick of his but remained standing; and his neat stack of charcoal was half-dismantled and fires were bursting forth from it. In a blaze of fury he turned upon the remaining huntsman and began to heap upon the man's head every insult he had ever heard.

But the huntsman had problems of his own. The reason that he had not ridden off with the others was that Blakeman was running, this way and that, beneath his horse's hooves, squealing all the while. Try as he might, the huntsman could not get free of him. The huntsman was very finely dressed in black, with boots of soft black leather and a jewelled harness. He was in fact John Uskglass (otherwise called the Raven King), King of Northern England and parts of Faerie, and the greatest magician that ever lived. But the Charcoal Burner (whose knowledge of events outside the woodland clearing was very imperfect) guessed nothing of this.

He only knew that the man would not answer him and this
than ever. "Say something!" he cried.

A stream ran through the clearing. John Uskglass glanc
Blakeman running about beneath his horse's hooves. He flung
Blakeman was transformed into a salmon. The salmon leapt throug
the brook and swam away. Then John Uskglass rode off.

The Charcoal Burner stared after him. "Well, now what am I going t
said.

He extinguished the fires in the clearing and he repaired the stack of cha
best he could. But a stack of charcoal that has been trampled over by hound
horses cannot be made to look the same as one that has never received such inju
and it hurt the Charcoal Burner's eyes to look at such a botched, broken thing.

He went down to Furness Abbey to ask the monks to give him some supper
because his own supper had been trodden into the dirt. When he reached the
Abbey he inquired for the Almoner whose task it is to give food and clothes to
the poor. The Almoner greeted him in a kindly manner and gave him a beautiful
round cheese and a warm blanket and asked what had happened to make his face
so long and sad.

So the Charcoal Burner told him; but the Charcoal Burner was not much
practised in the art of giving clear accounts of complicated events. For example
he spoke at great length about the huntsman who had got left behind, but he
made no mention of the man's fine clothes or the jewelled rings on his fingers,
so the Almoner had no suspicion that it might be the King. In fact the Charcoal
Burner called him "a black man" so that the Almoner imagined he meant a dirty
man—just such another one as himself.

The Almoner was all sympathy. "So poor Blakeman is a salmon now, is he?" he
said. "If I were you, I would go and have a word with Saint Kentigern. I am sure
he will help you. He knows all about salmon."

"Saint Kentigern, you say? And where will I find such a useful person?" asked
the Charcoal Burner eagerly.

"He has a church in Grizedale. That is the road over there."

So the Charcoal Burner walked to Grizedale, and when he came to the church
he went inside and banged on the walls and bawled out Saint Kentigern's name,
until Saint Kentigern looked out of Heaven and asked what the matter was.

Immediately the Charcoal Burner began a long indignant speech describing
the injuries that had been done to him, and in particular the part played by the
solitary huntsman.

"Well," said Saint Kentigern, cheerfully. "Let me see what I can do. Saints,
such as me, ought always to listen attentively to the prayers of poor, dirty, ragged

No matter how offensively those prayers are phrased. You are

said the Charcoal Burner, who was rather flattered to hear this.

entigern reached down from Heaven, put his hand into the church

ed out a salmon. He shook the salmon a little and the next moment

Blakeman, as dirty and clever as ever.

Charcoal Burner laughed and clapped his hands. He tried to embrace

n but Blakeman just ran about, squealing, with his customary energy.

ere," said Saint Kentigern, looking down on this pleasant scene with some

t. "I am glad I was able to answer your prayer.

Oh, but you have not!" declared the Charcoal Burner. "You must punish my

icked enemy!"

Then Saint Kentigern frowned a little and explained how one ought to forgive one's enemies. But the Charcoal Burner had never practised Christian forgiveness before and he was not in a mood to begin now. "Let Blencathra fall on his head!" he cried with his eyes ablaze and his fists held high. (Blencathra is a high hill some miles to the north of Grizedale.)

"Well, no," said Saint Kentigern diplomatically. "I really cannot do that. But I think you said this man was a hunter? Perhaps the loss of a day's sport will teach him to treat his neighbours with more respect."

The moment that Saint Kentigern said these words John Uskglass (who was still hunting), tumbled down from his horse and into a cleft in some rocks. He tried to climb out but found that he was held there by some mysterious power. He tried to do some magic to counter it, but the magic did not work. The rocks and earth of England loved John Uskglass well. They would always wish to help him if they could, but this power—whatever it was—was something they respected even more.

He remained in the cleft all day and all night, until he was thoroughly cold, wet and miserable. At dawn the unknown power suddenly released him—why, he could not tell. He climbed out, found his horse and rode back to his castle at Carlisle.

"Where have you been?" asked William of Lanchester. "We expected you yesterday."

Now John Uskglass did not want any one to know that there might be a magician in England more powerful than himself. So he thought for a moment. "France," he said.

"France!" William of Lanchester looked surprised. "And did you see the King? What did he say? Are they planning new wars?"

John Uskglass gave some vague, mystical and magician-like reply. Then he went up to his room and sat down upon the floor by his silver dish of water. Then he spoke to Persons of Great Importance (such as the West Wind or the Stars) and asked them to tell him who had caused him to be thrown into the cleft. Into his dish came a vision of the Charcoal Burner.

John Uskglass called for his horse and his dogs, and he rode to the clearing in the wood.

Meanwhile the Charcoal Burner was toasting some of the cheese the Almoner had given him. Then he went to look for Blakeman, because there were few things in the world that Blakeman liked as much as toasted cheese.

While he was gone John Uskglass arrived with his dogs. He looked around at the clearing for some clue as to what had happened. He wondered why a great and dangerous magician would chose to live in a wood and earn his living as a charcoal burner. His eye fell upon the toasted cheese.

Now toasted cheese is a temptation few men can resist, be they charcoal burners or kings. John Uskglass reasoned thus: all of Cumbria belonged to him—therefore this wood belonged to him—therefore this toasted cheese belonged to him. So he sat down and ate it, allowing his dogs to lick his fingers when he was done.

At that moment the Charcoal Burner returned. He stared at John Uskglass and at the empty green leaves where his toasted cheese had been. "You!" he cried. "It is you! You ate my dinner!" He took hold of John Uskglass and shook him hard. "Why? Why do you these things?"

John Uskglass said not a word. (He felt himself to be at something of a disadvantage.) He shook himself free from the Charcoal Burner's grasp, mounted upon his horse and rode out of the clearing.

The Charcoal Burner went down to Furness Abbey again. "That wicked man came back and ate my toasted cheese!" he told the Almoner.

The Almoner shook his head sadly at the sinfulness of the world. "Have some more cheese," he offered. "And perhaps some bread to go with it?"

"Which saint is it that looks after cheeses?" demanded the Charcoal Burner.

The Almoner thought for a moment. "That would be Saint Bridget," he said.

"And where will I find her ladyship?" asked the Charcoal Burner, eagerly.

"She has a church at Beckermet," replied the Almoner, and he pointed the way the Charcoal Burner ought to take.

So the Charcoal Burner walked to Beckermet and when he got to the church he banged the altar plates together and roared and made a great deal of noise until Saint Bridget looked anxiously out of Heaven and asked if there was any thing she could do for him.

The Charcoal Burner gave a long description of the injuries his silent enemy had done him.

Saint Bridget said she was sorry to hear it. "But I do not think I am the proper person to help you. I look after milkmaids and dairymen. I encourage the butter to come and the cheeses to ripen. I have nothing to do with cheese that has been eaten by the wrong person. Saint Nicholas looks after thieves and stolen property. Or there is Saint Alexander of Comana who loves Charcoal Burners. Perhaps," she added hopefully, "you would like to pray to one of them?"

The Charcoal Burner declined to take an interest in the persons she mentioned. "Poor, ragged, dirty men like me are your special care!" he insisted. "Do a miracle!"

"But perhaps," said Saint Bridget, "this man does not mean to offend you by his silence. Have you considered that he may be mute?"

"Oh, no! I saw him speak to his dogs. They wagged their tails in delight to hear his voice. Saint, do your work! Let Blencathra fall on his head!"

Saint Bridget sighed. "No, no, we cannot do that; but certainly he is wrong to steal your dinner. Perhaps it might be as well to teach him a lesson. Just a small one."

At that moment John Uskglass and his court were preparing to go hunting. A cow wandered into the stable-yard. It ambled up to where John Uskglass stood by his horse and began to preach him a sermon in Latin on the wickedness of stealing. Then his horse turned its head and told him solemnly that it quite agreed with the cow and that he should pay good attention to what the cow said.

All the courtiers and the servants in the stable-yard fell silent and stared at the scene. Nothing like this had ever happened before.

"This is magic!" declared William of Lanchester. "But who would dare . . . ?"

"I did it myself," said John Uskglass quickly.

"Really?" said William. "Why?"

There was a pause. "To help me contemplate my sins and errors," said John Uskglass at last, "as a Christian should from time to time."

"But stealing is not a sin of yours! So why . . . ?"

"Good God, William!" cried John Uskglass. "Must you ask so many questions? I shall not hunt today!"

He hurried away to the rose garden to escape the horse and the cow. But the roses turned their red-and-white faces towards him and spoke at length about his duty to the poor; and some of the more ill-natured flowers hissed, "Thief! Thief!" He shut his eyes and put his fingers in his ears, but his dogs came and found him and pushed their noses in his face and told him how very, very disappointed they were in him. So he went and hid in a bare little room at the top of the castle. But all that day the stones of the walls loudly debated the various passages in the Bible that condemn stealing.

John Uskglass had no need to inquire who had done this (the cow, horse, dogs, stones and roses had all made particular mention of toasted cheese); and he was determined to discover who this strange magician was and what he wanted. He decided to employ that most magical of all creatures—the raven. An hour later a thousand or so ravens were despatched in a flock so dense that it was as if a black mountain were flying through the summer sky. When they arrived at the Charcoal Burner's clearing, they filled every part of it with a tumult of black wings. The leaves were swept from the trees, and the Charcoal Burner and Blakeman were knocked to the ground and battered about. The ravens searched the Charcoal Burner's memories and dreams for evidence of magic. Just to be on the safe side, they searched Blakeman's memories and dreams too. The ravens looked to see what man and pig had thought when they were still in their mothers' wombs; and they looked to see what both would do when finally they came to Heaven. They found not a scrap of magic anywhere.

When they were gone John Uskglass walked into the clearing with his arms folded, frowning. He was deeply disappointed at the ravens' failure.

The Charcoal Burner got slowly up from the ground and looked around in amazement. If a fire had ravaged the wood, the destruction could scarcely have been more complete. The branches were torn from the trees and a thick, black layer of raven feathers lay over everything. In a sort of ecstasy of indignation, he cried, "Tell me why you persecute me!"

But John Uskglass said not a word.

"I will make Blencathra fall on your head! I will do it! You know I can!" He jabbed his dirty finger in John Uskglass's face. "You—know—I—can!"

The next day the Charcoal Burner appeared at Furness Abbey before the sun was up. He found the Almoner, who was on his way to Prime. "He came back and shattered my wood," he told him. "He made it black and ugly!"

"What a terrible man!" said the Almoner, sympathetically.

"What saint is in charge of ravens?" demanded the Charcoal Burner.

"Ravens?" said the Almoner. "None that I know of." He thought for a moment. "Saint Oswald had a pet raven of which he was extremely fond."

"And where would I find his saintliness?"

"He has a new church at Grasmere."

So the Charcoal Burner walked to Grasmere and when he got there he shouted and banged on the walls with a candlestick.

Saint Oswald put his head out of Heaven and cried, "Do you have to shout so loud? I am not deaf! What do you want? And put down that candlestick! It was expensive!" During their holy and blessed lives Saint Kentigern and Saint Bridget had been a monk and a nun respectively; they were full of mild, saintly patience.

But Saint Oswald had been a king and a soldier, and he was a very different sort of person.

"The Almoner at Furness Abbey says you like ravens," explained the Charcoal Burner.

" 'Like' is putting it a little strong," said Saint Oswald. "There was a bird in the seventh century that used to perch on my shoulder. It pecked my ears and made them bleed."

The Charcoal Burner described how he was persecuted by the silent man.

"Well, perhaps he has reason for behaving as he does?" said Saint Oswald, sarcastically. "Have you, for example, made great big dents in his expensive candlesticks?"

The Charcoal Burner indignantly denied ever having hurt the silent man.

"Hmm," said Saint Oswald, thoughtfully. "Only kings can hunt deer, you know."

The Charcoal Burner looked blank.

"Let us see," said Saint Oswald. "A man in black clothes, with powerful magic and ravens at his command, and the hunting rights of a king. This suggests nothing to you? No apparently it does not. Well, it so happens that I think I know the person you mean. He is indeed very arrogant and perhaps the time has come to humble him a little. If I understand you aright, you are angry because he does not speak to you?"

"Yes."

"Well then, I believe I shall loosen his tongue a little."

"What sort of punishment is that?" asked the Charcoal Burner. "I want you to make Blencathra fall on his head!"

Saint Oswald made a sound of irritation. "What do you know of it?" he said. "Believe me, I am a far better judge than you of how to hurt this man!"

As Saint Oswald spoke John Uskglass began to talk in a rapid and rather excited manner. This was unusual but did not at first seem sinister. All his courtiers and servants listened politely. But minutes went by—and then hours—and he did not stop talking. He talked through dinner; he talked through mass; he talked through the night. He made prophesies, recited Bible passages, told the histories of various fairy kingdoms, gave recipes for pies. He gave away political secrets, magical secrets, infernal secrets, Divine secrets and scandalous secrets—as a result of which the Kingdom of Northern England was thrown into various political and theological crises. Thomas of Dundale and William of Lanchester begged and threatened and pleaded, but nothing they said could make the King stop talking. Eventually they were obliged to lock him in the little room at the top of the castle so that no one else could hear him. Then, since it was inconceivable that a king should talk without someone listening, they were obliged to stay with him, day after day. After exactly three days he fell silent.

Two days later he rode into the Charcoal Burner's clearing. He looked so pale and worn that the Charcoal Burner was in high hopes that Saint Oswald might have relented and pushed Blencathra on his head.

"What is that you want from me?" asked John Uskglass, warily.

"Ha!" said the Charcoal Burner with triumphant looks. "Ask my pardon for turning poor Blakeman into a fish!"

A long silence.

Then with gritted teeth, John Uskglass asked the Charcoal Burner's pardon. "Is there any thing else you want?" he asked.

"Repair all the hurts you did me!"

Immediately the Charcoal Burner's stack and hut reappeared just as they had always been; the trees were made whole again; fresh, green leaves covered their branches; and a sweet lawn of soft grass spread over the clearing.

"Any thing else?"

The Charcoal Burner closed his eyes and strained to summon up an image of unthinkable wealth. "Another pig!" he declared.

John Uskglass was beginning to suspect that he had made a miscalculation somewhere—though he could not for his life tell where it was. Nevertheless he felt confident enough to say, "I will grant you a pig—if you promise that you will tell no one who gave it to you or why."

"How can I?" said the Charcoal Burner. "I do not know who you are. Why?" he said, narrowing his eyes. "Who are you?"

"No one," said John Uskglass, quickly.

Another pig appeared, the very twin of Blakeman, and while the Charcoal Burner was exclaiming over his good fortune, John Uskglass got on his horse and rode away in a condition of the most complete mystification.

Shortly after that he returned to his capital city of Newcastle. In the next fifty or sixty years his lords and servants often reminded him of the excellent hunting to be had in Cumbria, but he was careful never to go there again until he was sure the Charcoal Burner was dead.

DELIA SHERMAN is the author of the novels *Through a Brazen Mirror, The Porcelain Dove,* and *The Fall of the Kings* (with Ellen Kushner). She has also written two novels for young adults: *Changeling* and *The Magic Mirror of the Mermaid Queen. The Freedom Maze,* a middle-grade historical novel about time travel and slavery, is coming out from Big Mouth Press in 2011. Her short fiction has appeared in *The Magazine of Fantasy & Science Fiction* and in numerous anthologies, and she has new stories forthcoming in the teen vampire anthology *Teeth* and Ellen Datlow's urban fantasy anthology *Naked City.*

Sherman has only written one other story about a wizard—the Duke of Malvoeux in *The Porcelain Dove,* who was truly pure, mad evil, and preyed on small children. This story, too, is about an evil wizard, or it is according to the eponymous wizard, anyway.

"No matter what I try to write about," Sherman says, "somehow it always, on some level or other, boils down to finding and making family outside of the ties of blood."

And this story is no exception. In it, Nick Chanticleer finds himself in need of a safe haven and finds it in an unlikely place when he becomes the accidental apprentice to a self-proclaimed evil wizard who runs a bookshop called Evil Wizard Books.

For some people there is no place more magical than a bookstore. A bookstore is bigger on the inside than the outside, because it contains entire populations and worlds that exist only between the pages of the books within.

In bookstores, we are reminded not to judge a book by its cover—advice that applies as well to the volumes on the shelves as to the people who man the stacks.

WIZARD'S APPRENTICE
DELIA SHERMAN

There's an evil wizard living in Dahoe, Maine. It says so, on the sign hanging outside his shop:

EVIL WIZARD BOOKS
Z. SMALLBONE, PROP.

His shop is also his house, which looks just like an Evil Wizard's house ought to look. It's big and tumble-down, with a porch all around it and fancy carving around the eaves. It even has a tower in which a light glows balefully red at hours when an ordinary bookseller would be asleep. There are shelves and shelves of large, moldy-smelling, dusty leather books. Bats nest in its roof and ravens and owls nest in the pines that huddle around it.

The cellar is home to a family of foxes.

And then there's the Evil Wizard himself. Zachariah Smallbone. I ask you, is that any kind of name for an ordinary bookseller? He even looks evil. His hair is an explosion of dirty grey; his beard is a yellow-white thicket; his eyes glitter behind little iron-rimmed glasses. He always wears an old-fashioned rusty black coat and a top hat, furry with age and broken down on one side.

There are rumors about what he can do. He can turn people into animals, they say: and vice versa. He can give you fleas or cramps or make your house burn down. He can hex you into splitting your own foot in two instead of a log into kindling. He can kill with a word or a look, if he has a mind.

It's no wonder, then, that the good people of Dahoe, Maine make a practice of leaving Mr. Smallbone pretty much alone. Tourists, who don't know any better, occasionally go into his shop to look for bargains. They generally come out faster than they went in, and they never come back.

Every once in a blue moon, Mr. Smallbone employs an assistant. A scruffy-haired kid will appear one day, sweeping the porch, bringing in wood, feeding the chickens. And then, after a month or a year, he'll disappear again. Some say Smallbone turns then into bats or ravens or owls or foxes, or boils their bones for his evil spells. Nobody knows and nobody asks. It's not like they're local kids, with families people know and care about. They all come from away foreign—Canada or Vermont or Massachusetts, and they probably deserve whatever happens to them. If they were good boys, they wouldn't be working for an Evil Wizard, would they?

Well, it all depends what you call a good boy.

According to his uncle, Nick Chanticleer was anything but. According to his uncle, Nick Chanticleer was a waste of three meals a day and a bed: a sneak, a liar, a lazy good-for-nothing.

To be fair to Nick's uncle, this was a fair description of Nick's behavior. But since Nick's uncle waled the tar out of him at least once a day and twice on Sundays no matter what, Nick couldn't see any reason to behave any better. He stole hot dogs from the fridge because his uncle didn't feed him enough. He stole naps behind the woodpile because his uncle worked him too hard. He lied like a rug because sometimes he could fool his uncle into hitting someone else instead of him.

Whenever he saw the chance, he ran away.

He never got very far. For someone with such low opinion of Nick's character, his uncle was strangely set on keeping him around. Family should stick together—which meant he needed Nick to do all the cooking. For a kid, Nick was a pretty good cook. He also liked having somebody around to bully. In any case, he always tracked Nick down and brought him back home.

On Nick's eleventh birthday, he ran away again. He made a bologna and Wonder Bread sandwich and wrapped it in a checked handkerchief. When his uncle was asleep, he let himself quietly out the back door and set out walking.

Nick walked all through the night, cutting through the woods and staying away from towns. At dawn, he stopped and ate half the bologna and Wonder Bread. At noon, he ate the rest. That afternoon, it began to snow.

By nightfall, Nick was freezing, soaked, and starving. Even when the moon rose, it was black dark under the trees, and full of strange rustlings and squeakings. Nick was about ready to cry from cold and fear and weariness when he saw a red light, high up and far away through the snow and bare branches.

Nick followed the light to a paved road and a mailbox and a wooden sign, its words half-veiled with snow. Beyond the sign was a drive way and a big, shadowy house lurking among the pine trees. Nick stumbled up the porch steps and banged on the heavy front door with hands numb with cold. Nothing happened for what seemed a very long time. Then the door flew open with a shriek of unoiled hinges.

"What do you want?"

It was an old man's voice, crotchety and suspicious. Given a choice, Nick would have turned right around and gone somewhere else. As it was, Nick said, "Something to eat and a place to rest. I'm about frozen solid."

The old man peered at him, dark eyes glittering behind small round glasses. "Can you read, boy?"

"What?"

"Are you deaf, or just stupid? Can you *read*?"

Nick took in the old guy's wild hair and wilder beard, his old-fashioned coat and his ridiculous top hat. None of these things made Nick willing to part with even a little piece of truth about himself. "No. I can't."

"You sure?" The old man handed him a card. "Take a look at this."

Nick took the card, turned it upside down and around, then handed it back to the old man with a shrug, very glad that he'd lied to him.

The card said:

Evil Wizard Books
Zachariah Smallbone, Proprietor
Arcana, Alchemy, Animal Transformation
Speculative Fiction
Monday-Saturday. By Chance and by Appointment

Mr. Smallbone peered at him through his round glasses. "Humph. You're letting the cold in. Close the door behind you. And leave your boots by the door. I can't have you tracking up the floor."

That was how Nick came to be the Evil Wizard's new apprentice.

At first he just thought he was doing some chores in return for food and a night's shelter. But next morning, after a breakfast of oatmeal and maple syrup, Mr. Smallbone handed him a broom and a feather duster.

"Clean the front room," he said. "Floor and books and shelves. Every speck of dirt, mind, and every trace of dust."

Nick gave it his best, but sweep as he might, the front room was no cleaner by the end of the day than it was when he started.

"That won't do at all," said the Wizard. "You'll have to try again tomorrow. You'd best cook supper—there's the makings for scrapple in the icebox."

Since the snow had given way to a breath-freezing cold snap, Nick wasn't too unhappy with this turn of events. Mr. Smallbone might be an Evil Wizard, ugly as home-made sin, and vinegar-tongued. But a bed is a bed and food is food. If things got bad, he could always run away.

After days of sweeping, the front room was, if anything, dirtier than it had been.

"I've met dogs smarter than you," Smallbone yelled. "I should turn you into one, sell you at the county fair. You must have some kind of brain, or you wouldn't be able to talk. Use it, boy. I'm losing patience."

Figuring it was only a matter of time before Mr. Smallbone started to beat up on him, Nick decided it was time to run away from Evil Wizard Books. He took some brown bread and home-cured ham from the icebox, wrapped it and his flashlight in his checked handkerchief, and crept out the back door. The driveway was shoveled, and Nick tiptoed down it, towards the main road . . .

And found himself on the porch again, going in the back door.

At dawn, Mr. Smallbone found him walking in the back door for the umpteenth time.

"Running away?" Mr. Smallbone smiled unpleasantly, his teeth like hard yellow tiles in his bushy beard.

"Nope," Nick said. "Just wanted some air."

"There's air inside the house," Mr. Smallbone said.

"Too dusty."

"If you don't like the dust," Mr. Smallbone said, "you'd best get rid of it, hadn't you?"

Desperate, Nick used his brain, as instructed. He started to look into the books he was supposed to be cleaning to see if they held any clues to the front room's stubborn dirt. He learned a number of interesting things, including how to cast fortunes by looking at a sheep's liver, but nothing that seemed useful for cleaning dirty rooms. Finally, behind a chair he'd swept under a dozen times before, he found a book called *A Witch's Manual of Practical Housekeeping.*

He stuffed it under his sweater and smuggled it upstairs to read. It told him not only that there was a spell of chaos on the front room, but how to break it. Which he did, taking a couple of days over it, and making a lot of noise with brooms and buckets to cover up his spell-casting.

When the front room sparkled, he showed it to Mr. Smallbone. "Humph," said Mr. Smallbone. "You did this all yourself, did you?"

"Yep."

"Without help?"

"Yep. Can I leave now?"

Mr. Smallbone gave Nick the evilest smile in his repertoire. "Nope. The woodbox is empty. Fill it."

Nick wasn't at all surprised when the woodbox proved as impossible to fill as the front room had been to clean. He found the solution to that problem in a volume shoved out of line with the books around it, which also taught him about carrying water in colanders and filling buckets with holes in them.

When the woodbox was full, Mr. Smallbone found other difficult tasks for Nick to do, like sorting a barrel of white and wild rice into separate jars, building a stone wall in a single day, and turning a branch of holly into a rose. By the time

Nick had mastered these skills, it was spring and he didn't want to run away any more. He wanted to keep learning magic.

It's not that he'd gotten to like Mr. Smallbone any better—Nick still though he was crazy and mean and ugly. But if Mr. Smallbone yelled and swore, there were always plenty of blankets on Nick's bed and food on his plate. And if he turned Nick into a raven or a fox when the fit took him, he never raised a hand to him.

Over Summer and Fall, Nick taught himself how to turn himself into any animal he wanted. November brought the first snows and Nick's twelfth birthday. Nick made his favorite meal of baked beans and franks to celebrate. He was just putting the pot to bake when Mr. Smallbone shuffled into the kitchen.

"I hope you made enough for three," he said. "Your uncle's on his way."

Nick closed the oven door. "I better move on, then," he said.

"Won't help," said Mr. Smallbone. "He'll always find you in the end. Blood kin are hard to hide from."

Round about dusk, Nick's uncle pulled into the driveway of Evil Wizard Books in his battered old pick-up. He marched up the front steps and banged on the door fit to knock it down. When Mr. Smallbone answered, he put a beefy hand on the old man's chest and shoved him back into the shop.

"I know Nick's here," he said. "So don't go telling me you ain't seen him."

"Wouldn't think of it," said Mr. Smallbone. "He's in the kitchen."

But all Nick's uncle saw in the warm, bright kitchen, was four identical black Labrador puppies tumbling under the wooden table.

"What in tarnation is going on here?" Nick's uncle face grew red and ugly. "Where's my nephew at?"

"One of these puppies is your nephew," said Mr. Smallbone. "If you choose the wrong puppy, you go away and don't come back. If you choose the right one, you win two more chances to recognize him. Choose right three times in a row, and you can have him."

"What's to stop me from taking him right now?"

"Me," said Mr. Smallbone. His round glasses glittered evilly; his bushy beard bristled.

"And who are you?"

"I'm the Evil Wizard." Mr. Smallbone spoke quietly, but his words echoed through the uncle's brain like a thunder-clap.

"You're a weird old geezer, is what you are," said the uncle. "I oughta turn you in to the county authorities for kidnapping. But I'll be a sport." He squatted down by the puppies and started to rough-house with them. The puppies nipped at his hands, wagging their tails and barking—all except one, which cringed away from him, whining. Nick's uncle grabbed the puppy by the scruff of the neck and it turned into a wild-looking boy with black hair and angry black eyes.

"You always was a little coward," his uncle said. But he said it to thin air, because Nick had disappeared.

"Once," Mr. Smallbone said.

Next he took Nick's uncle to a storeroom full of boxes, where four identical fat spiders sat in the centers of spun four identical fine, large webs.

"One of these spiders is your nephew."

"Yeah, yeah," said Nick's uncle. "Shut up and let me concentrate." He studied each spider and each web carefully, once and then a second time, sticking his nose right up to the webs for a better look and muttering angrily under his breath. Two of the spiders curled their legs into knots. The third ignored him.

Nick's uncle laughed nastily. "This one."

Nick appeared, crouched beneath the web, looking grim. His uncle made a grab for him, but he was gone.

"Twice," Mr. Smallbone said.

"What's next?" demanded Nick's uncle. "I ain't got all night."

Mr. Smallbone lit an oil lamp and led him outside. It was cold and dark, now, and the wind smelled of snow. In a pine tree near the woodpile was a nest of four fine young ravens, just fledged and ready to fly. The big man looked them over. Nick's uncle tried to bring his face up close, but the young ravens cawed raucously and pecked at him with their strong, yellow beaks. He jerked back, cursing, and pulled his hunting knife out of his pocket.

Three of the ravens kept cawing and pecking; the fourth hopped onto the edge of the nest and spread its wings. Nick's uncle grabbed it before it could take off.

"This one," he said.

Nick struggled to shake off his uncle's embrace. But when Mr. Smallbone gave a tiny sigh and said, "Thrice. He is yours," he stopped struggling and stood quietly, his face a mask of fury.

Nick's uncle insisted on leaving right away, refusing to stay for the baked beans. He dragged him out to his battered pick-up, threw him inside, and drove away.

The first town they came to, there was a red light. They stopped and Nick made a break for it. His uncle jerked him back inside, slammed the door, whipped out a length of rope, and tied Nick's hands and feet. They drove on, and suddenly it began to snow.

It wasn't an ordinary snowstorm—more like someone had dumped a bucket of snow onto the road in front of them, all at once. The truck swerved, skidded, and stopped with a crunch of metal. Cursing blue murder, Nick's uncle got out of the cab and went around front to see what the damage was.

Quick as thinking, Nick turned himself into a fox. A fox's paws being smaller than a boy's hands and feet, he slipped free of the rope without trouble. He leaned on the door handle with all his weight, but the handle wouldn't budge. Before he could think what to do next, his uncle opened the door. Nick nipped out under his arm and made off into the woods.

When Nick's uncle saw a young fox running away from him into the trees, he didn't waste any time wondering whether that fox was his nephew. He just grabbed his shotgun and took off after him.

It was a hectic chase through the woods in the dark and snow. If Nick had been used to being a fox, he'd have lost his uncle in no time flat. But he wasn't really comfortable running on four legs and he wasn't woodwise. He was just a twelve-year-old boy in a fox's shape, scared out of his mind and running for his life.

The world looked odd from down so low and his nose told him things he didn't understand. A real fox would have known he was running towards water. A real fox would have known the water was frozen hard enough to take his weight, but not the weight of the tall, heavy man crashing through the undergrowth behind him. A real fox would have led the man onto the pond on purpose.

Nick did it by accident.

He ran across the middle of the pond, where the ice was thin. Hearing the ice break, he skidded to a stop and turned to see his uncle disappear with a splash and a shout of fury. The big man surfaced and scrabbled at the ice, gasping and waving his shotgun. He looked mad enough to chew up steel and spit out nails.

Nick turned tail and ran. He ran until his pads were sore and bruised and he ached all over. When he slowed down, he noticed that another fox was running beside him—an older fox, a fox that smelled oddly familiar.

Nick flopped down on the ground, panting.

"Well, that was exciting," the fox that was Mr. Smallbone said dryly.

"He was going to shoot me," Nick said.

"Probably. That man hasn't got the brain of a minnow, tearing off into the dark like that. Deserves whatever happened to him, if you ask me."

Nick felt a most un-foxlike pinch of horror. "Did I kill him?"

"I doubt it," Mr. Smallbone said. "Duck pond's not more than a few feet deep. He might catch his death of cold, though."

Nick felt relief, then a new terror. "Then he'll come after me again!"

Mr. Smallbone's foxy grin was sharp. "Nope."

After a little pause, Nick decided not to ask Mr. Smallbone if he was sure about that. Mr. Smallbone was an Evil Wizard, after all, and Evil Wizards don't like it if their apprentices ask too many questions.

Mr. Smallbone stood up and shook himself. "If we want to be back by sunrise, we'd best be going. That is, if you want to come back."

Nick gave him a puzzled look.

"You won your freedom," Mr. Smallbone said. "You might want to use it to live with somebody ordinary, learning an ordinary trade."

Nick stood up and stretched his sore legs. "Nope," he said. "Can we have oatmeal and maple syrup for breakfast?"

"If you cook it," said Mr. Smallbone.

There's an Evil Wizard living in Dahoe, Maine. It says so on the sign hanging outside his shop. Sometimes tourists stop by, looking for a book on the occult or a cheap thrill.

In the kitchen, two men bend over a table strewn with books, bunches of twigs and bowls of powder. The younger one has tangled black hair and bright black eyes. He is tall and very skinny, like he's had a recent growth-spurt. The older man is old enough to be his father, but not his grandfather. He is clean-shaven and his head is bald.

The doorbell clangs. The younger man glances at the older.

"Don't look at me," says the older man. "I was the Evil Wizard last time. And my rheumatism is bothering me. You go."

"What you mean," says Nick, "is that you're half-way through a new spell and don't want to be interrupted."

"If you won't respect my authority, apprentice, I'm going to have to turn you into a cockroach."

The bell clangs again. Mr. Smallbone the older bends over his book, his hand already reaching for a pile of black dust. Nick grabs a top hat with a white wig attached to it and crams it over his black curls. He hooks a bushy beard over his ears and perches a pair of steel-rimmed glasses on his nose. Throwing on a rusty black coat, he rushes to the front room, where he hunches his shoulders and begins to shuffle. By the time he reaches the door, he looks about a hundred years old.

The door flies open with the creak of unoiled hinges.

"What do you want?" the Evil Wizard Smallbone snaps.

JEFFREY FORD is the author of several novels, including *The Physiognomy*, *The Portrait of Mrs. Charbuque*, *The Girl in the Glass*, and *The Shadow Year*. He is a prolific author of short fiction, whose work has appeared in *The Magazine of Fantasy & Science Fiction*, *SCI FICTION*, and in numerous anthologies, including my own *The Living Dead*. Three collections of his short work have been published: *The Fantasy Writer's Assistant and Other Stories*, *The Empire of Ice Cream*, and *The Drowned Life*. He is a six-time winner of the World Fantasy Award, and has also won the Nebula and Edgar awards.

Not even the most powerful wizards can shoulder life's burdens alone, which is why most of them find it expedient to employ some good help. First of all, you'll need someone with a strong back. (Wizards are typically far too busy contemplating the numinous to spend much time at the gym.) After all, someone's got to do all that stomping about under the full moon yanking up mandrake root, or digging up all those graves to supply bits and pieces for necromantic recipes, or lugging that cauldron up to the top of the tower.

It also really helps to have some sort of animal servant—a cat, a bat, a snake, whatever suits your style. It's just a fact that everyone looks more dashing with an owl perched on one shoulder, and animals are always good for doing a little spying, or passing along messages, or offering wry advice.

So, just procure yourself an animal and an assistant with a strong back, like the wizard in our next story, and you'll be good to go. Just be sure to treat them well. In the wizarding world, disgruntled employees can be a real nightmare.

The Sorcerer Minus
Jeffrey Ford

Minus was considered the most evil of all sorcerers because his sorcery was backwards. He didn't enchant. He beckoned no wretches from the dead. He commanded no shadow people, slipping along the corridors of night. His work was to seize the day by the hair, pull back its head and slit its throat to let the last glistening drop of magic pulse out and reveal the grisly carcass of reality. He then read those stark remains of the day as a soothsayer might the entrails of a chicken and offered shrewd advice to the rudely awakened about what was left.

Sorcerers feared him, knowing he could sap their art and leave them mere men and women. Wealthy families hired him to cause a conversion in a patriarch gone grandiose with the family fortune.

"He's lost touch," they'd say to Minus.

"Do you want him to see reality or your reality?" the sorcerer always asked.

"Anything you could do would be fine," they usually said and then Minus went to work with the diligence of a crooked banker. There was no detail too small to obscure.

Sorcerers usually control spirits of the dead; instead Minus had two living creatures in his employ. One was a tall, gaunt man, in a black hat and raincoat, named Bill Mug. The other was Axis, an ingenious rat, whose loyalty was perfect to the cheese in the sorcerer's hand. When Mug took the job, Minus put certain spells on him to slowly leach away all but one single drop of his self-delusion. As for Axis, Minus knew he could never rival the rat's dedication to reality. He spent a mountain of cheese to learn the rodent's secrets.

What the sorcerer prized most about Bill Mug was his slowness, not physically—rumor was he could rapidly punch a man in the face for a solid hour without stopping—but mentally. Mug liked to mull things over, scratching his chin, forgetting what it was he'd been thinking. His conclusions, when they came, were like smoke becoming nothing. It was a constant reminder to Minus that illusion begets speed because illusion begets need. The pointless maunderings of Bill Mug were a tonic to the quicksilver of private Dreamlands. When Minus needed assistance, though, he always called first for the rat.

Given but a single name at birth, Minus found himself making a concession to the times in which he lived and attached a first name to his title so that he could move easily among the magically unendowed. A popular moniker of the day was Skip. Movie stars, singers, athletes had that name, and so he became Skip Minus. He drove a fast yellow car, wore sunglasses, and was known as an easy going guy. He could mix a drink and play a hand of Whist; he could cut a rug. He could shovel snow, smoke a pipe, or recite in its entirety "The Hall of the Mountain Springs" by Miss Stattle Dees.

Underneath all of this, though, at his very core, he was an evil sorcerer. It was whispered that a fair number of his human "patients," for whom he was paid to rub their noses in harsh reality, didn't survive the treatment. Of those that perished in pursuit of stark enlightenment, ninety percent committed suicide and one curious case could have been construed as murder. The victim was a Martin Aswidth.

Aswidth was found in a garbage dump, his face caved in, beaten to a shattered, bloody pulp. The last to have seen him alive was his maid who happened upon her employer and Minus and a drab, long fellow in a hat and raincoat. It was in Aswidth's bedchamber, amid the purple curtains. Skip Minus stood at his bedside, frantically gesticulating and rhythmically grunting. The prostrate Aswidth shivered and cried, "No, no, no . . . " like a child from a nightmare. The sorcerer called over his shoulder, "Bill, come and see if you can work your magic with Mr. Aswidth. He's a stubborn fellow."

Then Minus noticed the maid, a witness to it all, and he commanded her to leave. When Aswidth's body was discovered, she did come forward to tell the police what she'd seen and heard, but she only told them once. Two days later she disappeared from her locked bedroom in the middle of the afternoon on a clear day and was never seen or heard from again.

It's surmised that after she'd left the room that night, ordered out by Minus, Bill Mug went to work, beating the enchantment out of Aswidth's brain. The hardest punch is one thrown by a wiry man with thick wrists. Aswidth, for his part, was besotted with delusion like a fruit cake soaked in rum. He was, after all, a writer of genre stories.

At the trial, Minus told the jury that it was Axis who'd engineered the disappearance of the maid. "For a block of cheese," confessed the sorcerer, "he brought me a mercenary army of his brethren. They took her out through a mouse hole." The jury was aghast. "Those rats could be right now in the walls of this courthouse, laying dynamite charges," he said. He waited for a small panic to brew throughout the court, and then added, "But I wouldn't let that happen, of course."

Bill Mug was then called to the stand. The prosecutor asked, "How many times did you strike Mr. Aswidth on the night in question?" Mug mulled it over for two hours which gave Minus time to work a spell. He let it out slowly into the courtroom, a barely discernible gray miasma that spread and wafted over everything. Eventually, Mug answered, "I didn't strike him on the night in question, I struck him in the face. I lost count at three hundred." Both defendants were convicted and sentenced to the death penalty.

That's when Skip Minus rose, combed his hair, and bellowed for everyone to sit down and be quiet. The commotion that had been sparked by the reading of the verdict instantly ceased. Minus looked around. "I've had enough of this. I'm leaving and you won't want to stop me. If anyone raises a finger, I'll steal the magic from your children. I already have your self-confidence; perhaps I'll return it someday if I learn to forgive you. Come, Mug," said Minus and the two of them strode out of the courthouse, got in the yellow sports car, and sped away.

Humans could complicate his life and in the gnat storm of their complications his distraction could open him to truly dangerous attacks from other sorcerers. Minus knew he had to lay low. They fled to a rented cabin in the mountains where they met Axis. The place, a hunting lodge, was enormous and well stocked with provisions. They lit a fire in the stone fireplace and hunkered down for winter.

It wasn't long before Mug started to get on Minus's nerves. That gray scarecrow of a form, plodding endlessly from one end of the lodge to the other, occasionally stopping by the back door to smoke a cigarette. Even through the night, he struggled around, never sleeping. They had few conversations. Once they talked about how cold the wind was, and another time, after Minus had broken into the whiskey, he tried to explain to Mug the difference between objective and subjective reality. It was like talking to slate. Mug simply walked away, returning to his pointless rounds.

Later, over a piece of cheese and more whiskey, Minus confided to Axis, "Mug's a real pain in the ass."

"The right weight from that wheel of Gouda you have stashed away will make Bill Mug disappear," said the rat. "I'll need to contract a sizeable army to bring him down."

"No, no," said Minus. "I mean, come on, I have to show some restraint."

"As you wish," said Axis, contemplating the wheel of cheese.

"I have other work for you," whispered Minus.

The rat crawled closer across the white linen table cloth and sat on the edge of the cheese plate. He lifted an errant crumb, bit into it and said, "Tell me."

"That town where they put us on trial. I'm going to do them a favor. You must return to that place with your mercenaries, and I want you to bite each of the human inhabitants just once. You must puncture the flesh so that the magic can drain out, and the delusion can seep into the atmosphere and become a harmless gas. I want them all to be facing cold hard reality before the first snow."

"What will you pay?" asked Axis.

"The entire wheel of Gouda."

"Deal," said the rat and they shook on it, Minus using only his thumb and forefinger. Axis left that very evening to martial his forces for the raid. Also that very evening, Minus, unable to sleep for Mug's pacing, noticed that the lights were flickering in unison with the howling of the wind. He went into a spare bedroom they weren't using to look for an extra oil lamp should the electricity go out. He found one there and also a stack of board games and a small book shelf filled with mildewed paperbacks.

Minus scanned the titles, and the last book on the bottommost shelf was a novel, *Night and Day* by Martin Aswidth. He laughed as he pulled it off the shelf. The cover showed two faces side by side, very simply drawn. The eyes were open on one face and closed on the other. The awake face was rendered in white on a black background and the sleeping face in black on a white background. On the back cover there was a photo of Aswidth, his arms folded, his head held high, his eyes gazing into the distance. "This ought to be good," said Minus and slipped it into his back pocket.

He poured himself a whiskey, lit a fire in the den, and sat down with the book in hand. As he opened to the first page and started reading, a chill came into the air. A moment later, Mug passed through like a sleepwalker. His monumental lack of purpose could not be ignored. Minus closed the book, stared into the flames, and wondered how to get rid of him. The fire told him to empty his glass.

Mug lurched by three times, and on the fourth pass, Minus stopped him in his tracks by saying, "Mug, I've got a job for you."

"Now we're talking," grumbled Mug and approached his employer.

Minus held the copy of *Night and Day* out to Mug and said, "I want you to read this novel in the next three hours, and then I want you to take a rifle, and whatever other provisions you think you'll need, and strike out into the world, hunting for the very spirit of this book. When you find it, I want you to shoot it and bring it to me."

Mug stood still, staring.

"Do you get it?" yelled Minus, and in that shout he released a spell that reached into Mug and stole back the one drop of self-delusion he'd long afforded his employee.

Mug said, "Yeah, okay." He took the book, and paced away, opening to the first page. The sorcerer lifted his glass, and looked at the fire through the last drop of Mug's self-delusion. The fire told him to empty his glass, so he did.

By that night, Bill Mug had left on his quest. *Good riddance*, thought Minus and smiled when he noticed the air smelled like snow. He'd heard on the radio a blizzard was coming. It wasn't until the next morning when he went to the pantry for eggs that the sorcerer realized his mistake. There was no food left and Mug had taken the car.

It came to him instantly that he should never have taken Mug's last drop. He pictured his gray employee, devoid of self-delusion, in the yellow sports car: top down, speeding across the continent with one hand on the steering wheel and the rifle in the other. "God help the spirit of *Night and Day*," said Minus. And that's when it began to snow.

It snowed hard and constant, the drifts slowly burying the lodge, and Minus grew ravenously hungry.

Not until the dark afternoon of the second day did he remember the wheel of Gouda. He'd kept it separate from the other provisions, in a locked trunk in his room. Even as he feverishly dialed the lock's combination, he pictured what might happen when Axis returned and demanded payment. He thought of the rats taking Aswidth's maid out through the mouse hole and shuddered, but by then he'd already opened the trunk, taken the cheese from its burlap sack, and bitten through the outer wax of the wheel.

Surely the rat will understand, he thought each time he sliced the golden cheese. "Just a touch to keep body and soul together. Who could argue with it?" he'd say aloud and then listen long and hard to the howling of the wind. The snow rose, the days passed, the wheel, slice by slice, rolled into his stomach. All that Gouda and the loneliness and the dark days, the windows all covered by drifts, made Minus simple. He'd sit for hours before the fireplace, staring until it was dark and cold, his mind in an uproar from the effects of that indigestible drop of self-delusion.

He thought of Mrs. Aswidth, who'd hired him to relieve Martin of some of his "bullshit," as she put it. She was a statuesque, dark haired woman with a small chin. She wore tremendously high heels and met him for lunch at an egg and waffle place in the low-rent district.

"Do you want him to see reality or *your* reality?" asked Minus.

"He couldn't see reality if it sat on his face," she said. "Just do him."

Minus nodded. And woke later, shivering in the dark, wrapped in a blanket in the chair before the fireplace. His mind slipped and swirled into possible plots for Aswidth's *Night and Day*. He saw space travel, a story of an alien world, a giant cave filled with cryogenic cocoons, and a dangerous creature at the mouth of that cave. He imagined deeply into this scenario—saw the star-studded black velvet of space, imagined a caretaker of the cocoons falling in love with one of the frozen sleepers, gazing on her face through an icy window—until Gouda cravings commanded him to rise.

On the day after he ate the last half sliver of cheese, he looked up and noticed he was standing in a beam of sunlight coming through the front window of the lodge. He saw trees and grass outside, and upon seeing them, the howling of the wind abruptly disappeared from between his ears. He opened the door and breathed deeply, a warm breeze powdered with the scent of blossoms. He went to his room and dressed in one of his best Skip Minus get-ups, checkered slacks and a mohair cardigan, with Oxford loafers. Later that afternoon, as he sipped the last of the whiskey, sitting before the fireplace, he heard what at first he believed to be a hard rain. He looked to the window but the sun still shone.

Axis appeared then, standing on the table, leaning against the sorcerer's whiskey glass. "Mission accomplished."

Minus started at the sound of the rat's voice. It took a moment to recover his composure. "Did you bite them all?"

"Every one," said the rat. "Reality is backhanding them as we speak."

"Were there any problems?" asked Minus.

"They set some cats on us. We killed and ate them and took their fur for our nests."

"How was the weather . . . ?"

"Forget the weather, I've got hungry troops to feed. The wheel of Gouda, please."

"The wheel of Gouda is elsewhere," said Minus.

"Where?"

"I ate it. I was trapped by the snow. Mug took all of our provisions. "

Axis shook his head and smiled, "Your strategy is weak, sorcerer, but you've still got a lot of meat on you. As I said, my troops are starving." The rat nonchalantly gave the command and a furry wave of paws and teeth and tails rushed forward from the rafters to devour the flesh of Minus. The sorcerer, screaming, remained conscious through much of the repast and each bite was a sharp spell of agony.

The eyes were reserved for Axis, and he had them served with mustard when the day was done. Their jellied reflection told him that Minus could have used enchantment to save himself but chose not to. "Fool," said the rat. He bit down on the first eye and dust exploded into his mouth. "They didn't call him Minus for nothing," he said, spitting into the puddle of mustard and wiping his snout. The second eye, when bitten, gushed the drop of self-delusion and tasted sweet as a pineapple candy.

Years passed and the hunting lodge was forgotten by whoever had owned it. The picked-clean skeleton of Minus sat in its chair before the fireplace. On the day ten years later when Bill Mug finally captured the spirit of *Night and Day* and minutes later willingly released it before blowing his brains out, the sorcerer's jawbone fell off into his lap. On the evening when Axis was devoured by a swarm of locusts during the Battle of the Great Plains in the Insect/Rodent Wars, the rotted front chair legs gave out and dumped Minus's skeleton in a jumble on the floor before the fireplace. The mohair cardigan was eaten, over a decade of summer evenings, by white moths. Weeds grew up through what remained of the planks and sprouted from the skull's left eye socket. The roof collapsed, the rains came, the drifts of snow and weeds again.

Everyone who remembered the sorcerer Minus eventually died. His bones were pulverized to dust by the tread of Time. It's hard now to remember if he ever really existed or was merely some spell of enchantment, perhaps the dream of a space traveler asleep in a cryogenic cocoon. Or something far less: an act of subtraction, diminishing into the future.

CHARLES COLEMAN FINLAY is the author of the novels *The Prodigal Troll, The Patriot Witch, A Spell for the Revolution,* and *The Demon Redcoat.* Finlay's short fiction—most of which appears in his collection, *Wild Things*—has been published in several magazines, such as *The Magazine of Fantasy & Science Fiction, Strange Horizons,* and *Black Gate,* and in anthologies, such as *The Best of All Flesh* and my own *By Blood We Live* and *The Living Dead 2.* He has twice been a finalist for the Hugo and Nebula awards, and has also been nominated for the Campbell Award for Best New Writer, the Sidewise Award, and the Theodore Sturgeon Award.

This next story draws us into Colonial America, a time and place where piracy ruled—even in the provincial government. After all, it's a well-known fact that most flamboyant of American forefathers, John Hancock, made his fortune as a privateer.

When Proctor Brown and Deborah Walcott, two young Quaker witches, set out on a mission for General Washington, they expect to use their powers to catch a spy, not a pirate. But when magic goes awry, the pair find themselves pulled into a pocket world of oceans, islands, and never-ending night. In this alternate corner of reality, nothing is as it seems, and while they have found their quarry, he proves just as enigmatic as the strange world they've entered. Is he another victim of this place's magic, or a magician himself? And how can Proctor and Deborah discover a way out of a land that just might be . . . hell?

In this tale, C.C. Finlay gives us new piece of his *Traitor to the Crown* milieu. It's magic on the high seas—in a realm as dark as a pirate's heart.

LIFE SO DEAR OR PEACE SO SWEET
C.C. FINLAY

"Is life so dear or peace so sweet as to be purchased at the price of chains and slavery? Forbid it, Almighty God! I know not what course others may take, but as for me, give me liberty, or give me death!"—Patrick Henry

The Thimble Islands
off the coast of Connecticut
May, 1776

"I don't know how we're supposed to see anything in this mist," Proctor Brown said in the bow of the boat. The little one-sail wherry bobbed like a cork in a milky morning fog that obscured everything around them, including the British spy ship they were seeking.

"If you shout a little louder, maybe they'll hear you and call out where they are," Deborah Walcott answered quietly behind him.

Proctor bit his tongue on a reply. The implication to be quiet was a good one, especially since other searchers had gone missing when they chased the mysterious spy ship.

Deborah's sharp wit was one of the things that he simultaneously loved and found deeply frustrating. The other was not knowing where he stood with her. The murder of her parents before the Battle of Bunker Hill had complicated things between them, and the friends of her mother who had appointed themselves guardians and chaperones did their best to keep Proctor and Deborah apart.

The tone of her voice had made it hard to tell if she was amused at him or angry, so he turned to read the clues in her face. It didn't help. Even though only a few feet away in the middle of the boat, she was little more than a gray shadow.

"Eyes forw'd, eh," said the third passenger from the rear of the boat—a weathered privateer named Esek O'Brian. Like Proctor and Deborah, he'd been personally selected by General George Washington for this mission, though the three of them hadn't met until Esek picked up Deborah and Proctor on a beach this morning. He was built like an iron anvil, equally suited to shape good purposes as ill, and had been a privateer and smuggler in these waters for thirty years. But all sorts of men had joined the Revolution, so Proctor hesitated to judge him.

"Eyes forward," Proctor answered. He leaned over the gunwale to watch for the dangerous rocks that lurked just beneath the slate-colored waves.

A British warship had been seen several times lurking among the rocky Thimble Islands just off the coast of Connecticut. There was concern that the British were landing spies there, maybe even preparing to land troops. The American colonies had still not officially declared their independence from England and a dramatic victory by the British could bring it all to end.

The colonies had sent several fishing boats and sloops out to find the elusive ship, but four of them had disappeared now without a trace. There were no sounds of battle, no signs of wreckage. People whispered that it was like magic, that even the fog was unnatural. Diverting more and larger ships to search would leave other parts of the coast unprotected.

So General Washington decided that one small ship, too swift to catch, maybe too small to notice, might succeed where larger ships had failed.

And just in case the whispers of magic were true, he sent along two witches to deal with it. Proctor and Deborah had already used their special talents to counter black magic in Boston before the Battle of Bunker Hill.

A wave splashed over the side, the cold water soaking Proctor's face, salt stinging his eyes. He was wiping his eyes when just yards ahead of them the water broke over barely submerged boulders.

"Left!" he shouted, then remembered Deborah's earlier comment about lowering his voice. "*Rocks on the left.*"

"Port," O'Brian said, not bothering to hide the contempt in his voice. "It's *port*. Look out, miss." He tugged on the sail-lines with the same ease that Proctor steered a team of oxen on the farm.

Proctor turned to help Deborah, but she ducked easily under the spritsail as it swung over her head. He was chiding himself for always wanting to protect her—she had proven more than capable of looking after herself—when the boat tilted sharply and he had to hold on to keep from going overboard. As the boat skimmed past the hazard, O'Brian let the sail fall slack and they drifted where they were.

"Fog's a getting thicker, not burning off," O'Brian said quietly. "Used to be able to see the islands here in the fog from the shadow of the trees. But the army cut down all the trees so there wouldn't be any place to hide a mast. It didn't help them, and now it's not helping us." He shifted in his seat, rocking the small boat, and the waves slapped harder at the sides for a moment. "So I understand that the two of you are folks with talents, eh?"

Proctor tensed. Witchcraft was still a dangerous thing to discuss with strangers. "I can play *Yankee Doodle* on the fipple flute."

O'Brian snorted.

"What were you told about us, Mr. O'Brian?" Deborah asked.

"Esek," he said. "Like Esek Hopkins, the privateer. I was named for . . . you've never heard of him, have you?" Before Deborah or Proctor could answer, he said, "Never mind. It's Esek. Mister is for those what think they're better than other folks."

He spat over the side of the boat. "I hear you're a witch and he's a wizard, or some such, but I shouldn't be afraid of you because you're both Christian. But not good Christians, 'cause you're Quakers. Though either way, don't make no difference to me. I've seen things you wouldn't believe. Saw a Chinaman in Macau who could make the cards in your hand change colors and move the gold in your pocket to his. Though that last part wasn't magic as much as it was just playing cards. So call up a demon if you need to, as long as we find this British ship and I get paid."

"There will be no summoning of demons," Deborah promised. "But I have been working on a focus for a finding spell."

Of course, Proctor thought. He figured they would find the ship first, then figure out the magic. Deborah planned more and improvised less. If he had to create a finding spell in a hurry, what would he use? "Is there anything I can do to help?"

"Keep your eyes open," she said.

She bowed her head and folded her hands in prayer. Silence radiated outward from her and across the craft until even the waves lapping the wherry were hushed. "We hold this need in the Light," she said. "Bring to light the hidden things of darkness."

She opened her palms like a flower and sat quietly.

"Is that all there is to it?" Esek said. " 'Cause the Chinaman, he—"

"Give it a moment," Proctor said.

Deborah was powerful enough that she needed to speak a spell only once, and then hold it in her mind in silence. Proctor still needed a physical focus to channel his spells and needed to repeat it. Though he recognized the verse she had chosen from Corinthians, he was more familiar with the Old Testament and would have crafted a spell from Isaiah. As he stared at Deborah, waiting for her spell to take effect, he made a discreet drawing gesture with his hand for a focus and silently repeated the verse. *Give us the treasures of darkness and the hidden riches of secret places, give us the treasures of darkness and the hidden riches of secret places.*

As the words ran through his head, a light—supernatural and numinous—

bloomed like a spring flower in Deborah's cupped hands. Esek flinched despite his earlier assurances, and the boat rocked. But Deborah breathed a little sigh of relief and poured her power into the tiny sphere of light.

Proctor watched her, trying to follow how she did it. But faster than he could track, the light swelled and enveloped Deborah, clinging tightly to her body. Then, just when he thought that was all it would do, it speared outward from the boat like the mirrored beam shining from a lighthouse. It swept through the fog, casting light on one low-lying rocky island after another, each covered with tree stumps and waste, but nothing that could conceal a ship. As it came around the boat, the light, pearlescent and cool, passed over Proctor's shoulder, setting all his hair on end, leaving its touch like dew on his skin even after it moved on. The light completed one circumference of the boat, then blinked out of existence as completely and abruptly as it had entered.

Deborah sagged, exhausted. "Did you see anything?"

"Um." Proctor realized he'd been watching her more closely than the beam.

"I never seen anything like that before," Esek said, and it was hard to tell if he was impressed or frightened as he craned his head around warily, but he rested one hand on the pistol tucked in his belt.

"Better than card tricks?" Proctor asked.

"I dunno 'bout that," Esek said. "I still don't see any ship."

"Maybe the flashing light scared it off," he said, trying to lighten the mood.

He regretted it immediately. Deborah looked at him from under the brim of her plain bonnet, and he could see the tension in the way she held herself. The spell hadn't gone quite as she had expected, after all. But then, when you worked with supernatural forces, that was often the result. You never really controlled the power, you only channeled it. And like any channel, sometimes it overflowed.

"We'll be getting back to the old way of searching then," Esek said, standing up to adjust the sail.

"Maybe we should give Deborah another chance," Proctor said.

"These have been pirate waters for a hundred years," Esek said. "Every pirate who was anyone has sailed these waters. I hid a cargo of smuggled tea here from British tax collectors once. But there are only so many places to hide, depending on your ship. Did they say if it was full-rigged or fore-and-aft—?" He stopped as the boat lurched beneath them. "What witchery is this?"

The sail was slack but the boat moved against the current. Beneath the cold breeze coming off the water and the clammy touch of the fog, Proctor felt a tingle across his skin that told him wizard's work was being done nearby.

"It is not my doing," Deborah said, and that worried Proctor more than anything.

The sail snapped tight as it caught the wind, then shuddered loudly as the boat continued to push against it. Esek pulled out his revolver, but before he could do anything with it, the fog suddenly lifted.

It should have revealed the clear sky of morning, but as it shredded and fell away like pieces of lace, darkness fell around them.

Night. And a sky filled with stars.

As their eyes adjusted from gray to black, broad-shouldered islands of rock emerged from the murky shade like footpads stepping out of a dark alley.

"What's going on here?" Esek said. He didn't seem to know whether to point the pistol at them or at the water. Proctor calculated his chances of tackling him. The boat was too long, too unsteady, and there were too many things between them. Proctor loosened the tomahawk at his belt. He had trained with it for the militia. One good throw . . .

"Look," Deborah said. "There's the ship."

The ship, anchored nearby, and more.

Distant islands, which had been clear cut, were now covered once again with trees.

But that fact was less remarkable than the structures occupying the two islands dead ahead of them. One smaller island was occupied by a tiny shack made of shipwreck and driftwood. The larger island was filled from edge to edge with a white marble palace, onion-domed with minarets, like something from an oriental picture book.

A rope bridge connected the two islands.

Proctor's skin usually tingled in the presence of magic, but at this moment it crawled and itched and twitched as if he were wearing a blanket of ants. Deborah crouched in the middle of the boat, appearing just as surprised as he felt.

The boat continued its motion, drifted around the two islands the way water spiraled down a drain. They passed the bigger island with the palace, the smaller island with the shack, and moved on past the anchored ship. It looked old to Proctor, almost ancient. The wood was gray and worm-eaten, cut with deep gouges. The paint had long faded so that it was impossible to tell what colors it had once been and the sails were so thin they were nearly transparent. Frayed lines had been knotted again and again beyond count. There were twenty cannons poking out the gunports on one side, but they were rusted and draped with bits of seaweed and other windblown debris.

"That can't be the British spy ship," Proctor said.

"That can't be . . . " Esek said from the back of the little boat. "The devil, it is."

"Fancy that," Deborah murmured.

Proctor followed her gaze. Although nearly all the paint had faded, the ship's name could still be read across the stern. *Fancy.*

It didn't mean anything to Proctor. Deborah caught his eye and it didn't seem to mean anything to her either. But Esek leaned forward eagerly.

" 'Hoy," came a voice from the island, startling them all.

A thin man with short-cropped hair and hollow, haunted eyes had stepped out of the shack. He was wearing a dress coat, as gray and dusty as the rocks, threads hanging from the hem. He wore a pair of breeches but no stockings or shoes. He took a hesitant step toward them, then dodged back into the shack.

"Hello," Proctor shouted. "Where are we?"

The man came back out, tugging a ratty old wig onto his head and slapping an outrageous feathered hat atop that. He ran across the rocks and grabbed hold of a rope-line that connected the island to the ship. " 'Hoy," he shouted again. "You don't want to drift past the ship there."

Proctor looked past the ship. Another island, mounded with white rocks atop the gray, waited ahead of them. "Why not?" he called back.

But the man was pulling himself hand over hand across the line to the *Fancy.* He had a knife clenched in his teeth so he was unable to answer.

"I can stop her," Esek called back. "There's no wind, she won't steer out of the current."

Their boat floated past the *Fancy,* too quickly to be drifting. It was like they were a fish on a line that someone was reeling in. Now that they were around the ship, Proctor could see the shore of the third island was covered with wreckage, bits of spar and plank and flotsam. The flag of Massachusetts drooped from a broken mast.

The missing ships.

Proctor was about to say as much when a dark shape stirred on the top of the white mound. One of the rocks rolled loose and tumbled with a hollow sound down to the water's edge, where it came to rest—a skull. The mound was made of bones and skulls.

The dark silhouette stood and stretched like a housecat waking from a nap. But it was too large, the largest cat that Proctor had ever seen. A tiger. Its paws were the size of paddles.

Esek had grabbed an oar from the bottom of the boat and was alternately trying to steer or paddle clear. The boat teetered under Proctor's feet as he twisted, searching for another oar.

"Here," shouted the stranger. His feet thumped across the deck of the *Fancy* as he ran to the bow. He used the knife to saw through one of the sail-lines. Fabric tumbled behind him. He swung the rope once, twice, and let go on the third loop.

It arced through the air toward the little boat. Proctor leaned over the side and stretched out his arm.

The rope fell well short, hitting the water with a sad splash.

"Damn," said the man, softly. "Not as strong as I used to be."

"Grab it," Esek shouted. He swatted at it with the oar, tipping the boat precariously, and Proctor flung himself to the other side to keep from falling in. The rope was already beyond them.

The stranger stood in the bow of the *Fancy*, hand cupped to his mouth. "Been a long time since I had any company. But it was good to know you."

Esek yelled at the man on the ship. "Try again—throw another rope—it's not too late—"

Proctor glanced at Deborah—rigid with fear in the middle of the boat—and glanced once over his shoulder. The tiger climbed down from its mound of bones and batted the skull into the water.

Proctor's head snapped back to the rope that dangled from the ship.

He didn't have Deborah's talent, or her skill, but he had used his magic on the farm. And one of the things he had done was learn to feed a rope through a pulley without climbing to the top of the barn.

"Spare not, lengthen thy cords, and strengthen thy stakes," he said.

Nothing happened. He stretched his hand out to the rope. On the farm he used a smaller piece, cut from the same length, drawn through his hand for a focus. He made the motion of drawing the rope through his hands. *"Spare not, lengthen thy cords, and strengthen thy stakes."*

The rope lashed out of the water like the end of a whip. It cut a slash across Proctor's hand but he grabbed it and held on tight. It was just barely long enough to reach them, and the boat twisted under his feet.

"Don't go overboard," Esek ordered, rocking the boat so much that he nearly pitched Proctor over the edge. Proctor braced himself, hunkered down, and pulled.

They came a few inches closer to the ship. He could feel the boat trying to pull away from him, like a team of oxen leading a plow. He drew a breath, reached forward, and pulled again. The nose of the boat dipped toward the water, but he drew them a few inches closer.

Deborah scooted over behind him, grabbing the loose end of the rope and pulled with him. Feeling her presence next to him, her breath at his back, lent him extra will. Only the strength of his arms stood between her safety and a likely death. It was enough.

Hand over hand, he dragged them in to the ship.

Deborah gathered up the rope behind him and passed it back to Esek, who quickly tied it off. When they came alongside the *Fancy*, he lashed them together.

Only then did Proctor look back. The tiger seemed to be watching them curiously. When their eyes met, it opened its mouth and roared. The sound echoed over the water, making all Proctor's hair stand on end and his knees turn to jelly.

A thump sounded behind him. The stranger had dropped a ladder over the side of the ship.

"That's Old Scratch," he said, cheerfully. "Don't pay no attention to her."

"Are you all right?" Deborah asked. Her fingertips rested on his forearm. Proctor glanced down and saw the blood streaming over his wrist. The slash in his palm had been gouged deeper with each pull on the rope.

"I'm fine," he said, snatching his hand away and squeezing it shut. The sting, which must have been there all along, finally reached him and he winced. "Are you—?"

"I'm fine," she said.

The look on her face must have mirrored his own. There was no way either of them could be fine. "Where are we?"

She stepped in close to him and whispered. "It's like a hidden room off the main room of the house. These are still the Thimble Islands, maybe the very same place we were before. But we've passed through a door into a private room."

"Your doing?" he asked.

"I think what I did with the light must have attracted the attention of a witch far more powerful than we've ever seen. Even more powerful than the Widow Nance."

"The stranger," Proctor whispered, deliberately not glancing up at the ship. "But then why did he try to save us?"

"That question troubles me also," she said.

"Come on." Esek had climbed up the ladder to the deck of the ship and was gesturing for them to follow. Proctor steadied the ladder for Deborah. In a normal tone of voice, he said, "Be careful."

Esek reached out with one arm and hoisted her onto the deck. Proctor followed and soon stood beside them.

Up close, the stranger looked like a madman. He stank, like a man who had not bathed or washed his clothes in a lifetime. His eyes were rimmed red and the sockets beneath them were as dark as a bruise. There were four pale parallel scars beneath the stubble that covered his sunken cheek. His clothes had once been very fine, better even than Proctor had seen the governor wearing, but they were old and covered with stains. Buttons were missing and the lace trim hung as loose as autumn leaves, waiting for a strong wind to set them adrift. A sword hung at his waist, on a belt that had been notched so many times it nearly wrapped around him twice.

But none of those things, alone or together, marked him as mad, merely as unfortunate, like a castaway lost for years on some desert island. He seemed mad because of his grin, which was as wide as the Atlantic, revealing teeth as dark as stormclouds.

His grin, and his eyes. The smile did not touch his eyes, which were dark and dangerous and fixed on Proctor. "That was a most remarkable feat," he said, with a nod toward the island with the tiger. "Old Scratch hasn't been frustrated like that in a very long time."

"Is the tiger your . . . pet?" Deborah asked.

The smile returned to the stranger's face, though not as broad and now slightly uncertain. "No, no, definitely not my pet." He glanced toward the island and licked his lips nervously, giving an impression wholly at odds with the capable man of action who pulled himself across the rope and ran to attempt their rescue. "But where are my manners? Will you be so kind as to join me in my somewhat humble residence?"

"Do you live in the shack or the palace?" Esek asked. He had tucked the pistol back in his belt, but he rested his hand on his waist close to it.

"Oh, it's more than a shack, very comfy, really," the stranger said. "But we mustn't go in the palace. No, that's not for us."

"Who's it for?" Proctor asked.

The madman grinned and rubbed his hands together. "Who wants to go first?"

The crossing from the ship to the island was done by the way of ropelines, one for hands and one for feet. "I would prefer to go first," Deborah said. "If those ropes are as old as those on the ship, they're likely to break under the weight of the gentlemen."

Without waiting for permission, she stepped out onto one rope and grabbed hold of the other at shoulder height. Though not quick, she made her way confidently and deliberately across the line. Proctor caught himself suppressing a smile. She could be surprisingly practical. When she had gone about half way, and dangled so low that her hem nearly touched the water, the stranger leaned over to Proctor.

"She's the kind who'll put on pants if you're not careful," he said.

The comment offended Proctor. In fact, Deborah had worn pants on several occasions when they were fighting the witches of the Covenant the year before and it didn't bother him in the least. But he wasn't going to give credit to the stranger's remark, nor defend her actions to someone who didn't know her. "She values her independence, as all good Americans do," he said. "It is a trait I admire in her."

His use of *good Americans* was intended as a shiny minnow on the end of a hook, by which he hoped to draw out the stranger's reaction to the war. But he failed to take the bait. In fact, he was so busy glancing back at the island with the tiger that he scarcely seemed to hear them at all.

"Oh, believe me, I know the type," he mumbled. "I very well know the type."

Deborah had reached the other side and hopped down onto the rocky shore. She turned and waved at Proctor, who lifted his hand in answer. While he waved, Esek climbed out on the rope. "I'll be getting over next," he said.

"Are you sure that's wisest?" Proctor asked, looking at his size and thinking about what Deborah had said.

"Sure. I'm bigger than either of you, so if it'll hold me, you can cross no problem, eh?"

He started across. The tiger roared again, a sound followed by a loud splash. The stranger ran back to the other side of the boat and peered down. He reached over and thumped the wood, screaming at the tiger.

"Do tigers swim?" Proctor said.

The stranger spun around, his eyes wide with mad delight. "Oh, yes. And they are also excellent climbers."

The deep gouges on the side of the ship that he had taken for worm-marks took form again in a different light. Proctor turned back to Esek, who moved quickly for a man his size. Still he was heavy enough that the rope drooped all the way down into the waves, soaking his boots. "You best hurry up," Proctor called.

Esek gave no reply, but the mad stranger rubbed his hands a bit too gleefully. "They don't swim that fast. No, it's you who best hurry when it comes your turn."

"Can't the tiger just climb onto your island? Why would we be any safer there?"

The madman patted the hilt of his sword. "We've reached an agreement over the years. She doesn't come on my island and I don't interfere with hers."

This talking of the tiger as if it were a person worried Proctor. Though the man looked mad, his words and actions had all been lucid. Everything except his behavior toward the beast. "Didn't you interfere by rescuing us before we wrecked?"

"Ah, that I did now, didn't I?" he said, laughing. He clapped Proctor on the shoulder. "I would go now if I were you."

Esek had climbed ashore across the water and stood at the far edge of the island, staring at the white palace. Deborah stood halfway between him and Proctor, near the entrance of the small hut.

Proctor climbed out on the rope, finding it harder than it looked. His feet swayed back and forth, nearly toppling him into the water. The raw sound of claws scraping wood echoed from the far side of the ship. Terror wriggled into Proctor's heart, and he hurried, but the more he hurried, the more he swayed until he lost his feet entirely and dangled by his arms while the rope whipped back and forth beneath him. He had one eye looking for purchase for his feet and the other watching for the tiger coming around the edge of the boat.

The madman stood at the side of the ship and cupped his hands to his mouth. "Hurry."

His crazed laughter brought Proctor cold resolve that the circumstances did not provide alone. His feet found the rope and he made his way calmly and deliberately to the other side, where Deborah waited for him.

"I don't see how he survives here," Deborah said. "Clearly he lives here—there's a pile of old rags that serves as either a rat's nest or a bed, though given the size, I suspect the latter. But there's no sign of food, only a little bit of water—"

"Do you think he's a ghost?" Proctor asked quietly. His arms were still shaky from the strain of dragging their boat to safety and then pulling himself across the ropes, and he tried to rub feeling back into them while they spoke.

"He doesn't smell like a ghost," Deborah said.

"That's the truth," Proctor said. "And I don't feel like one either, so we didn't die to get here. He's certainly mad. Are we?"

"No," she said. "Because I want to get back in our boat and find a way back home, and there's nothing mad in that."

The stranger's laughter rose in pitch with the sound of splashing. He dangled over the water with the tiger swimming beneath him. The beast lunged upward, swiping at him with its huge paw. He pulled his legs up out of the way and then snapped one down to try to kick the animal's nose.

Esek had approached them and barked out rough laughter at the sight. "Now that's a man other men would follow to hell," he said. Then realizing his own words, "Do you think we're in hell?"

Proctor shook his head in reply.

The madman swung like a monkey over to the shore and hopped down. As soon as he landed, he snatched up a rock and threw it at the tiger. Without waiting to see if it hit, he turned to his guests. "After all this time, you'd be surprised that there are any rocks remaining, wouldn't you? But every time I come out here I find some more. Oh . . . that's too bad."

"What?" Proctor asked, but then he saw.

Their little boat was adrift. It floated past the shift, picking up speed, and rammed into the island with enough speed to snap the mast. The waves pulled back and then surged, casting it up on the rocks a second time, this time snapping its keel like the spine of a small animal. Proctor reached out to give Deborah's arm a reassuring squeeze.

The tiger, treading water just offshore, shook the spray off its head and then paddled away.

"Where is it going?" Proctor asked.

"Back where she came from, just as she always does," the madman said. "Old Scratch, she's devious, but predictable." Then he laughed and clapped his hands. "Well now, who wants some tea?"

The madman walked away from them and checked a variety of tins and broken crockery set out on the rocks.

"We'll find some way out of here," Proctor said. "I s—"

"Don't swear to it," Deborah said.

Ever the Quaker. It almost made him smile. "I wasn't going to. I was going to say, I sense magic here, but I haven't seen him use any yet."

"I do too, and neither have I. But we should be on our guard. Remember how the Widow Nance tricked us."

"Too well," he said. The scars on his arms from that misadventure were still pink and healing. "Can you put a binding spell on him if we need to?"

She opened her hand to reveal several knotted strings. She had been tying them as a focus for a spell. "But not before we find a way off the island."

Nearby, the madman sniffed at a cracked pitcher. "This one's fresh," he said, carrying it over to a circle of rocks outside his shack. "Rainwater." He piled up pieces of driftwood and knelt to strike a fire. The crack of flint on steel sounded several times before the spray of tiny orange sparks caught hold in the tinder.

The steel and flint puzzled Proctor. If the stranger was a wizard why didn't he just speak a word and start the fire? Everyone had different talents, but anyone who could open this room off the side of world had incredible power. With the fire going, the madman stood and looked around, puzzled. "Now where did I leave those tea leaves?"

Esek blocked his way. "I know who you are," he said.

"I'm sure you don't," the madman said. His grin was weak.

"You're Henry Every."

"Never heard of him."

"Henry Every, Long Ben, Captain of the *Fancy*."

"He's been dead a long time," the madman said.

"He's been *gone* a long time," Esek corrected. "He disappeared, never to be seen again. And now I know where you went and why you've never been seen."

"I have tea leaves around here, somewhere, I'm sure," the madman said, as if they hadn't spoken. He walked away and examined various plates and fragments of bowls that had been left out on the rocks.

Esek turned to Proctor and Deborah. "Henry Every. I bet you've never heard of him either, no more than you've heard of Captain Esek Hopkins."

"No . . . " Proctor said. As if he should have heard of every pirate who had ever lived.

"Should we have?" Deborah asked.

Esek shook his head in disbelief. He raised one thick arm and pointed it at the shambling wreck of a man who shuffled around the tiny island lifting and sniffing various plates. "Yes, you should have. That man is the greatest pirate who ever lived. He taught Captain Kidd everything he knew, and . . . you haven't heard of Captain Kidd either, I suppose?"

"Him, I've heard of," Proctor said. Captain Kidd was a piece of New England history. There wasn't a boy in Massachusetts who hadn't heard of him. "Some say he buried his treasure near Boston, and some say in the Thimble Islands."

"Captain Kidd sailed through the Thimble Islands," Esek said. "But it wasn't to bury his own treasure, it was to dig up Henry Every's."

Proctor saw the gleam of greed in Esek's eyes, and he exchanged a worried glance with Deborah. One madman was more than enough to deal with if they hoped to escape. He tried to interrupt the smuggler, but now that he had started, there was no slowing him down. He paced, using his arms in excitement as he spoke.

"Henry Every is the king of the pirates. He sailed the *Fancy* in the Indian Sea, where he came across the treasure ship of the emperor of Hindoostan. The treasure ship was huge—it had sixty guns and four hundred soldiers onboard. But Long Ben—that's what his men called him—laid alongside her in the *Fancy*, crippled her with the cannons, and then boarded her for some of the bloodiest hand-to-hand fighting any man or devil ever seen. The captain of the ship ran down and hid among the whores—"

Proctor flinched at the harsh word, for Deborah's sake, though she didn't show any reaction.

"When Every's men finally took the ship, they found more than a million dollars in gold and jewels aboard that ship. Each and every man who survived the battle got a thousand pounds in coins and a sack full of rubies and emeralds and diamonds." He pounded his fist in his palm. "They were as rich as any gentleman in England, and that's where most of them went, where the authorities arrested them because the emperor of Hindoostan complained to the King. But not Henry Every. He had friends in Massachusetts and Connecticut, and he came here, where a free man has always been welcome. Then he disappeared."

"The women," Deborah said.

"What?" Esek seemed confused by her interruption.

"The whores," she said. "What happened to them?"

"What do you think? The pirates took them aboard for their amusement, those that didn't kill themselves right away and weren't killed. . . ." Esek realized what he was saying and the sentence stammered to an end. "I'm sorry, miss. I didn't mean to—"

"Didn't mean to what?" Proctor asked.

"Didn't mean to speak so freely, I'm sure," Deborah said. "Though free men should always speak freely, don't you think?"

Esek was eager to change the subject. "What I'm trying to tell you is this man is the greatest pirate who ever lived. He stole the treasure ship of Hindoostan and captured all the emperor's wives. And he got away with it."

Proctor looked over his shoulder at the sad raggedy man walking barefoot over the cold wet rocks. "It doesn't look like he got away with it to me."

Esek gestured to Proctor to step aside. "A word between men," he said.

"Please feel free," Deborah said. "I know how men can be . . . delicate sometimes."

Proctor stepped aside with the privateer. "Distract Every for me if you can," Esek said in a hushed tone. "I want to explore that larger island. We need a boat, and there may be one hidden on the far side."

"I can do that," Proctor said.

"Here we go," the madman announced cheerfully. Proctor turned to see him grinning as he held up a wooden plate.

They gathered around the fire.

"I don't often acquire fresh tea leaves here, so I have to dry them," the madman said, scraping them off into the boiling water. "We better let it steep a while."

Deborah sat on a nearby rock. When Proctor chose his own seat among the weathered stones, he made sure to choose one so that if the madman were looking at him, his eyes would be turned away from the marble palace.

"Are you?" Deborah asked.

"Am I?" the madman said.

"Are you who he said you are? Henry Every, the pirate captain."

He shook his head. "I'm just a poor sinner. A man who's had a long time to regret a few . . . rash actions."

"Is your ship the one that's been spotted around the Thimble Islands of late?" Proctor said. "Can it sail us back there again?"

"If it could sail anywhere else, do you think I'd still be here?" Every fidgeted, frequently stirring the leaves in the pot and looking everywhere but never making eye contact.

"A sinner might still be here, a man with something to repent," Deborah said.

"I said I was a sinner, not a saint." Every stood abruptly and entered his shack. He came back with a tall pipe of the sort that Proctor had sometimes seen used to smoke tobacco. Every sucked at a mouthpiece and then threw it down on the rocks, where it hit with a sharp crack. "Useless. Since the opium has gone, it's been useless."

His voice trembled.

Proctor was putting all the pieces together. Every wasn't a wizard: he was cursed, cursed for his piracy and the evil deeds he had done. He could sail his ship back to the other world, but only to taunt him with the things he had lost. "You can sail your ship back to the real world, to our world," Proctor said. "That's why we've seen your ship so frequently of late, lurking among the islands. But you can't stay there. You're drawn back here, the same way our little boat was drawn through the fog. That's why they can never find you."

"Perhaps," Every said quietly. With that one word, he seemed to Proctor to become both sad and even worthy of pity. He had four chipped cups, which he dipped into his pitcher of steeping water. "Would you care for some tea? I'm afraid I can offer you neither cream nor sugar."

Proctor accepted a cup and tried not to wince when he sipped. The tea was so weak and dirty it tasted like dishwater. Deborah saw his reaction and set her cup down without tasting it. "What happened to you?" Proctor asked.

"I overheard your friend. He had much of it right. My ship and crew attacked a musselman off the coast of Malabar. It was the moghul's ship, headed for Mecca, carrying his gift to the imans and his wife and all his concubines on holy pilgrimage. The hold was filled with treasure—chest after chest of gold coins and cut jewels, bolts of silk, blocks of pure opium." He licked his lips nervously. "But it wasn't enough. When greed takes a man—when it takes a crew of men—no glut of prizes is ever enough. We tortured the crew members and wom—" He glanced at Deborah. "We tortured the crew members. One by one in search of more treasure. For thirteen days, we made sport of them, forcing them to reveal their secrets, little treasures they may have hidden, on their person or aboard the ship. And on the thirteenth day, we found the greatest treasure of all: the moghul's sorcerer." He paused. "He gave up his secrets, but the secrets came with a curse." He held out his hands. "And now here I am. Have you ever heard the expression 'to grab a tiger by the tail'? Once you grab hold, you can never let go or they will—hey, your friend really shouldn't venture over there."

He jumped to his feet. Esek dangled from the ropes midway between Every's island and the island with the palace.

"He's our companion, but not our friend," Proctor said.

Every didn't hear a word that Proctor said. He was already running down to shore to shout at Esek.

Deborah came to Proctor's side. "Every is an evil man who has done evil things," Proctor said. "There's much he's not telling us, particularly about the emperor's wives."

"I know," Deborah said. "But his judgment will be up to God, not us."

Proctor had a terrible realization. "Unless Esek was right and this *is* hell."

"Don't think that thought hasn't crossed my mind," Deborah said.

"If this is hell, or even if it isn't . . . " Proctor said. He regretted the words as soon as they escaped his mouth. Not knowing how to pull them back in, he opened the stall doors and chased the rest of them out. "I need to know whether . . . " *Whether you love me.* He couldn't make himself say it aloud. "Whether you still have feelings for me."

Deborah took a step away from him, her face revealing and then masking a whole book full of emotions he wasn't literate enough to read. Having grown up as a witch, in a country that killed witches, she was used to keeping her talents secret, a skill that extended to her thoughts. And he couldn't blame her. But he wanted to know.

She could tell. She looked up at his face and knew he needed something from her. A word. A sign. She reached out and brushed her fingers against the back of his hand.

"Ask me again once we've escaped this place, wherever it is," she said. "Until we escape, it doesn't matter."

Every, ragged and miserable, stretched beyond the normal span of days, stood at the edge of the island and raged at Esek.

"I don't know," Proctor said. "If we don't escape, it may matter even more. Esek told me he would search the big island for a boat."

Deborah pointed at the *Fancy*. "We have a boat. Or rather a ship. Maybe it's Every who's drawn back here and not the vessel. If we were aboard it without Every, would you know how to get it under sail?"

"I might be able to figure it out, given time," Proctor said. "But even then, I don't know that I could steer it through these treacherous channels. How would we break the spell that smashes everything on the rocks? How would we open the door back into our world?"

"I am already thinking of a focus and a spell," Deborah said.

He nodded, mind racing, eager to help. "What verse will you use? There's *Job. The gates of death have been opened unto thee. Thou hast seen the doors of the shadow of death.*"

"You're too fond of the Old Testament," she said.

"What do you expect?" he said. "I was raised by Puritans."

"I believe this is not hell and we are not yet dead," she said. "I was thinking about something from *Acts*: *The angel of the Lord by night opened the prison doors and brought them forth.*"

"What can I do to help?"

The voices of argument rose to a new pitch. "This is the last time I'll warn you," Every screamed, froth flying from his lips like spume from the tip of a wave. "If you don't come back now, I'll chase you down and cut out your bloody heart."

Esek stood on the other island, dripping to the waist. His pistol pointed across the water at Every. "Try it and I'll finish the job that time did not. You've got no claim on a treasure you have not spent in a hundred years, dead man."

He shuffled backwards toward to the palace. Every screamed in blind incomprehensible rage, put his knife in his teeth, and reached up to grab the ropelines. Esek laughed at him and turned to run to the palace.

"Are you sure we need Esek to escape the island?" Deborah asked.

Proctor looked at the time-worn ship with its puzzle of lines and masts and sails. "Most likely."

"Then you better go save him. If you cannot save them both."

Every had already reached the far shore where he dropped nimbly to the rocks and chased Esek into the marble palace. Proctor checked the tomahawk, hung at his belt, the only weapon from his militia days that he carried with him. Then he spit on his hands, reached up, and grabbed the ropelines.

He let his weight hang on the unfamiliar ropes and felt them sag.

This passage was much wider than the one between the ship and Every's island, and the drooping ropelines dunked Proctor in the waves until he was soaked halfway to his waist. When he reached the far shore, he saw two sets of wet footprints. Esek's heavy boots followed by the faint and fading print of Every's bare feet, converging on the large and ornate archway of the marble palace.

Proctor paused before it.

The building itself was wrong. Up close there was no sign of workmanship in the stone, and the ornate details seemed vague and fuzzy whenever he tried to focus on them. It was less a building than it was someone's memory of a building. And it felt less like a palace and more like a tomb. The finial on the dome was topped with a crescent moon. The real moon, also a crescent, hung in the sky behind it. Proctor realized it had not moved since their arrival.

The sooner they escaped from here, the better.

"Esek, Every," he shouted. "Come on out—we can work through our differences."

He heard their voices arguing far away, as if down a long corridor. With a glance back over his shoulder at Deborah, he loosened the tomahawk in his belt, and went inside.

There were no fires, no candles or lamps of any kind, but the broad interior corridors were suffused with a cool light that emanated from the marble walls. Less like natural light and more like someone's memory of a lit room. The building was large outside, but certainly not much larger than the Old North Church in Boston. And yet the corridor led him on and on, appearing straight in front of him, though whenever he looked behind it twisted and turned.

He ignored the side doors and passages as he followed the voices toward the center of the building. Just ahead he spied a transept, a crossing of major corridors. He heard a cough around one of the corners, and he ran forward. "Esek, is that you? Proclaim yourself—"

The command died on his tongue as he rounded into the new hall.

The tiger stood at his feet, dripping a pool of water on the floor. It stared at Proctor curiously, as if its deep yellow-brown eyes were taking the measure of his soul. It leaned forward and licked the dried blood from the cut on his hand.

Raspy tongue had barely touched bare skin when Proctor spun away and sprinted into the other hall. He dodged into the first side door that opened for him, and then again into a narrow stairway, which he climbed three steps at a time. Every time he glanced back, he saw shadows moving on the wall and heard the soft pad of feet, until he was running blind, not looking back at all. The corridors were narrower here, and darker, with many more branches, and several of the rooms were dead-ends. He stopped in the third of these, braced himself in a corner, and fumbled at his belt for his tomahawk. He held the weapon before him, twitching in anticipation of an attack that might come at any moment or never.

After a while, his panic subsided and he caught his breath.

He was lost. His shifted his feet and felt them squish in wet socks. At first the noise seemed impossibly loud, a trumpet blaring his location. But then he realized it might be his rescue. He dropped to the floor to trace the breadcrumb trail of water drops back to the original entrance.

Hope faded like dew in the sun. The floors felt unreal, like a plaster model of barely remembered floors. There were no drops to follow, not even in the corner where he'd just been standing. The surface swallowed them up the way sand swallowed water.

He stood and peered cautiously around each dim corner. He made his way slowly, choosing the wider corridor every time paths diverged, looking for a staircase down to the first floor again. But the labyrinth frustrated him, and he found himself back in the narrowest of hallways which ended in a plain arched doorway. When he looked back, all the other doors and passages were gone.

He wracked his brain for a verse that he could use as a spell. But all he could think of was First Samuel, *And the asses of Kish Saul's father were lost . . .*

Maybe the only way out was through. He tiptoed forward, as quietly as he could in wet shoes, paused in the door, and peered into the room.

A person dressed from head to foot in dark robes, knelt before an eastward facing window, with forehead, nose, and palms touching the ground. Though he could not understand the words, the voice was unmistakably that of a woman.

"Alaahumma baarik 'ala Muhammadin wa 'alaa ali Muhammadin. Kaama baarakta 'alaa Ibraaheema wa 'alaa ali Ibraaheema. Innaka hammedun Majeed." She glanced over her right shoulder. "As Salaamu 'alaikum wa rabmatulaah." She glanced over her left shoulder. "As Salaamu 'ala—"

She noticed Proctor there and faltered. He held up his hands to indicate his peaceful intent.

Only one of his hands was clutching a tomahawk.

He quickly slipped it back into his belt.

"—ikum wa rabmatulaah," she finished.

With her hands cupped, palm up, at chest level, she said something that only she herself could hear. She had to be one of the women Every had kidnapped. When Esek called them whores, Proctor had imagined exotic women in shameful clothing, flaunting themselves. But this woman reminded him of a pious goodwife or some popish nun. He wanted to speak to her, but something told him it would be wrong to interrupt. Finally, she wiped her face with her palms and stood. She turned to face him. Her skin was dark but her features delicate and perfectly formed. Her amber eyes considered him, thoughtfully but fearlessly.

"You must be a most earnest and good-hearted man to find your way through these corridors," she said in lilted English. "In all this time, no other man has found me here."

"To be honest I wasn't looking," Proctor said.

"That explains it," she said. "If you were, you would never have succeeded."

"Do you know the way out?"

"Of course. That is why you came, to escort me away from this place. Come, we must hurry." She walked past him, and he turned to follow her, his head spinning with questions.

But the questions quickly disappeared. The corridors that had been twisting and ever-changing before were now straight and solid. She paused and pressed a finger to her lips. "We must stop somewhere on our way out," she said softly. "There are dangerous men here, and we must be careful to escape their notice."

Contradictory choices raced through Proctor's head. On the one hand, they still needed Esek in order to escape. On the other hand, if this poor woman wanted to avoid the notice of a pirate and a smuggler, he felt obligated to help.

She led him down a narrow stairway into a room that looked like the nave of an old church, ringed with high arches. A balcony arcade circled the second story. In the middle of the floor sat a box that Proctor would have taken for an altar had not the top been knocked off to reveal an empty casket. The rest of the room was filled with the emperor's treasure, or what was left of it. Bolts of brightly colored silk, silver plates and statues, casks of coins and jewels lined the walls. Many were cracked open, or lay empty, the pieces scattered.

The woman held a small bag on a cord. She pulled it open and began to fill it with gold coins and gems.

Proctor felt an itch on the back of his neck. Something wasn't right. "Are you sure—"

A roar as a shadow passed over his head, and then a heavy weight slammed into his shoulders, knocking him to the ground. He thought that the tiger had found him, pouncing from the balcony above, but then he saw Esek rise beside him.

"The treasure's mine!" Esek said. "And Every's whore too."

Proctor saw the knife in Esek's hand but he was unprepared for how quickly the smuggler moved to cut his throat. He twisted away just in time to feel the blade slash his cheek. The big sailor's fist followed a split second later, connecting with his temple and snapping Proctor's head against the floor.

"Hold still, damn you," Esek said. "There's no reason this can't be quick."

Proctor had no intention of letting it be quick. His left hand fumbled at his belt for his tomahawk, but it was twisted under him as he tried to roll away from Esek. His right hand grabbed blindly for a weapon, but all his fingers found was a bolt of silk. It was better than nothing, and Proctor whipped it around just as Esek slashed at him again. This time the knife bit into the fabric, which Proctor twisted, knocking the knife out of Esek's hand; he then shoved the bolt into the smuggler to tangle his arms and knock him down. Esek grabbed a handful of coins and flung them in Proctor's face, then rose and charged at Proctor again.

The tomahawk came out. Esek warded off the first blow with his forearm. The second split his skull and stuck there like a maul in a piece of wood. Esek toppled to the ground, pulling the weapon out of Proctor's hand as he fell.

Proctor stood there shaking from the suddenness of the attack, the sharpness of the pain across his face, and the thought of having killed a man he knew so quickly, so easily.

"You had to do it," the woman said, slipping the cord around her neck and tucking the bag inside her robes.

"We needed him to sail the ship," he said.

"No we don't," she answered. "We only need to cut it loose and go. Follow me."

"Wait a moment," he said. He had to put his boot on Esek's face to pull free his tomahawk, and then he stopped to wipe it on the bolt of silk before slipping it back into his belt. "Now I'm ready."

They exited the palace in just a few moments and crossed the rocky shore toward the ropelines. Deborah rose eagerly from her seat.

"Are you all right?" she called. "You've been gone a long time."

"I'm fine," Proctor said. "This is—"

"I am the moghul's wife," the woman said softly.

"—a friend," Proctor called back. To the woman, he said, "Can you make your way across the ropes?"

"I can," she said, and climbed up on them as one who'd had some practice. Proctor watched her make her way across and then glanced back at the palace, where he thought he saw a face briefly at one of the upper balconies. Every would not let this treasure go lightly. Not if he had sacrificed so much to keep her here. The woman was barely halfway across the ropes when Proctor followed her. He moved more quickly than she did, and was catching up to her in the middle, when he heard Every scream behind him.

"You can't have her!"

Proctor was twisting around to reply with reason, such as it was, when a pistol cracked and a ball whistled past him. The moghul's wife gasped and slipped from the rope.

Every stood on the shore with Esek's pistol in his hand.

"Hurry," Proctor said. "Before he can reload or follow."

"I don't . . . think . . . I can," the woman said. A dark stain spread across her robes. Her hand slipped off the ropes and she fell into water.

Proctor let go and dropped after her. The water was ice cold, worse than he expected, and he swallowed a mouthful. He floundered for a moment, gagging on the salt and trying to catch his breath, when he saw her robes. He swam over and grabbed them, intending to drag her to safety. He went to hook an arm around her, but he found the robes were empty—he had mistaken their waterlogged weight for a body.

"Proctor—"

Deborah's voice called his attention to shore. Her extended arm carried it back out to the water. In the channel between the islands he saw the tiger.

He looked frantically in either direction for the moghul's wife and then he swam desperately for the shore. When he looked over his shoulder, the tiger paddled after him. His arms and legs were going numb from the cold when his knee banged against a rock, and he realized he had made it. Slipping and stumbling, he pulled himself up onto the rocks. He was shivering from the cold and his fingers refused to grab hold of anything. Deborah clutched a fistful of his jacket and dragged him to higher ground.

It was not far enough or quick enough. The tiger splashed ashore only yards behind him.

He grabbed Deborah's arm and choked out words through chattering teeth. "The moghul's wife is—"

But there was no time for anything more. The tiger surged out of the water and climbed up the rocks behind him. He rolled over onto his back, reaching for his tomahawk. He could grab the beast by the scruff of its neck . . . maybe blind it . . . give Deborah a chance to escape . . .

The tiger was wounded. Blood poured from its side.

It took another step toward Proctor and he reached out to grab it.

His hand missed . . .

. . . and the tiger transformed into a naked woman, her body shivering with the cold, her face contorted in pain, and she fell across him, gasping.

"The moghul's wife is the moghul's sorcerer," Deborah said.

Deborah had put on her heavy coat against the fog that morning. Now she pulled it off and quickly wrapped the other woman in it.

Proctor's brain felt sluggish, as if he were only now putting together the pieces of a puzzle that was obvious to everyone else. The moghul's wife was also the moghul's sorcerer. When Every had captured her and tortured her, he had brought her here with him, to his hideaway. She built the palace for herself, a place where she could hide from him. But from time to time she had to come out, and when she did, she took a form that was not so easy for him to abuse.

And now Every came for her again across the ropelines.

The tomahawk was already in Proctor's hand. He scrambled to his feet and hacked at the lines where they were knotted to a post. The sound of the iron striking wood was answered by a cry of rage. Proctor struck again and again.

The top rope parted and Every fell into the waves.

Proctor hacked at the lower rope and cast it also into the water.

"He cannot swim very well," the moghul's wife said. Deborah's coat was wrapped around her, and Deborah's arms were wrapped around the coat. "We must hurry and cut loose his ship."

"I have to treat your wound," Deborah said.

"Aboard the ship," the other woman answered. She looked at Proctor. "I was in too much of a hurry. You appeared at my left shoulder, and not my right. It was an evil sign. But I had been here too long already."

She tried to stand on her own and fell. Proctor scooped her up in his arms and lifted her. She barely weighed anything.

Behind them, Every had floundered back to the far shore. "You can't have her. Do you hear me? She's mine."

The woman shuddered. "Please. Please help me get aboard the ship. I want to see sunshine again . . . "

"Can you wrap your arms around my neck and hold on tight?" Proctor asked.

"Yes, I can," she answered with grim determination.

"Then I will get you aboard. Deborah?"

"I'll go first," she said.

"Good. I don't want you here if he makes it ashore." Deborah climbed back up to the ship as quickly as she had climbed down. Proctor followed deliberately, holding on tight to the injured woman with one arm as he slid along the ropelines up to the rotting ship. They could see the island of skulls and bones from the deck. It was impossible not to recall the sight of the tiger atop that pile of bones.

"I am most sorry," the moghul's wife said. "I was only trying to frighten you away. Those are the bones of every man Every has killed. All his crew members, all the men from the ships caught in his trap designed to bring them here so he might scavenge the things he needed. He liked to pretend that he was trying to save people, then watch them crash—"

She caught her breath in pain.

"Is this place your work or his?" Deborah asked. She opened the coat and examined the gunshot wound. She didn't say anything of it, but Proctor could read the worry on her face.

"The building was my work, an attempt to protect myself, a place to remember. I formed it from my memories of the Taj Mahal, a tomb built by Shah Jehan for his love of Mumtaz. I made mine in memory of my dear husband, lost to me forever." She lifted her head, but her skin had begun to look dusty gray. "All the rest, Every created to keep me here. One night forever, the night we landed here, locked in a room outside of time. I taught him, I taught him everything, because I was too weak to let him kill me instead," she said to Deborah with a sob.

"You only did what you had to do," Deborah said, stroking her face.

"How do we get away?" Proctor asked, glancing back to the island.

"Just set the ship adrift," the moghul's wife answered. "It will want to return to its proper place."

Proctor ran to the anchor rope. He looked at the means for winding it in, and then decided it was easier to simply cut it loose. He began to chop at it with his tomahawk, but the rope was old and thick and strong.

There was a thump against the side of the ship, and then clawing and scratching.

Proctor chopped harder but the rope refused to part.

One big black paw came over the side of the ship and then another. A panther's snout followed, its ears laid back.

The moghul's wife cried out. She spoke rapidly in a different language, probably trying to transform, but whatever she did wasn't working.

The panther pulled itself onto the deck and shook itself, spraying water everywhere. His chest was heaving, and Proctor could see that he had struggled to swim this far.

It was Every.

Something in the way it stood, something in the ribs showing at its sides—he couldn't say why, but he *knew*. This was the source of all those bones piled up on the shipwreck island. Proctor turned and brought down the tomahawk with all his force.

The panther snarled and came at him.

The anchor rope separated and the ship lurched into motion, throwing them all off-balance. As the rope-end slithered across the deck, tethered to the anchor left behind, Proctor said, *"Spare not, lengthen thy cords, and strengthen thy stakes."*

The rope slipped through the anchor port and disappeared. The panther squatted, ready to pounce.

With all his focus, Proctor drew his hands in the air as if he were making a knot.

The rope whipped up over the side of the ship, wrapped around the panther's ankle and tied itself into a knot. The panther lunged at Proctor—

—and came up short.

As the boat started to move, the anchor stayed put, and the panther was dragged across the deck. He snarled and bit at the rope, clawed at it, and then, as the ship began to pick up speed, he transformed. Every was naked, flat on his stomach, sliding toward the water. He spun over, grasping at his ankle, but he was a split second too late. He slammed into the side of the ship, flipped up, and was pulled over.

His hand snapped out to snag the ship's railing.

"I'll never let you go," he shouted. "I'll never let you go!"

The railing snapped.

Proctor ran to the edge of the ship. Every was dragged under screaming, water flooding into his mouth, and then dark water and silence swallowed him.

"The ship is moving," Deborah said quietly to the moghul's wife.

She nodded understanding. "Maraja al-bahrayni yaltaqiayni," she said.

Deborah wrapped her hands around the other woman's. "Here, draw on my power."

"Maraja al-bahrayni yaltaqiayni," she repeated, the words coming with longer pauses between them. "Do you understand? The two seas flow freely so they meet together."

"I understand," Deborah said.

Proctor watched. This is what Deborah did well, forming a circle and sharing power with another. Above them, the stars and the moon faded. The sky grew light. For Proctor it was like seeing the transformation from night to dawn to noon, all collapsed into a few seconds. The fog had burned off and it was a clear and sunny day on the ocean. The cries of gulls filled the air, and the smell of saltwater and the sound of waves.

"It's been so long since I felt sunshine," the moghul's wife whispered. She reached up and took the bag from around her neck and handed it to Deborah. "This was to buy my passage home."

Deborah tried to push it away. "I can't take that."

But the woman forced it over Deborah's head. "I do not think that I will need it now."

"Don't say that—"

"I am at peace." Her voice faltered and the next words were faint. "It is very sweet."

Deborah squeezed the cords in her fist. "What is your name? We would remember your name."

But the answer was forever beyond her. Her face turned toward the sun, which bathed it in warm and gentle light.

The ship shuddered beneath their feet and tilted to one side. Proctor looked over and noticed they were low in the water. "Deborah . . . "

Deborah was still cradling the other woman in her lap, tears streaming down her cheeks. "Not now," she said.

"Deborah, the ship is sinking."

More than sinking. It was coming apart at the seams beneath them. The sides were splitting, the planks in the deck slowly separating. The mast cracked and toppled toward the deck. Proctor wrapped an arm around Deborah and pulled her out of the way. Wood and sail and rigging crashed into the deck just behind them.

"Thank y—" she started to say.

The words were cut off as she slipped out of Proctor's hand. The deck tilted beneath them as the ship capsized. Proctor slid down the deck toward Deborah, both of them chased by a vast net of tangled wreckage. He had just enough time to take a deep breath before he hit the water. If they didn't get clear of the wreckage they would be dragged under with it.

His momentum carried him deep, so deep he thought his lungs would burst, but he kicked and pushed his arms and somehow rose again. When his head broke the surface he was gasping for air. He spun in the water, searching for Deborah, and saw her floundering nearby.

He swam to her side. "Here, take hold of me," he said. "I'll n—"

The words formed in his mouth, but he had just moments before heard them come from Every's lips, and he couldn't say them.

Deborah had no such reservation. "I won't let go of you," she said.

With a gladder heart than he'd had a moment before, he pulled them through the waves to a floating mast and they clung to it like shipwreck survivors. A sail appeared in the distance, perhaps even the ship scheduled to rendezvous with them when they had set out that morning with Esek. They would only need to hang on a little while. But Deborah looked despondent.

"We know now there is no British spy ship," he told her, as they began to shiver in the cold. "And no more ships will disappear in the fog, no more men will die at Every's hand."

Deborah nodded reluctantly. Then she let go of the mast with one hand to grab the bag at her throat. "And we have this."

A thousand uses for that money ran through Proctor's head in an instant. If nothing else, they could donate it to the war, use it to help the fight for independence.

"With this we can build a real school for women with talent, a place where they can learn to use magic safely and not have to be afraid of men," she said, and her face began to brighten.

Proctor didn't even think twice. "I'll help any way I can."

RAJAN KHANNA is a writer living in Brooklyn, NY. His stories have appeared in (or are forthcoming from) *Shimmer Magazine*, *Greatest Uncommon Denominator*, *Steampunk Tales*, *Shadows of the Emerald City*, and *Dreams of Decadence*. He also writes about a variety of geeky topics for *Tor.com*, and about wine, beer, and spirits for *FermentedAdventures.com*. His writing has received Honorable Mentions in the prestigious anthology series *The Year's Best Fantasy & Horror*, and he is a graduate of the Clarion West Writing Workshop. In addition to writing, he has also narrated stories for the podcasts PodCastle and Starship Sofa. Learn more at www.rajankhanna.com.

Our next story takes us to the American south, a land of riverboats, muddy water, and playing cards.

Whether it's card tricks and sleight of hand, telling the future or constructing a house of cards—since their invention, playing cards have been put to uses that transcend the simple games they were created for. Once, only the wealthy and powerful owned them—each deck a hand-painted commission, a sign of their status. In Quentin Ketterly's world, however, it is the possession of a deck of cards that makes a person powerful in the first place.

Quentin is a gambler with a very special deck of cards and an appetite for vengeance. But, as the author says, we all deal with limitations, in whatever worlds we inhabit, and in particular, the choice between serving yourself and serving others can be a struggle. And when you're caught between love, loyalty, and revenge, making the wrong decision can be a deadly one.

Here we give you a new take on the wizard's spellbook, in which a single ace can beat a royal flush—if it's the right ace, played at the right time.

CARD SHARP
RAJAN KHANNA

By the time Quentin reached the Ketterly Riverboat, he was down to thirty-seven cards, not counting the two Jokers. He ran his index finger along the edge of the deck, tucked securely in his waistcoat pocket.

He was unarmed, not the kind of man who ever felt comfortable with a pistol, though he had once regularly carried a knife on his hip. Back then, his playing cards had been as disposable as everything else in his life: his women, his possessions, his inheritance.

But he mourned the loss of each of *these* cards. Eight had been lost to his training—the Twos and the Threes. He lost two during the trouble in Missoula when he'd been caught with that Ace—a normal Ace, mind you—up his sleeve. Another went escaping a mudslide. And in Odessa, Texas he'd lost three fending off thieves.

But that had been all prelude. To *this*. The riverboat.

He reached into his pocket and withdrew the Seven of Diamonds. The card flared like phosphorous in his hand, then disappeared in a wisp of smoke. He felt an ephemeral film coat his body. He moved from his hiding place behind some trees and moved down the walkway and to the ramp leading up to the riverboat.

He could feel the stares of the riverboat guards on him, even though he knew they could not see him. Using the Seven of Diamonds might have been overkill, but better safe than sorry. Still, his neck hair prickled at the idea that at the moment, their rifles could be trained on him, preparing to fire.

He made for a small washroom near the center of the main deck. As he approached it, the riverboat's great paddlewheel began to move, churning the water in a great roar. With a lurch, the riverboat began to move, taking Roland Ketterly and his men down the Mississippi.

Quentin slipped through the washroom door, taking care to close it quietly and minimize his noise. Whatever concealment the first card had provided was visual alone.

He drew the next two cards in his pocket. They were at the front, exactly how he'd arranged them. He removed the Jack of Diamonds and the Jack of Hearts, cupping them in his hands as if in a card game. It pained him to have to play two face cards, especially a Heart that could be used for healing, but he needed to ensure that the card he played had enough power to hold and convince the boat's occupants. Quentin threw down the pair of Jacks.

He stifled a moan as his face seemed to turn to wax. The Diamond alone would have given him the disguise he wanted, but that wouldn't have fooled anyone, especially with his voice and manner of walking unchanged. The Heart ensured the change was physiological, and though it disgusted Quentin to assume that hateful form, it was his best chance to move freely aboard the riverboat.

When the transformation was completed, he looked into the mirror, noting how eerily alike he looked to Roland Ketterly, the man he had come to kill.

Quentin could still remember the hands he'd played in that game in Tombstone. He had been having a glorious ride, the majority of the table's chips arranged in a jagged mass in front of him. The old man he was playing against, however, was clearly irritated and with each hand—and each lost ridge of chips from the once great reef in front of him—his bitter scowl deepened.

Feeling flushed from his winnings and surrounded by ladies, Quentin had started showing off, demonstrating his legerdemain with the cards and chips, making them dart and dance and disappear. With each trick the women cooed and leaned closer. With every flourish, the old man's displeasure grew.

In the end, he had taken almost everything. He packed away his winnings and retired to his room, leaving it unlocked should any of the ladies wish to join him. The old man, however, appeared, uninvited.

"What do you want?" Quentin said, thinking of the knife that now rested next to the room's wash basin.

"I need that money," the old man said.

"I won it fair."

"I know. But I can offer you something for it. Something more important. Something more valuable."

"What's more valuable than money?"

The old man flashed a smile. "Power."

Quentin kept his gait regular and his senses alert as he climbed the riverboat's stairs to the upper decks. He'd long ago realized that anxiety and panic could be bigger threats than anything external. He'd managed to overcome them in card games and sleight of hand, but *this*, this was still relatively new to him.

The chatter from the crew below was swallowed by the roar of the paddlewheel. The sickly sweet mushroom smell of the Mississippi filled the air.

On the staircase he passed a member of the riverboat's crew heading down. The man tipped his hat to him. Quentin grunted back in Roland's voice, the way he had seen Roland do many times before. His heart beat faster in his chest. The man continued on his way, paying him no mind.

He thought of Roland on the highest deck, in his private rooms. The rest of the riverboat was given over to business—to passengers or cargo, traditional operations. But the top of the boat was Roland's domain, it was from there he ran his empire. The empire that had once belonged to Quentin's father.

Between shuddering breaths he reached the top deck, one hand on the polished wooden banister, the other, fingers outstretched, hovering over his waistcoat pocket. A man came out of one of the rooms, bearded, wearing a white coat. "Ah, there you are, Mr. Ketterly," he said. "I wonder if you could come with me for a moment."

Quentin could hear his pulse pound in his ears. "I'm in a hurry," he said, in Roland's voice.

"Please," the man said. "It's your wife."

At this, a river of ice flooded his blood. "Very well," he said, and followed the man into one of the rooms.

And there, on a bed, covered in blankets, her face damp and drawn, lay Quentin's mother.

"It's a very old tradition," the old man said. "As old as the cards."

"But why cards?" Quentin asked.

"Because you need a way to focus the energy, a way to shape it. I guess some people use words written down on paper. We use the cards. They work well—numbers and symbols all tied up together. And they're portable. Light. They travel well."

"I guess that makes a kind of sense," Quentin said.

"There are two main things you need to know," the old man said. "The suit of the card determines the effect—so Hearts are good for anything involving the body, Diamonds are good for things involving money, and ways to fool the eye, and so forth. The number of the card determines the size or power of the effect. The higher the number, the more powerful the effect will be."

Quentin frowned. "Then why not just use the highest cards all the time?"

The old man gave a wicked grin. "Oh, didn't I mention that already? Because you can only use each card once."

"What?"

"That's right. Each card is one-time only. Once you burn through your deck, you're done."

Quentin sank into a wooden chair. "Well that takes some of the fun out of it," he said.

"Don't it just?"

"How do you know what number to use, then?"

"Ah, y'see that's the trick," the old man said, holding up his index finger. "It's a kind of gamble. You just have to lay it all out there and hope that you figured right. You'll get a feel for it after a while."

"But by then I'll have lost those cards."

"That's the truth of it, yes."

Quentin flipped through the cards of the deck in front of him. "What about the Jokers?" he asked. "Do those count, too?"

"Of course they do," the old man said, smiling wider, his face shining. "The Jokers are wild."

Quentin stared at his mother, pained by the way she drew in shallow breaths, by the wispiness of her. She used to be so solid. But that was back when she was married to his father. Before she had taken up with Roland Ketterly.

He reached for her dry and thin hand and held it. "How is she doing?" he asked the doctor.

"Frankly, not good," the doctor said, wiping his forehead with one of his sleeves. "Her illness is progressing. She falls in and out of lucidity. There's not much I can do except keep giving her the morphine."

Quentin held back tears. He wouldn't cry for her now, not with Roland's eyes. He acutely felt the weight of the cards in his pocket. He flipped through them until the found the card he wanted. He pulled the Queen of Hearts and held it between shaking fingers. The card could heal her. He pinched it tight. One thought, and it would come to life. One thought. The card vibrated, but did not burn.

At last, he tucked it back into his pocket. He was here, on Roland's doorstep. That card might be the difference between him winning, or dying.

And she had stayed with Roland, after all.

He turned away from her, letting her hand drop. "Do what you can," he told the doctor, then left to find Roland.

He would wash away his guilt in blood and fire.

Quentin wiped the sweat from his forehead. He had just played his first card, throwing the Two of Clubs, creating a small flame and making it dance in the air before him. "How do you know which number to use? How do you know how long the play will last or if it will do what you want it to do?"

"You don't," the old man said, shaking his head. "They're cards. It's all a gamble.

Sometimes, it's a bluff. But as with everything else, you learn to feel out the cards and you'll get better at all of that."

The old man held up another card, the Two of Diamonds, in his arthritic hands. "Now, another one."

Quentin took it, still unsure of the old man and his motives. He still didn't know the man's name, not after two weeks of training, of poring over books and flipping through cards and learning the histories and associations of them all. The man had said to call him Hoyle, though Quentin doubted that was his real name.

Quentin looked at his nearly but not quite full deck, face down on the table. The maroon backs bore the image of a circle, or wheel. He had started with fifty-four. Now he was down to fifty-three. He looked at the old man. "How many?" he said.

"What?"

"How many cards do you have left?"

The old man blinked and lowered his eyes. "Only five."

Quentin saw the regret, the loss in the old man's eyes. But he pushed that aside. He had almost a full deck, and when he was finished learning how to use them, he would go after Roland.

Yet as he lifted the next card, he winced as he willed it to life, knowing that it would forever be lost to him thereafter. Diamonds was the suit of illusion, of trickery, and Quentin conjured up an image of the old man, as if it had stepped from a mirror to stand next to him. But despite his concentration, the image never took on lifelike proportions. It appeared, hazy and flat, indistinct. A ghost and nothing more.

"What happened?" he asked.

"You tried for something beyond the value of the card," the old man said. Even as he spoke, the image faded away to nothingness.

"This is horseshit," Quentin said. "I just wasted a card. I don't see why I have to keep doing this."

"That's precisely why you need to get the feel for the cards. There are those who don't practice. They go out with full decks, don't want to waste none. They always get smoked sooner or later. They don't have the feel for the cards. You gotta learn to judge. You don't just sit down at a card game and start bluffing seasoned players before you know the game, do you? You have to learn how to order them in the deck, know what to draw and when to draw it. Hell, we haven't even talked about combining cards yet."

Quentin sighed, but he could see the old man's point. All of this was preparation. The practice would be worth it, because it would give him Roland.

"What about the Jokers, though? Can you feel them out?"

Hoyle shrugged. "They're unpredictable. No suit, no value. We call the red one The Magician. The black one's The Fool." Quentin was becoming used to the names some cards had—the Death Card for the Ace of Spades, the Laughing Boy for the Jack of Diamonds, The False King, the King of Hearts.

"If I were you, I'd put them Jokers somewhere out of the way where they can't muck things up for you. I keep mine tucked into my boots. One in my left, one in my right. They're there if you need them, but me, I don't trust anything I can't predict."

"And you can predict me?"

"Maybe not in a card game," Hoyle said, "but in everything else you're a bull seeing red. Ain't nothing to predict."

He held up the next card.

Quentin headed for the inner rooms of the upper level, where he knew Roland would be. He ignored the riverboat crew, striding forward with purpose. He reached for the door to the inner rooms, pulled it open, and stared into the face of Roland Ketterly.

They looked at each other for a moment, both surprised. Then, as Quentin reached for a card, Roland yelled and ducked behind the wall. Men, heavily armed, appeared behind him.

Quentin ducked behind the wall, away from the door and fished in his pocket for another card. Fingers trembling, he pulled out the Nine of Spades and visualized the shield taking shape around him. Moments later, a hail of bullets bounced off of it, and Quentin exhaled.

He could barely see through the gunsmoke and muzzle flare, but he pulled cards from his pocket, Spades and Clubs, Diamonds and Hearts, each one sparking to life before it felled one of the men. He used all of the meanings he could call up, all of the effects he had practiced—fire for Clubs, earth for Diamonds, water for Hearts, air for Spades. And then the other meanings, Spades for offense, Hearts to affect the body. Card after card after card.

With each one, another man fell. But not the right man. Not Roland Ketterly.

Not Quentin's uncle.

Quentin stood by the old man's bed and mopped perspiration from his brow with a cloth. "I need you to do something for me," Hoyle said.

Quentin had been expecting that. The old man was going to ask him to use one of his Hearts. He'd thought long and hard on that and decided that it was worth it. The old man had given him the deck, after all.

"Go on."

"I have a son. One I haven't seen in a while. We're not . . . we're not close. This kinda life don't lend itself well to family."

"You want me to give him some money?"

The old man shook his head. "I been giving him money. That's what I needed it for in the first place. No, I want you to give him his own cards."

"What?"

"I don't want him to have the life that I did. Boy's in a spot of trouble. Comes from not having anyone around to teach him. But they can help him. You can show him how."

"But I don't even know how to make the deck," Quentin said.

"I made it already," Hoyle said. "You just have to give it to him and show him how it works."

"Hoyle-"

"Please. I haven't been able to face him. Not after all that's happened. But you can. You can give him all I have left to give. Please, say you'll do it."

Quentin thought about his own father, and about all the trouble he'd gotten into running away from the family business. He would give anything for a connection to the man, something passed down that wasn't a stake in the family empire. Something that didn't stink of Roland.

"Okay, I'll do it. But you needn't die. I have cards. I can help fix you up."

Hoyle shook his head. "I done that before. Fixed myself up so much I've outlived my life. Only I'm all dried up now. Worn out. It's time for me to go. Do what I asked," he said. "Please."

Later, after Quentin had said goodbye, he'd taken the new deck of cards, so full and fresh, and placed them in his case. They wouldn't work for him—he knew that—but he would try to pass them on.

But first there would be a reckoning.

The smell of smoke and gunpowder filled Quentin's nostrils. Bodies littered the floor. But his attention was fixed on the door at the end of the hall, where Roland had fled. The deck felt thin between his fingers as he drew the next card. But he was close to Roland. That had to be worth the loss of the cards.

He flexed the card between his fingers, then walked up to the door and kicked it open. He felt a thrill as the impact ran up his shin and thigh. He paused for a moment.

Nothing.

Then he caught a glimpse of a large form through the door. The card burned away in his hand and six glittering blades flew through the air. He felt the smile curl his lips as he moved forward.

But the man, tall and corpulent, still stood. And it was his turn to smile, playing cards fanned out in his hands.

Quentin reached for another card, for one that was higher—in duels the high card won. He pulled out the Queen of Hearts. A potent card, but then he remembered his mother, and hesitated.

A card flashed in the fat man's hand. Invisible fists pushed at Quentin until his back slammed against the wall of the room. And he couldn't move. He couldn't reach his cards.

The fat man moved forward. Behind him, Roland sat in a chair, one leg crossed over the other.

"You have your own cards," Quentin said.

The other card sharp smiled. "You think you're the only one?"

Quentin gritted his teeth.

"Course my deck is a bit thinner than it used to be," the fat man said. "That's the rub, ain't it? The more you use it, the shorter it gets. It's a good thing cocks ain't like that." He smiled again and Quentin longed to punch the man's yellowed teeth in. Quentin flexed at his invisible bonds but they didn't give.

The fat man withdrew a partially smoked cigar from his pocket and lit it with a brass lighter, puffing on the end until it glowed red. "He's all yours, Ketterly."

Roland stepped forward until he was just a few paces before Quentin. He had aged some, was a little thinner, but he still stood rod straight.

"So you came for me," Roland said. "I have to admit I didn't think you had it in you. I figured you to be as toothless as your father."

"Better toothless than fanged"

"Well," Roland said. "We know which your mother preferred."

Quentin snarled and tried to move. "She may have swallowed your lies. But I didn't."

Roland's eyes widened. "Such fire. You really are a changed man. But you've failed."

"I made short work of your men," Quentin said.

"Men are replaceable." He smiled, showing all of his teeth.

Quentin reflexively tried to curl his hands into fists and was thwarted by the fat man's play. But this time, the tips of his fingers wavered in the air. Quentin blinked. Was the play weakening? If the fat man had only a limited deck, then maybe the power of his cards was limited. Or maybe he misjudged?

"You bought yourself some time, is all," Quentin said. "I *will* kill you."

"Ha," Roland said. "You do believe that, don't you? You are caught. Like a fish, floundering in a bucket. And my earlier generosity is all dried up. Soon, Lacroix here will kill you and nothing will change. Your momma already considers you dead. All I can say is you had your chance. I was happy to let you leave, have a life, find your own happiness. But you couldn't let go, could you?"

Roland walked away, then turned back. "You know, I said that you took after your father before. And maybe you do, in your blundering. But . . . I was thinking that if your father had the power you had, the . . . the magic, he wouldn't have spent it on blood, on violence. He would have tried to help people. Used it for one of his saintly pursuits." He stepped forward and cupped Quentin's face. Quentin couldn't flinch away. "No, Quentin. The truth is, in that respect at least, you're more like me."

Quentin wanted to scream, to grab Roland and claw out his eyes. But the play held him tight. All except for his fingers, which he could now wiggle. Just a little longer.

Roland smiled serenely. "I think it's time to say goodbye now, Quentin." He slapped Quentin's cheek. "Say hello to my brother for me." He stepped away and drew a pistol from his belt.

Quentin could now move his whole fingers and part of his hand.

Roland cocked back the hammer.

Quentin's wrist flexed.

And the Ace up his sleeve flipped into his hand.

Clubs, the suit of fire.

As it flared to life, so did Lacroix, catching fire like a sheaf of kindling. The fat man's cards, held tight in his hands, fluttered to the floor.

Lacroix screamed and Quentin felt the force holding him drop away. Roland fired, but Quentin was already moving, skirting the burning man, the card in his right sleeve, the Ace of Spades, falling into his hand.

The gun flashed again and burning streaks of pain speared through Quentin as the air filled with thunder. He fell backward and to the floor, the Ace falling from his hand as the world fragmented and blurred.

Roland stepped on the card, then bent over him and pulled the rest of the deck from his vest. He tossed them behind him. "I didn't think you'd get the drop on Lacroix," he said. "But it didn't help you in the end."

Quentin clutched at his wounds. He had none of the cards in his waistcoat, and had lost the two he'd had up his sleeves.

Roland raised the pistol. "You fool."

Memory flared, as brightly as one of the cards. Quentin reached for the card clipped into his right boot.

The Black Joker.

The Fool.

He pulled it out.

Roland's finger jerked back on the trigger.

The card flared in front of him, dazzling his eyes.

The sound of the world cracking reverberated in his ears.

And the moment passed. Quentin was unharmed. The Joker remained in his hand, but the bullet lay in two pieces, cut in two by the card.

Quentin batted the pistol away, and punched Roland in the groin. As his uncle reeled, Quentin reached for the card still lying on the ground.

The Ace of Spades.

The card blazed in his hand.

Quentin sat in the sleeper car, looking at the road ahead. In his left waistcoat pocket was his deck, or what was left of it, twenty-something. After all of the cards he had used at the hotel, he'd been forced to use another, the Seven of Hearts, to heal his gunshot wounds. Then the Queen of Hearts, on his mother. He didn't know if it would work, if the magic was that strong, but he left her in the doctor's care. He couldn't face her after everything he'd done.

His reason for learning how to use the cards was now gone. Half of them had been spent on justice. But he still had the other half left.

All the way from the hotel, Roland's words had echoed in his head. About his father. And how he would have used the cards. And how right that was.

But first he had a promise to keep. A new card sharp to bring in to the fold. Maybe *he* would choose the right path.

Quentin had played the Fool and luck had carried him through.

Now was his time to make a new play.

Now he would be the Magician.

GENEVIEVE VALENTINE's first novel, *Mechanique: A Tale of the Circus Tresaulti*, is forthcoming from Prime Books in 2011. Her short fiction has appeared in the anthology *Running with the Pack* and in the magazines *Strange Horizons*, *Futurismic*, *Clarkesworld*, *Journal of Mythic Arts*, *Fantasy Magazine*, *Escape Pod*, and more. Her work can also be found in my anthologies *Federations* and *The Living Dead 2*, and in my online magazine *Lightspeed*. In addition to writing fiction, Valentine is a columnist for *Tor.com* and *Fantasy Magazine*.

For most people, global warming is an incipient but still-academic issue, a bogey man still hiding beneath the bed. For the Inuit, whose land is being revealed inch by inch, summer by ever warmer summer, global warming is as real as an uninvited house guest snoring on the couch. As the great ice sheets melt, new opportunities and remarkable challenges arise for these northern people. This next story dives into the glacial slush—and finds magic treading the waters.

Anna Sitiyoksdottir is an Inuit shaman living in last four acres of protected Inuit territory. Her home of Umiujaq is a paved and peopled land, a land whose magic is bleeding out with every last drop of glacial melt. It's easier for Anna to do her job as a marine biologist, studying a dying sea, than it is to cope with the broken state of natural magic in such an unhealthy world.

No one knows how humanity will survive in a world of massive climate change. This story asks: How will we find magic in such a changed world? And how will we ever deserve it?

So Deep That the Bottom Could Not Be Seen
Genevieve Valentine

Anna woke up knowing the last narwhal had died.

It was a note in the air as she dressed; when she opened her door, the wind sighed it into her face, across her fingers.

(She didn't bother with gloves any more. Winters weren't what they used to be.)

It was still dark as she walked over the dirt flats to the observation post, her shadow dotted by the fence that marked the last four acres of protected Inuit territory.

Nauja Marine Observatory had been a three-room school, back when. After the new state schools had swallowed up all the students, the government cleared out the building for Anna ("A gesture of goodwill," the representative said with a straight face). Now it housed third-hand equipment gifted from the territorial government.

The observatory was on the water's edge. When Anna went down the embankment in summer, she could look past the electric green shallows to where the shore fell into the sea and left nothing but fathomless black water and slabs of milky ice. The sheet ice was already turning greasy and breaking, rotting through as it melted.

The creeping spring made Anna ill; she didn't look.

Inside, she pulled up the computer and was registering the date of death when the knock came.

The man at the door was in a parka and gloves and a hat and was still shivering.

"Anna Sitiyoksdottir?"

Her State name.

After a second, she said, "Sure."

This seemed to cheer him up. He checked his handheld. "Miss Sitiyoksdottir, my name is Stephens. I'm here to invite you to the First International Magical Congress."

She snorted.

He glanced at his handheld to find his place. "The United Nations has called a task force of magic-users to discuss our rapidly changing magical and environmental climate, and to begin cooperation on future initiatives. As a shaman with natural magic, your input will be invaluable. The conference begins tomorrow and goes for two days."

"No," she said.

He smiled and went on as if she hadn't spoken. "I will be your escort and aide while you're a delegate. We can go now, if you're ready. I'll wait while you pack."

"I'm not a shaman," she said. "And when the last one was alive, spellcasters and the UN didn't find her input valuable in the least. Pass."

His smile thinned out. "Miss Sitiyoksdottir, you're the last Inuit with any shaman status on record, and the government of the Northern States insists you be present. Please reconsider. I have authorization to involve the police if necessary."

So it was the usual sort of government invitation.

"I need an hour," she said finally. "Narwhals became extinct last night. I have to find the body on radar and send a report in to the Wildlife Council."

He blinked. "How do you know they're extinct if you didn't see anything?"

She looked at him and didn't answer. After a moment, he had the good manners to blush.

The narwhal had thrown itself onto the shore to die. Anna saw that the sand around it was undisturbed—it hadn't fought to get back to the water, hadn't so much as tossed its head to call out.

"Are you going to move it?" Stephens was breathing heavily from the scramble over the rocks. When he pulled off his cap to fan his face, she saw that his hair was thinning.

Narwhals, like winters, weren't what they used to be, but the carcass still weighed six hundred kilograms.

"No," she said, then added, "It's right that the birds have it."

"Oh," he said slowly, as if he was in the presence of great and terrible magic.

She wished the sea would swallow him.

The whale's skin was pale grey and utterly smooth, like a pup, even though it was adult. Anna knew it meant something, but she couldn't sense what. She stepped forward and touched it with a flat hand, waiting. Listening. She rested her forehead on the cool, clammy hide.

Talk to me. Talk to me. What should I do?

"Miss Sitiyoksdottir, if you're not planning to move the animal, we should get you to the airport."

It was an answer of sorts.

So Anna went. It wasn't like narwhals would be less extinct in two days.

Her mother, Sitiyok, had moved to Umiujaq as soon as the rest of the province began to fill up with refugees from the Lower States.

Everyone thought Sitiyok was a worrier and a coward to go. She was the shaman; how could she leave them? The land had been given to them; the land was theirs. Nothing would happen. Just because the Southern States were warming up didn't mean anything. Let some people move north. Who wanted to live in the South anyway, if they could help it?

Sitiyok had smiled at them all, and had moved as far north as she could.

It was not a comfort to know, years later, that she had been right. Her parents' cities were concreted over to make room for newcomers from the south.

Most Inuit tried to live off the new landscape as they had tried to live off the old one. They gave up hunting and waited tables; they gave up tanning hides and minded stores. They became government workers, or hotel managers, or pilots. Around them the air got warmer; winter was carved away from the land a little more each spring, and Southerners filled in the cracks like a rockslide.

In Umiujaq, Sitiyok took dogs out onto the ice to hunt for seal. She sold the skins she could spare; eventually she sold the dogs. When the sea warmed up and the seals didn't return, the others in Umiujaq moved inland to find work, one family at a time.

"You can't stay," they said. "Come with us."

Sitiyok smiled, and stayed where she was.

She and a few others remained in the ghost town, slowly starving out on their homeland. Sitiyok learned how to hunt rabbit; how to snare fish; how to go hungry.

One winter, she had a child, and named her Annakpok—the one who is free.

The Congresse Internationale du Magique was held in the Amphitheatre at Aventicum, in Switzerland; it avoided any question about the host country unduly influencing the proceedings.

As they left the hotel and the morning hit her, Anna frowned against the baking sun. "And we're meeting in the amphitheatre because?"

"For the magic," Stephens said, waving one hand vaguely before he caught himself. "No disrespect. It's just—my faith is in science. I studied biology."

She said, "So did I."

He coughed. "Here's our car."

The Amphitheatre was ringed with police. Under a sign that read PLEASE KEEP ALL AMULETS VISIBLE, two security guards were peering at talismans, necklaces, and tattoos. Inside the Amphitheatre, food stands and souvenir booths had been set up, and the vendors were shouting over one another in their attempts to reach the milling crowd.

The tiers above the gladiatorial floor were marked off by country. She saw signs for Kenya, Germany, the Malaysian Republic, Russia. (She wondered if the Nenets still had real winter.)

"How long did it take to find enough natural magicians to fill the quota? Are there decoys? You can tell me."

Stephens said, "Please keep your voice down."

Her name was at the Canadian United Republic table, beside a man whose nameplate read James Standing Tall. He was older—as old as her mother would have been—and when he saw her approaching he blinked.

"I didn't know there were still shamans in the Northern States," he said by way of greeting.

"There aren't," she said as she sat. "They'll take anyone these days."

The sorcerer Adam Maleficio, Greater Britain delegate, was the last of them to arrive—under a suddenly-dark sky, in a single crack of lightning and a plume of smoke.

Several of the spellcasters stood and pointed their wands, canes, and open palms at the source of the disruption.

"Hold!" one shouted, and another cried, "Pax!"

Adam Maleficio held up his hands. "Friends, hold back your spells! I come among you as a brother, to speak with you of future friendship." Absently, he brushed off his cape and his lapels. "*Absit iniuria verbis*, no?"

A handful of sorcerers laughed. He laughed as well, his eyes glinting red, his teeth glinting white.

From behind Anna's chair, Stephens leaned forward and translated, "May our words not injure."

Anna said, "We'll see about that."

The Congress Director called for comments before the floor opened for debate.

Maleficio stood up with great ceremony and said, "I have been elected to deliver a statement on behalf of all users of magic."

James Standing Tall looked at Anna. "Too late to opt out?"

"Eight hundred years too late," she said.

Maleficio delivered an erudite and lengthy Statement of Brotherhood to the assembled. (There was no telling who had elected him to speak, since some spellcasters' wands stayed pointed at him the whole time he read.)

After the first twenty minutes, Anna and James wrote notes to each other on their programs.

She learned he was Cree, one of the last of his nation. He had remained in the Southern States even after Canada had annexed them. He would come home to a spring of 130 degrees.

I can call the wind with prayer, he wrote. *It's better than leaving.*

She didn't question why he stayed. Anna had no questions to ask about where people dug the trenches for their last stands.

Instead she wrote, *Why did you come?*

He wrote, *I wanted a voice.*

What are you fighting for? she wrote.

He wrote, *Everything. We will have to fight everything, if we are to have any power.*

After a moment she wrote, *My mother was the shaman, not me. I have no real magic.*

On the floor of the amphitheatre, Adam Maleficio was saying, "Unity is more important now than ever, when magic users are taking a unique and visible position in a changing world. Let us not forget this is a place we made. This is a place of magic. This is a place *for* magic. And without unity, we weaken."

James wrote, *As long as you can fight.*

Maleficio was still going, enjoying the podium and trying to drown out the translators for good measure. "This is a place for those who know true magic to meet with respect and understanding, to come together with a single vision, and, *conjunctis viribus*, we shall succeed in all we try to do on this sacred ground."

"With united powers," Stephens translated.

"May this be a milestone of a new era," Maleficio finished.

He crushed the pages in his hands and threw his arms wide; the paper turned into six doves and flew away.

The day was boiling hot and fruitless, and during the Magic-Assisted Environment Preservation referendum Anna decided she would leave. There was no reason for her to pretend she had a voice in a council full of wand-wavers.

Then one of the delegates from Japan stood up to address the assembly.

She was wrapped in a fox stole so long that half a dozen fox heads knocked against one another as she stood. Under the stole her suit was the grey of rotting ice; the grey of the narwhal.

Anna sat up in her chair.

"While I can't speak for all natural magicians," the woman said, her voice carrying over the hum of translation, "I know my own magic has already been compromised by the problem that you ask us to solve. Without a natural world for us to call upon, we are powerless."

Maleficio called, "Don't pretend you're powerless, foxwitch!"

Her stole rippled as the six fox heads lifted and hissed at the crowd.

"No magic, *no* speaking out of turn," called the Congress Director. "Delegate Hana, thank you, you may sit down—no magic, ladies and gentlemen, *please*!"

The woman sat, amid a chorus of derisive laughter from the spellcasters.

James said, "If they had to call their spells from the grass, they wouldn't be laughing."

"If they had to call their spells from the grass," Anna said, "we'd still have grass."

The first thing Annakpok had done as shaman was build a bier for her mother's body and sing as it burned down to ashes.

It was still cold enough that Annakpok walked out onto the sea, scattering the ashes around the holes in the ice where her mother had hunted—a gift to the seals, in return for what they had given.

(It was an empty gesture; there were no more seals.)

There would be a feeling of light, her mother had told her. Annakpok would take a breath and know her purpose as shaman, and her power would move through her blood.

The closest Annakpok had come to feeling like a shaman was when she was twelve, and a government agent came to get her mother's blood sample and register Sitiyok as a natural magician.

The deep-winter sun had already set, and without her mother Annakpok was alone in Umiujaq. Besides the moon on the empty ice, there was no light at all.

The wind stole the ashes from the bowl as she walked; when Annakpok reached land again, she was empty-handed.

That was the last thing Annakpok had done as shaman.

Anna put herself in the Japanese woman's way as everyone filed out of the theatre at sunset. The woman didn't look surprised to see her.

("Kimiko Hana," Stephens told her. "*Tsukimono-suji*. They hold power over magic fox familiars. It's inherited."

"Is that spellcasting or natural magic?"

Stephens shrugged.)

Anna watched the fox heads watching her. "Do you kill them to get their power?"

The fox heads shrank back and hissed; Kimiko rested her hand on the stole to quiet them.

"No," she said, when they were still again. Her voice was carefully neutral. "It's to remember them after they leave our family. Their children are close to us." She looked askance at Anna. "Do you . . . have a familiar?"

Anna wondered if a dead narwhal counted. "No," she said, and then, recklessly, "I don't even have magic."

Kimiko raised an eyebrow, kept walking.

Anna followed her down the stairs and across the amphitheatre, waiting for a reciprocation that never came.

Finally she asked, "What sort of magic have you got?"

"It serves me better not to explain," Kimiko said. Her dark eyes flashed red. "If you don't have power, pretend otherwise. If you *do*, pretend otherwise."

She stroked the foxes' heads; under her hand, they sighed.

"What is your power?" Kimiko asked.

Anna said, "I'm great with funerals."

A woman outside the hotel was selling amulets from a card table.

"Magicked by the sorcerers from the Congress," she called, holding out a stamped clay bead on a string. "Talismans and charms! Witch-blessed! Shaman-approved!"

Anna didn't know what the symbols meant, but she could tell they were empty of power. The seller had dusted them all in cinnamon; the smell choked the air.

As Anna passed, the woman thrust it at her brightly. "Need a little magic, miss?"

Yes, Anna thought, and kept walking.

Anna dreamed of the narwhal, stark and pale against the black rocks. When she walked across the ice to meet it (she was so far away, she should not have wandered), she slipped. She remembered the ice was rotten, and was afraid. She stood where she was, too frightened to move another step and risk falling through the ice and into the water.

On the beach, the narwhal had turned to face her. Its mouth gaped open, revealing Sitiyok inside, standing and waving, gesturing to the shore.

Annakpok could not move, she was so frightened—even when the ice she was standing on sank under her, she stayed where she was. She looked down at the water lapping at her knees—so cold she couldn't feel herself drowning, so deep that the bottom could not be seen.

The ice gave way under her, and she tilted her face upwards, fighting for her last breath. The sun above her gleamed fox-red.

As the water swallowed her, she opened her hands and felt something slip from them; she had been holding tight to something she could not see.

There is always more than we can see, her mother said.

Her mother was unafraid.

Her mother was waving.

"You look horrible," Stephens said as they took their seats. "Didn't you sleep? The papers will think you're a refugee."

"And *that's* why they recruited you into the Diplomatic Corps," Anna said.

The environmental referendum ended with spellcasters insisting that they could not possibly be to blame for a weakening of natural magic they did not even use.

"We make a study of the art," said Maleficio. "Our magic is the result of scholarship. If anything, we begin at a disadvantage, because natural magic rarely chooses us. We are powerless, though we may pretend otherwise."

Anna looked up. The tips of her fingers itched as if she were stroking fur.

Maleficio threw his arms wide. "Natural magicians have the authority of the ages—they have inherited magic!"

"We have to register like livestock!" someone from the Kenyan delegation called.

Maleficio ignored him. "We spellcasters have to read and practice, and must make the best we can of lesser circumstances, to create what power we can."

The spellcasters nodded sadly. Anna and James exchanged a look.

Kimiko said, "Then in your infinite scholarship and wisdom, suggest a solution that will enable natural magicians to find enough magic for ourselves without robbing powerless, impoverished spellcasters of all their hard work."

"No magic!" cried the Congress Director, as a dark rumble spread through the Amphitheatre.

The air crackled, and heat rose from the dozens of angry sorcerers. Adam Maleficio seemed angriest of all, his arm trembling, the air rippling around him.

For a moment, his blue eyes glinted fox-red.

There is always more than we can see.

In the pause between debates, Anna slid into place behind Maleficio. Across the amphitheatre she could see James and Stephens frowning at her. She ignored them and leaned in. This close, Maleficio smelled of sulfur.

"Tsukimono-suji," she whispered.

He startled, stiffened. "Who are you?" he asked without looking.

"I'm natural magic. And so are you, foxwitch."

"I'm a sorcerer," he hissed. Around them, people were caught up in arguments over who was responsible for making natural magic possible for those who practiced it; no one heard him. "I studied at Stonehenge. I *spellcast*."

"You have a fox at home," she said. "The rest is party tricks."

She felt, rather than saw him flinch. "What do you want?"

"Force a vote," she said. "In our favor."

He sniffed. "Forget it. I'm not about to switch sides. Besides, the others won't care if I'm foxblood. I put in the work on spellcasting."

"Oh sure," she said. "It's heartwarming. We'll wrap up with that story, then," and she moved as if to rise.

He flailed one arm behind him. "Stop, stop, come back, you horror. What am I putting to a vote?"

In a surprise turnaround, Adam Maleficio made an eloquent case for the responsibility of the magical community to support its own.

"Natural magic was the earliest magic," he said. "It deserves our respect, our support, and our devotion. I, for one, will be voting to create a coalition that will work to discover a magic strong enough to shield the natural from the ravages it has suffered, and shame, *shame*, on those who do not join me!"

The spellcasters drew wands, and voted (barely) yes.

As Anna walked the ring of the amphitheatre back to her seat, she passed the Japanese table. Kimiko caught her eye and beckoned her over.

"What did you do to him? You must have more power than you thought."

Anna smiled. "I had no power," she said. "I just pretended otherwise."

One of the fox heads looked up and grinned.

When she got back to her seat, the note paper was waiting for her. James was looking straight ahead; he didn't even acknowledge she had come back.

Under *I have no real magic*, James had drawn a question mark.

She folded the paper carefully, rested both hands on it like a talisman.

At home, she waited for dark to go down to the water.

A hundred yards out, in the dim moonlight, she could still see that the narwhal was gone.

She ran.

As she lurched over the rocks, she saw it was not really gone; it hadn't sprung to life again and swum out to sea (as she had half-hoped).

It was devoured.

The narwhal was eaten clean down to the bones (impossible for birds to manage in three days), and the bones themselves were intact, despite the wind (impossible, impossible). The ribs rose sharply white against the green-black sky, the skin curling like parchment against the black ground as if the wind itself had pulled it gently from the flesh.

Annakpok looked in the sand for tracks. No animal tracks (she expected none), but she was surprised that only her own footprints came out this far.

She walked slowly, tracing the edge of the laid-out hide with her feet as she went, trying to still her pounding heart. She had to listen; she needed to see.

There was no flesh left on the bones at all; she would have suspected that she had been trapped in time, at the summit for a hundred years, except that the bones had not yet begun to dry. They were pearl-white still, the ribs like joyful hands, the tailbones pointing mournfully to the sea.

Anna knelt and plucked the smallest tailbone from the hide. It was the length of her palm, and hollow. She slid it over one finger.

She made rings out of ten vertebrae. They warmed against her skin; when she curled her hands they shifted against one another like she wore gloves of bone.

The ice under her feet was slippery, rotten, but she stepped where the moon reflected thickest. The bones in her hands thrummed as she breathed.

She walked across the sheet ice, out and on, past the light from shore, past her mother's old hunting grounds, to the edge of the ice-veiled sea. There she stopped, and trembled. The ice rocked gently under her feet, and she knew if she slipped here the sea would swallow her.

It might swallow her in any case. (She thought of her mother inside the mouth of the narwhal, beckoning her home.) It was great magic, what she was attempting. It was beyond her power.

She would be the sacrifice.

Around her the world was flat and black; the wind slid mournfully against her face.

Annakpok held out her open hands before she could be afraid. If she was a shaman, the sea would bring them back to her as narwhals. She had only to wait, and be worthy.

(*What are you fighting for?*

Everything.)

The bones fell into the water, ten white sparks that disappeared into a black so deep that the bottom could not be seen.

When she turned for the shore, the narwhal's bones looked like a doorway, like an open hand waving her home.

NNEDI OKORAFOR is the author of the novels *Zahrah the Windseeker*, *The Shadow Speaker*, and *Who Fears Death*. Her book for children, *Long Juju Man*, won the Macmillan Writer's Prize for Africa. She is also the winner of the Wole Soyinka Prize for Literature and the Carl Brandon Society's Parallax Award, and has been a finalist for the NAACP Image Award, Andre Norton Award, and the *Essence Magazine* Literary Award. Forthcoming books include *Akata Witch* and *Iridessa the Fire-Bellied Dragon Frog*. Her short fiction has appeared in *Strange Horizons*, *Clarkesworld*, and in anthologies such as *Eclipse Three*, *Seeds of Change*, *So Long Been Dreaming*, and *Dark Matter: Reading the Bones*.

Our next tale is about wizardry in modern-day Africa. Africa is a less common setting for fantasy stories, but there are some notable works out there for readers who are interested in the continent. Among the best known are the adventure tales of H. Rider Haggard, including *She* and *King Solomon's Mines* (starring the character Alan Quatermain, who also appeared in Alan Moore's graphic novel series *League of Extraordinary Gentlemen*). Charles Saunders has written a series of sword and sorcery tales starring African characters, beginning with the collection *Imaro*. Octavia E. Butler's *Wild Seed* begins in ancient Africa and follows the lives of two immortals as they attempt to come to terms with their unusual abilities. Alan Dean Foster's *Carnivores of Light and Darkness* follows an African tribesman who sets out on a quest to rescue a princess and who faces off against all manner of magical obstacles. And *Lion's Blood* by Steven Barnes is an alternate history in which Africa is the most powerful continent on earth.

In addition to her interest in Africa, another of Nnedi Okorafor's passions is strange creatures. Her work is full of wild and colorful animals, such as the very unusual birds in this next story.

THE GO-SLOW
NNEDI OKORAFOR

It was Nigerian style gridlock. The worst kind of traffic. It was a carnival of vehicles from cars to supersize trucks, nose to ass for miles, oozing, spewing, dribbling exhaust into the weighted heat under the hot penetrating African sun. Only the *okada* were on the move. The motorbikes snaked clumsily between cars and trucks, with their one, two, even *three* passengers hanging on for dear life. The *okada* dodged opportunistic hawkers and occasionally scraped the fenders of a vehicles. They always kept right on going.

The go-slow was especially sluggish today and Nkem was smoldering with irritation. All he'd meant to do was drive from one part of Owerri to another, a matter of miles. Instead, for the last two hours, he'd been stuck behind a smoke-belching truck and beside a rusty van full of choir members from some fanatical church. He'd turned off his car an hour and half ago, despite the heat. If he didn't die from inhaling the truck's noxious fumes, he was going to go mad from the women's high-pitched singing. Just then, the women started yet another verse of "Washed in the Blood of Christ."

"God Dammit," Nkem shouted, slamming his hands down on the steering wheel in frustration. Several of the women stopped singing to glare at him. He considered giving them the finger or cursing at them with such fury that they'd either think he had Tourette's syndrome or been possessed by some ungodly spirit, but then he imagined how appalled his mother would be with him. She was always in his head at the wrong times. "The goddamn church can kiss my ass, man," he muttered. "Psychos, all of them. The crippling force of this country."

But he said nothing to the women and he kept all his fingers wrapped around the steering wheel. He gnashed his teeth. It was amazing how slowly time moved in certain situations, especially ones of deep annoyance. Go-slows were like getting stuck in time warps. He shielded his eyes, looked into the sky and spotted a large eagle soaring by. Leisurely, free, ruler of the sky.

"Goddamn bird," he muttered.

He'd been on his way to a good fuck. He deserved it; he'd finished shooting his latest film, *No Boundaries*, yesterday. He owed himself the distraction and he wasn't going to get it from his wife. Besides, what he wanted was a *destructive* distraction. He'd met the girl, Agnes, at a club four months ago. Of course, she'd been ecstatic to get a phone call from Nigeria's sexiest actor. She was ready and waiting for him at a hotel twenty minutes away.

Nkem smacked the steering wheel again and pulled at his budding dreadlocks. Why had he taken this way? At this time of day? The go-slow was *always* bad here. There was no rhyme or reason. It wasn't the beginning or end of the work day. There were no especially large potholes. If it was an accident then there must have been an accident here at the same time every day. There were simply a lot of vehicles that came through here at this time. *And I* knew *this,* he thought. His blood pressure rose from just thinking about it.

Two hours of his life wasted. He picked up his cell phone and then put it down. Agnes would wait. She'd wait all day for him. Any woman would.

"Fuck it," Nkem grumbled. He rolled up the window, started the car and cranked up the air conditioner. His Jaguar guzzled fuel, but if he ran out, what did it matter? No car was going anywhere anyway. He sat back and shut his eyes as the refreshing, cool air blew against his sweaty face. Closing the window, combined with the roar of the AC, made the singing of the traveling choir in the van beside him significantly more bearable. He leaned back, moaning with the pleasure of the icy-cold air and relative quiet. He shivered and laughed to himself, amazed that he could feel any pleasure at all in a situation of such grand *dis*pleasure. Life was complicated like that sometimes.

He opened his eyes just as the truck in front of him belched out a fresh plume of black greasy smoke. He laughed again and thought *I'm going to die out here.*

That would be right in line with the way he felt. He was running to Agnes because he needed to *pound* something. He wanted to revel in the badness of the act and the sweetness of her flesh. Fake people and fake bullshit, he was surrounded by it. And he was slowly growing convinced that he wasn't for this world.

Nkem looked out the window. To his left was a busy market from which colorfully-dressed hawkers emerged to sell items like bagged plantain chips, chin chin, and cashews, skewers of spicy beef suya, and tiny plastic bags of cold "pure" water. But out of the corner of his eye, he spotted something beyond the market— something large and white and heading toward him. He blinked, wondering what it could possibly be. Too large to be a bird. A car maybe?

Whatever it was was coming fast. He slowly turned his head toward it. His eyes grew very, very wide: A large, white long-horned bull was galloping right at him. There was no time to get out. No time to run. This was it. The crazed beast was going to smash right into his side of the car and impale him with its sharp horns. Then Nkem spotted the animals' eyes; they were a milky white. Every hair on Nkem's body stood up. He took in a sharp shocked breath. He hadn't seen this since he was a kid. Since one of *them* had last tried to kill him.

Nkem tried to jump into the passenger seat. Finally, a shout of wild horror escaped his mouth as the steer bore down upon him.

But at the very last moment, the steer shook its head and changed direction. *SCREEEEEE*! Its left horn scratched hard across Nkem's window. The sound was worse than running one's nails across a chalkboard. It was a wonder that the glass didn't shatter. *"Awo!"* Nkem exclaimed, clapping his hands over his ears. After veering away from his car, the beast trotted between the other vehicles, across the street and into a patch of trees on the other side of the road.

Nkem slowly sat up, staring at the deep foot-long scratch in his window. He'd nearly died like this three times as a kid. When he was three a group of hens had tried to peck him to death. He still remembered how the chickens had all had milky eyes and been shaking their heads like they had an itch in their skulls that they could not scratch. Thankfully his mother had been nearby. That night every one of those chickens was killed, cooked and eaten. No one said anything about the chickens having weird eyes.

When he was seven, a mad milky-eyed goat had tried to butt him with its horns. Nkem had only escaped it because he was a fast and quick runner. Like the chickens, this beast also had been shaking its head. The last time was when Nkem was twelve years old. He'd been walking home alongside a busy street when a crazed, milky-eyed horse bearing an empty saddle had come running at him.

The horse shook its head violently and, a few feet before reaching Nkem, galloped into the road right in front of an overcrowded bus. The bus ran over the horse and then veered and smashed into a truck just in time for them both to career over the bridge down the road. There were mangled bodies all over the road and in the bushes. In the small river that the vehicles had splashed into, more bodies floated and people screamed for help. Nkem had just stood there, physically untouched but mentally touched deeper than he'd ever been.

This was the defining moment of twelve-year-old Nkem's life. Just before it all happened, Nkem had been thinking about his growling stomach. He hadn't eaten for days. His parents had bought him school books which meant days without food. He was the insignificant seventh son of a poor yam farmer and a crippled mother and all these people had just died because of him. Because the horse would rather run into the street than obey whatever had temporally captured its brain.

The gruesome scene of the resulting accident had been such a visual spectacle. So impressive that he'd forgotten his hunger. This moment made him yearn to go into film instead of doing medicine. He never learned where the horse came from or where its rider had gone. But aside from everything else, he never forgot the horse's completely white eyes, not blind, but *occupied*. The very look he'd just seen now, twenty years later.

He turned the car off, got out, and ran his fingertips over the scratch. They came away coated with grated glass. The scratch was deep, as if the animal was actually pushing as it turned, purposely scraping his window. The women in the car beside him had stopped singing and were staring at Nkem as if he were Lazarus himself. The man in the truck in front of him leaned out. "The Lord protects you, o! Dat animal de craze!"

Three shabbily-dressed and winded-looking boys with sticks came running between the cars. "It went that way!" one of the choir women said, pointing at the patch of trees. The boys nodded, too breathless to respond as they ran in the beast's direction. Nkem slumped in his seat with a relieved sigh, vaguely wondering how much it would cost to replace the window.

An hour later, the traffic thinned and began to move. Nkem didn't care. The image of the insane white-eyed steer was branded to his mind. He kept thinking about the way it was shaking its head. Nkem's urge to fuck was gone, not that he wanted to return to his wife back in Aba, either.

He drove three fast miles before he came to yet another patch of "go-slow" congestion. As he decelerated, he launched into a string of Igbo and English curses. He had such a terrible headache. He shouldn't have bothered leaving his hotel room. It would have been better to relax on his balcony, with a glass of cold beer and a good book. He laughed loudly. He didn't want that either. "I don't know *what* I want anymore!" he said to himself. What he did know was that he wasn't going to get sucked into yet another go-slow.

Before the cars came to a full halt, he spotted a break in a patch of palm trees. A side road. Did he dare? There had been a terrible storm last night. Was the dirt still wet? It was a hot day. The sun was high in the sky, so most likely not.

"Fuck it," he mumbled and pulled the car onto the dirt road. As soon as he did, he wished he hadn't. What if he got stuck in some mud? Last thing he needed was to really mess up his car. But he didn't want to turn around, either. He was always making impulsive errors of rebellion like this. It was how he found himself walking down the aisle—his family had had the nerve to object and that made him marry her that much faster.

The dirt road was wide enough for two cars and it was fairly smooth. After five minutes of driving, he had yet to encounter any mud spots. Miraculously, the road seemed to run right alongside the highway. Nkem was sure that eventually there would be an opening for him to get back onto the main road. The forest flanking the sides of the street looked dense and mysterious, the highway visible on the other side about an eighth of a mile away. He smiled to himself; he was moving while the traffic was stagnant. The story of his life. He pushed his car to move faster.

As he sped on, he again noticed something in his peripheral vision. *"Ah ah! What in hell is going on today?"* he whispered.

Running along the left side of his car was a large, ostrich-like bird with shaggy black feathers that made him immediately think of a masquerade, the kind that danced and was made of packed raffia. Nkem was going about thirty miles per hour and the bird was easily keeping up. The speed at which it was moving caused its soft, fine feathers to flatten as it ran. It turned its head to look at Nkem, and when it did, he saw its small, red eyes flash like jewels. Clear eyes. *Good. At least there's that,* he thought. And it wasn't shaking its head either.

Nkem looked away from the creature only to find yet another bird approaching from the right. *"Chineke!"* he whispered then returned his eyes to the road so that he didn't swerve off to the side. And that was when he saw *yet another* one standing in the middle of the road staring right at him. Even from afar, for some reason, he could see right into the bird's eyes. They were a glowing brown color, like Chocolate with the sun shining through it. Nkem heard a ringing in his ears, his heart danced in his chest, and a terrible, intense brightness momentarily blinded him.

WHAM! Whump whump!

Nkem felt the impact as if he himself had been run over. All the air left his lungs and everything went white just for a moment. Then the pain was gone. Somehow he was able to get his foot to hit the break. His tires bit into the road's dirt and he came to a silent stop. From nearby, he could hear the slow, slow traffic of the highway.

No time to consider the situation. The other birds were coming toward his car. He glared at them then turned to look at the body in the middle of the road. A heap of feathery meat. Definitely dead. One of the birds ran up to his window and tapped it with its short but strong black beak. *Tick, tick, tick,* just below the scratch from the steer's horn. Nkem let out a short breath and sat back for a moment.

"Since when are there goddamn *ostriches* in Imo State?" he wondered, leaning his head back and looking up at the black roof of his car. He considered calling his friend Festus, who was an amateur birdwatcher. He grabbed his cell phone then put it down, knowing he'd sound like a lunatic if he told Festus any of this.

One of the birds brought its head closer to the window. "What do you want, bird?" he asked. It ambled off. Nkem turned to the dead creature again, his leather seat creaking as he strained for a better look. Whatever the fuck they were, what were they doing *here*? And if they could run that fast, why *stand* in the middle of the fucking road and get run over?

An idea came to mind, and Nkem pinched and tugged at his short beard. He laughed to himself. Should he do it? "Why not," he said. He had an old sheet covering the bottom of his trunk. The boy he'd once been, the one who never wasted an ounce of food because he never had food to waste, was alive and well within him, despite his now lavish lifestyle. Why waste good meat? He laughed again. No, he wasn't going to go see Agnes. He would go see his mother who lived an hour away. *She'd* appreciate this huge amount of meat.

Nkem backed up to the dead bird and, leaving the car running, slowly got out. All the loitering birds raised their long-necked heads at attention.

"You all," he muttered. "Stay back. *Stay* back."

The birds kept their distance. Some of them, he couldn't tell how many, started making a loud booming sound in their throats. It almost sounded like deep drum beats. *That is creepy*, he thought. He looked down at the dead creature. This one was bigger than the others and looked somewhat different. There was a bright blue tint along its broken neck and deep red shadowing above its eyes. Its long neck was plumed with fluffy white feathers, and the top of its head was crowned with three long black ones. It was an attractive beast.

Thing's going to be heavy, Nkem thought, but he was tall and lifted weights daily—he was a strong guy. Even if the bird weighed more than a hundred pounds, he'd still be able to get it into the car's trunk. But goddamn, what a huge bird! It would feed everyone in the village for days. He bent down and scooped his arms underneath it. His white silk shirt would be ruined if the bird was dirty or oily, he realized, but then thought *Fuck it, I can afford another*. He lifted. It *was* heavy, easily over a hundred and twenty pounds. Something fell to the ground from between the bird's thick feathers as he lifted it. It looked like a small piece of ice.

The bird's head hung limply, like a piece of boiled cassava, and bumped against his leg. Nkem glanced at the other birds, hoping they didn't take notice of what he was doing. There were now at least ten of them standing around, blank faced, turning their heads this way and that, eying him.

Nkem placed the dead bird in the trunk then knelt down and scooped up the thing that had fallen from the bird's feathers. Some kind of gemstone? He turned it over and held it before his eyes. Quartz, maybe. He put it into the pocket of his jeans and got into the car.

For about two miles, the huge wingless birds ran beside the car on the dirt path as he drove. It was oddly exhilarating. He almost felt like one of them as he pushed the car to drive faster and, for a while, they kept up. Eventually, his car outran them, leaving them in the dust.

About a mile later, dead bird in his trunk, he got back on the highway. He was free and clear.

Or so he thought. Ten minutes after returning to the highway, Nkem pulled over after hearing a repetitive thumping sound coming from the back of the car. "How can I have a flat tire?!" he groaned. But as he pulled off the road, he began to wonder if it was something else. The thumping wasn't the rhythmic *thud-thud-thud* that a flat tire typically makes. As a matter of fact, the thumping was quite erratic.

Thump, thump!

There it was again. He rolled to a stop and listened.

THUMP!

Shit! he thought. It was coming from the trunk. The bird was still alive. Even as a kid, he'd never liked wringing even a chicken's neck. Now he'd have to wring the neck of a gigantic half-dead mystery bird.

THUMP! THUMP, THUMP!

The front of his car was already slightly dented from the impact, and now the damn thing was going to dent his trunk too if he didn't do something about it fast. He jumped out of the car and walked around to the back, then stood looking at the closed trunk, his knuckles on his hips. The afternoon sun beat against his neck and sweat trickled down his armpits.

THUMP THUMP!

He could see the metal of his trunk dome up each time. *THUMP THUMP!* "Okay, let's do this," he said, and quickly ran his finger over the sensor on his key to pop the trunk. The trunk flew open and out leapt a figure, graceful as an ostrich, shaggy feathery coat undulating with every movement. Nkem jumped back, nearly screaming. He instinctively raised his fists, ready to battle like hell.

A *woman*. His eyes had to be deceiving him. But he didn't dare blink. She was tall with strong, long legs and she wore a dress that resembled the bird's feathery hide. A *woman*. Not a giant bird. She dug her foot into the dirt, keeping her arms close to her sides.

"What do you think you are doing?" she demanded, in a hard, deep authoritative voice. "Do you think you can fight me, now?"

The bird-woman was taller than him and looked to be about thirty years old. She had strings of chunky red glass beads and white-brown cowry shells woven into her thick, tightly-braided hair. Her lips were painted dark with black lipstick and her entire dress was made of silky bird feathers. Her beaded braids clicked and clacked as she awkwardly walked around him.

"What are you?" Nkem finally asked, his fists still up.

"What is wrong with you?" she asked.

Nkem lowered his fists. "N . . . nothing."

"Why didn't you leave me to die?"

"I thought you *were* dead," he started to say, then paused, catching himself. Why was he acting like this woman was the bird he'd run over?

Before he could say more, *they* came out of the bushes. One, two, *ten*, *sixteen* big birds! *I guess they didn't stop following*, he thought. They surrounded him like a group of strange curious women.

A car driving by blew its horn. "*Nah woooooow!*" the driver exclaimed out the window, staring. Several more cars slowed down to look.

"*Chineke!*" someone else shouted.

A man held a cell phone out of the passenger seat window. Nkem could even see its camera lens adjusting to capture him in perfect high definition focus. "Snap it, now!" the driver said. "Snap it and send, o! Then broadcast live!"

"Look at *that*!"

Up close the birds had a bitter, grapefruit-like scent. They were all making that low, booming drum beat noise now and the woman was looking at them thoughtfully. Then she looked at Nkem and said something that made his heart flip: "I wanted to *die*," she whispered, then moved close to him. "I . . . I led some to freedom but too many to death. I should die for not saving them all."

Nkem blinked, suddenly far too aware of all the cars and people around him. People would certainly recognize him; he was a celebrity, Nigeria's "Sexist Man Alive." With so many witnesses, could it be long before the paparazzi showed up?

"Get in the car," he said.

She looked at him like he was crazy. "These are my friends."

"Just get in! Let them follow."

Nkem wasn't sure if this would deflect attention from him, but it was better than just standing there. He got in the Jaguar and opened the door for the bird-woman. She slowly climbed in, folding her long legs and keeping her eye on Nkem.

He felt ill but at the same time, utterly exhilarated. This was something new. This was unexpected and insane. "Who are you?" he asked as he pulled the car onto the street in front of the rubbernecking traffic. He kept to the outer lane of the street so that the herd of birds could run alongside the car. "*What* are you?"

"Ogaadi," she said, looking out the window at the running birds. "That is my name."

Nkem glanced at her but didn't say anything else.

"It is 2013," she proclaimed.

He frowned, looking at her. "Yes."

"*Chey*! How time flies. Felt more like no time was passing at all." She opened the window. "I am an *amusu*, I admit that. My uncle initiated me when I was ten. What was I supposed to do? Say no?!" She glared accusingly at Nkem.

"Uh . . . I didn't . . . you're a witch?"

"I listened to my uncle," she continued. "He taught me great things. He was the real thing, *sha*. He taught me how to eat poison and live, force plants to grow, how to cause my father to become rich in the stock market. Juju is not all bad, you know. But then my . . . my mother and my sister . . . " She swallowed hard. Nkem glanced at her with a frown as she closed her eyes and clenched her fists. He turned his eyes back to the road, feeling a shiver creep up his spine. "What happened to your mother and sister?" Nkem carefully asked.

"They died. And I don't know why! Some sort of flu," she said, after a moment. "*I* didn't do it!"

Nkem remained silent, waiting for her to continue.

"My . . . my uncle was wild with grief when they died," she said. "He had to blame someone, so he cursed me. He was so close to all of us." She took a deep breath. "Maybe ten miles from here, just outside of Owerri, my uncle had a farm, raising emu."

Emu, Nkem thought. *That's what they're called.*

"He changed me into one and threw me in with them," she continued. "Twenty years he left me there."

Nkem was having a hard time concentrating on the road. The damn emu herd running alongside the car wasn't helping, nor was the growing crowd of gawkers on the road to his left. He tightened his grip on the steering wheel and took a deep breath. *Nonsense*, he thought. *This is all nonsense! Maybe someone slipped a mild sweetie into my breakfast or something. Maybe one of the cooks hated my films.* It was a possibility. Such a thing had happened to another actor some years ago. But the strange thing was that Nkem *believed* every word this woman said. Somehow he just KNEW all that she was saying was true.

"Twenty years I hid and avoided my uncle," she said. "Business was good for him. Owerri's a good place to sell emu meat." She glanced out the open window at the running emu. She lowered her voice. "People like it. Most don't even know it's emu. They think it's beef. My uncle thought that I had long ago been slaughtered and sold as meat like the other birds. But he taught me well. I had ways of hiding in there. But I could not escape; there was an electrical fence."

Nkem felt another chill. "Last night—did the storm do something . . . ?"

"To the fence, yes," she said. "It was struck by lightning. The minute I saw our chance, I got all the emu to stampede. The fence was still sparking and many of us were killed. I . . . I didn't know that would happen. It was terrible." Tears welled up in her eyes. "So, you see, when I saw you speeding toward me, I thought fate was providing me an opportunity. I wanted to end my life . . . "

Her words touched him in an odd way. Although her story was fantastic and strange compared to Nkem's, on some basic level, how she felt was how he felt too.

He wasn't of this world. Maybe he didn't want to die but he wanted to leave this life of his behind.

"The sacrifice must have broken my uncle's juju," she said.

As they drove, more vehicles around them slowed down. Soon, Nkem found he could barely drive faster than twelve miles per hour. Neither Ogaadi nor the rest of the herd liked this. The birds began angrily making that strange drum beat sound in their chests. Ogaadi grew more and more anxious as she looked at the crowd of gawkers.

"Why do these people do this?"

"Come on," Nkem snapped. "Who *wouldn't* come and look?"

Up ahead, the traffic stopped in what looked like another very annoying bit of go-slow. Suddenly, Ogaadi looked at Nkem with bulging eyes and hollered, "You're working with him!"

"Eh? Who? What?"

"He can stop everything! I know his ways!" She suddenly grabbed at the steering wheel.

"What are you doing?" Nkem screamed.

They narrowly missed two cars as they whipped to the right, careening off the road. Nkem heard the hiss of grass as they rolled into the foliage and thankfully came to a stop without hitting anything. Ogaadi opened the door and leaped out; the emu, meanwhile, did the opposite and lunged at the car, pecking and kicking. Nkem's mind was in a muddle. "*Stop it!*" he screamed, jumping out of the car.

Nkem was shaking so badly that he fell to the ground. He got up and clumsily ran at one of the emu. He tried to push it away from his car but it was too heavy and strong. It snapped its beak at him and he jerked his head back just in time to save his nose. "What is this? Oh my god what *is* all this?!" he shouted, pulling at his hair.

Arms suddenly encircled his waist and pulled him backward. "Don't you bring harm to my people!" Ogaadi hissed in his ear as she dragged him away from the car.

They tumbled to the ground. Nkem tried to roll away but she held him there. With all his might, he kicked forward with both his legs, bucking himself out of her arms. She came at him again and next thing Nkem knew, he was grappling with the bird-woman in the grass.

"Stop it!" he cried, breaking free of her at last.

"He sent you!" she screamed. "You think I'm stupid?" She lunged at him and they fell to the ground again. Nkem was sweating profusely as dirt mashed into his locks and shirt. He was beginning to panic. Ogaadi was immensely strong. She rolled him over, straddling him with her long legs and holding his arms above his head. He was helpless.

"What is wrong with you!?" he bellowed, looking up into her wild face.

Stinging sweat dripped into his eyes caused them to tear up. He blinked them away.

Like the birds, she smelled strongly of grapefruit and she too was sweating. She was looking into his eyes with her "chocolate in front of the sun" eyes as she breathed heavily. Her face began to relax into a stunned frown.

"He didn't send you, did he?" she asked.

"No!" Nkem said, and they both fell silent.

"Isn't that Nkem Chukwukadibia?" he heard someone say.

Nkem and Ogaadi both looked toward the road. Cars had stopped and people had gotten out to watch the spectacle. No one came to help. Nkem wasn't surprised. He and Ogaadi were yards into a grassy area. The place could be full of snakes. Nkem cursed and feebly tried to kick at one of the birds, despite Ogaadi sitting on him. The bird was so focused on pecking his vehicle that it didn't notice.

"Oh God," he moaned, giving up and laying back. "My life is such shit." He looked at the sky, begging it to fall on him. There was the damn eagle again, probably watching the whole incident from above. Ogaadi just looked down at him, disgusted.

"I hate weakness," she said.

"I don't care what you hate!" he snapped.

"Weakness doesn't suit you."

"What do you know about me?" He shoved at her. "Get off me, goddammit!"

As if he'd personally insulted it, one of the birds turned to Nkem and stared at him. Nkem looked back at it frowning. It made the deep booming sound in its chest. Then it shook its head. Its eyes were white orbs.

"Oh . . . oh shit," he whispered as the bird lowered its head and started angrily strutting toward him. Nkem eyed its three-toed long-nailed powerful feet as it came at him. Perfect for stomping, raking and disemboweling a human to death. He resumed his escape efforts, frantically wriggling and thrashing. "Get off of me! *Biko!* Look at it! Its . . . "

Ogaadi didn't budge as she pensively watched the approaching emu. She held up a hand. "Leave her," she said to the emu. The bird shook its head and then clumsily sat down. Nkem gasped as the bird's eyes cleared, regaining their deep red color. He felt prickly, as if he were on the verge of understanding something very, very important. He heard blood pulse in his ears and sweat trickling down the sides of his face.

Ogaadi looked down at him and leaned close to his face.

"What did you do to it?" he asked. "Did you see its eyes? Something in the eyes . . . "

She sniffed him. "I . . . I can *smell* it on you," she said. She frowned. "You don't belong here."

"What?" he whispered.

She leaned closer, bringing her face close to his, their lips nearly touching. He didn't move. This close, she smelled sweeter, more like the inside of a grapefruit tree's flower than the actual grapefruit. She sniffed his breath again. "Ogbanje," she whispered. She sat straight up. "You?"

He wanted to speak but his throat felt heavy and useless.

"Don't you even know?" she asked.

He slowly shook his head. He felt a mosquito bite him on the leg and more sweat trickle down his back. "How? . . . " He shut his eyes for a moment, trying to collect his thoughts. "I nearly died three times as a kid for three different reasons, animals, crazy animals," he said, his eyes still closed. If he looked at her or the damn emus or the gathering crowd, he'd lose his train of thought. "My . . . my . . . my mother used to make jokes but . . . "

"Always seeking to return to the spirit world," she said, vaguely. "Yes." She nodded. "Now it makes sense. You are no coincidence." Suddenly, Ogaadi reached out and felt Nkem's pocket.

"Hey!" he said, slapping her hand away. "What are you—"

"What is this thing in your pocket?" she asked, poking at it again. He slapped her hand away and she slapped his hand hard. "Stop it!" she snapped.

"*I'll* get it!" He reached in and pulled out the piece of quartz. But it wasn't transparent as it had been when he first found it. It was gold, pure gold. She snatched it from him and held it close to her face. "What the—!" she whispered. Then she stared at him as if seeing him for the first time. She touched her tongue to the golden shard and humphed. "Where did you get this?"

"It fell off you when I picked you up," he said. "When you were still an emu, a *dead* emu."

"What did you do to it?"

"Nothing."

"Nothing?"

He rolled his eyes.

She looked down at him disgusted again. "You?"

Behind them, the crowd had grown to more than thirty people, watching, snapping photos and broadcasting with their net phones, and commenting to each other and online.

"What is that?" Nkem asked. "Why's it gold now?"

"Is this some sort of joke? You're not a child," she said. "I'm supposed to have a child."

Nkem looked at her blankly. "Uh . . . I can't . . . I mean . . . "

"I'm supposed to get a child!" she shouted. She slapped him hard across the face.

"Hey, stop it!" Nkem shouted, trying to buck her off him. If she did that again, he didn't care who was watching, he was going to beat the hell out of her . . . once he got up.

"I'm . . . sorry." She looked at the gold stone again. "I didn't mean to. You?"

"Me *what*?" He pounded his fist in the dirt and winced as his back ground against a stone. "Fuck! Get *off* me!"

"Ogbanjes seek freedom," she said, not budging. "Always seeking freedom. My uncle was one, too. That's what I sensed about you. If I could find him . . . and I will, the first thing I will do is make him very, very small and imprison him in a very small iron cage." She clenched her fist. "You're an ogbanje, too. If animals have been trying to kill you, they are possessed by your spirit friends who want you home. They sense your weakness. They can always sense when one of you wants to die."

There it was. He was an ogbanje.

He'd been hearing it all his life but only now did he really take it in. And as he let it sink in, it was as if his entire life started to make sense. *I was a lucky* kid, he realized. *They'd been trying to kill me.*

The "friends" of ogbanje children were rarely true friends. They were spirits who'd been his companions in the spirit world. And they were envious and territorial beings who ached to experience the physical world for themselves. Since they could not, they didn't want him to enjoy life, either.

So whenever he was weak, they would try to pull him back into the spirit world. When the chickens had attacked, he'd had malaria. When the goat attacked, he'd been deeply depressed because his dog had died that morning. When the horse attacked, he'd been weak from not eating for two days. Since he'd found his calling, the day of the spectacular accident, he could not remember when he'd last been sick, depressed, or deeply distraught. It had all been good. Until today.

Nkem glanced at the crowd. Then at the emus. Then at his beat-to-shit car. "Jesus." He licked his lips. He couldn't believe what he was thinking but there it was.

He and Ogaadi spoke at the same time: "You want to leave your life for a while," she said, as he said, "Can . . . can you change me?"

Again, they spoke simultaneously. "I can," she said, as he said, "You can't make me do anything."

She held a hand up. "Listen for a second," she said. "When we reach a certain age . . . "

"Who's 'we'?"

"People like me, *amusu*," she said. "We take on one we will teach. We have a stone that changes when we meet our student."

"And I'm your 'student'?"

She nodded. "The stone changes to gold when it is touched by the student."

He laughed hysterically. "You're barely older than me," he said. "Look at you." He gazed up at her. Her skin was smooth and her thighs were firm and muscular and she smelled like grapefruit and flowers. Suddenly he had to get her off him. He glanced at the crowd. There had to be close to fifty people now. He sat up but she didn't move. "We need to get out of here," he said.

She climbed off of him and they both stood. All Nkem had to do was look at the crowd and his growing erection disappeared from whence it came.

"I thought you wouldn't be so . . . . old," she said.

"Hey, I'm only twenty-five!"

"Students are usually only five or six! I was only under that spell for twenty years!"

"Maybe time works differently for birds," he said, then frowned, wondering where he'd come up with the idea.

She turned away from him. "Twenty years trapped and I have no time to be free before a student is thrust on me. Nonsense," she mumbled.

He heard a woman chuckle and say, "I wonder what his wife will think of this. *Na wow.*" He wanted to pick up a stone and throw it at her.

Ogaadi looked at the woman, bent down, picked up a stone and threw it at the woman. It landed right at her feet. "*Chineke!*" the woman exclaimed as she jumped back and bumped into a man beside her. Several people beside her all exclaimed at the same time, "Heeey!" But none of them moved to leave.

Ogaadi made the deep booming sound in her chest and all the emu stopped pecking at Nkem's car and instead ran at the crowd. People screamed and ran, losing shoes, net phones, and purses. They hopped in cars, SUVs, and trucks and screeched away. Others ran down the road pursued by the large birds. Soon Nkem and Ogaadi were alone.

"Don't mind them," she said.

He chuckled. "You don't know who I am. All of Nigeria will know about this in an hour."

She waved a hand. "Nonsense." She looked him up and down. "So did you mean what you said?"

Nkem walked over to his car and ran his hand over the scratches and dents. No one would believe this. Even *with* all the pictures and live footage. The emus had even cracked the glass of two of his back windows and windshield. Still his wife would be on the war path. He turned to Ogaadi. "Can you protect me from my spirit 'friends'?"

"Only if I am there."

Well, I've escaped them four times so far, he thought.

"What exactly . . . "

"I can't tell you until you accept," she said.

He looked at the now empty road. "How long will I be . . . gone?"

"That depends," she said with a sigh as she looked at her jagged nails. "You'll return to acting in your movies when I finish with you and your movies will be . . . something else." She paused. "You said you needed some free time. I could use some, too. Do you still want that?"

"Yes."

She laughed and nodded. "Ogbanjes are all the same. Irresponsible as hell."

Even before the word escaped his lips, he felt his body changing. Pulling in on itself, shifting, breaking. It hurt but not in a terrible way. He felt like sobbing but soon he was not able to do even that. But on the inside, he cried; he was leaving all that he held dear behind: his wife, his family, his career, the goddamn gossiping crowd. He was leaving them all behind. He was leaving the road full of congested traffic to sneak down a side road. For a while.

Ogaadi's voice sounded sharp and full. "You come back to me when I call you. Then we'll get started." She laughed. "Today is a good day. We're both free! But beware of your spirit friends."

Nkem knew.

When Nkem flew into the sky, it was like flying over a fence. She'd turned him into an eagle. He'd been afraid she'd turn him into an emu. She must have read his mind. The eagle was a creature he'd envied since he was a boy. They made meals out of chickens and easily soared above even the most insane goats and horses.

She was a powerful *amusu*, indeed. He was so elated that he opened his beak and shrieked with joy. He flew higher and higher. And then Nkem flew away.

KRISTA HOEPPNER LEAHY's fiction has appeared in *Writers of the Future, Vol. XXV*, *Shimmer*, and *flashquake*. She has an MFA in Theater, and is a graduate of the Odyssey Fantasy Writing Workshop. Her poetry has appeared in *Free Lunch*, *Raritan*, and *Tin House*.

The Odyssey is one of the great stories of Western civilization—an epic tale of one man's determination to triumph against all odds. By the end of the saga, it's apparent that those odds are steeper than he could have imagined. After all, Odysseus sets out on his journey with a full complement of warriors and shipmates, but he is the only one to arrive home.

Our next story digs into the untold life of Elpenor, a figure best remembered for his untimely death on Circe's island. As the author says, "Elpenor, in my opinion, gets kind of a raw deal. Through the ages, his death has been held up as an example of the recklessness and drunken foolery of youth. I asked myself, what might have driven him to drink, to lose himself so completely that he would fall off the roof?"

Her answer to that question takes us into the heart of a man haunted by his experience of war's hell—and tormented by a sorcery that made his ghosts seem only more real. This tale will make you wonder: What does it *really* mean to be a beast?

Too Fatal a Poison
Krista Hoeppner Leahy

Being a pig *changed* me.

The smells like fists punching my snout, the pent-up power in my haunches, the ground right there, inches from my chin, begging me to plow it with my snout, to dig to find its treasures, *now* and *now* and *now*. Wood mushroom, cheese, acorns, dried honeycomb, apple cores, corncob, I can't remember all that I ate that one transporting day, but everything tasted like hot, fresh *now*. Such immediacy, right there, under me, hot and sweet and begging me in all my pigness to devour it, consume it, *possess* it, eat it up, snort it down, roll around in it until I smelled like it and it smelled like me and we were one as we had always been meant to be, me and this earth, this earth and me.

Most of the crew shrugged it off, like a dog shaking dry after a swim. Some of the dafter ones, well, I don't think they even noticed.

But me—it had *changed* me, and Elpenor as well.

At first, I didn't think we'd be friends. Underneath, Elpenor was sensitive—too sensitive in fact—but outside he was classic warrior: tall, powerfully muscled, a bit of a brute and a hell of a fighter. He was young in age, not in skills, and had more deaths to his name than anyone but Odysseus himself. I, on the other hand, was the runt of the crew and possessed a distinct tendency to run rather than fight. With my wiry black hair, I had the look and temperament of a neurotic terrier.

Elpenor tried to distance himself from me, but the war was long and we were often thrown together, pressed into service for the dirtiest of work because we were the babies of the crew. Disposing of corpses, cleaning latrines, scrubbing the deck after punishments—Elpenor and I bonded over blood and human excrement, and we found ourselves talking to take our minds off the stench in front of us.

Soon we discovered we were both the youngest of large families, both pressured into fighting and sailing by older brothers who wanted us to be "men"—to kill and to wench and to sweat and to curse. Elpenor had handled the pressure by learning to fight, and fight well; I had responded by figuring out how not to fight, until this damnable war came along and I'd felt the need to prove myself.

Somewhere in the long middle of the war, there came a day when Odysseus ordered the two of us to collect all the eyes from the dead.

We never talked about that day.

But that was the day we became brothers.

That night we got drunk, confessed we both hated the captain, missed our sisters more than we missed our brothers, and right then and there we took a blood oath to survive, make it home, and never, ever touch a sword again.

Elpenor had been fine, more or less, during the war, but now that we were headed home he'd brood for hours about the men he'd killed. Who they'd been, who they could have been. Late at night swinging in our hammocks, I'd try to distract him with stories of our future. I came up with a plan to open a winery— marry some nice smart girls, raise kids, plant vines, and run the best winery in Greece. Once, drunk, I told him I could actually conjure vines out of the night air, vines that were green and full of life, which stretched all the way from our hammocks, all the way across the wide sea, all the way home. He laughed and told me to lay off the wine. But I could tell I'd managed to snag a bit of hope, for after that, on the truly bad nights, he'd always ask about my "damn vines."

Elpenor and I had been standing next to each other when beautiful Circe en-sorcelled us—not that any of us understood that at the time. Most of the rest of the crew started munching happily at the hay in the pigsties. But not Elpenor. He'd always been brave, whether as man or pig, and he barreled right past the hay, punching a hole out the back of the pigsty. Before I knew it, I too was through the jagged wood, following him out the hole, surprised at my own speed and power and fearlessness. Elpenor and I raced off in different directions, explosions of heat and hunger hunting in the forest.

Gods, I loved the wild freedom, the rooting visceralness of it. I was huge, hot, hungry desire and as soon as I saw something I ate it. Or gored it. Or rolled in it. Or gored it, rolled it, and *then* ate it. If I gored something, I didn't feel bad, and if I ate something I didn't feel bad, and if I rolled in something, no matter how smelly or disgusting, I didn't feel bad. I didn't worry about the war or my homesickness or my lost sense of morality. Rutting with wild sows, devouring acorns, splashing in rivers, the feel of mud drying on my skin—I simply *was*, I simply *experienced*, I simply *wanted*. What I didn't do was *think*.

How I wanted that day to last forever.

Towards dusk, exhausted by our adventure, Elpenor and I met up again, familiar to each other even as pigs, and we collapsed in a clearing: two pigs, covered in layers of earth and pine needles, and two happier animals there had never been.

I was drifting off to sleep when the change happened. It didn't feel like much, just a sudden shiver, and a weird sensation, like someone else was stretching your muscles for you, stretching them wildly far; oddly, it didn't hurt.

Odysseus had convinced Circe to release the crew, for suddenly we were men again. Dirty men, tired from our strange adventure. I was filthier than I'd ever been in my life, nauseous, and Elpenor looked at me with such loss and puzzlement in his eyes, I didn't know what to say. I shook my head. The cold knot within my chest beat its old familiar bruise. We brushed the worst of the dirt off and headed back to Circe's palace.

That night, Odysseus and Circe went at each other with abandon, and the rest of the crew plunged their newly restored human bodies into a frenzy of debauchery. Rather than deal with the taunts of "How many nymphs can you handle, baby-face?"—and "Need someone to show you how?"—Elpenor and I retreated to the roof with a large rhyton of honey mead.

The night was clear and crisp, scented by pine and salt, and the stars were just coming out as we reclined, shirtless, on the roof tiles. The hair rippled on my torso, but I couldn't feel the wind against my skin. My heart beat cold and distant as the stars piercing the night sky. I wondered if pigs were ever lost enough to look at the stars.

"Gods, I *liked* it," I said, keeping my eyes on the night sky. Elpenor didn't say anything, already stewing in a drunken brood. I wondered if his skin was flushing red the way I felt my own heating up. I took a long gulp of mead, its warmth tickling my throat.

"I liked it *a lot*," I said, louder this time. I couldn't come right out and say I wanted to be a pig again. It seemed disloyal somehow. "I want *today* again."

"Today? You want *today* again? Time to go backwards?" he said, slurring.

"You know what I mean. I want—"

"Doesn't matter what we want, don't you get that?" He was in a worse mood than I'd thought—not a typical brood, but mean, more like I'd seen him in battle. He grabbed the mead and stood up.

"Hey, save some for me," I said, rising with him, chucking him on the shoulder, trying to lighten the mood.

He stumbled back from the shoulder tap, reeling slightly. "Leave me alone." He took another big swig, then stepped towards me, lowered his head, and started . . . snorting.

It should have been ludicrous, but instead it was frightening. He'd refused to bathe earlier, and in the starlight, the forest mud on his naked chest could have been the blood of battle. He was mad and drunk enough to brawl, and I didn't want to fight him, especially in the dark, on a slippery roof.

"Come on, Elpenor, ease up."

He snorted thick guttural grunts, too low for a human.

"Stop that." I took a step backwards. "Stop it! Speak like a man."

He answered with bursts of gravelly breath so violent, spit and mucus sprayed out of his nose.

"Elpenor! Like a man!"

"Okay—Oink, oink!" he said. "You happy? That what you wanted? Come on—oink, oink. Say it like a *man*."

I didn't respond.

"Can't even say it, can you?" He took a last swallow, tossed the rhyton off the roof. A wolf howled as the ceramic rhyton shattered against the stone courtyard below. Elpenor howled back, circling me, oinking and howling.

"Stop it, Elpenor!"

"You're the one who liked it so much, come on, why don't you join me, say a little oink oink? Oink, oink. Why not? Too human?" He snorted like a pig again, snot oozing out of his nostrils.

I jumped backwards, almost slipping. "Stop it!"

His arms behind his back, he lunged towards me, head first, snorting and wheezing like a pig.

"Cerberus take you, Elpenor!" I covered my head with my arms, but he rammed into me, snorting wildly. I pushed him, hard, but he kept attacking. I couldn't tell if he was growling, crying, howling—gods, what sounds—but he was beginning to hurt me, so mad as hell, I took a deep breath and snorted back. Loudly.

One more head-butt, but then he grabbed me in a fierce hug and—thank the gods—stopped making those sounds. I felt stupid, my face smashed into his chest, his dirty sweat slick and hot against my forehead, but I was glad he'd stopped attacking me. For the first time since I'd become human again, I could feel my heart beating wildly against my ribcage.

Finally he broke our embrace. "So, a pig at heart, eh?"

I rubbed my muscles where Elpenor's hug had been a bit too tight. "Let's just say it was the first time I've felt lucky to be under the captain's command."

He snorted, but more human than pig this time.

"Elpenor? You okay?"

He licked the snot off his upper lip, as if he were sampling a delicacy. "I liked not remembering, you know?"

"Uh-huh."

"But now I remember."

I didn't know what to say. My own unwelcome memories had flooded back after the change from pig to man, but I'd managed an uneasy peace with the hellish bits, a trick my friend had never mastered. "Well, someone has to remember, right?"

"Think that's what the crew's doing downstairs? Remembering?" His mouth curved into a harsh smile. "Think the captain remembers anything about what *we've* been through? What *we've* seen?"

"No, but I remember. You remember."

"Yeah, that's my point. You wanna remember?"

"No, but—"

"But . . . you wish we were pigs." His strange grin faded.

I chuckled. Snorted softly at him.

He snorted once, choked, turned away. He walked to the edge of the roof. "How about you get us some more mead."

"A vine night?"

"Get the mead."

I nodded, noticing the thickness in his voice, and the strained slope of his shoulders. Tears, then. The human kind of howls.

I walked to the far edge, saw a few wolves and lions pacing around the smashed remnants of the rhyton, and carefully lowered myself through the top floor window. Everyone was passed out inside, nymphs and men alike. I tiptoed my way through the sleeping house, down to the ground floor where the kitchen was.

I was bundling up a skin of mead and food, when, all at once, like a cry to battle, the wolves howled and the lions roared. Grabbing a kitchen knife, I ducked outside to see what the alarm was about. The beasts were clumped around the side of the palace, and I elbowed my way to the center.

Must have been something human left in the wolves and lions, for they backed away and left me alone, kneeling by my friend. Except for the blood running out of his mouth, Elpenor looked like he was resting. The slackness of his jaw, the lack of tension in the muscles around his eyes, he looked . . . not at war. My mind was stupid molasses, thick and slow-moving, unwilling to understand.

I put my head on his chest, hoping for a sign of life, but there was nothing. Unasked, air rushed in and out of my lungs; my chest rose and fell in response. The motion of breath never seemed grotesque until next to my friend's stillness.

I stayed there all night long, hoping I could trade my breath for his. Hoping I could summon his life back from the underworld. Hoping he would lift his head, smile crazily and snort through the blood and spit. But he never did.

He never did.

Now it is the dead of night, three weeks to the day that Elpenor died, and I have just finished preparing two cups of spiced mead for Odysseus and Circe. I will place the cups beside their bed, and they will drink them in the morning, as is their habit. His with hemlock, hers without.

I will poison him, as he poisoned Elpenor. His was a double dose of venom: his toxic orders for brutality, followed by the whiplash of Circe's enchantment.

Being a pig was too fatal a poison for my friend.

I approach the bed, tray steady, feet sure. Elpenor is with me, guiding me through the darkness of their bedchamber. They are both asleep. I place the hemlock cup on the table by his side of the bed. He does not stir. I cross quietly to Circe's side, setting the innocent cup within easy reach.

I begin to leave, but stumble. There must be bed-clothes on the floor. I try to shuffle my feet free, but the bed-clothes rise higher. Or are they ropes? I kick, but the ropes tighten around my ankles, beginning to climb my calves. I want to scream, but force myself not to panic. Something skein-like, soft and warm, now reaches nearly to my waist. I pray silently to the gods: *Help, for the love of my friend, someone help me.*

The room lightens; the heat of flame warms my back. Turning, I see Circe, awake, her eyes aglow—a forest beast hunting in the night. Long fingers of green light tie me to her hands. I shake my head, try to clear my vision. Long, living threads have wrapped themselves tightly around my feet, my legs, my waist, up to my chest, trapping me by the bed. Behind her, prone, lays Odysseus. He is as dark as she is light.

"What shall I do with such a sad little murderer?" the sorceress says.

I struggle against her strange finger-threads.

"Don't be so impatient." Sparks fly out of her eyes, and the cords around my body squeeze once, twice. Warmth rushes through me, relaxing me. "Why do you seek to murder my beloved?"

Circe's face blurs as the floor seesaws, as if I'm on the ship again. Her damn hands must be drugging me. The skein of fingers tightens, forcing my gaze upwards. Sea-green hair flows down her back, intertwining with her finger-threads as if she were a waterfall. I am a small raft floating helplessly towards the cascade of her. "He killed my friend, like he's killed so many others."

"He's killed many men, but not your friend."

"If Elpenor had never been a pig, he wouldn't have . . . fallen off that roof."

"But I am the one who enchanted you and your friend."

"Odysseus is the one responsible. He's the one who made you change us back into men."

"Your friend longed to be a pig?" Her eyes flash at the question. "Why?"

"He . . . " I hesitate, not certain of the true answer, not wanting to betray his memory. "He loved not being human," I finally say. Close enough to the truth.

"And you?"

"I loved . . . being a pig," I whisper.

"That is different than loving not being human?"

I hesitate again. The pressure of the cords increases, and the words tumble out of my mouth. "Elpenor liked forgetting he was human, forgetting he'd *ever* been human. I loved . . . the pleasure, the freedom, the chance to experience without having to think. I loved how there was no separation between me and my senses, and no division between good me and bad me. Gods, to be a pig again." The wish falls easily out of my mouth, even though I have not once named my desire since that night on the roof.

"True or false. You seek your death. As your friend sought his."

"No," I struggle to raise my voice, but can't. I am cocooned in calm. "False, he—" I do not know how to finish the sentence of what he sought, or didn't seek. "I seek—I want to be a pig."

How odd to see my heartbeat, pulsing in her watery skin.

"You long for my punishment. But what you wish for will not bring your friend back."

"I know." I swallow. For the first time since I've been drugged, shame rises within me. Tears burn the edges of my eyes. Her strange, strong embrace grows even stronger and the shame subsides. "But maybe pigs don't remember their friends are dead," I say.

I'm not sure why I'm crying, all I feel is numb. Her finger-threads reach out and catch my tears before they can spill, as if thirsty for them. "Think carefully."

I do. I think about running hot and wild through the woods, devouring golden mushrooms, nuts, sweet fruits of trees. Sleek and powerful, seeking pleasure after pleasure, rolling in the damp peat, the cold river, the loamy underwood. Nothing between me and my sweet earth. No separation, no worries, no confusion, no sense of right or wrong, no memory. *No memory.* The phrase sticks and repeats in my mind. No memory. What Elpenor longed for. But do I?

"I won't remember being human?" I say. "I won't remember my friend?"

"True. Beasts do not have human memories." Odysseus stirs in the bed beside her, his darkness shifting like a small mountain. "You must choose now, mortal. Odysseus will wake soon, and he will kill you outright should he find you here. If you want death, do nothing. But if you seek life, you must choose. You can choose to be a pig, or you can choose to be a man, but you must choose *now*."

I hesitate.

"Your hesitation chooses for you. Good-bye and good-bye to your friend."

"His name was Elp—"

Before I finish his name, she mumbles some words. My skin shivers and shrinks, stretches and tears, and all the time her finger-threads cradle me, keeping me paralyzed as wave after wave of emotion and memory and longing hit. In her strange woven-hands, she lifts me out the window and down towards the stone courtyard. Her hands unfurl like living green vines.

I gasp for breath, as I glimpse the heady wildness soon to be mine. Smells so rich they're food in my mouth: the thick honey of crushed flowers; the salt air needles pricking the back of my throat; the forest's mushroom succulence begging me to plunge and rip and flee into its darkness.

The air is cold candy to my skin; my blood rises hot in response. I struggle violently against Circe's hold, thrashing towards the sweet forgetful earth beckoning me.

I smell freedom.

I smell oblivion.

I smell *now*.

I taste hot salt-sweet blood; I see the howling eyes of Circe's beasts; I hear the dull click of my hooves against stone; the world overflows with *now* and *now* and *now*.

ORSON SCOTT CARD is the best-selling author of more than forty novels, including *Ender's Game*, which was a winner of both the Hugo and Nebula Awards. The sequel, *Speaker for the Dead*, also won both awards, making Card the only author to have captured science fiction's two most coveted prizes in consecutive years. His most recent books include another entry in the Enderverse, *Ender in Exile*, and a sequel to his near-future political thriller *Empire*, *Hidden Empire*. He is currently working on *The Lost Gates*, the first volume of a new fantasy series.

One of Card's recurrent themes in his fiction is precocious children whose superior intellect isolates them from their peers and brings them into conflict with dull-witted adult authorities, and whose exceptional abilities destine them for world-changing actions about which they may be reluctant or ignorant. (Most famously in *Ender's Game* and its many sequels and companion novels.)

And in today's storytelling landscape, in which parents are all too often kidnapped, deceased, or otherwise out of the picture—all the better to free up the kids to go adventuring—Card is resolute about writing about family and community and the ways in which those things shape us.

Card's 2005 novel *Magic Street* is one such story, set in the Baldwin Hills section of Los Angeles. It tells the tale of a very unusual boy named Mack Street who must face a lurking evil that has invaded his neighborhood. (A story set in this milieu, "Waterbaby," is available on the author's website.)

Our next story also involves many of Card's storytelling signatures—an exceptionally bright young man, some very strange abilities, and a special destiny.

JAMAICA
ORSON SCOTT CARD

AP Chemistry was a complete scam and Jam Fisher knew it. Riddle High School was the cesspool of the county school system. Somebody in the superintendent's office came up with a completely logical solution: Since statistics proved that high schools with the highest enrollment in Advanced Placement courses showed the highest rates of graduation and college placement, they would make *all* the students at Riddle High take AP courses.

How dumb do you have to be to believe something like *that?* Dumb enough, apparently, to go to college, get an Ed.D., and then work in the Riddle County School System.

Jam was one of the few kids at Riddle who would have taken AP Chemistry anyway. But now, instead of studying with other kids who were serious about learning something, he was stuck in a class with a bunch of goof-offs, dumbasses, and idiots.

Which he knew wasn't fair. They weren't actually dumb, they were simply out of their depth. *They* didn't have a college-grad Mom like Jam did, or have a small shelf of books in the living room which were written by relatives (but read by almost nobody).

Fair or not, the result was predictable. In order to have a hope of teaching anybody anything, they were dumbing down the curriculum, and so Jam would have to work twice as hard to educate himself in order to do decently on the AP tests. Mom would go ballistic if he didn't ace them all and come out of high school with a whole year of college credits. "If you don't have a full ride scholarship you'll be at Riddle Tech and that means you'll be qualified—barely—for janitorial work."

And here he was on the first day of class in his junior year, listening to some overly-chummy teacher making chemistry into a joke.

"What I have here," said Mr. Laudon, "is a philosopher's stone. Supposedly it could change any common metal into gold, back in the days of alchemy." He handed it to Amahl Piercey in the first row. "So before we go any further, I want every one of you to hold it—squeeze it, taste it, stick it up your nose, I don't care—"

"If I'm spose to taste it, I don't want it up Amahl's nose," said Ceena Robles. Which provoked laughter. Meanwhile, Amahl, not much of a clown, had merely squeezed it, shrugged, and passed it back.

The stone was passed hand to hand up and down the rows. Jam saw that it looked like amber—yellowy and translucent. But nobody seemed to notice anything special about it, till it got to Rhonda Jones. She yelped when she got it handed to her and dropped it on the floor. It rolled crookedly under another desk.

"It burned me!" she said.

Shocked you, you mean, thought Jam. Amber builds up an electric charge. That's the trick Mr. Laudon must mean to play on us.

But Jam kept his thoughts to himself. The last thing he needed was to have Laudon as an enemy. He'd done a year where he antagonized a teacher and it wasn't fun—or good for the grades.

"Pick it up," said Laudon. "No, not you, her. The one who dropped it."

"My name is Rhonda," she said, "and I'm not picking it up."

"Rhonda." Laudon scanned the roll sheet. "Jones. Yes you *will* pick it up, and now, and squeeze it tightly."

Rhonda got that stubborn look and folded her arms across her chest.

And with a resigned feeling, Jam spoke up to take the heat off her. "Is this an experiment or something?" asked Jam.

Laudon glared at him. Good start, Jam. "I'm talking to Miz Jones here."

"I'm just wondering what's so important," said Jam. "It's not as if there's such a thing as a philosopher's stone. It's just amber that builds up an electric charge and it shocked her when she got it."

"Oh, excuse me," said Laudon, looking at the roll. "Yep, I checked, and right here it says that *I'm* the teacher here. Who are *you?*"

"Jam Fisher."

"Jam? Oh, I see. That's a nickname for *Jamaica* Fisher. I've never heard of a *boy* named Jamaica."

Some titters from the class, but not many, because in the lower grades Jam had been through bloody fights with anybody who said Jamaica was a girl's name.

"And yet you have the evidence right there in your hands," said Jam. "Doesn't the roll have a little M or F by our names?"

"It's gallant of you, Mr. Fisher, to try to rescue Miz Jones, but she *will* pick up that stone."

Jam knew he was committing academic suicide, but there was something in him that would not tolerate a bully. He got up, strode forward. Laudon backed away a step, probably afraid Jam intended to hit him. But all Jam did was reach down under the desk where the stone had rolled and reach out to pick it up.

The next thing he was aware of was somebody slapping his face. It stung, and Jam lashed out to slap back. Only has hand barely moved. He was so weak he couldn't lift his arm more than an inch before it fell back to the floor, spent.

The floor? What was he doing, lying on his back on the floor?

"Open your eyes, Mr. Fisher," commanded Laudon. "I need to see if your pupils are dilated."

What is this, a drug test?

Jam *meant* to say it. But his mouth didn't move.

Another slap.

"Stop it!" he shouted.

Or, rather, whispered.

"Open your eyes."

With some fluttering, Jam finally complied.

"No concussion. No doubt your brain is in its original condition, despite having hit the floor. You—the two of you—help him stand up."

"No thanks," murmured Jam.

But the two students delegated to help him were more afraid of Laudon's glare than Jam's protest.

"I'll throw up," Jam said. Or started to say. But the last part came out in a gush of lunch. By good fortune, it landed between desks, but it still got all over Jam's shoes, and the shoes and pantlegs of everyone near him.

"I think he needs to go to the nurse," said Rhonda.

"Need to lie down," Jam said. Whereupon he fainted again, which accomplished his stated objective.

He woke up the next time in the nurse's office. He heard her talking on the phone. "I can call an ambulance for him," the nurse was saying, "but school policy does not allow us to transport a sick or injured student in private vehicles. Yes, I know you wouldn't sue me, but I'm not worried about getting sued, I'm worried about losing my job. You don't have a job for a fired nurse, do you? Then let's not argue about the policy. Either I call an ambulance, or you come get him, Miz Fisher, or I keep him here to infect every other student who comes in here."

"I'm not sick," murmured Jam.

"Now he's saying he's not sick," said the nurse, "even though he still has puke on his shoes. Yes, ma'am, 'puke' is official nurse lingo for vomitus. We speak English nowadays, even in the best nursing schools."

"Tell her not to come I'm okay," whispered Jam.

"He says for you not to come, he's okay. Weak as a baby, probably delirious, but by no means should you leave work to come get him."

Within twenty minutes, Mother was there.

So was Mr. Laudon. "Before you take him, I want it back," he said to Jam.

"Want what?" asked Mother. "Are you accusing my son of stealing?" Jam didn't even have to open his eyes to see his mother right up in Laudon's face.

"He picked up something of mine from the floor and he still has it."

Jam noticed that Laudon didn't seem to want to tell Mother or the nurse that what he was looking for was a stone. "Search me," Jam whispered.

Mother immediately was stroking his head, cooing at him. "Oh, Jamaica, baby, don't you try to talk, I know you don't have it."

"He offered to let me search," said Mr. Laudon.

"So this boy of mine, this straight A student who comes home from school every day and takes care of his handicapped brother and prepares dinner for his mother, *this* is the boy you want to treat like a criminal?"

"I'm not saying he stole it," said Mr. Laudon, backing down—but not giving up, either. "He might not even know he has it."

"Search me," Jam insisted. "I don't want your philosopher's stone."

"What did he say?" said Mother.

"He's delirious," said Laudon. Jam could feel his hands now, patting his pockets.

Jam opened his hands to show they were empty.

"I'm so sorry," said Mr. Laudon. "I could have sworn he had it. It wasn't in the room when they carried him out."

"Then I suggest you take a good hard look at some *other* child," said Mother. "Jamaica, baby, can you sit up? Can you walk? Or shall I have Mr. I-Lost-My-Rock-So-Somebody-Must-Have-Stolen-It help you out to the car?"

Rather than have Laudon touch him again, Jam rolled to one side and found he could do it. He could even push himself into an upright position. He wasn't so weak anymore. But he wasn't strong, either. He leaned heavily on his mother as she helped him out to the car.

"What a great first day of school," he said.

"Tell me the truth now," said Mother. "Did somebody hit you?"

"Nobody hits me anymore, Mama," said Jam.

"Damn well better not. That teacher—what was that about?"

"He's an idiot," said Jam.

"Why is he an idiot who's already on your case on the first day of school? Answer me, or I'll tell the principal he touched you indecently when he was patting you down and that'll get his ass fired."

"Don't say 'ass,' Mama," said Jam.

"Ass ass ass," said Mother. "Who's the parent here, you or me?"

It was an old ritual, and Jam finished it. "Must be me, cause it sure ain't you."

"Now get in that car, baby."

By the time they got home, Jam was recovered enough that he didn't have to lean on anybody. "Maybe you should take me back to school, Mama, I feel a lot better."

"So does that mean you were faking it before?" asked Mother. "What's so bad that you want to get out of it and jeopardize your whole future by skipping school, not to mention jeopardizing my job by making me leave all in a rush to take you home?"

"If I could've talked I would have told the nurse not to call you."

"Answer my question, Jamaica."

"Mama, he was passing around a stupid stone, talking about alchemy as the forerunner of chemistry, and claiming it was a philosopher's stone. Only it picked up a static charge and zapped Rhonda Jones's hand and she dropped it, and Mr. Laudon was having a hissy fit, trying to *make* her pick it up even though she had already touched it and what's the point *anyway*, he was just going to tell us that alchemy doesn't work but chemistry does, so why should we all touch the stupid rock?"

"Let me guess. You saw injustice being done so you had to put your face right in it."

"I just bent over to pick up the stone and I must have passed out because I woke up on the floor."

"You didn't pick it up?"

"No, Mama. *You* accusing me of stealing now?"

"No, I'm accusing you of having something seriously wrong with your health and having visions of getting called out of work next time because you turned out to have a faulty valve in your heart or something and you keeled over dead on a basketball court."

"The only way I'll ever get on a basketball court is if I'm already dead and they're using me for a freethrow line."

"I got too many hopes pinned on you, you poor boy. If only—I should have killed him instead of marrying him."

"Don't go off on Daddy now, Mama."

"Don't you call him Daddy. He's nothing to you or to me."

"Then don't bring him up whenever anything goes wrong."

"He's the reason *everything* goes wrong. He's the reason I have to work like a slave every day. He's the reason you have to earn a scholarship to get to college. He's the reason your poor brother is in that house on his bed for the rest of his life, your brother who once had such . . . so much . . . "

And then, of course, she cried, and refused to let him comfort her until he made her let him hug her, and then it was *him* helping her into the house, making her lie down, bringing her a damp washcloth to put on her forehead so she could calm down and get control of herself so she could get back to work.

He closed the blinds and closed the door as he left her room. Only then did he go into the living room where Gan's bed was, in front of the television, which he didn't really watch, even though it was on all day. The neighbor lady who supposedly looked in on him several times a day would set the channel and leave it.

"How you doin', Gan?" said Jam, sitting down on the bed beside his brother. "Anything good on? Watch Dr. Phil? I already got myself in trouble with a teacher—chemistry teacher, and a complete idiot of course—and then I passed out and smacked my head on the floor and threw up. You should have been there."

Then, even though Gan didn't say anything or even make a sound, Jam knew that he needed his diaper changed. It was one of the weird things that Jam had been able to do since he was nine, and Gan got brain-damaged—Jam knew what Gan wanted. He learned not to bother telling Mother or anyone else—they just thought it was cute that "Jamaica thinks he knows what Ghana wants, isn't that sweet? Always looking out for his brother." Jam simply did whatever it was Gan needed done. It was simpler. And it gave Jam a reputation among the neighborhood women as the best son and brother on God's green earth, when he was no such thing. It's just that he knew what Gan wanted and nobody else did, and nobody would believe him, so what *else* was there to do?

Jam got a clean diaper from the box and brought the wipes and pulled down his brother's sheet. He pulled loose the tabs and then rolled his brother over. And this was the other weird thing that had started when Jam began taking care of his brother: His skin never actually touched the diaper or anything in it. It was like his fingers hovered in the air just a micron away, so close that you couldn't fit a hair between, and he could pick things up and move them as surely as if he had an iron grip on them. But there was never any friction. Never any contact.

All that Mother noticed was that Jam was tidy and never soiled his hands. She still made him wash. Once, defiant, Jam had gone through the whole handwashing ritual without ever letting the soap or water actually touch his skin. But it took real effort to repel the water, not like fending off solid objects. So he didn't bother pretending, when washing was so easy. Didn't bother defying anybody, either. Except when somebody was being a bully. If he'd stood up to Daddy, got between him and Gan, maybe things would have been different. Daddy never hit Jam, it was only Gan he lit into, even at his angriest.

The diaper was a real stinker but it made no difference to Jam. It didn't soil his hands, and he had stopped minding the smell years ago. Dealing with anybody else's poop would make him sick, but it was Gan's, so it was just a thing that needed doing. Jam cleaned off his butt—it took three wipes—and then folded the diaper into a wad and dumped it into the garbage can with the anti-odor bag in it.

Then he opened the clean diaper, slipped it into position, and rolled Gan back onto it. Now that everything was clean again, he didn't bother fending—his hand touched the bare skin of his brother's hip. He was about to fasten the diaper closed when suddenly Gan's hand flashed out and gripped Jam's wrist.

For a moment all Jam felt was the shock of being grabbed. But then he was flooded with emotion. Gan *grabbed* him. Gan *moved*. Was it a reflex? Or did it mean Gan was getting better?

Jam tried to pry Gan's hand from his wrist, but he couldn't—his grip was like iron. "Come on, Gan, I can't fasten the diaper if you—"

"Show me," said Gan.

Jam looked at his face, looked close. Had Gan really said it? Or was it in his mind, the way Jam always knew what Gan wanted? Gan's eyes were still closed. He looked completely unchanged. Except for the grip on Jam's wrist, which grew tighter.

"Show you what?"

"The stone," said Gan.

A shudder ran through Jam's body. He hadn't told Gan anything about the stone. "I don't *have* it."

"Yes you do," said Gan.

"Gan, let me go get Mama, she has to know you're talking."

"No, don't tell her," said Gan. "Open your hand."

Jam opened the hand that Gan was gripping.

"Other hand."

Jam's right hand was still holding the tab on the diaper, preparing to fasten it. So he finished the action, closing one side of the diaper, and then opened his hand.

Right in the middle of his palm, half buried in the skin, was the stone. And it was shining.

"Power in the stone," said Gan.

"Is it the stone that healed you?"

"I'm not healed," said Gan.

Then, as Jam watched, the stone receded into his palm and the skin closed over it as if it had never been opened.

"It wasn't there before, Gan. How will I know when it's there?"

"It's always there. If you know how to see."

"How'd I get it? I never touched it. How'd it get inside me like that?"

"Your chem teacher. He serves the enemy who trapped me like this. He gathers power for him and stores it in the stone. Steals it from the children. When he has to tell his master that he lost it. . . ." Gan smiled, a mirthless, mechanical smile, as if he were controlling his body from the outside, making himself smile by pulling on his own cheeks. "He'll want it back."

"Well, *yeah*," said Jam.

"Don't touch him," said Gan. "Don't let him touch you."

"Who's his master?"

"If he ever finds out you're involved in this, Jam, you'll end up like me. Or dead."

"So it wasn't Daddy?"

"Daddy hit me, yes, like he hit me a hundred times before. Do you think I'd ever let *him* hurt me? No, my enemy struck me at the same moment. And Daddy got blamed for it." Then, as if he could read Jam's thoughts, he added, "Don't go feeling sorry for Daddy. He *meant* to hurt me every time."

"Is it the stone that's letting you talk?"

"The power stored up in the stone. When you stop touching me, I'll be trapped again."

"Then I'll never let go. Can you get up and walk?"

"I'd use up everything in that stone within an hour."

"What's going on, Gan? Who's your enemy? Are you in a gang?"

Gan's body trembled with grim laughter. "A gang? You could say that. Yes, a gang. The gangs that secretly rule the world. The turf wars that are invisible to people who have no nose for magic. Sorcerers with deep power. This is the price I pay for being uppity."

"Isn't there anybody who can help you?"

"There's nobody we can trust. You never know who is a servant of the Emperor."

"There's no emperor in America."

"In the *real* world, there's no America. Only the wizards and their toys and playthings in the natural world. What's a president or an army or money compared to someone who controls the laws of physics at their root? Now let go of me, before we use up the stone. We'll need its power."

"Are you under a spell? Like in a book?" But there was no answer, for Gan had let go, and now skin was not touching skin. Gan lay there as he had for all these years, slack-faced, inert, unable to move or speak or even show that he recognized you. But he *was* inside that body, just as Jam had always believed, just as Mother pretended to believe but didn't anymore. Gan was alive and he had spoken and . . .

Jam sank to the floor beside Gan's bed and cried.

Mama came into the room. Jam stopped himself from crying, but it was too late, she had seen.

"Oh, baby," she said, "are you really sick? Or is there something wrong at school?"

"Gan," said Jam. And then she thought she understood, and sat beside him on the floor, and cried with him for her great strong son Ghana, who had once been her friend and protector, and now lay on a bed in her living room like a corpse in a coffin, so her life was one long endless funeral. Jam understood now, and longed to tell her what was really going on. But Gan had told him not to, and so he didn't. He just wept with his mother until they were worn out with weeping.

Then she went to work, and Jam went outside and watered the tomatoes and sprayed them for the fungus that wiped them out last year. They'd already had so many tomatoes this year, what with Jam spraying them every two weeks, that they'd been sharing with half the neighborhood. And Jam and Mother were so sick of tomatoes that they were giving them *all* away now. But Jam couldn't stop watering and spraying them. It was as if having too many tomatoes this year made up for having almost none the last.

Jam thought about what Gan had told him. An emperor. Wizards. Gan involved in a war—a revolution?—and nobody knew it. How futile it was that Jam had worked so hard last year to learn the name and capital and location of every nation in the world—only to find that they don't even matter. He wondered what the map would look like, if the cartographers knew who really ran things.

And yet the government still took taxes and controlled the cops and the army—that was power, it wasn't *nothing*. Did the wizards meddle in the wars of ordinary people? Fiddle with the laws that Congress or the city council passed? Mess with zoning laws? Or bigger stuff, like the weather. Could they stop global warming if they felt like it? Or had the caused it? Or merely caused people to believe it was happening? What was real, now that a small part of the secret world had been revealed?

I have a stone in my hand.

Mr. Laudon showed up so soon after school let out that Jam suspected he dismissed class early. Or maybe his last period was free. Anyway, if he knocked on the door, Jam didn't hear it. The first he knew Laudon was there was when he saw him standing near the gate to the front yard, watching as Jam pick the ready beans off the tall vines. Jam was carrying the picked beans in his shirt, holding the bottom of it out like a basket.

Jam couldn't think of a thing to say. So he said, "Want some tomatoes?"

Laudon looked at the beans in his shirt. "That what you call a tomato?"

"No, we just got plenty of tomatoes. We ain't sick of beans yet."

He could see Laudon wince at "ain't." Laudon was the kind of teacher who would never catch on that whenever he wanted to, Jam spoke in the same educated accents and careful grammar as his mother. The kind of teacher who thought there was something morally wrong with speaking in the vernacular.

"I came for the stone," said Laudon.

Jam rolled up the front of his shirt to hold the beans, then pulled it off over his head and set it on the back lawn. He pried off his shoes. Pulled off his socks. Pulled off his pants and tossed them to Laudon. Wearing only his jockeys, he said, "You want to sniff these, too, Mr. Laudon? That what you came over for?"

Laudon glared—but he went through the pockets of the pants. "This proves nothing. You've been home long enough to hide it anywhere."

As if I'd let it out of my sight, now that I know what it can do. "What's so important about this stone, Mr. Laudon?"

"It's an antique."

"A genuine philosopher's stone."

"A stone that people in the middle ages genuinely believed to be one."

"That's such a lie," said Jam.

"Watch what you say to me."

"You're in my back yard, watching me strip my clothes off. I'll say what I want, or you'll be explaining to the cops what you're doing here."

Laudon threw the pants back at him. "I didn't ask you to take your clothes off."

"There were a lot of kids in that room, Mr. Laudon. I'm the one who was unconscious, remember? Why not search among the ones who were awake? What about Rhonda Jones? She's the one who dropped it. Whatever's in that stone, it bothered her, didn't it? Maybe she took it."

"You know she didn't," said Laudon. "You think I don't know how to track the stone? Where it is, and who has it?"

"And yet you checked the pockets of my pants."

Laudon glared. "Maybe I should go ask your brother."

"Go ahead," said Jam. But inside, he was wondering: Was Laudon the enemy who did this to Gan? Would he harm Gan, lying there helpless in bed?"

Laudon smirked. "You haven't given it to him, I know that much. You don't know how."

Jam wondered what would happen if he touched Laudon. Not *hit* him, just touched him. Would Laudon get a jolt of power the way Gan did? Or would Jam have power over Laudon? How did this stuff work?

"You've got the fire in your eyes," said Laudon. "Ambition. You're wondering if you can use the power in the stone. The answer is, you can't. It's a collector.

A battery of magic. Only someone with power can draw on it. And that's not you."

He said "you" with such contempt that it made Jam angry. He bent over and plunged both hands into the muddy soil around the tomatoes. But he did it while fending, so that when he pulled his hands out, they were clean—not a speck of dirt or mud clung to them. He showed his hands to Laudon and then walked toward him. "Does this look like 'no power' to you?"

"You can fend?" asked Laudon, glancing around. "Then why did you let me. . . . " He clamped his mouth shut.

Why did I let him in here? Interesting. So the fending he did was supposed to work farther than just a micron's depth of air surrounding his body. Jam had never tried to push things farther away than that. He tried to do it, to use the fending to push outward.

It was like when he decided to try to wiggle his ears. He had already noticed that when he grinned, his ears went up. So he stood in front of the mirror, grinning and then letting his face go slack, trying to feel the muscles that moved his ears. Then he worked at moving only those muscles, worked for days on it, and pretty soon he could do it—move either ear up and down, without stirring a muscle on the front of his face.

This was the same thing, in a way—not a muscle, but he did know how to fend a little. Now he isolated the feeling, the thing he did to make the fending happen, and pushed it outward from himself. At first he had to move his arms a little, but quickly he realized that this had nothing to do with it.

His shirt, twisted up on the ground with the beans inside, began to roll away from him. The garden hose snaked across the grass. Laudon took a step back. "You don't know what you're doing here, Jam. Don't attract the attention of powers you don't understand."

"You're the one who doesn't understand," said Jam. "You said the stone was nothing but a collector, but that's not true. That's what *you* are, gathering whatever magical power your students have. Rhonda had a lot of it, didn't she? But you don't know what I have."

"I know you fainted when you touched it."

"I never touched it," said Jam.

"And I know it's here. Somewhere close."

Jam gathered his fending power and made a thrust toward Laudon.

Laudon staggered back. He looked frightened. Now Jam was sure that Laudon himself was no wizard. He tried to bully Jam only as long as he thought Jam was powerless, just a kid who stole something. Now that he knew Jam had some power—apparently more than Jam himself had guessed—it was a different story. Laudon was frightened.

"The emperor will hear of this."

"As if you ever met the emperor," said Jam contemptuously. "All you're good for is gathering power for somebody else. And *not* the emperor."

"A servant of the emperor," said Laudon. "The same thing."

"Unless it isn't. Didn't you take history? Don't you know how this works? How do you know the one you serve, the one you've been gathering power for, how do you know he's really loyal to the emperor? How do you know he isn't gathering power to try to challenge him?" Jam gave Laudon another shove, which knocked him off his feet this time.

This is cool, thought Jam.

He flung the hose at Laudon now, and it went after him like a flying snake, hitting him, splashing him with the dregs of water left in the hose.

"I'll report this!"

"What can you do to me that's worse than was already done? My brother's lying in there like a *vegetable,* and you think I'm worried about the treasonous wizard you serve?"

"He's not treasonous!" But Laudon looked worried now—about a lot more than a garden hose or a few grass stains on his butt. "You don't know who you're messing with!"

Which was true enough. Jam had no idea who the emperor was, or who Laudon's master was, or anything but this: He had a stone inside his skin, and now when he touched Gan, his brother came to life under his hand.

He also knew that when he made wild accusations about Laudon's master, he got more anxious and fearful. So maybe there was some truth to it.

I shouldn't mess with this, thought Jam. I'm out of my depth. Whatever Laudon's afraid of, I should be afraid of it too.

Or maybe not. Maybe I shouldn't let fear decide what I'm going to do. Gan never showed fear of *anything.*

Then again, Gan ended up as a vegetable for all these years, trapped inside a body that couldn't do anything. What might happen to me?

What will happen to me—and Gan, and Mother—if I don't do anything?

"Who is your master?" demanded Jam.

Laudon rolled his eyes. "As if I'd tell you."

"I'll ask Gan."

"Yes, yes, go ahead," said Laudon, taunting him now. "If he *knew,* do you think he would have let down his guard? You don't know anything, little boy."

"I know that *you* don't know anything, either. In fact, you know less than nothing, because the things you think you know are wrong."

"It's the madness of power on you, boy. You think you're the first? You realize you've got something that nobody else has, you realize you've got your hands on something powerful, and suddenly you think you're omnipotent. But go look at your brother. See what you think about *his* omnipotence!"

"No, I don't think I'm powerful," said Jam. "Just more powerful than *you*."

"But not more powerful than the one I serve. Never more powerful than that. And every word you say, every push you make with that fending power of yours will only draw attention to you. Attention you truly *do not want*."

"But I do want it," said Jam. "I want the emperor to come here! I want the emperor to judge between us!"

Where had that idea come from?

Gan? Was it Gan, telling him what to say?

"You tell the emperor who your master is, and how he trapped Gan, and how he's using you to gather power."

"It's for the emperor, I told you, *all* the power I've gathered."

"Then let the emperor come, and I'll give the stone to him!"

"So you do have it."

Jam rolled his eyes. "Duh."

"That's all I needed to hear," said Laudon. He stood up. Started walking toward Jam.

Jam fended him. Laudon didn't even pause. "I can feel your little pushes, boy," he said. "That made it easy to pretend you had power over me. But you don't. You're like a baby with a squirt gun." Laudon reached out and took Jam by the throat. "Where is it? Not in your head—though that wouldn't stop me, I'd have your head, it belongs to my master just like everything else does."

"Nothing belongs to your master!" cried Jam. "It all belongs to the emperor!" Or at least it would if this magic society worked like feudalism.

"Do you think the emperor cares what happens to you?" Laudon ran a finger down Jam's neck and chest until it rested directly over his heart. "Which arm?" he asked. Then his finger traced out and down to Jam's right hand. "I'll have that back now, thanks."

"No you won't," said Jam. He rammed his knee into Laudon's groin.

"Owie owie," said Laudon, sarcastically.

"I should have known," said Jam. "You gave your balls to your master along with everything else."

"Open your hand."

"Open it yourself."

"Right down to the bone if I have to," said Laudon. Then he pulled a sharp piece of obsidian from his pocket and prepared to slice Jam's palm open.

So all his bravado had come to nothing. And yet there *was* a power that could save him—or destroy him—but what else could he call upon? He had only just learned that there *was* an emperor, and yet somehow he knew all about him. No, he knew nothing about him but his true title—and the only other thing that mattered. That Jam could trust him.

He pulled away from Laudon and fended him with all his might. "I call upon the Emperor of the Air, to come and judge between you and me!"

His fending was more powerful than Jam had dared to hope—Laudon flew away from him clear to the fence and fell into the cucumbers.

"Oh, master!" cried Laudon, reaching out his arms beseechingly.

Oh. It wasn't Jam's power that had thrown Laudon so far. Jam had called on an outside power, but it wasn't the emperor who had come.

Jam turned to see Mother standing in the back door. "Why did you come back here!" she demanded of Laudon.

"He has it," Laudon said. "I told you he had it."

"I would have known," she said. "Do you think he could have it, and I not know?"

"He admitted it! And he can fend. He has power."

"He has no power," said Mother. "Do you think I can't tend my own house?"

Jam's mind reeled. Was it possible that his own mother was his enemy?

"No, baby," said Mother. "This man is a fool. He has no business here."

"You know about all this," said Jam. "About the stone, and collecting power, and Gan being enchanted."

"I only know that my boy is standing in the back yard in his underwear while a high school teacher is lying in the cucumbers," said Mother. "That's enough for me to call the cops."

Laudon chimed in. "He already called somebody."

"Do you think *he'd* waste his time?"

"Are you still loyal to him?" demanded Laudon. "I haven't been helping you commit treason, have I?"

"Shut up, Laudon," said Mother. "Nobody wants to hear what you have to say."

Jam turned to see how Laudon would react, but saw instead that Laudon had no mouth. Just a smooth expanse of skin from nose to jaw.

Mother reached out her arms to Jam. "Come on inside, baby."

"He was going to cut me with this," said Jam, holding up the obsidian blade.

She held out her hand for it. "That's too dangerous for you to play with it."

"Dangerous for me, Mama? Or you?"

"Come inside."

"Are you the one who locked Gan inside his body? Are you the one that made him a vegetable?"

"A talky vegetable, judging from your attitude right now. Jamaica, don't make me cross with you. We're too close for such a spat between us."

"You haven't denied it yet."

"Oh, how television of you. No, darling, I didn't hurt Gan. But if I *had* hurt him, would I tell you? So why bother asking a question that has only one possible answer, whether it's true or not?"

"Has it all been an act? All your tears for Gan?"

"An act? Gan is my son! Gan owns my heart. Do you think I could do this to him?"

"I don't know," said Jam. "I don't know anything. Nobody's who I thought they were. Nothing's what it seemed like up to now."

"My love for you is real."

"Are you Laudon's master?"

"Jam, I'm not anybody's master."

"You've got Gan on a bed where he can't do anything, not even speak."

"And that is the greatest tragedy of my life," said Mother, starting to cry. "Are you going to find a way to blame me for that?"

Arms closed around Jam from behind. "I've got him now, Master," said Laudon.

Jam fended him viciously, and abruptly he was free. He glanced over his shoulder and saw Laudon sprawled on the grass.

"Oh, very nice," said Mother. "Is that how I taught you to treat company?"

"What I want to know is, does Father have any of this power? Are we all magicians?"

"You're not, and your father isn't, and Gan *was* but now he's not," said Mother.

"But if you have so much power, Mother, why don't you *heal* Gan?"

"*Heal* him? He chooses to be the way he is."

"Chooses!"

"He was not a dutiful son," said Mother.

"And what about me?" said Jam.

"There has never been a better boy than you."

"Unless I refuse to give you the stone."

Her face grew sad. "Ah, Jamaica, baby, are you going to be difficult too?"

"Was that what happened to Daddy? He got 'difficult'?"

"Your father is an animal who doesn't deserve to be around children. Or anybody, for that matter. Now come here and open your hand to me."

"It doesn't show," said Jam.

"Then open your hand so I can see for myself that I can't see it."

Jam walked to her, his hand open.

"Don't try to deceive me, Jamaica," said Mother. "Where is it?"

"This is the hand it's in," said Jam.

"No, it's not," said Mother. Then she pressed her ear against Jam's chest. "Oh, Jamaica, baby," she said. "Why did you have to do that?"

"Do what?"

"Swallow it."

"But I didn't."

"I'm going to get it from you," said Mother. "One way or another." She reached out a hand toward Laudon. In a moment, the obsidian knife was in her grasp and she was singing something so softly that Jam couldn't catch a single word of it.

She reached out with the obsidian blade toward Jam's bare chest. "It always hides in the heart," she said. "I'll have it now."

"Are you going to kill me, now, Mother?" asked Jam.

"It's not my fault," she said. "You could give it to me freely, though—then I wouldn't have to cut."

"I don't control the thing," said Jam.

"No," said Mother sadly. "I didn't think so."

The obsidian flashed forward and she drew it down sharply.

But there wasn't a mark on Jam's skin.

"Don't try to outmagic *me*," she said. "Your father tried it, and look where he is."

"He's better off than Gan."

"Because he's not so dangerous to me. I trusted Gan before he turned against me. Now stop fending."

"It's a reflex," said Jam. "I can't help it."

"That's all right," said Mother. "I can get inside your fending."

"Not if don't let you."

"You're part of me, Jam. You belong to me, like Gan."

"As you told me growing up, if I can't take care of my toys, I'm not entitled to have them."

"You're not my toy. You're my son. If you serve me loyally, then I'll be good to you. Haven't I always been till now?"

"Till now I didn't know what you did to Gan."

"I must have that stone!" she said. "It's mine!"

"That's all I needed to hear."

Mother and Jam both turned to see who had spoken—the voice certainly wasn't Laudon's.

In the middle of the back yard, standing on the lawn, was a slim, young-looking man with flashing eyes.

"Who are you?" asked Jam.

"I'm the one you called," said the Emperor of the Air. "Now your mother has admitted that the stone is for her."

"For me to give to *you*," she said, sinking to her knees.

"What would *I* do with it?" he asked.

"Why, how *else* do you get your vast powers?"

"Virtue," said The Emperor of the Air. "You hid your deeds for years, but you should have known you couldn't hide forever."

"I could have, if this boy hadn't—"

"She's not really your mother," the Emperor of the Air said to Jam. "No more than Gan is your brother. She took you, as she took Gan, because you had the power. She tried to use Gan's power as a wizard, but he rebelled and she punished him. You're the substitute. She stole you when Gan was confined to bed."

"She's not my mother?"

The Emperor of the Air waved his hand and suddenly the dam inside Jam's mind broke and he was flooded with memory. Of another family. Another home. "Oh, God," he cried, thinking now of his real father and mother, of his sisters. "Do they think I'm dead?"

"That was not right," said Mother—no, *not* Mother—she was Mrs. Fisher now. "We were so close."

"Not so close you weren't willing to tear his heart out to get at the stone. But you wouldn't have found it," said the Emperor of the Air. "Because you never knew what he was—and is."

"What is he?" demanded mother.

"His whole body is a philosopher's stone. He gathers power from everyone he touches. The stone flew to him the way magnets do. It went inside him because it was of the same substance. You can't get it out of him. And that knife of yours can never cut him."

"Why are you doing this to me?" she cried out from her heart.

"What am I doing to you?" asked the Emperor of the Air.

"Punishing me!"

"No, my love," said the Emperor. "You only *feel* punished because you know you deserve it." He held out a hand to Jam.

Wordlessly, Jam took his hand, and together they passed Mrs. Fisher by, entering the house without even glancing at her.

The Emperor led Jam to Gan's bed. "Touch the lad, would you, Jamaica?"

Jam leaned down and touched Gan.

Gan's eyes opened at once. "My lord," he said to the Emperor of the Air.

"My good servant," said the Emperor. "I've missed you."

"I called out to you."

"But you were weak, and I didn't hear your voice, among so many. Only when your brother called did I hear—his voice is very loud."

Jam wasn't sure if he was being teased or not.

"Take me home," said Gan.

"Ask your brother to heal you."

Jam shook his head. "I can't heal anybody."

"Well, technically, that's true. But if you let your brother draw on the power stored up inside you, he can heal himself."

"Whatever I have," said Jam, "belongs to him, if he needs it."

"That's a good brother," said the Emperor.

Jam felt the tingle, the flow, like something liquid and cold flowing through his arm and out into Gan's body. And in a few moments he was out of breath, as if he had been running for half an hour.

"Enough," said the Emperor. "I told you to heal yourself, not make yourself immortal."

Gan sat up, swung his legs off the bed, rose to his feet, and put his arm around Jam's shoulders. "I had no idea you had so much strength in you."

"He's been collecting it his whole life," said the Emperor of the Air. "Everyone he meets, every tree and blade of grass, every animal, any living thing he has ever encountered gave a portion of their power to him. Not all—not like that trivial stone—but a portion. And then it grew inside him, nurtured by his patience and wisdom and kindness."

Patience? Wisdom? Kindness? Had anyone every accused Jam of such things before?

Gan hugged Jam. "We can go home now," he said. "I to the Emperor's house, and you to your true family. But you're always my brother, Jamaica."

Jam hugged him back. And with that, Gan was gone. Vanished. "I sent him home," the Emperor explained. "He has a wife and children who have needed him for long years now."

"What about Mother? I mean Mrs. Fisher? What she did to Gan. To *me*. Taking away even my memories of my family!"

The Emperor nodded gravely, then gestured toward Gan's bed.

Mrs. Fisher lay there, helpless, her eyes open.

"I'm kinder to her than she was to Gan," said the Emperor. "Gan did no wrong, yet she took from him everything but life. I've left her eyes and ears to her, and her mouth. She can talk."

Then Mr. Laudon stood beside the bed. "And *that* will be Laudon's punishment, won't it, dear lad? To take care of her as Jam once cared for Gan—only you get to hear what she has to say." The Emperor turned to Jam. "Tell me, Jamaica. Am I just? Is this equitable?"

"It's poetic," said Jam.

"Then I have achieved even beyond my aspirations. Go home now, Jam, and be a great wizard. Live with kindness, as you have done up to now, and the power that flows to you will be well-used. You have my trust. Do I have your loyalty?"

Jam sank to his knees. "You had it before you asked."

"Then I give you these lands, to be lord where once this poor thing ruled."

"But I don't want to rule over anybody."

"The less you rule, the happier your people will be. Assume your duties only when they demand it. Feel free to continue high school, though not at Riddle High, alas. Now go home."

And at that moment the house disappeared, and Jam found himself on the sidewalk in front of the home where in fact he had lived for the first twelve years of his life. He remembered now, how he met Mrs. Fisher. She came to the house as a pollster, asking his parents questions about the presidential election. But when Jam came into the room, she rose to her feet and reached for his hand and at that moment he was changed, he remembered growing up with *her* as his mother, and being Gan's brother, and the tragic incident where "father" knocked him down and damaged his brain. None of it true. Nothing. She stole his life.

But the Emperor of the Air had given it back, and more besides.

The door to the house opened. His real mother stood there, her face full of astonishment. "Michael!" she cried out. "Oh, praise God! Praise him! You're here! You came home!"

She ran to him, and he to her, and they embraced on the front lawn. As she wept and kissed him and called out to everyone in the neighborhood that her son was home, he came back, Jam—no, Michael—murmured his thanks to the Emperor of the Air.

ROBERT SILVERBERG—four-time Hugo Award-winner, five-time winner of the Nebula Award, SFWA Grand Master, SF Hall of Fame honoree—is the author of nearly five hundred short stories, nearly one hundred-and-fifty novels, and is the editor of in the neighborhood of one hundred anthologies. Among his most famous works are *Lord Valentine's Castle, Dying Inside, Nightwings,* and *The World Inside.* Learn more at www.majipoor.com.

For most people, learning magic is no easy feat. It's not really the sort of thing you can just puzzle out for yourself in your spare time. I mean, what are the chances that anyone's going to accidentally stumble across just the right incantation or just right quantity of eye of newt? Sure, you might be one of the lucky ones who gets invited to some sort of amazing wizard academy, but most practitioners of the arts are just going to have to suck it up and apprentice themselves to some crotchety old coot.

Being a sorcerer's apprentice typically involves a lot of scut work—sweeping floors, emptying chamber pots, polishing beakers. And the most frustrating thing is, you've probably learned just enough magic to get an enchanted broom to do the job for you, but not enough to actually make it stop.

Our next story points out that while fiction would have us believe that most wizarding masters are ancient graybeards, some aspiring magicians may in fact find themselves apprenticed to attractive female wizards. However, for an amorous young man, this can be a mixed blessing. This story also points out that the ways of the heart can be as tricky, mysterious, and potent as any other form of enchantment.

The Sorcerer's Apprentice
Robert Silverberg

Gannin Thidrich was nearing the age of thirty and had come to Triggoin to study the art of sorcery, a profession for which he thought he had some aptitude, after failing at several for which he had none. He was a native of the Free City of Stee, that splendid metropolis on the slopes of Castle Mount, and at the suggestion of his father, a wealthy merchant of that great city, he had gone first into meat-jobbing, and then, through the good offices of an uncle from Dundilmir, he had become a dealer in used leather. In neither of these occupations had he distinguished himself, nor in the desultory projects he had undertaken afterward. But from childhood on he had pursued sorcery in an amateur way, first as a boyish hobby, and then as a young man's consolation for shortcomings in most of the other aspects of his life—helping out friends even unluckier than he with an uplifting spell or two, conjuring at parties, earning a little by reading palms in the marketplace—and at last, eager to attain more arcane skills, he had taken himself to Triggoin, the capital city of sorcerers, hoping to apprentice himself to some master in that craft.

Triggoin came as a jolt, after Stee. That great city, spreading out magnificently along both banks of the river of the same name, was distinguished for its huge parks and game preserves, its palatial homes, its towering riverfront buildings of reflective gray-pink marble. But Triggoin, far up in the north beyond the grim Valmambra Desert, was a closed, claustrophobic place, dark and unwelcoming, where Gannin Thidrich found himself confronted with a bewildering tangle of winding medieval streets lined by ancient mustard-colored buildings with blank facades and gabled roofs. It was winter here. The trees were leafless and the air was cold. That was a new thing for him, winter: Stee was seasonless, favored all the year round by the eternal springtime of Castle Mount. The sharp-edged air was harsh with the odors of stale cooking-oil and unfamiliar spices; the faces of the few people he encountered in the streets just within the gate were guarded and unfriendly.

He spent his first night there in a public dormitory for wayfarers, where in a smoky, dimly lit room he slept, very poorly, on a tick-infested straw mat among fifty other footsore travelers. In the morning, waiting on a long line for the chance to rinse his face in icy water, he passed the time by scanning the announcements on a bulletin board in the corridor and saw this:

Apprentice Wanted

Fifth-level adept offers instruction for serious student, plus lodging. Ten crowns per week for room and lessons. Some household work required, and assistance in professional tasks. Apply to V. Halabant, 7 Gapeligo Boulevard, West Triggoin.

That sounded promising. Gannin Thidrich gathered up his suitcases and hired a street-carter to take him to West Triggoin. The carter made a sour face when Gannin Thidrich gave him the address, but it was illegal to refuse a fare, and off they went. Soon Gannin Thidrich understood the sourness, for West Triggoin appeared to be very far from the center of the city, a suburb, in fact, perhaps even a slum, where the buildings were so old and dilapidated they might well have dated from Lord Stiamot's time and a cold, dusty wind blew constantly down out of a row of low, jagged hills. 7 Gapeligo Boulevard proved to be a ramshackle lopsided structure, three asymmetrical floors behind a weatherbeaten stone wall that showed sad signs of flaking and spalling. The ground floor housed what seemed to be a tavern, not open at this early hour; the floor above it greeted him with a padlocked door; Gannin Thidrich struggled upward with his luggage and at the topmost landing was met with folded arms and hostile glance by a tall, slender woman of about his own age, auburn-haired, dusky-skinned, with keen unwavering eyes and thin, savage-looking lips. Evidently she had heard his bumpings and thumpings on the staircase and had come out to inspect the source of the commotion. He was struck at once, despite her chilly and even forbidding aspect, with the despairing realization that he found her immensely attractive.

"I'm looking for V. Halabant," Gannin Thidrich said, gasping a little for breath after his climb.

"I am V. Halabant."

That stunned him. Sorcery was not a trade commonly practiced by women, though evidently there were some who did go in for it. "The apprenticeship—?" he managed to say.

"Still available," she said. "Give me these." In the manner of a porter she swiftly separated his bags from his grasp, hefting them as though they were weightless, and led him inside.

Her chambers were dark, cheerless, cluttered, and untidy. The small room to the left of the entrance was jammed with the apparatus and paraphernalia of the professional sorcerer: astrolabes and ammatepilas, alembics and crucibles, hexaphores, ambivials, rohillas and verilistias, an armillary sphere, beakers and retorts, trays and metal boxes holding blue powders and pink ointments and strange seeds, a collection of flasks containing mysterious colored fluids, and much more that he was unable to identify. A second room adjacent to it held an overflowing bookcase, a couple of chairs, and a swaybacked couch. No doubt this room was for consultations. There were cobwebs on the window and he saw dust beneath the couch, and even a few sandroaches, those ubiquitous nasty scuttering insects that infested the parched Valmambra and all territories adjacent to it, were roaming about. Down the hallway lay a small dirty kitchen, a tiny room with a toilet and tub in it, storeroom piled high with more books and pamphlets, and beyond it the closed door of what he supposed—correctly, as it turned out—to be her own bedroom. What he did not see was any space for a lodger.

"I can offer one hour of formal instruction per day, every day of the week, plus access to my library for your independent studies, and two hours a week of discussion growing out of your own investigations," V. Halabant announced. "All of this in the morning; I will require you to be out of here for three hours every afternoon, because I have private pupils during that time. How you spend those hours is unimportant to me, except that I will need you to go to the marketplace for me two or three times a week, and you may as well do that then. You'll also do sweeping, washing, and other household chores, which, as you surely have seen, I have very little time to deal with. And you'll help me in my own work as required, assuming, of course, your skills are up to it. Is this agreeable to you?"

"Absolutely," said Gannin Hidrich. He was lost in admiration of her lustrous auburn hair, her finest feature, which fell in a sparkling cascade to her shoulders.

"The fee is payable four weeks in advance. If you leave after the first week the rest is refundable, afterwards not." He knew already that he was not going to leave. She held out her hand. "Sixty crowns, that will be."

"The notice I saw said it was ten crowns a week."

Her eyes were steely. "You must have seen an old notice. I raised my rates last year."

He would not quibble. As he gave her the money he said, "And where am I going to be sleeping?"

She gestured indifferently toward a rolled-up mat in a corner of the room that contained all the apparatus. He realized that that was going to be his bed. "You decide that. The laboratory, the study, the hallway, even. Wherever you like."

His own choice would have been her bedroom, with her, but he was wise enough not to say that, even as a joke. He told her that he would sleep in the study, as she seemed to call the room with the couch and books. While he was unrolling the mat she asked him what level of instruction in the arts he had attained, and he replied that he was a self-educated sorcerer, strictly a novice, but with some apparent gift for the craft. She appeared untroubled by that. Perhaps all that mattered to her was the rent; she would instruct anyone, even a novice, so long as he paid on time.

"Oh," he said, as she turned away. "I am Gannin Thidrich. And your name is—?"

"Halabant," she said, disappearing down the hallway.

Her first name, he discovered from a diploma in the study, was Vinala, a lovely name to him, but if she wanted to be called "Halabant," then "Halabant" was what he would call her. He would not take the risk of offending her in any way, not only because he very much craved the instruction that she could offer him, but also because of the troublesome and unwanted physical attraction that she held for him.

He could see right away that that attraction was in no way reciprocated. That disappointed him. One of the few areas of his life where he had generally met with success was in his dealings with women. But he knew that romance was inappropriate, anyway, between master and pupil, even if they were of differing sexes. Nor had he asked for it: it had simply smitten him at first glance, as had happened to him two or three times earlier in his life. Usually such smitings led only to messy difficulties, he had discovered. He wanted no such messes here. If these feelings of his for Halabant became a problem, he supposed, he could go into town and purchase whatever the opposite of a love-charm was called. If they sold love-charms here, and he had no doubt that they did, surely they would sell antidotes for love as well. But he wanted to remain here, and so he would do whatever she asked of him, call her by whatever name she requested, and so forth, obeying her in all things. In this ugly, unfriendly city she was the one spot of brightness and warmth for him, regardless of the complexities of the situation.

But his desire for her did not cause any problems, at first, aside from the effort he had to make in suppressing it, which was considerable but not insuperable.

On the first day he unpacked, spent the afternoon wandering around the unprepossessing streets of West Triggoin during the stipulated three hours for her other pupils, and, finding himself alone in the flat when he returned, he occupied himself by browsing through her extensive collection of texts on sorcery until dinnertime. Halabant had told him that he was free to use her little kitchen, and so he had purchased a few things at the corner market to cook for himself. Afterward, suddenly very weary, he lay down on his mat in the study and fell instantly asleep. He was vaguely aware, sometime later in the night, that she had come home and had gone down the hallway to her room.

In the morning, after they had eaten, she began his course of instruction in the mantic arts.

Briskly she interrogated him about the existing state of his knowledge. He explained what he could and could not do, a little surprised himself at how much he knew, and she did not seem displeased by it either. Still, after ten minutes or so she interrupted him and set about an introductory discourse of the most elementary sort, beginning with a lecture on the three classes of demons, the untamable valisteroi, the frequently useful kalisteroi, and the dangerous and unpredictable irgalisteroi. Gannin Thidrich had long ago encompassed the knowledge of the invisible beings, or at least thought he had; but he listened intently, taking copious notes, exactly as though all this were new to him, and after a while he discovered that what he thought he knew was shallow indeed, that it touched only on the superficialities.

Each day's lesson was different. One day it dealt with amulets and talismans, another with mechanical conjuring devices, another with herbal remedies and the making of potions, another with interpreting the movements of the stars and how to cast spells. His mind was awhirl with new knowledge. Gannin Thidrich drank it all in greedily, memorizing dozens of spells a day. ("To establish a relationship with the demon Ginitiis: Iimea abrasax iabe iarbatha chramne" .... "To invoke protection against aquatic creatures: Lomazath aioin acthase balamaon" .... "Request for knowledge of the Red Lamp: Imantou lantou anchomach" . . . .) After each hour-long lesson he flung himself into avid exploration of her library, searching out additional aspects of what he had just been taught. He saw, ruefully, that while he had wasted his life in foolish and abortive business ventures, she had devoted her years, approximately the same number as his, to a profound and comprehensive study of the magical arts, and he admired the breadth and depth of her mastery.

On the other hand, Halabant did not have much in the way of a paying practice, skillful though she obviously was. During Gannin Thidrich's first week with her she gave just two brief consultations, one to a shopkeeper who had been put under a geas by a commercial rival, one to an elderly man who lusted after a youthful niece and wished to be cured of his obsession. He assisted her in both instances, fetching equipment from the laboratory as requested. The fees she received in both cases, he noticed, were minimal: a mere handful of coppers. No wonder she lived in such dismal quarters and was reduced to taking in private pupils like himself, and whoever it was who came to see her in the afternoons while he was away. It puzzled him that she remained here in Triggoin, where sorcerers swarmed everywhere by the hundreds or the thousands and competition had to be brutal, when she plainly would be much better off setting up in business for herself in one of the prosperous cities of the Mount where a handsome young sorceress with skill in the art would quickly build a large clientele.

It was an exciting time for him. Gannin Thidrich felt his mind opening outward day by day, new knowledge flooding in, the mastery of the mysteries beginning to come within his grasp.

His days were so full that it did not bother him at all to pass his nights on a thin mat on the floor of a room crammed with ancient acrid-smelling books. He needed only to close his eyes and sleep would come up and seize him as though he had been drugged. The winter wind howled outside, and cold drafts broke through into his room, and sandroaches danced all around him, making sandroach music with their little scraping claws, but nothing broke his sleep until dawn's first blast of light came through the library's uncovered window. Halabant was always awake, washed and dressed, when he emerged from his room. It was as if she did not need sleep at all. In these early hours of the morning she would hold her consultations with her clients in the study, if she had any that day, or else retire to her laboratory and putter about with her mechanisms and her potions. He would breakfast alone—Halabant never touched food before noon—and set about his household chores, the dusting and scrubbing and all the rest, and then would come his morning lesson and after that, until lunch, his time to prowl in the library. Often he and she took lunch at the same time, though she maintained silence throughout, and ignored him when he stole the occasional quick glance at her across the table from him.

The afternoons were the worst part, when the private pupils came and he was forced to wander the streets. He begrudged them, whoever they were, the time they had with her, and he hated the grimy taverns and bleak gaming-halls where he spent these winter days when the weather was too grim to allow him simply to walk about. But then he would return to the flat, and if he found her there, which was not always the case, she would allow him an hour or so of free discourse about matters magical, not a lesson but simply a conversation, in which he brought up issues that fascinated or perplexed him and she helped him toward an understanding of them. These were wonderful hours, during which Gannin Thidrich was constantly conscious not just of her knowledge of the arts but of Halabant's physical presence, her strange off-center beauty, the warmth of her body, the oddly pleasing fragrance of it. He kept himself in check, of course. But inwardly he imagined himself taking her in his arms, touching his lips to hers, running his fingertips down her lean, lithe back, drawing her down to his miserable thin mat on the library floor, and all the while some other part of his mind was concentrating on the technical arcana of sorcery that she was offering him.

In the evenings she was usually out again—he had no idea where—and he studied until sleep overtook him, or, if his head was throbbing too fiercely with newly acquired knowledge, he would apply himself to the unending backlog of housekeeping tasks, gathering up what seemed like the dust of decades from under the furniture, beating the rugs, oiling the kitchen pots, tidying the books, scrubbing the stained porcelain of the sink, and on and on, all for her, for her, for love of her.

It was a wonderful time.

But then in the second week came the catastrophic moment when he awoke too early, went out into the hallway, and blundered upon her as she was heading into the bathroom for her morning bath. She was naked. He saw her from the rear, first, the long lean back and the narrow waist and the flat, almost boyish buttocks, and then, as a gasp of shock escaped his lips and she became aware that he was there, she turned and faced him squarely, staring at him as coolly and unconcernedly as though he were a cat, or a piece of furniture. He was overwhelmed by the sight of her breasts, so full and close—set that they almost seemed out of proportion on such a slender frame, and of her flaring sharp-boned hips, and of the startlingly fire-hued triangle between them, tapering down to the slim thighs. She remained that way just long enough for the imprint of her nakedness to burn its way fiercely into Gannin Thidrich's soul, setting loose a conflagration that he knew it would be impossible for him to douse. Hastily he shut his eyes as though he had accidentally stared into the sun; and when he opened them again, a desperate moment later, she was gone and the bathroom door was closed.

The last time Gannin Thidrich had experienced such an impact he had been fourteen. The circumstances had been somewhat similar. Now, dizzied and dazed as a tremendous swirl of adolescent emotion roared through his adult mind, he braced himself against the hallway wall and gulped for breath like a drowning man.

For two days, though neither of them referred to the incident at all, he remained in its grip. He could hardly believe that something as trivial as a momentary glimpse of a naked woman, at his age, could affect him so deeply. But of course there were other factors, the instantaneous attraction to her that had afflicted him at the moment of meeting her, and their proximity in this little flat, where her bedroom door was only twenty paces from his, and the whole potent master-pupil entanglement that had given her such a powerful role in his lonely life here in the city of the sorcerers. He began to wonder whether she had worked some sorcery on him herself as a sort of amusement, capriciously casting a little lust—spell over him so that she could watch him squirm, and then deliberately flaunting her nakedness at him that way. He doubted it, but, then, he knew very little about what she was really like, and perhaps—how could he say?—there was some component of malice in her character, something in her that drew pleasure from tormenting a poor fish like Gannin Thidrich who had been cast up on her shore. He doubted it, but he had encountered such women before, and the possibility always was there.

He was making great progress in his studies. He had learned now how to summon minor demons, how to prepare tinctures that enhanced virility, how to employ the eyebrow of the sun, how to test for the purity of gold and silver by the laying on of hands, how to interpret weather omens, and much more. His head was swimming with his new knowledge. But also he remained dazzled by the curious sort of beauty that he saw in her, by the closeness in which they lived in the little flat, by the memory of that one luminous encounter in the dawn. And when in the fourth week it seemed to him that her usual coolness toward him was softening—she smiled at him once in a while, now, she showed obvious delight at his growing skill in the art, she even asked him a thing or two about his life before coming to Triggoin—he finally mistook diminished indifference for actual warmth and, at the end of one morning's lesson, abruptly blurted out a confession of his love for her.

An ominous red glow appeared on her pale cheeks. Her dark eyes flashed tempestuously. "Don't ruin everything," she warned him. "It is all going very well as it is. I advise you to forget that you ever said such a thing to me."

"How can I? Thoughts of you possess me day and night!"

"Control them, then. I don't want to hear any more about them. And if you try to lay a finger on me I'll turn you into a sandroach, believe me."

He doubted that she really meant that. But he abided by her warning for the next eight days, not wanting to jeopardize the continuation of his course of studies. Then, in the course of carrying out an assignment she had given him in the casting of auguries, Gannin Thidrich inscribed her name and his in the proper places in the spell, inquired as to the likelihood of a satisfactory consummation of desire, and received what he understood to be a positive prognostication. This inflamed him so intensely with joy that when Halabant came into the room a moment later Gannin Thidrich impulsively seized her and pulled her close to him, pressed his cheek against hers, and frantically fondled her from shoulder to thigh.

She muttered six brief, harsh words of a spell unknown to him in his ear and bit his earlobe. In an instant he found himself scrabbling around amidst gigantic dust-grains on the floor. Jagged glittering motes floated about him like planets in the void. His vision had become eerily precise down almost to the microscopic level, but all color had drained from the world. When he put his hand to his cheek in shock he discovered it to be an insect's feathery claw, and the cheek itself was a hard thing of chitin. She had indeed transformed him into a sandroach.

Numb, he considered his situation. From this perspective he could no longer see her—she was somewhere miles above him, in the upper reaches of the atmosphere—

nor could he make out the geography of the room, the familiar chairs and the couch, or anything else except the terrifyingly amplified details of the immensely small. Perhaps in another moment her foot would come down on him, and that would be that for Gannin Thidrich. Yet he did not truly believe that he had become a sandroach. He had mastered enough sorcery by this time to understand that that was technically impossible, that one could not pack all the neurons and synapses, the total intelligence of a human mind, into the tiny compass of an insect's head. And all those things were here with him inside the sandroach, his entire human personality, the hopes and fears and memories and fantasies of Gannin Thidrich of the Free City of Stee, who had come to Triggoin to study sorcery and was a pupil of the woman V. Halabant. So this was all an illusion. He was not really a sandroach; she had merely made him believe that he was. He was certain of that. That certainty was all that preserved his sanity in those first appalling moments.

Still, on an operational level there was no effective difference between thinking you were a six-legged chitin-covered creature one finger-joint in length and actually being such a creature. Either way, it was a horrifying condition. Gannin Thidrich could not speak out to protest against her treatment of him. He could not restore himself to human shape and height. He could not do anything at all except the things that sandroaches did. The best he could manage was to scutter in his new six-legged fashion to the safety to be found underneath the couch, where he discovered other sandroaches already in residence. He glared at them balefully, warning them to keep their distance, but their only response was an incomprehensible twitching of their feelers. Whether that was a gesture of sympathy or one of animosity, he could not tell.

The least she could have done for me, he thought, was to provide me with some way of communicating with the others of my kind, if this is to be my kind from now on.

He had never known such terror and misery. But the transformation was only temporary. Two hours later—it seemed like decades to him, sandroach time, all of it spent hiding under the couch and contemplating how he was going to pursue the purposes of his life as an insect—Gannin Thidrich was swept by a nauseating burst of dizziness and a sense that he was exploding from the thorax outward, and then he found himself restored to his previous form, lying in a clumsy sprawl in the middle of the floor. Halabant was nowhere to be seen. Cautiously he rose and moved about the room, reawakening in himself the technique of two-legged locomotion, holding his out-spread fingers up before his eyes for the delight of seeing fingers again, prodding his cheeks and arms and abdomen to confirm that he was once again a creature of flesh. He was. He felt chastened and immensely relieved, even grateful to her for having relented.

They did not discuss the episode the next day, and all reverted to as it had been between them, distant, formal, a relationship of pure pedagogy and nothing more. He remained wary of her. When, now and then, his hand would brush against hers in the course of handling some piece of apparatus, he would pull it back as if he had touched a glowing coal.

Spring now began to arrive in Triggoin. The air was softer; the trees grew green. Gannin Thidrich's desire for his instructor did not subside, in truth grew more maddeningly acute with the warming of the season, but he permitted himself no expression of it. There were further occasions when he accidentally encountered her going to and fro, naked, in the hall in earliest morning. His response each time was instantly to close his eyes and turn away, but her image lingered on his retinas and burrowed down into his brain. He could not help thinking that there was something intentional about these provocative episodes, something flirtatious, even. But he was too frightened of her to act on that supposition.

A new form of obsession now came over him, that the visitors she received every afternoon while he was away were not private pupils at all, but a lover, rather, or perhaps several lovers. Since she took care not to have her afternoon visitors arrive until he was gone, he had no way of knowing whether this was so, and it plagued him terribly to think that others, in his absence, were caressing her lovely body and enjoying her passionate kisses while he was denied everything on pain of being turned into a sandroach again.

But of course he did have a way of knowing what took place during those afternoons of hers. He had progressed far enough in his studies to have acquired some skill with the device known as the Far-Seeing Bowl, which allows an adept to spy from a distance. Over the span of three days he removed from Halabant's flat one of her bowls, a supply of the pink fluid that it required, and a pinch of the grayish activating powder. Also he helped himself to a small undergarment of Halabant's—its fragrance was a torment to him—from the laundry basket. These things he stored in a locker he rented in the nearby marketplace. On the fourth day, after giving himself a refresher course in the five-word spell that operated the bowl, he collected his apparatus from the locker, repaired to a tavern where he knew no one would intrude on him, set the bowl atop the garment, filled it with the pink fluid, sprinkled it with the activating powder, and uttered the five words.

It occurred to him that he might see scenes now that would shatter him forever. No matter: he had to know.

The surface of the fluid in the bowl rippled, stirred, cleared. The image of V. Halabant appeared. Gannin Thidrich caught his breath. A visitor was indeed with her: a young man, a boy, even, no more than twelve or fifteen years old.

They sat chastely apart in the study. Together they pored over one of Halabant's books of sorcery. It was an utterly innocent hour. The second student came soon after: a short, squat fellow wearing coarse clothing of a provincial cut. For half an hour Halabant delivered what was probably a lecture—the bowl did not provide Gannin Thidrich with sound—while the pupil, constantly biting his lip, scribbled notes as quickly as he could. Then he left, and after a time was replaced by a sad, dreamy-looking fellow with long shaggy hair, who had brought some sort of essay or thesis for Halabant to examine. She leafed quickly through it, frequently offering what no doubt were pungent comments.

No lovers, then. Legitimate pupils, all three. Gannin Thidrich felt bitterly ashamed of having spied on her, and aghast at the possibility that she might have perceived, by means of some household surveillance spell of whose existence he knew nothing, that he had done so. But she betrayed no sign of that when he returned to the flat.

A week later, desperate once again, he purchased a love-potion in the sorcerers' marketplace—not a spell to free himself from desire, though he knew that was what he should be getting, but one that would deliver her into his arms. Halabant had sent him to the marketplace with a long list of professional supplies to buy for her—such things as elecamp, golden rue, quicksilver, brimstone, goblin-sugar, mastic, and thekka ammoniaca. The last item on the list was maltabar, and the same dealer, he knew, offered potions for the lovelorn. Rashly Gannin Thidrich purchased one. He hid it among his bundles and tried to smuggle it into the flat, but Halabant, under the pretext of offering to help him unpack, went straight to the sack that contained it, and pulled it forth. "This was nothing that I requested," she said.

"True," he said, chagrined.

"Is it what I think it is?"

Hanging his head, he admitted that it was. She tossed it angrily aside. "I'll be merciful and let myself believe that you bought this to use on someone else. But if I was the one you had in mind for it—"

"No. Never."

"Liar. Idiot."

"What can I do, Halabant? Love strikes like a thunderbolt."

"I don't remember advertising for a lover. Only for an apprentice, an assistant, a tenant."

"It's not my fault that I feel this way about you."

"Nor mine," said Halabant. "Put all such thoughts out of your mind, if you want to continue here." Then, softening, obviously moved by the dumbly adoring way in which he was staring at her, she smiled and pulled him toward her and brushed his cheek lightly with her lips. "Idiot," she said again. "Poor hopeless fool." But it seemed to him that she said it with affection.

Matters stayed strictly business between them. He hung upon every word of her lessons as though his continued survival depended on committing every syllable of her teachings to memory, filled notebook after notebook with details of spells, talismans, conjurations, and illusions, and spent endless hours rummaging through her books for amplifying detail, sometimes staying up far into the night to pursue some course of study that an incidental word or two from her had touched off. He was becoming so adept, now, that he was able to be of great service to her with her outside clientele, the perfect assistant, always knowing which devices or potions to bring her for the circumstances at hand; and he noticed that clients were coming to her more frequently now, too. He hoped that Halabant gave him at least a little credit for that too.

He was still aflame with yearning for her, of course—there was no reason for that to go away—but he tried to burn it off with heroic outpourings of energy in his role as her housekeeper. Before coming to Triggoin, Gannin Thidrich had bothered himself no more about household work than any normal bachelor did, doing simply enough to fend off utter squalor and not going beyond that, but he cared for her little flat as he had never cared for any dwelling of his own, polishing and dusting and sweeping and scrubbing, until the place took on an astonishing glow of charm and comfort. Even the sandroaches were intimidated by his work and fled to some other apartment. It was his goal to exhaust himself so thoroughly between the intensity of his studies and the intensity of his housework that he would have no shred of vitality left over for further lustful fantasies. This did not prove to be so. Often, curling up on his mat at night after a day of virtually unending toil, he would be assailed by dazzling visions of V. Halabant, entering his weary mind like an intruding incubus, capering wantonly in his throbbing brain, gesturing lewdly to him, beckoning, offering herself, and Gannin Thidrich would lie there sobbing, soaked in sweat, praying to every demon whose invocations he knew that he be spared such agonizing visitations.

The pain became so great that he thought of seeking another teacher. He thought occasionally of suicide, too, for he knew that this was the great love of his life, doomed never to be fulfilled, and that if he went away from Halabant he was destined to roam forever celibate through the vastness of the world, finding all other women unsatisfactory after her. Some segment of his mind recognized this to be puerile romantic nonsense, but he was not able to make that the dominant segment, and he began to fear that he might actually be capable of taking his own life in some feverish attack of nonsensical frustration.

The worst of it was that she had become intermittently quite friendly toward him by this time, giving him, intentionally or otherwise, encouragement that he had become too timid to accept as genuine. Perhaps his pathetic gesture of buying that love potion had touched something in her spirit. She smiled at him frequently now, even winked, or poked him playfully in the shoulder with a finger to underscore some point in her lesson. She was shockingly casual, sometimes, about how she dressed, often choosing revealingly flimsy gowns that drove him into paroxysms of throttled desire. And yet at other times she was as cold and aloof as she had been at the beginning, criticizing him cruelly when he bungled a spell or spilled an alembic, skewering him with icy glances when he said something that struck her as foolish, reminding him over and over that he was still just a blundering novice who had years to go before he attained anything like the threshold of mastery.

So there always were limits. He was her prisoner. She could touch him whenever she chose but he feared becoming a sandroach again should he touch her, even accidentally. She could smile and wink at him but he dared not do the same. In no way did she grant him any substantial status. When he asked her to instruct him in the great spell known as the Sublime Arcanum, which held the key to many gates, her reply was simply, "That is not something for fools to play with."

There was one truly miraculous day when, after he had recited an intricate series of spells with complete accuracy and had brought off one of the most difficult effects she had ever asked him to attempt, she seized him in a sudden joyful congratulatory embrace and levitated them both to the rafters of the study. There they hovered, face to face, bosom against bosom, her eyes flashing jubilantly before him. "That was wonderful!" she cried. "How marvelously you did that! How proud I am of you!"

This is it, he thought, the delirious moment of surrender at last, and slipped his hand between their bodies to clasp her firm round breast, and pressed his lips against hers and drove his tongue deep into her mouth. Instantly she voided the spell of levitation and sent him crashing miserably to the floor, where he landed in a crumpled heap with his left leg folded up beneath him in a way that sent the fiercest pain through his entire body.

She floated gently down beside him.

"You will always be an idiot," she said, and spat, and strode out of the room.

Gannin Thidrich was determined now to put an end to his life. He understood completely that to do such a thing would be a preposterous overreaction to his situation, but he was determined not to allow mere rationality to have a voice in the decision. His existence had become unbearable and he saw no other way of winning his freedom from this impossible woman.

He brooded for days about how to go about it, whether to swallow some potion from her storeroom or to split himself open with one of the kitchen knives or simply to fling himself from the study window, but all of these seemed disagreeable to him on the esthetic level and fraught with drawbacks besides. Mainly what troubled him was the possibility that he might not fully succeed in his aim with any of them, which seemed even worse than succeeding would be.

In the end he decided to cast himself into the dark, turbulent river that ran past the edge of West Triggoin on its northern flank. He had often explored it, now that winter was over, in the course of his afternoon walks. It was wide and probably fairly deep, its flow during this period of springtime spate was rapid, and an examination of a map revealed that it would carry his body northward and westward into the grim uninhabited lands that sloped toward the distant sea. Since he was unable to swim—one did not swim in the gigantic River Stee of his native city, whose swift current swept everything and everyone willy-nilly downstream along the mighty slopes of Castle Mount—Gannin Thidrich supposed that he would sink quickly and could expect a relatively painless death.

Just to be certain, he borrowed a rope from Halabant's storeroom to tie around his legs before he threw himself in. Slinging it over his shoulder, he set out along the footpath that bordered the river's course, searching for a likely place from which to jump. The day was warm, the air sweet, the new leaves yellowish-green on every tree, springtime at its finest: what better season for saying farewell to the world?

He came to an overlook where no one else seemed to be around, knotted the rope about his ankles, and without a moment's pause for regret, sentimental thoughts, or final statements of any sort, hurled himself down headlong into the water.

It was colder than he expected it to be, even on this mild day. His plummeting body cut sharply below the surface, so that his mouth and nostrils filled with water and he felt himself in the imminent presence of death, but then the natural buoyancy of the body asserted itself and despite his wishes Gannin Thidrich turned upward again, breaching the surface, emerging into the air, spluttering and gagging. An instant later he heard a splashing sound close beside him and realized that someone else had jumped in, a would-be rescuer, perhaps.

"Lunatic! Moron! What do you think you're doing?"

He knew that voice, of course. Apparently V. Halabant had followed him as he made his doleful way along the riverbank and was determined not to let him die. That realization filled him with a confused mixture of ecstasy and fury.

She was bobbing beside him. She caught him by the shoulder, spun him around to face her. There was a kind of madness in her eyes, Gannin Thidrich thought. The woman leaned close and in a tone of voice that stung like vitriol she said, "Iaho ariaha . . . .aho ariaha . . . .bakaksikhekh! Ianian! Thatlat! Hish!"

Gannin Thidrich felt a sense of sudden forward movement and became aware that he was swimming, actually swimming, moving downstream with powerful strokes of his entire body. Of course that was impossible. Not only were his legs tied together, but he had no idea of how to swim. And yet he was definitely in motion: he could see the riverbank changing from moment to moment, the trees lining the footpath traveling upstream as he went the other way.

There was a river otter swimming beside him, a smooth sleek beautiful creature, graceful and sinuous and strong. It took Gannin Thidrich another moment to realize that the animal was V. Halabant, and that in fact he was an otter also, that she had worked a spell on them both when she had jumped in beside them, and had turned them into a pair of magnificent aquatic beasts. His legs were gone—he had only flippers down there now, culminating in small webbed feet—and gone too was the rope with which he had hobbled himself. And he could swim. He could swim like an otter.

Ask no questions, Gannin Thidrich told himself. Swim! Swim!

Side by side they swam for what must have been miles, spurting along splendidly on the breast of the current. He had never known such joy. As a human he would have drowned long ago, but as an otter he was a superb swimmer, tireless, wondrously strong. And with Halabant next to him he was willing to swim forever: to the sea itself, even. Head down, nose foremost, narrow body fully extended, he drilled his way through the water like some animate projectile. And the otter who had been V. Halabant kept pace with him as he moved along.

Time passed and he lost all sense of who or what he was, or where, or what he was doing. He even ceased to perceive the presence of his companion. His universe was only motion, constant forward motion. He was truly a river otter now, nothing but a river otter, joyously hurling himself through the cosmos.

But then his otter senses detected a sound to his left that no otter would be concerned with, and whatever was still human in him registered the fact that it was a cry of panic, a sharp little gasp of fear, coming from a member of his former species. He pivoted to look and saw that V. Halabant had reverted to human form and was thrashing about in what seemed to be the last stages of exhaustion. Her arms beat the air, her head tossed wildly, her eyes were rolled back in her head. She was trying to make her way to the riverbank, but she did not appear to have the strength to do it.

Gannin Thidrich understood that in his jubilant onward progress he had led her too far down the river, pulling her along beyond her endurance, that as an otter he was far stronger than she and by following him she had exceeded her otter abilities and could go no farther. Perhaps she was in danger of drowning, even. Could an otter drown? But she was no longer an otter. He knew that he had to get her ashore. He swam to her side and pushed futilely against her with his river-otter nose, trying in vain to clasp her with the tiny otter flippers that had replaced his arms. Her eyes fluttered open and she stared into his, and smiled, and spoke two words, the counterspell, and Gannin Thidrich discovered that he too was in human form again. They were both naked. He found that they were close enough now to the shore that his feet were able to touch the bottom. Slipping his arm around her, just below her breasts, he tugged her along, steadily, easily, toward the nearby riverbank. He scrambled ashore, pulling her with him, and they dropped down gasping for breath at the river's edge under the warm spring sunshine.

They were far out of town, he realized, all alone in the empty but not desolate countryside. The bank was soft with mosses. Gannin Thidrich recovered his breath almost at once; Halabant took longer, but before long she too was breathing normally. Her face was flushed and mottled with signs of strain, though, and she was biting down on her lip as though trying to hold something back, something which Gannin Thidrich understood, a moment later, to be tears. Abruptly she was furiously sobbing. He held her, tried to comfort her, but she shook him off. She would not or could not look at him.

"To be so weak—" she muttered. "I was going under. I almost drowned. And to have you see it—you—you—"

So she was angry with herself for having shown herself, at least in this, to be inferior to him. That was ridiculous, he thought. She might be a master sorcerer and he only a novice, yes, but he was a man, nevertheless, and she a woman, and men tended to be physically stronger than women, on the average, and probably that was true among otters too. If she had displayed weakness during their wild swim, it was a forgivable weakness, which only exacerbated his love for her. He murmured words of comfort to her, and was so bold to put his arm about her shoulders, and then, suddenly, astonishingly, everything changed, she pressed her bare body against him, she clung to him, she sought his lips with a hunger that was almost frightening, she opened her legs to him, she opened everything to him, she drew him down into her body and her soul.

Afterward, when it seemed appropriate to return to the city, it was necessary to call on her resources of sorcery once more. They both were naked, and many miles downstream from where they needed to be. She seemed not to want to risk returning to the otter form again, but there were other spells of transportation at her command, and she used one that brought them instantly back to West Triggoin, where their clothing and even the rope with which Gannin Thidrich had bound himself were lying in damp heaps near the place where he had thrown himself into the river. They dressed in silence and in silence they made their way, walking several feet apart, back to her flat.

He had no idea what would happen now. Already she appeared to be retreating behind that wall of untouchability that had surrounded her since the beginning. What had taken place between them on the riverbank was irreversible, but it would not transform their strange relationship unless she permitted it to, Gannin Thidrich knew, and he wondered whether she would. He did not intend to make any new aggressive moves without some sort of guidance from her.

And indeed it appeared that she intended to pretend that nothing had occurred at all, neither his absurd suicide attempt nor her foiling of it by following him to the river and turning them into otters nor the frenzied, frenetic, almost insane coupling that had been the unexpected climax of their long swim. All was back to normal between them as soon as they were at the flat: she was the master, he was the drudge, they slept in their separate rooms, and when during the following day's lessons he bungled a spell, as even now he still sometimes did, she berated him in the usual cruel, cutting way that was the verbal equivalent of transforming him once again into a sandroach. What, then, was he left with? The taste of her on his lips, the sound of her passionate outcries in his ears, the feel of the firm ripe swells of her breasts against the palms of his hands?

On occasions over the next few days, though, he caught sight of her studying him surreptitiously out of the corner of her eye, and he was the recipient of a few not so surreptitious smiles that struck him as having genuine warmth in them, and when he ventured a smile of his own in her direction it was met with another smile instead of a scowl. But he hesitated to try any sort of follow-up maneuver. Matters still struck him as too precariously balanced between them.

Then, a week later, during their morning lesson, she said briskly, "Take down these words: Psakerba enphnoun orgogorgoniotrian phorbai. Do you recognize them?"

"No," said Gannin Thidrich, baffled.

"They are the opening incantation of the spell known as the Sublime Arcanum," said Halabant.

A thrill rocketed down his spine. The Sublime Arcanum at last! So she had decided to trust him with the master spell, finally, the great opener of so many gates! She no longer thought of him as a fool who could not be permitted knowledge of it.

It was a good sign, he thought. Something was changing.

Perhaps she was still trying to pretend even now that none of it had ever happened, the event by the riverbank. But it had, it had, and it was having its effect on her, however hard she might be battling against it, and he knew now that he would go on searching, forever if necessary, for the key that would unlock her a second time.

WENDY N. WAGNER's first novel, *Her Dark Depths*, is forthcoming from the small press Virtual Tales. Her short fiction has appeared in the anthology *2012 A.D.* and in the online magazine *Crossed Genres*. In addition to her fiction writing, she has conducted interviews for horror-web.com. She shares her Portland, Oregon, home with one painting husband, one brilliant daughter, and no zombies. Her website is winniewoohoo.com.

When most of us think of dwarves, we think of Snow White's seven friends, adorable and friendly. Or perhaps the noble lords of the underground that Tolkien portrayed in *The Lord of the Rings*. But the ancient Norse myths painted an image of a darker, subterranean race, a race firmly linked with stone and greed and evil. Of all the origin-tales, the dwarf in our next story is closest to these ancient dwarves—and yet nothing like them at all.

Rugel is the last of his kind, a dwarf alone in the world and lost from his moorings. He's a thief and a trickster, a murderer and an unwilling wizard. Now his wanderings have brought him back to his childhood home, where he must confront himself and the shambles of his life.

Wagner says that this story is about a man who spends his whole life running away from incredible pain and loss, a man who is afraid to make a life for himself. "But luckily," she says, "it's also about the transformative power of love and the ways it can give even the most desperate person courage and power."

Now *that's* magic.

The Secret of Calling Rabbits
Wendy N. Wagner

The breeze shifted as Rugel ran, and he caught a scent upon it, sweet and strong, a scent that reached into the depths of his memories and twanged them. He lost his footing at the power of it, and he threw himself into a bush beside the path, gasping. He preferred running to hiding, but he couldn't run with that scent thickening the air.

His pursuer shouted again. "Wait! Show me how you did that!" Her voice distracted him from the smell of the past; it focused his mind on the pressing problem of survival. He should have never come back to this place.

She came closer, and Rugel peeked out at the little girl on the path. Her knees, bared by her too-short shift, were scabbed and grass-stained as she spun a slow searching circle. Rugel crouched further down inside the currant bush. He was a dwarf—though "dwarf" was a generous measure of someone his size—and he had a gift for going unseen; perhaps the girl would lose sight of him.

"Please!" the girl cried. She stopped in front of the bush, picking out his gnarled face from the tangle of undergrowth. "I saw you call the rabbit."

Rugel cursed to himself. He should never have summoned the hare, or, having called it, he ought to have killed it. Now he'd go hungry, and this Big creature had seen him. But it was a child Big, he thought with a measure of hope, and children were easily scared.

"Go away!" he growled.

She stood solid, brown eyes fierce.

He tried again. "I'll kill ya!"

Her lip trembled at his words, but not much. She had seen him pet the hare. Now she could not imagine him performing violence. He had killed before, both animals and humans—although never children, only grown men bent on harm—but she did not know that. She had only seen a very small man, tiny as herself, running his fingertips over the calm back of a brown rabbit.

He straightened himself up out of the currant bush. "You've got to have dwarf magic to call animals, girl," he called. "You don't have it."

"Can't I learn it?"

"No." He barked the word. Two hundred years of running and hiding and sneaking around the edges of the world had given him a voice as leathery and tough as his face. It should have sent her home crying.

And it did. Or it did start her crying, anyway. Even dripping tears she stood fast, staring at him while her shoulders quaked without sound. He could hardly stand to look at all that mute unhappiness.

Face half-twisted away, he grumbled: "Why are you crying?"

"I'm so lonely," she whispered. "Peter's sick and Mama's milk dried up so they had to sent the baby to Auntie Relda's. And Papa's farming all day and hunting all night to pay the witching bill. I'm all alone." The tears grew larger and the quaking grew stronger. A tiny sound came up in her throat, barely audible.

The sound pained his ears. He didn't like the sounds children made when they were unhappy, and he didn't understand her story. But he knew alone. He stepped away from the currant bush. "Who's Peter?"

She swiped the snot from her face with her sleeve. "My brother. He stepped on a nail last week and then he couldn't move his leg. So Eva the Witch put him on a cot in her house and bound his ankles with magic cord and rubbed his whole body with tincture of mandrake root."

Mandrake. That was the smell. Rugel shivered.

He should have never come back to this place.

The girl had caught her breath and now added, in a pleased voice, "I'm going to be a witch like her when I grow up."

He examined her face and could tell by looking that she was right. There was human magic pricking in the back of her eyes. Right now if she put her mind to it, she probably could call that hare out of the bush. But he wasn't going to tell her that.   •

His silence did not discourage her. "Papa says our village is cursed."

"Yes?" Feeling a story coming, Rugel sat down to take the weight off his feet. They ached sometimes. He'd like a better pair of boots, but he was only a so-so shoemaker. Maybe he would steal a pair, the next village.

The girl squatted so she could still see his face. "It rained so much this winter the rye fields washed away. That's something bad." She lowered her voice. "And I heard Papa tell Eva he thought there was something in the woods stealing our luck. Maybe something as bad as a hobgoblin."

With his wizened brown face, Rugel had been called worse things. And he'd stolen plenty. Once his people had practiced the arts of calling ore from the dark places of the earth, of spinning straw into gold, but this was great earth-magic, and he, the last of the dwarves, did not dare such workings. He made do with safer, minor talents: animal charming, theft, invisibility. But not here. Even those shabby excuses for magic were too risky in this forest that reeked with the stink of mandrake.

The little girl settled onto her bottom, stretching her legs in front of her with a sound of contentment.

"I'm Rachel," she announced.

He grunted. Her eyes were as round as a hare's as she stared at him. She expected him to introduce himself, he realized. And for the first time since he was very young, he was tempted to tell someone—this girl—his name. He hadn't heard his name spoken in another's voice in so, so long.

He jumped to his feet. "I've got to go."

"Will I see you again?" She sounded excited, tangling her legs in her hurry to catch up with him.

"Maybe, maybe not," he called over his shoulder, and drawing on all his woods-craft, disappeared into the bracken. An odd piece of him wanted to hide and watch her enjoy his disappearing act. But instinct and habit kept him running. Instinct, and a breeze carrying the graveyard smell of mandrake.

Rugel didn't want to see the girl again. He told himself that as he followed the game trails, fouling the wires of any un-sprung rabbit snares he found. It was a tiny revenge undersized for its risk. The men of village were already on-edge. If they caught him, they'd tip to violence.

He pinched a wire between his fingers, feeling a fading warmth. The trap was freshly sprung, the rabbit twitching when Rugel came across it. He could use magic to melt that wire, heat it until it boiled in the palm of his hand. It would be easy; there was so much power waiting in the rich earth of this place. It called to him and the quiet coals of magical talent hidden within him.

He struggled to resist the temptation to soak up power and blast every last wire snare in the forest. He was painfully close to the village. If he scaled the boulder beside him, he could see the roofs of the little town. It was smaller than the dwarven village they'd built it over. He refused to look at it. And if he allowed himself to use magic now, he'd never get away from that sight.

Slipping the rabbit into his pack, he looked at the warren entrance hidden in the lee of the boulder. The trapper had sought it out, placing his snare where the rabbits would pass it going in and out of their burrow. Placing death where an animal expected only the security of home.

That was humans, all right.

There was a bitter taste in Rugel's mouth as he picked his way back to his little camp. He moved every night, caching his gear before setting out for the day's errands. He'd never stayed so long in one place. But he'd never come back to this place before, never seen Bigs in the forest his people had replanted and nurtured. Stealing their catch and breaking their traps felt too right for him to just move on without doing so.

Rugel pulled the rabbit's hind-leg loose of its flop-limbed body and began to gnaw it. Once he had eaten meat cooked well, spiced and sauced by his mother, the best cook in his village. But he'd learned early on not to risk fire. There'd been times men had found him, had taken one look at his lumpy face and tried to capture him.

They always wanted something. Gold, usually, the famed dwarven gold of all the stories, never mind that his people never had any use for that too-soft stone. And the Bigs that didn't want gold wanted his luck. His little hands, his little feet, anything tiny and portable was fair game for a trophy, just like the rabbit's foot he was carefully nibbling around; its claws were sharp.

He cast the paw deep into the brush. Soon enough something would clean it up. He had no fears humans would connect it to him. In the stories, dwarves never ate rabbit.

Rugel eyed the other rabbit leg, its lucky foot still hairy and dirty, and couldn't bring himself to bite into it. He was *old*. He was sick of the taste of raw meat. And there wasn't a soul alive who knew his name. He got to his feet. Maybe he'd try tickling trout for a real dinner.

The creek was cool, shadowed by thickets of willow grown tightly together, made impenetrable with lashings of vine and ivy. Here, where it meandered into a curve, the creek made a pool, deep and dark, overhung by an enormous alder. The alder's pale trunk was lapped all over by the green tongues of lungwort. Rugel made a note to come back and collect the viridian lichen; it was good for bandaging wounds.

He was ashamed that such herblore was the extant of his healing practice, but life on the run precluded the use of greater magics. Once as a child, he had assisted his father as he healed a deer, its shoulder singed down to the muscle by the same wildfire that had swallowed the forest. Once he had helped his mother push disease out of an oak tree weakened by lightning strikes. But that was all earth magic, fed by the land itself. Every bit a dwarf used bound him more tightly to the soil he drew it from. When the Elders worked their great works, they became as rooted to the land as the alder with its lungwort.

He blinked up at the tree, and wondered who had planted it after the wildfires, which dwarf dead and gone. He had tried to keep all of their names fresh in his memory, but they had faded out one by one, till even his little sister's name eluded him. It was something like Lily, he thought. He wished he could remember.

He hunkered at the edge of the pool, sharpening an alder stick in readiness as a spear. He was not a good trout tickler, and expected the need to fall back on the spear to supplement his fish dinner. It would be bloody and ugly, but he was used to that.

A scream from the willow thickets made him jerk his knife and jab the palm of his hand.

With a curse, he dropped the stick. He snapped off a strip of lungwort and pressed it against the cut, listening again for the voice in the willows. He didn't need to hear it a second time to know it was the girl's voice.

She was crying. The first sound had been a shriek of pain, but now she was sobbing, whimpering. She sounded badly hurt.

"Stay away from her," he whispered to himself. "It'll just be trouble. Look at all those fish, waiting for you to catch them." He forced his eyes to the pond. A fish struck; he saw the ripples of it.

But the girl was still crying.

He put his knife in his belt pouch and ran into the thicket.

The willows grew densely, impenetrable for someone without Rugel's woodcraft, but he barely noticed the branches clawing at his face or the vines twisting around his ankles. A sense of urgency pulled him forward. The image of the girl as he had seen her last rose up in his memory. She had stood there in her homespun shift, as eager and nervous on the forest path as a young hare, with the same dark and liquid eyes. Curiosity had made her brave back there. Curiosity had probably gotten her hurt.

He felt certain of it as he slipped through the last tangle of willow. He stood in a small bright space, a pocket meadow made when an ancient oak toppled, its body flattening the tender ash saplings around it. He couldn't help noticing the fire scars on its aged trunk. It was older even than he.

The girl lay at the edge of the clearing in a snarl of the oak tree's exposed roots. She had stopped shrieking. Instead, she was silent, and still.

"Girl?"

It came out in a whisper. He cleared his throat, surprised to find it so dry. "Girl?"

She moaned.

He dropped to his knees beside her. "What happened?"

She moaned again, and he let his eyes answer the question. Where the earth had been lifted by the upturned oak's roots were dozens of small holes. Some had torn open, revealing tunnels the right size for burrowers, and when he looked at her hands, they were dark with soil. The right was particularly dirty and dark purple, with two red marks staring up at him like angry eyes. Or like the impressions made by a snake's fangs.

He touched the girl's face and was startled by how cold it was.

"Girl? Can you speak?" He tapped her shoulder with no response. He tapped again. "Rachel?"

"I saw a bunny," she whispered. "But something bit me."

He squeezed his eyes shut. She could have called that rabbit if she knew the trick. If he'd taught it to her. When he opened them again, the red bite mark stared back at him, reproachful.

Rugel knew a great deal about surviving in the woods. He knew lungwort for cuts and he knew clay mud for bee stings. He had once set his own broken leg with a yew stave and deer sinews. But snakebites were beyond his medical skills. He knew nothing beyond binding the bitten limb and prayer. He ripped a strip from the bottom of his tunic and knotted it just above her wrist, remembering those healings he had helped work as a child. Magic beat prayer when the gods he knew were as dead as his people.

He hesitated, his throat tight. He could not imagine using magic so close to the village. He would be trapped here. His spirit would blend with the spirit of the stones and soil and he would never get the stink of mandrake out of his nose.

No. He couldn't do that.

The girl whimpered. He stared at her pale face, where the freckles stood out like flecks of dirt on white stone. She was dying. If he did nothing and just left her here, the snake's poison would work its way through her body, turning it silent and swollen. She might die even if he managed to get her to the witch. Snakebites were beyond most witches' power.

He imagined what would happen if he took her to her village. He was small and gnarled and ugly, as bad as a hobgoblin to people afraid of ill-luck creatures. She was just a little girl, gray and still and close to death. The humans would think the worst. He could still smell the mandrake-scent on the breeze. She might die anyway, he reminded himself. He didn't need to face all of that. He could just run away.

Her eyes fluttered and she saw him. "Little man," she said. It was almost a croak. Something in his gut twisted in response. She already looked worse than when he had burst into the clearing, the purple swelling moving up her arm.

A witch who could cure a brother with a paralyzed leg might be able to cure a snake bite, Rugel thought.

He squatted beside the girl and lifted her into his arms. Her feet hung close to the ground as he held her. He shifted his grip, and something quivered inside his chest, a phantom hand trembling against his heart.

He took a step into the forest, in the direction of Rachel's village, and behind them he heard a rabbit drum an "all clear" on the side of the oak. Rugel broke into a run.

Despite the weight in his arms, it felt just like the run he had made from the creek to the village two hundred years ago. His feet still knew the trail, the little ridges of rock beneath the soil speaking in their same old tongue. For a moment he was running through charred tree trunks and drifts of ash, his body a lad's again, running toward his village with screams reverberating in his ears.

No one had seen him when he reached the village, he remembered. He had crouched in the shadow of a boulder—maybe even the rabbit-snare boulder—and watched them cut down the women. His young power, still small and fragile inside him, flared with the force of his rage. He reached into the land to raise a wall of fire against the Bigs, and felt the sick earth shudder. There was no strength in its scorched soil. His power, overspent, unfueled, sputtered out. His vision grayed, but he could still see his sister, running with her shift pulled up over her grass-stained knees. Darkness still hadn't taken him when he saw the scythe rip through her belly in an explosion of blood.

Tears welled up as Rugel remembered it all, obscuring his vision as he ran. His hands were full of the girl, and he could not wipe his eyes clear. He stumbled on, remembering.When the elders tried to speak, the Big men screamed over the words. They struck down the old men even as the Elders struggled to draw power from the deep bones of the earth.

"They thought we were stealing their luck," he whispered to the little girl, whose head only rattled against his chest. "They wouldn't listen. They were sure we were evil."

He almost dropped Rachel then, as he crossed the invisible boundary he'd set for himself since his arrival in the forest. He'd never come this close to her village before. For a second, he wondered if he should drop her and just keep running as long as he could.

The scent of mandrake was so strong now . . . too strong for him to think clearly.

He thought of the first time he had smelled it, sitting on the fresh graves of his mother and father and all the rest, the brilliant green of new mandrake shoots pushing up through the ash-stained soil. He had watched them grow far faster than any ordinary mandrake, sending out leaves to stretch for the sun. Little buds revealed white flowers like tiny eyes in the thickets of green leaves. Such a strange and horrible smell and now so strong he almost choked on the air.

Rugel passed the wattle fence of the first cottage. He had arrived at the village.

The girl's breathing was very slight; her skin almost gray. He felt a pang. If only he could have prayed for her. If only he had taught her the secret for calling rabbits. But it was too late for that. Already, as he lowered her to the ground, he could hear voices coming from the cottage behind him.

He might have a few seconds. He could still run, like he'd run the last long years of his life. He *would* run. He'd run far away from this place, maybe as far as Ireland. But not until he made things right. She wouldn't be here, almost dead, if it hadn't been for him.

He owed her.

Rugel pressed his creased brown lips close to the little girl's ear, and he whispered: "This is the secret of calling rabbits, girl."

Her eyelids trembled. He couldn't be certain she had heard him. He added anyway: "Call to them while you think rabbit thoughts. You've got the magic. All you need is the knowledge. Like calling to like."

He wished she knew his name.

Then it was suddenly too late to run. Great hands closed on his arms and pulled him away from her, lifting him as easily as a child even as he kicked and screamed.

On the ground, Rachel went rigid, her back bending like a bow and foam spraying from her lips. Time slowed for Rugel as he felt a fist connect with his face, felt the skin above his eyebrow split, but he saw only the little girl's face as it went red, then purple, then dark.

She was dying. It was too late for the witch's cure.

And Rugel knew. The time for running was over. He reached down inside himself for the little spark of magic he'd kept banked all these years. The only way to feed it was to reach out to the earth, the stones and soil of this village. There would be no leaving once he touched that energy. He felt his body becoming hotter with the strength of his growing power.

"Rachel," he whispered. He could barely see her beyond the crowd, jerking and twitching on the pale grass. He had forgotten how to break down the venom in her blood, but he could give her air, could shield her heart from the poison's progress. He could buy time for the witch. Rugel stretched his magical grasp wider, drawing energy from the soil beneath the village, the boulder by the rabbit warren, the banks of the stream.

And then his heat was too much for his captors. There were shouts, and Rugel was flying through the air, his body launched from furious hands. He struck the edge of the mandrake patch with a horrible jolt.

He lay there for a second, feeling the magic catch hold of Rachel's lungs, sensing her heart beating normally again, and then he forced himself to get up. He pushed deeper into the mandrake patch, knowing he ran over graves he'd dug himself. He might not be able to flee this place, but there was a still a chance he could escape the angry mass of villagers if he could just make it through this field.

He'd just spurred himself into a full run when he felt the first of the rocks strike his back.

He ran on and felt a bigger stone, as large as a man's two fists joined, smash into his back and send him sprawling. In his memory, he saw his father, face down in the thin young soil with the fletching of an arrow between his shoulder blades.

Rugel lay on his belly in the soft loam, his arms and legs still pumping, still running, a reflex after two hundred years. The rocks kept coming, big and small, some thrown with greater accuracy than others. The back of his skull leaked hot trickles down into his collar, and when a stone smashed his shoulder blade he gasped with agony, sucking in humus and leaf bits. But his legs kept running.

The soil churned away under the motion of his legs and he felt himself burrowing down into the earth. After all that running, he'd forgotten. Dwarves were creatures of the earth, expert diggers, and safety to a dwarf always meant underground. It was so easy to forget, alone. After he'd buried his dead, all forty-eight men and women and children and elders, he had begun to run. He'd gotten good at running away.

He put effort into it now, concentrating power into his treading arms, and while he could still feel the rocks, he moved away from them; they were glancing off the muscle of his buttocks, hardly painful at all. The cool softness of soil pressed against his face. The cut above his eye no longer stung. He hoped the witch could take away Rachel's pain the way the soil took away his.

Laughter bubbled up, exhilarated laughter—he was escaping, he was getting away, and he breathed in grit and loam with the ease of breathing air. It felt good, sliding into his lungs. Even the wriggle of the earthworms in his throat was no more irritating than the passage of air bubbles inside the intestines.

His arms slowed now, pressing up against stone immovable and massive, attenuating into slender coils that worked themselves into the stone's crannies. There was shelter there, shelter and something tangy and mineral he found himself craving. His legs trembled as a soil creature, a nematode or wood louse, brushed bristles against sensitive skin.

Movement ground into such slowness it became near immobility, and Rugel felt his thoughts slow with it. His mind constricted to a single point of focus, so intense it was like a ray of brilliant green light, and stones, pain, villagers, and yes, even the little girl child, were forgotten entirely. There was only green and the peace of settling into the soil and the sense that up above there was something warm and vital he would someday reach up to touch with new green leaves.

Rachel sat with her knees clasped, staring at the spray of stones surrounding a pushed-up mound of soil. The little man had gone down in there. The villagers left, but he didn't come out, not even later that night when Rachel snuck out of the witch's hut to search for him. She watched the mound, intent for any movement. Some of the stones around it were stained blood-brown.

Someone patted her shoulder. It was Eva, the witch, and she squeezed the shoulder kindly before crossing to the mound and dropping to her knees. Her gnarled old hands seized a rock and tucked it quickly into the pocket of her apron.

"Well, what are you waiting for?"

The little girl shook her head. She didn't understand the woman's impatient tone or the brisk movements of her hands collecting stones.

The old woman waved her hand, indicating the field full of plants with white flowers. "The stones will slow the growth of new seedlings. They're not as bad as weeds, but they'll make the roots grow in crooked."

The girl reached out for one of the rocks, her movements slow and uncertain. Eva smiled broadly.

"That's my girl. Got to take good care of the mandrake plants. They're precious rare, and there aren't many villages with a patch like ours." Eva smoothed the soil over the mound, tamping it down like a farmer planting garlic.

The light of memory fired in Rachel's eyes. "You used tincture of mandrake root when you helped my brother."

"I did. It saved his life. And I used it to cure your snakebite."

Rachel closed her fingers over a stone and felt its weight in her hand. In her mind's eye, she saw the dwarf's wrinkled face, coarse as a carved turnip a week after Samhain, his body as small and twisted as a mandrake root.

"The roots look like little men, don't they?" Rachel asked, and she looked over the field, as big as her father's field of peas and every foot lush with the green foliage of mandrake plants.

"Yes. Strange, isn't it? How one of the best plants for curing a man looks like one? That's the way things work, though. Like will call to like." The old woman eased herself to her feet and gave Rachel's shoulder another pat. "You come see me any time now, little Rachel. I've got plenty to teach you."

The little girl sat alone on the edge of the mandrake field, the red-stained stone folded in her fist, finally certain that the little man was gone. She closed her eyes, and tears soaked her eyelashes until they traced courses like rivers, like questing roots, down the soft slopes of her cheeks.

Rachel let the tears dry on her face before she opened her eyes again. When she pried her salt-crusted lids apart, she was surprised to see a hare browsing between the mandrake tops. It looked nervous at her presence, but it merely munched with one eye on her, momentarily content.

She watched it for a few minutes, its awkward hops more endearing than any other rabbit she had ever seen. And somehow, she knew what to do, just as if someone whispered the instructions in her ear.

"Come," she called. She focused her mind on rabbit thoughts, soft and welcoming as fresh-turned soil. Inside her, she could feel a strange flickering, as warm and welcome as a candle flame. She focused her mind and felt the flickering steady and grow even warmer.

The rabbit hopped right to her.

Rachel laughed as she stroked its soft, humped back. Its fur beneath her fingertips felt luxuriant and warm, softer than anything she'd ever touched. She scooped the little creature up and rested her cheek on its side.

Around her, the flowers of the mandrakes nodded on their stalks like tiny sleepy eyes. Beneath the soil, a new root began to reach toward the sun—nameless but not alone.

KELLY LINK is a short fiction specialist whose stories have been collected in three volumes: *Stranger Things Happen*, *Magic for Beginners*, and *Pretty Monsters*. Her stories have appeared in *The Magazine of Fantasy & Science Fiction*, *Realms of Fantasy*, *Asimov's Science Fiction*, *Conjunctions*, and in anthologies such as *The Dark*, *The Faery Reel*, and *Best American Short Stories*. With her husband, Gavin J. Grant, Link runs Small Beer Press and edits the 'zine *Lady Churchill's Rosebud Wristlet*. Her fiction has earned her an NEA Literature Fellowship and won a variety of awards, including the Hugo, Nebula, World Fantasy, Stoker, Tiptree, and Locus awards.

A common issue that comes up when discussing wizard stories is this: Why don't wizards rule the world? After all, wizards supposedly wield immense magical powers, and yet most fantasy kingdoms still seem to be governed by kings and dukes and lords, whereas the wizards are relegated to being merely advisors, or else they're off skulking in some humble tower or hovel or cave. Why don't any of these so-called wizards aim a little higher? Where's their ambition? Couldn't they just march into town, toss around a few fireballs, and declare themselves boss?

Of course, many of them are probably happier contemplating arcane mysteries, but surely some must take an interest in local affairs? Can't they use their powers for good? In Peter S. Beagle's *The Last Unicorn*, Molly Grue admonishes Schmendrick the Magician, "Then what is magic for? What is the use of wizardry, if it cannot even save a unicorn?" Answer: "That's what heroes are for."

But why? Our next story, which originally appeared in the young adult anthology *Firebirds Rising*, is built around this basic conundrum: Why don't those darn wizards ever get off their butts and actually do something for a change?

THE WIZARDS OF PERFIL
KELLY LINK

The woman who sold leech grass baskets and pickled beets in the Perfil market took pity on Onion's aunt. "On your own, my love?"

Onion's aunt nodded. She was still holding out the earrings which she'd hoped someone would buy. There was a train leaving in the morning for Qual, but the tickets were dear. Her daughter Halsa, Onion's cousin, was sulking. She'd wanted the earrings for herself. The twins held hands and stared about the market.

Onion thought the beets were more beautiful than the earrings, which had belonged to his mother. The beets were rich and velvety and mysterious as pickled stars in shining jars. Onion had had nothing to eat all day. His stomach was empty, and his head was full of the thoughts of the people in the market: Halsa thinking of the earrings, the market woman's disinterested kindness, his aunt's dull worry. There was a man at another stall whose wife was sick. She was coughing up blood. A girl went by. She was thinking about a man who had gone to the war. The man wouldn't come back. Onion went back to thinking about the beets.

"Just you to look after all these children," the market woman said. "These are bad times. Where's your lot from?"

"Come from Labbit, and Larch before that," Onion's aunt said. "We're trying to get to Qual. My husband had family there. I have these earrings and these candlesticks."

The woman shook her head. "No one will buy these," she said. "Not for any good price. The market is full of refugees selling off their bits and pieces."

Onion's aunt said, "Then what should I do?" She didn't seem to expect an answer, but the woman said, "There's a man who comes to the market today, who buys children for the wizards of Perfil. He pays good money and they say that the children are treated well."

All wizards are strange, but the wizards of Perfil are strangest of all. They build tall towers in the marshes of Perfil, and there they live like anchorites in lonely little rooms at the top of their towers. They rarely come down at all, and no one is sure what their magic is good for. There are wobbly lights like balls of sickly green fire that dash around the marshes at night, hunting for who knows what, and sometimes a tower tumbles down and then the prickly reeds and marsh lilies that look like ghostly white hands grow up over the tumbled stones and the marsh mud sucks the rubble down.

Everyone knows that there are wizard bones under the marsh mud and that the fish and the birds that live in the marsh are strange creatures. They have got magic in them. Boys dare each other to go into the marsh and catch fish. Sometimes when a brave boy catches a fish in the murky, muddy marsh pools, the fish will call the boy by name and beg to be released. And if you don't let that fish go, it will tell you, gasping for air, when and how you will die. And if you cook the fish and eat it, you will dream wizard dreams. But if you let your fish go, it will tell you a secret.

This is what the people of Perfil say about the wizards of Perfil.

Everyone knows that the wizards of Perfil talk to demons and hate sunlight and have long twitching noses like rats. They never bathe.

Everyone knows that the wizards of Perfil are hundreds and hundreds of years old. They sit and dangle their fishing lines out of the windows of their towers and they use magic to bait their hooks. They eat their fish raw and they throw the fish bones out of the window the same way that they empty their chamber pots. The wizards of Perfil have filthy habits and no manners at all.

Everyone knows that the wizards of Perfil eat children when they grow tired of fish.

This is what Halsa told her brothers and Onion while Onion's aunt bargained in the Perfil markets with the wizard's secretary.

The wizard's secretary was a man named Tolcet and he wore a sword in his belt. He was a black man with white-pink spatters on his face and across the backs of his hands. Onion had never seen a man who was two colors.

Tolcet gave Onion and his cousins pieces of candy. He said to Onion's aunt, "Can any of them sing?"

Onion's aunt indicated that the children should sing. The twins, Mik and Bonti, had strong, clear soprano voices and when Halsa sang, everyone in the market fell silent and listened. Halsa's voice was like honey and sunlight and sweet water.

Onion loved to sing, but no one loved to hear it. When it was his turn and he opened his mouth to sing, he thought of his mother and tears came to his eyes. The song that came out of his mouth wasn't one he knew. It wasn't even in a proper language and Halsa crossed her eyes and stuck out her tongue. Onion went on singing.

"Enough," Tolcet said. He pointed at Onion. "You sing like a toad, boy. Do you know when to be quiet?"

"He's quiet," Onion's aunt said. "His parents are dead. He doesn't eat much, and he's strong enough. We walked here from Larch. And he's not afraid of witchy folk, begging your pardon. There were no wizards in Larch, but his mother could find things when you lost them. She could charm your cows so that they always came home."

"How old is he?" Tolcet said.

"Eleven," Onion's aunt said and Tolcet grunted.

"Small for his age." Tolcet looked at Onion. He looked at Halsa, who crossed her arms and scowled hard. "Will you come with me, boy?"

Onion's aunt nudged him. He nodded.

"I'm sorry for it," his aunt said to Onion, "but it can't be helped. I promised your mother I'd see you were taken care of. This is the best I can do."

Onion said nothing. He knew his aunt would have sold Halsa to the wizard's secretary and hoped it was a piece of luck for her daughter. But there was also a part of his aunt that was glad that Tolcet wanted Onion instead. Onion could see it in her mind.

Tolcet paid Onion's aunt twenty-four brass fish, which was slightly more than it had cost to bury Onion's parents, but slightly less than Onion's father had paid for their best milk cow, two years before. It was important to know how much things were worth. The cow was dead and so was Onion's father.

"Be *good*," Onion's aunt said. "Here. Take this." She gave Onion one of the earrings that had belonged to his mother. It was shaped like a snake. Its writhing tail hooked into its narrow mouth, and Onion had always wondered if the snake were surprised about that, to end up with a mouthful of itself like that, for all eternity. Or maybe it was eternally furious, like Halsa.

Halsa's mouth was screwed up like a button. When she hugged Onion good-bye, she said, "Brat. Give it to me." Halsa had already taken the wooden horse that Onion's father had carved, and Onion's knife, the one with the bone handle.

Onion tried to pull away, but she held him tightly, as if she couldn't bear to let him go. "He wants to eat you," she said. "The wizard will put you in an oven and roast you like a suckling pig. So give me the earring. Suckling pigs don't need earrings."

Onion wriggled away. The wizard's secretary was watching, and Onion wondered if he'd heard Halsa. Of course, anyone who wanted a child to eat would have taken Halsa, not Onion. Halsa was older and bigger and plumper. Then again, anyone who looked hard at Halsa would suspect she would taste sour and unpleasant. The only sweetness in Halsa was in her singing. Even Onion loved to listen to Halsa when she sang.

Mik and Bonti gave Onion shy little kisses on his cheek. He knew they wished the wizard's secretary had bought Halsa instead. Now that Onion was gone, it would be the twins that Halsa pinched and bullied and teased.

Tolcet swung a long leg over his horse. Then he leaned down. "Come on, boy," he said, and held his speckled hand out to Onion. Onion took it.

The horse was warm and its back was broad and high. There was no saddle and no reins, only a kind of woven harness with a basket on either flank, filled with goods from the market. Tolcet held the horse quiet with his knees, and Onion held on tight to Tolcet's belt.

"That song you sang," Tolcet said. "Where did you learn it?"

"I don't know," Onion said. It came to him that the song had been a song that Tolcet's mother had sung to her son, when Tolcet was a child. Onion wasn't sure what the words meant, because Tolcet wasn't sure either. There was something about a lake and a boat, something about a girl who had eaten the moon.

The marketplace was full of people selling things. From his vantage point Onion felt, for a moment, like a prince: as if he could afford to buy anything he saw. He looked down at a stall selling apples and potatoes and hot leek pies. His mouth watered. Over here was an incense seller's stall, and there was a woman telling fortunes. At the train station, people were lining up to buy tickets for Qual. In the morning a train would leave and Onion's aunt and Halsa and the twins would be on it. It was a dangerous passage. There were unfriendly armies between here and Qual. When Onion looked back at his aunt, he knew it would do no good, she would only think he was begging her not to leave him with the wizard's secretary, but he said it all the same: "Don't go to Qual."

But he knew even as he said it that she would go anyway. No one ever listened to Onion.

The horse tossed its head. The wizard's secretary made a *tch-tch* sound and then leaned back in the saddle. He seemed undecided about something. Onion looked back one more time at his aunt. He had never seen her smile once in the two years he'd lived with her, and she did not smile now, even though twenty-four brass fish was not a small sum of money and even though she'd kept her promise to Onion's mother. Onion's mother had smiled often, despite the fact that her teeth were not particularly good.

"He'll eat you," Halsa called to Onion. "Or he'll drown you in the marsh! He'll cut you up into little pieces and bait his fishing line with your fingers!" She stamped her foot.

"Halsa!" her mother said.

"On second thought," Tolcet said, "I'll take the girl. Will you sell her to me instead?"

"What?" Halsa said.

"What?" Onion's aunt said.

"No!" Onion said, but Tolcet drew out his purse again. Halsa, it seemed, was worth more than a small boy with a bad voice. And Onion's aunt needed money badly. So Halsa got up on the horse behind Tolcet, and Onion watched as the wizard's servant and his bad-tempered cousin rode away.

There was a voice in Onion's head. It said, "Don't worry, boy. All will be well and all manner of things will be well." It sounded like Tolcet, a little amused, a little sad.

There is a story about the wizards of Perfil and how one fell in love with a church bell. First he tried to buy it with gold and then, when the church refused his money, he stole it by magic. As the wizard flew back across the marshes, carrying the bell in his arms, he flew too low and the devil reached up and grabbed his heel. The wizard dropped the church bell into the marshes and it sank and was lost forever. Its voice is clappered with mud and moss and although the wizard never gave up searching for it and calling its name, the bell never answered and the wizard grew thin and died of grief. Fishermen say that the dead wizard still flies over the marsh, crying out for the lost bell.

Everyone knows that wizards are pigheaded and come to bad ends. No wizard has ever made himself useful by magic, or, if they've tried, they've only made matters worse. No wizard has ever stopped a war or mended a fence. It's better that they stay in their marshes, out of the way of worldly folk like farmers and soldiers and merchants and kings.

"Well," Onion's aunt said. She sagged. They could no longer see Tolcet or Halsa. "Come along, then."

They went back through the market and Onion's aunt bought cakes of sweetened rice for the three children. Onion ate his without knowing that he did so: since the wizard's servant had taken away Halsa instead, it had felt as if there were two Onions, one Onion here in the market and one Onion riding along with Tolcet and Halsa. He stood and was carried along at the same time and it made both of him feel terribly dizzy. Market-Onion stumbled, his mouth full of rice, and his aunt caught him by the elbow.

"We don't eat children," Tolcet was saying. "There are plenty of fish and birds in the marshes."

"I know," Halsa said. She sounded sulky. "And the wizards live in houses with lots of stairs. Towers. Because they think they're so much better than anybody else. So above the rest of the world."

"And how do you know about the wizards of Perfil?" Tolcet said.

"The woman in the market," Halsa said. "And the other people in the market. Some are afraid of the wizards and some think that there are no wizards. That they're a story for children. That the marshes are full of runaway slaves and deserters. Nobody knows why wizards would come and build towers in the Perfil marsh where the ground is like cheese and no one can find them. Why do the wizards live in the marshes?"

"Because the marsh is full of magic," Tolcet said.

"Then why do they build the towers so high?" Halsa said.

"Because wizards are curious," Tolcet said. "They like to be able to see things that are far off. They like to be as close as possible to the stars. And they don't like to be bothered by people who ask lots of questions."

"Why do the wizards buy children?" Halsa said.

"To run up and down the stairs," Tolcet said, "to fetch them water for bathing and to carry messages and to bring them breakfasts and dinners and lunches and suppers. Wizards are always hungry."

"So am I," Halsa said.

"Here," Tolcet said. He gave Halsa an apple. "You see things that are in people's heads. You can see things that are going to happen."

"Yes," Halsa said. "Sometimes." The apple was wrinkled but sweet.

"Your cousin has a gift, too," Tolcet said.

"Onion?" Halsa said scornfully. Onion saw that it had never felt like a gift to Halsa. No wonder she'd hidden it.

"Can you see what is in my head right now?" Tolcet said.

Halsa looked and Onion looked too. There was no curiosity or fear about in Tolcet's head. There was nothing. There was no Tolcet, no wizard's servant. Only brackish water and lonely white birds flying above it.

It's beautiful, Onion said.

"What?" his aunt said, in the market. "Onion? Sit down, child."

"Some people find it so," Tolcet said, answering Onion. Halsa said nothing, but she frowned.

Tolcet and Halsa rode through the town and out of the town gates onto the road that led back towards Labbit and east, where there were more refugees coming and going, day and night. They were mostly women and children and they were afraid. There were rumors of armies behind them. There was a story that, in a fit of madness, the king had killed his youngest son. Onion saw a chess game, a thin-faced, anxious, yellow-haired boy Onion's age moving a black queen across the board, and then the chess pieces scattered across a stone floor. A woman was saying something. The boy bent down to pick up the scattered pieces. The king was laughing. He had a sword in his hand and he brought it down and then there was blood on it. Onion had never seen a king before, although he had seen men with swords. He had seen men with blood on their swords.

Tolcet and Halsa went away from the road, following a wide river, which was less a river than a series of wide, shallow pools. On the other side of the river, muddy paths disappeared into thick stands of rushes and bushes full of berries. There was a feeling of watchfulness, and the cunning, curious stillness of something alive, something half-asleep and half-waiting, a hidden, invisible humming, as if even the air was saturated with magic.

"Berries! Ripe and sweet!" a girl was singing out, over and over again in the market. Onion wished she would be quiet. His aunt bought bread and salt and hard cheese. She piled them into Onion's arms.

"It will be uncomfortable at first," Tolcet was saying. "The marshes of Perfil are so full of magic that they drink up all other kinds of magic. The only ones who work magic in the marshes of Perfil are the wizards of Perfil. And there are bugs."

"I don't want anything to do with magic," Halsa said primly.

Again Onion tried to look in Tolcet's mind, but again all he saw was the marshes. Fat-petaled waxy white flowers and crouching trees that dangled their long brown fingers as if fishing. Tolcet laughed. "I can feel you looking," he said. "Don't look too long or you'll fall in and drown."

"I'm not looking!" Halsa said. But she *was* looking. Onion could feel her looking, as if she was turning a key in a door.

The marshes smelled salty and rich, like a bowl of broth. Tolcet's horse ambled along, its hooves sinking into the path. Behind them, water welled up and filled the depressions. Fat jeweled flies clung, vibrating, to the rushes and once in a clear pool of water Onion saw a snake curling like a green ribbon through water weeds soft as a cloud of hair.

"Wait here and watch Bonti and Mik for me," Onion's aunt said. "I'll go to the train station. Onion, are you all right?"

Onion nodded dreamily.

Tolcet and Halsa rode further into the marsh, away from the road and the Perfil market and Onion. It was very different from the journey to Perfil, which had been hurried and dusty and dry and on foot. Whenever Onion or one of the twins stumbled or lagged behind, Halsa had rounded them up like a dog chasing sheep, pinching and slapping. It was hard to imagine cruel, greedy, unhappy Halsa being able to pick things out of other people's minds, although she had always seemed to know when Mik or Bonti had found something edible; where there might be a soft piece of ground to sleep; when they should duck off the road because soldiers were coming.

Halsa was thinking of her mother and her brothers. She was thinking about the look on her father's face when the soldiers had shot him behind the barn; the earrings shaped like snakes; how the train to Qual would be blown up by saboteurs. She had been supposed to be on that train, she knew it. She was furious at Tolcet for taking her away; at Onion, because Tolcet had changed his mind about Onion.

Every now and then, while he waited in the market for his aunt to come back, Onion could see the pointy roofs of the wizard's towers leaning against the sky as if they were waiting for him, just beyond the Perfil market, and then the towers would recede, and he would go with them, and find himself again with Tolcet and Halsa. Their path ran up along a canal of calm tarry water, angled off into thickets of bushes bent down with bright yellow berries, and then returned. It cut across other paths, these narrower and crookeder, overgrown and secret looking. At last they rode through a stand of sweet-smelling trees and came out into a hidden, grassy meadow that seemed not much larger than the Perfil market. Up close, the towers were not particularly splendid. They were tumbledown and lichen-covered and looked as if they might collapse at any moment. They were so close together one might have strung a line for laundry from tower to tower, if wizards had been concerned with such things as laundry. Efforts had been made to buttress the towers; some had long, eccentrically curving fins of strategically piled rocks. There were twelve standing towers that looked as if they might be occupied. Others were half in ruins or were only piles of rocks that had already been scavenged for useful building materials.

Around the meadow were more paths: worn, dirt paths and canals that sank into branchy, briary tangles, some so low that a boat would never have passed without catching. Even a swimmer would have to duck her head. Children sat on the half-ruined walls of toppled towers and watched Tolcet and Halsa ride up. There was a fire with a thin man stirring something in a pot. Two women were winding up a ball of rough-looking twine. They were dressed like Tolcet. More wizards' servants, Halsa and Onion thought. Clearly wizards were very lazy.

"Down you go," Tolcet said and Halsa gladly slid off the horse's back. Then Tolcet got down and lifted off the harness and the horse suddenly became a naked, brown girl of about fourteen years. She straightened her back and wiped her muddy hands on her pants. She didn't seem to care that she was naked. Halsa gaped at her.

The girl frowned. She said, "You be good, now, or they'll turn you into something even worse."

"Who?" Halsa said.

"The wizards of Perfil," the girl said, and laughed. It was a neighing, horsey laugh. All of the other children began to giggle.

"Oooh, Essa gave Tolcet a ride."

"Essa, did you bring me back a present?"

"Essa makes a prettier horse than she does a girl."

"Oh, shut up," Essa said. She picked up a rock and threw it. Halsa admired her economy of motion, and her accuracy.

"Oi!" her target said, putting her hand up to her ear. "That hurt, Essa."

"Thank you, Essa," Tolcet said. She made a remarkably graceful curtsey, considering that until a moment ago she had had four legs and no waist to speak of. There was a shirt and a pair of leggings folded and lying on a rock. Essa put them on. "This is Halsa," Tolcet said to the children and to the man and women. "I bought her in the market."

There was silence. Halsa's face was bright red. For once she was speechless. She looked at the ground and then up at the towers, and Onion looked too, trying to catch a glimpse of a wizard. All the windows of the towers were empty, but he could feel the wizards of Perfil, feel the weight of their watching. The marshy ground under his feet was full of wizards' magic and the towers threw magic out like waves of heat from a stove. Magic clung even to the children and servants of the wizards of Perfil, as if they had been marinated in it.

"Come get something to eat," Tolcet said, and Halsa stumbled after him. There was a flat bread, and onions and fish. Halsa drank water which had the faint, slightly metallic taste of magic. Onion could taste it in his own mouth.

"Onion," someone said. "Bonti, Mik." Onion looked up. He was back in the market and his aunt stood there. "There's a church nearby where they'll let us sleep. The train leaves early tomorrow morning."

After she had eaten, Tolcet took Halsa into one of the towers, where there was a small cubby under the stairs. There was a pallet of reeds and a mothy wool blanket. The sun was still in the sky. Onion and his aunt and his cousins went to the church where there was a yard where refugees might curl up and sleep a few hours. Halsa lay awake, thinking of the wizard in the room above the stairs where she was sleeping. The tower was so full of wizard's magic that she could hardly breathe. She imagined a wizard of Perfil creeping, creeping down the stairs above her cubby, and although the pallet was soft, she pinched her arms to stay awake. But Onion fell asleep immediately, as if drugged. He dreamed of wizards flying above the marshes like white lonely birds.

In the morning, Tolcet came and shook Halsa awake. "Go and fetch water for the wizard," he said. He was holding an empty bucket.

Halsa would have liked to say *go and fetch it yourself*, but she was not a stupid girl. She was a slave now. Onion was in her head again, telling her to be careful.

"Oh go away," Halsa said. She realized she had said this aloud, and flinched. But Tolcet only laughed.

Halsa rubbed her eyes and took the bucket and followed him. Outside, the air was full of biting bugs too small to see. They seemed to like the taste of Halsa. That seemed funny to Onion, for no reason that she could understand.

The other children were standing around the fire pit and eating porridge. "Are you hungry?" Tolcet said. Halsa nodded. "Bring the water up and then get yourself something to eat. It's not a good idea to keep a wizard waiting."

He led her along a well-trodden path that quickly sloped down into a small pool and disappeared. "The water is sweet here," he said. "Fill your bucket and bring it up to the top of the wizard's tower. I have an errand to run. I'll return before nightfall. Don't be afraid, Halsa."

"I'm not afraid," Halsa said. She knelt down and filled the bucket. She was almost back to the tower before she realized that the bucket was half empty again. There was a split in the wooden bottom. The other children were watching her and she straightened her back. *So it's a test,* she said in her head, to Onion.

You could ask them for a bucket without a hole in it, he said.

I don't need anyone's help, Halsa said. She went back down the path and scooped up a handful of clayey mud where the path ran into the pool. She packed this into the bottom of the bucket and then pressed moss down on top of the mud. This time the bucket held water.

There were three windows lined with red tiles on Halsa's wizard's tower, and a nest that some bird had built on an outcropping of stone. The roof was round and red and shaped like a bishop's hat. The stairs inside were narrow. The steps had been worn down, smooth and slippery as wax. The higher she went, the heavier the pail of water became. Finally she set it down on a step and sat down beside it. *Four hundred and twenty-two steps,* Onion said. Halsa had counted five hundred and ninety-eight. There seemed to be many more steps on the inside than one would have thought, looking at the tower from outside. "Wizardly tricks," Halsa said in disgust, as if she'd expected nothing better. "You would think they'd make it fewer steps, rather than more steps. What's the use of more steps?"

When she stood and picked up the bucket, the handle broke in her hand. The water spilled down the steps and Halsa threw the bucket after as hard as she could. Then she marched down the stairs and went to mend the bucket and fetch more water. It didn't do to keep wizards waiting.

At the top of the steps in the wizard's tower there was a door. Halsa set the bucket down and knocked. No one answered and so she knocked again. She tried the latch: the door was locked. Up here, the smell of magic was so thick that Halsa's

eyes watered. She tried to look *through* the door. This is what she saw: a room, a
window, a bed, a mirror, a table. The mirror was full of rushes and light and water.
A bright-eyed fox was curled up on the bed, sleeping. A white bird flew through
the unshuttered window, and then another and another. They circled around and
around the room and then they began to mass on the table. One flung itself at
the door where Halsa stood, peering in. She recoiled. The door vibrated with peck
and blows.

She turned and ran down the stairs, leaving the bucket, leaving Onion behind
her. There were even more steps on the way down. And there was no porridge left
in the pot beside the fire.

Someone tapped her on the shoulder and she jumped. "Here," Essa said,
handing her a piece of bread.

"Thanks," Halsa said. The bread was stale and hard. It was the most delicious
thing she'd ever eaten.

"So your mother sold you," Essa said.

Halsa swallowed hard. It was strange, not being able to see inside Essa's head,
but it was also restful. As if Essa might be anyone at all. As if Halsa herself might
become anyone she wished to be. "I didn't care," she said. "Who sold you?"

"No one," Essa said. "I ran away from home. I didn't want to be a soldier's
whore like my sisters."

"Are the wizards better than soldiers?" Halsa said.

Essa gave her a strange look. "What do you think? Did you meet your wizard?"

"He was old and ugly, of course," Halsa said. "I didn't like the way he looked
at me."

Essa put her hand over her mouth as if she were trying not to laugh. "Oh dear,"
she said.

"What must I do?" Halsa said. "I've never been a wizard's servant before."

"Didn't your wizard tell you?" Essa said. "What did he tell you to do?"

Halsa blew out an irritated breath. "I asked what he needed, but he said
nothing. I think he was hard of hearing."

Essa laughed long and hard, exactly like a horse, Halsa thought. There were
three or four other children, now, watching them. They were all laughing at Halsa.
"Admit it," Essa said. "You didn't talk to the wizard."

"So?" Halsa said. "I knocked, but no one answered. So obviously he's hard of
hearing."

"Of course," a boy said.

"Or maybe the wizard is shy," said another boy. He had green eyes like Bonti
and Mik. "Or asleep. Wizards like to take naps."

Everyone was laughing again.

"Stop making fun of me," Halsa said. She tried to look fierce and dangerous. Onion and her brothers would have quailed. "Tell me what my duties are. What does a wizard's servant do?"

Someone said, "You carry things up the stairs. Food. Firewood. Kaffa, when Tolcet brings it back from the market. Wizards like unusual things. Old things. So you go out in the marsh and look for things."

"Things?" Halsa said.

"Glass bottles," Essa said. "Petrified imps. Strange things, things out of the ordinary. Or ordinary things like plants or stones or animals or anything that feels right. Do you know what I mean?"

"No," Halsa said, but she did know. Some things felt more magic-soaked than other things. Her father had found an arrowhead in his field. He'd put it aside to take to the schoolmaster, but that night while everyone was sleeping, Halsa had wrapped it in a rag and taken it back to the field and buried it. Bonti was blamed. Sometimes Halsa wondered if that was what had brought the soldiers to kill her father, the malicious, evil luck of that arrowhead. But you couldn't blame a whole war on one arrowhead.

"Here," a boy said. "Go and catch fish if you're too stupid to know magic when you see it. Have you ever caught fish?"

Halsa took the fishing pole. "Take that path," Essa said. "The muddiest one. And stay on it. There's a pier out that way where the fishing is good."

When Halsa looked back at the wizard's towers, she thought she saw Onion looking down at her, out of a high window. But that was ridiculous. It was only a bird.

The train was so crowded that some passengers gave up and went and sat on top of the cars. Vendors sold umbrellas to keep the sun off. Onion's aunt had found two seats, and she and Onion sat with one twin on each lap. Two rich women sat across from them. You could tell they were rich because their shoes were green leather. They held filmy pink handkerchiefs like embroidered rose petals up to their rabbity noses. Bonti looked at them from under his eyelashes. Bonti was a terrible flirt.

Onion had never been on a train before. He could smell the furnace room of the train, rich with coal and magic. Passengers stumbled up and down the aisles, drinking and laughing as if they were at a festival. Men and women stood beside the train windows, sticking their heads in. They shouted messages. A woman leaning against the seats fell against Onion and Mik when someone shoved past her. "Pardon, sweet," she said, and smiled brilliantly. Her teeth were studded with gemstones. She was wearing at least four silk dresses, one on top of the other. A man across the aisle coughed wetly. There was a bandage wrapped around his throat, stained with red. Babies were crying.

"I hear they'll reach Perfil in three days or less," a man in the next row said.

"The King's men won't sack Perfil," said his companion. "They're coming to defend it."

"The King is mad," the man said. "God has told him all men are his enemies. He hasn't paid his army in two years. When they rebel, he just conscripts another army and sends them off to fight the first one. We're safer leaving."

"Oooh," a woman said, somewhere behind Onion. "At last we're off. Isn't this fun! What a pleasant outing!"

Onion tried to think of the marshes of Perfil, of the wizards. But Halsa was suddenly there on the train, instead. *You have to tell them,* she said.

Tell them what? Onion asked her, although he knew. When the train was in the mountains, there would be an explosion. There would be soldiers, riding down at the train. No one would reach Qual. *Nobody will believe me,* he said.

You should tell them anyway, Halsa said.

Onion's legs were falling asleep. He shifted Mik. *Why do you care?* he said. *You hate everyone.*

I don't! Halsa said. But she did. She hated her mother. Her mother had watched her husband die, and done nothing. Halsa had been screaming and her mother slapped her across the face. She hated the twins because they weren't like her, they didn't *see* things the way Halsa had to. Because they were little and they got tired and it had been so much work keeping them safe. Halsa had hated Onion, too, because he *was* like her. Because he'd been afraid of Halsa, and because the day he'd come to live with her family, she'd known that one day she would be like him, alone and without a family. Magic was bad luck, people like Onion and Halsa were bad luck. The only person who'd ever looked at Halsa and really seen her, really known her, had been Onion's mother. Onion's mother was kind and good and she'd known she was going to die. *Take care of my son,* she'd said to Halsa's mother and father, but she'd been looking at Halsa when she said it. But Onion would have to take care of himself. Halsa would make him.

Tell them, Halsa said. There was a fish jerking on her line. She ignored it. *Tell them, tell them, tell them.* She and Onion were in the marsh and on the train at the same time. Everything smelled like coal and salt and ferment. Onion ignored her the way she was ignoring the fish. He sat and dangled his feet in the water, even though he wasn't really there.

ᑫᓄ

Halsa caught five fish. She cleaned them and wrapped them in leaves and brought them back to the cooking fire. She also brought back the greeny-copper key that had caught on her fishing line. "I found this," she said to Tolcet.

"Ah," Tolcet said. "May I see it?" It looked even smaller and more ordinary in Tolcet's hand.

"Burd," Tolcet said. "Where is the box you found, the one we couldn't open?"

The boy with green eyes got up and disappeared into one of the towers. He came out after a few minutes and gave Tolcet a metal box no bigger than a pickle jar. The key fit. Tolcet unlocked it, although it seemed to Halsa that she ought to have been the one to unlock it, not Tolcet.

"A doll," Halsa said, disappointed. But it was a strange-looking doll. It was carved out of a greasy black wood and when Tolcet turned it over, it had no back, only two fronts, so it was always looking backwards and forwards at the same time.

"What do you think, Burd?" Tolcet said.

Burd shrugged. "It's not mine."

"It's yours," Tolcet said to Halsa. "Take it up the stairs and give it to your wizard. And refill the bucket with fresh water and bring some dinner, too. Did you think to take up lunch?"

"No," Halsa said. She hadn't had any lunch herself. She cooked the fish along with some greens Tolcet gave her, and ate two. The other three fish and the rest of the greens she carried up to the top of the stairs in the tower. She had to stop to rest twice, there were so many stairs this time. The door was still closed and the bucket on the top step was empty. She thought that maybe all the water had leaked away, slowly. But she left the fish and she went and drew more water and carried the bucket back up.

"I've brought you dinner," Halsa said, when she'd caught her breath. "And something else. Something I found in the marsh. Tolcet said I should give it to you."

Silence.

She felt silly, talking to the wizard's door. "It's a doll," she said. "Perhaps it's a magic doll."

Silence again. Not even Onion was there. She hadn't noticed when he went away. She thought of the train. "If I give you the doll," she said, "will you do something for me? You're a wizard, so you ought to be able to do anything, right? Will you help the people on the train? They're going to Qual. Something bad is going to happen if you won't stop it. You know about the soldiers? Can you stop them?"

Halsa waited for a long time, but the wizard behind the door never said anything. She put the doll down on the steps and then she picked it up again and put it in her pocket. She was furious. "I think you're a coward," she said. "That's why you hide up here, isn't it? I would have got on that train and I know what's going to happen. Onion got on that train. And you could stop it, but you won't. Well, if you won't stop it, then I won't give you the doll."

She spat in the bucket of water and then immediately wished she hadn't. "You keep the train safe," she said, "and I'll give you the doll. I promise. I'll bring you other things too. And I'm sorry I spit in your water. I'll go and get more."

She took the bucket and went back down the stairs. Her legs ached and there were welts where the little biting bugs had drawn blood.

"Mud," Essa said. She was standing in the meadow, smoking a pipe. "The flies are only bad in the morning and at twilight. If you put mud on your face and arms, they leave you alone."

"It smells," Halsa said.

"So do you," Essa said. She snapped her clay pipe in two, which seemed extravagant to Halsa, and wandered over to where some of the other children were playing a complicated looking game of pick-up sticks and dice. Under a night-flowering tree, Tolcet sat in a battered, oaken throne that looked as if it had been spat up by the marsh. He was smoking a pipe too, with a clay stem even longer than Essa's had been. It was ridiculously long. "Did you give the poppet to the wizard?" he said.

"Oh yes," Halsa said.

"What did she say?"

"Well," Halsa said. "I'm not sure. She's young and quite lovely. But she had a horrible stutter. I could hardly understand her. I think she said something about the moon, how she wanted me to go cut her a slice of it. I'm to bake it into a pie."

"Wizards are very fond of pie," Tolcet said.

"Of course they are," Halsa said. "And I'm fond of my arse."

"Better watch your mouth," Burd, the boy with green eyes, said. He was standing on his head, for no good reason that Halsa could see. His legs waved in the air languidly, semaphoring. "Or the wizards will make you sorry."

"I'm already sorry," Halsa said. But she didn't say anything else. She carried the bucket of water up to the closed door. Then she ran back down the stairs to the cubbyhole and this time she fell straight asleep. She dreamed a fox came and looked at her. It stuck its muzzle in her face. Then it trotted up the stairs and ate the three fish Halsa had left there. *You'll be sorry*, Halsa thought. *The wizards will turn you into a one-legged crow.* But then she was chasing the fox up the aisle of a train to Qual, where her mother and her brothers and Onion were sleeping uncomfortably in their seats, their legs tucked under them, their arms hanging down as if they were dead—the stink of coal and magic was even stronger than it had been in the morning. The train was laboring hard. It panted like a fox with a pack of dogs after it, dragging itself along. There was no way it would reach all the way to the top of the wizard of Perfil's stairs. And if it did, the wizard wouldn't be there, anyway, just the moon, rising up over the mountains, round and fat as a lardy bone.

The wizards of Perfil don't write poetry, as a general rule. As far as anyone knows, they don't marry, or plow fields, or have much use for polite speech. It is said that the wizards of Perfil appreciate a good joke, but telling a joke to a wizard is dangerous business. What if the wizard doesn't find the joke funny? Wizards are sly, greedy, absent-minded, obsessed with stars and bugs, parsimonious, frivolous, invisible, tyrannous, untrustworthy, secretive, inquisitive, meddlesome, long-lived, dangerous, useless, and have far too good an opinion of themselves. Kings go mad, the land is blighted, children starve or get sick or die spitted on the pointy end of a pike, and it's all beneath the notice of the wizards of Perfil. The wizards of Perfil don't fight wars.

It was like having a stone in his shoe. Halsa was always there, nagging. *Tell them, tell them. Tell them.* They had been on the train for a day and a night. Halsa was in the swamp, getting farther and farther away. Why wouldn't she leave him alone? Mik and Bonti had seduced the two rich women who sat across. There were no more frowns or handkerchiefs, only smiles and tidbits of food and love, love, love all around. On went the train through burned fields and towns that had been put to the sword by one army or another. The train and its passengers overtook people on foot, or fleeing in wagons piled high with goods: mattresses, wardrobes, a pianoforte once, stoves and skillets and butter churns and pigs and angry-looking geese. Sometimes the train stopped while men got out and examined the tracks and made repairs. They did not stop at any stations, although there were people waiting, sometimes, who yelled and ran after the train. No one got off. There were fewer people up in the mountains, when they got there. Instead there was snow. Once Onion saw a wolf.

"When we get to Qual," one of the rich women, the older one, said to Onion's aunt, "my sister and I will set up our establishment. We'll need someone to keep house for us. Are you thrifty?" She had Bonti on her lap. He was half-asleep.

"Yes, ma'am," Onion's aunt said.

"Well, we'll see," said the woman. She was half-in-love with Bonti. Onion had never had much opportunity to see what the rich thought about. He was a little disappointed to find out that it was much the same. The only difference seemed to be that the rich woman, like the wizard's secretary, seemed to think that all of this would end up all right. Money, it seemed, was like luck, or magic. All manner of things would be well, except they wouldn't. If it weren't for the thing that was going to happen to the train, perhaps Onion's aunt could have sold more of her children.

Why won't you tell them? Halsa said. *Soon it will be too late.*

You tell them, Onion thought back at her. Having an invisible Halsa around, always telling him things that he already knew, it was far worse than the real Halsa had been. The real Halsa was safe, asleep, on the pallet under the wizard's stairs. Onion should have been there instead. Onion bet the wizards of Perfil were sorry that Tolcet had ever bought a girl like Halsa.

Halsa shoved past Onion. She put her invisible hands on her mother's shoulders and looked into her face. Her mother didn't look up. *You have to get off the train,* Halsa said. She yelled. *Get off the train!*

But it was like talking to the door at the top of the wizard's tower. There was something in Halsa's pocket, pressing into her stomach so hard it almost felt like a bruise. Halsa wasn't on the train, she was sleeping on something with a sharp little face.

"Oh, stop yelling. Go away. How am I supposed to stop a train?" Onion said.

"Onion?" his aunt said. Onion realized he'd said it aloud. Halsa looked smug.

"Something bad is going to happen," Onion said, capitulating. "We have to stop the train and get off." The two rich women stared at him as if he were a lunatic. Onion's aunt patted his shoulder. "Onion," she said. "You were asleep. You were having a bad dream."

"But—" Onion protested.

"Here," his aunt said, glancing at their traveling companions. "Take Mik for a walk. Shake off your dream."

Onion gave up. The rich women were thinking that perhaps they would be better off looking for a housekeeper in Qual. Halsa was tapping her foot, standing in the aisle with her arms folded.

Come on, she said. *No point talking to them. They just think you're crazy. Come talk to the conductor instead.*

"Sorry," Onion said to his aunt. "I had a bad dream. I'll go for a walk." He took Mik's hand.

They went up the aisle, stepping over sleeping people and people stupid or quarrelsome with drink, people slapping down playing cards. Halsa always in front of them: *Hurry up, hurry, hurry. We're almost there. You've left it too late. That useless wizard, I should have known not to bother asking for help. I should have known not to expect you to take care of things. You're as useless as they are. Stupid good-for-nothing wizards of Perfil.*

Up ahead of the train, Onion could feel the gunpowder charges, little bundles wedged between the ties of the track. It was like there was a stone in his shoe. He wasn't afraid, he was merely irritated: at Halsa, at the people on the train who didn't even know enough to be afraid, at the wizards and the rich women who thought that they could just buy children, just like that. He was angry, too. He was angry at his parents, for dying, for leaving him stuck here. He was angry at the king, who had gone mad; at the soldiers, who wouldn't stay home with their own families, who went around stabbing and shooting and blowing up other people's families.

They were at the front of the train. Halsa led Onion right into the cab where two men were throwing enormous scoops of coal into a red-black, boiling furnace. They were filthy as devils. Their arms bulged with muscles and their eyes were red and inflamed. One turned and saw Onion. "Oi!" he said. "What's he doing here? You, kid, what are you doing?"

"You have to stop the train," Onion said. "Something is going to happen. I saw soldiers. They're going to make the train blow up."

"Soldiers? Back there? How long ago?"

"They're up ahead of us," Onion said. "We have to stop now."

Mik was looking up at him.

"He saw soldiers?" the other man said.

"Naw," said the first man. Onion could see he didn't know whether to be angry or whether to laugh. "The fucking kid's making things up. Pretending he sees things. Hey, maybe he's a wizard of Perfil! Lucky us, we got a wizard on the train!"

"I'm not a wizard," Onion said. Halsa snorted in agreement. "But I know things. If you don't stop the train, everyone will die."

Both men stared at him. Then the first said, angrily, "Get out of here, you. And don't go talking to people like that or we'll throw you in the boiler."

"Okay," Onion said. "Come on, Mik."

Wait, Halsa said. *What are you doing? You have to make them understand. Do you want to be dead? Do you think you can prove something to me by being dead?*

Onion put Mik on his shoulders. *I'm sorry,* he said to Halsa. *I don't want to be dead. But you see the same thing I see. You see what's going to happen. Maybe you should just go away. Wake up. Catch fish. Fetch water for the wizards of Perfil.*

The pain in Halsa's stomach was sharper, as if someone was stabbing her. When she put her hand down, she had hold of the wooden doll.

What's that? Onion said.

Nothing, Halsa said. *Something I found in the swamp. I said I would give it to the wizard, but I won't! Here, you take it!*

She thrust it at Onion. It went all the way through him. It was an uncomfortable feeling, even though it wasn't really there. *Halsa,* he said. He put Mik down.

Take it! she said. *Here! Take it now!*

The train was roaring. Onion knew where they were; he recognized the way the light looked. Someone was telling a joke in the front of the train, and in a minute a woman would laugh. It would be a lot brighter in a minute. He put his hand up to stop the thing that Halsa was stabbing him with and something smacked against his palm. His fingers brushed Halsa's fingers.

It was a wooden doll with a sharp little nose. There was a nose on the back of its head, too. *Oh, take it!* Halsa said. Something was pouring out of her, through the doll, into Onion. Onion fell back against a woman holding a birdcage on her lap. "Get off!" the woman said. It *hurt.* The stuff pouring out of Halsa felt like *life,* like the doll was pulling out her life like a skein of heavy, sodden, black wool. It hurt Onion, too. Black stuff poured and poured through the doll, into him, until there was no space for Onion, no space to breathe or think or see. The black stuff welled up in his throat, pressed behind his eyes. "Halsa," he said, "let go!"

The woman with the birdcage said, "I'm not Halsa!"

Mik said, "What's wrong? What's wrong?"

The light changed. *Onion,* Halsa said, and let go of the doll. He staggered backward. The tracks beneath the train were singing *tara-ta tara-ta ta-rata-ta.* Onion's nose was full of swamp water and coal and metal and magic. "No," Onion said. He threw the doll at the woman holding the birdcage and pushed Mik down on the floor. "No," Onion said, louder. People were staring at him. The woman who'd been laughing at the joke had stopped laughing. Onion covered Mik with his body. The light grew brighter and blacker, all at once.

Onion! Halsa said. But she couldn't see him anymore. She was awake in the cubby beneath the stair. The doll was gone.

Halsa had seen men coming home from the war. Some of them had been blinded. Some had lost a hand or an arm. She'd seen one man wrapped in lengths of cloth and propped up in a dog cart which his young daughter pulled on a rope. He'd had no legs, no arms. When people looked at him, he cursed them. There was another man who ran a cockpit in Larch. He came back from the war and paid a man to carve him a leg out of knotty pine. At first he was unsteady on the pine leg, trying to find his balance again. It had been funny to watch him chase after his cocks, like watching a wind-up toy. By the time the army came through Larch again, though, he could run as fast as anyone.

It felt as if half of her had died on the train in the mountains. Her ears rang. She couldn't find her balance. It was as if a part of her had been cut away, as if she was blind. The part of her that *knew* things, *saw* things, wasn't there anymore. She went about all day in a miserable deafening fog.

She brought water up the stairs and she put mud on her arms and legs. She caught fish, because Onion had said that she ought to catch fish. Late in the afternoon, she looked and saw Tolcet sitting beside her on the pier.

"You shouldn't have bought me," she said. "You should have bought Onion. He wanted to come with you. I'm bad-tempered and unkind and I have no good opinion of the wizards of Perfil."

"Of whom do you have a low opinion? Yourself or the wizards of Perfil?" Tolcet asked.

"How can you serve them?" Halsa said. "How can you serve men and women who hide in towers and do nothing to help people who need help? What good is magic if it doesn't serve anyone?"

"These are dangerous times," Tolcet said. "For wizards as well as for children."

"Dangerous times! Hard times! Bad times," Halsa said. "Things have been bad since the day I was born. Why do I see things and know things, when there's nothing I can do to stop them? When will there be better times?"

"What do you see?" Tolcet said. He took Halsa's chin in his hand and tilted her head this way and that, as if her head were a glass ball that he could see inside. He put his hand on her head and smoothed her hair as if she was his own child. Halsa closed her eyes. Misery welled up inside her.

"I don't see anything," she said. "It feels like someone wrapped me in a wool blanket and beat me and left me in the dark. Is this what it feels like not to see anything? Did the wizards of Perfil do this to me?"

"Is it better or worse?" Tolcet said.

"Worse," Halsa said. "No. Better. I don't know. What am I to do? What am I to be?"

"You are a servant of the wizards of Perfil," Tolcet said. "Be patient. All things may yet be well."

Halsa said nothing. What was there to say?

She climbed up and down the stairs of the tower, carrying water, toasted bread and cheese, little things that she found in the swamp. The door at the top of the stairs was never open. She couldn't see through it. No one spoke to her, although she sat there sometimes, holding her breath so that the wizard would think she had gone away again. But the wizard wouldn't be fooled so easily. Tolcet went up the stairs, too, and perhaps the wizard admitted him. Halsa didn't know.

Essa and Burd and the other children were kind to her, as if they knew that she had been broken. She knew that she wouldn't have been kind to them, if their situations had been reversed. But perhaps they knew that too. The two women and the skinny man kept their distance. She didn't even know their names. They disappeared on errands and came back again and disappeared into the towers.

Once, when she was coming back from the pier with a bucket of fish, there was a dragon on the path. It wasn't very big, only the size of a mastiff. But it gazed at her with wicked, jeweled eyes. She couldn't get past it. It would eat her, and that would be that. It was almost a relief. She put the bucket down and stood waiting to be eaten. But then Essa was there, holding a stick. She hit the dragon on its head, once, twice, and then gave it a kick for good measure. "Go on, you!" Essa said. The dragon went, giving Halsa one last reproachful look. Essa picked up the bucket of fish. "You have to be firm with them," she said. "Otherwise they get inside your head and make you feel as if you deserve to be eaten. They're too lazy to eat anything that puts up a fight."

Halsa shook off a last, wistful regret, not to have been eaten. It was like waking up from a dream, something beautiful and noble and sad and utterly untrue. "Thank you," she said to Essa. Her knees were trembling.

"The bigger ones stay away from the meadow," Essa said. "It's the smaller ones who get curious about the wizards of Perfil. And by curious, what I really mean is hungry. Dragons eat the things that they're curious about. Come on, let's go for a swim."

Sometimes Essa or one of the others would tell Halsa stories about the wizards of Perfil. Most of the stories were silly, or plainly untrue. The children sounded almost indulgent, as if they found their masters more amusing than frightful. There were other stories, sad stories about long-ago wizards who had fought great battles or gone on long journeys. Wizards who had perished by treachery or been imprisoned by ones they'd thought friends.

Tolcet carved her a comb. She found frogs whose backs were marked with strange mathematical formulas, and put them in a bucket and took them to the top of the tower. She caught a mole with eyes like pinpricks and a nose like a fleshy pink hand. She found the hilt of a sword, a coin with a hole in it, the outgrown carapace of a dragon, small as a badger and almost weightless, but hard, too. When she cleaned off the mud that covered it, it shone dully, like a candlestick. She took all of these up the stairs. She couldn't tell whether the things she found had any meaning. But she took a small, private pleasure in finding them nevertheless.

The mole had come back down the stairs again, fast, wriggly, and furtive. The frogs were still in the bucket, making their gloomy pronouncements, when she had returned with the wizard's dinner. But other things disappeared behind the wizard of Perfil's door.

The thing that Tolcet had called Halsa's gift came back, a little at a time. Once again, she became aware of the wizards in their towers, and of how they watched her. There was something else, too. It sat beside her, sometimes, while she was fishing, or when she rowed out in the abandoned coracle Tolcet helped her to repair. She thought she knew who, or what it was. It was the part of Onion that he'd learned to send out. It was what was left of him: shadowy, thin, and silent. It wouldn't talk to her. It only watched. At night, it stood beside her pallet and watched her sleep. She was glad it was there. To be haunted was a kind of comfort.

She helped Tolcet repair a part of the wizard's tower where the stones were loose in their mortar. She learned how to make paper out of rushes and bark. Apparently wizards needed a great deal of paper. Tolcet began to teach her how to read.

One afternoon when she came back from fishing, all of the wizard's servants were standing in a circle. There was a leveret motionless as a stone in the middle of the circle. Onion's ghost crouched down with the other children. So Halsa stood and watched, too. Something was pouring back and forth between the leveret and the servants of the wizards of Perfil. It was the same as it had been for Halsa and Onion, when she'd given him the two-faced doll. The leveret's sides rose and fell. Its eyes were glassy and dark and knowing. Its fur bristled with magic.

"Who is it?" Halsa said to Burd. "Is it a wizard of Perfil?"

"Who?" Burd said. He didn't take his eyes off the leveret. "No, not a wizard. It's a hare. Just a hare. It came out of the marsh."

"But," Halsa said. "But I can feel it. I can almost hear what it's saying."

Burd looked at her. Essa looked too. "Everything speaks," he said, speaking slowly, as if to a child. "Listen, Halsa."

There was something about the way Burd and Essa were looking at her, as if it were an invitation, as if they were asking her to look inside their heads, to see what they was thinking. The others were watching, too, watching Halsa now, instead of the leveret. Halsa took a step back. "I can't," she said. "I can't hear anything."

She went to fetch water. When she came out of the tower, Burd and Essa and the other children weren't there. Leverets dashed between towers, leaping over each other, tussling in midair. Onion sat on Tolcet's throne, watching and laughing silently. She didn't think she'd seen Onion laugh since the death of his mother. It made her feel strange to know that a dead boy could be so joyful.

The next day Halsa found an injured fox kit in the briar. It snapped at her when she tried to free it and the briars tore her hand. There was a tear in its belly and she could see a shiny gray loop of intestine. She tore off a piece of her shirt and wrapped it around the fox kit. She put the kit in her pocket. She ran all the way back to the wizard's tower, all the way up the steps. She didn't count them. She didn't stop to rest. Onion followed her, quick as a shadow.

When she reached the door at the top of the stairs, she knocked hard. No one answered.

"Wizard!" she said.

No one answered.

"Please help me," she said. She lifted the fox kit out of her pocket and sat down on the steps with it swaddled in her lap. It didn't try to bite her. It needed all its energy for dying. Onion sat next to her. He stroked the kit's throat.

"Please," Halsa said again. "Please don't let it die. Please do something."

She could feel the wizard of Perfil, standing next to the door. The wizard put a hand out, as if—at last—the door might open. She saw that the wizard loved foxes and all the wild marsh things. But the wizard said nothing. The wizard didn't love Halsa. The door didn't open.

"Help me," Halsa said one more time. She felt that dreadful black pull again, just as it had been on the train with Onion. It was as if the wizard were yanking at her shoulder, shaking her in a stony, black rage. How dare someone like Halsa ask a wizard for help. Onion was shaking her too. Where Onion's hand gripped her, Halsa could feel stuff pouring through her and out of her. She could feel the kit, feel the place where its stomach had torn open. She could feel its heart pumping blood, its panic and fear and the life that was spilling out of it. Magic flowed up and down the stairs of the tower. The wizard of Perfil was winding it up like a skein of black, tarry wool, and then letting it go again. It poured through Halsa and Onion and the fox kit until Halsa thought she would die.

"Please," she said, and what she meant this time was *stop*. It would kill her. And then she was empty again. The magic had gone through her and there was nothing left of it or her. Her bones had been turned into jelly. The fox kit began to struggle, clawing at her. When she unwrapped it, it sank its teeth into her wrist and then ran down the stairs as if it had never been dying at all.

Halsa stood up. Onion was gone, but she could still feel the wizard standing there on the other side of the door. "Thank you," she said. She followed the fox kit down the stairs.

The next morning she woke and found Onion lying on the pallet beside her. He seemed nearer, somehow, this time. As if he weren't entirely dead. Halsa felt that if she tried to speak to him, he would answer. But she was afraid of what he would say.

Essa saw Onion too. "You have a shadow," she said.

"His name is Onion," Halsa said.

"Help me with this," Essa said. Someone had cut lengths of bamboo. Essa was fixing them in the ground, using a mixture of rocks and mud to keep them upright. Burd and some of the other children wove rushes through the bamboo, making walls, Halsa saw.

"What are we doing?" Halsa asked.

"There is an army coming." Burd said. "To burn down the town of Perfil. Tolcet went to warn them."

"What will happen?" Halsa said. "Will the wizards protect the town?"

Essa laid another bamboo pole across the tops of the two upright poles. She said, "They can come to the marshes, if they want to, and take refuge. The army won't come here. They're afraid of the wizards."

"Afraid of the wizards!" Halsa said. "Why? The wizards are cowards and fools. Why won't they save Perfil?"

"Go ask them yourself," Essa said. "If you're brave enough."

"Halsa?" Onion said. Halsa looked away from Essa's steady gaze. For a moment there were two Onions. One was the shadowy ghost from the train, close enough to touch. The second Onion stood beside the cooking fire. He was filthy, skinny, and real. Shadow-Onion guttered and then was gone.

"Onion?" Halsa said.

"I came out of the mountains," Onion said. "Five days ago, I think. I didn't know where I was going, except that I could see you. Here. I walked and walked and you were with me and I was with you."

"Where are Mik and Bonti?" Halsa said. "Where's Mother?"

"There were two women on the train with us. They were rich. They've promised to take care of Mik and Bonti. They will. I know they will. They were going to Qual. When you gave me the doll, Halsa, you saved the train. We could see the explosion, but we passed through it. The tracks were destroyed and there were clouds and clouds of black smoke and fire, but nothing touched the train. We saved everyone."

"Where's Mother?" Halsa said again. But she already knew. Onion was silent. The train stopped beside a narrow stream to take on water. There was an ambush. Soldiers. There was a bottle with water leaking out of it. Halsa's mother had dropped it. There was an arrow sticking out of her back.

Onion said, "I'm sorry, Halsa. Everyone was afraid of me, because of how the train had been saved. Because I knew that there was going to be an explosion. Because I didn't know about the ambush and people died. So I got off the train."

"Here," Burd said to Onion. He gave him a bowl of porridge. "No, eat it slowly. There's plenty more."

Onion said with his mouth full, "Where are the wizards of Perfil?"

Halsa began to laugh. She laughed until her sides ached and until Onion stared at her and until Essa came over and shook her. "We don't have time for this," Essa said. "Take that boy and find him somewhere to lie down. He's exhausted."

"Come on," Halsa said to Onion. "You can sleep in my bed. Or if you'd rather, you can go knock on the door at the top of the tower and ask the wizard of Perfil if you can have his bed."

She showed Onion the cubby under the stairs and he lay down on it. "You're dirty," she said. "You'll get the sheets dirty."

"I'm sorry," Onion said.

"It's fine," Halsa said. "We can wash them later. There's plenty of water here. Are you still hungry? Do you need anything?"

"I brought something for you," Onion said. He held out his hand and there were the earrings that had belonged to his mother.

"No," Halsa said.

Halsa hated herself. She was scratching at her own arm, ferociously, not as if she had an insect bite, but as if she wanted to dig beneath the skin. Onion saw something that he hadn't known before, something astonishing and terrible, that Halsa was no kinder to herself than to anyone else. No wonder Halsa had wanted the earrings—just like the snakes, Halsa would gnaw on herself if there was nothing else to gnaw on. How Halsa wished that she'd been kind to her mother.

Onion said, "Take them. Your mother was kind to me, Halsa. So I want to give them to you. My mother would have wanted you to have them, too."

"All right," Halsa said. She wanted to weep, but she scratched and scratched instead. Her arm was white and red from scratching. She took the earrings and put them in her pocket. "Go to sleep now."

"I came here because you were here," Onion said. "I wanted to tell you what had happened. What should I do now?"

"Sleep," Halsa said.

"Will you tell the wizards that I'm here? How we saved the train?" Onion said. He yawned so wide that Halsa thought his head would split in two. "Can I be a servant of the wizards of Perfil?"

"We'll see," Halsa said. "You go to sleep. I'll go climb the stairs and tell them that you've come."

"It's funny," Onion said. "I can feel them all around us. I'm glad you're here. I feel safe."

Halsa sat on the bed. She didn't know what to do. Onion was quiet for a while and then he said, "Halsa?"

"What?" Halsa said.

"I can't sleep," he said, apologetically.

"Shhh," Halsa said. She stroked his filthy hair. She sang a song her father had liked to sing. She held Onion's hand until his breathing became slower and she was sure that he was sleeping. Then she went up the stairs to tell the wizard about

Onion. "I don't understand you," she said to the door. "Why do you hide away from the world? Don't you get tired of hiding?"

The wizard didn't say anything.

"Onion is braver than you are," Halsa told the door. "Essa is braver. My mother was—"

She swallowed and said, "She was braver than you. Stop ignoring me. What good are you, up here? You won't talk to me, and you won't help the town of Perfil, and Onion's going to be very disappointed when he realizes that all you do is skulk around in your room, waiting for someone to bring you breakfast. If you like waiting so much, then you can wait as long as you like. I'm not going to bring you any food or any water or anything that I find in the swamp. If you want anything, you can magic it. Or you can come get it yourself. Or you can turn me into a toad."

She waited to see if the wizard would turn her into a toad. "All right," she said at last. "Well, goodbye then." She went back down the stairs.

The wizards of Perfil are lazy and useless. They hate to climb stairs and they never listen when you talk. They don't answer questions because their ears are full of beetles and wax and their faces are wrinkled and hideous. Marsh fairies live deep in the wrinkles of the faces of the wizards of Perfil and the marsh fairies ride around in the bottomless canyons of the wrinkles on saddle-broken fleas who grow fat grazing on magical, wizardly blood. The wizards of Perfil spend all night scratching their flea bites and sleep all day. I'd rather be a scullery maid than a servant of the invisible, doddering, nearly blind, flea-bitten, mildewy, clammy-fingered, conceited marsh-wizards of Perfil.

Halsa checked Onion, to make sure that he was still asleep. Then she went and found Essa. "Will you pierce my ears for me?" she said.

Essa shrugged. "It will hurt," she said.

"Good," said Halsa. So Essa boiled water and put her needle in it. Then she pierced Halsa's ears. It did hurt, and Halsa was glad. She put on Onion's mother's earrings, and then she helped Essa and the others dig latrines for the townspeople of Perfil.

Tolcet came back before sunset. There were half a dozen women and their children with him.

"Where are the others?" Essa said.

Tolcet said, "Some don't believe me. They don't trust wizardly folk. There are some that want to stay and defend the town. Others are striking out on foot for Qual, along the tracks."

"Where is the army now?" Burd said.

"Close," Halsa said. Tolcet nodded.

The women from the town had brought food and bedding. They seemed subdued and anxious and it was hard to tell whether it was the approaching army or the wizards of Perfil that scared them most. The women stared at the ground. They didn't look up at the towers. If they caught their children looking up, they scolded them in low voices.

"Don't be silly," Halsa said crossly to a woman whose child had been digging a hole near a tumbled tower. The woman shook him until he cried and cried and wouldn't stop. What was she thinking? That wizards liked to eat mucky children who dug holes? "The wizards are lazy and unsociable and harmless. They keep to themselves and don't bother anyone."

The woman only stared at Halsa, and Halsa realized that she was as afraid of Halsa as she was of the wizards of Perfil. Halsa was amazed. Was she that terrible? Mik and Bonti and Onion had always been afraid of her, but they'd had good reason to be. And she'd changed. She was as mild and meek as butter now.

Tolcet, who was helping with dinner, snorted as if he'd caught her thought. The woman grabbed up her child and rushed away, as if Halsa might open her mouth again and eat them both.

"Halsa, look." It was Onion, awake and so filthy that you could smell him from two yards away. They would need to burn his clothes. Joy poured through Halsa, because Onion had come to find her and because he was here and because he was alive. He'd come out of Halsa's tower, where he'd gotten her cubby bed grimy and smelly, how wonderful to think of it, and he was pointing east, towards the town of Perfil. There was a red glow hanging over the marsh, as if the sun were rising instead of setting. Everyone was silent, looking east as if they might be able to see what was happening in Perfil. Presently the wind carried an ashy, desolate smoke over the marsh. "The war has come to Perfil," a woman said.

"Which army is it?" another woman said, as if the first woman might know.

"Does it matter?" said the first woman. "They're all the same. My eldest went off to join the King's army and my youngest joined the General Balder's men. They've set fire to plenty of towns, and killed other mothers' sons and maybe one day they'll kill each other, and never think of me. What difference does it make to the town that's being attacked, to know what army is attacking them? Does it matter to a cow who kills her?"

"They'll follow us," someone else said in a resigned voice. "They'll find us here and they'll kill us all!"

"They won't," Tolcet said. He spoke loudly. His voice was calm and reassuring. "They won't follow you and they won't find you here. Be brave for your children. All will be well."

"Oh, please," Halsa said, under her breath. She stood and glared up at the towers of the wizards of Perfil, her hands on her hips. But as usual, the wizards of Perfil were up to nothing. They didn't strike her dead for glaring. They didn't stand at their windows to look out over the marshes to see the town of Perfil and how it was burning while they only stood and watched. Perhaps they were already asleep in their beds, dreaming about breakfast, lunch, and dinner. She went and helped Burd and Essa and the others make up beds for the refugees from Perfil. Onion cut up wild onions for the stew pot. He was going to have to have a bath soon, Halsa thought. Clearly he needed someone like Halsa to tell him what to do.

None of the servants of the wizards of Perfil slept. There was too much work to do. The latrines weren't finished. A child wandered off into the marshes and had to be found before it drowned or met a dragon. A little girl fell into the well, and had to be hauled up.

Before the sun came up again, more refugees from the town of Perfil arrived. They came into the camp in groups of twos or threes, until there were almost a hundred townspeople in the wizards' meadow. Some of the newcomers were wounded or badly burned or deep in shock. Essa and Tolcet took charge. There were compresses to apply, clothes that had already been cut up for bandages, hot drinks that smelled bitter and medicinal and not particularly magical. People went rushing around, trying to discover news of family members or friends who had stayed behind. Young children who had been asleep woke up and began to cry.

"They put the mayor and his wife to the sword," a man was saying.

"They'll march on the king's city next," an old woman said. "But our army will stop them."

"It *was* our army—I saw the butcher's boy and Philpot's middle son. They said that we'd been trading with the enemies of our country. The king sent them. It was to teach us a lesson. They burned down the market church and they hung the pastor from the bell tower."

There was a girl lying on the ground who looked Mik and Bonti's age. Her face was gray. Tolcet touched her stomach lightly and she emitted a thin, high scream, not a human noise at all, Onion thought. The marshes were so noisy with magic that he couldn't hear what she was thinking, and he was glad.

"What happened?" Tolcet said to the man who'd carried her into the camp.

"She fell," the man said. "She was trampled underfoot."

Onion watched the girl, breathing slowly and steadily, as if he could somehow breathe for her. Halsa watched Onion. Then: "That's enough," she said. "Come on, Onion."

She marched away from Tolcet and the girl, shoving through the refugees.

"Where are we going?" Onion said.

"To make the wizards come down," Halsa said. "I'm sick and tired of doing all their work for them. Their cooking and fetching. I'm going to knock down that stupid door. I'm going to drag them down their stupid stairs. I'm going to make them help that girl."

There were a lot of stairs this time. Of course the accursed wizards of Perfil would know what she was up to. This was their favorite kind of wizardly joke, making her climb and climb and climb. They'd wait until she and Onion got to the top and then they'd turn them into lizards. Well, maybe it wouldn't be so bad, being a small poisonous lizard. She could slip under the door and bite one of the damned wizards of Perfil. She went up and up and up, half-running and half-stumbling, until it seemed she and Onion must have climbed right up into the sky. When the stairs abruptly ended, she was still running. She crashed into the door so hard that she saw stars.

"Halsa?" Onion said. He bent over her. He looked so worried that she almost laughed.

"I'm fine," she said. "Just wizards playing tricks." She hammered on the door, then kicked it for good measure. "Open up!"

"What are you doing?" Onion said.

"It never does any good," Halsa said. "I should have brought an axe."

"Let me try," Onion said.

Halsa shrugged. *Stupid boy*, she thought, and Onion could hear her perfectly. "Go ahead," she said.

Onion put his hand on the door and pushed. It swung open. He looked up at Halsa and flinched. "Sorry," he said.

Halsa went in.

There was a desk in the room, and a single candle, which was burning. There was a bed, neatly made, and a mirror on the wall over the desk. There was no wizard of Perfil, not even hiding under the bed. Halsa checked, just in case.

She went to the empty window and looked out. There was the meadow and the makeshift camp, below them, and the marsh. The canals, shining like silver. There was the sun, coming up, the way it always did. It was strange to see all the windows of the other towers from up here, so far above, all empty. White birds were floating over the marsh. She wondered if they were wizards; she wished she had a bow and arrows.

"Where is the wizard?" Onion said. He poked the bed. Maybe the wizard had turned himself into a bed. Or the desk. Maybe the wizard was a desk.

"There are no wizards," Halsa said.

"But I can feel them!" Onion sniffed, then sniffed harder. He could practically smell the wizard, as if the wizard of Perfil had turned himself into a mist or a vapor that Onion was inhaling. He sneezed violently.

Someone was coming up the stairs. He and Halsa waited to see if it was a wizard of Perfil. But it was only Tolcet. He looked tired and cross, as if he'd had to climb many, many stairs.

"Where are the wizards of Perfil?" Halsa said.

Tolcet held up a finger. "A minute to catch my breath," he said.

Halsa stamped her foot. Onion sat down on the bed. He apologized to it silently, just in case it was the wizard. Or maybe the candle was the wizard. He wondered what happened if you tried to blow a wizard out. Halsa was so angry he thought she might explode.

Tolcet sat down on the bed beside Onion. "A long time ago," he said, "the father of the present king visited the wizards of Perfil. He'd had certain dreams about his son, who was only a baby. He was afraid of these dreams. The wizards told him that he was right to be afraid. His son would go mad. There would be war and famine and more war and his son would be to blame. The old king went into a rage. He sent his men to throw the wizards of Perfil down from their towers. They did."

"Wait," Onion said. "Wait. What happened to the wizards? Did they turn into white birds and fly away?"

"No," Tolcet said. "The king's men slit their throats and threw them out of the towers. I was away. When I came back, the towers had been ransacked. The wizards were dead."

"No!" Halsa said. "Why are you lying? I know the wizards are here. They're hiding somehow. They're cowards."

"I can feel them too," Onion said.

"Come and see," Tolcet said. He went to the window. When they looked down, they saw Essa and the other servants of the wizards of Perfil moving among the refugees. The two old women who never spoke were sorting through bundles of clothes and blankets. The thin man was staking down someone's cow. Children were chasing chickens as Burd held open the gate of a makeshift pen. One of the younger girls, Perla, was singing a lullaby to some mother's baby. Her voice, rough and sweet at the same time, rose straight up to the window of the tower, where Halsa and Onion and Tolcet stood looking down. It was a song they all knew. It was a song that said all would be well.

"Don't you understand?" Tolcet, the wizard of Perfil, said to Halsa and Onion. "There are the wizards of Perfil. They are young, most of them. They haven't come into their full powers yet. But all may yet be well."

"Essa is a wizard of Perfil?" Halsa said. Essa, a shovel in her hand, looked up at the tower, as if she'd heard Halsa. She smiled and shrugged, as if to say *Perhaps I am, perhaps not, but isn't it a good joke? Didn't you ever wonder?*

Tolcet turned Halsa and Onion around so that they faced the mirror that hung on the wall. He rested his strong, speckled hands on their shoulders for a minute, as if to give them courage. Then he pointed to the mirror, to the reflected Halsa and Onion who stood there staring back at themselves, astonished. Tolcet began to laugh. Despite everything, he laughed so hard that tears came from his eyes. He snorted. Onion and Halsa began to laugh, too. They couldn't help it. The wizard's room was full of magic, and so were the marshes and Tolcet and the mirror where the children and Tolcet stood reflected, and the children were full of magic, too.

Tolcet pointed again at the mirror, and his reflection pointed its finger straight back at Halsa and Onion. Tolcet said, "Here they are in front of you! Ha! Do you know them? Here are the wizards of Perfil!"

NEIL GAIMAN's most recent novel, the international bestseller *The Graveyard Book*, won the prestigious Newbery Medal, given to great works of children's literature. Other novels include *American Gods*, *Coraline*, *Neverwhere*, and *Anansi Boys*, among many others. In addition to his novel-writing, Gaiman is also the writer of the popular *Sandman* comic book series, and his books *Coraline* and *Stardust* were recently made into feature films. Gaiman's short fiction has appeared in numerous magazines and anthologies, including my own *The Living Dead*, *By Blood We Live*, and *The Improbable Adventures of Sherlock Holmes*. Most of his short work has been collected in the volumes *Smoke and Mirrors*, *Fragile Things*, and *M is for Magic*. His latest book is a hardcover edition of his poem, *Instructions*, illustrated by Charles Vess.

Most Americans have probably heard someone say, "If you believe that, I've got a bridge to sell you," referring to New York's Brooklyn Bridge. It's just taken for granted that handing over your money to a con man who offers to "sell" you such a famous landmark would be the ultimate example of gullibility. Believe it or not though, this old cliche is based on a real scam that was perpetrated over and over again on naive immigrants whose heads were filled with exaggerated notions of America as a land of opportunity. Con artists would memorize the routes of the beat cops and then set up signs saying "Bridge for sale" when they knew the police would be out of sight. Police repeatedly had to evict people who had been swindled and were attempting to charge tolls for crossing "their" bridge. As newcomers to the city gradually become more sophisticated, the con died away, but lived on in movies such as *Every Day's a Holiday* and even in a Bugs Bunny cartoon ("Bowery Bugs").

Our next tale, about a gentleman's club for con artists, provides a new twist on this old idea, albeit one involving a much grander bridge and a much grander swindle.

How to Sell the Ponti Bridge
Neil Gaiman

My favorite rogues' club is the oldest and still the most exclusive in all the Seven Worlds. It was formed by a loose association of rogues, cheats, scoundrels, and confidence men almost seventy thousand years ago. It has been copied many times in many places (there was one started quite recently, within the last five hundred years at any rate, in the City of London), but none of the other clubs matches the original Rogues' Club, in the city of Lost Carnadine, for atmosphere. No other club has quite so select a membership.

And the membership of the Lost Carnadine Rogues' Club is particularly select. You will understand the kind of person who makes it to membership if I tell you that I myself have seen, walking or sitting or eating or talking, in its many rooms, such notables as Daraxius Lo (who sold the Kzem a frog-bat on a holy day), Prottle (who sold the palace of the King of Vandaria to the King of Vandaria), and the self-styled Lord Niff (who, I have heard it whispered, was the original inventor of the fox twist, the cheat that broke the bank at the Casino Grande). In addition, I have seen Rogues of interuniversal renown fail to gain admittance to even discuss their membership with the secretary—on one memorable day I passed a famous financier, in company with the head of the Hy-Brasail mafia and a preeminent prime minister on their way down the back stairs with the blackest of expressions upon their faces, having obviously been told not even to think about returning. No, the ones who make it into the Rogues' Club are a high bunch. I am sure that you will have heard of each of them. Not under those names, of course, but the touch is distinctive, is it not?

I myself gained membership by means of a brilliant piece of creative scientific research, something that revolutionized the thinking of a whole generation. It was my disdain for regular methodology and, as I have said, creative research that gained me membership, and when I am in that part of the cosmos I make a point of stopping off for an evening, taking in some sparkling conversation, drinking the club's fine wines, and basking in the presence of my moral equals.

It was late in the evening and the log fire was burning low in the grate, and a handful of us sat and drank one of the fine dark wines of Spidireen in an alcove in the great hall. "Of course," one of my new friends was saying, "there are some scams that no self-respecting rogue would ever touch, they are so old and classless and tired. For example, selling a tourist the Ponti Bridge."

"It's the same with Nelson's Column, or the Eiffel Tower, or the Brooklyn Bridge, back on my home-world," I told them. "Sad little con games, with as much class as a back-alley game of Find the Lady. But look on the good side: Nobody who sold the Ponti Bridge would ever get membership in a club like this."

"No?" said a quiet voice from the corner of the room. "How strange. I do believe it was the time I sold the Ponti Bridge that gained me membership in this club." A tall gentleman, quite bald and most exquisitely dressed, got up from the chair in which he had been sitting, and walked over to us. He was sipping the inside of an imported rhûm fruit, and smiling, I think at the effect that he had created. He walked over to us, pulled up a cushion, and sat down. "I don't believe we've met," he said.

My friends introduced themselves (the gray-haired deft woman, Gloathis; the short, quiet dodger Redcap) as did I.

He smiled wider. "Your fame precedes each of you, I am honored. You may call me Stoat."

"Stoat?" said Gloathis. "The only Stoat I ever heard of was the man who pulled the Derana Kite job, but that was . . . what, over a hundred years ago. What am I thinking? You adopted the name as a tribute, I presume."

"You are a wise woman," said Stoat. "It would be impossible for me to be the same man." He leaned forward on his cushion. "You were talking about the sale of the Ponti Bridge?"

"Indeed we were."

"And you were all of the opinion that selling the Ponti Bridge is a measly scam, unworthy of a member of this club? And perhaps you are right. Let us examine the ingredients of a good scam." He ticked off the points on the fingers of his left hand as he spoke. "Firstly, the scam must be credible. Secondly, it must be simple—the more complex the more chance of error. Thirdly, when the sucker is stung he must be stung in such a way as to prevent him from ever turning to the law. Fourthly, the mainspring of any elegant con is human greed and human vanity. Lastly, it must involve trust—confidence, if you will."

"Surely," said Gloathis.

"So you are telling me that the sale of the Ponti Bridge—or any other major landmark not yours to sell—cannot have these characteristics? Gentlemen. Lady. Let me tell you my story.

"I had arrived in Ponti some years ago almost penniless. I had but thirty gold crowns, and I needed a million. Why? I am afraid that is another story. I took stock of myself—I had the gold crowns and some smart robes. I was fluent in the aristocratic Ponti dialect, and I am, I pride myself, quite brilliant. Still, I could think of nothing that would bring me the kind of money I had to have in the time by which I needed it. My mind, usually teeming and coruscating with fine schemes, was a perfect blank. So, trusting to my gods to bring me inspiration, I went on a guided tour of the city . . . "

Ponti lies to the south and to the east, a free city and port at the foot of the Mountains of Dawn. Ponti is a sprawling city, on either side of the Bay of Dawn, a beautiful natural harbor. Spanning the bay is the bridge, which was built of jewels, of mortar, and of magic nearly two thousand years ago. There were jeers when it was first planned and begun, for none credited that a structure almost half a mile across could ever be successfully completed, or would stand for long once erected, but the bridge was completed, and the jeers turned to gasps of awe and civic pride. It spanned the Bay of Dawn, a perfect structure that flashed and shone and glinted in myriad rainbow colors beneath the noon sun.

The tour guide paused at the foot of it. "As you can see, ladies and gentlemen, if you will examine closely, the bridge is built entirely of precious stones—rubies, diamonds, sapphires, emeralds, chryolanths, carbuncles, and such—and they are bound together with a transparent mortar which was crafted by the twin sages Hrolgar and Hrylthfgur out of a primal magic. The jewels are all real—make no mistake about that—and were gathered from all five corners of the world by Emmidus, King of Ponti at the time."

A small boy near the front of the group turned to his mother and announced loudly, "We did him in school. He's called Emmidus the Last, because there weren't any more after him. And they told us—"

The tour guide interrupted smoothly. "The young man is quite correct. King Emmidus bankrupted the city-state obtaining the jewels, and thus set the scene for our current beneficent Ruling Enclave to appear."

The small boy's mother was now twisting his ear, which cheered the tour guide up immensely. "I'm sure you've heard that confidence tricksters are always trying to play tourists for mugs by telling them that they are representing the Ruling Enclave, and that as the owners of the bridge they are entitled to sell it. They get a hefty deposit, then scarper. To clarify matters," he said, as he said five times each day, and he and the tourists chuckled together, "the bridge is definitely not for sale." It was a good line. It always got a laugh.

His party started to make its way across the bridge. Only the small boy noticed that one of their number had remained behind—a tall man, quite bald. He stood at the foot of the bridge, lost in contemplation. The boy wanted to point this out to everybody, but his ear hurt, and so he said nothing.

The man at the foot of the bridge smiled abruptly. "Not for sale, eh?" he said aloud. Then he turned and walked back to the city.

They were playing a game not unlike tennis with large heavy-strung racquets and jeweled skulls for balls. The skulls were so satisfying in the way they thunked when hit cleanly, in the way they curved in great looping parabolas across the marble court. The skulls had never sat on human necks; they had been obtained, at great loss of life and significant expense, from a demon race in the highlands, and, afterward jeweled (emeralds and sweet rubies set in a lacy silver filigree in the eye sockets and about the jawbone) in Carthus's own workshops.

It was Carthus's serve.

He reached for the next skull in the pile and held it up to the light, marveling at the craftsmanship, in the way that the jewels, when struck by the light at a certain angle, seemed to glow with an inner luminescence. He could have told you the exact value and the probable provenance of each jewel—perhaps the very mine from which it had been dug. The skulls were also beautiful: bone the color of milky mother-of-pearl, translucent and fine. Each had cost him more than the value of the jewels set in its elegant bony face. The demon race had now been hunted to the verge of extinction, and the skulls were well-nigh irreplaceable.

He lobbed the skull over the net. Aathia struck it neatly back at him, forcing him to run to meet it (his footsteps echoing on the cold marble floor) and—thunk—hit it back to her.

She almost reached it in time. Almost, but not quite: the skull eluded her racquet and fell toward the stone floor and then, only an inch or so above the ground, it stopped, bobbing slightly, as if immersed in liquid or a magnetic field.

It was magic, of course, and Carthus had paid most highly for it. He could afford to.

"My point, lady," he called, bowing low.

Aathia—his partner in all but love—said nothing. Her eyes glinted like chips of ice, or like the jewels that were the only things she loved. Carthus and Aathia, jewel merchants. They made a strange pair.

There was a discreet cough from behind Carthus. He turned to see a white-tuniced slave holding a parchment scroll. "Yes?" said Carthus. He wiped the sweat from his face with the back of his hand.

"A message, lord. The man who left it said that it was urgent."

Carthus grunted. "Who's it from?"

"I have not opened it. I was told it was for your eyes and the eyes of the Lady Aathia, and for no other."

Carthus stared at the parchment scroll but made no move to take it. He was a big man with a fleshy face, sandy receding hair, and a worried expression. His business rivals—and there were many, for Ponti had become, over the years, the center of the wholesale jewel business—had learned that his expression held no clue to his inner feelings. In many cases it had cost them money to learn this.

"Take the message, Carthus," said Aathia, and when he did not, she walked around the net herself and plucked the scroll from the slave's fingers. "Leave us."

The slave's bare feet were soundless on the chill marble floor.

Aathia broke the seal with her sleeve knife and unrolled the parchment. Her eyes flicked over it once, fast, then again at a slower pace. She whistled. "Here . . . " Carthus took it and read it through.

"I—I really don't know what to make of it," he said in a high, petulant voice. With his racquet he rubbed absentmindedly at the small crisscross scar on his right cheek. The pendant that hung about his neck, proclaiming him one of the High Council of the Ponti Jewel Merchants' Guild, stuck briefly to his sweaty skin, and then swung free. "What do you think, my flower?"

"I am not your 'flower.' "

"Of course not, lady."

"Better, Carthus. We'll make a real citizen of you yet. Well, for a start, the name is obviously false. 'Glew Croll' indeed? There are more men named Glew Croll in Ponti than there are diamonds in your storehouses. The address is obviously rented accommodation in the Undercliffs. There was no ring mark on the wax seal. It's as if he has gone out of his way to maintain anonymity."

"Yes. I can see all that. But what about this 'business opportunity' he talks about? And if it is, as he implies, Ruling Enclave business, why would it be carried on with the secrecy he requests?"

She shrugged. "The Ruling Enclave has never been averse to secrecy. And, reading between the lines, it would appear that there is a great deal of wealth involved."

Carthus was silent. He reached down to the skull pile, leaned his racquet against it, and placed the scroll beside it. He picked up a large skull. He caressed it gently with his blunt, stubby fingers. "You know," he said, as if speaking to the skull, "this could be my chance to get one up on the rest of the bleeders on the Guild High Council. Dead-blood aristocratic half-wits."

"There speaks the son of a slave," said Aathia. "If it wasn't for my name you would never have made council membership."

"Shut up." His expression was vaguely worried, which meant nothing at all. "I can show them. I'm going to show them. You'll see."

He hefted the skull in his right hand as if testing the weight of it, reveling in and computing the value of the bone, the jewels, the fine-worked silver. Then he spun around, surprisingly fast for one so big, and threw the skull with all his might at a far pillar, well beyond the field of play. It seemed to hang in the air forever and then, with a painful slowness, it hit the pillar and smashed into a thousand fragments. The almost-musical tinkling sounds it made as it did so were very beautiful.

"I'll go and change and meet this Glew Croll then," muttered Carthus. He walked out of the room, carrying the scroll with him. Aathia stared at him as he left, then she clapped her hands, summoning a slave to clear up the mess.

The caves that honeycomb the rock on the north side of the Bay of Dawn, down into the bay, beneath the bridge, are known as the Undercliffs. Carthus took his clothes off at the door, handing them to his slave, and walked down the narrow stone steps. His flesh gave an involuntary shiver as he entered the water (kept a little below blood temperature in the aristocratic manner, but still chill after the heat of the day), and he swam down the corridor into an anteroom. Reflected light glimmered across the walls. On the water floated four other men and two women. They lounged on large wooden floats, elegantly carved into the shapes of waterbirds and fish.

Carthus swam over to an empty float—a dolphin—and hauled his bulk up onto it. Like the other six he wore nothing but the Jewelers' Guild High Council pendant. All the High Council members, bar one, were there.

"Where's the president?" he asked of no one in particular.

A skeletal woman with flawless white skin pointed to one of the inner rooms. Then she yawned and twisted her body, a rippling twist, at the end of which she was off the float—hers was carved into the shape of a giant swan—and into the water. Carthus envied and hated her: that twist had been one of the twelve so-called noble dives. He knew that, despite having practiced for years, he could not hope to emulate her.

"Effete bitch," he muttered beneath his breath. Still, it was reassuring to see other council members here. He wondered if any of them knew anything he didn't.

There was a splashing behind him, and he turned. Wommet, the council president, was clutching Carthus's float. They bowed to each other, then Wommet (a small hunchback, whose ever so many times great-grandfather had made his fortune finding for King Emmidus the jewels that had bankrupted Ponti, and had thus laid the foundations for the Ruling Enclave's two-thousand-year rule) said, "He will speak to you next, Messire Carthus. Down the corridor on the left. It's the first room you come to."

The other council members, on their floats, looked at Carthus blankly. They were aristocrats of Ponti, and so they hid their envy and their irritation that Carthus was going in before them, although they did not hide it as well as they thought they did; and, somewhere deep inside, Carthus smiled.

He suppressed the urge to ask the hunchback what this business was all about, and he slipped off his float. The warmed seawater stung his eyes.

The room in which Grew Croll waited was up several rock steps, and was dry and dark and smoky. One lamp burned fitfully on the table in the center of the room. There was a robe on the chair, and Carthus slipped it on. A man stood in the shadows beyond the lamplight, but even in the murk Carthus could see that he was tall and completely bald.

"I bid you good day," said a cultured voice.

"And on your house and kin also," responded Carthus.

"Sit down, sit down. As you have undoubtedly inferred from the message I sent you, this is Ruling Enclave business. Now, before another word is said, I must ask you to read and sign this oath of secrecy. Take all the time you need." He pushed a paper across the table: it was a comprehensive oath, pledging Carthus to secrecy about all matters discussed during their meeting on pain of the Ruling Enclave's "extreme displeasure"—a polite euphemism for death. Carthus read it over twice. "It—it isn't anything illegal, is it?"

"Sir?" The cultured voice was offended. Carthus shrugged his great shoulders and signed. The paper was taken from his fingers and placed in a trunk at the far end of the hall. "Very good. We can get down to business then. Something to drink? Smoke? Inhale? No? Very well."

A pause.

"As you may have already surmised, Glew Croll is not my name. I am a junior administrative member of the Ruling Enclave." (Carthus grunted, his suspicions confirmed, and he scratched his ear.) "Messire Carthus, what do you know of the Bridge of Ponti?"

"Same as everyone. National landmark. Tourist attraction. Very impressive if you like that sort of thing. Built of jewels and magic. Jewels aren't all of the highest quality, although there's a rose diamond at the summit as big as a baby's fist, and reportedly flawless . . . "

"Very good. Have you heard the term 'magical half-life'?"

Carthus hadn't. Not that he could recall. "I've heard the term," he said, "but I'm not a magician, obviously, and . . . "

"A magical half-life, messire, is the nigromantic term for the length of time a magician, warlock, witch, or whatever's magic lasts after his or her death. A simple hedge witch's conjurations and so on will often vanish and be done with on the moment of her death. At the other end of the scale you have such phenomena as the Sea Serpent Sea, in which the purely magical sea serpents still frolic and bask almost nine thousand years after the execution of Cilimwai Lah, their creator."

"Right. That. Yes, I knew that."

"Good. Then you will understand the import when I tell you that the half-life of the Ponti Bridge—according to the wisest of our natural philosophers—is little more than two thousand years. Soon, perhaps very soon, messire, it will begin to crumble and collapse."

The fat jeweler gasped. "But that's terrible. If the news got around . . . " He trailed off, weighing up the implications.

"Precisely. There would be panic. Trouble. Unrest. The news cannot be allowed to leak out until we are ready, hence this secrecy."

"I think I will have that drink now, please," said Carthus.

"Very wise." The bald nobleman unstoppered a crystal flagon and poured clear blue wine into a goblet. He passed it across the table and continued. "Any jeweler—and there are only seven in Ponti and perhaps two others elsewhere who could cope with the volume—who was permitted to demolish and keep the materials of the Ponti Bridge would regain whatever he paid for it in publicity alone, leaving aside the value of the jewels. It is my task to talk to the city's most prestigious wholesale jewelers about this matter.

"The Ruling Enclave has a number of concerns. As you can imagine, if the jewels were all released at once in Ponti, they would soon be almost worthless. In exchange for entire ownership of the bridge, the jeweler would have to undertake to build a structure beneath it, and as the bridge crumbles he or she would collect the jewels, and would undertake to sell no more than half a percent of them within the city walls. You, as the senior partner in Carthus and Aathia, are one of the people I have been appointed to discuss this matter with."

The jeweler shook his head. It seemed almost too good to be true—if he could get it. "Anything else?" he asked. His voice was casual. He sounded uninterested.

"I am but a humble servant of the Enclave," said the bald man. "They, for their part, will wish to make a profit on this. Each of you will submit a tender for the bridge, via myself, to the Ruling Enclave. There is to be no conferring among you jewelers. The Enclave will choose the best offer and then, in open and formal session, the winner will be announced and then—and only then—will the winner pay any money into the city treasury. Most of the winning bid, as I understand things, will go toward the building of another bridge (out of significantly more mundane materials, I suspect) and to paying for a ferry for the citizens while there is no bridge."

"I see."

The tall man stared at Carthus. To the jeweler it seemed as if those hard eyes were boring into his soul. "You have exactly five days to submit your tender, Carthus. Let me warn you of two things. Firstly, if there is any indication of collaboration between any of you jewelers, you will earn the Enclave's extreme displeasure. Secondly, if anybody finds out about the spell fatigue, then we will not waste time in finding out which of you jewelers opened his mouth too wide and not too well. The High Council of the Ponti Jewelers' Guild will be replaced with another council, and your businesses will be annexed by the city—perhaps to be offered as prizes in the next Autumn Games. Do I make my meaning plain?"

Carthus's voice was gravel in his throat. "Yes."

"Go then. Your tender in five days, remember. Send another in."

Carthus left the room as if in a dream, croaked "He wants you now," to the nearest High Council member in the anteroom, and was relieved to find himself outside in the sunlight and the fresh air. Far above him the jeweled heights of the Ponti Bridge stood, as they had stood, glinting and twinkling and shining down on the town, for the last two thousand years.

He squinted: Was it his imagination, or were the jewels less bright, the structure less permanent, the whole glorious bridge subtly less magnificent than before? Was the air of permanence that hung about the bridge beginning to fade away?

Carthus began to calculate the value of the bridge in terms of jewel weight and volume. He wondered how Aathia would treat him if he presented her with the rose diamond from the summit; and the High Council would not view him as a nouveau riche upstart, not him, not if he was the man who bought the Ponti Bridge.

Oh, they would all treat him better. There was no doubt of that.

One by one, the man who called himself Glew Croll saw the jewel merchants. Each reacted in his or her own way—shock or laughter, sorrow or gloom—at the news of the spell fatigue in the binding of the Ponti Bridge. And, beneath the sneers or the dismay, each of them began to judge profits and balance sheets, mentally judge and guess possible tenders, activate spies in rival jewelers' houses.

Carthus himself told no one anything, not even his beloved, unattainable Aathia. He locked himself in his study and wrote tenders, tore them up, wrote tenders once again. The rest of the jewelers were similarly occupied.

The fire had burned out in the Rogues' Club, leaving only a few red embers in a bed of gray ash, and dawn was painting the sky silver. Gloathis, Redcap, and I had listened to the man called Stoat all night. It was at this point in his narrative that he leaned back on his cushion, and he grinned.

"So there you have it, friends," he said. "A perfect scam. Eh?"

I glanced at Gloathis and Redcap, and was relieved to see that they looked as blank as I felt.

"I'm sorry," said Redcap. "I just don't see . . . "

"You don't see, eh? And what about you, Gloathis? Do you see? Or are your eyes covered with mud?"

Gloathis looked serious. She said, "Well . . . you obviously convinced them all that you were a representative of the Ruling Enclave—and having them all meet in the anteroom was an inspired idea. But I fail to see the profit in this for you. You've said that you need a million, but none of them is going to pay anything to you. They are waiting for a public announcement that will never come, and then the chance to pay their money into the public treasury . . . "

"You think like a mug," said Stoat. He looked at me and raised an eyebrow. I shook my head. "And you call yourself rogues."

Redcap looked exasperated. "I just don't see the profit in it! You've spent your thirty gold coins on renting the offices and sending the messages. You've told them you're working for the Enclave, and they will pay everything to the Enclave . . . "

It was hearing Redcap spell it out that did it. I saw it all, and I understood, and as I understood I could feel the laughter welling up inside me. I tried to keep it inside, and the effort almost choked me. "Oh, priceless, priceless," was all I could say for some moments. My friends stared at me, irritated. Stoat said nothing, but he waited.

I got up, leaned in to Stoat, and whispered in his ear. He nodded once, and I began to chortle once again.

"At least one of you has some potential," said Stoat. Then he stood up. He drew his robes around him and swept off down the torch-lined corridors of the Lost Carnadine Rogues' Club, vanishing into the shadows. I stared after him as he left. The other two were looking at me.

"I don't understand," said Redcap.

"What did he do?" begged Gloathis.

"Call yourself rogues?" I asked. "I worked it out for myself. Why can't you two simply . . . Oh, very well. After the jewelers left his office he let them stew for a few days, letting the tension build and build. Then, secretly, he arranged to see each of the jewelers at different times and in different places—probably lowlife taverns.

"And in each tavern he would greet the jeweler and point out the one thing that he—or they—had overlooked. The tenders would be submitted to the Enclave through my friend. He could arrange for the jeweler he was talking to—Carthus, say—to put in the winning tender.

"For of course, he was open to bribery."

Gloathis slapped her forehead. "I'm such an oaf! I should have seen it! He could easily have raked in a million gold coins' worth of bribes from that lot. And once the last jeweler paid him, he'd vanish. The jewelers couldn't complain—if the Enclave thought they'd tried to bribe someone they thought to be an Enclave official, they'd be lucky to keep their right arms, let alone their lives and businesses. What a perfect con."

And there was silence in the Hall of the Lost Carnadine Rogues' Club. We were lost in contemplation of the brilliance of the man who sold the Ponti Bridge.

CHRISTIE YANT is a software tester by day, a science fiction/fantasy writer by night. She is also an assistant editor with *Lightspeed Magazine* and the podtern for *The Geek's Guide to the Galaxy* podcast. This story is her first fiction publication. In addition to writing fiction, she has also narrated several stories for the *Starship Sofa* podcast, and reviews audiobooks for Audible. com. She lives on the central coast of California with her two amazing daughters and assorted four-legged nuisances. Her website is inkhaven.net.

Fiction often seems more real to us than reality, and many of us wish that we could climb right into a book and inhabit the world it describes, or that the characters could step right off the page and join us for a drink.

Our next tale is about two characters named Miles and Audra. "They were inspired by and loosely based on two real artists for whom I have a great deal of respect," says Yant, "They each have a very unique and public persona and weave a twisted kind of artistic magic of their own."

The book of fairy tales described in this story is also based on a real book. "It was given to me by my paternal grandmother and dates from the 1930s. It's a book of fairy tales called *Through Fairy Halls*. I read it over and over as a child, and from it I learned that fairy tales exist all over the world, and are unique little realities unto themselves. That book is where I learned to love them, and it makes perfect sense to me that the stories between its covers are true, and that maybe one is missing."

THE MAGICIAN AND THE MAID AND OTHER STORIES
CHRISTIE YANT

She called herself Audra, though that wasn't her real name; he called himself Miles, but she suspected it wasn't his, either.

She was young (how young she would not say), beautiful (or so her Emil had told her), and she had a keen interest in stories. Miles was old, tattooed, perverted, and often mean, but he knew stories that no one else knew, and she was certain that he was the only one who could help her get back home.

She found him among the artists, makers, and deviants. They called him Uncle, and spoke of him sometimes with loathing, sometimes respect, but almost always with a tinge of awe—a magician in a world of technicians, they did not know what to make of him.

But Audra saw him for what he truly was.

There once was a youth of low birth who aspired to the place of King's Magician. The villagers scoffed, "Emil, you will do naught but mind the sheep," but in his heart he knew that he could possess great magic.

The hedge witches and midwives laughed at the shepherd boy who played at sorcery, but indulged his earnestness. He learned charms for love and marriage (women's magic, but he would not be shamed by it) and for wealth and luck, but none of this satisfied him, for it brought him no nearer to the throne. For that he needed real power, and he did not know where to find it.

He had a childhood playmate named Aurora, and as they approached adulthood Aurora grew in both beauty and cleverness. Their childhood affection turned to true love, and on her birthday they were betrothed.

The day came when the youth knew he had learned all that he could in the nearby villages and towns. The lovers wept and declared their devotion with an exchange of humble silver rings. With a final kiss Emil left his true love behind, and set out to find the source of true power.

It was not hard to meet him, once she understood his tastes. A tuck of her skirt, a tug at her chemise; a bright ribbon, new stockings, and dark kohl to line her eyes.

She followed him to a club he frequented, where musicians played discordant arrangements and the patrons were as elaborately costumed as the performers. She walked past his booth where he smoked cigarettes and drank scotch surrounded by colorful young women and effeminate young men.

"You there, Bo Peep, come here."

She met his dark eyes, turned her back on him, and walked away. The sycophants who surrounded him bitched and whined their contempt for her. He barked at them to shut up as she made her way to the door.

Once she had rejected him it was easy. She waited for his fourth frustrated overture before she joined him at his table.

"So," she said as she lifted his glass to her lips uninvited, "tell me a story."

"What kind of story?"

"A fairy tale."

"What—something with elves and princes and happily-ever-after?"

"No," she said and reached across the corner of the table to turn his face toward her. He seemed startled but complied, and leaned in until their faces were just inches apart. "A real fairy tale. With wolves and witches, jealous parents, woodsmen charged with murdering the innocent. Tell me a story, Miles—" she could feel his breath against her cheek falter as she leaned ever closer and spoke softly into his ear "—tell me a story that is true."

Audra was foot-sore and weary when they reached the house at dawn. She stumbled on the stone walk, and caught Miles's arm to steady her.

"Are you sure you don't need anything from home?" he asked as he worked his key in the lock.

At his mention of *home,* she remembered again to hate him.

"Quite sure," she said. He faced her, this time with a different kind of appraisal. There was no leer, no suspicion. He touched her face, and his habitual scowl relaxed into something like a smile.

"You remind me of someone I knew once, long ago." The smile vanished and he opened the front door, stepping aside to let her pass.

His house was small and filled with a peculiar collection of things that told her she had the right man. Many of them where achingly familiar to Audra: a wooden spindle in the entryway, wound with golden thread; a dainty glass shoe on the mantle, almost small enough to fit a child; in the corner, a stone statue of an ugly, twisted creature, one arm thrown protectively over its eyes.

"What a remarkable collection," she said and forced a smile. "It must have taken a long time to assemble."

"Longer than I care to think of." He picked a golden pear off the shelf and examined it. "None of it is what I wanted." He returned it to the shelf with a careless toss. "I'll show you the bedroom."

The room was bare, in contrast with the rest of the house. No ornament hung on the white plaster walls, no picture rested on the dresser. The bed was small, though big enough for two, and covered in a faded quilt. It was flanked by a table on one side, and a bent wood chair on the other.

Audra sat stiffly at the foot of the bed.

The mattress creaked as Miles sat down beside her. She turned toward him with resolve, and braced herself for the inevitable. She would do whatever it took to get back home.

She had done worse, and with less cause.

He leaned in close and stroked her hair; she could smell him, sweet and smoky, familiar and foreign at the same time. She lifted a hand to caress his smooth head where he lingered above her breast. He caught her wrist and straightened, pressed her palm to his cheek—eyes closed, forehead creased in pain—then abruptly dropped her hand and rose from the bed.

"If you need more blankets, they're in the wardrobe. Sleep well," he said, and left Audra to wonder what had gone wrong, and to consider her next move.

Aurora was as ambitious as Emil, but of a different nature. She believed that the minds of most men were selfish and swayed only by fear or greed. In her heart there nestled a seed of doubt that Emil could get his wish through pure knowledge and practice. She resolved in her love for him to secure his place through craft and wile.

Aurora knew the ways of tales. She planted the seed of rumor in soil in which it grew best: the bowry; the laundry; anywhere the women gathered, she talked of his power.

But word of the powerful sorcerer had to reach the King himself, and to get close enough she would need to use a different craft.

The hands of guards and pikemen were rougher than Emil's; the mouths of servants less tender. She ignited the fire of ambition in their hearts with flattery, and fanned it with promises that Emil, the most powerful sorcerer in the kingdom, would repay those who supported him once he was installed in the palace.

And if she had regrets as she hurried from chamber to cottage in the cold night air, she dismissed them as just a step on the road toward realizing her lover's dream.

Audra woke at mid-day to find a note on the chair in the corner of the room.

In deep black ink and an unpracticed hand was written:

"Stay if you like, or go as you please. I am accountable to only one, and that one is not you. If that arrangement suits you, make yourself at home. – M."

It suited her just fine.

She searched the house. She wasn't sure what she was looking for, but she was certain that any object of power great enough to rip her from her own world would be obvious somehow. It would be odd, otherworldly, she thought—but that described everything here. Like a raven's hoard, every nook contained some shiny, stolen object.

On a shelf in the library she found a clear glass apothecary jar labeled "East Wind." *Thief,* she thought. Audra hoped that the East Wind didn't suffer for the lack of the contents of the jar. She would keep an eye on the weather vane and return it at the first opportunity.

Something on the shelf caught her eye, small and shining, and her contempt turned to rage.

Murderer.

She pocketed Emil's ring.

Miles seemed to dislike mirrors. There were none in the bedroom; none even in the washroom. The only mirror in the house was an ornate, gilded thing that hung in the library. She paused in front of it, startled at her disheveled appearance. She smoothed her hair with her fingers and leaned in to examine her blood-shot eyes—and found someone else's eyes looking back at her.

The gaunt, androgynous face that gazed dolefully from deep within the mirror was darker and older than her own.

"Hello," she said to the Magic Mirror. "I'm Audra."

The Mirror shook its head disapprovingly.

"You're right," she admitted. "But we don't give strangers our true names, do we?"

She considered her new companion. The long lines of its insubstantial face told Audra that it had worn that mournful look for a long time.

"Did he steal you, as well? Perhaps we can help each other find a way home. The answer is here somewhere."

The face in the Mirror brightened, and it nodded.

Audra had an idea. "Would you like me to read to you?"

Emil travelled a bitter road in search of the knowledge that would make his fortune. By day he starved, by night he froze. But one day Luck was with him, and he caught two large, healthy hares before sunset. As he huddled beside his small fire, the hares roasting over the flames, a short and grizzled man came out of the forest, carrying a sack of goods.

"Good evening, Grandfather," Emil said to the little man. "Sit, share my fire and supper." The man gratefully accepted. "What do you sell?" Emil asked.

"Pots and pans, needles, and spices," the old man said.

"*Know you any magic?*" Emil asked, disappointed. *He was beginning to think the knowledge he sought didn't exist, and he was losing hope.*

"*What does a shepherd need with magic?*"

"*How did you know I'm a shepherd?*" Emil asked in surprise.

"*I know many things,*" the man said, *and then groaned, and doubled over in pain.*

"*What ails you?*" Emil cried, *rushing to the old man's side.*

"*Nothing that you can help, lad. I've a disease of the gut that none can cure, and my time may be short.*"

Emil questioned the man about his ailment, and pulled from his pack dozens of pouches of herbs and powders. He heated water for a medicinal brew while the old man groaned and clutched his stomach.

The man pulled horrible faces as he drank down the bitter tea, but before long his pain eased, and he was able to sit upright again. Emil mixed another batch of the preparation and assured him that he would be cured if he drank the tea for seven days.

"*I was wrong about you,*" the man said. "*You're no shepherd.*" *He pulled a scroll from deep within his pack.* "*For your kindness I'll give you what you've traveled the world seeking.*"

The little man explained that the scroll contained three powerful spells, written in a language that no man had spoken in a thousand years. The first was a spell to summon a benevolent spirit, who would then guide him in his learning.

The second summoned objects from one world into another, for every child knew that there were many worlds, and that it was possible to pierce the veil between them.

The third would transport a person between worlds.

If he could decipher the three spells, he would surely become the most powerful sorcerer in the kingdom.

Emil offered the old man what coins he had, but he refused. He simply handed over the scroll, bade Emil farewell, and walked back into the forest.

Audra filled her time reading to the Mirror. The shelves were filled with hundreds of books: old and new, leather-bound and gilt-edged, or flimsy and sized to be carried in a pocket.

She devoured them, looking for clues. How she got here. How she might get back.

On a bottom shelf in the library, in the sixth book of a twelve-volume set, she found her story.

The illustrations throughout the blue, cloth-bound book were full of round, cheerful children and curling vines. She recognized some of her friends and enemies from her old life: there was Miska, who fooled the Man-With-The-Iron-Head and whom she had met once on his travels; on another page she found the fairy who brought the waterfall to the mountain, whom Audra resolved to visit as soon as she got home.

She turned the page, and her breath caught in her throat.

"The Magician and the Maid," the title read. Beneath the illustration were those familiar words, "Once upon a time."

A white rabbit bounded between birch trees toward Audra's cottage. Between the tree tops a castle gleamed pink in the sunset light, the place where her story was supposed to end. Audra traced the outline of the rabbit with her finger, and then traced the two lonely shadows that followed close behind.

Two shadows: one, her own, and the other, Emil's.

Audra was reading to the Mirror, a story it seemed to particularly like. It did tricks for her as she read, creating wispy images in the glass that matched the prose.

She had just reached the best part, where the trolls turn to stone in the light of the rising sun, when she heard footsteps outside the library door. The Mirror looked anxiously toward the sound, and then slipped out of sight beyond the carved frame.

The door burst open.

"Who are you talking to?" Miles demanded. "Who's here?" He smelled of scotch and sweat, and his overcoat had a new stain.

"No one. I like to read aloud. I am alone here all day," she said.

"Don't pretend I owe you anything." He slouched into the chair and pulled a cigarette from his coat. "You might make yourself useful," he said. "Read to me."

The room was small, and she stood no more than an arm's length away, feeling like a school girl being made to recite. She opened to a story she did not know, a tale called "The Snow Queen," and began to read. Miles closed his eyes and listened.

"Little Kay was quite blue with cold, indeed almost black, but he did not feel it; for the Snow Queen had kissed away the icy shiverings, and his heart was already a lump of ice," she read.

She glanced down at him when she paused for breath to find him looking at her in a way that she knew all too well.

Finally, an advantage.

She let her voice falter when he ran a finger up the side of her leg, lifting her skirt a few inches above her knee.

She did not stop reading—it was working, something in him had changed as she read. Sex was a weak foothold, but it was the only one she had, and perhaps it would be a step toward getting into his mind.

"He dragged some sharp, flat pieces of ice to and fro, and placed them together in all kinds of positions, as if he wished to make something out of them. He composed many complete figures, forming different words, but there was one word he never could manage to form, although he wished it very much. It was the word 'Eternity.' "

He fingered the cord tied at her waist, and tugged it gently at first, then more insistently. He leaned forward in the chair, and unfastened the last hook on her corset.

"Just at this moment it happened that little Gerda came through the great door of the castle. Cutting winds were raging around her, but she offered up a prayer and the winds sank down as if they were going to sleep; and she went on till she came to the large empty hall, and caught sight of Kay; she knew him directly; she flew to him and threw her arms round his neck, and held him fast, while she exclaimed, "Kay, dear little Kay, I have found you at last.' "

His fingers stopped their manipulations. His hands were still on her, the fastenings held between his fingertips.

She dared not breathe.

Whatever control she had for those few minutes was gone. She tried to reclaim it, to keep going as if nothing had happened. She even dropped a hand from the book and reached out to touch him. His hand snapped up and caught hers; he stood, pulling hard on her arm.

"Enough." He left the room without looking back. She heard the front door slam.

Audra straightened her clothes in frustration and wondered again what had gone wrong.

It took only a moment's thought for Audra to decide to follow him. She peered out into the street: there he was, a block away already, casting a long shadow in the lamp light on the wet pavement.

Her feet were cold and her shoes wet through by the time he finally stopped at a warehouse deep in a maze of brick complexes. He manipulated a complex series of locks on the dented and rusting steel door, and disappeared inside.

So this was where he went at night? Not to clubs and parlors as she had thought, but here, on the edge of the inhabited city, to a warehouse only notable for having all its window glass.

The windows were too high for her to see into, but a dumpster beneath one of them offered her a chance. The metal bin was slick with mist, and she slipped off it twice, but on her third try she hoisted herself on top and nervously peered through the filthy glass of the window.

In the dim light she could just make out the shape of Miles, rubbing his hands fiercely together as if to warm them, then unrolling something—paper, or parchment—spreading it out carefully in front of him on the concrete floor. He stood, and began to speak.

The room grew brighter, and a face appeared in front of him, suspended in the air—a familiar face made of dim green light; Audra could see little of it through the dirty glass. She could hear Miles's voice, urgent and almost desperate, but the words he shouted at the thing made no sense to her.

She shifted her weight to ease the pain of her knee pressing against the metal of the dumpster, and slipped. She fell, and cried out in pain as she landed hard on the pavement. She didn't know if Miles had heard, but she did not wait to find out. She picked herself up—now wet, filthy, and aching—and ran.

When she reached the house she went straight to the library. Audra shifted the books on the shelf so that the remaining volumes were flush against each other, and she hid her book in the small trunk where she kept her few clothes.

The Mirror's face emerged from its hiding place behind the frame, looking worried and wan.

"It's my story, after all," she told it. "I won't let him do any more damage. What if he takes the cottage? The woods? Where would I have to go home to? No, he can't have any more of our story."

The language of the scroll was not as impossible as the little man had said—while it was not his own, it was similar enough that someone as clever as Emil could puzzle it out. He applied himself to little else, and before long Emil could struggle through half of the first spell. But when he thought of arriving home after so long, still unable to execute even the simplest of the three, the frustration in him grew.

Surely, he thought, he should begin with the hardest, for having mastered that the simpler ones will come with ease.

So thinking, he set out to learn the last of the three spells before he arrived home.

When Miles finally returned the following evening at dusk, he looked exhausted and filthy, as if he had slept on the floor of the warehouse. She met him in the kitchen, and didn't ask questions.

He brooded on a chair in the corner while she chopped vegetables on the island butcher block, never taking his eyes off her, then stood abruptly and left the room.

The hiss and sputter of the vegetables as they hit the pan echoed the angry, inarticulate hiss in her mind. She had been here for days, and she was no closer to getting home.

The knife felt heavy and solid in her hand as she cubed a slab of marbled meat. She imagined Miles under the knife, imagined his fear and pain. She would get it out of him—how to get home—and he would tell her what he had done to her Emil before the miserable bastard died.

Sounds from the next room were punctuated with curses. The crack of heavy books being unshelved made her flinch.

"Where is it?" he first seemed to ask himself; then louder, "*Where?*" he demanded of the room at large; then a roar erupted from the doorway: "*What have you done with it, you vicious witch?*"

A cold wash of fear cleared away her thoughts of revenge.

"What are you talking about?"

"My book," he said. "Where is it? What have you done with it?"

He came at her hunched like an advancing wolf. They circled the butcher block. She gripped the knife and dared not blink, for fear that he would take a split second advantage and lunge for her.

"You have many books."

"*And I only care about one!*" His hand shot out and caught her wrist, bringing her arm down against the scarred wood with a painful shock. The knife fell from her hand.

He dragged her into the library. "There," he said, pointing to the shelf where her book had been. "Six of twelve. It was there and now it's not." He relaxed his grip without letting go. "If you borrowed it, it's fine. I just want it back." He released her and forced a smile. "Now, where is it?"

"You're right," she said, "I borrowed it. I didn't realize it was so important to you."

"It's very special."

"Yes," she said, her voice low and hard, "it is."

And with that, she knew she had given herself away.

Miles shoved her away from him. She fell into the bookcase as he left the small library and shut door behind him. A key turned in the lock.

It was too late.

She rested with her forehead against the door and caught her breath. She tried to pry open the small window, but it was sealed shut with layers of paint. She considered breaking the glass, and then thought better of it; she could escape from this house, it was true, but not from this world. For that, she still needed Miles.

She watched the sun set through the dirty window, and tried to decide what to do when he let her out. She heard him pacing through the house, talking to himself with ever greater stridency, but the words made no sense to her. It gave her a headache.

The sound of the key in the door woke her. She grabbed at the first thing that might serve as a weapon, a sturdy hardcover. She held in front of her like a shield.

Miles stood in the doorway, a long, wicked knife in his hand.

"Who are you?" he finally asked, his eyes narrowed with suspicion. "And how did you know?"

"Someone whose life you destroyed. Liar. Thief. Murderer." She produced Emil's ring.

He seemed frozen where he stood, his eyes darting back and forth between the ring in her hand and her face. "I am none of those things," he said.

"You took all of this," she gestured around the room. "You took him, and you took me. And what did you do with the things that were of no use to you?"

She had been edging toward him while he talked. She threw the book at his arm and it struck him just as she had hoped. The knife fell to the floor and she dove for it, snatching it up before Miles could stop her.

She had him now, she thought, and pressed the blade against his throat. He tried to push her off but she had a tenacious grip on him and he ceased his struggle when the knife pierced his thin skin. She felt his body tense in her hands, barely breathing and perfectly still.

"You still haven't told me who you are."

"Where is he?" she demanded.

"Where is who?" His voice was smooth and controlled.

"The man you stole, like you stole me. Like you stole all of it. Where is he?"

"You're obviously very upset. Put that down, let me go, and we'll talk about it. I don't know about any stolen man, but maybe I can help you find him."

He voice was calm, slightly imploring, asking for understanding and offering help. She hesitated, wondering what threat she was really willing to carry out against an enemy who was also her only hope.

She waited a moment too long. Miles grabbed a heavy jar off the shelf and hurled it at the wall.

The East Wind ripped through the room, finally free.

Fatigued and half-starved, Emil made his way slowly toward his home, and tried to unlock the spell. Soon he had three words, and then five, and soon a dozen. He would say them aloud, emphasizing this part or that, elongating a sound or shortening it, until the day he gave voice to the last character on the page, and something happened: a spark, a glimmer of magic.

He had ciphered out the spell.

Finally, on the coldest night he could remember, with not a soul in sight, he raised his voice against the howling wind, and shouted out the thirteen words of power.

As weeks turned into months the stories of Emil the Sorcerer grew, until finally even the King had heard, and wanted his power within his own control.

But Emil could not be found.

The angry vortex threw everything off the shelves. Audra ducked and covered her head as she was pummeled by books and debris. Miles crouched behind the trunk, which offered little protection from the gale.

There was a crash above Audra's head; her arms flew up to protect her eyes; broken glass struck her arms and legs, some falling away, some piercing her skin.

The window broke with a final crash and the captive wind escaped the room. The storm was over. Books thumped and glass tinkled to the ground.

Audra opened her eyes to the wreckage. Miles was already sifting through the pages and torn covers.

"No," he said, "no! It has to be here, my story has to be here . . . " He bled from a hundred small cuts but he paid them no mind. Audra plucked shards of dark glass out of her flesh. The shards gave off no reflection at all.

A cloud drifted from where the Mirror had hung over the wreckage-strewn shelves, searching. On the floor beside Audra's trunk, the lid torn off in the storm, it seemed to find what it was looking for. It slipped between the pages of a blue cloth-bound volume and disappeared.

"Here!" Audra said, clutching the volume to her chest. He scrambled toward her until they kneeled together in the middle of the floor, face to face.

Smoke curled out of the pages, only a wisp at first. Then more, green and glowing like a sunbeam in a mossy pond, crept out and wrapped itself around both them.

"The Guide you sought was always here," a voice whispered. "Your captive, Emil, and your friend, Aurora." Audra—Aurora—looked at the man she had hated and saw what was there all along: her Emil, thirty years since he had disappeared, with bald head and graying beard. Miles, who kept her because she looked like his lost love, but who wouldn't touch her, in faith to his beloved.

Emil looked back at her, tears in the eyes that had seemed so dead and without hope until now.

"Now, Emil, speak the words," the voice said, "and we will go home."

So should you happen across a blue cloth-bound book, the sixth in a set of twelve, do not look for "The Magician and the Maid," because it is not there.

Read the other stories, though, and in the story of the fairy who brought the waterfall to the mountain, you may find that she has a friend called Audra, though you will know the truth: it is not her real name.

If you read further you may find Emil as well, for though he never did become the King's magician, every story needs a little magic.

According to *Locus Magazine*, MIKE RESNICK has won more awards for short fiction than any other science fiction writer, living or dead. He is perhaps best known for his critically-acclaimed *Kirinyaga* series of short stories, but is also the author of more than fifty novels. In addition to his work as a writer, Resnick has also edited dozens of anthologies and served as executive editor for the online magazine *Jim Baen's Universe*. Recent work includes a new collection, *Blasphemy*, just out from Golden Gryphon, and a new novel, *The Buntline Special*, from Pyr, due in December. Also, earlier this year, a nonfiction book, *The Business of Science Fiction* (written with Barry Malzberg), was released. Learn more at mikeresnick.com.

Perhaps the most famous wizard of them all is Merlin the magician, a staple of Arthurian legend. The character goes all the way back to Geoffrey of Monmouth in the twelfth century, and the story has been embellished over the years by numerous other authors, such as Thomas Malory (*Le Morte d'Arthur*), T. H. White (*The Once and Future King*), and Mary Stewart (*The Crystal Cave*). Though there are many variations, Merlin is generally remembered as having been sired by an incubus (a demon), which gave him supernatural powers. He tutored Arthur and helped him become king, and was eventually imprisoned in a crystal cave by the Lady of the Lake.

"I wrote this story the day I learned that my late mother-in-law had Alzheimer's," Resnick says. "I tried to imagine what it was like for her, going to bed each night and knowing she'd wake up a little less intelligent each morning. I knew I needed to work it out fictionally. Then I remembered that the Merlin of *The Once and Future King*, my favorite fantasy novel, lived backward in time, and I decided I could use that as a metaphor."

Winter Solstice
Mike Resnick

It is not easy to live backwards in time, even when you are Merlin the Magnificent. You would think it would be otherwise, that you would remember all the wonders of the future, but those memories grow dim and fade more quickly than you might suppose. I know that Galahad will win his duel tomorrow, but already the name of his son has left me. In fact, does he even have a son? Will he live long enough to pass on his noble blood? I think perhaps he may, I think that I have held his grandchild upon my knee, but I am not sure. It is all slipping away from me.

Once I knew all the secrets of the universe. With no more than a thought I could bring Time to a stop, reverse it in its course, twist it around my finger like a piece of string. By force of will alone I could pass among the stars and the galaxies. I could create life out of nothingness, and turn living, breathing worlds into dust.

Time passed—though not the way it passes for you—and I could no longer do these things. But I could isolate a DNA molecule and perform microsurgery on it, and I could produce the equations that allowed us to traverse the wormholes in space, and I could plot the orbit of an electron.

Still more time slipped away, and although these gifts deserted me, I could create penicillin out of bread mold, and comprehend both the General and Special Theories of Relativity, and I could fly between the continents.

But all that has gone, and I remember it as one remembers a dream, on those occasions I can remember it at all. There was—there someday will be, there may come to you—a disease of the aged, in which you lose portions of your mind, pieces of your past, thoughts you've thought and feelings you've felt, until all that's left is the primal *id*, screaming silently for warmth and nourishment. You see parts of yourself vanishing, you try to pull them back from oblivion, you fail, and all the while you realize what is happening to you until even that perception, that realization, is lost. I will weep for you in another millennium, but now your lost faces fade from my memory, your desperation recedes from the stage of my mind, and soon I will remember nothing of you. Everything is drifting away on the wind, eluding my frantic efforts to clutch it and bring it back to me.

I am writing this down so that someday someone—possibly even *you*—will read it and will know that I was a good and moral man, that I did my best under circumstances that a more compassionate God might not have forced upon me, that even as events and places slipped away from me, I did not shirk my duties, I served my people as best I could.

They come to me, my people, and they say, It hurts, Merlin. They say, Cast a spell and make the pain go away. They say, My baby burns with fever, and my milk has dried up. Do something, Merlin, they say; you are the greatest wizard in the kingdom, the greatest wizard who has ever lived. Surely you can do something.

Even Arthur seeks me out. The war goes badly, he confides to me; the heathen fight against baptism, the knights have fallen to battling amongst themselves, he distrusts his queen. He reminds me that I am his personal wizard, that I am his most trusted friend, that it was I who taught him the secret of Excalibur (but that was many years ago, and of course I know nothing of it yet). I look at him thoughtfully, and though I know an Arthur who is bent with age and beaten down by the caprices of Fate, an Arthur who has lost his Guinevere and his Round Table and all his dreams of Camelot, I can summon no compassion, no sympathy for this young man who is speaking to me. He is a stranger, as he will be yesterday, as he will be last week.

An old woman comes to see me in the early afternoon. Her arm is torn and miscolored, the stench of it makes my eyes water, the flies are thick around her.

I cannot stand the pain any longer, Merlin, she weeps. It is like childbirth, but it does not go away. You are my only hope, Merlin. Cast your mystic spell, charge me what you will, but make the pain cease.

I look at her arm, where the badger has ripped it with his claws, and I want to turn my head away and retch. I finally force myself to examine it. I have a sense that I need something, I am not sure what, something to attach to the front of my face, or if not my whole face then at least across my nose and mouth, but I cannot recall what it is.

The arm is swollen to almost twice its normal size, and although the wound is halfway between her elbow and her shoulder, she shrieks in agony when I gently manipulate her fingers. I want to give her something for her pain. Vague visions come to mind, images of something long and slender and needlelike flash briefly before my eyes. There must be something I can do, I think, something I can give her, some miracle that I employed when I was younger and the world was older, but I can no longer remember what it is.

I must do more than mask her pain, this much I still know, for infection has set in. The smell becomes stronger as I probe and she screams. *Gang*, I think suddenly: the word for her condition begins with *gang*—but there is another syllable and I cannot recall it, and even if I could recall it I can no longer cure it.

But she must have some surcease from her agony, she believes in my powers and she is suffering and my heart goes out to her. I mumble a chant, half-whispering and half-singing. She thinks I am calling up my ethereal servants from the Netherworld, that I am bringing my magic to bear on the problem, and because she needs to believe in something, in *anything*, because she is suffering such agony, I do not tell her that what I am really saying is God, just this one time, let me remember. Once, years, eons from now, I could have cured her; give me back the knowledge just for an hour, even for a minute. I did not ask to live backward in Time, but it is my curse and I have willingly borne it—but don't let this poor old woman die because of it. Let me cure her, and then You can ransack my mind and take back my memories.

But God does not answer, and the woman keeps screaming, and finally I gently plaster mud on the wound to keep the flies away. There should be medicine too, it comes in bottles—(bottles? Is that the right word?)—but I don't know how to make it, I don't even remember its color or shape or texture, and I give the woman a root, and mutter a spell over it, and tell her to sleep with it between her breasts and to believe in its healing powers and soon the pain will subside.

She believes me—there is no earthly reason why she should, but I can see in her eyes that she does—and then she kisses my hands and presses the root to her bosom and wanders off, and somehow, for some reason, she *does* seem to be in less discomfort, though the stench of the wound lingers long after she has gone.

Then it is Lancelot's turn. Next week or next month he will slay the Black Knight, but first I must bless his sword. He talks of things we said to each other yesterday, things of which I have no recollection, and I think of things we will say to each other tomorrow.

I stare into his dark brown eyes, for I alone know his secret, and I wonder if I should tell Arthur. I know they will fight a war over it, but I do not remember if I am the catalyst or if Guenivere herself confesses her infidelities, and I can no longer recall the outcome. I concentrate and try to see the future, but all I see is a city of towering steel and glass structures, and I cannot see Arthur or Lancelot anywhere, and then the image vanishes, and I still do not know whether I am to go to Arthur with my secret knowledge or keep my silence.

I realize that it has all happened, that the Round Table and the knights and even Arthur will soon be dust no matter what I say or do, but they are living forward in Time and this is of momentous import to them, even though I have watched it all pass and vanish before my eyes.

Lancelot is speaking now, wondering about the strength of his faith, the purity of his virtue, filled with self-doubt. He is not afraid to die at the hands of the Black Knight, but he is afraid to face his God if the reason for his death lies within himself. I continue to stare at him, this man who daily feels the bond of our friendship growing stronger while I daily find that I know him less and less, and finally I lay a hand on his shoulder and assure him that he will be victorious, that I have had a vision of the Black Knight lying dead upon the field of battle as Lancelot raises his bloody sword in victorious triumph.

Are you sure, Merlin, he asks doubtfully.

I tell him that I am sure. I could tell him more, tell him that I have seen the future, that I am losing it as quickly as I am learning the past, but he has problems of his own—and so, I realize, have I, for as I know less and less I must pave the way for that youthful Merlin who will remember nothing at all. It is *he* that I must consider—I speak of him in the third person, for I know nothing of him, and he can barely remember me, nor will he know Arthur or Lancelot or even the dark and twisted Modred—for as each of my days passes and Time continues to unwind, he will be less able to cope, less able to define even the problems he will face, let alone the solutions. I must give him a weapon with which to defend himself, a weapon that he can use and manipulate no matter how little he remembers of me, and the weapon I choose is superstition. Where once I worked miracles that were codified in books and natural law, now as their secrets vanish one by one, I must replace them with miracles that bedazzle the eye and terrify the heart, for only by securing the past can I guarantee the future, and I have already lived the future. I hope I was a good man, I would like to think I was, but I do not know. I examine my mind, I try to probe for weaknesses as I probe my patients' bodies, searching for sources of infection, but I am only the sum of my experience, and my experience has vanished and I will have to settle for hoping that I disgraced neither myself nor my God.

After Lancelot leaves I get to my feet and walk around the castle, my mind filled with strange images, fleeting pictures that seem to make sense until I concentrate on them and then I find them incomprehensible. There are enormous armies clashing, armies larger than the entire populace of Arthur's kingdom, and I know that I have seen them, I have actually stood on the battlefield, perhaps I even fought for one side or the other, but I do not recognize the colors they are wearing, and they use weaponry that seems like magic, *true* magic, to me.

I remember huge spacefaring ships, ships that sail the starways with neither canvas nor masts, and for a moment I think that this must surely be a dream, and then I seem to find myself standing at a small window, gazing out at the stars as we rush by them, and I see the rocky surfaces and swirling colors of distant worlds, and then I am back in the castle, and I feel a tremendous sense of poignancy and loss, as if I know that even the dream will never visit me again.

I decide to concentrate, to force myself to remember, but no images come to me, and I begin to feel like a foolish old man. Why am I doing this, I wonder. It was a dream and not a memory, for everyone knows that the stars are nothing but lights that God uses to illuminate the night sky, and they are tacked onto a cloak of black velvet, and the moment I realize this, I can no longer even recall what the starfaring ships looked like, and I know that soon I will not even remember that I once dreamed of them.

I continued to wander the castle, touching familiar objects to reassure myself: this pillar was here yesterday, it will be here tomorrow, it is eternal, it will be here forever. I find comfort in the constancy of physical things, things that are not as ephemeral as my memories, things that cannot be ripped from the Earth as easily as my past has been ripped from me. I stop before the church and read a small plaque. It is written in French, and it says that *This Church was* something *by Arthur, King of the Britains.* The fourth word makes no sense to me, and this distresses me, because I have always been able to read the plaque before, and then I remember that tomorrow morning I will ask Sir Hector whether the word means *built* or *constructed*, and he will reply that it means *dedicated*, and I will know that for the rest of my life.

But now I feel a sense of panic, because I am not only losing images and memories, I am actually losing words, and I wonder if the day will come when people will speak to me and I will understand nothing of what they are saying and will merely stare at them in mute confusion, my eyes as large and gentle and devoid of intelligence as a cow's. I know that all I have lost so far is a single French word, but it distresses me, because in the future I will speak French fluently, as well as German, and Italian, and . . . and I know there is another language, I will be able to speak it and read it and write it, but suddenly it eludes me, and I realize that another ability, another memory, yet another integral piece of myself has fallen into the abyss, never to be retrieved.

I turn away from the plaque, and I go back to my quarters, looking neither right nor left for fear of seeing some building, some artifact that has no place in my memory, something that reeks of permanence and yet is unknown to me, and I find a scullery maid waiting for me. She is young and very pretty, and I will know her name tomorrow, will roll it around on my mouth and marvel at the melody it makes even coming forth from my old lips, but I look at her and the fact dawns upon me that I cannot recall who she is. I hope I have not slept with her—I have a feeling that as I grow younger I will commit more than my share of indiscretions—only because I do not wish to hurt her feelings, and there is no logical way to explain to her than I cannot remember her, that the ecstasies of last night and last week and last year are still unknown to me.

But she is not here as a lover, she has come as a supplicant, she had a child, a son, who is standing in the shadows behind my door, and now she summons him forth and he hobbles over to me. I look down at him, and I see that he is a clubfoot:

his ankle is misshapen, his foot is turned inward, and he is very obviously ashamed of his deformity.

Can you help him, asks the scullery maid; can you make him run like other little boys? I will give you everything I have, anything you ask, if you can make him like the other children.

I look at the boy, and then at his mother, and then once more at the boy. He is so very young, he has seen nothing of the world, and I wish that I could do something to help him, but I no longer know what to do. There was a time when I knew, there will come a time when no child must limp through his life in pain and humiliation, I know this is so, I know that someday I will be able to cure far worse maladies than a clubfoot, at least I think I know this, but all that I know for sure is that the boy was born a cripple and will live a cripple and will die a cripple, and there is nothing I can do about it.

You are crying, Merlin, says the scullery maid. Does the sight of my child so offend you?

No, I say, it does not offend me.

Then why do you cry, she asks.

I cry because there is nothing else I can do but cry, I reply. I cry for the life your son will never know, and for the life that I have forgotten.

I do not understand, she says.

Nor do I, I answer.

Does this mean you will not help my son, she asks.

I do not know what it means. I see her face growing older and thinner and more bitter, so I know that she will visit me again and again, but I cannot see her son at all, and I do not know if I will help him, or if I do, exactly *how* I will help him. I close my eyes and concentrate, and try to remember the future. *Is* there a cure? Do men still limp on the Moon? Do old men still weep because they cannot help? I try, but it has slipped away again.

I must think about this problem, I say at last. Come back tomorrow, and perhaps I will have a solution.

You mean a spell, she asks eagerly.

Yes, a spell, I say.

She calls the child to her, and together they leave, and I realize that she will come back alone tonight, for I am sure, at least I am almost sure, that I will know her name tomorrow. It will be Marian, or Miranda, something beginning with an M, or possibly Elizabeth. But I think, I am really almost certain, that she will return, for her face is more real to me now than it was when she stood before me. Or is it that she has not stood before me yet? It gets more and more difficult to separate the events from the memories, and the memories from the dreams.

I concentrate on her face, this Marian or Miranda, and it is another face I see, a lovely face with pale blue eyes and high cheekbones, a strong jaw and long auburn hair. It meant something to me once, this face, I feel a sense of warmth and caring and loss when I see it, but I don't know why. I have an instinctive feeling that this face meant, will mean, more to me than any other, that it will bring me both happiness and sorrow beyond any that I've ever known. There is a name that goes with it, it is not Marion or Miriam (or is it?), I grasp futilely for it, and the more franticly I grasp the more rapidly it recedes.

Did I love her, the owner of this face? Will we bring joy and comfort to one another, will we produce sturdy, healthy children to comfort us in our old age? I don't know, because my old age has been spent, and hers is yet to come, and I have forgotten what she does not yet know.

I concentrate on the image of her face. How will we meet? What draws me to you? There must be a hundred little mannerisms, foibles as often as virtues, that will endear you to me. Why can I not remember a single one of them? How will you live, and how will you die? Will I be there to comfort you, and once you're lost, who will be there to comfort me? Is it better than I can no longer recall the answers to these questions?

I feel if I concentrate hard enough, things will come back to me. No face was ever so important to me, not even Arthur's, and so I block out all other thoughts and close my eyes and conjure up her face (yes, *conjure*; I am Merlin, am I not?)—but now I am not so certain that it *is* her face. Was the jaw thus or so? Were her eyes really that pale, her hair that auburn? I am filled with doubt, and I imagine her with eyes that were a deeper blue, hair that was lighter and shorter, a more delicate nose—and I realize that I have never seen this face before, that I was deluded by my self-doubts, that my memory has not failed me completely, and I attempt to paint her portrait on the canvas of my mind once again, but I cannot, the proportions are wrong, the colors are askew, and even so I cling to this approximation, for once I have lost it I have lost her forever. I concentrate on the eyes, making them larger, bluer, paler, and finally I am pleased with them, but now they are in a face that I no longer know, her true face as elusive now as her name and her life.

I sit back on my chair and I sigh. I do not know how long I have been sitting here, trying to remember a face—a woman's face, I think, but I am no longer sure—when I hear a cough, and I look up and Arthur is standing before me.

We must talk, my old friend and mentor, he says, drawing up his own chair and seating himself on it.

Must we, I ask.

He nods his head firmly. The Round Table is coming apart, he says, his voice concerned. The kingdom is in disarray.

You must assert yourself and put it in order, I say, wondering what he is talking about.

It's not that easy, he says.

It never is, I say.

I need Lancelot, says Arthur. He is the best of them, and after you he is my closest friend and advisor. He thinks I don't know what he is doing, but I know, though I pretend not to.

What do you propose to do about it, I ask.

He turns to me, his eyes tortured. I don't know, he says. I love them both, I don't want to bring harm to them, but the important thing is not me or Lancelot or the queen, but the Round Table. I built it to last for all eternity, and it must survive.

Nothing lasts for eternity, I say.

Ideals do, he replies with conviction. There is Good and there is Evil, and those who believe in the Good must stand up and be counted.

Isn't that what you have done, I ask.

Yes, says Arthur, but until now the choice was an easy one. Now I do not know which road to take. If I stop feigning ignorance, then I must kill Lancelot and burn the queen at the stake, and this will surely destroy the Round Table. He pauses and looks at me. Tell me the truth, Merlin, he says, would Lancelot be a better king than I? I must know, for if it will save the Round Table, I will step aside and he can have it all—the throne, the queen, Camelot. But I must be sure.

Who can say what the future holds, I reply.

You can, he says. At least, when I was a young man, you told me that you could.

Did I, I ask curiously. I must have been mistaken. The future is as unknowable as the past.

But everyone knows the past, he says. It is the future that men fear.

Men fear the unknown, wherever it may lie, I say.

I think that only cowards fear the unknown, says Arthur. When I was a young man and I was building the Table, I could not wait for the future to arrive. I used to awaken an hour before sunrise and lay there in my bed, trembling with excitement, eager to see what new triumphs each day would bring me. Suddenly he sighs and seems to age before my eyes. But I am not that man anymore, he continues after a thoughtful silence, and now I fear the future. I fear for Guenivere, and for Lancelot, and for the Round Table.

That is not what you fear, I say.

What do you mean, he asks.

You fear what all men fear, I say.

I do not understand you, says Arthur.

Yes, you do, I reply. And now you fear even to admit to your fears.

He takes a deep breath and stares unblinking into my eyes, for he is truly a brave and honorable man. All right, he says at last. I fear for *me*.

That is only natural, I say.

He shakes his head. It does not *feel* natural, Merlin, he says.

Oh, I say.

I have failed, Merlin, he continues. Everything is dissolving around me—the Round Table and the reasons for it. I have lived the best life I could, but evidently I did not live it well enough. Now all that is left to me is my death—he pauses uncomfortably—and I fear that I will die no better than I have lived.

My heart goes out to him, this young man that I do not know but will know someday, and I lay a reassuring hand on his shoulder.

I am a king, he continues, and if a king does nothing else, he must die well and nobly.

You will die well, my lord, I say.

Will I, he asks uncertainly. Will I die in battle, fighting for what I believe when all others have left my side—or will I die a feeble old man, drooling, incontinent, no longer even aware of my surroundings?

I decide to try once more to look into the future, to put his mind at ease. I close my eyes and I peer ahead, and I see not a mindless babbling old man, but a mindless mewling baby, and that baby is myself.

Arthur tries to look ahead to the future he fears, and I, traveling in the opposite direction, look ahead to the future *I* fear, and I realize that there is no difference, that this is the humiliating state in which man both enters and leaves the world, and that he had better learn to cherish the time in between, for it is all that he has.

I tell Arthur again that he shall die the death he wants, and finally he leaves, and I am alone with my thoughts. I hope I can face my fate with the same courage that Arthur will face his, but I doubt that I can, for Arthur can only guess at his while I can see mine with frightening clarity. I try to remember how Arthur's life actually does end, but it is gone, dissipated in the mists of Time, and I realize that there are very few pieces of myself left to lose before I become that crying, mindless baby, a creature of nothing but appetites and fears. It is not the end that disturbs me, but the knowledge of the end, the terrible awareness of it happening to me while I watch helpless, almost an observer at the disintegration of whatever it is that has made me Merlin.

A young man walks by my door and waves to me. I cannot recall ever seeing him before.

Sir Pellinore stops to thank me. For what? I don't remember.

It is almost dark. I am expecting someone, I think it is a woman, I can almost picture her face. I think I should tidy up the bedroom before she arrives, and I suddenly realize that I don't remember where the bedroom is. I must write this down while I still possess the gift of literacy.

Everything is slipping away, drifting on the wind.

Please, somebody, help me.

I'm frightened.

CINDA WILLIAMS CHIMA is the best-selling author of the young adult fantasy series the *Heir Chronicles*, consisting of (so far) *The Warrior Heir*, *The Wizard Heir*, and *The Dragon Heir*. Two more books in the series are forthcoming. Meanwhile, Chima recently started publishing a new series (also young adult)—the *Seven Realms* quartet—which began with *The Demon King* in 2009 and was followed by *The Exiled Queen* earlier this year. Learn more at cindachima.com.

Lord Acton said, "Power corrupts, and absolute power corrupts absolutely," and that certainly seems to be the case with a lot of wizards one could name. In J.R.R. Tolkien's *The Lord of the Rings*, the Dark Lord Sauron creates an evil master ring in order to enslave the wearers of the other rings of power. In *The Black Cauldron*, the wicked Horned King uses the eponymous cookware to call forth an army of zombie slaves. And in the novel *Azure Bonds* by Jeff Grubb and Kate Novak, an amnesiac warrior awakens to discover that her arm has been tattooed with magical sigils, and when they glow, she falls under the mental domination of a cadre of sinister conspirators.

So why can't wizards ever try to get what they want by just asking nicely? It's always enslavement this and domination that. The heroine of our next piece also finds herself an unwilling pawn to a cruel wizard; those familiar with Chima's *Heir Chronicles* series will recognize her as the enchantress Linda Downey. The story began life as a deleted scene from the second book in the trilogy, *The Wizard Heir*, which Chima says it broke her heart to cut. So when I contacted her about writing a story for the anthology, she reworked it into this fine standalone story.

The Trader and the Slave
Cinda Williams Chima

The house by the sea was always cold, and the light never more than tentative. The gloom held fast in the corners, by day or night, and sometimes Linda fancied that things crouched there, watching her. But there was never any need to conjure monsters beyond the ones she knew for real: There could be none more terrifying. After all, the imagination had its limits.

The broker, Garlock, was talking when Linda entered the hall, waving his arms expansively, pitching like a barker at a traveling show. It was meant to inspire condescension in his clients, to make them underestimate him.

The stranger was listening, head cocked a little to one side, one hand grasping his other forearm. This trader—another wizard, of course—was tall and lean, with large hands and unimportant clothes, and a face that hinted he had stories of his own. A ring set with a large stone glittered on his right hand. It seemed out of place, somehow, given the nondescript nature of the rest of his clothes. Was it a heartstone? Linda couldn't tell.

As was usual with wizards, it was difficult to tell how old he was. He reminded her of a leopard, taut and high strung, not a bit of unnecessary flesh on him. A predator. His long coat had been soaked with rain on the long walk up from the drive, and now it steamed, as if he gave off heat. Or perhaps he had purposely smudged his appearance with a glamour.

Well, Linda thought, *he must be powerful, or he'd be dead already*. And Garlock wouldn't have sent for her at all.

All this she noticed, although she had trained herself to display nothing. All of Garlock's clients were engaged in the Trade. They were dealers in misery, one much like another. It was not her job to stop it, but to stay alive.

It would be a blessing if they killed each other off.

The trader's head came up as Linda entered the room, although her feet made no sound on the stone floor.

She drifted to a stop in front of the trader, keeping her eyes on the floor, her arms relaxed at her sides. The dress she wore was silk—loose and slip-like, and she'd wrapped a gauzy scarf around her neck to hide the silver collar beneath.

In truth, it didn't matter what she wore—her real power sizzled under her skin, and her eyes were windows to that gift. A strong, wary wizard could resist, but most chose not to. Most were willing to risk ensnarement for the pleasure of connection.

She looked up, then, into the trader's eyes. They were green, and sheltered under thick black brows. His nose was on the large side, and the skin of his face tightly drawn over high cheekbones. An oddly handsome face, given the unlikely parts of it.

When their eyes met, the trader took an involuntary step back, putting more distance between them, and shifted his gaze to Garlock. His voice was as cold and complex as a November day. "An enchanter? I thought I had made myself clear. I represent a syndicate that wishes to field a player in the Game. We are looking for Weirlind—for a warrior."

"Of course, Mr. Renfrew," Garlock said, dry-washing his hands. "And you shall have one, if we can come to terms. But we are brokers for a spectrum of talent in the underguilds—sorcerers, warriors, seers, and enchanters. I thought it would do no harm to display her. If not your group, perhaps you know of someone else who would be interested."

After a moment, Renfrew reached out and put his fingers under Linda's chin, lifting her head so she looked into his eyes again. He studied her, either assessing her value or perhaps assessing his own ability to resist. She put her shoulders back and met his gaze boldly, spinning out the spider silk of attraction. She was what she was, and it was not her fault that wizards made the rules.

"She's young," Renfrew said, releasing her chin and running a hand through his dark curls, looking a bit clouded. "How old is she, anyway?"

Garlock rested a proprietary hand on Linda's shoulder. "Youth is an advantage, some would say, given that enchanters do not live so long as wizards."

"What's her name?" Renfrew asked, still directing his questions to Garlock, as if she were a pony or a pet bird.

Or as if he didn't dare engage her in conversation.

"Linda Downey," Garlock replied. The broker was confident now, convinced the client had been redirected. Linda wasn't so sure. If she'd entangled him, she couldn't tell it. She couldn't read this wizard at all.

"What about the boy? The warrior I came to see?" Renfrew raked back his sleeve and looked at his watch. "Given the weather, I'll be late getting back to York as it is."

For an instant, Garlock looked slapped, but he quickly rearranged his face.

"Ah, yes," he said, clearing his throat. "Tomorrow. You can see the warrior tomorrow."

Renfrew took a step toward Garlock, and the broker raised both hands, palms outward, as if to ward off a blow.

Garlock's words spilled out like marbles from a bag. "It isn't often a warrior comes available, and I had to be sure you were a serious bidder. You must understand that, given the current shortage of Weirlind, it isn't wise to keep such a valuable asset on site."

Though Garlock sounded conciliatory, Linda had trained herself to read his moods. She could tell he was furious, and she would pay the price. She shuddered, biting her lip, trying to control her thrashing heart. Then looked up to find Renfrew staring at her, eyes narrowed.

He turned back to Garlock. "Well, no, I *don't* understand," Renfrew said, each word a spike of glacier ice. "I did not travel all this distance out of York only to be told 'tomorrow.' I need to know whether you can deliver." He paused, then added softly, "Or not."

Linda slid out from under Garlock's hand. If flames began to fly, she had no intention of being caught in the crossfire of wizard politics.

Garlock noticed, of course. He glowered at Linda before turning back to Renfew.

"Did *you* bring the piece we spoke of?" Garlock blustered. "The heartstone you offered in trade?"

Renfrew nodded brusquely. "Unlike you, I came prepared to deal." He opened his fist to reveal the heartstone, centered on his palm. It was about the size of a deck of cards, carved of stone, polished by centuries of wizard hands. It gleamed softly as if it made its own light.

The heartstone disappeared as quickly as it appeared. "You can examine it more closely once I know *you* are serious," Renfrew said.

Linda stared at the floor. Damn! Renfrew had it on his person. That sealed it. The trader would die tonight, and Garlock would get what he wanted.

Garlock still focused on where he had last seen the stone. "Very well. I will send for the boy. He will be here tomorrow morning and we will make the trade."

"I'll return midmorning tomorrow, then," Renfrew said. "I will call before I come, so as to avoid another wasted trip." He took a step back, toward the door, but didn't turn his back on Garlock.

Renfrew was smart, then. Smarter than most. He must be very interested in this deal.

"Please—stay with us tonight," Garlock said, as if seized by a spasm of affability. "As you said, it's a long way back to York. Hours there, and hours back again, and the weather is abysmal. Perhaps our hospitality can make up for this inconvenience."

Renfrew took another step back. "Thank you, no. Driving clears my head." He had that distracted look again, his breathing quick and ragged.

Perhaps Linda was getting to him after all. She was putting considerable effort into it, bringing all of her power to bear.

Smelling blood in the water, Garlock gave Linda a rough push toward the trader. "Stay with us, and Linda will serve you supper. Perhaps we can yet convince you to do a second deal." He smiled, and everyone knew he was promising more than supper. A promise Linda hoped she wouldn't have to keep.

Linda knew her role by heart. She wrapped her fingers around Renfrew's arm, smiled at him, feeling the ripple of power through layers of fabric—hers and his. "Please," she whispered, her voice yet another web of magic. "I would like to hear more about how you play the Game."

He froze, as if pinned by her touch, and stood looking down at her. "Do you take me for a fool?" he said, raising an eyebrow.

Young as she was, Linda was a master at making smart men foolish. Pushing up on her toes, she reached up and pressed her free palm against his cheek.

His eyes widened and he flinched back, knocking her hand away. But then he stopped, his eyes fixed on her face.

Taking a deep breath, he released it. "All right," he said. "Against my better judgment, I will stay."

"Good, good," Garlock said. "I'll show you to your room while Linda puts your supper together." The broker scowled at Linda before he turned away. He'd have words for her later. More than words. Sliding her fingers under the scarf, she pried at the metal against her skin, swearing under her breath.

The two wizards headed toward the bedroom wing, and Linda the other direction, to the kitchen. Unlocking the sideboard with a key at her belt, she set the silver tray on the counter, brought down the crystal carafe used for such occasions, and two glasses. She chose a bottle from the rack on the sideboard. A merlot or cabernet was best for this purpose; the tannins hid a multitude of sins. Drawing a small pouch from the drawer, she ripped it open with her teeth, and emptied it into the carafe, tapping it to free the last grains. Then she deftly uncorked the bottle, filled the carafe, stoppered it, and swirled the contents, like blood washing against the glass.

Now for dinner. Wizards were used to eating well.

She had just covered the tray when a slight sound behind her told her she was no longer alone. As she turned, the collar around her neck sent red-hot pain into her spine. She went down on her knees, tearing at the collar with her fingertips, her kneecaps and the heels of her hands stinging where they struck the floor. Garlock crouched in front of her. He grabbed a fistful of her hair and yanked her head back, arching her body so he could see her face.

"Don't you think you could try a little harder with our guests, girl? I thought enchanters were supposed to be enticing." As if to emphasize the last word, the collar constricted again, searing her skin. It never got any easier to bear.

She gasped, sucking in air, but then closed her mouth firmly on the scream. She needed to calm him, not remind him of his power to hurt.

She put her hands on his shoulders, looking into his muddy eyes, soothing him, taking the edge off his anger. Keeping it subtle, so he wouldn't notice. Garlock hated being manipulated.

"He wouldn't respond . . . as well . . . to an aggressive approach. Did you want to scare him off?" She took a deep breath. "This is what I do. Let me handle it. He stayed, didn't he?"

Garlock stared at her a moment, then nodded slowly, chewing on his lip. He sat back on his heels, and she knew she had him. Finally he stood, extended his hand and helped her to her feet.

"Just see you get that wine into him and let's have this business behind us." He jerked her towards him and kissed her roughly, the stubble on his chin and cheeks abrading her skin. He smiled in his sloppy way. "You drive me crazy sometimes," he whispered, licking his lips as if to recapture the kiss. That was his idea of an apology.

You were crazy before I ever got here, she thought, running her fingers through her hair, adjusting her scarf, and twitching her dress back into place. She picked up the tray and put back her shoulders. This was always the way. Garlock was a coward, with limited magical talent. Linda was the one who would suffer if the plan went wrong.

It would be up to her to defang the dragon.

Renfrew was in the guest room, a roughly square stone chamber beneath Garlock's second floor study. The stage was set with a huge, ornately carved bed, wardrobe, desk and chair and a small round table and chairs.

The trader had pulled the shutters open, and was standing, looking out the window at the driving rain. The wind stirred his hair, and rain splattered on the stones at his feet, but he didn't seem to notice. Somewhere, far below, the North Sea flung itself against the rocks. The fire was laid, but he hadn't lit it despite the chill.

"Here's your supper," she said, setting the tray on the small table. He continued to look out the window. Indifferent.

"You're going to freeze with the window open." She stepped in front of him to pull the shutters to, and his hand closed on her wrist. It seemed fragile in his grasp.

"Leave it open," he said hoarsely. "I need the air."

"If you say so," she said softly, making no move to free herself. He released her then, and turned back to the rain.

"Why don't you pour us some wine, while I light the fire?" she suggested, crossing the room to the fireplace and kneeling next to the hearth. Though it would make more sense for a wizard to light the fire, they were always less suspicious when they poured the wine themselves, if they both drank from the carafe.

She'd grown skilled at lighting fires.

When she turned away from the fireplace, she saw that Renfrew had moved to the table with the dinner tray and was pouring wine from the carafe. Only one glass. He crossed the room and extended it to her. She took it, after a moment. "Won't you join me?"

"I don't care for any, thank you." And he stood, one hand grasping the other forearm, as he had before. A smile ghosted across his face, as if he'd made his move and was waiting for her counter.

There was no point in drinking alone. It wouldn't do to still her magic while his was unimpaired. This match was unequal enough as it was.

Linda set her glass down next to the plate. "Please—go ahead and eat. It's a cold supper, I'm afraid, but it won't improve on standing. I'll keep you company."

Perhaps he would wash his dinner down with the wine.

Perhaps she should have chosen something spicier.

She might convince him to do her bidding if she could just get her hands on him, but knew that might dispel any thoughts of supper. So Linda sat in one of the chairs at the table. She rested her feet on the crossbrace, elevating her knees so her skirt slipped back along her thighs.

The wizard made no move to sit. "I think you'd better take your wine and go." He tilted his head toward the door.

He knows it's a trap, Linda thought. *He's known all along.*

But if so, then why did he stay?

Linda shivered, panic closing her throat. If she failed, Garlock would skin her alive. She smothered a twinge of guilt. Renfrew was just another wizard, and a trader at that. She would do whatever it took to survive until she could find a way out.

She stood, moved towards him, close enough that she had to tilt her head back to look up at him. "You are not hungry at all?" And she stood on tiptoe, leaned into him and twined her arms around his neck. She used her small weight to pull his head down toward her and kissed him.

Just for a moment, he returned the kiss. She could feel his desire for her, an explosion of power so potent it nearly slammed her to the floor. Then he pushed her away, both hands against her chest until he realized what they were pushing against. He yanked his hands back like they were burnt.

"You are hardly more than a child," he said, breathing hard, eyes glittering. "You should not be involved in this."

"I am *not* a child, I am eighteen," she said hotly, automatically adding a year to her age. She moved towards him again, pressing her advantage.

He extended his hands, as if to embrace her, but instead spoke a charm that froze her to the floor in midstride. He flung his arms up, and brought them down, in quick, angry strokes, describing an image in the air, muttering charms all the while. She thought she heard something about "Eighteen! Ha!" among the rest.

The room was split with a curtain of light too bright to look upon, on either side, behind and in front of them. When he was finished, they were secluded in a small chamber of light, perhaps six by six feet.

"Now, then," he said. "It's just you and me. Your partner won't be able to help you in here. Or hear you if you scream," he added.

"He is not my partner!" Linda snapped.

Renfrew smiled, the kind of smile that raises gooseflesh. "If not, you'd better convince me of it now. I'm not a patient man."

Garlock, you idiot, Linda thought. *You've snared a lion in your rabbit trap.*

"Promise to behave and I'll unleash you," Renfrew said.

Reluctantly, she nodded, and the invisible bonds dissolved. She experimentally pushed her hand against the wall of light behind her. It gave slightly, but not much.

"Well," she said, almost to herself. "Garlock won't be happy. He likes to watch." She rolled her eyes up, toward the ceiling. He would be above them, in the study.

Renfrew followed her gaze. "You can start by telling me what the real game is."

Linda couldn't say what made her decide to tell the truth. Maybe it was the threat that hung in the air between them. She was the bird in this wizard's hand.

Yet there was something almost unsullied about him—compared to Garlock, at least. He was self-contained, direct and deadly. It was like being penned up close with a wolf.

Perhaps it was the unrelenting nature of the dance—the boards she trod over and over again, like a long-running play, with all the players the same, save one.

Linda was sick of herself, and sick of the game. Sick and tired.

And reckless.

"Garlock's game is bait and switch," she said, looking Renfrew in the eye. "He means to kill you and steal the heartstone you brought. He is not really a Broker. I'm the only talent he has. He's just a dealer in magical pieces."

Renfrew considered this, massaging his forehead with the heel of his hand. "What's in the wine?"

"Weirsbane, to disable your Weirstone," she said, resting her hand on her chest, "and something to make you sleep, so you'll be easy to kill."

"How do you do it?" he asked acidly. "A dagger to the heart? A carafe to the head? Perhaps you . . . "

"Not me," Linda interrupted. "I always leave. Before. My job is to get the wine into them." Tears burned her eyes. *No!* She was done with crying. She would not cry in front of this man.

"How many?" he asked, relentless as the driving rain.

The tears spilled over. *Damn!* She turned away, swiping at her face with the sleeve of her robe. "In the past year, perhaps ten or twelve."

Eighteen, actually.

There was a brief pause in the interrogation. "Then he doesn't even have a warrior?" he asked then, wearily.

"He did, but Jared died six months ago. He killed himself." Garlock's warrior had been physically strong, but never the survivor that Linda was.

"Dead," Renfrew said quietly. He toyed with the ring on his finger, looking unaccountably sad, as if it were a personal loss.

"So you and your syndicate will have to look elsewhere, I'm afraid."

"Yes, of course," he said, lost in thought.

"So. Now what? Do you plan to kill me?" She stood, hands on hips, one knee forward. "I might prefer it over what Garlock will do to me." She was matter-of-fact.

He refocused on her. "There is another option. You can leave with me, if you choose." He spread his fingers. "And then go wherever you like."

As if a wizard could be believed. If she stayed, she might not survive her punishment. But there was no way out for her. Not yet.

"I . . . I can't," she said finally, looking up at him, the words thick in her mouth.

"So—you *choose* to stay?" Renfrew's hands closed into fists, and Linda heard surprise and possibly disappointment in his voice.

Yanking at the scarf at her neck, she pulled it free, lifting her chin so he could see. She tapped the silver collar, inscribed with runes. "It's a dyrne sefa. A heartstone. When I try to leave . . . " She shuddered. She *had* tried, twice. She would never forget it.

"A slaver."

The look on his face made Linda take a step backwards, pressing up against the magical wall.

"We'll have to do a deal, then," he said.

"He won't make a trade for me," she said. Garlock had told her as much. He was crazy. He was obsessed. He would never let her go.

"He'll like my terms," Renfrew said calmly. "Not many people say no to me."

Could she trust this ruthless stranger? There was no reason for him to do a deal unless he had his own plans for her. Was she trading the devil she knew for the one she didn't?

Truth be told, she was ready for a different devil. It wasn't like she owed any loyalty to Garlock.

"All right," she said. But she had to ask the question that had been dogging her. "But I don't get it. If you knew it was a trap all along, why did you stay?"

The wizard smiled, a long, slow smile that improved his looks considerably. "I thought it was obvious," he said. "I stayed for you."

He brought his hands apart quickly, and the walls of light shattered, the shards drifting to the floor like sunlight. Then he flung his arms up towards the ceiling of the chamber, palms up. He muttered a charm, and the wood and plaster above their heads seemed to dissolve, glittering into the darkness.

And there was Garlock, suspended in the air, his eye to the peephole that no longer existed. As Renfrew lowered his hands, the broker settled gently to the floor at their feet.

Garlock lay there a moment, as if he thought he might go unnoticed. Then he scrambled to his feet, brushing nervously at his unfortunate clothing. His face was pale as putty.

"Mr. Garlock, thank you for . . . dropping in," Renfrew said with a smile. "I'm interested in the enchanter after all. I won't wait to see the warrior. I'll trade the heartstone for her."

Garlock's eyes darted from Linda to Renfrew. She knew what he was thinking. This dragon was hardly defanged, and the fault was hers. "The heartstone for Linda," he said, wetting his lips. "I'll have to think about it."

"What's to think about? Surely a win for you. A warrior is worth more than an enchanter in the markets, and you said you were willing to do that deal for him." Renfrew's voice had acquired a distinct chill.

Garlock glared at Linda, suspicious. "You! Get over here." She shook her head, and remained at Renfrew's side.

Suspicion turned to fury. It was done, now. There was no going back.

"I understand you hold her with a slaver," Renfrew said. "I'll want the key to that as well."

"A slaver!" Garlock wiped his hands on his shirt. "I don't know what this slut has told you, but we both know lying comes as naturally to an enchanter as breathing." Garlock was trying, in his way, to be charming, wizard to wizard.

"This offer is available for a limited time," Renfrew said, as if Garlock hadn't spoken. "I'm going to count to three, and then it will be withdrawn. My next offer will be . . . considerably less appealing."

Garlock blinked at him.

"One." The trader extended his arms, straight in front of him, palms out. The air shimmered, solidified, raced away from him. When it struck the wall, the concussion nearly blew the three of them off their feet. When Linda uncovered her eyes, one entire side of the room was gone, the wall on the ocean side. The rain poured in, the wind lifted papers from the desk and spun them out into space.

Linda could hear the ocean clearly now, crashing far below. She took a step away from Renfrew, the back of her hand across her mouth. What had she done? The charms Garlock used were personal, small time nasties. She had never seen anything like this before. From any wizard.

Garlock's mouth opened, then closed, and his fingers knotted themselves together.

"Two." Renfrew lifted his hands, and white-hot flame spiraled from his fingers, blasting upwards, driving the color from the room with its brilliance, running like rivulets over the stone, finding the opening in the ceiling, gathering there. With a blaze of heat, the ceiling was gone, and the roof three stories up, everything between incinerated or blown away.

When Linda looked up, squinting her eyes against the wet, she could see only darkness, and the rain arrowing down. In moments, she was soaked through and shivering, her hair plastered to her head, water running down her neck, the wet fabric of her dress sticking to her flesh. They were entirely out in the weather, clinging to the edge of a cliff that was being taken apart, piece by piece around them.

Renfrew smiled, a flash of white teeth in the gloom. He extended his arms toward Garlock, opening his hands. It was clear what the next target would be. Or who, rather.

"Wait!" Garlock screamed to be heard above the clamor of the gale and the roar of the angry ocean. "I'll make the deal!" he shrieked. "I'll make the deal," he repeated, to make sure Renfrew got the message. "Only I . . . I have to go get the key." He was shaking, hands opening and closing helplessly. He had made no move to launch a counter-attack. He was out-classed, and knew it.

"Tell her where it is." Renfrew nodded at Linda. "She'll fetch it."

"He keeps it on him," Linda said. "Night and day."

Garlock pressed his lips together. His gaze shifted from Renfrew to the door, as if he were judging his chances of making his escape. Finally, shoulders slumping in defeat, he slid his fingers into his neckline and pulled a chain from under the collar of his jacket. He lifted it over his head and thrust it towards Linda. A large gold key dangled from it.

"It had better not be jinxed," Renfrew said. "That would be most unfortunate."

Garlock shook his head, his eyes fixed on Linda. She closed her hand over the key, jerking the chain out of his hand.

She thought of simply taking it and running away, somewhere wizards couldn't find her. But she needed to get the collar off first, or she wouldn't get far. She dropped the key onto Renfrew's palm. She'd been passed from one wizard to another. Was this progress?

"Watch him," Renfrew said to Linda, tipping his head toward Garlock. Facing her, he slid his fingers under the torc around her neck, turning it. Linda's breath hissed out as the metal pressed against her blistered skin. "Sorry," he murmured, his breath warming her frozen hair.

Sorry? *Sorry?* Wizards never say they're sorry.

Renfrew found the joining and inserted the key into the lock. A soft click, and he opened the collar, lifting it away from her. Then swore under his breath. Looking into her eyes, he brushed his fingertips over the inflamed skin, more gently than she would have thought possible.

Linda tilted her face up into the rain, to wash her tears away. *Don't give in*, she thought. *Don't trust him. He's a wizard.*

Renfrew lifted the slaver in one hand, raising it high. It took on a glow, was too bright to look at. Then it slumped, lost its shape, seemed to dissolve. Molten metal dripped from his fingers and hissed and sizzled as it hit the wet floor. Finally, it was gone.

"What . . . what about the heartstone?" Garlock asked, startling Linda. She'd nearly forgotten he was there.

Renfrew turned to Garlock. "You are fortunate," he said, "that I am better at controlling my temper than I used to be. I've left you alive, and I've—ah—left you a wall and a door to go in and out of." A smile tugged at the corners of his mouth. "I think you should count yourself fortunate. Unless you want me to propose another trade." He raised an eyebrow.

Garlock shook his head wordlessly.

Renfrew gripped Linda's shoulder, turning her away from the cliff. Surprisingly, very little heat came through. With a thrust of the other hand, he drove a pathway through the rubble to the outside.

Garlock looked down at the puddle of metal on the stone floor, and then up at the trader. "Renfrew," he said softly. "Why have I not heard of you?"

"Renfrew?" The trader smiled. "You must have misunderstood. My name is Hastings."

"Hastings?" It came out strangled, a mix of dread and sudden understanding. "*Leander* Hastings?"

Hastings, Linda thought. Jared had shared a rumor about a wizard named Leander Hastings who had single-handedly disrupted a tournament at Raven's Ghyll and spirited away one of the warriors. At first, everyone assumed it was a simple robbery—that the warrior would resurface in the Trade, at a fancy price. But it never happened.

Instead, there were more raids—on tournaments, on auctions, on the network of wizard slavers known as the Trade. And the members of the underguilds who disappeared—some said they were working with Hastings now, joining in his dangerous and hopeless quest.

Linda didn't believe it for a moment. Why would a wizard risk his life for the underguilds? It was just a fairytale the powerless told each other to prevent despair. Or a lie spread by the powerful in order to convince the underguilds to wait for a rescue that would never come.

But now, confronted with the man instead of the legend—a tiny spark of belief kindled within Linda.

As Hastings propelled her through the ruins ahead of him, Linda thought, *All right, Leander Hastings, if that's your real name—you'll not be rid of me so easily. I'm going to find out if any of those stories are true. And if they are, I'm going to show you what I can do.*

Linda glanced over her shoulder and saw Garlock crossing himself. For a murderer and a thief, he had always been devout. For years after, she held that incongruous picture of Garlock in her mind. But she never saw him again.

Life is a series of trades—a heartstone for an enchanter. New stories for old. Sin for redemption. The devil you knew for the one you didn't.

Perhaps an ending for a new beginning.

ADAM-TROY CASTRO's work has been nominated for several awards, including the Hugo, Nebula, and Stoker. His novels include *Emissaries from the Dead* and *The Third Claw of God*. He has also collaborated on two alphabet books with artist Johnny Atomic: *Z Is for Zombie*, and *V Is for Vampire*, which are due to come out next year. Castro's short fiction has appeared in such magazines as *The Magazine of Fantasy & Science Fiction*, *Science Fiction Age*, *Analog*, *Cemetery Dance*, and in a number of anthologies. I previously included his work in *The Living Dead*, *The Living Dead 2*, and in *Lightspeed Magazine*. His story collections include *A Desperate, Decaying Darkness* and *Tangled Strings*.

The oldest and most primal form of storytelling is fantasy—tales of gods and monsters, heroes and magic—and the most fundamental form of fantasy is the quest narrative. In his highly influential work *The Hero with a Thousand Faces*, Joseph Campbell identifies what he calls the "monomyth," a story that is told and retold in every human society—that of a young man who sets out from his village on a great quest. He faces steadily escalating challenges and acquires magical talismans and helpful companions—often including a talking animal and a wise old man. Finally he faces his greatest fears and returns home to share the wisdom and power he's acquired. In many quest stories, the hero must also rescue a beautiful princess. Video games frequently evoke this motif, with games like *Super Mario* and *Zelda* building long-running franchises around the idea of princess-rescuing. Contemporary fantasies, such as *The Stepsister Scheme* by Jim C. Hines, often turn this idea on its head, featuring princesses who are more than capable of rescuing themselves, if the need arises. Our next tale also features an unconventional take on the idea of a quest to rescue a beautiful woman.

CERILE AND THE JOURNEYER
ADAM-TROY CASTRO

The journeyer was still a young man when he embarked on his search for the all-powerful witch Cerile.

He was bent and gray-haired a lifetime later when he found a map to her home in the tomb of the forgotten kings.

The map directed him halfway across the world, over the Souleater mountains, through the Curtains of Night, past the scars of the Eternal War, and across a great grassy plain, to the outskirts of Cerile's Desert.

The desert was an ocean of luminescent white sand, which even in the dead of night still radiated the killing heat it swallowed during the day. He knew at once that it could broil the blood in his veins before he traveled even half the distance to the horizon. It even warned him: "Turn back, journeyer. I am as sharp as broken glass, and as hot as open flame. I am filled with soft shifting places that can open up and swallow you without warning. I can drive you mad and leave you to wander in circles until your strength sinks into the earth. And when you die of thirst, as you surely shall if you attempt to pass, I can ride the winds to flay the skin from your burnt and blistered bones."

He proceeded across the dunes, stumbling as his feet sank ankle-deep into the sand, gasping as the furnace heat turned his breath to a dry rasp, but hesitating not at all, merely continuing his march toward the destiny that could mean either death or Cerile.

When the desert saw it couldn't stop him, the ground burst open in a million places, pierced by a great forest that with the speed known only by miracles shot up to scrape the sky. The trees were all hundreds of arm-lengths across, the spaces between them so narrow that even an uncommonly thin man would have had to hold his breath to pass. It was a maze hat could exhaust him utterly before he traveled even halfway to the horizon. It even warned him: "Turn back, journeyer. I am as dark as the night itself, and as threatening as your worst dreams. I am rich with thorns sharp enough to rip the skin from your arms. And if you die lost and alone, as you surely shall if you attempt to pass, I can dig roots into your flesh and grow more trees on your bones."

He entered the woods anyway, crying out as thorns drew blood from his arms and legs, gasping as the trees drew close and threatened to imprison him, but hesitating not at all: merely continuing to march west, toward the destiny that could mean either death or Cerile.

When the forest saw that it couldn't stop him, then the trees all around him merely withered away, and the ground ahead of him rose up, like a thing on hinges, to form a right angle with the ground at his feet. The resulting wall stretched from one horizon to the other, rising straight up into the sky to disappear ominously in the clouds. He knew at once that he did not have the skill or the strength to climb even halfway to the unseen summit. It even warned him: "Turn back, journeyer. I am as smooth as glass and as treacherous as an enemy. I am poor with handholds and impossible to climb. And if you fall, as you surely will if you attempt to pass, then the ground where I stand will be the resting place of your shattered corpse."

He proceeded to climb anyway; moaning as his arms and legs turning to lead from exhaustion, gasping as the temperature around him turned chilly and then frigid, but hesitating not at all: merely continuing to climb upward, toward the destiny that could mean either death or Cerile.

When the cliff saw that it couldn't stop him, then warm winds came and gently lifted him into the sky, over the top of the wall, and down into a lush green valley on the other side, where a frail, white-haired old woman sat beside a still and mirrored pond.

The winds deposited him on his feet on the opposite side of the pond, allowing him to see himself in the water: how he was bent, and stooped, and white-haired, and old, with skin the texture of leather, and eyes that had suffered too much for too long.

He looked away from his reflection, and faced the crone across the water. "You are Cerile?"

"I am," she croaked, in a voice ancient and filled with dust.

"I have heard of you," he said, with the last of his battered strength. "How you have mastered all the secrets of the heavens and the earth, and can make the world itself do your bidding. How you've hidden yourself in this place at the edge of the world, and sworn to grant the fondest wish of any soul clever and brave enough to find you. I have spent my entire life journeying here, Cerile, just to ask this of you. I wish—"

The old woman shushed him, softly but emphatically, and painfully pulled herself to her feet; her bent back forcing her to face the ground as she spoke to him again. "Never mind your wish. Meet me in the water, journeyer."

And with that she doffed her clothes and lowered her withered, emaciated frame into the water, disturbing its mirrored surface not at all. By the time she was knee-deep, her white hair darkened, turning raven black; by the time she was hip-deep, the wrinkles in her face had smoothed out, becoming perfect, unblemished skin; by the time she was shoulder-deep, her rheumy, unfocused eyes had unclouded, revealing a shade of green as brilliant and as beautiful as the most precious emerald.

By then, of course, the journeyer had also descended naked into the magical pond, to feel the weight of years lifted from his flesh; to feel his weathered skin smooth out, growing strong and supple again; to feel his spine grow straight and his eyes grow clear and his shoulders grow broad, as they had been before he started his quest, more years ago than he could count.

When they met, at the deepest part of the pond, she surprised him with an embrace.

"I am Cerile," she said. "I have been awaiting your arrival for longer than you can possibly know."

He couldn't speak. He knew only that she was right, that he had known her for an age far beyond the limited reach of his memory, that they had loved each other once, and would now love each other again.

They kissed, and she led him from the water, to a small cottage that had not been standing on the spot a heartbeat before. There were fine clothes waiting for him, to replace those torn to rags by his long journey. There was a feast, too, to fill the yawning void in his belly. There were other wonders too, things that could only exist in the home of a miracle-worker like Cerile: things he had not the wit to name, that glittered and whirred in odd corners, spinning soft music unlike any he had ever heard. He would have been dazzled by them had Cerile not also been there, to dazzle him even more.

But still, something gnawed at him.

It wasn't the wish, which seemed such a trivial little thing, now, a trifle not even worth mentioning, because Cerile in her love gave him everything any man could possibly want . . . and yet, yes, damn him, it was the wish, the miracle he'd waited his entire life to see, and had marched across kingdoms to find.

It had something to do with all those oceans he'd crossed, all those monsters he'd fought, all the winters he'd endured.

It was pride.

He stayed with her for a year and a day, in that little valley where the days themselves seemed written for them, where the gardens changed colors daily to fit their moods, and the stars danced whimsical little jigs to accompany the musical way she laughed at night. Even troubled as he was, he knew a happiness that he hadn't known for a long time, maybe not ever, certainly not for as far back as his limited memory recorded: not since sometime before the day, a lifetime before, when he'd found himself a stranger in a small fishing village, wholly unable to remember who he was or how he'd come to that place.

Then, late one night, at the end of their year together, he awoke tormented by the strange restlessness in his heart, and rose from their bed to walk alone by the edge of her private fountain of youth. The water had always reflected the stars, every other night he'd looked upon it; it had always seemed to contain an entirely self-contained universe, as filled with endless possibility as the one where he and Cerile lived and walked and breathed. But tonight, though there were plenty of stars in the sky, none were reflected on the pond surface. The water showed only a dark, inky blackness that reflected not possibility but the cold finality of a prison.

Cerile's beautiful voice rang out from somewhere in the darkness that suddenly surrounded him. "What is wrong, my love?"

"I was thinking," he said, without turning to face her. "That I journeyed all this distance and spent all this time here and never got around to asking you to grant my Wish."

"Is there any point?" she asked—and for the first time since he arrived, he heard in a voice an unsettling note of despair. "What could you possibly wish for that would be of any value to you here? Health? Strength? Eternal youth and beauty? You already have that, here. Love? Happiness? I've given you those, too. Riches? Power? Stay here and you can have as much of either as any man could possibly want."

"I know," he said. "They were all things I once thought I'd wish for when I found you. You gave them to me without waiting for me to wish for them. But my Wish is still hanging over my head, demanding to be used."

"You don't have to listen to it."

"I do. It's the only thing I own that I earned myself, that I can truly say you didn't give me. And if I don't use it, then everything I've done means nothing."

"Why don't you just wish that you can be content to always stay here with me, and love me forever, as I'll love you forever?"

He turned and faced her, seeing her forlorn and lost by the door of their cottage, wanting her more than everything he'd ever wanted before, feeling his own heart break at the knowledge that he'd caused the sorrow welling in her eyes. And for the first time he understood that they'd endured this moment hundreds or even thousands of times before, for as long as the sun had been a fire in the sky.

He said, "I'm sorry. I can't wish for that. I wish for the one thing I lost when I came here. A purpose. Something to struggle for. A reason to deserve everything you give me, whenever I manage to find my way back."

She granted his Wish, then fell to her knees and sobbed: not the tears of an omnipotent creature who controlled the earth and the stars, and could have had everything she ever wanted, but the tears of a lonely little girl who couldn't.

When she rose again, she approached the waters of eternal youth, and sat down beside them, knowing that she wouldn't feel their touch again until the inevitable day, still a lifetime away, when he would, all too briefly, return to her.

Someday, she swore, she'd make him so happy that he'd never Wish to leave.

Until then—

The journeyer was still a young man when he embarked on his search for the all-powerful witch Cerile.

He was bent and gray-haired a lifetime later when he found a map to her home in the tomb of the forgotten kings . . .

YOON HA LEE's work has appeared in *Lightspeed, The Magazine of Fantasy & Science Fiction, Clarkesworld, Fantasy Magazine, Ideomancer, Lady Churchill's Rosebud Wristlet, Farrago's Wainscot, Beneath Ceaseless Skies, Electric Velocipede,* and *Sybil's Garage.* She's also appeared in the anthologies *Twenty Epics, Japanese Dreams, In Lands That Never Were, Year's Best Fantasy #6,* and *Science Fiction: The Best of 2002.* Her poetry has appeared in such venues as *Jabberwocky, Strange Horizons, Star*Line, Mythic Delirium,* and *Goblin Fruit.* Learn more at yoonhalee.com.

Our next story involves some math. Wait, don't go! It's also got demon armies, a lie-detecting magic sword, bitter family drama, and all that good stuff, we promise. But there's some math too, or at least, mathematical concepts.

Yoon Ha Lee is a former high school math teacher, and her work often incorporates aspects of her training. Most of us tend to imagine magic as an easy path to power, a way of getting something for nothing, and we're enticed by the notion of flying through the air and hurling fireballs the moment we pick up our first wand. We tend to think of magic as something at which we would be naturally and effortlessly talented. But what if learning magic was a lot like learning math? What if you actually did have to learn a lot of math in order to perform magic? How many of us would stick with it?

Our next story presents a world in which magic and mathematics are inextricably linked, and in which solving equations is a matter of life or death. But don't worry, you won't need any calculus or trigonometry to enjoy this story. And no, this won't be on the test.

COUNTING THE SHAPES
YOON HA LEE

How many shapes of pain are there?
  Are any topologically equivalent?
  And is one of them death?

Biantha woke to a heavy knocking on the door and found her face pressed against a book's musty pages. She sat up and brushed her pale hair out of her face, trying to discern a pattern to the knocking and finding that the simplest one was impatience. Then she got to her feet and opened the door, since her warding spell had given her no warning of an unfriendly presence outside. Besides, it would be a little longer before the demons reached Evergard.

"Took your time answering the door, didn't you, Lady Biantha?" Evergard's gray-haired lord, Vathré, scowled at her. Without asking for permission, which he never did anyway, he strode past her to sweep his eyes over the flurry of papers that covered her desk. "You'd think that, after years of glancing at your work, I'd understand it."

"Some of the conjectures are probably gibberish anyway." She smiled at him, guessing that what frustrated him had little to do with her or the theorems that made her spells possible. Vathré visited her when he needed an ear detached from court intrigues. "What troubles you this time, my lord?"

He appropriated her one extra chair and gestured for her to sit at the desk, which she did, letting her smile fade. "We haven't much longer, Biantha. The demons have already overrun Rix Pass. No one agrees on when they'll get here. The astrologer refused to consult the stars, which is a first—claimed he didn't want to see even an iffy prediction—" Vathré looked away from her. "My best guess is that the demons will be here within a month. They still have to march, overwhelming army or no."

Biantha nodded. Horses barely tolerated demon-scent and went mad if forced to carry demons. "And you came to me for battle spells?" She could not keep the bitterness from her voice. The one time she had killed with a spell had been for a child's sake. It had not helped the child, as far as she knew.

"Do you have any battle spells?" he asked gravely.

"Not many." She leaned over and tapped the nearest pile of paper. "I was in the middle of this proof when I discovered that I'd have to review one of Yverry's theorems. I fell asleep trying to find it. Give me a few days and I can set up a battle spell that will kill any demons you've already managed to wound." Biantha saw the weariness in the lord's green eyes and flushed. "It isn't much, I know."

"That helps, but it isn't what I came for."

Dread opened at the pit of her stomach. "The Prophecy."

Vathré inclined his head.

"I've tried to pry some sense out of it ever since I learned of it, you know." She rubbed her eyes. "The poetry translates into shapes and equations that are simply intractable. I've tried every kind of analysis and transformation I know. If there's any hope in the rhymes, the rhythms, the ambiguities, don't ask me to show you where it is. You'd do better consulting the minstrels for a lecture on symbolism."

"I don't *trust* the minstrels." His brows drew together. "And any time I consult the other magicians, I get too many uncertainties to untangle. The seers and healers are hopeless. The astrologer gets headaches trying to determine where to start. The cartomancer gives me a dozen different *possibilities* each time she casts the cards. As far as the Prophecy is concerned, yours is the only kind of magic I can trust."

Biantha smiled wanly. "Which is why, of course, it's so limited." Sometimes she envied the astrologer, the cartomancer, the enchanters, the healers, the seers—magicians whose powers were less reliable but more versatile. "I'll work on it, my lord."

"A month," he reminded her.

She hesitated. "Have you declared your heir yet?"

Vathré eyed her. "Not you, too?"

She swallowed. "If you die, my lord, someone must carry on. Don't leave the succession in doubt. A problem may have several solutions, but some solutions can still be wrong."

"We've been over this before," he said. "Considering the current state of affairs, I'd have to declare a chain of succession down to the apprentice cook. If anyone survives, they can argue over it. My advisors can rule by council until then."

Biantha bowed her head and watched him leave.

Usually Biantha avoided Evergard's great hall. It reminded her of her former home, the demon emperor's palace, though the scents of lavender and lilacs drifted through the air, not the smell of blood; people smiled at her instead of bowing or curtsying rigidly. Musicians played softly while nobles chattered, idle soldiers gambled for pittances, and children scampered in and out, oblivious to the adults' strained voices. A few of the boys were fair-haired, like herself. Biantha closed her eyes briefly before turning along the walls, partly to avoid thinking about a particular fair-haired boy, partly because she had come to study the tapestries for inspiration.

The tapestries' colors remained as vibrant as they had been when she first swore fealty to Lord Vathré upon the Blade Fidora. Biantha had long ago determined the logic by which the tapestries had been arranged, and did not concern herself with it now. Instead, she inspected the scenes of the Nightbreak War.

Here was the Battle of Noiren Field, where webs of starlight blinded a thousand soldiers and angular silhouettes soared above, ready for the massacre. Here was General Vian on a blood bay destrier, leading a charge against a phalanx of demons. Here was amber-eyed Lady Chandal weeping over a fallen young man whose closed eyes might also have been amber, flowers springing up where her tears splashed onto the battlefield. Biantha swallowed and quickened her steps. One by one she passed the tapestries until she found what she sought.

Unlike the other Nightbreak tapestries, its border had been woven in rust rather than Evergard's colors, blue and black: rust for betrayal. She stared at the dispassionate face of Lord Mière, enchanter and traitor to Evergard. His had been a simpler magic than her own, drawing upon ritual and incantation. With it he had almost defeated the Watchlanders; only his daughter's knife had saved them.

Symmetry, she sighed. The one thing she had pried from the Prophecy was that it possessed a twisted symmetry. It hinted at two wars between the demons' empire and the Watchlands, and because records of the first war—the Nightbreak War—were scant, Biantha had yet to understood certain cantos, certain equations, that dealt with it. Hours with Evergard's minstrels and historians hadn't helped. Other than herself, only Vathré knew that there might be a second traitor among them.

Or that, because they had won the first war, they might lose the second, in a cruel mirroring transformation of history.

"Lady Biantha?"

She turned. "Yes?"

The captain—she did not know his name—bowed slightly. "It isn't often that we see you down here, my lady."

Biantha smiled wryly. "A bit too much noise for my work, and on occasion I test spells that might go wrong, sometimes fatally so. My chambers are shielded, but out here . . ."

In the demon emperor's court, her words would have been a veiled threat. Here, the captain nodded thoughtfully and gestured at the tapestry. "I was wondering why you were looking at this. Most people avoid it."

"I was thinking about the Prophecy," she said, retracing the intractable equations in her mind. There had to be a way to balance term against term, solve the system and read Evergard's future, but it continued to escape her. "I'm worried."

"We all are."

Biantha paused. "You said 'most people.' Does that include yourself?"

His mouth twisted. "No. It's a useful reminder. Do you ever wish you had stayed at the demon emperor's palace?"

She read honest curiosity in the captain's expression, not innuendo. "Never." She breathed deeply. "I started learning mathemagic there because magicians, even human magicians, are protected unless they do something foolish. Otherwise I would have been a slave or a soldier; I had no wish for the former and no heart, no talent, for the latter."

Such a small word, *foolish*, when the penalty it carried had given Biantha nightmares for years. She had seen the demon emperor touch his serpent-eyed scepter to a courtesan's perfumed shoulder, as if in blessing; had been unable to avert her gaze before she saw the woman's eyes boiling away and splinters of bone erupting through the rouged skin.

The captain looked down. "I'm sorry to have reminded you, my lady."

"A useful reminder," she echoed. "And what does this portrait of Lord Mière remind you of, if I may ask?"

"Honor, and those who lose it," he said. "Lord Mière was my great-grandfather."

Biantha blinked and saw that there was, indeed, a resemblance in the structure of his face. Her eyes moved to the tapestry's rust border. What had driven Mière to betrayal? It occurred to her, not for the first time, that she herself had fled the demon emperor's court—but the symmetry here seemed incomplete. "Do you think there's hope for us?" she asked the captain.

He spread his hands, studying Biantha's face as she had his just a moment before. "There are those of us who say we must have a chance, or you would have returned to the demons."

She felt herself flush—and then laughed, though that laughter came perilously close to tears. "I have rarely known demons to forgive. Neither have they forgiven Evergard their defeat in the Nightbreak War."

"More's the pity," said the captain, frowning thoughtfully, and took his leave.

For us or the demons? Biantha thought.

Symmetry. The word haunted Biantha through the days and nights as she struggled with the Prophecy. She had wondered, after meeting the captain, if it meant something as simple as her flight from the demons, the fact that one of Lord Mière's descendants survived here. The ballads said Mière had but a single daughter, named Paienne, but they made no mention of her after she saved the Watchlands.

The secret eluded her, slipped away from her, sent her into dreams where dizzying shifts in perspective finally drove her to awaken. Biantha turned to her tomes, seeking clues in others' mathemagical speculations; when she tired of that, she memorized her battle spells, bowing to the heartless logic of war. And went back to the tomes, their treasury of axioms and theorems, diagrams and discussions.

She was leafing through Athique's *Transformations* when someone imitated thunder on her door. Biantha put down the book and opened the door. "Yes?"

The herald bowed elaborately. "A meeting of the court, my lady. Lord Vathré wishes you to attend."

"I'll be there." Firmly, she shut the door and changed into her formal robes as swiftly as she could. Biantha had attended few court meetings: at first, because Vathré had been uncertain of her loyalties, then because of her awkwardness as a foreigner, and finally because she rarely had anything to contribute to matters of state and found her time better spent working on her magic. That Vathré should summon her now was unusual.

She was right. For once the attendants and servants had been cleared out, and the court had arrayed itself along the sides of the throne room while Vathré and his advisers sat at the head. She took her place between the astrologer and Lady Iastre. The astrologer wore his habitual frown, while the lady's face was cool and composed, revealing nothing. Biantha knew better, after playing draughts or rithmomachia against Iastre once a week in less hectic times: Iastre's face only went blank when she anticipated trouble.

"We have a guest today," said Vathré at his driest. His eyes might have flicked to Biantha, too briefly for her to tell for certain.

On cue, the guards led in a man who wore black and red and gold, stripped of his sword—she knew there had been a sword, by the uniform. The style of his clothing spoke of the demons' realm, and the only one besides the emperor who dared appear in those colors was his champion. The emperor's champion, her son.

A challenge? Biantha thought, clenching her hands so they would not shake. *Has Marten come to challenge Vathré?* But surely the emperor knew Evergard held different customs and would hardly surrender the Watchlands' fate to a duel's outcome.

Hopelessly, she studied the man who had so suddenly disrupted her memories of the child who hid flowers and leaves between the pages of her books, who climbed onto her desk to look out the window at the soldiers drilling. He had her pale hair, a face very like hers. His hands, relaxed at his sides, were also hers, though deadlier; Biantha knew of the training an emperor's champion underwent and had little faith that the guards could stop him from killing Vathré if he wished. But Marten's eyes belonged to a man Biantha had tried to forget, who had died attempting to keep her from leaving the palace with their child.

Silence descended upon the throne room. Vathré's court noted the resemblance, though Marten had yet to spot his mother. He looked straight ahead at Evergard's lord.

Vathré stood and drew the Blade Fidora from its sheath. It glimmered like crystal, like the first light of morning, like tears. The lords and ladies glanced at each other, but did not set whispers spinning through the room. Biantha, too, kept silent: a word spoken false in the unsheathed sword's presence would cause it to weep or bleed; the magic had driven men and women mad, and no lord of Evergard used it lightly.

"I am trying to decide whether you are very thoughtless or very clever," Vathré said softly. "Who are you and why are you here?"

"I was the sword at the emperor's side," he answered, "and that sword was nameless." The pale-haired man closed his eyes, opened them. "My name is Marten. I came because the emperor has thousands of swords now, to do his bidding; and I no longer found that bidding to my taste."

Vathré glanced down at the Blade Fidora. Its color remained clear and true. "An interesting time to change your loyalties—if, indeed, they've changed. You might have found a better way to leave than by showing up here in full uniform, scaring the guards out of their wits."

"I left when the demons were . . . subduing a village," Marten said flatly. "I don't know the village's name. I hardly had time to find more suitable attire, my lord, and on campaign one dresses in uniform as a matter of course. To do otherwise would have aroused suspicion."

"And you weren't afraid of being caught and killed on the spot?" one of the advisers demanded.

He shrugged. "I was taught three spells in my training. One allowed me to walk unharmed through the palace wards. One calls fire from blood. And the last lets me pass by like the dream of a ghost."

Biantha glanced at the Blade Fidora and its unwavering light.

Lady Iastre coughed. "Forgive me if I'm less well-informed than I ought to be," she said, "and slow to react as well—but you mentioned being 'on campaign.' Is this a common thing, that 'the sword at the emperor's side' should be out in the field?"

Marten's eyes moved toward the source of the voice, and so he caught sight of Biantha. He inhaled sharply. Biantha felt her face freeze, though she longed to smile at the stranger her son had become. *Answer,* she wished him. *Say you've come to me after so many years—*

Marten gathered himself and said, "I came to warn you, if nothing else; death is a price I have taken from many." His voice shook, but he continued to face Vathré squarely. "The demon emperor has come, and your battles will be the harder for it." Then the whispers began, and even Iastre cast troubled eyes toward

Biantha; the light of the Blade Fidora reflected all the shades of fear, all the colors of despair, that were voiced. "Please," Marten said, raising his voice but slightly, "let me help. My lord, I may be slow in learning that there is more to war than following orders. That there are people who die for their homes or their families—"

"Families," Biantha repeated, tasting bitterness. So calm, his face, like polished metal. She felt Iastre's hand on her arm and forced a smile.

The whispers had died down, and Marten faltered. "I know how the emperor thinks," he said at last. "Let me help you there, my lord, or have me killed. Either way, you will have taken the emperor's champion from him."

So pale, his face, like Fidora's light. Biantha caught her breath, waiting for Vathré to speak.

Lines of strain etched the lord's face as he left the throne to stand before Marten. "Will you swear fealty to the Watchlands and their lord, then?"

Marten did not flinch. "Yes."

Yes, echoed Biantha, doubt biting her heart. She had not known, when she first came to Evergard, what powers the Blade Fidora possessed. A magician-smith had died in its forging, that there might never again be a traitor like Lord Mière. Vathré had questioned Biantha, as he had just questioned Marten, and the first part of the sword's virtue had been plain to her, a mirror of spoken minds.

Only later had Vathré told her the second part, that a false oath sworn upon the sword killed the oath-taker. Once an heir to Evergard had sworn guardianship to the Watchlands and their people and fallen dead. Once a weary soldier had woken Evergard's lady three hours before dawn to confess a betrayal planned, and then committed suicide. Biantha had no desire to find her son the subject of another story, another song. How had Paienne felt, she wondered suddenly, when her father's treachery became part of the Nightbreak War's history?

Marten laid his hand upon the glass-clear blade. "I swear it." Then, swallowing, he looked directly at Biantha.

She could not bring herself to trust him, even after the long years, when he wore a uniform like his father's. This time, she did turn away.

"There's something sinful," said Iastre, fingers running round and round a captured draughts piece, "in sitting here playing a game when our world is falling apart."

Biantha smiled uncertainly and considered her options. "If I stayed in my room and fretted about it all the time, I should go mad." She nudged one of her pieces to a new square, musing on how the symmetry of the game—red on black, black on black—had soon been spoiled by their moves.

"I hear it was Marten's planning that kept the demons from overrunning Silverbridge so far."

She looked up and saw Iastre's worried expression. "A good thing, I suppose—especially considering that the emperor now has a personal reason for wanting to humble the Watchlands."

"Surely you don't think he should have stayed in the emperor's service," Iastre protested.

Oh, but he did once, Biantha did not say. "It's your move."

A snort. "Don't change the subject on me now. You fled the emperor's palace too, if you'll recall."

"Too well," she agreed. She had slept poorly the first few years at Evergard, hearing danger in the footfalls that passed by her door and dreaming of the emperor's serpent-eyed scepter upon her own shoulder. "But I left in a time of peace, and as terrible a crime as I had committed, I was only a human mathemagician. Besides,"—and Biantha drew in a shaky breath—"they knew they had my son: punishment enough."

Iastre shook her head and finally made her move. "He's here now, and he may be our only hope."

"That," she said, "is what worries me."

Even here, playing draughts, Biantha found no escape from Marten. She had spotted him once in the courtyard, sparring against Evergard's best soldiers while a healer and several enchanters looked on, lest the former champion seek a life instead of a touch. At mealtimes in the great hall she took to eating at the far end of the high table; yet over the clinking glasses and silverware, the tense voices and rustling clothes, Biantha heard Marten and Vathré speaking easily with each other. Evergard's lord trusted Marten—they all trusted Marten now, while she dared not.

Like a pendulum, her thoughts swung between her son and Paienne, her son and Lord Mière. Late at night, when she walked the battlements listening vainly for the footfalls of marching soldiers, feeling betrayal's cold hand in every tremor of the wind, she remembered tales of the Nightbreak War. Biantha had never put much faith in the minstrels' embellished ballads, but the poetry preyed upon her fears.

Working with fragments of history and the military reports that came in daily, she attempted to map past onto future, battle onto battle . . . betrayal onto betrayal. And failed, over and over. And cursed the Prophecy, staring at the worn and inscrutable pages, alone in her room. It was during one of those bouts that a familiar knocking startled her from her work.

Marten? thought Biantha involuntarily. But she had learned the rhythm of

Vathré's tread, and when she opened the door she knew who waited behind it. The twin edges of relief and disappointment cut her heart.

The gray-haired man looked her up and down, and scowled. "I thought you might be overworking yourself again."

She essayed a smile, stepping aside so he could enter. "Overwork, my lord? Tell that to the soldiers who train, and fight, and die for it, or see their friends die for it. Tell that to the cook or the servants in the keep."

"There are ways and ways of work, my dear." He paced around the chamber, casting a curious eye over her bookcase and her cluttered desk, then rested a hand on her shoulder. "Perhaps I should come back later, when you've rested—and I do mean rest, not sitting in bed to read your books rather than sitting at your desk."

Biantha craned her head back to glance at him. "At least tell me why you came."

"Marten," he said bluntly, releasing her shoulder.

She flinched.

"You're hurting the boy," Vathré said. "He's been here quite a while and you haven't said a word to him."

She arched an eyebrow. "He's not the boy I left behind, my lord." Her voice nearly broke.

"I'm old enough to call you a girl, Lady Biantha. Don't quibble. Even I can't find cause to mistrust him, and the years have made me paranoid."

"Oh?" She ran her fingers over her copy of the Prophecy, worn smooth by years of on-and-off study. By all accounts, Marten's advice was sound—but the demons kept coming.

"I'm sending him to command at Silverbridge." Vathré shook his head. "We've held out as long as we can, but it looks like our efforts have been no more than a delaying action. I haven't told the council yet, but we're going to have to withdraw to Aultgard." He exhaled softly. "Marten will keep the demons occupied while the bulk of the army retreats."

Biantha stared at him.

"The soldiers are coming to trust him, you know," he remarked. "He's perhaps the best tactician Evergard has seen in the past couple generations, and I want to see if that trust is justified."

She closed her eyes and said, "A gamble, my lord. Wouldn't you do better to put someone else in charge?"

Vathré ignored her question. "I thought you should know before I announce it."

"Thank you, my lord." Biantha paused, then added, "Do you know where Marten might be at the moment?"

He smiled sadly. "Haunting the battlements, hoping you will stop by."

She bowed her head and, after he had left, went to search for her son. Biantha found him by the southern tower, a sword sheathed at his back. Even now it disconcerted her to see him in the dress of Evergard's soldiers, as if her mind refused to surrender that first image of Marten standing before the court in red and black and gold.

"Mother," he said, clasping his hands behind his back.

Slowly, reluctantly, she faced him. "I'm here."

Moonlight pooled in his eyes and glittered in the tears that streaked his face. "I remember," he said without accusation. "I was seven years old and you told me to pack. You were arguing with Father."

Biantha nodded. Marten had nearly reached the age where he would have to begin training as either a magician or a soldier, or forfeit what little protection his parents' status gave him. Over the years, as their son grew older, she spoke to her husband of leaving the demons' empire to seek refuge in the Watchlands or the realms further east. He always treated her kindly, without ever turning an eye to the courtesans—demon and human both—who served those the emperor favored.

Yet Biantha had never forgotten her husband's puzzlement, molting slowly into anger, that she should wish to leave a court that sheltered them, though it did nothing to shelter others. She could not reconcile herself to the demons' casual cruelty: one of the emperor's nieces sent, after an ill-advised duel, to redeem her honor by riding a horse to the mines of Sarmont and back, five days and back forcing a terrified beast to carry her. The pale-eyed assassin who had fallen from favor after killing the rebellious lady of Reis Keep, solely because he had left evidence of his work. Children drowned after a plague blinded them and clouded their wits. If anything, the demons were as cruel to each other as to the humans who lived among and below them, but Biantha had found less and less comfort in that knowledge.

"I stood in the doorway," Marten went on, "trying to understand. Then Father was weeping—"

She had said to her husband, *If you will not come, then I must go without you.*

"—and he drew his sword against you."

"And I killed him," Biantha said, dry-mouthed. "I tried to get you to come with me, but you wouldn't leave him. You started to cry. I had little time, and there were ever guards nearby, listening for anything amiss. So I went alone. It would have been my death to stay after murdering one of the emperor's officers. In the end, the emperor's trust meant more to him than you or I."

"Please don't leave me again," Marten whispered. He stood straight-backed in the darkness, the hilt of the sword at his back peering over his shoulder like a sleepy eye, but his face was taut. "I am leaving for Silverbridge tomorrow."

"Will you be at the forefront?"

"It would be unwise." His mouth tightened for a moment. "I will be giving orders."

"To kill." *And, perhaps, be killed,* she wanted to say, but the words fluttered in her throat.

Marten met her gaze calmly. "It is war, Mother."

"It is now," she agreed, "but it wasn't before. I know what it is to be the emperor's champion. 'The sword at the emperor's side,' you said. The others heard the words only; they have never lain awake and sleepless for memory of bloodstains on a pale rug, or because of the sudden, silenced cries at night. How many fell to your blade, Marten?"

"I came to follow you when I started losing count." His eyes were dry, now, though Biantha saw the shapes of pain stirring behind them. "When the numbers started slipping out of my grasp."

Biantha held silence before her like a skein of threads that wanted words to untangle it.

He lifted a hand, hesitated, let it drop. "I wanted to talk to you once, if never again. Before I go to Silverbridge where the demons await."

She smiled at him, then. But always the suspicion remained that he had some way of breaking his oath to Vathré, that the demon emperor had sent him to ensure the Watchlands' downfall through some subtle plan—or, more simply, that he had come to betray the mother he had abandoned, who had abandoned him; she no longer knew which.

"Go, then," said Biantha, neither promise nor peril in her voice, and left him to await dawn alone.

Four days later, Biantha stood before her bookcase, eyes roaming aimlessly over her collection of mathemagical works, some in the tight, angular script of the demon empire, others in the ornate writing common to the Watchlands' scholars. *There has to be something useful,* she told herself, even after having scoured everything that looked remotely relevant. Now, more than ever, she wished she had talent for another of the magical disciplines, which did not rely on memorized proofs or the vagaries of inspiration, though none of them had ever seemed to get far with the Prophecy.

Would that it were a straightforward problem—

Biantha froze. The Prophecy did not describe the idealized spaces with which she had grown accustomed to dealing, but the tangles of truth, the interactions of demons and humans, the snarls of cause and effect and relation. Even the astrologer admitted privately that his predictions, on occasion, failed spectacularly where people were involved. She had been trying to linearize the cantos: the wrong approach.

Evergard's treasurer had once teased her about the cost of paper, though she took care to waste as little as possible. She located a pile of empty sheets in a drawer and set them on her desk, opening her copy of the Prophecy to the first page. After a moment, Biantha also retrieved Sarielle's *Speculations, Spells and Stranger Sets*, sparing a glance for the 400-line poem in the back; Sarielle of Rix had fancied herself a poet. She had passed evenings lingering over the book's carefully engraved figures and diagrams, curves that Sarielle had labeled "pathological" for their peculiarities.

Symmetry. That which remained changeless. Red pieces upon black and black upon black at the start of a draughts match. A ballad that began and ended with the same sequence of measures; and now that Biantha turned her thoughts in this direction, she remembered a song that traveling minstrels had performed before the court, voice after voice braiding into a whole that imitated each part. Her image in the mirror. And now, Sarielle's pathological curves, where a segment of the proper proportion spawned yet more such segments.

Methodically, she went through the Prophecy, searching for these other symmetries, for the solution that had eluded her for so long. Late into the night, throat parched because she had drained her pitcher and dared not break her concentration by fetching another or calling a servant, Biantha placed *Speculations, Spells and Stranger Sets* to one side and thumbed through the appendix to Athique's *Infinities*. Athique and Sarielle, contemporaries, had been opposites as far as titles went. She reached the approximations of various shapes, sieves and flowers, ferns and laces, that no mortal hand could craft.

One page in particular struck her: shapes built from varying polygons with various "pathologies," as Athique dubbed them in what Biantha suspected had been a jab at Sarielle's would-be wordsmithing, repeating a procedure to the borders of infinity. The Prophecy harbored greater complexities, but she wondered if her solution might be one of many algorithms, many possibilities. Her eyes flooded: a lifetime's work that she had uncovered, explored briefly by mathemagicians before her, and she had little time in which to seek a solution that helped the Watchlands.

Even after she had snuffed the lamp and curled into bed, a headache devouring her brain, words still burned before her eyes: *Symmetry. Pathologies. Infinity.*

Only a few weeks later, Biantha found herself walking aimlessly down a corridor, freeing her mind from the Prophecy's tyrannous grip, when Lady Iastre shook her shoulder. "They're back, Biantha," she said hurriedly. "I thought you'd like to be there to greet them."

"Who's back?"

"Your son. And those who survived Silverbridge."

Those who survived. Biantha closed her eyes, shaking. "If only the demons would leave us alone—"

The other woman nodded sadly. "But it's not happening. The emperor will soon be at Evergard itself, is the news I've been hearing. Come on."

"I can't," she said, and felt as though the keep were spinning around her while pitiless eyes peered through the walls. "Tell him—tell Marten—I'm glad he's back." It was all she could think to say, a message for her son—a message that she would not deliver in person, because the urgency of the situation had jarred her thoughts back to the Prophecy.

"Biantha!" Iastre cried, too late to stop her.

In bits and pieces she learned the rest of the story, by eavesdropping benignly on dinner conversations and the servants' gossip. The emperor had indeed forsaken his court for the battlefield, perhaps because of Evergard's stubborn resistance. None of this surprised her, except when a curly-haired herald mentioned the serpent-eyed scepter. To her knowledge that scepter had never left the empire—unless, and the thought sickened her, the demons had begun to consider Evergard part of their empire. It had turned Silverbridge, the shining bridge of ballad, into rust and tarnish, and even now the demons advanced.

Vathré gave a few permission to flee further east with their families, those whose presence mattered little to the coming siege. Others prepared to fight, or die, or both; the mock-battles that Biantha sometimes watched between the guards grew more grim, more intent. She and Iastre agreed that the time for draughts and rithmomachia had passed, as much as she would have welcomed the distraction.

As for Marten—she saw almost nothing of him except the terrible weariness that had taken up residence in his face, as though he had survived a torture past bearing. Biantha grieved for him as a mother; as a mathemagician, she had no comfort to offer, for her own helplessness threatened to overwhelm her. Perhaps he in his turn sensed this, and left her alone.

Day by day the demons came closer, to the point where she could stand on the battlements and see the baleful lights in the distance: the orange of campfires, the gold and silver of magefires. Day by day the discussions grew more frantic, more resigned.

At last, one morning, the horns blazed high and clear through the air, and the siege of Evergard began. Biantha took her place on the parapets without saying any farewells, though some had been said to her, and watched while archers fired into the demons' massed ranks. Not long after, magefire rolled over their hastily raised shields, and she prepared her own spells. Only when the demons began to draw back and prepare a second attack did she call upon powers that required meticulous proofs, held in her mind like the memory of a favorite song—or a child in her arms.

She gathered all the shapes of pain that afflicted the demons and twisted them into death. Red mists obscured her vision as the spell wrenched her own soul, sparing her the need to watch the enemy falling. Yet she would have to use the spell again and again before the demons' mathemagicians shaped a ward against it. Those who shared her art rarely ventured into battle, for this reason: it often took too long to create attacks or adapt to them. A theorem needed for a spell might take years to discover, or turn out to be impossible; and inspiration, while swift, was sometimes unreliable. She had seen mathemagicians die from careless assumptions in spellcasting.

By midday Biantha no longer noticed the newly fallen corpses. She leaned against the wall's cold stone—and glimpsed black and red and gold in the distance: the demon emperor, carrying the serpent-eyed scepter that she remembered too clearly. For a moment she thought of the Blade Fidora and cursed the Prophecy's inscrutable symmetry. "No," she whispered. Only if the emperor were certain of victory would he risk himself in the front lines, and a cold conviction froze her thoughts.

Marten. He's counting on Marten to help him.

She had to find Vathré and warn him. She knew where he would be and ran, despite the archers' protests that she endangered herself. "My lord!" she cried, grieving already, because she saw her fair-haired son beside gray-haired Vathré, directing the defense. "My lord! The emperor—" Biantha nearly tripped, caught herself, continued running.

Vathré turned, trusting her, and then it happened.

The emperor raised his scepter, and darkness welled forth to batter Evergard's walls. In the darkness, colors moved like the fire of dancing prisms; silence reigned for a second, strangely disturbing after the clamor of war. Then the emperor's spell ended, leaving behind more dead than the eye could count at a glance. Broken shapes, blood, weapons twisted into deadly metal flowers, a wind like the breath of disease.

Biantha stared disbelievingly over the destruction and saw that the demons who had stood in the spell's path had died as well; saw that the emperor had come forward to spare his own soldiers, not—she hoped not—because he knew he had a traitor in the Watchlanders' ranks. So much death, and all they had been able to do, she and the other magicians, was watch.

"Mercy," Vathré breathed.

"The scepter," Marten said harshly. "Its unspoken name is Decay."

She looked across at the gates and sneezed, dust stinging her nostrils. Already those who had fallen were rotting, flesh blackening and curling to reveal bone; Evergard's sturdy walls had become cracked and mottled.

Marten was shouting orders for everyone to abandon that section of wall before it crumbled. Then he looked at her and said, "We have to get down. Before it spreads. You too, my lord."

Vathré nodded curtly and offered Biantha his arm; Marten led the way down, across footing made newly treacherous. The walls whispered dryly behind them; she flinched at the crash as a crenel broke off and plummeted.

"—use that scepter again?" she heard the lord asking Marten as she concentrated on her footing.

"No," she and her son both said. Biantha continued, "Not so far from the seat of his power and without the blood sacrifices. Not against wood or stone. But a touch, against living flesh, is another matter."

They had reached safety of sorts with the others who had fled the crumbling section of wall. "What of the Prophecy?" Vathré asked her, grimacing as he cast his gaze over the morning's carnage.

"Prophecy?" Marten repeated, looking at them strangely.

Perhaps he had not heard, or failed to understand what he heard, in the brief time he had been at Evergard. Biantha doubted he had spent much time with the minstrels. At least he was not—she prayed not—a traitor, as she had thought at first. Breath coming hard, she looked around, listened to the cries of the wounded, and then, all at once, the answer came to her, one solution of several.

Perspective. Time and again she had brooded over the Prophecy and the second war it foretold. *The rhymes, the rhythms, the ambiguities,* she had said to Vathré not long ago. She had thought about the strange symmetry, the Nightbreak War's traitor—but failed to consider that, in the Prophecy's second war, the corresponding traitor might betray the demons. The demons, not the Watchlands.

Last time, Lord Mière had betrayed the Watchlands, and died at Paienne's hand—father and daughter, while Biantha and Marten were mother and son. But the mirror was imperfect, as the twisted symmetry already showed her. Marten did not have to die, and there was still hope for victory.

"The emperor is still down there," said Vathré quietly. "It seems that if someone were to stop him, we could hold the keep. Hold the keep, and have a chance of winning."

"A challenge," Biantha breathed, hardly aware that those around them were listening avidly, for on this hung Evergard's fate. "Challenge the emperor. He has his honor, strange as it may seem to us. He lost his champion; will he turn down an opportunity to slay, or be slain by, that champion?"

Had there been such a challenge in the Nightbreak War? The ballads, the histories, failed to say. No matter. They were not living a ballad, but writing their own lines to the song.

Vathré nodded, seeing the sense in her words; after all, she had lived in the demons' realm. Then he unfastened the sheath of his sword from his belt and held it out to Marten. "Take the sword," he said.

If she was wrong, giving the Blade Fidora to him was unrivaled folly. But they no longer had a choice, if they meant to take advantage of the Prophecy's tangled possibilities.

He blanched. "I can't. I don't even know who the heir is——" probably because Vathré *still* had not declared the succession. "I haven't the right."

Biantha gazed at the gates, now twisted into rusty skeins. The captain of the guard had rallied the remaining troops and was grimly awaiting the demons' advance.

The lord of Evergard said, exasperated, "I *give* you the right. This isn't the time for questions or self-recriminations. *Take the sword.*"

Resolutely, Marten accepted the Blade Fidora. He grasped the sword's hilt, and it came clear of the scabbard, shining faintly. "I'm sorry for what I have done in the past," he whispered, "even though that doesn't change what was done. Help me now."

"Hurry," said Biantha, guessing the battle's shape. "The emperor will soon come to claim his prize, *our* home, and you must be there to stop him." She stood on her toes and kissed him on the cheek: a mother's kiss, which she had not given him for too many years. She called to mind every protective spell she could think of and forged them together around him despite her exhaustion. "Go with my blessing." *And please come back to me.* After losing him once, Biantha did not mean to lose him again.

"And go with mine," Vathré echoed.

He ducked his head and moved away at a run. Shivering, Biantha tried to gather the strength for more magic against the demons, to influence the Prophecy in their favor. She felt as if she were a formula in an old book, a creature of faded ink and yellowed paper.

As she and Vathré watched, Marten shoved through the soldiers at the gate, pausing only to exchange a few words with some of his comrades. They parted for him, wondering that he and not Vathré held the Blade Fidora; Vathré waved at them in reassurance. Past the gates were the emperor and his elites, dressed in rich colors, standing in near-perfect formation.

"Traitor," said the emperor to Marten in the cool voice that had never revealed anything but mockery; demon and human both strained to hear him. "Do you think Evergard's blade will protect you?"

In answer Marten swung the sword toward the emperor's exposed throat, where veins showed golden through the translucent skin. The elites reacted by moving to surround him while the emperor brought his serpent-eyed scepter up in a parry. The soldiers of Evergard, in their turn, advanced in Marten's defense. Biantha felt a hysterical laugh forming: the soldiers of both sides looked as though they had choreographed their motions, like dancers.

Now, straining to see what was happening, she realized why the emperor had chosen her son for his champion. Several of the elites saw clearly the blows that would kill them, yet failed to counter in time. Yet her eyes were drawn to the emperor himself, and she sucked in her breath: the emperor appeared to be aiming at a woman who had crippled one of the elites, but Biantha saw the twist in the scepter's trajectory that would bring it around to strike Marten. Even a traitor champion could not survive a single touch of the scepter; it would weaken him beyond his ability to recover.

"Marten!" she screamed. He was all she had left of her old home and its decadent intrigues; of a man with gentle hands who had loved her within the narrow limits of court life; of her family. The emperor had stolen him from her for so long—

Mathemagical intuition launched her past the meticulous lemmas and lines of a proof, panic giving her thoughts a hawk's wings. Biantha spun one more spell. Symmetry: the emperor's attack became Marten's, in spaces too strange for the mind to imagine. The Blade Fidora went true to its target, while the scepter missed entirely, and it was the emperor's golden blood that showered Marten's hands.

I'm sorry for everything, Marten, thought Biantha, and folded out of consciousness.

The minstrels who survived the Siege of Evergard made into song the deaths, the desperation, the duel between the demon emperor and he who was now heir to the Watchlands. Biantha, for her part, listened and grieved in her own way for those who had died . . . for Mière's great-grandson. There was more to any story, she had learned, than what the minstrels remembered; and this was as true of herself, her husband, her son.

Biantha wrote only two lines in the margin of an unfinished book—a book of her own theorems.

There are too many shapes of love to be counted.
   One of them is forgiveness.

It was a conjecture, not a proof, but Biantha knew its truth nonetheless. After the ink had dried, she left her room with its well-worn books and went to the great hall where Vathré and Iastre, and most especially Marten, expected her for dinner.

for Ch'mera, and for those who teach math

LEV GROSSMAN is the author of three novels: *Warp, Codex,* and *The Magicians.* He is also a world-renowned critic and technology writer, having been published in such venues as *The New York Times, Salon.com, Entertainment Weekly, The Wall Street Journal,* and *The Village Voice.* He is also the long-time book reviewer for *Time Magazine.* He is currently working on a sequel to *The Magicians,* which is due out in 2011. Learn more at levgrossman.com.

Grossman's recent novel *The Magicians* takes a jaded look at magical tales in the Harry Potter/Narnia mode. Grossman's protagonist Quentin Coldwater is a shy, bright high school senior with an interest in fantasy novels and stage magic who one day finds himself transported to a secretive magical academy called Brakebills. But this is no delightful voyage of wonder and discovery. Magic, it turns out, is mind-numbingly tedious to learn, and what do you do with your life after you graduate? The instructors at Brakebills are unhinged and often callous, and getting along with the other students is as painful and complicated as in the real world. Finally Quentin begins to believe that he can find a way into a real fantasy world—one full of quests and talking animals—but that doesn't exactly go according to plan either.

George R.R. Martin says, "*The Magicians* is to *Harry Potter* as a shot of Irish whiskey is to a glass of weak tea." Our next tale is set in the same universe as *The Magicians,* and shows what some young wizards get up to when they're done with studying.

ENDGAME
LEV GROSSMAN

It was morning rush hour and the subway station was packed. The platform was choked with people: they bunched up at the stairs and wherever construction made the space too narrow and they had to walk in single file. Some of them had thought it necessary to bring an umbrella and some of them hadn't.

They were all trying to hurry while at the same time not touch each other or look directly at each other or acknowledge in any way that there was anybody else on the platform with them. They made themselves human black holes: no information about their interior lives, if they had any, escaped through their faces. A train pulled in, and everybody raised their hands to their ears in unison at the scream of metal on metal.

A pretty young woman with short dark hair stood by a metal pylon at the edge of the platform, just short of the nubby yellow warning strip. She kept her back to the tracks, watching the crowd shuffle by her. Trains came and went, but she didn't get on any of them. She just stood there. The only other person doing the same thing was an old man in a dashiki sitting on a milk crate under the stairs, who was playing "Margaritaville" over and over again on a steelpan.

The young woman had been excited when she first arrived, but she'd been standing there for two hours now, starting at six in the morning, and her excitement was starting to pall. It was separating out into boredom and jitteriness, the way the frosting on a birthday cake that's been left out too long separates into butter and sugar. She wasn't especially enjoying "Margaritaville," which the old man in the dashiki rendered slowly and lovingly, with a lot of swelling tremolos and rallentandos. She leaned back against the iron pillar, bumpy with hundreds of coats of burnt-orange house paint, thinking bored and jittery thoughts, and let the waves of people wash past her. Here they were, the winners of humanity's great historical lottery, living in the richest city in the world, in the richest period of human civilization ever, and they were trudging to work in a rat-infested cement cavern on their way to stare at computer screens for eight hours. What happened here? Whose fault was it? Who had betrayed whom? And yes, real live rats. She'd seen six so far.

She just wanted it to start already. She looked at her watch. The fug in the air was rich and capricious—steam, sweat, machine oil, cheese, shit—Jesus, you took your life in your hands every time you breathed in. It was only about the third time she'd ever even *been* in a subway station.

She glanced down the platform to where Rob was standing, his gawky curly head bobbing and swiveling above the crowd like an ostrich's, his mouth never quite completely closed. They were supposed to make eye contact every five minutes. That was part of the system. Sean would be somewhere down the other end. The three of them were the stoppers. She looked at her watch, then back at the crowd.

The thing was, it was taking too long. It had already taken too long. Way too long. She looked at her watch again: 8:07.

Possibly they hadn't come, or they hadn't come this way, but she didn't believe it. They had to come this way; tactically it was over-determined ten times over, and plus they had good intel. But the thing was, they didn't have all that far to come, and they wouldn't have waited this long. They must have slipped through the net. Maybe their guises were better than anticipated. Something new. They'd be at the goal soon if somebody didn't chase them down. Probably they were already there, except that then the turn would have ended.

If she could just find them she could take them. She knew she could. It might already be too late. Anyway she had to pee.

She bit her lip and looked at Rob again, gave him the OK sign. Then, when he looked away, she stepped back from the pylon, ditched her prop purse in the trash—*if you see something, say something*—and joined the crowd that was slowly trying to feed itself up the stairs. She was going off *piste*, Sean would say. Off the reservation. They would murder her if she was wrong, *destroy* her, but wasn't that why she was a stopper? She took the big chances nobody else would. So.

Anyway if she was wrong she'd be back in position in a couple of minutes. No harm no foul. As she passed the man in the dashiki, he stopped covering Jimmy Buffett and stood up abruptly. She made a curious, contorted sign with her fingers and whispered a word in Farsi. He sat down again and face-planted gently into his steelpan, his sticks clattering on the cement. *Some people claim that there's a woooooooooman to blame* . . .

Now she was moving around and in play it was all different. The scene had unfrozen, it was no longer a photograph but a movie—starring her. She could breathe again; it was like she'd taken a hit off an inhaler. The early morning fog was burning off. This was the good part. And when the going was good, nobody was better at it than she was. She tried to keep her eyes glazed and empty like everybody else, but she was full of crazy energy. She wanted to grin like a loon.

Everybody else looked so *normal*. Even the freaks were freaky in a normal way. She slowed her pace with an effort. *Walk like a regular person, asshole.*

The flow of the crowd bore her up the iron-shod cement stairs to the concourse level. At the turnstiles she did a mirror-image buck-and-wing dance with a guy wearing Prada and a novelty beard who wanted to come in the same turnstile she was going out. That took an amazingly long time to sort out, by which time the clock in the token booth already read 8:11.

The hallways of the concourse radiated out around her in all directions. She counted five exits and they all looked wrong. No time. Pick one. She stopped. The crowd was thinning out around her. No one was giving up any obvious tells. The turnstiles clattered and chirped incessantly in the background, at slightly different pitches, like a chorus of peeping frogs.

She felt a stab of panic. She could double back to the platform, it wasn't too late. But the turn would be over soon. There were rules.

"Shee-it," she said out loud.

She lifted the brass and mother-of-pearl opera glasses that hung on a chain around her neck, so tiny they looked like a toy, and scanned the crowd.

And you know what? She'd been one hundred percent right. Young man, mid-twenties, sandy hair, olive houndstooth jacket with leather elbow patches, could pass for a pussy-chasing editorial assistant at Simon & Schuster except for the crowd of glowing icons over his head, bobbing along in time with his steps: numbers and Greek letters and sundry more obscure symbols in fluorescent green. He was trudging up the concourse with the rest of the straights, not a care in the world.

And on the same bearing, about ten feet in back of him: an upper east side matron, complete with pearls and fur jacket. Full civilian drag. A dense configuration of ochre italic writing hovered above her quaffed, steel-grey head, with two satellite stars spinning in place over her shoulders. They'd sent a captain.

They couldn't be working together. It was practically impossible. There were rules, rules, rules. Well, either way they only had two options from where they were: stairs up to the street or revolving doors to the left, which led into the basement lobby of an office building. Houndstooth stepped into the revolving doors, and bless his pussy-chasing heart because she *loved* revolving doors. Her heart was racing now, but she could step back from it—it was like she pressed some mental clutch, disengaging it from the drive train, while her fingers calmly did the walking. Throw in some archaic Dutch expletives and just like that the door jammed with Houndstooth inside. He did a hilarious involuntary mime-trapped-in-a-box routine, made all the more hilarious by the fact that *he actually was trapped in a box.*

The crowd began backing up against the jammed door, murmuring discontentedly. It would take him a minute to figure out what she'd done, because she hadn't done it the way you'd think, which why would she have? But it always took them a minute to figure it out. And a minute was all she needed. The Matron knew something was up, she had turned around, still walking but backwards, trying to spot her in the crowd, but she didn't have the benefit of those fancy glasses. There was a moment's grace. She began to put the Matron to sleep the same way she had the busker: a Persian fainting charm, it only stings for a second. But this was apparently a much more senior magician than Jimmy Buffett back there because before she could finish, something invisible hit her hard in the chest and she went right down on her ass.

Maybe she actually should have *read* that writing over the Matron's head. That woman was a captain at least. Probably more. Shocked commuters went to help her up, but she shrugged them off, taking deep breaths and massaging her breastbone. The Matron was already off and running, sprinting up the stairs like a champion, surprisingly spry in those heels. She should give chase. But first, what to do with Houndstooth? She could feel him unpicking her charm, loop by loop. A little of the rough stuff, she decided. With a gust of force she blew the whole revolving door off its axle and back into the office building basement. The crash it made was incredible.

That would hold him for a minute or two more. No broken bones, but it would shake him up and tie him up. Maybe even knock him out. Crude but effective, and most important, legal. The crowd went shrieking crazy. The noise faded as she pounded up the steps into the sunlight. The Matron was heading for the same office building that Houndstooth was now in the basement of, a monolith with a double-height green glass lobby. The game was well and truly afoot.

Fast-walking in parallel, on opposite sides of the street, she and the Matron tried to trip each other, then make each other forget where they were going, then give each other heart palpitations. They messed with each others' vision and steered pedestrians into each others' way, which was somewhat off the reservation ruleswise but they were both doing it so call it a wash. Then, on a lark, she reached out to the lights on an idling town car and made them flash, much too brightly, so brightly that the older woman had to stop for a minute and press the heels of her hands against her eyes and lean on the hood.

Set and match. She darted across the street, between the cars and right past the wilting Matron and straight at the green glass and through it and there—the most beautiful sight she had ever seen—was Houndstooth coming up the escalator, right on time, still rubbing his head and arguing with a security guard over whether or not he was okay.

She could capture him and go for the tie, or try to follow him to the goal and go for the win. The next best thing to knowing where something was was knowing who knew where it was, and she knew that Houndstooth knew. Though what beyond-asshole had decided to hide the Blue Cube in a midtown office building? Just a lot of extra hassle and cleanup for everybody.

Precognition was sort of like body English in pool: there was no good reason why it should work but sometimes it did anyway. With her eyes closed, groping around with some nameless mental extremity in some nameless direction, she dredged one simple fact out of where it lay mired ninety seconds in the future: an elevator number. So she was ready, right behind him, when Houndstooth stepped into it. Just as the doors were closing she karate-chopped her hand in between them, they shuddered back open, and she marched into the little box with him with a shit-eating grin all over her face.

Let's be honest: the ride up was awkward. She really did feel sorry for him. He was a rookie, and it was just dawning on him who she was. He made the Pax sign with thumb and forefinger, indicating that they could dispense with hostilities. Like downing a football at the twenty. He wasn't going to fight. Disappointed Houndstooth! With his narrow face and his wavy chestnut hair that was just getting thin at the temples.

God, it was taking forever. For whatever reason Houndstooth had not thought it necessary to choose the express elevator. The artificial respite was giving her time to think. Too much time—her mind had been spinning at maximum speed, and now that it wasn't getting traction on anything the thoughts were piling up on each other. She tried to count up points but kept getting lost. The formulae were complex, and some of the variables were still in play. But she would keep her seeding, anyway. Youngest number one since they'd been keeping records. Five months straight. She was a prodigy, a talent so out of scale that it would have smacked of witchcraft if it wasn't witchcraft they were all doing in the first place.

She sighed, and Houndstooth gave her a searching look, possibly flirtatious, but she blanked him. It's not that she was worried about it. It's not like she was going to *lose*. She was just—it hurt to admit it—a little bit tired of the whole wargaming scene. Being a magician, it turned out, wasn't so much like it was in books. You thought there'd be a Sauron or a White Witch or a Voldemort waiting for you when you graduated, but you know what? Those fuckers could never be bothered to show up. Didn't get the memo.

Their final betrayal, their ultimate evil, was their refusal to exist. So there she was, a newly minted sorceress, spoiling for a fight, but there was nobody to fight and precious little to fight for. Wargaming wasn't the adventure she'd been waiting for, and training for, and living for. But it was pretty much the only game in town.

And she was good at it. But they'd been at it for three weeks, with another four to go, and suddenly that seemed like a fuck of a long time, a hell of a slog. Crashing at a new squat every night, in a new time zone, living on junk food, five raids a week, awake twenty hours a day on speed. People got so obsessed with it. She hadn't had breakfast this morning, and she was getting weak at the knees from too much adrenaline on an empty stomach. Where next? Vilnius, probably. Maybe Perth. There were a lot of Envelopes still left to open. This would keep her numbers up though. There would be an Artifact in the cube. But you know what it was? It's that she was way too young to be this bored.

Ping, the doors opened. She gestured grandly—after you—because why not be as much of a bitch about it as absolutely possible? Houndstooth looked at her emptily, like a man cursed from birth, then walked over and buzzed himself in through the glass doors into the office. Give him some credit, he'd cased the security ahead of time. She followed.

It was an office floor. Fluorescent lights, gray carpets, incurious employees in cubicles. They looked up as she passed, then back down at their screens, unaware that they were in the presence of two living gods, two angelic emissaries from the secret world that lay all around them, if they only had eyes to see it. The silence was like chloroform. It was freezing, the air was conditioned to death.

She trailed after her quarry, ten paces back. He wouldn't be taking her right to it, he wasn't *that* scared. He probably didn't know where he was taking her. Not a big deal. She could wait while he decided. There was still some time left to play with. This was endgame stuff. Queen takes pawn.

The civilians stared at their flickering, incandescent spreadsheets. A woman listened on the phone, a shoe dangling from her stockinged toe, a lock of chocolate-colored hair tucked in her mouth. The cubicles were like a maze. Funny how the walls were carpeted with the same stuff as the floor. Like just in case the room suddenly changes its orientation, Escher-wise, we can all walk comfortably on the walls. A soft labyrinth. Maybe there would be a plushy carpeted minotaur in the middle.

God, it really was cold in here. Houndstooth turned right, then right again, then left. What's your hurry? A gaggle of office cuties excused themselves past her. She took a jogging sidestep.

Hang on, where was he? She'd lost track. She stopped and hopped up and down to see over the cubicles. Nothing. If only she were as tall as Rob. She listened. Silence.

She breathed out, and her breath showed white in the air.

No no no no no! She raised the opera glasses to her eyes. The entire floor was a forest of invisible writing, green and ochre, so dense as to be illegible. This wasn't an office. And there were no civilians here.

She dropped to a squat and slapped the rough carpet, hard, with both hands, and shouted a phrase in Russian. A wave of force blew out in all directions. The cubicle dividers went down in a ring around her, as if they were fir trees and she were the epicenter of a Siberian meteor strike. Somebody shrieked, and a window cracked.

Well, she could only do that once. Wards, wards, wards—she threw them up one after the other, even as a tide of magical energy threatened to swamp her from all sides, neon scribbles in the air, trying to pick her shields apart and tear them down again. But nobody worked as fast as she did. It was a gift. In college she'd had to slow her hands down for her professors, they couldn't follow. (And what was her hurry? What was she trying so hard to stay ahead of, exactly?) Everybody was probably expecting her to Pax out now, but she'd never done that in her life. This was survivable. It had to be. At least until it wasn't. The cubicle walls began re-erecting themselves behind her, cutting off her retreat. But she didn't want to retreat.

She blew on her knuckles and gave herself the Hard Hand—her right hand became big and heavy and tough and numb. She loved the Hard Hand. You couldn't cast spells with it, but there were plenty of enchantments she could work with her left hand only. She advanced behind her huge, glittering right fist. *Boom,* she punched down the wall in front of her. A lanky kid with a shaved head yelped and went down under it. They were always surprised, right out of Brakebills, how much rough stuff people got up to. Whatever. We can all have a tea ceremony together later.

A wild wind was raging through the office now, and the air was full of reams of copier paper. Ward and shield, ward and shield, she moved ahead under a hail of fire—you could actually see the invisible curve of her shield in the air, outlined by the glow of the spellwork shattering against it. Mostly boring kinetic stuff, whatever. Some of them were doing computer magic, automated spells: weak stuff, but you could churn it out in bulk. Most of the casters were smart enough not to try to get too near to her physically, but a distractingly handsome blond guy stepped out of an office and squared off with her, tricked out with all kinds of martial-arts type enhancements. She slipped past him, leaving behind an image of herself frozen with fear, then belted him in the back of the head with the last fading moments of the Hand.

From their point of view she was speeding up and slowing down now at random intervals, and fading in and out of view. It made her hard to catch and hard to target and sort of queasy-making to look at. But other things were coming at her that weren't covered by her general defenses and dismissals. Crazy atmospheric effects, fog and smoke and cold and plasma, radiation too, stuff even she wouldn't have tried in a populated area. The carpet was slithering fast under her feet, flowing like lava, trying to upend her. And somebody had been choking off her air, gradually, for the past twenty seconds or so, and she couldn't quite make out who or how. They must have been laying this trap since yesterday.

She had spotted the Matron now, watching from the corner office. The minotaur in the maze. Stupid—should have known she wouldn't go down that easy. The cold was coming from there, and it was numbing her fingers, locking her jaw. That along with the choking. She'd almost forgotten about it. Her vision was going all gray and psychedelic at the edges.

There was no possible way this was happening. It just wasn't possible. Most of the people in this hex weren't within four levels of her! She gambled and spent some of her dwindling energy on a Maximal Dismissal, snuffing everything within ten yards. At least it brought her trachea back online. She sucked wind.

Paper was thick in the air around her. Some of it was on fire, and somebody kept trying to form it into a kind of golem-shape, which wanted to wrap its papery arms around her. She ripped up the carpet, wrapped people up in it, blocked them off. Between them they were tearing the place apart, right down to the reinforced concrete. The Matron was blitzing her with the whole spellbook, major and minor, smart and stupid, presumably with the idea that something would get through and it didn't really matter what. She was strong, really strong. Not a captain. Higher than that.

Sweat was freezing on her face. This was not sustainable. She had to stop it, all the bullshit. Make it go away. The hair was rising on the back of her neck, static fuzz bristled on the carpeting. Something shorted out in the cubicle next to her. Computer monitors ruptured with a sound like busting piñatas. Frost crystals bloomed wildly on glass surfaces all around her, and snow condensed out of the air. The Matron was building up to her big finale.

But at the same time she was having a ridiculous idea. Really wonderfuckingly ridiculous. And impossible. But listen: there was a clock on the wall. There was a clock in every computer and every phone and printer and fax on this floor. Clocks were wild magic—not much by themselves, but put them together and gather all the threads and cut them . . . desperate times call for batshit insane measures.

Adding a couple of magical feet to her vertical leap, she vaulted into the air and snatched a fluorescent tube out of the ceiling and made it into a Griggs' Scepter, hard and magnesium-bright. She whipped it in a series of intricate patterns, tracing letters and sigils and wards in the air around her, then stabbed it down into the floor in front of her, with both hands. Something rippled out from around it.

Time snagged on something, got stuck. Groaning and complaining, it jerked to a halt.

Silence. She breathed hard, raggedly, resting her forehead against the rough carpet. Time hadn't really stopped, of course. They were all breathing and their hearts were beating. But they couldn't perceive it. Or time couldn't perceive them. Or something—in the heat of the moment her spellcraft had leapt ahead of whatever theory was supposed to be underpinning it. But it worked. They would spend years adjudicating the legality of it, but meantime it would just add to her legend. And she would have the Blue Cube. Possession. Nine tenths of something. Now to find it.

And, looking up, she found it. It was in the right hand of a tall, skinny stranger who was strolling down the aisle toward her, between the shattered cubicles. Stray papers were hanging in the air, suspended; he batted one aside with his free arm. His clothes were odd. Fancy embroidery. If she had to describe his expression she'd say it was melancholy and humorous.

Well, she'd give him something to be melancholy and humorous about. She would lay him out flat. She still had the Scepter for a few more minutes.

But then she didn't. He'd made it go away somehow—put it away somewhere she couldn't get at. Really, it was the most eyebendingly strange casting she could ever remember seeing. Totally alien gramarye. She could have followed up with the fainting charm—her standard second serve—but she didn't. Something told her it was pointless. And anyway if he was unconscious she couldn't ask him how the hell he'd just done that.

In that same foreign style of magic, he immobilized her. Not in a mean way, but thoroughly. Like he meant it. She could try and cast something vocally, but she didn't feel like having her mouth bound too. And she still had to pee.

"Annie," he said. "Poppy Muller."

She shrugged, as best she could under the circumstances. Yeah, and?

He spun the cube cleverly on one finger. Not a magic trick, just old-fashioned fingersmithing. His clothes really were odd. Old-timey and yet not. He might have been twenty-five, twenty-seven at most. Whose side was he on?

"You're ranked number one in the world. Overall."

"And in three individual categories."

"I'm Quentin." He sniffed at the air, wrinkled his nose. Yeah, lot of toxic smoke in here. Burning plastic. "I haven't seen a Griggs' Scepter for years."

She wasn't afraid of him exactly, but he was talking very slowly, and her time spell wouldn't hold much longer. She needed to move. She had to make him let her. Mentally she ran through angles, looked for points of leverage. She didn't find much.

"You don't really want to spend the rest of your life playing games, do you?" he said.

"I don't know," she said. Keep it flip. "Maybe. It's not like I had anything else planned."

"I understand. Would you like to see a real magic trick, Poppy?"

She frowned. Her eyes stayed glued to the cube.

"What do you mean, real?" she said.

She'd gone really off *piste* now. He let the spell dissipate. Just like that she was free. Watching her carefully, as if she were a small wild rodent of some kind, prone to unpredictable behavior, Quentin put his hand on her shoulder, and with the other hand he reached inside his jacket.

Then he must have touched something, something quite small and extremely magic, because the ruined office vanished from around them. And just before a new world arrived to replace it (she really hoped they had bathrooms there) and everything changed forever, she had time to think: this is really going to fuck up my average.

But the funny thing was, she really didn't care.

SIMON R. GREEN is the best-selling author of dozens of novels, including several long-running series, such as the *Deathstalker* series and the *Darkwood* series. Most of his work over the last several years has been set in either his *Secret History* series or in his popular *Nightside* milieu. Recent novels include *The Good, the Bad, and the Uncanny* and *The Spy Who Haunted Me*. A new series, *The Ghost Finders*, is forthcoming. Green's short fiction has appeared in the anthologies *Mean Streets, Unusual Suspects, Wolfsbane and Mistletoe, Powers of Detection*, and in my anthology *The Living Dead 2*.

Our lives are ruled by routines: wake up, take a shower, eat breakfast, go to work, eat lunch, and so on, always the same, day after day. We may move to a new city, a new country, and tell ourselves that we'll break the routine, discover something new every day, but pretty quickly we inevitably find ourselves frequenting the same shops, following the same routes to and fro.

In a wide world full of endless possibilities, why do we find ourselves doing the same things in the same way day after day? We're creatures of habit, as the saying goes, and of course there's a certain comfort to be found in the familiar, the predictable, the everyday. When we read stories about wizards, we tend to see them at moments of high drama: exploring a dungeon or preparing to work some grand casting. But of course wizards, like everyone else, must have their average days, their normal routines. What would it be like, a day in the life of a wizard? That's what our next tale explores. Though of course there's quite a bit more to the life of a modern urban wizard than cubicles and commutes.

Street Wizard
Simon R. Green

I believe in magic. It's my job.

I'm a street wizard, work for London City Council. I don't wear a pointy hat, I don't live in a castle, and no one in my line of work has used a wand since tights went out of fashion. I'm paid the same money as a traffic warden, but I don't even get a free uniform. I just get to clean up other people's messes, and prevent trouble when I can. It's a magical job, but someone's got to do it.

My alarm goes off at nine o'clock sharp every evening, and that's when my day begins. When the sun's already sliding down the sky towards evening, with night pressing close on its heels. I do all the usual things everyone else does at the start of their day, and then I check I have all the tools of my trade before I go out: salt, holy water, crucifix, silver dagger, wooden stake. No guns, though. Guns get you noticed.

I live in a comfortable enough flat, over an off-license, right on the edge of Soho. Good people, mostly. But when the sun goes down and the night takes over, a whole new kind of people move in. The tourists and the punters and every other eager little soul with more money than sense. Looking for a good time, they fill up the streets with stars in their eyes and avarice in their hearts, all looking for a little something to take the edge off, to satisfy their various longings.

Someone has to watch their backs, to protect them from the dangers they don't even know are out there.

By the time I'm ready to leave, two drunken drag queens are arguing shrilly under my window, caught up in a slanging match. It'll all end in tears and wig-pulling, but I leave them to it, and head out into the tangle of narrow streets that make up Soho. Bars and restaurants, night clubs and clip joints, hot neon and cold hard cash. The streets are packed with furtive-eyed people, hot on the trail of everything that's bad for them. It's my job to see they get home safely, or at least that they only fall prey to the *everyday* perils of Soho.

ᥱᢣ

I never set out to be a street wizard. Don't suppose anyone does. But, like music and mathematics, with magic it all comes down to talent. All the hard work in the world will only get you so far; to be a Major Player you have to be born to the Craft. The rest of us play the cards we're dealt. And do the jobs that need doing.

I start my working day at a greasy spoon caff called *Dingley Dell*. There must have been a time when I found that funny, but I can't remember when. The caff is the agreed meeting place for all the local street wizards, a stopping off place for information, gossip and a hot cup of tea before we have to face the cold of the night. It's not much of a place, all steamed-up windows, Formica-covered tables, plastic chairs, and a full greasy breakfast if you can stomach it. There's only ever thirteen of us, to cover all the hot spots in Soho. There used to be more, but the budget's not what it used to be.

We sit around patiently, sipping blistering tea from chipped china, while the Supervisor drones on, telling us things he thinks we need to know. We hunch our shoulders and pretend to listen.

He's not one of us. He's just a necessary intermediary between us and the Council. We only put up with him because he's responsible for overtime payments.

A long miserable streak of piss, and mean with it, Bernie Drake likes to think he runs a tight ship. Which basically means he moans a lot, and we call him Gladys behind his back.

"All right, listen up! Pay attention and you might just get through tonight with all your fingers, and your soul still attached." That's Drake. If a fart stood upright and wore an ill-fitting suit, it could replace our Supervisor and we wouldn't even notice. "We've had complaints! *Serious* complaints. Seems a whole bunch of booze demons have been possessing the more vulnerable tourists, having their fun and then abandoning their victims at the end of the night, with really bad hangovers and no idea how they got them. So watch out for the signs, and make sure you've got an exorcist on speed dial for the stubborn ones. We've also had complaints about magic shops that are there one day and gone the next, before the suckers can come running back to complain the goods don't work. So if you see a shop front you don't recognize, call it in. And, Jones, stay away from the wishing wells! I won't tell you again. Padgett, *leave the witches alone*! They've got a living to make, same as the rest of us.

"And, if anybody cares—apparently something's been eating traffic wardens. All right, all right, that's enough hanging around. Get out there and do some good. Remember, you've a quota to meet."

ᥱᢣ

We're already up and on our feet and heading out, muttering comments just quietly enough that the Supervisor can pretend he doesn't hear them. It's the little victories that keep you going. We all take our time about leaving, just to show we won't be hurried. I take a moment to nod politely to the contingent of local working girls, soaking up what warmth they can from the caff, before a long night out on the cold, cold streets. We know them, and they know us, because we all walk the same streets and share the same hours. All decked out in bright colors and industrial strength makeup, they chatter together like gaudy birds of paradise, putting off the moment when they have to go out to work.

Rachel looks across at me, and winks. I'm probably the only one there who knows her real name. Everyone else just calls her Red, after her hair. Not much room for subtlety, in the meat market. Not yet thirty, and already too old for the better locations, Red wears a heavy coat with hardly anything underneath it, and stilettos with heels long enough to qualify as deadly weapons. She crushes a cigarette in an ashtray, blows smoke into the steamy air, and gets up to join me. Just casually, in passing.

"Hello, Charlie boy. How's tricks?"

"Shouldn't I be asking you that?"

We both smile. She thinks she knows what I do, but she doesn't. Not really.

"Watch yourself out there, Charlie boy. Lot of bad people around these days."

I pay attention. Prossies hear a lot. "Anyone special in mind, Red?"

But she's already moving away. Working girls never let themselves get close to anyone. "Let me just check I've got all my things; straight razor, knuckle duster, pepper spray, condoms and lube. There; ready for anything."

"Be good, Red."

"I'm always good, Charlie boy."

I hold the door open for her, and we go out into the night.

I walk my beat alone, up and down and back and forth, covering the streets of Soho in a regular pattern. Dark now, only artificial light standing between us and everything the night holds. The streets are packed with tourists and punters, in search of just the right place to be properly fleeced, and then sent on their way with empty pockets and maybe a few nice memories to keep them going till next time. Neon blazes and temptation calls, but that's just the Soho everyone sees. I see a hell of a sight more, because I'm a street wizard. And I have the Sight.

When I raise my Sight, I can See the world as it *really* is, and not as most people *think* it is. I See all the wonders and marvels, the terrors and the nightmares, the glamour and magic and general weird shit most people never even know exists. I raise my Sight and look on the world with fresh eyes, and the night comes alive, bursting with hidden glories and miracles, gods and monsters. And I See it all.

Gog and Magog, the giants, go fist-fighting through the back streets of Soho; bigger than buildings, their huge misty forms smash through shops and businesses without even touching them. Less than ghosts, but more than memories, Gog and Magog fight a fight that will never end till history itself comes stumbling to a halt. They were here before London, and there are those who say they'll still be here long after London is gone.

Wee-winged fairies come slamming down the street like living shooting stars, darting in and out of the lamp-posts in a gleeful game of tag, leaving long shimmering trails behind them. Angels go line-dancing on the roof of St Giles' Church. And a handful of Men in Black check the details of parked vehicles, because not everything that *looks* like a car *is* a car. Remember the missing traffic wardens?

If everyone could See the world as it really is, and not as we would have it—if they could See everything and everyone they share the world with—they'd shit themselves. They'd go stark staring mad. They couldn't cope. It's a much bigger world than people think, bigger and stranger than most of them can imagine. It's my job to see that the hidden world stays hidden, and that none of it spills over into the safe and sane everyday world.

I walk up and down the streets, pacing myself, covering my patch. I have a lot of ground to cover every night, and it has to be done the traditional way, on foot. They did try cars, for a while. Didn't work out. You miss far too much, from a car. You need good heavy shoes for this job, strong legs and a straight back. And you can't let your concentration slip, even for a moment. There's always so much you have to keep an eye out for. Those roaming gangs of Goths, for example, all dark clothes and pale faces. Half of them are teenage vampires, on the nod and on the prowl, looking for kicks and easy blood. What better disguise? You can always spot the real leeches, though. They wear ankhs instead of crucifixes. Long as they don't get too greedy, I let them be. All part of the atmosphere of Soho.

And you have to keep a watchful eye on the prossies, the hard-faced working girls on their street corners. Opening their heavy coats to flash the passing trade, showing red, red smiles that mean nothing at all. You have to watch out for new faces, strange faces, because not everything that *looks* like a woman *is* a woman. Some are sirens, some are succubae, and some are the alien equivalent of the praying mantis. All of it hidden behind a pleasing glamour until they've got their dazzled prey somewhere nice and private; then they take a lot more than money from their victims.

I pick them out and send them packing. When I can. Bloody diplomatic immunity.

Seems to me there's a lot more homeless out and about on the streets than there used to be: the lost souls and broken men and gentlemen of the road. But some have fallen further than most. They used to be Somebody, or Something, living proof that the wheel turns for all of us. If you're wise you'll drop the odd coin in a cap, here and there, because karma has teeth; all it takes is one really bad day, and we can all fall off the edge.

But the really dangerous ones lurk inside their cardboard boxes like tunnel spiders, ready to leap out and batten onto some unsuspecting passerby in a moment, and drag them back inside their box before anyone even notices what's happened. Nothing like hiding in plain sight. Whenever I find a lurker, I set fire to its box and jam a stake through whatever comes running out. Vermin control, all part of the job.

From time to time I stop to take a breath, and look wistfully at the more famous bars and night clubs that would never admit the likes of me through their upmarket, uptight doors. A friend of mine who's rather higher up the magical food chain, told me she once saw a well-known sitcom star stuck half way up the stairs, because he was so drunk he couldn't remember whether he was going up or coming down. For all I know, he's still there. But that's Soho for you: a gangster in every club bar, and a celebrity on every street corner doing something unwise.

I stoop down over a sewer grating, to have a chat with the undine who lives in the underground water system. She controls pollution levels by letting it all flow through her watery form, consuming the really bad stuff and filtering out the grosser impurities. She's been down there since Victorian times, and seems happy enough. Though like everyone else she's got something to complain about; apparently she's not happy that people have stopped flushing baby alligators down their toilets. She misses them.

"Company?" I ask.

"Crunchy," she says.

I laugh, and move on.

Some time later, I stop off at a tea stall, doing steady business in the chilly night. The local hard luck cases come shuffling out of the dark, drawn like shabby moths to the stall's cheerful light. They queue up politely for a cup of tea or a bowl of soup, courtesy of the Sally Army. The God botherers don't approve of me any more than I approve of them, but we both know we each serve a purpose. I always make a point to listen in to what the street people have to say. You'd be amazed what even the biggest villains will say in front of the homeless, as though they're not really there.

I check the grubby crowd for curses, bad luck spells, and the like, and defuse them. I do what I can.

Red turns up at the stall, just as I'm leaving. Striding out of the night like a ship under full sail, she crashes to a halt before the tea stall and demands a black coffee, no sugar. Her face is flushed, and she's already got a bruised cheek and a shiner, and dried blood clogging one nostril.

"This punter got a bit frisky," she says, dismissively. "I told him; that's extra, darling. And when he wouldn't take the hint, I hit him in the nads with my knuckle-duster. One of life's little pleasures. Then when he was down I kicked him in the head, just for wasting my time. Me and a few of the girls rolled him for all he had, and then left him to it. Never touch the credit cards, though. The filth investigate credit cards. God, this is bad coffee. How's your night going, Charlie boy?"

"Quiet," I say, and work a simple spell to heal her face. "You ever think of giving this up, Red?"

"What?" she says. "And leave show business?"

More and more drunks on the street now, stumbling and staggering this way and that, thrown out of the clubs and bars once they run out of money. I work simple spells, from a safe distance. To sober them up, or help them find a safe taxi, or the nearest Underground station. I work other protections too, that they never know of. Quietly removing weapons from the pockets of would-be muggers, driving off mini-cab drivers with bad intent by giving them the runs, or breaking up the bigger street gangs with basic paranoia spells, so they turn on each other instead. Always better to defuse a situation than risk it all going bad, with blood and teeth on the pavement. A push here and a prod there, a subtle influence and a crafty bit of misdirection, and most of the night's trouble is over before it's even started.

I make a stop at the biggest Chinese Christian Church in London, and chat with the invisible Chinese demon that guards the place from trouble-makers and unbelievers. It enjoys the irony of protecting a Church that officially doesn't believe in it. And since it gets to eat anyone who tries to break in, it's quite happy. The Chinese have always been a very practical people.

❧

Just down the street is an Indian restaurant once suspected of being a front for Kali worshippers on the grounds that not everyone who went in came back out again. Turned out to be an underground railroad, where people oppressed because of their religious beliefs could pass quietly from this dimension to another. There's an Earth out there for everyone, if you only know where to look. I helped the restaurant put up an avoidance spell, so only the right kind of people would go in.

I check out the dumpsters round the back, while I'm there. We've been having increasing problems with feral pixies, just likely. Like foxes, they come in from the countryside to the town, except foxes can't blast the aura right off you with a hard look. Pixies like dumpsters; they can play happily in them for hours. And they'll eat pretty much anything, so mostly I just leave them to get on with it. Though if the numbers start getting too high, I'll have to organize another cull.

I knock the side of the dumpster, but nothing knocks back. Nobody home.

After that, it's in and out of all the pokey little bars in the back streets, checking for the kind of leeches that specialize in grubby little gin joints. They look human enough, especially in a dimly-lit room. You know the kind of strangers, the ones who belly up to the bar next to you with an ingratiating smile, talking about nothing in particular, but you just can't seem to get rid of them. It's not your company, or even your money, they're after. Leeches want other things. Some can suck the booze right out of you, leaving you nothing but the hangover. Others can drain off your life energy, your luck, even your hope.

They usually run when they see me coming. They know I'll make them give it all back, with interest. I love to squeeze those suckers dry.

Personal demons are the worst. They come in with the night, swooping and roiling down the narrow streets like leaves tossed on the breeze, snapping their teeth and flexing their barbed fingers. Looking to fasten on to any tourist whose psychic defenses aren't everything they should be. They wriggle in, under the mental barricades, snuggle onto your back and ride you like a mule. They encourage all their host's worst weaknesses—greed or lust or violence, all the worst sins and temptations they ever dreamed of. The tourists go wild, drowning themselves in sensation—and the demons soak it all up. When they've had enough they let go, and slip away into the night, fat and engorged, leaving the tourists to figure out where all their money and self respect went. Why they've done so many things they swore they'd never do. Why there's a dead body at their feet, and blood on their hands.

I can See the demons, but they never see me coming. I can sneak up behind them and rip them right off a tourist's back. I use special gloves that I call my emotional baggage handlers. A bunch of local nuns make them for us, blessed with special prayers, every thread soaked in holy water, and backed up with nasty silver spurs in the fingertips. Personal demons aren't really alive, as such, but I still love the way they scream as their flimsy bodies burst in my hands.

Of course, some tourists bring their own personal demons in with them, and then I just make a note of their names, to pass on to the Big Boys. Symbiosis is more than I can handle.

I bump into my first group of Grey aliens of the night, and make a point of stopping to check their permits are in order. They look like ordinary people to everyone else, until they get up close, and then they hypnotize you with those big black eyes, like a snake with a mouse, and you might as well bend over and smile for the probe. Up close, they smell of sour milk, and their movements are just *wrong*. Their dull grey flesh slides this way and that, even when they're standing still, as though it isn't properly attached to the bones beneath.

I've never let them abduct anyone on my watch. I'm always very firm; no proper paperwork, no abduction. They never argue. Never even react. It's hard to tell what a Grey is thinking, what with that long flat face and those unblinking eyes. I wish they'd wear some kind of clothes, though. You wouldn't believe what they've got instead of genitals.

Even when their paperwork is in order, I always find or pretend to find something wrong, and send them on their way, out of my area. Just doing my bit, to protect humanity from alien intervention. The Government can stuff their quotas.

Round about two or three a.m., I run across a Street Preacher, having a quiet smoke of a hand-rolled in a back alley. She's new, Tamsin MacReady. Looks about fifteen, but she must be hard as nails or they'd never have given her this patch. Street Preachers deal with the more spiritual problems, which is why few of them last long. Soon enough they realize reason and compassion aren't enough, and that's when the smiting starts, and the rest of us run for cover. Tamsin's a decent enough sort, disturbed that she can't do more to help.

"People come here to satisfy the needs of the flesh, not the spirit," I say, handing her back the hand-rolled. "And we're here to help, not meddle."

"Oh, blow it out your ear," she says, and we both laugh.

It's not long after that I run into some real trouble; someone from the Jewish Defense League has unleashed a Golem on a march by British Nazi skinheads.

The Golem is picking them up and throwing them about, and the ones who aren't busy bleeding or crying or wetting themselves are legging it for the horizon. I feel like standing back and applauding, but I can't let this go on. Someone might notice. So I wade in, ducking under the Golem's flailing arms, until I can wipe the activating word off its forehead. It goes still then, nothing more than lifeless clay, and I put in a call for it to be towed away. Someone higher up will have words with someone else, and hopefully I won't have to do this again. For a while.

I take some hard knocks and a bloody nose before I can shut the Golem down, so I take time out to lean against a stone wall and feel sorry for myself: My healing spells only work on other people. The few skinheads picking themselves up off the pavement aren't sympathetic. They know where my sympathies lie. Some of them make aggressive noises, until I give them a hard look, and then they remember they're needed somewhere else.

I could always turn the Golem back on, and they know it.

I head off on my beat again, picking them up and slapping them down, aching quietly here and there. Demons and pixies and golems, oh my. Just another night, in Soho.

Keep walking, keep walking. Protect the ones you can, and try not to dwell on the ones you can't. Sweep up the mess, drive off the predators, and keep the world from ever finding out. That's the job. Lots of responsibility, hardly any authority, and the pay sucks. I say as much to Red, when we bump into each other at the end of our shifts. She clucks over my bruises, and offers me a nip from her hip flask. It's surprisingly good stuff.

"Why do you do it, Charlie boy? Hard work and harder luck, with nothing to show but bruises and bad language from the very people you're here to help? It can't be the money; I probably make more than you do."

"No," I say. "It's not the money."

I think of all the things I See every night that most of the world never knows exists. The marvelous and the fantastic, the strange creatures and stranger people, gods and monsters and all the wonders of the hidden world. I walk in magic and work miracles, and the night is full of glory. How could I ever turn my back on all that?

"You ever think of giving this up, Charlie boy?" says Red.

"What?" I say. "And leave show business?"

T.A. PRATT (also known as Tim Pratt) is the Hugo Award-winning author of several novels featuring the sorcerer Marla Mason: *Blood Engines*, *Poison Sleep*, *Dead Reign*, and *Spell Games*. Additionally, two Marla Mason novels, *Bone Shop* and *Broken Mirrors* are available as online serials on Pratt's website, timpratt.org. Another novel, *The Strange Adventures of Rangergirl*, is a standalone, "cowpunk" fantasy. Pratt is also the author of many short stories, which have appeared in such venues as *Subterranean*, *Realms of Fantasy*, *Asimov's Science Fiction*, and *Strange Horizons*, and reprinted in *Best American Short Stories*, *The Year's Best SF*, and *The Year's Best Fantasy & Horror*. His short work has been collected in *Little Gods* and *Hart & Boot & Other Stories*.

Our next tale concerns Pratt's above-mentioned series character Marla Mason, the tough, no-nonsense sorcerer who presides over the fictional city of Felport. (Each city needs a wizard to keep it safe, and the wizards of each city are constantly vying for the top spot.) In this universe, every sort of magic you've ever heard of (and many you haven't) is real—sympathetic magic, necromancy, pyromancy, etc. (Not to mention—memorably—"pornomancy.")

When it comes to magic, Marla is a jack-of-all-trades-master-of-none, which makes her supremely adaptable but also means she's often outclassed in the magic department—forcing her to scrape by with guile and a little help from her ultra-powerful cloak, which can turn her into an unstoppable killing machine (but it grows in power with each use and is always angling to overthrow her mind and take over her body).

Marla has already had to deal with an Aztec god, a woman whose dreams become reality, and an army of zombies. This next story is another action-packed tale in which Marla, early in her career, faces off against several colorful foes.

Mommy Issues of the Dead
T.A. Pratt

"It's not an assassination, precisely." Viscarro, the subterranean sorcerer who dwelt in the tunnels and vaults beneath the seen-better-days city of Felport, tinkered with an oddly beautiful contraption on his desk, all brass gearwheels and copper spheres on articulated arms, all together no bigger than a football. "It's more that I want you to physically inconvenience someone by tricking him into putting high explosives inside his chest cavity. But it's not murder, because Savery Watt is already dead."

Marla Mason propped her feet up on Viscarro's desk, because it annoyed him. "I've got nothing against the dead. Dead people don't bother anybody. You, on the other hand . . . "

Viscarro bared his hideous teeth at her. "Do you want to engage in pointless banter, or do you want to find out about the *job*, you insolent child?" He had the patience of a trapdoor spider when it came to plotting, planning, and scheming, but he got irritated quickly when dealing with people who didn't just nod and say "Yes, master." He had about fifty apprentices, pale cowed creatures who filed his vast archives, sorted the mountains of junk he bought from auction houses and estate sales in search of magical artifacts for his collection, and—for all Marla knew—competed for the honor of giving him nightly massages complete with happy endings. Of all the sorcerers she'd worked with in Felport, Viscarro was her least favorite—and competition for that spot was *fierce*—but he paid well for her mercenary services. Marla didn't ask money for these jobs: she asked for knowledge and power, and Viscarro had promised to teach her a trick and tell her a secret in exchange for this job. She knew what trick she wanted. She was still thinking about the secret.

"Lay it on me, old man."

Viscarro nodded. "It's simple. I want you to blow up Watt's body. But don't worry—it won't violate your silly moral code. He can always get another body, you see. Watt is a lich."

"Which ones are liches again? Do they drink blood or eat corpses? I forget."

Viscarro sniffed. "Neither. A lich is essentially a corpse animated by its own ghost. For some reason—genetics, a curse, something else—conventional paths to sorcerous immortality were closed to Watt, so in order to cheat death he performed a dark ritual. He put his soul into a phylactery—some small object, traditionally a gem—committed suicide, and awakened as an undead creature. His original body was recently destroyed in an explosion, so he's building a new one. He *thinks* he's buying a power source for his new body—I gather it's a junkpile robot sort of thing—but he's actually buying . . . well. Kaboom." Viscarro tapped the weird little engine on his desk to set it spinning, and it whirred away, generating a low hum, as its spheres orbited and gears interlocked.

"So that thing's a bomb?"

"It is both a perpetual motion machine *and* a bomb."

"There's no such thing as perpetual motion."

"Of course not. This device steals small quantities of velocity and momentum from various other sources—passing cars, grandfather clocks, merry-go-rounds, even the rotation of the Earth. Built by a mad technomancer named Canarsie a century ago. With this, Watt won't need to recharge his batteries."

"It's not your style to blow up some fancy old magical thing. Won't it leave a hole in your collection?"

Viscarro waved a hand, though it was more shriveled and clawlike than most things people called hands. Marla didn't know how old he was, but "ancient" was a good guess. "I have two other examples of Canarsie's engines. Besides, Watt is going to trade me for a certain . . . item I require."

"So why the explodey double-cross?"

"Hmm? Oh, because he's planning to cheat me, of course. He knows I won't go in person—" Viscarro had agoraphobia, though Marla thought it was weird he found the outside world scary, since most of the outside world would be scared of *him*—"and he plans to kill my messenger, claim she never arrived, and keep the engine *and* the snow globe for himself."

"Snow globe? You're sending me to bomb a guy and steal his snow globe?"

"It's a very special snow globe. Nothing *you'd* want—it's more cursed than magical. But it has a great deal of sentimental value for me," Viscarro said, entirely straight-faced. He was about as sentimental as a liver fluke, but as long as he paid her, what did she care? As far as selling her services went, she drew the line at murder, but if Watt was a lich, it wasn't murder, anyway—it was monster-killing.

"How do you know he's planning to screw you over?"

Viscarro frowned. "Because I've known him a long time, and we are much alike, and it's what *I* would do, if our positions were reversed."

"Okay. The price is right. I'm up for it. Where am I going?" Her mercenary gigs had taken her to Los Angeles, Las Vegas, and Chicago so far, and she hoped this one was somewhere closer, Boston or Pittsburgh, so she wouldn't have to spend much time out of Felport. She hated traveling. This city was her home.

"Just outside a wide place in the road called Sweetwater, in the North Carolina mountains. Beautiful, especially in autumn. The colors of the leaves, you know. I haven't been there in a long time, but I can remember."

"What's a sorcerer doing there? Aren't the southern Appalachians all . . . " She waved her hands vaguely. "I don't know. Black bears and straw hats and moonshine and inbreeding?"

"Provincial little bigot," Viscarro said. "I was born in the South. I remember Lexington-style barbecue quite fondly, though no one makes it right up here. And, no, Mr. Watt does not make moonshine." Viscarro paused. "He makes methamphetamine these days, mostly."

"Oh, *that's* reassuring."

Viscarro finished tinkering with the engine and passed it over. "One other thing. You can't take your cloak with you on this trip."

Marla touched the silver stag beetle pin that held her white-and-purple cloak around her shoulders. "What are you, my mother? Why should you get a say in my fashion decisions?"

Viscarro bared his teeth. "That cloak isn't an item of fashion, it's a *weapon*."

"Okay, fine—then why should I let you dictate which weapons I bring with me?" Marla was not a big fan of stipulations and limitations. Her life wasn't a sonnet; it didn't benefit from the rigors of a restrictive form. She liked having lots of options on a mission, and the cloak she'd found hanging in a thrift store on her twentieth birthday was her ultimate option: while wearing it, any wounds she received healed rapidly, and if she needed to, she could unleash the cloak's destructive powers, and become a one-woman massacre.

Viscarro shook his head. "The cloak *reeks* of magic. I want Watt to think you're merely a messenger. If he sees you arrive in *that* thing, he'll know you're a true operative. Besides, I want to see how you handle a situation *without* that advantage. A lot of people say you're a talentless little hack, you know, who just lucked into finding a potent magical weapon. Sometimes when people want to hire you, they don't say, 'I should hire Marla,' they say, 'I should hire the girl with the cloak.' How does that make you feel?"

She snorted. "Feelings are stupid. But I don't need the cloak. I can bust heads just fine on my own." And maybe she *was* too dependent on her artifact. She didn't like the way using the cloak made her feel, anyway—it was much older than her, and quite possibly smarter, and absolutely more malevolent, and sometimes when she was wearing it, she felt almost like the cloak was wearing *her* instead.

"If you'd like to leave it with me, in, ah, storage—" Viscarro began.

"What, so you can lock it in a vault and give me back a duplicate cloak with some shitty temporary enchantments and hope I don't notice?" Viscarro's covetousness in regard to magical artifacts was legendary, and he didn't scruple when it came to acquiring new toys for his vast collection. Obsession like that wasn't healthy. Doubtless indicative of some deeper psychological flaw. Probably something to do with his upbringing. "I'll make my own arrangements."

Marla caught a pre-dawn flight to the airport in Greensboro North Carolina, and one of Viscarro's local contacts drove her the two hours or so into the mountains near Sweetwater. The driver was a fairly attractive guy with short blond hair, about Marla's age, but he had his jaw wired shut, so his conversation was limited mostly to grunts. Marla wondered if the wiring was due to an injury or if Viscarro was just worried about the guy saying things he shouldn't.

She'd never been to the mountains before, and she had to admit, the drive had some beautiful moments—the side of the road dropping away to reveal vast chasms of green, with hazy blue mountains in the distance—but for the most part it just made her uncomfortable, especially when hillsides hemmed the road in tight on both sides, exposed rock faces looking like avalanches waiting to happen, and even the scenic lookouts grew disturbing as she contemplated all that . . . *nature*—just sitting there, empty and waiting. Marla lived in the heart of a city and loved it, and the only green she saw on a regular basis these days was the occasional windowsill garden and grass growing up through cracks in the asphalt. She felt a little better when they passed antique malls and Christmas tree farms—crass humanity and consumerism made her feel more at home.

The driver stopped the car in the middle of a curving road crowded by pine trees and pointed at a nearly-hidden steep driveway that wound up the side of a wooded hill. "Bet that driveway's a bitch to get up in the winter," she said. "My guy's up there?"

The driver nodded and held up two stopwatches, each set for one hour. He pressed their start buttons simultaneously.

"You'll be back for me here in an hour, when this runs out?" Marla said.

Another nod.

"And if I'm not here, you'll come back every hour after that until I *am* here."

He couldn't frown, exactly, but he tried to, winced at however it felt, and shook his head.

Marla grinned, reached into her knapsack, and withdrew her favorite dagger. The blade was old, but she kept it sharp. "That wasn't a question, Jaws. You *will* be here every hour, or I *will* come find you after I'm forced to make my own way out of this place. I know all kinds of magic—how to start fires with a word, how to insinuate myself into dreams, how to make myself unseen—but I won't bother with any of that stuff. I'll just cut your balls off with this knife. After I do some whittling first to make the blade duller. Understood?"

Wide-eyed, he nodded, rather more vigorously this time.

"Excellent. Maybe pick up some doughnuts or something for the drive back, too, huh?" She slipped out of the car and headed up the driveway, and though she was in good shape, she soon felt a burn in muscles she didn't often use. She'd have to start running up and down stadium bleachers or something—just traveling the relatively flat streets of Felport wasn't sufficient conditioning, obviously.

Birds sang, a cool breeze blew—that first nip of autumn in the air—and she had to admit, the fall foliage was pretty, where it peeked out from the zillions of evergreens that mostly surrounded her. The driveway petered out next to a low cinderblock foundation that had probably once supported a mobile home, and she sighed, looked around, and followed what might have been a deer path deeper into the woods. The perpetual motion machine in her bag was heavy as hell, and every time it bumped and shifted she got more anxious, even knowing the ball of plastic explosive at its heart wouldn't explode until she pressed the button on the garage door opener in her jacket pocket.

The trail opened into a clearing with two structures: an old-school vaguely oval-shaped silver RV, and a cozy little log cabin, some serious Abe Lincoln shit. The door of the RV banged open and two simian-looking skinheads in denim overalls bounded out, followed by an invisible cloud of chemical stink. The men held new-looking black scatterguns at ready position. They were both potential medalists in the Olympics of Ugliness, but the one on the right showed him her teeth, and they were green where they weren't yellow, and yellow where they weren't black, and black where they weren't entirely absent, so he won the gold medal by the skin of his nasty teeth. "She don't look like the law," Silver Medal Ugly said.

"Looks like a college girl who got lost," Gold Medal said.

"I'm here to see Mr. Watt. I've got a delivery for him from Felport."

Silver grunted. "Go on in then." He gestured at the cabin's front door.

"Just like that? You don't want to search me for weapons or anything?"

Gold laughed. "You pull a weapon on Mr. Watt and he'll take it away from you and stick it where God split you."

"The ladies must love you guys," Marla said, and went for the front steps. She wondered if she'd have to fight those two after she blew up their boss, or if the confusion would cover her escape. Maybe the explosion would make the silver trailer, which doubtless held a meth lab full of assorted inflammables, go up in flames too. She didn't murder people, but if they turned out to be collateral damage, well, they were in a dangerous line of work, and she wouldn't feel guilty.

She knocked, and a voice that sounded like air whistling through pipes and blowing over bottle tops, and puffing out of a bellows said, "Come."

Marla opened the door and stepped inside, but she didn't see anybody, just a bunch of junk. The cabin was small, crowded with shelves that held a godawful profusion of knick-knacks and gimcrackery, including—she was dismayed to note—at least forty or fifty snow globes lined up on several shelves. A table made out of a big cable spool held a half-dissected car engine, and a low workbench along one wall was scattered with bits of metal shavings and fragments of wire, various tools hanging on the wall above it. And right in the middle of the floor there was a heap of junk almost as tall as her, car grilles and a refrigerator door and shiny hubcaps and long hinged metal bars and fist-sized glass fuses and rubber hoses and—

The top of the junk pile turned toward her, two amber lights glowing, and that fluting voice emerged in a puff of diesel-scented air, saying, "You brought me the engine?"

Viscarro had told her Watt was a "a junkpile robot," but she'd expected something more robot and less junkpile. "Yes, sir. You have the snow globe?"

A few puffs of high-pitched air emerged, and Marla assumed it was his version of evil laughter, because evil sorcerers enjoyed their evil laughter. "I do have it. But first let me inspect your merchandise."

Marla shrugged, removed the engine from her knapsack, and held it out to him. Watt extended a multi-hinged arm that terminated in a profusion of crazily jointed fingers and grasped the engine, flicked it into motion, and watched as it spun. "Marvelous." He reached into his . . . chest—Marla guessed—and opened what appeared to be a circuit breaker panel. While he was absorbed in putting the engine into his chest and attaching it to various cables, Marla eyeballed the snow globes. Typical souvenir junk: snowman, Santa Claus, Eiffel Tower, Hollywood sign—like it ever snowed *there*—clowns, polar bears, Christmas tree, a menorah, mountains, a pyramid, sailing ships . . .

But they were all currently snow-free, since no one had shaken them up recently. All but one. One snow globe on the top shelf—about the size of a baseball mounted on a round black base—was full of swirling snow, nothing in view but churning whiteness. Now, maybe it was some fancy wind-up or battery-powered snow globe or something—Marla didn't keep up with the cutting edge in snow globe technology—but so far it was the likeliest one to be magic. She stepped closer, peered in at the glass, and saw what looked to be a tiny shapeless black figure moving in among the whiteness, disappearing and reappearing in swirls of snow.

"I'll be taking this." She stood on tiptoe and snatched the snow globe down.

"No, you won't." Savery Watt's eyes began to glow more intensely. "I think I'll wipe your mind and sell you to some gentlemen I know in the next valley instead."

"Praesidium," Marla said, though she thought using incantatory trigger words in Latin was dumb—why couldn't she just say "protection" or "force field" or something? But Viscarro had woven the spell, so she was stuck with his technique. She felt the spell click into place, the room around her becoming faintly shimmery as if seen through warped glass, and then triggered the garage door opener in her pocket.

No explosion. She jammed the button harder, to similar lack of effect. Shit. Was it a double cross? No, Viscarro wanted the snow globe, she believed that, and the spell he'd designed to protect her from the explosion was working, after all. He'd probably just had one of his idiot apprentices put the bomb together and not bothered to double-check the work.

Fortunately the magical shell protected her just fine against the jagged lances of lightning that sprayed from Watt's body. Marla ran as fast as she could—"run like your ass is on fire and your head is catching," her mother used to say—and the force field bobbed around her like an impregnable soap bubble. Which was fine as far as that went, but the bubble wouldn't last for more than a few minutes. Watt bellowed behind her—high pitched bellowing, yes, but still loud—and Gold and Silver Ugly popped out and started firing at her, shots bouncing harmlessly off her shield . . . for the moment.

She pulled the stopwatch out of her pocket. The whole thing, walk and all, had taken only twenty-eight minutes, so even if she hauled ass down the driveway, Jaws wouldn't be there waiting to pick her up yet. She had to lose her pursuit first, so Marla veered into the trees and started looking for a place to go to ground. For the first minute her force field snapped tree branches all around her, leaving a clear trail, no doubt, but then the field sputtered out and she started stepping more carefully, trying to cover her tracks, though she was crap as a woodsman.

The noise of Watt crashing around behind her was still audible, but getting quieter. She was about to cast a look-away spell to make herself less noticeable—it probably wouldn't fool Watt, but it might work for his meth monkeys—when she jumped over a big log and found a steep drop-off on the other side. Her mom always said "Look before you leap," which invariably pissed Marla off, both because it was a stupid cliché and because her mother liked having one-night-stands with abusive rednecks and was thus hardly qualified to counsel caution, but this was a situation where the advice could have helped.

Marla managed to snag the stem of a bush as she fell instead of rolling down the hill. As far as upsides went, she'd had better. And to make matters worse, as Marla clung halfway down a muddy hillside in the Blue Ridge mountains of North Carolina, she couldn't stop thinking about her mother. She hadn't seen the woman in almost seven years, since running away at fifteen, and she didn't miss her much at all, but she had to admit, life with her was better than waiting for a junkyard robot to come kill you. Marla's mom had been most tolerable during her occasional forays into 12-step programs, though she usually hit a wall right around step 4: making a searching and fearless moral inventory. Marla's mom wasn't much for introspection. In that respect, mother and daughter had something in common.

Marla decided to do a fearless personal inventory of her own, though—not of her morals, but of her resources.

In the hand not clutching the bush, she held a battered leather knapsack, which had slid off her shoulder and nearly tumbled down the hill—it seemed a lot more like a mountainside than a hillside to her, but she was from Felport by way of Indiana, so what did she know from mountains?—which would have been bad, since the bag contained various valuable things, fragile and otherwise, including:

A pair of knives: an antique dagger her mentor had given her, and another balanced for throwing that she'd purchased herself;

A coil of thin, strong line fifty feet long, attached to a clever collapsible grappling hook;

A pair of brass knuckles with a wicked inertial enchantment worked into the metal, perfect for face-punching;

Spare socks;

A rain poncho;

A slightly-rusty Altoids tin that contained a survival kit in miniature, consisting of a small signal mirror, waterproof matches, flint and a little hacksaw blade, cotton balls, a tiny (non-magical) compass, a brass wire small animal snare, a twist of nylon fishing line with fishhooks, a bit of candle, a flashlight the size of a lipstick, a plastic bag for carrying water, and iodine tablets;

And, of course, a cursed snow globe. Everything else would be more or less useful if she had to hide out in the woods overnight—hideous thought—but she wasn't sure what good the snow globe could possibly do her.

For now, if she could get the grappling hook out and snag it on the bush she was clinging to, then she could lower herself down this slope, hoping it didn't end in a river or leg-breaking deadfall or something, and from there maybe hike to high ground, climb a tree, figure out which way the road was, hike that way, and maybe possibly get to her extraction point before—

"She's down there!" shouted a voice up on the ridgeline. Sounded like one of the meth-lab-monkeys.

"So go down and *get* her," Watt said, his voice weirdly high and fluting and artificial, but his annoyance and impatience still coming through loud and clear.

Oh well, Marla thought. *Let's go, gravity.* She relinquished her grip on the bush. Marla bumped and slid and rolled along, collecting a full suite of bruises. *Damn I wish I had my cloak*, she thought, and then she rolled over an especially big rock and went airborne.

Marla sailed through the air, though not far, since falling human bodies are not especially aerodynamic. She landed in a mound of damp leaves at the base of the hill and sat up groaning, but nothing was broken, just generally battered. Marla tore open her knapsack, slipped on her brass knuckles, considered her knives, and finally just lifted out the snow globe. Running away hadn't worked so well, and from the sound of things Watt and his imps were coming down the hill in a more controlled way than she had, so it was time to make some kind of stand.

The scatterguns came sliding down the hill first, no doubt lost in transit, and Marla grinned. That was a bit of luck. She snatched up one gun and chucked the other behind her into the trees. The meth monkeys landed a moment later, covered in mud and not too happy about it, and they looked less happy when Marla pointed the gun at them, low, and fired. They both collapsed, their legs riddled with shot, howling. They'd live, but their injuries probably hurt badly enough they wished they wouldn't.

Marla tossed the gun down. Shooting the junkyard golem where Savery Watt's spirit resided wouldn't even piss him off. It'd be like tossing snowballs at the sun.

Watt trundled down the hill on a combination of tanklike treads and spidery articulated multi-jointed legs. "College girl. Give me the snow globe, and I'll kill you fast."

"How about you let me go, or I smash the globe?"

"It's *magical*, fool. You can't just crack the glass."

Marla lifted her metal-wrapped hand. "Not even with brass knuckles enchanted for extra smashy-ness? I can punch through a bank vault with these."

"Try it."

Uh oh. Marla smashed her fist into the top of the snow globe, and, predictably, nothing happened except the *tink* of metal tapping glass. "Huh." So that was no good. But now that she looked closer, this was clearly not a mass-produced snow globe, with the glass top glued on—it was more homemade looking, and the base appeared to just be a jar lid painted black, which meant maybe . . .

Marla twisted the glass top one way, and the base the other way, and at first it didn't want to give, but she was a champion opener of pickle jars, so she strained, and *then*—

"No!" Watt screamed, and the woods filled with swirling whiteness, deadening sound and reducing visibility to no more than a foot or two at most.

"You rescued me," came a voice from within the whiteness.

A woman dressed in ragged black furs stood before Marla, who still held both pieces of the now-empty snowglobe in her hands. She was tall, black-haired, black-eyed, still strikingly beautiful despite being at least twice Marla's age, and when she spoke, arctic puffs of air emerged from her mouth. She shivered. "I've been walking in that snowstorm for . . . how long? Time is strange in there. What year is it?"

Marla told her. The woman's lips quirked in a half-smile. "That means I missed the 1936 World Series then. I don't suppose you know who won?"

"Uh. I don't really follow sports."

"No matter. I can look it up." She waved a hand in front of her face, and the snow that filled the air sizzled and turned to steam, replacing the opaque whiteness with merely misty vapor . . . allowing them to see Savery Watt, who was trying without much success to trundle his way back up the hill.

"Son," the woman said, and Watt stopped, then slowly rolled backwards and rotated on his treads to face her.

"Mother," he fluted.

"Oh hell," Marla said. "Did I step into a family thing?"

The woman approached her son and touched his robot face. "Oh, Savery, you naughty boy. What have you done with your body?"

"I . . . it was destroyed in a fire, Mother. An explosion in a, uh, factory I owned."

"That breaks my heart, baby. I carried that body in my own body, I gave birth to it, and you let it be destroyed? In a *fire*, no less? I take that as a personal insult."

"It was an accident."

"How about trapping me in a jar for all those decades? Was that an accident?"

"I didn't do that! It was Leland! I just held onto—"

"Do you remember the Robert Frost poem I read to you when you were a boy?" she said. "The one that starts 'Some say the world will end in fire / Some say in ice'? Do you recall how it ends?"

"No, Mother."

"It ends, 'I think I know enough of hate / To know that for destruction ice / Is also great / And would suffice."

"*Please*, Mother," Watt said.

She shook her head, sadly. "You had your fire already, my darling. And now . . ." Ice flowed from her fingers, covering him in a frosty shell, and his amber lights dimmed. She glanced at the two terrified meth monkeys, waved her hand casually, and they froze in place, transformed into ice sculptures of themselves.

She turned to look at Marla, smiling. "Now, dear, what's your name?"

"Uh. Marla Mason. And you are . . . ?"

"I call myself Regina Queen."

Marla blinked. "Doesn't that mean, like, 'Queen Queen'?"

She smiled indulgently. "Some people need to be told things twice before they understand them, dear. I've been married to two men—bore them both sons—but I didn't want to keep either of their last names, so I made up my own, suitable to my station. Some called me the Snow Queen, though I'm not from a fairy tale." She stretched her arms overhead, turning her face up to the sun. "Oh, it's so nice to be out and about. I love the winter, but that was too much of a good thing. Now. Why did you set me free?"

Marla considered lying, but who knew which lie would keep her from being turned into an icicle? "I was sent to, ah, blow that guy up. Your son. No offense."

"Of course, of course."

"And to steal the snow globe, though I didn't know there was anybody *in* it."

"Mmm." Regina sat cross-legged on the dirt, produced a hairbrush from somewhere not entirely obvious, and began brushing out her long black hair. "Who hired you?"

"A sorcerer in Felport, named Viscarro."

"I see. I mentioned I was married twice. My second husband was the Reverend Reginald Watt, poor Savery's father. My *first* husband, father of my firstborn, was Captain Antonio Viscarro. So I assume your employer is my son Leland? And that my boys had some sort of falling out?"

Viscarro's name was *Leland*? He didn't look like a Leland, but then, he didn't look like anything except maybe Methuselah. "He didn't tell me his family history. Ma'am. Just sent me with a dud bomb and orders to steal a snow globe."

She finished brushing her hair and stood up. "All right. I have no intention of being imprisoned again, which means, as much as it pains me, I'll have to go kill my son Leland."

"Is that totally necessary?"

"I'm afraid so. You'll take me to him, of course."

"That's maybe not such a good idea."

"If you aren't with me, Miss Mason, then you are, by definition, against me." She walked over to one of the meth monkeys and kicked his arm, the limb snapping off and shattering into chunks of ice. "Which is it?"

"Right." Marla had no great love for Viscarro, but he was a ranking sorcerer on Felport's council, and if some outsider came into the city and murdered him there would be consequences. Chaos, retaliation, all-out magical warfare, and other disruptive, city-wrecking unpleasantness, and if Marla was on *either* side of the conflict, it would be bad for her. Plus, Marla wouldn't be able to get paid if Regina killed Viscarro. "So, you want revenge against your son, or . . . ?"

"Of course not. I love my boys. They had their reasons for imprisoning me. But once Leland realizes I'm no longer in the snow globe, he'll come after me, to kill me, or trap me again, and . . . I can't abide that. I don't know for sure if I'll win a fight against my son, but with the element of surprise on my side, and your help getting in to see him, it's possible. I'd prefer to go somewhere up north and avoid the whole ordeal, but what choice do I have?"

Marla thought furiously. "What if Viscarro didn't know you'd escaped?"

"The snow globe is empty, dear. That will be readily apparent when you deliver it. And while we could, I suppose, kidnap some hill person and trap them in the globe, they would soon perish in the snow there, and the ruse would be revealed. Only someone with certain . . . immortal qualities . . . can survive inside that sphere."

"Yeah, okay, but what if we put *him* in the globe?" She pointed to the frozen junk sculpture that was Savery Watt. "Getting your other son out of the way too?"

Regina shook her head. "That's not my son. That's just a pile of junk. His soul isn't in that body, he was just *using* it. His soul resides in some object—probably an egg, or stone, or jewel, but a lich's phylactery can be almost anything. I grant you, your plan works in theory, but without the phylactery, we *can't* trap him. No, I'm afraid war is the only solution."

"Come on," Marla said. "I know where Savery lives. You're his mother. Are you saying you don't know your son well enough to guess where he might have hidden his soul?"

Regina shook her head as she surveyed the interior of the cavern. "Savery, you hoarder. You're almost as bad as your brother. I got them started collecting baseball cards—I love baseball, it's funny, you'd think I'd prefer winter sports, but I don't—and from there they both started collecting *everything*." She walked along the shelves, peering at porcelain dogs, ceramic unicorns, and, of course, the profusion of snow globes.

Marla, meanwhile, found a metal safe, punched it open with her brass knuckles, and scooped out several banded bundles of crumpled cash. She traded her services to sorcerers for knowledge, not money—so she had to make money where she could.

"Oh," Regina said softly. "I can't believe he kept this." Marla walked over as she lifted a metal toy monkey from the shelf. "It's a tin toy from England. I bought him this, for his collection, the same Christmas he and his brother . . . Well. They gave me a snow globe that year." She cocked her head. "This. This is his phylactery."

"You sure?"

She shrugged. "If I'm wrong, we can just try sticking everything else in this house into the snow globe, until I grow too bored, and decide to go to war instead."

"Gotcha." Marla took the two halves of the snow globe from her bag. Regina set the toy monkey on the globe's base and started screwing on the top. It didn't look like it should fit—the monkey was too big—but the glass sphere fit over it easily, and when Regina screwed it down, the globe filled with whiteness . . . and there, in the center, a black shape ran in wild circles.

"That's it, then," Regina said. "Seems a shame to trap my son this way, but it's more merciful than destroying his soul."

"Just think of it as putting your kid in time out," Marla said, and Regina looked at her blankly. Right. She came from a time when disciplining your child meant sending him out to cut the switch you intended to beat him with. "Never mind. Can you help me get that frozen junkpile body up here? I need to cover my tracks."

Marla checked her watch, figured the timing was right, and said, "Let's do it." She and Regina stood well back and watched as the meth lab exploded, a simple fire spell combining with the chemicals inside to make a big ugly boom that engulfed Savery Watt's robot body in fire. Regina whispered down a ring of ice to contain the fire and keep the woods from burning, which was considerate of her, Marla thought.

If Viscarro sent someone to check up on her story, he'd find a smoking ruin and a bunch of scrap metal to support Marla's version of events. Sure, he might start wondering when he never heard from his brother again, but with luck he'd just assume Savery was in hiding. Viscarro was arrogant. He'd be fine believing he'd utterly overpowered his brother.

"So where are you going now?" Marla asked.

"Better you don't know, Marla. Thank you for saving me, even if it was unintentional. I'll find a peaceful place and catch up on everything that's happened since I was trapped."

"Wait'll you hear about global warming," Marla said. "You're going to hate it." She waved goodbye and went down the hill, and the car pulled up soon after she reached the bottom. The driver was a full two minutes late, which spoiled the perfectly-timed arrival she'd envisioned, but she was feeling magnanimous, so she didn't even threaten him, just said, "Home, Jaws."

They passed a fire engine and two cop cars on the way, and the scream of sirens made Marla homesick.

"Fine, fine," Viscarro said when Marla finished her tale, in which things went much as planned, unlike in real life. He held up the snow globe to the light, grunted, and placed it on a shelf behind his desk. "You did well. I suppose you'd like to be paid. What trick did you want me to teach you?"

"I thought it would be cool to learn to summon an incubus," she said.

Viscarro shuddered. "Youth is disgusting. The young and their urges and fluids repulse me. Fine. Return to me on the next new moon and I'll show you the ritual. Are we done?"

"Ah, ah." Marla waved her forefinger at him. "You still owe me a secret."

"Yes, *fine*. Do you want to know the true identity of Kaspar Hauser? Where Ambrose Bierce ended up? What happened to the Lost Colony?"

"I was thinking more, I want you to tell me who's trapped inside that snow globe, and why."

Viscarro's hands curled into configurations even more clawlike than usual. "Those are secrets that touch on me, Marla."

She shrugged. "You didn't say no personal questions. I like to know about the people I work for." She knew Viscarro would keep his promise. Sorcerers would twist, lie, and deceive all day and all night, but if they said they'd do something, they did it—a sorcerer's word was one of his most valuable currencies.

"Fine." He spun in his desk chair, looking at the snow globe, which stood between a blue glass bottle and a Faberge egg, on a shelf full of similarly dissimilar bric-a-brac. "If you must know, my mother, Regina Viscarro Watt, is trapped inside the snow globe. As for why? Because she's incredibly dangerous."

"How so?"

"I'm sure your sense of history is as stunted as those of every other person in their twenties, but perhaps you've heard of the Blizzard of 1899? No? Well. It snowed in the South, that year. It snowed in Florida—the only time in recorded history Florida has ever experienced sub-zero weather. It snowed in Louisiana. There were ice floes in the gulf of Mexico. Where we lived, in Erasmus Tennessee, the temperature dropped to thirty below zero. And do you know what caused that cold? My mother did. She was a weather witch with ice water in her veins. And do you know *why* she froze the South? Because my stepfather wouldn't take her on vacation. She was angry, and she threw a fit, and the world paid the price. It was not the first time she did something like that, nor the last." He shook his head, and swiveled his chair back to her. "The man you took the snow globe from is my half-brother, and he has been . . . unreliable since his body was destroyed. The ordeal drove him a bit mad. I felt I would be a better choice for custodianship of our mother. He disagreed. So I sent you to press the issue. I am a dangerous person, Marla, as you well know, but I am nothing—nothing—compared to my mother. The world is a better place with her on this shelf."

"Wow," Marla said. "That's, uh . . . Wow." What had she set free? Hell. It wasn't *her* fault. Viscarro should have given her a bomb that worked.

"Leave me now," Viscarro said, and turned in his chair to stare at the snow globe.

Marla walked out of Viscarro's catacombs, past hurrying apprentices, down narrow corridors, through brick-lined tunnels, and climbed a ladder to emerge from a manhole not far from her apartment. Autumn was getting a grip on Felport, and there was a definite nip in the air. Winters here were always hard, but did it seem . . . colder than usual, for October?

"Ice will suffice," she muttered, and wrapped her cloak more tightly around herself, and set off for home. Maybe this year she'd send her mother a Christmas card. All things considered, maybe the old lady wasn't so bad.

JEREMIAH TOLBERT's fiction has appeared in *Fantasy Magazine, Interzone, Ideomancer,* and *Shimmer,* as well as in the anthologies *Seeds of Change, Federations,* and *Polyphony 4.* He's also been featured several times on the *Escape Pod* and *Podcastle* podcasts. In addition to being a writer, he is a web designer, photographer, and graphic artist—and he shows off each of those skills in his Dr. Roundbottom project, located at www.clockpunk.com. He lives in Colorado, with his wife and cats.

In everyday life, when people use the word "wizard," they're almost always talking about a "computer wizard," and that's no accident. There are many striking parallels between the wizards of old and our modern-day IT folks. Both are conversant in inscrutable languages full of strange symbols where even the tiniest error can spell disaster, both spend hours locked away in rooms full of books and equipment, and both can produce dazzling effects.

In fact, to most people computers seem like magic. In one *Too Much Coffee Man* comic, the hero's computer attempts to explain to him how it works, in terms of RAM and binary numbers and machine code. A skeptical Too Much Coffee Man tears the computer apart only to reveal what he's always suspected—inside is nothing but a tiny devil standing on a flaming pentagram.

It's no surprise then that many fantasy writers have speculated about how sorcery and computers might intersect. Our next tale is one of a series in which Tolbert utilizes his formidable knowledge of computers to present a world in which hackers and geeks are also wizards and witches, where a "sprog" ("spell" + "program") can do almost anything, and where spam can be deadly.

ONE-CLICK BANISHMENT
JEREMIAH TOLBERT

STUCK THREAD * Six Lessons Learned in MAA's Captive Servitude

Posted by Hidr at 7:42 PM Yesterday

Yeah, the rumors are true. Big Mother caught me (note the past-tense, indicating that it happened in the *past* and it's *no longer the case*. Isn't language fun?). Before I get started, I want to make one thing *very* clear—anyone who asks me when Tometracker will be back online will be banned from the board and cursed with a sprog that turns your dick into a cactus. If you don't believe I own that sprog, just ask @DedJonny. The word on Tometracker is, I'm working on moving the servers. It takes time when they're located on an astral plane.

Some of you kids might not know who I am. I've stayed away from the general forums for a long time because I can't stand the crap you nerds talk about. Check my two-digit user ID and tremble, n00bs. But I've come in here to share with you some very important lessons.

Everybody's got a talent, and mine's damned useful when you're a m4g1ck pirate (yarr). My handle is Hidr for a reason. I make things *very* hard to find. I've been evading the MAA's goons and daemons for almost a decade. Yes, by your standards I'm an old geezer. When I joined up, we downloaded sprogs on 28.8 baud modems. My 8086 barely had enough processing power to cast even the most simple cantrips. Also, I walked to school uphill both ways without an energy boost sprog. Oh, and our music was better than the crap you kids listen to.</old fart>

You are using defensive or obfuscation sprogs that I crunched from tomes or coded myself. I've personally developed a toolbox of tricks that Big Mother has not been able to beat. Until a few days ago.

Your MAA countermeasures are only as good as your own personal paranoia. MAA has been slow to catch on to our tactics and methodology (you learn slower when your organization is made up of immortal wizards born in the time of cave people, I guess), but they had someone new, younger, working in their Anti-Piracy division. I was not expecting to be taken out by a fucking social engineering hack.

I won't go into the personal details. It's too embarrassing. Let's just say that

Big Mother never would have caught me if it wasn't for my weakness for nerdy redheads. Stay off of Craigslist, boys and girls. They are probably still planting honey pots in the form of geeky love interests that don't exist. Well, they might exist, but they're not posting in the "casual encounters" area of Craigslist.

They tagged me because I was running a minor glamour on my jailbroken iPhone, covering up some acne scars from my misbegotten youth. Even something small, low-mojo-using, makes you stand out in a crowded restaurant to their scryers. Lesson number one: run obfuscation at *all* times. You should have enough mojo to do that, and if you don't, better start collecting it. (Plenty of files in the FTP for you to put on tracker sites with a personalized collector sprog.)

So the worst of it is, they weren't even trying to catch a higher-up like myself. They were canvassing for any m4g1ck pirates they could find and got lucky. Go figure. But you want to hear all the gory details, huh. Here we go.

So the ordeal starts with MAA agents sucking me into a Box sprog running on what looked like a pretty necklace worn by the undercover MAA agent. Turns out to be a mini-computer the size of a USB stick. It's pretty awesome. I'll tell you more about it later—

—*Hold on, I need to reboot a router. I'll pick this up in the next post.*

Posted by Hidr at 8:14 PM Yesterday

Time's funny in a Box. I lose track of it banging on the glass-smooth walls and screaming obscenities. I burn through a gig of mojo trying to crack my way out. Enough time goes by that I can write a sprog in Aleph-code to try to overwrite the Box's World-Object-Model. But I'm Hidr, not Escapr. I carry just about every defensive sprog ever cracked, but I don't carry escape tools when I go out on a date. Paranoia FAIL. That's lesson number two. You can never be paranoid enough with the MAA around.

When they crack open the Box, I slurp out into an interrogation cell with two MAA pirate hunters. These assholes are *so* stereotypical. They're in black suits and dark shades, all business, but the menacing Fed look is ruined by the unkempt gray beards and pointed wizard caps. So yeah, I can finally say that I have seen not one but two agents in person. I'm just guessing here, but they probably don't wear the hats in public. Which is where I would like to be right about now: in public.

Before I can even hit "Run" on my *Get Out of Jail Free* sprog, Agent #1 tasers me.

If someone ever offers you the chance to be tasered, pass. While I lay on the floor convulsing like a meth addict in need of a hit, Agent #2 rummages through my pockets and takes my phone, my backup PDA, my USB sticks, and a couple of sentimental charms that probably don't do shit (and definitely don't protect against Box sprogs or fucking taser guns).

They sit me up in the chair and chain me down with the Manacles of Morteus. Good sprog, actually. We bootlegged that one a few years back. Chained up, this is when I expect the beating and shouting to begin, but Agent #1 just smiles real funny while Agent #2 waves his hand over my belongings and they vanish in a puff of purple smoke.

The agents move kind of weird, almost like marionettes. They talk in clipped tones. I wonder if they're from another world, or if they're imps in disguise. Something ain't right. Maybe it's just the way MAA stooges are.

They call me by my True Name, and that scares the hell out of me. I can only figure that they did a records search once they had me in the Box. "Mr. [True Name Deleted], please be patient and remain calm," they said. "Magister Atretius will be with you momentarily."

(Oh, there's no way I'm posting my True Name here for you bastards. The last time one of you got ahold of it, I was RickRolled in my sleep for a month. Do you know how disturbing it is to be about to get it on with some hot girl and have her transform into a singing, dancing Rick Astley? I'm sending the therapy bills to whoever was responsible just as soon as I track you down. I've got daemons on your trail armed with sprogs full of vengeance. I hope you like peeing rainbows. Literally.

Good hack though, I have to admit.)

So another MAA agent I assume to be the Magister 'ports into the chamber. He's—okay, he's younger than me—wearing ill-fitting blue jeans and a size XXL black t-shirt for HackCon IV. He's kind of a lard ass, but who spends sixteen hours a day behind a keyboard and isn't, right?

The Magister doesn't seem to notice me. He fiddles with a mojo-charged gadget that I swear is some kind of hacked *Zune*. It figures that one evil empire would be using the products of another. That's what cube jockeys call *synergy*.

He looks up as if surprised to find himself in the dank concrete cell with a surprisingly untortured prisoner, then smiles and nods. He waves to the agents, and they port out leaving only the smell of grandpa farts.

I wiggle a bit to confirm that my chair is bolted to the floor. When I do, I notice that the pendant that launched the Box sprog is still on the table. The stone table rises in a seamless piece from the cell floor between the chairs. I palm the pendant as quick as I can, hoping that the Magister doesn't notice. Thank Cthulhu, he doesn't seem to.

Magister Atretius slumps into the chair across from me, sighing. I readjust my age estimate downward. This kid looks like he's barely out of high school. "I really hate to bring you in, Hidr. I'm a big fan. I've been reverse engineering your sprogs since I was in junior high."

I try to muster up some spit, but my mouth is dry from all the shouting in the Box. "So you're a turncoat."

He shrugs. "Piracy doesn't pay. Literally, in money or power, and I don't mean 'mojo.' Pirates are like children playing with firecrackers. The MAA has nuclear warheads. I'm just the kind of guy who wants access to the biggest bombs." He taps his finger on the screen of his gadget, reading something. "I'm sure you know why you're here," Atretius says after a moment.

"Yeah I know why, but your goons didn't bother to read me my rights. I think I can get this case thrown out. Plus, it was entrapment or something."

"Or something." He sighs again. "We can charge you with as many counts of spell copyright infringement as we want, aiding spell copyright violation, facilitating the avoidance of MAA authorities, and a dozen other charges you've never even heard of."

Only one of those words really mattered to me. " '*Can?*' Not '*will*'?"

"I've been kissing my superior's asses all day to get you this deal, so I want you to listen to me before you get sarcastic and all 'down with the man!' "

"Big Mother can suck Donkey Kong's dong." My heart's not really in the insult, but I feel it's expected. (Don't you *even* ask me who Donkey Kong is, or I will not be responsible for my actions.)

The Magister shakes his head, tsking. " 'The Magical Association of Atlantis is an organization made up of numerous individuals and as such cannot comply with your demand.' Would you believe that's verbatim from a memorandum on 'prisoner relations' I got yesterday? Look, I'm not asking you to turn in anyone. We haven't even managed to take down your distribution network. Even with all your gear, we still can't crack your obfuscation. Routing the connections through routers in Chaos Space and the Outer Realms is brilliant, by the way. Oh, and it's your skill with server obfuscation that is one of the reasons you are perfect for this job."

I laugh just a little hysterically. "You're offering me a *job?*" Before I can explain how I wouldn't work for MAA if my balls were on fire and they had the last glass of water in the world, he interrupts.

"Piracy is *not* the only concern of the organization. Before both our times, the MAA was primarily tasked with knowledge control—keeping dangerous stuff out of the hands of people too stupid to know how to use it. The relaxed attitude your upstart cabals have about recruiting means stopping piracy and controlling access to the lore is the same thing now."

I nod. I think I remember having read that somewhere before, maybe in Captain Bl00d's manifesto. Ancient history.

"We have a problem that our most technically-inclined mages are unable to solve. Have you heard of 1CB?"

It sounds Web 2.0 trendy, but doesn't ring a bell. I shake my head.

"One-Click Banishment. An unknown party has put up a website that allows users to enter the True Name of anyone and with the click of a button, send the target immediately to the Gray Fields."

I stare at him. "How is that even possible?"

"I don't know, but I assure you it is. We have been overwhelmed with transport work. Do you know how much mana it costs to bring them back and wipe their memories? We need a better tactic. We need to shut it down."

"It shouldn't be hard to take down a website," I say. "A denial of service attack can do it, and I know you guys know about those. You've tried them on TomeTracker. And *failed*, of course." I allow myself a smirk.

"Guy before me. Real idiot. Our zombie nets do come in handy, but not for dealing with the likes of you. I could see right from the start that your obfuscation techniques would protect from DoS attacks. They don't work on your sites and they do not work on 1CB for the same reason. But because my superiors are idiots, over half the world's bandwidth is being taken up by a MAA DoS attack on 1CB. The server's load times have not been effected one millisecond."

"Huh," I say. Even I can be at a loss for words sometimes. "A sprog capable of transporting mundanes to another plane costs terabytes of mojo, or mana, or whatever you call it. That should make it easier to track down. Who has that kind of juice?"

"We can only account for registered, legal stores of mojo, and while they are taxed by our relocation project, every focule of energy is accounted for."

I mentally run through a list of what underground groups might come close to having enough stored mojo to power the 1CB sprog. The Spam Kings, maybe. They powered the *unduplicatus* spell that our fellow Buccaneers used to escape the MAA a couple of years back, and that thing was a mojo hog. Of course, the Pornomancers have mojo to spare, but 'porting eyeballs away from screens would run contrary to their whole gig. I check off our Order right away. Since Captain Bl00d was routed to dev/dead, we've been too disorganized to pull off anything like this, and besides, I would have heard about it. (You kids can't keep a secret. Soon as you learn something juicy, you're on the forums spouting off.)

The Socialistas *can* keep a secret, but they probably haven't accumulated that kind of mojo. They burn it as fast as they get it on lovey-dovey good-will crap. The HardC0re have buckets of juice, but are worse than us about agreeing on anything. They dissolve into a Playstation vs. Xbox flame war any time they try to make a group decision.

"Any idea what kind of traffic the site has seen?" I ask. "It hasn't appeared on the social news sites, has it?"

The Magister shakes his head. "Our moles are limiting the public knowledge of 1CB. We're blocking emails, tweets, and SMS that include the url by retasking Project Echelon. Yeah, we can do that. But we can't control the spread through person-to-person communications, not with our mojo taxed rescuing the targets from eternal boredom. Our last count put the number of banished at over fifty thousand."

"How the hell do fifty thousand mundanes disappear without it being noticed by the media?" I can't help myself—I'm getting into the mystery.

He stares at me, waiting for me to remember who I am dealing with."Like I said, the cover-up is a considerable drain on our resources. I don't have an agent I can put on this. I'm the ideal candidate, but I'm busy keeping my superiors from doing anything . . . drastic. Which brings us to you. You're more skilled than most of my agents anyway."

"Uh, thanks. So we can be sure that this is a major power play by an unknown. Also, *nobody* offers this kind of power for free. There's a catch somewhere," I scratch my chin, thinking. "I can see why you guys are worried, I guess."

He runs a finger across the screen of his device and the Manacles sprog vanishes. I rub my wrists.

"We have of course been interested in apprehending you for some time. It seems like a coincidence that we caught you in Operation LittleHeadThinker when we did, but perhaps the Fates have conspired to bring you to us. I noticed similarities in the hosting methods of 1CB and your illicit site early on in our investigation. And when I saw your name on the containment roster, I pulled strings, and here we are." Despite his apparent enthusiasm, for a moment he does not look happy. I wonder why he isn't accusing *me* of building the damned thing, but I'm not going to bring it up if he isn't. Something must have proved my innocence.

I evaluate my options. I don't have many. I'm caught up in the situation whether I want to be or not. Whoever is running 1CB is using my bag of tricks. The routers are, you guys have to admit, one of my moments of brilliance. Routing data traffic through the Chaos plane and then the Outer Realms makes it impossible for anyone to find the servers. Do a traceroute and you end up at some tiny ISP in Argentina. You'll get anything *but* the route to the actual servers. It as much a matter of pride now as anything else.

Plus, I don't want to be banished or executed just yet. "Fine," I say. "I'm in."

Okay, so, my stomach is going to strangle me with my intestines if I don't get something to eat right now, so hold tight. The story is just starting to get crazy.

☙

Posted by Hidr at 11:14 PM Yesterday

Say what you will about the Magical Association of Atlantis and the graybeards. The Noodly One knows I have. But they have some awesome toys.

After letting me out of the cell, Atretius gives me supervised access to part of their store of High Artifacts.

That's right, nerds: I totally got to play with Artifacts.

You might not be familiar with the term if you haven't been in the cabal long. Artifacts are ancient implements from before the time of mechanical or digital processors, like hundreds of years old at least. They look like mundane junk, but their platonic representations in the World Object Model have been overwritten by Elder Gods, aka They Whose Awesome Powers Will Make You Shit Yourself. We're talking beings with intellect so vast and calculating that they can work through sprog equations as easily as you add 2+2. *Their* mojo comes from the millions of *human souls* (the old school mojo source of choice) that they acquired through the centuries by trading with mages for processing time on their intellects. If you think a bored kid playing a Flash game is a good source of mojo, imagine what you get from that bored teen playing a flash game for one-hundred thousand years.

Luckily for us, the giant evil bastards were banished, bound, or annihilated when the computer revolution hit and they were no longer a "necessary evil" of m4gick. Hard to believe, but at one point the MAA were the good guys. You have to give them some credit for insuring that we aren't all sex toys of Cthulhu as trade for a few m4gickal tricks.

The first *totally awesome* m4gickal trick and artifact the Magister hooks me up with is a silver medallion to protect against banishment. Passive, grounding me to the material plane like a cosmic paperweight. It scans oddly dull for energy, but Atretius assures me that's part of how it works.

"Our mystery party may try to banish you if they find out you're onto them," he says. "This will stop them. All our agents are wearing them right now."

The second thing he gives me is a broom. No sleek sports car for this MAA agent apparently. Thank the Noodly One, it doesn't work by flying. For a moment I was honestly shitting myself at the idea of flying through the air at Mach 2 sitting on something barely wider than my thumb. Instead, it teleports me from one place to another via the Dusty meta-plane. I arrive at my destination looking like a vacuum cleaner bag had exploded in my face, but I get there in one piece.

Lastly, they returned my miscellaneous personal belongings, in particular my iPhone, newly loaded with documents pertaining to the case.

"So, what's your plan?" Atretius asks as he escorts me through processing. It turns out I'm in some kind of massive subterranean detainment center. I'm so excited to be getting out, I don't even hesitate to tell him.

"Inspect the site, look for clues to who is behind it. After that, we'll see."

"Headed back to your lair then? Good. Well, keep me informed," he says sternly. I flip him the bird and with that, I'm outta there and back to my Bat Cave.

Now my cat needs to go out. BRB

Posted by Hidr at 12:41 AM Today

Back at my lair, I spend the first fifteen minutes checking on my servers. At this point, they're still up (but of course. I run Linux *only in my sanctum*), but something really odd is showing up in the admin logs. I notice weird packets transferring through my routers that aren't originating from me or my servers. They shouldn't be there. If I could spare the time to pick them apart, I would, but they don't seem to be causing any downtime. Their volume doesn't match what I would expect from 1CB, and they're not on the right port for a web server anyway. I file it away for later inspection and turn to the MAA files.

They don't tell a different story from what the Magister had explained, and I get bored reading them less than halfway through.

My first real action as an agent of the MAA is to poke at the 1CB server.

Traceroute sure enough pointed at an internet café in Hong Kong. Ha, not likely. I used a sprog to look through the monitors at the café's clientele, but it's just a bunch of kids playing video games.

I take a look at the site in a custom version of Mozilla I wrote for investigating things like this. The site is one page, with a very simple, clean design style. It's not running any presentation-layer sprog code, so it's not trying to bespell the user.

It consists of a form field for the name and a button labeled "Banish" and that's it. The submit action on the form looks like a 256-bit encrypted Aleph symbol-set. Not a workable lead there. It would take literally all eternity to decrypt it and identify the processing sprog.

Time to test the site then. Who to use as my victim? I take an old high school yearbook from my bookshelf and flip pages until I see Danny de Marco. All my tortured nerd pain comes rushing back. Oh yes. He will do nicely.

I enter his name, checking it for typos (very carefully!) and click "Banish." A modal window pops up with a user agreement. Ha! *So* not "one-click." I move my mouse to click "accept" without thinking like I always do but then . . . I have a hunch and I have to pry my mouse finger back with my left hand. It goes against every computer-using instinct I have to not click through.

Must. Not. Succumb. To. Legalese.

I scroll through twelve pages of the usual "you can't sue us" garbage before I find what I'm looking for.

BY ACCEPTING THIS AGREEMENT, USER WILL BEQUEATH USER'S METAPHYS-
ICAL-ESSENCE ENERGY, HEREAFTER REFERRED TO AS "SOUL" TO THE ENTITY
KNOWN AS BAALPHORUM. THIS IS A NONREFUNDABLE TRANSACTION. ALL
HAIL HIS DEMONIC VISAGE. HE WILL RETURN TO TAKE WHAT IS RIGHTFULLY
HIS AND ALL SHALL TREMBLE BEFORE HIS GLORY.

And then the doc runs back to legal-speak standard bullshit. One paragraph of pure contractual evil buried in legal cruft. Clever. Nobody ever reads the user agreement text before checking the box and continuing. I've heard people *joke* that we were giving away our souls in the damned things, but I'd never seen anyone actually try it.

Here in the U.S., the user agreement constitutes a legal contract—the parties being the site user and this entity Baalphorum, who I have never heard of but I am pretty certain is one of the lesser Elder Gods. Those entities have always codified their arrangements with humans in contracts. Guess modern contract law has provided them a few new loopholes and tricks since the days of Mephistopheles.

I click "cancel" and close my browser. I consider setting fire to my computer, just to be sure. Giving away your soul in exchange for a *single* banishment is what we in the m4gick game call a sucker's deal.

(That's lesson number three. If you are going to trade your soul for anything, it's got to at least involve a computer with more processor cores than a hydra has heads. Not what amounts to an annoying, even if amusing and powerful, prank.)

I Skype a contact of mine in the Socialistas, an old-school pagan New Ager who likes reading the dusty books even if they don't have spells in them. Me, I could never be bothered. Her name is Cristina. No handle. That's how boring the Socialistas are.

The call beeps for five minutes (I'm patient) before Cristina answers in a mush of words I can't make out.

"What?"

"I said, 'Do you have any fucking idea what time it is?'"

I look out my window. "Uh . . . dark?" I don't even know what day it is. I glance at my system clock and see that it's been a week since I was captured, and, oh, it is currently 4 AM.

"What do you need now, Hidr?" I hear another feminine voice in the back-ground asking a question. Christina covers the mic and I can't make out his reply. I hear a giggle as she comes back on. "Make it quick, I have company."

"You always have company, you lucky girl. This won't take long and I'll send you a gig of mojo for your trouble. I need to know if you've heard of an Elder God named Baalphorum."

Christina *hmms*. "Maybe. Hold on." The call goes quiet, then I can hear the fwit-fwit of pages flipping. " 'Classified as a lesser Arch-Demon. He is the Prince of Journeys Gone Afoul. A patron demon to highwaymen and cutthroats.' The MAA banished him in the late '40s, locked him up in a deep Outer Realm. You know, I think I've read somewhere that cultists over the years have made several attempts to free him. Apparently, he was an easy date back in the day. What's going on?"

I sigh. "It looks like someone has found a new way to bust him out." I explain 1CB and ask if it could free the demon somehow.

"Promised souls are souls 'in the hand' for some spells. He would need to quickly reap the souls or face a mystic backlash that would slingshot his thorny ass past Andromeda, but it would work."

I file that tidbit away for later use. "How many souls would it take for a demon of Baalphorum's stature to break out?"

"I have no idea. Math's your game, pal."

"Give me a guess. Less than fifty thousand?"

I can almost hear her shrug. "Probably more than that. Say, one-hundred thousand? Isn't this what the MAA is supposed to take care of when they're not harassing us?"

I stammer, but there's no sense in lying to a Socialista. They always know, especially Cristina. "They've got me freelancing on this problem. Their resources are tied up in getting the mundanes back."

A long pause. "Well, we're all doomed then."

"Gotta go, Christina. Thanks for the vote of confidence."

I disconnect and call Atretius, who helpfully loaded his contact info into my phone before returning it. I start talking as soon as the call connects.

"This whole thing is a sucker deal in disguise. It's in the EULA."

There's a long enough pause that I think maybe I've dropped the call, but then: "Shit. I can't believe nobody read this thing. Do you know who or what this 'Baalphorum' is?"

I give him the details. He swears again.

"So we know where the mojo's coming from to power the banishments," Atretius says. "Baalphorum probably has mana stores in his prison. He shouldn't be able to get anything out from the prison, but the MAA containment budgets have been slimmer since we've redirected our resources, so maybe there are some cracks showing. At least we know what Baalphorum is getting in exchange."

"Someone has to be helping him on this side, but fuck if I know who," I say.

Something is bothering me that I can't quite place. "I verified that they're hiding the server with the same trick of Chaos space that I used on mine. The only way to trace it would be to have the actual astral encryption keys that were used to create the routing table, but I don't have the ones used to hide 1CB, so the site itself is a dead end."

"You better think of something quickly because . . . " I hear the clackity-clack of a classic IBM keyboard. "The fecal matter just hit the fan. The link is out in the wild. The site just made Digg. It'll be posted again to Metafilter and Reddit in minutes."

"*What*!" I nearly shout. "How did they get through?"

"Someone set up a redirect engine. It's being submitted with different URLs every time. *Someone's* been busy registering domain names. I'm transferring our DoS bots to take down all the social networking sites, but it's going to take a bit.

"You've got to get out there and find who's responsible for the site and shut them down," Artetius says. "It's our best chance of stopping this."

"Yeah, sure. There's just the one thing. I've got *zero leads*! Well, other than that whoever put the site up knows my methods of obfuscating a server. I explained how to maybe six people in the world, but I don't know who they really are or where they live. We're all anonymous in Bl00d's Cabal."

My phone dinged to announce new email.

"I've just sent you dossiers on your cabal mates."

"Holy shit! You have this information?"

Atretius yells something unintelligible in the background. "Can't talk any longer, I need to manage things on this end. Start kicking in doors." Click.

I scan the files, take a look at the first name and address. Before I go, I try to equip myself better, just in case. I ransack my place for gear and I turn up my old smartphone. It has a processor slower than a turd and a whole 128 megabytes of space. But it's better than nothing. I pocket it and then broom-port to my first "interviewee."

I arrive in a cramped basement apartment, coughing, eyes watering, gray all over with dust. A teenager, not a second older than fourteen, lies slumped over a keyboard snoring. The file says this is DedJonny, but I can't believe it. It makes me feel so much older.

I scroll through my selection of curses and prepare to squeeze him for info.

DedJonny nearly pisses himself when I clap my hands and wake him. He babbles. "Oh shit, oh man, I didn't do it, please, don't—"

"Shut up," I say calmly. "I'm Hidr. I have some questions."

He looks relieved. "How'd you get through my defensive sprogs? Oh right— you wrote them, must have put in backdoors huh? That's so chill."

"I'm offended you would think that. I have ethical standards," I snap, putting on my best "angry adult" voice. "What do you know about One Click Banishment?"

"One-what?" He blinks unconvincingly. Even an under socialized geek can see he's lying.

I swipe the screen on my phone and select the cactus-dick curse (see the first post in this thread). I pour 100k of mojo into the spell and hit him with it.

It won't last long, and the effect isn't as pronounced as it would be with a few megabytes, but it does the job. He screams and paws his crotch, and *that* doesn't make things any better.

"I've got worse than that here. Do you want to see how much worse?"

"No! It was me, okay? We go to school together, and he, he—started dating my girlfriend after we broke up—augh, why is my junk covered in needles?"

Hmm. Not the confession I was looking for. "Who?"

"OneEyedPete. I used the site on OneEyedPete. Isn't that why you're here? I knew he'd get back somehow, I just wanted to teach him a lesson is all."

That has the ring of truth. I dispel the curse. And by the way, DedJonny, if you're reading this, sorry about that, man. You'll understand why I had to do it by the end of this. I owe you some mojo.

I don't waste any time apologizing (I did that by writing the above). I move on to the next name on my list. And another, and so on until each one convinces me they have no idea who is behind One Click Banishment and it definitely isn't any of them.

It's only when I come to the end of my list when I realize that one name is missing: "LongDongSilver." Some of you may remember him. He was initiated into the Cabal a little bit after Bl00d's death. He was really eager to get to know everyone then. Check his posting history. He was crude and a little naïve, but he really got the nuts and bolts of networking protocols, so I brought him in on the private networking forums.

So how can the MAA have records on us so thorough, but be missing *one* Cabal member, who just happens to have access to my private forum?

I haven't wanted to consider the possibility, not really. It means we've been infiltrated for a long time now. And it explains the detailed records.

Just as it all makes sense, I am force-shifted across planes to the Gray Fields. It happens in a blink, without even a sound. One minute I am on the street outside a San Francisco apartment watching the sun rise, the next I am in the empty, barren wasteland of the Fields, surrounded by thousands of confused douchebags. Jocks, corrupt cops, snitches, power-hungry teachers—anyone who had ever pissed of a computer savvy geek is here, and more are arriving every minute.

They bitch and moan like the worst has happened to them but *they're* just being inconvenienced; their pranksters are going to pay for it with their souls.

I tear off the obviously fake medallion and throw it to the ground. I walk for ten minutes until I'm away from the smell of Old Spice and sit down. I swear by the Noodly One, I will fucking *pwn* Magister Atretius for this.

My phone rings. Impressive to receive a signal here, especially for AT&T. "Guess where I am?" says Atretius, a/k/a "LongDongSilver," calling to gloat.

I suggest something about carnal relations with a capybara.

"Wrong. I'm in your inner sanctum, stealing your IP tablez."

"How the fuck?" Of course he bugged me, probably via phone. See, n00bs? Not paranoid enough.

"Why do you want my tables?" I think I know, but I want him to say it.

"You haven't figured it out yet?" He laughs. "You are getting slow in your old age."

"Why don't you explain it to me, junior. It must be killing you not to share your genius plan with someone."

He sniffs. "Do you realize how much power the Elder Ones have? He's taught me so much already in little messages."

"But how has he been talking to you?"

"I have you to thank for that. One of your routers was close enough metaphysically for him to connect to your little ethereal network. Even a 'lesser' being like Baalphoruum has a mind capable of more processing than every computer on the planet. They're the original super computers. And I'm gonna have sole access to it."

"This is about *hardware*? What a nerd." I am beginning to rethink my open-mindedness towards the socially inept.

"Of course it is! In return for freeing him, Baalphoruum has promised me twenty years of Elder-processing time. Do you know what I can accomplish with that? I could create my own pocket universe!"

"There's no way he's going to let you get away with that. The Elder Ones always get the upper hand. Duh, they're smarter than the entire planet?"

"They are bound by laws, and my uncle's this big-time contract lawyer. When I found his messages in your router packets—"

"Yeah, yeah. We've covered this. So you were a plant in our organization from the beginning? They brought you into the MAA to infiltrate us, I bet. But you had bigger plans than being a MAA stooge. Hell, the MAA gave you the tools to make sure your stupid scheme didn't backfire on you. And then my idiot self gave you the basic principles of my network protocols so you could make sure nobody could put a stop to your soul collector. You probably even planned to pin it all on me. That about right?"

His silence was enough confession for me.

"What I can't figure though, and yeah, maybe it's because I'm *old* and *slow*, but why in the hell would you let me out and send me to track your own scheme down? You had me locked up. I was the only person who could possibly stop you."

I stopped, hit with revelation. "But you needed my IP tables to free him. You're bringing him back *through* the routers."

"If there had been any other way, I would have used it. Even having captured you, there was no way you would hand over your IP tables. And finding the great Hidr's inner sanctum didn't work, never did. But you talked enough on the forums about your kind of girl, and dropped enough hints that I knew what city you were in, so I launched Project LittleHeadThinker. I brought you in and gave you just enough rope to run back home. Admit it, I'm just more clever than you."

Actually, he had just given me the means of my escape, so I guess, in a way, he was, but I sure as hell wasn't going to admit it.

"There, all done." He stopped typing. "Baalphoruum will soon be on his way. You were pretty hot shit once, Hidr, but I've taken the netgeek throne."

"You're just keeping my seat warm, you little shit," I shouted. I hung up, threw down the phone, and stomped it to bits. This served two purposes. It made me feel better, and it prevented the bastard from seeing what was coming next.

Which will have to come after I write a few emails. Stay tuned for the stunning conclusion.

Posted by Hidr at 2:15 AM Today

Having routers stashed all over the outer planes, it turns out, is not the best idea when it comes to the safety of the world, but it comes in handy when you find yourself stuck in one of said outer planes.

My back-up smartphone has just enough memory to run a scan sprog. I didn't personally deliver my routers to the outer realms, but I would be an idiot if I didn't have a way of locating them for repairs. If Baalphoruum was sending suckers to the Gray Fields, that meant I had a router along the way.

I push through the crowds, keeping an eye out for MAA agents, following the sub-etheric signal from my router. Sure, they could get me back home, but I'd be brainwashed in the process, and that isn't going to do anyone any good.

After what feels like days, I locate the router, locked in its protective field, humming with mojo tapped straight from my private cloud storage space.

I plug my piece of crap smartphone into the router with a USB cable and tap the mojo. It's barely enough, and using it will take down my sites, but it'll get me home.

I might be getting old, and I might be a little out of touch with the hip things these days, but I still can code Aleph like *nobody* else. I whip up a matter-to-data transportation sprog based on a teleportation spell insprog based on a teleportation spell in the *Maleficus*. It's probably something very similar to what Atretius is writing to bring Baalphoruum to him. I'm counting on my skills as a sprog hacker now to get me back before the demon does.

Let me just say to you kids that being made up of nothing but encrypted UDP packets is not all its cracked up to be. Worse, my code was a little buggy, and I'm missing a toe now. I should have written better error-handling. But I got back, even if it wasn't in entirely one piece.

I find Atretius in my Bat Cave, my inner sanctum. He's set up an altar that looks like it was made by Ikea. I can smell defensive sprogs thick in the air, I can taste the gigs of mojo burning up. Within a protective summoning circle of Cat-5 cables, Atretius sits coding at a laptop. He has discarded the casual wear for the traditional black robes of evil-doing. I think that the entities are kind of old-fashioned when it comes to formal wear or something. I'm determined not to let the bastard impress his master with his sense of fashion.

I launch every attack sprog I have, which isn't many given my crap phone. They error out immediately, stymied by the defense sprogs. Atretius doesn't even look up. I laugh and give my attack sprogs my backdoor passwords, counting on his arrogance.

Oh, yeah. Lesson number four: there's *always* a backdoor password.

Sure enough, he is using my own work to defend himself. They come down leaving him defenseless but also leaving me out of almost out of mojo.

Atretius looks up then . . . and smiles.

A rip in the fabric of space, like the universe's own dead pixel, forms before the altar. Something *huge* is trying to squeeze through. Distracted by this, I'm not ready when Atretius hits me with the Manacles again. I'm down. The Magister sighs and steps out of his circle.

"If you just pin your arms to your sides, I'll pull on your horns," Atretius says.

"That's something you know a lot about, huh? Jerking on demon horn," I say.

He lets loose of the demon and turns his full attention on me. I can sense him drawing mojo from his hacked Zune. But it's suddenly cut off by my inner sanctum's network defenses coming online.

"This is a nix-only house, asshole," I say with a grin which quickly fades to terror.

Baalphoruum exits the portal with a slurping sound, followed by a deep and teeth-shattering laugh. The demon fixes his hundreds of red eyes on Artetius. He frantically pushes buttons on his gadget to no effect.

"YOUR SERVICES WILL NO LONGER BE REQUIRED, BARRY," Baalphorum says in a voice like ten thousand babies crying. "I AM INVOKING THE TERMINATION CLAUSE OF OUR CONTRACT."

"What—what termination clause?" The "Barry formerly known as Artetius" stutters, but then his head is several feet from his neck. I guess his uncle wasn't such hot shit at contract law after all. With the turncoat deader than Kurt Cobain (Google him, kids), the manacles dispelled.

Unfortunately, now Baalphoruum has turned his attention to me. And it seems he's intent on killing me slowly. He wraps a six-fingered fist around my neck and lifts me into the air to stare at me with his many fiery eyes.

You know, I never watched *Buffy the Vampire Slayer*, so I don't know any badass moves to take out a demon. (I'm more old-school in my entertainment. I grew up watching a little movie called *Monster Squad*. You can catch it on cable every once and a while. Check it out.)

So, lesson number five: like a wolf man, arch-demons have 'nards.

A well-placed kick drops me to the floor and my vision fades back in around the edges. I had a plan before coming in, but I hadn't counted on physical contact with a demon. I'm a little winded, but then, so is Baalphorum. And he's still weak, overdrawn on soul mojo. That's when I point and execute the Box pendant.

Pwned. Now here is where things get tricky. The Box spell is good, but it won't keep a demon like Baalphorum trapped for long. After I catch my breath, I hack out a little old-fashioned web code and insert it into the Box sprog.

I didn't actually *see* this next part, but I imagine this is how things went:

Baalphorum stalks the small space of the Box spell, roaring with fury. He hammers on the walls and they crack ever so slightly. He could break free with time, but he wants to take what is his *now*.

A pair of buttons appear in the air before him, along with text:

"Do you wish to escape, my master? YES/NO"

Ahh, the mortal (me) has seen the error of its ways. He will escape and slaughter Earth more quickly now.

An endless, sprawling legal agreement appears, tiny text, miles of it. A checkbox labeled "Check here to continue." On the surface, it seems simple enough, and each moment he spends outside his prison without the souls, he grows weaker.

Even Elder Ones can't stand reading the damned things. Baalphorum checks the box and readies himself for a rampage. Instead, he is promptly hurled back into his prison across a thousand astral planes. I hope it hurts like hell.

And that's lesson number six: software user agreements will fuck you every time.

JONATHAN L. HOWARD is the author of the novels *Johannes Cabal the Necromancer* and *Johannes Cabal the Detective*. His short fiction has appeared in *Realms of Fantasy* and *H. P. Lovecraft's Magazine of Horror*. He has also worked in the computer games industry since the early '90s as a game designer and scriptwriter. He lives in Bristol, England.

If you were a necromancer, how would you feel if you found yourself in the middle of a zombie outbreak? One that threatened the future of the entire world? Well, if you're Johannes Cabal, you're not particularly worried—you're just a little put out.

Cabal has an unusual way of looking at the world, and it's not just because of his profession, although working with corpses might have colored his outlook. As quick on his feet as James Bond and as selfish as the worst comic book villain, Cabal is an unlikely savior of the world, but when he's confronted by a magician with more ability than brains, this wizard of the dead is our last and only hope. Unfortunately, all he's got on his side is one bumbling constable, a bit of rope, and top-notch reconnaissance.

This story fills the gap between the short story "Exeunt Demon King" and the first novel about Cabal, *Johannes Cabal the Necromancer*. Jonathan Howard says of this story's inspiration: "I myself halted a zombie apocalypse a couple of years ago, and I remember thinking at the time, 'This would make a good story.' "

We *think* he's joking.

THE ERESHKIGAL WORKING
JONATHAN L. HOWARD

This was not the first time a corpse had abruptly sat up on the mortuary slab and turned to face Johannes Cabal with murder in its eyes; it was, however, the first time one had done so without waiting to be formally reanimated. They stared at one another for a moment before the corpse, apparently unaware of the *faux pas*, made a cry like somebody receiving terrible news, and lunged at Cabal. Cabal, whose faults were mainly moral, grabbed the dead man by the scruff and threw it face first to the floor. While keeping it prone and thrashing with a foot to the back of its neck, he pulled a nearby wheeled trolley to him and reached into the brown leather Gladstone bag that lay open upon it.

The performance was observed in a baleful silence by a dishevelled police constable who sat against the wall, gagged and bound. He watched as Cabal drew a handgun of egregious aspect from the Gladstone, placed the muzzle at the junction between the occipital lobe and the atlas vertebrae, and completed the ad-hoc de-animation procedure with the introduction of a .577 bullet. The sound of the shot was deafening against the morgue's hard walls and floor, echoing harshly from the cold stone slabs. Cabal kept his foot in place and drew back the revolver's hammer in anticipation of further trouble. The corpse, however, showed no signs of attempting any further movement other than slumping. Cabal waited for a long moment in case it was a cunning zombie ruse, before gently thumbing the hammer back to rest. He glanced sideways as if sensing the policeman's accusing glare.

"I don't know why you're looking at me like that," said Cabal, a faint German accent just discernible in his clipped and clearly enunciated speech. "This has nothing to do with me."

Nor was he lying. Johannes Cabal had taken advantage of the town's annual carnival weekend to carry out a little specialist shopping. While the crowds gathered on the streets to see the parade go by—this year with the exciting new innovation of enormous hydrogen balloons rendered in the form of newspaper cartoon characters and advertising mascots—Cabal had quietly entered the municipal mortuary through a back window and sequestered himself in the morgue, wherein he had intended to remove some footling bits of offal necessary to his researches. This simple plan had almost foundered once already; an alert police officer had seen Cabal slide down a back alley and had become suspicious. This was not a startling piece of detectively intuition; Cabal was a tall blond man of wan complexion, wearing a black suit and carrying a brown leather Gladstone bag. Though he was only in his late twenties, Cabal's demeanour was not one of fun and frivolity, even on such an occasion. He had barely looked at the parade as it passed, beyond a glance at the great flying cartoon characters, and even these had only caused his lip to curl. Then he had looked both ways—failing to spot the policeman who had taken station in a doorway—before all but tip-toeing down the alley to the rear of the mortuary. Thus, while not quite wearing a striped shirt, mask, and carrying a bag marked "Swag," Cabal had not been as surreptitious as he had hoped.

The officer, a Constable Copeland, had investigated the alley and, finding a window jemmied open, had crept inside. Unhappily for him, his creeping was not so very surreptitious either, and he had been laid low by a scientifically applied crowbar. When he had recovered consciousness, it was to discover himself tied and gagged and witness to Cabal's attempted body part snatching . . . and the unexpected resurrection that thwarted it.

Cabal was most put out. First, the policeman turning up had put him off his stride, and now a dead man coming at him really was beyond the pale. "This is not normal," he commented. Most people would doubtless have agreed, but most people were not necromancers for whom "normal" is a much broader category.

A whispering groan from beneath a sheet on the furthermost slab drew his attention. He watched the form beneath it stirring into a semblance of life even as the occupant of the next-closest table also begun to wheeze air into lungs unused for a day or two. Cabal considered quickly; he had five rounds remaining in his Webley, and a further six in his pocket, bundled together with an elastic band to prevent them rattling. There were four occupied slabs in the morgue, all of whose occupants were showing uncalled for signs of activity. He could probably stay and fight, but there was something untoward occurring here and he might need the ammunition later. Discretion, as was usually the way, would stand in for valour.

In three long strides he was by the policeman, pulling him to his feet and pushing him through the swinging double doors. He let the bound man sprawl to the floor, taking the moment to draw a switchblade that snapped open with a perfunctory *clik*. He quickly knelt by the policeman, who was regarding the sharp blade with some trepidation and, fearing the worst, began to struggle. Cabal was having none of it, and slapped Constable Copeland. "Don't be a fool. If I wanted you dead, you would never have woken up." The blade went in and sliced, and the policeman suddenly found his hands free. Cabal stood up, the ropes in his left hand, the blade in his right. He snapped the blade shut and dropped it back into his jacket pocket.

Shadows fell across the frosted glass in the upper halves of the morgue doors as Cabal turned back to them. He jammed his foot against the base of the doors as he fed the rope through the handles and quickly knotted them tight. He stepped away as the doors were roughly shoved from the far side. Through the glass, four outlines crowded around the door, pushing.

The policeman had drawn his own penknife and was just finishing sawing through the ropes around his ankles. His gag, his own handkerchief, hung around his neck. "What's happening?" he demanded hoarsely. "What have you done?"

Cabal didn't turn, but continued to watch the activity of the shadows. "To answer your second question first, beyond saving your life, I have done nothing. To answer your first, I am not yet sure."

The shoving had quietened down, and Cabal was just wondering if they had given up when all four shapes rammed the door simultaneously. The rope grew tight under the impact, but held. The shadows became blurs, then sharpened as they rammed the door together again. The rope, tied with a knot that would distress Houdini, held firm. "Ah," Cabal said. "Now that is interesting."

"You," said the policeman, searching for a rock to base his sanity upon and settling upon duty, "are under arrest."

Cabal sighed, pulled his revolver from his bag and waggled it in a more or less threatening way. "You are being a fool again, officer. I truly am not only the least of your worries at present, but possibly your only chance for salvation. Listen . . ."

They listened, and beyond the rhythmic thump of undead bouncing off morgue doors could be heard distant screams. Cabal noted the policeman's expression of dawning realisation with a thin smile. "We are not the only ones having trouble with the walking dead."

From the topmost storey of the mortuary, they were able to look out across the town square, and the massacre that was occurring there. The carnival crowd had only recently become aware that there was something very horrible occurring within it. It had started when first a scattering of people across the town had collapsed, including many in the crowd. A doctor had struggled through to the nearest victim and done his best, but it was too late. Too late in all manner of ways as it turned out when the dead man's eyes had flickered open. The happy cries of his family sounded a lot less happy when he grabbed the doctor by the throat and throttled him in a few convulsive twists.

Then the doctor had gotten up too, and the bystanders decided they were not in the safest place. But, hemmed in by the surrounding crowd, there was nowhere to run.

"My God!" cried the policeman.

"Oh? Where?" replied Cabal, looking about with affected surprise.

The policeman glared at him. "I have to help!"

For his part, Cabal now leaned on the chest high windowsill with both arms flat, his chin resting on the uppermost, watching the chaos below with the detachment of an entomologist watching red ants fight black. The policeman waited a long moment for some sort of response before finally giving up and turning angrily on his heel.

"This *helping*," said Cabal, just loudly enough to be heard. He did not look away from the window. "This *helping* to which you refer, I assume you intend to help the living?" Cabal took the pause in footsteps to mean he had the policeman's attention. "It's just that your current course of action can only help the walking dead I see out there, by inevitably bolstering their numbers. Come here."

With some reluctance, the footfalls grew closer until the policeman joined him at the window.

Cabal lifted his head and made a small wave of his hand to take in the moiling mixture of violent dead and unhappy living. "Observe, constable. What do you see?"

"Carnage," said the policeman hoarsely. His mouth was dry and when he licked his lips, it didn't help at all. "Terror."

"Yes, yes," said Cabal impatiently. "Very picturesque terms but hardly scientific."

The constable breathed in sharply. "Oh, dear God, there are children out there!"

Cabal favoured him with a disapproving glance. "Of course there were children out there. There was a parade. Why wouldn't there . . . Oh." He nodded with realisation. "You mean there are children being murdered. Yes, there are, but that isn't the interesting thing."

"What kind of a man are you?"

"The kind who sneaks into mortuaries with the intention of stealing parts of human brains, and isn't especially put out by the appearance of the unquiet dead—beyond a sort of 'Oh, what a nuisance' sort of reaction, anyway." The two men glared at one another. "Those are all the hints you're getting," said Cabal. "I really can't see you making CID if you can't reach a conclusion based on them."

The constable had, in fairness, already reached a conclusion, but that didn't mean he had to like it. "You're a necromancer," he said, quietly repulsed.

"Yes, I am." Cabal was splendidly unconcerned with the constable's opinion one way or the other. "And we are a rare breed, which makes all this," he looked out the window again, "all the more interesting. I come here and the dead spontaneously rise. This really is not normal."

"Isn't it?" There was a distinct sneer in the words, and an irony that tottered into sarcasm. It could not have been calculated to irritate Cabal—a man notoriously prone to irritation—with more effectiveness.

"No," he snapped, rounding on the constable. "No, it isn't, and I have some actual experience in these areas, rather than that righteous unctuousness in your tone that you fondly believe substitutes for knowledge. Look!" And so saying he took hold of the constable's collar and pushed him to the window. "There!" Cabal pointed at one group of undead shambling across the road. "There!" He pointed out another group standing aimlessly in the churchyard on the southern side of the town square. "And there!" The mortuary was just off the square, but the town hall was still visible some two hundred yards away. "Do you see?"

The constable angrily shook Cabal's hand from his collar and glared out of the window. "Monsters," he said, finally. "Your monsters are everywhere, they . . . " He paused.

"You see?" asked Cabal, deciding to ignore the "your monsters" calumny.

"They're behaving differently," said the constable slowly, his eyes flickering from one group to the next. "Some are working together, others just stand there." There was a scream outside. The constable blanched. "Unless somebody gets too close. Why aren't they all doing the same things?"

Cabal didn't answer. Instead he had opened his Gladstone and was sorting through its contents. A moment later, he straightened up, snapped a small telescope out to length, and peered out across the town square.

The constable saw he wasn't going to be getting any immediate answers and ventured upon conjecture. "Are they . . . like bees? Workers and . . . drones and . . . "

"A gestalt hive mind," offered Cabal, not lowering his telescope.

"Yes!"

"No. Not least because drones sexually serve the queen, and the idea of those roles having analogies in a horde of walking dead is simply too distasteful to contemplate. More pertinently, however, they are not exhibiting different behaviour; only one area of the growing horde *is*, and that area is not fixed. These are not human bees; these are puppets of flesh. Observe, and you will note that the walkers become more active, more directed, in an area some thirty feet across. This signifies the area of the puppet master's attention."

"The puppet master? Somebody's controlling them? Who?"

"Yes, there is a puppet master. Yes, he is controlling them and . . . " he handed the constable the telescope and pointed across the square, " . . . he's the fat bastard on the roof of the town hall."

"Fat" was an overstatement, but the man visible on the town hall roof was certainly well-built. The constable could see an ursine form capering back and forth along the parapet edge of the flat-roofed building, gazing out across the chaos he had created now and then with what appeared to be a pair of army surplus field glasses.

"Why has he done this? All this death? All these innocent people? *Why?*"

Cabal took the telescope back, closed it up with a smart snap, and put it back into his bag. "At the risk of sounding conceited, I believe it's all about me. It really is too great a coincidence that this fellow decides to embark on such a clottish piece of amateur necromancy at the very same time that I just happen to be skull delving in the local mortuary."

"He's trying to impress you?" The idea horrified the constable. "What sort of . . . "

"No, no, no," said Cabal, and made a *haha* sort of noise that may have been a laugh, or it may have been a nervous tic. "He's trying to *kill* me. Not the most efficient way of setting about it, but I can imagine how all this might appeal to a certain type of personality. Not a very clever one, though."

"Amateur? He managed to raise an army of the dead!"

"Oh, that?" Cabal sniffed dismissively, as if this unknown enemy had raised an army of chinchillas. "Any fool can do that. In fact, only a fool *would* do that. That is a ritual known as the Ereshkigal Working, and no necromancer with an ounce of wit who isn't an avowed nihilist would want anything to do with it."

Constable Copeland was not overly interested in what was à la mode this year in necromancy. He was watching the quick legging it from the dead. "That's the last of the survivors out of the square. If they have any sense, they'll barricade themselves in their homes until the army gets here. Those things won't stand a chance then." He nodded with desperate assuredness at Cabal. "We can just sit this out, can't we?"

Cabal shook his head, and left the window to perch on the edge of a desk. He gestured for Copeland to sit by him, and this he did with a sense that Cabal had approximately a bathful of ice-cold water to throw on those hopes. As, indeed, he did.

"Constable," Cabal began, "this is a reasonably-sized town, yes? About two hundred thousand people?" Copeland nodded, and Cabal continued, "In a conurbation of this size, about twelve people die every day. Their bodies remain viable for Ereshkigalian resurrection for about a month. Assume that half are cremated within the first week after death, and that half of the remainder can't get out of their graves. That's optimistic, by the way. The dead are very good at exhuming themselves."

Copeland opened his mouth to ask how Cabal could know such a thing, before realising how foolish that would sound, so he closed it again.

"Therefore," continued Cabal, "in addition to the scattering of deaths that the Working caused, there are approximately another hundred and fifty five corpses around the place that will also be up and about by now. Each will attempt to kill the living. Every time that they succeed, the fresh corpse will be added to the sum of their army. If you have ever wondered what a geometrical progression looks like, you need only look out of that window. So, to answer your question, no, we cannot just 'sit this out.'"

There was a crash from downstairs that startled Copeland to his feet. "They're out of the morgue!"

"Right," said Cabal with an air of getting down to work. "First things first. Avoid being killed by undead. That's very important. Then, deal with that idiot before he inadvertently wipes out the human race. Also quite important."

"Wait." The constable took Cabal by the arm. "I can't take this in. You really mean this is . . . this could be Doomsday?"

Cabal looked pointedly at the constable's hand until he removed it from Cabal's bicep. "I mean what I say, Constable. What the hoi polloi sensationally and inaccurately call the *Zombie Apocalypse*, professionals such as myself refer to more soberly as the *Ereshkigal Working*. Nomenclature aside, the results are much the same. Humanity goes down beneath a tide of its own angry carcasses."

Below them they could hear the sound of the building being thoroughly if violently searched by the mortuary corpses. Cabal said that these were the ones most concentrated upon by their resurrector, and that he would certainly be watching through their eyes in the periods when he wasn't using his own through the field glasses. If they should see Cabal, the main force would be directed toward him instead of milling around the streets. Things would likely go badly for Cabal and the constable in such a case.

Thus, instead of descending to street level just yet, they climbed to the roof. "This is the plan, constable. We shall travel along this rooftop, drop to the next, go to the alleyway on its far side, descend via the fire escape . . . "

"How do you know it's got a fire escape?" interrupted the constable.

"Because I made it my business to know. It usually pays to have at least two escape routes planned; a fast one and an evasive one. This is the evasive. Now, once we reach street level, we cut across the road behind that overturned wagon. The dead are staying this side of it so far, so we had better use it before they spread out."

"That's insane. Why break cover that long? If we go in the other direction, we only have to cross two small alleyways."

Cabal drew a pair of dark glasses from his breast pocket, and made a small show of polishing the blue lenses. "That route has been considered and rejected." He put on the glasses with an air of finality.   •

"Rejected? But, why?" The constable scoffed incredulously. "Your route is madness. Mine is much safer, a couple of alleyways, and cut through the churchyard and . . . " He paused, a thought occurring. "Do you have a problem with churches?"

Cabal's expression was unreadable behind the glasses. Without a word, he turned and trotted off in a crouch to avoid being seen from the town hall. On reaching the end of the roof, he unhesitatingly stepped off into space. A moment later, the constable heard the crunch of sensible shoes on gravel and bitumen, and knew Cabal was safely on the next rooftop. Cursing under his breath, Constable Copeland followed.

With galling inevitability, Cabal turned out to be right about the fire escape, and the two men descended unseen to a narrow lane that opened out onto the main road. Cabal wasn't quite so accurate on the state of the road itself, however. A lone corpse had wandered past the overturned wagon and was standing aimlessly in the middle of the way, its back to them. Once upon a time, it had been a tobacconist, but now it was just a nuisance.

"What do we do? Can you shoot it?" The constable was trying hard to think of the figure as an object, and not Mr. Billings from whom he had bought a packet of Senior Service that very morning before going on duty. He thought of the cigarettes sitting in his locker at the police station; they seemed like an artefact of a bygone civilisation now. The Apocalypse had come, and here he was, PC Copeland, a parochial plod of the local constabulary, lurking down an alley in the company of a necromancer while avoiding the attentions of an undead tobacconist.

"They're dead, not deaf." Cabal took the switchblade from his pocket, and snapped out the blade. He searched around in an eddy pool of litter by the base of the wall and found a bottle top. "No, this calls for subtlety." Holding the knife so the blade was angled down, much like one might hold an ice pick, Cabal set off to demonstrate his personal definition of subtlety. Walking quietly but upright, trusting to the wagon to hide him from the main mass of walking dead, he approached the former Mr. Billings from the rear. On reaching him, Cabal paused and flipped the bottle top so it landed in front of Billings with a distinct musical *ting*, all glittery and eye-catching in the midday sunshine. Mr. Billings, who found the smallest things of infinite wonder ever since Mrs. Billings, about fifteen minutes earlier, had torn out his throat with her teeth, looked down at it and in so doing obligingly exposed the nape of his neck. Without the slightest hesitation, Cabal drove the knife in with an expertise that should worry any casual observer. Just as in the morgue, the spinal cord was transected between the occipital and the atlas—the strings were cut—and Mr. Billings' body fell forward heavily to lie in the middle of the High Street on carnival day.

Cabal leaned down, and Copeland momentarily thought he was going to check that the job had been done properly, but Cabal only wiped the blade on the back of Mr. Billings' coat before snapping it shut and dropping it back into his pocket. "Come on," said Cabal. "And bring my bag."

They made their way down the alleyway, across the High Street, and continued some little way down there until Cabal paused at the back door of a shop and forced his way in. It was a hardware store, which he seemed to expect, making Constable Copeland realise just how meticulous his unusual companion's reconnaissance had been. Cabal paused to steal a coil of half-inch rope, and Copeland didn't even bother to *tut* disapprovingly; things had moved beyond worrying about petty larceny. They reached the top floor where Cabal opened a locked skylight with the crowbar from his bag, and then they were on the rooftops again. They moved along a little way and then, from the shadow of a chimneystack, they observed the man on the town hall roof once again. He was still about a hundred feet away, but they could see him far more clearly now. This was not necessarily a bonus. The man wore a suit cut from the sort of tweed that weavers devise for a bet; brown lines against a yellow field, making the wearer look like an Ordnance Survey map of custard. He was a big bear of a man with a fine, Jovian beard and a collar-length mane of thick red hair of a shade too ruddy for any to call "ginger" and live.

"Are you that good a shot?" whispered Copeland.

"I'm not going to shoot him," replied Cabal. "Worst thing I could possibly do. Despite the brutal, painful, and lingering death that this idiot so richly deserves, I have to keep him alive for the moment."

"I don't understand."

"Since they don't teach necromantic theory at the police college, I'm hardly surprised. Very well—a crash course. You will notice that the undeads' behaviour falls into three categories. There are the very focussed examples in the morgue; these are the only ones that saw me, and so their master is keeping much of his attention on them, for the moment at least. Then there are the ones who are moving around as a flock; these are his secondaries and his attention upon them is vague. He has moved them up towards the mortuary in reserve should he still find me there. Finally, we have the vast majority, who stand around like that example in the road. They are at the edge of his awareness. He is overwhelmed by complexity here—he has far, far more subjects than he can effectively control. So, most are forgotten and are being fed no commands by the psychic links he has with the whole ugly crowd of them."

"How are they dangerous, then?"

"Because the force that animates them is atavistic and feral. Whenever an opportunity to kill is presented to them, they slip the vague control of this nominal puppet master until the killing has been done. The force is greedy—it craves more bodies to occupy." Cabal turned his telescope upon the man on the roof once more. "He is the means by which this animating force came into our world, and he holds its leash. That leash can never be more than a range of twenty-three *tirum*, an obsolete unit of measurement once used by the culture that created the Ereshkigal Working. Twenty-three equates to just under three miles. Twelve yards, seven point one six inches under, to be exact.

"But, what he is doing is mentally exhausting. Sooner or later, he will have to sleep. That is when they will kill him. The leash will evaporate, and the animating force will have free rein to extend its activities as far as it likes. Did I mention how greedy it is for more bodies? I believe I did."

All the talk of an apocalypse had seemed like so much hyperbole up to now, but now Constable Copeland could see the awful mechanism at play. "Won't . . . won't he stop if he gets you? Won't he send this force back where it came from?"

Cabal had been wondering how long it would be before a cloaked version of *What happens if I throw you to the zombies?* was aired, and he was ready for it. "The ritual is irreversible. He either doesn't realise that yet, or he just assumed he'd have a use for an army of the dead afterwards. As I said, the man's an idiot."

Copeland considered Cabal's words. "So you're saying, we only have a few hours before this all becomes unstoppable?"

"Exactly so." Cabal was looking around the square through his telescope. He considered the remains of the parade in front of the town hall; he considered the hydrogen-filled cartoon characters looking cheerfully down upon the scene of carnage; he considered the undead turning away from the mortuary as presumably the search there was abandoned; he considered the church across the way. "That church has a weathervane, so at least the wretched building is good for something."

"It has a clock, too," Copeland retorted without thinking, a feeling of guilty apostasy immediately settling upon him.

Cabal did not reply, but was looking at the bridge over the local river, just visible where the road in front of the town hall curved. "This town has a small harbour, does it not?"

"We're at the neck of the estuary here. The sea's less than a mile away. Why?" he said, then added a little bitterly: "Are you going to steal a boat?"

Cabal lowered the telescope and looked at him. It was an unreadable look, and Copeland had a strange sense that behind the blue-glass spectacles and behind the eyes themselves, there was something disarranged, something missing. "Perhaps I have not made my intentions clear, Constable. There is a brief period before this plague will spread, and the world as we know it is lost forever. I need that world, and I will not stand idly by or run while there is the slightest chance of preserving it."

Copeland grimaced. "How do you make something heroic sound so selfish?"

"You cut me to the quick," Cabal replied evenly. Then he said, "You're a policeman. I assume that means you carry useful pieces of equipment as well as that comedic helmet we left in the morgue? A truncheon? Handcuffs? A notebook? That sort of thing?"

Copeland narrowed his eyes—he liked his helmet—but nodded.

"Excellent. Well, if it is so necessary for heroism to save the day, and given that I am such a selfish person, then by a process of deduction . . . "

And Johannes Cabal smiled.

Being a mighty sorcerer was turning out to be a great deal easier than he had imagined. The hardest part of the whole plan had been tracking Cabal to this town, but after that it had been plain sailing. Admittedly, he had only intended the dead in the morgue to rise, and the resurrections in the carnival crowd had been a surprise—it seemed that the Ereshkigal Working was a more of a blunderbuss than he'd anticipated—but he had shrugged, taken it in his stride, and it all seemed to be going very well now. By allowing his consciousness to blur, he had put out a ring of drones to keep the area contained, and he was positive that it had not been breached. Now he just had to search every building within the cordon, and soon he would have his revenge. He hoped it *was* soon; all the extra work involved in controlling so many carcasses was astonishingly tiring.

It turned out to be even sooner than he'd expected. As he leaned on the town hall parapet and marshalled his forces to tear through shop after office, a voice spoke behind him, quiet and with a faint Teutonic accent.

"So," it said. "You are the one behind this ham-fisted attempt on my life, are you?"

He turned to see Cabal himself, the loathed object of his every waking thought for years past, standing before him, arrogant and unconcerned. "Johannes Cabal. You should be dead by now, and one of my meat puppets." He laughed, a very declamatory laugh of the kind normally associated with cloaks, thin moustaches, and a battered top hat. "Well, I'm glad that you have survived this long. I wouldn't want to miss the pleasure of your final destruction!"

"I haven't come to confront you, whoever you are. I've come to parlay. See?" Cabal took his switchblade from his pocket, showed it, and dropped it to the gravelled surface of the roof.

"You . . . don't know who I am?" The man's face twisted in an ugly admixture of fury and sneer. "I have hunted you for years, Cabal, and you didn't even know it. You fool!" Ideally there would have been a crack of thunder at this point.

"*Fool* is a strong term to be used by somebody who does such a thing to kill one man," said Cabal, nodding at the crowded corpses below them.

"You don't deserve a clean, quick death, Cabal. Not after what you have done." The man threw out his chest and drew himself up to his admittedly impressive full height. "You murdered my father!"

"Did I?" Cabal was glad that they had arrived at some sort of conclusion, although it didn't actually help him that much. "Oh."

Despite his profession and his laissez-faire attitude to the mortality of others, Cabal had not actually had cause to kill very many people who hadn't previously been dead anyway, and he doubted whether putting down an uppity revenant such as the very, very deceased Mr. Billings, to take a recent example, was technically murder at all. Then again, people often developed emotional attachments to sides of meat that had once been relatives, so who was to say that some experimental subject or another had not once been this buffoon's father?

"Well," Cabal continued, "obviously I'm very sorry about killing your father, whoever he was, but don't you, whoever *you* are, think causing the destruction of the human race for purposes of personal revenge is at least mildly disproportionate?"

"Whoever I am?" roared the man, the perceived insult rating far more highly in his world than accidental genocide. "I am your nemesis, Johannes Cabal! I am the architect of your destruction! I am . . . Rufus Maleficarus!"

"Who?"

"You dare? You killed my father!"

Cabal rolled his eyes. "So you keep saying, Mr . . . " And then the penny dropped. "Maleficarus . . . As in *Maleficarus the Magnificent*? The conjuror?" He laughed. This was simply too ludicrous. "You have the wrong man, sir. I didn't kill your father. He killed himself. Twice in fact, which shows a certain stoicism."

Maximilian Maleficarus "the Magnificent" had been a stage illusionist with delusions of magical competence beyond the vanishing of rabbits and the sawing in half of obliging young ladies. After an encounter in his early career with the lively, if technically dead, Maleficarus senior, Cabal had walked away with a broken scapula, and Maleficarus had not walked away at all. Given that the elder Maleficarus spent a considerable time dead before resurrecting himself, it seemed unlikely that his son could have known him as more than a blurry figure from childhood.

But, in much the same way that feuds and vendettas can run for generations without troubling themselves to find a decent *cassus belli*, it seemed to the outraged family pride of Maleficarus junior, a planet full of undead was a small price to pay for hurt feelings.

Or was it? Maleficarus' heavy brow folded with suspicion. "What did you mean just then, *the destruction of the human race?*"

"The Ereshkigal Working. You must remember it? That thing you did with the chalk circle and the incense? Well, all these dead people walking around, the two things are actually related. Did you know that?"

"Don't talk to me like I'm an idiot, Cabal!"

"You *are* an idiot, Maleficarus! Have you the vaguest idea why the Working has not been used in over four millennia? See! Over there on the far side of the square! See what you stupidity has created!"

Maleficarus looked, and saw nothing. Cabal was furious. "It is right there! Use your binoculars if you have to, but look!"

Maleficarus raised the binoculars to his eyes, and so he did not see Cabal's high passion fade instantly away, to be put into his inner jumble room of false emotions until it was next needed.

"I don't see anything unusual," muttered Maleficarus, already grown blasé to zombies. "What am I looking at?" For a reply, something narrow and metallic suddenly encircled his wrist. He tried to jerk his arm away, but not nearly quickly enough to stop Cabal from closing the ratchet on the handcuff. "What? What is this? What are you doing?"

"Saving the world. I can't take all the credit, mind you. Just most. Of course, a lot still depends on how capable the local police are." As he spoke, Cabal was backing away to the parapet over the town hall's rear courtyard. As he reached the edge, Cabal turned and looked down. "I hope you're ready, Constable," he shouted, "or we are all going to die."

Maleficarus looked at Cabal in bewilderment, and then looked at his handcuffed wrist. The other cuff was already locked shut and, unexpectedly, there was the end of a piece of rope tied tightly to it. He followed the rope with his gaze, across the rooftop and over the parapet by where Cabal was standing. He looked up and saw one of the great hydrogen-filled carnival balloons floating there, apparently anchored to its wagon in the courtyard. Then Maleficarus understood, and the colour drained from his face. "Oh, no. No, Cabal!"

Cabal looked back at him with an expression of rapacious anticipation. He did not have to wait long. Down in the courtyard, Constable Copeland took a moment away from kicking zombies off the wagon, said a silent prayer to the effect that his knots were at least as good as Cabal's, and severed the balloon's tether with a pair of bolt-cutters. Then, hefting the cutters, he turned back to the encroaching horde and smashed the undead husk of his chief inspector over the head with them. Even if he were to die now, he thought, at least he'd got one last life's ambition out of the way.

The balloon rose quickly, far too quickly to give Maleficarus any time to do more than ineffectually scrabble at the knotted end of the rope before the slack went and he was jerked off his feet and into the air. He swivelled and gibbered and screamed for help as he rose higher—the captive of a gigantic cartoon cat—begged Cabal to save him even as the prevailing wind caught the balloon and sent it in the direction of the sea.

But Cabal just stood with his hands in his pockets, and watched him go, muttering under his breath, "Goodbye, Rufus. I would be obliged if you could avoid dying until you are at least three miles away from land." When the sight of an idiot flying into the distance ceased to amuse him, he turned to the crowd of walking dead, and waited. Presently, they started to drop to the ground at the far end of the square, and smoothly collapsed in a wave that swept towards him, past him and behind him, as their creator moved out of range and off towards a clear horizon. It no longer mattered what happened to Maleficarus; as the final zombie toppled, the Ereshkigal Working lost its last subject, and quietly came to an end.

It seemed very quiet all of a sudden. Cabal looked down upon the hundreds of corpses that lay scattered across the town square, and he shook his head sadly. It was such an awful waste. All that fresh material just lying there, and he didn't have time to take advantage of any of it. It was heartbreaking. He walked across the flat roof to look down at PC Copeland, standing exhausted within a ring of bludgeoned bodies. Sensing himself watched, he raised his head to look at Cabal, shading his eyes against the sun.

"Still in the land of the living, eh, Constable?" called Cabal.

Copeland raised his bloody bolt cutters and pointed them at Cabal. "You," he managed to gasp out from between ragged breaths, "are bleeding nicked."

"Alas," said Cabal, "there are the practicalities to observe. Not only are your handcuffs currently floating away from here with a comical character attached to either end, but you are down there, and I am up here. By the time you get up here, I guarantee I shall have found an alternative route to down there, and will be fleeing the scene with practised rapidity. Feel free to attempt an arrest by all means, but please, don't be disappointed when you fail."

But, despite the warning, Copeland still was disappointed.

DAVID FARLAND is the author of the best-selling *Runelords* series, which began with *The Sum of All Men*, with the eighth and latest volume, *Chaosbound*, coming out last year. Farland, whose real name is Dave Wolverton, has also written several novels using his real name as his byline, such as *On My Way to Paradise*, and a number of *Star Wars* novels such as *The Courtship of Princess Leia* and *The Rising Force*. His short fiction has appeared in Peter S. Beagle's *Immortal Unicorn*, David Copperfield's *Tales of the Impossible*, *Asimov's Science Fiction*, *Intergalactic Medicine Show*, and *War of the Worlds: Global Dispatches*. He is a Writers of the Future winner and a finalist for the Nebula Award and Philip K. Dick Award.

In the movie *The Last Unicorn* (based on the classic novel by Beagle), Schmendrick the Magician warns, "And be wary of wousing a rizard's wrath . . . rousing a rizard's . . . be wary of making a magician angry!" That's really good advice since, when it comes to revenge, wizards have a dizzying array of unpleasant options at their disposal.

When Merlin incurs the wrath of the Lady of the Lake, he finds himself imprisoned in a crystal cave. In Robert Asprin's *Another Fine Myth*, an escalating practical joke contest between a pair of wizards leaves one of them permanently stripped of his sorcerous powers. And in the Stephen King novel *Thinner*, an obese man finds himself cursed by a witch to undergo an involuntary and unstoppable weight loss program. (In a similar—and somewhat lighter—vein, the movie *My Demon Lover* is about a man who is cursed by a sorceress to turn into a horrid monster whenever he becomes sexually aroused.)

Our next story also tells of an unfortunate fellow who finds himself in the crosshairs of a magic-user, and it reminds us once again why it's definitely not a good idea to rouse the wrath of a rizard . . . er, wizard.

FEEDING THE FERAL CHILDREN
DAVID FARLAND

Yan woke in the pre-dawn, sweat making her blouse cling to the hollow of her chest. She lay on her bed, unwilling to move, lest she waken her three-year-old sister who curled into her, her face close to Yan's breast. The little girl would be hungry when she woke; this one was *always* hungry, and Yan did not want to have to get up and steam the rice.

Lightning snarled softly in the distance, like a hunting tiger, and just outside the window the bamboo rustled in the wind.

Yan had dreamt of Huang Fa. Only a few years before, the Silk Road had been opened to Persia, and Huang Fa had dared to take it for her last spring. Winter was coming, and snow would soon fill the Himalayas. If Huang Fa did not return soon, the trails would be blocked until next year.

In Yan's dream, she'd seen his startlingly clear eyes under the moonlight, while the crickets sang their nightly hymns of longing and carp finned in the pond beside her cottage. "When I return," he'd said, "I will have much silver. Your father will surely agree to the match when he sees what I bring." Huang Fa was but a lowly merchant from a fishmonger's family, and he dared to hope to marry a landowner's daughter. He would have to rise much higher in station to do so; he would need to buy land himself.

His voice, soft and husky, seemed preternaturally clear in the dream, as if he stood over her bed. His image had left her feeling over-warm, with a soft fluttering in her womb. At fifteen, Yan was young and in love, and felt all of the longing and guilt and confusion that went with it. Her mother had once told her, "A girl's first love is always the most treasured. If you are fortunate, he will also be your last love."

Yan inhaled deeply, hoping that perhaps Huang Fa really had come in the night, that she might catch his scent. But the early morning sky outside smelled only of thunder. She wondered where Huang Fa might be, and as she did, she whispered a prayer to the Sun God. "Wherever he is, may he greet the morning with pleasant thoughts of me."

ᘓᗝ

The land was black in the Altai Mountains, black stone upon black stone, with only the sparest of grasses and shrubs cropping up here and there.

Huang Fa stalked through the cold pre-dawn in a sullen rage, and for a moment he tried to conjure an image of Yan. Walking a hundred li in single night can drive the humanity from a man, make him hard and cold. Fatigue had left him reeling, and the icy winds wafting down from the Altai Mountains over the barren gray stones had drained the warmth from him. He had only one sandal, and so he hobbled as best he could. In a jest of fate, his sandaled foot had developed blisters that bled, and so hurt more than his naked foot. But before the sun was even a sullen smudge on a smoke-gray sky, he spotted his roan horse, gazing down in a desultory stare at the barren rocks, its long dark mane and tail gusting in the wind. The barbarians that had stolen her had left her tied to the only tree within three li, and they'd fallen asleep under it. For ten hours Huang Fa had been wondering how best to kill them.

Huang Fa felt a touch on his elbow. "Are you sure you want to do this?" whispered the monk with no name.

Huang Fa paused, turned toward the young man in the pre-dawn. The monk was but a shadow in the darkness, with a bit of moonlight shining upon his clean-shaven head. The monk had no name, for he had renounced it. He whispered urgently, "These men are not killers. They were kind enough to merely sneak off with all your belongings, sparing your life. To take theirs would be to return compassion with brutality."

Huang Fa argued, "The barbarians only stole the horse before, but they won't make the same mistake again. Once they open my bags and find the dragon's tooth. . . . "

The monk did not dare argue. He knew that the barbarians would never relinquish such a great treasure. Yet the dragon's tooth meant little to Huang Fa. He had to save his mare. The barbarians could not guess the worth of such a fine mount. These men consumed horses as if they were chickens. Even if they did not butcher her, they would likely only wait until she bore her foal and then harvest her mare's milk to make liquor.

Huang Fa was determined to get his mare back at any cost, and he could not let them live.

Dread clenched his stomach. He wasn't sure how many men he might have to face. He was determined to use the wizard warrior Jiang Ziya's wolf strategy of battle—to attack when least expected, at the weakest point.

Stepping carefully now, Huang Fa strode over the sparse prairie, with only the barest of grass. There was no rustling of feet, no brush of his pants woven from silky China grass as he rushed into the camp.

One barbarian, wearing a hairy vest of musk ox hide and a fur cap, sat on guard, but had fallen asleep with his back to a nearly leafless saxaul tree. Another lay nearby rolled in a blanket. The two had camped without a fire.

In the gloom, Huang Fa heard a sound and dully registered that a snow pheasant was already up, thundering down from a rocky summit to take cover in the rocks. To the south, in the hills beyond a glacial river, a wolf howled.

Huang Fa strode angrily to the young barbarian on guard duty, grabbed his own bronze battle ax from the young man's sleeping hands, and smashed the man's face before he had even a chance to rouse. Blood blackened the man's chin, and he choked out a "Gah!" as he tried to hold himself upright. Huang Fa struck another blow to the skull to finish him.

The thief's bow-legged friend must have heard the skirmish, for he gave a yelp of warning and hopped out of his blanket, then leapt over the stones like a jerboa.

Want to race? Huang Fa thought. He hurled his ax. A blow to the right lung knocked the barbarian to the ground, and there was no fight left in him. Huang Fa went to the man. "You think it funny to steal a man's horse and his sandal too? Laugh now." He split the man's skull with his bronze ax.

The deed would haunt him. He might make a joke while killing another, but it was a foul thing to have to do. Damn the horse thieves.

He flipped the man over to make sure that he was not breathing. What he saw sickened him. It was not a man, but a boy—barely thirteen, just gaining his adult size. He lay back, gazing blankly at the pre-dawn gray, and his eyes were fixed. His teeth had all been filed down to points, and a tattoo upon his chin showed the trunk of a tree in black, rising up to his forehead. Branches from it spread out upon either side of his cheeks and forehead, creating the holy symbol of the Tree of Life.

Huang Fa wished that he had never seen that face. He wondered if the boy was a shaman. He went to the other barbarian, found that he too was nothing more than a child, and that his teeth had been filed to points, and that he bore the same tribal markings.

Only five years ago, Huang Fa thought, I was their age.

No words could adequately describe how much their faces disturbed him. Though his stomach was empty, he lurched away from camp and did not return until his heart quit pounding. He avoided peering into the faces of the dead.

"Bojing," Huang Fa softly called to his mare. "Are you all right?" He stepped close to let her catch his scent. She nuzzled the hollow beneath his chin, and he stroked her neck gratefully. She was the finest horse he'd ever seen. He had bought her from an Arab band, and now he stroked her side fondly. For weeks now he had only walked her over the mountains, afraid that the hard journey might cause her to lose the foal.

It would have been a shame to let the barbarians eat such a majestic horse.

Huang Fa checked his saddle packs, where he retrieved his left sandal. "Ha, ha," he said to the dead barbarians.

His paltry supplies were intact, except that the boys had eaten the last of his wrinkled apples. But the silver was there, with precious ointments of frankincense for Yan, and opium tar and a single dragon's fang to sell to the apothecaries.

The Taoist crept up to the camp at last. "May I fix us some beans?" he asked humbly.

Huang Fa fumed. The monk was not a coward. He was heading back from Persia, where the Emperor Qin would likely cut out his tongue because of his religious views. The emperor hated Taoists and Buddhists.

But the monk had refused to fight the barbarians. A man who would not kill animals, who would not even eat meat, could not be counted on in a fight. Right now, Huang Fa did not feel any more tolerant of the Taoist than the emperor did. Damn the Taoist and his compassion.

"No, you may not," Huang Fa said.

The monk merely bowed in acquiescence.

Satisfied at last, Huang Fa built a small fire. Fuel was scarce, so he settled on dried dung from a wild ass that had ranged this far north in the spring. Soon the fire blazed like a gem. The skull of a giant ox, bleached by the sun, lay in the golden grass beneath the tree, its broad black horns faded like ash. A poem was scrawled on it in charcoal.

> A cold moon sets
> below these holy mountains.
> My hands are so cold.
> Is this where the gods
> come to die?

Huang Fa glanced down toward the skirts of the mountain and saw that, indeed, from here the full moon was setting far below him in the southwest, so that he seemed to look at it above as if he were a god in the clouds. It floated in the lavender dawn like a glowing pearl beneath the water, slowly descending into the mists. The mountainside was covered in black and barren stone for many li. Huang Fa hoped to glimpse lights—the twinkling of campfires. He and the monk had been chasing the season's last caravan; it could not be more than a few days ahead.

As weary as the dead, Huang Fa rolled himself in the barbarian boy's blanket and tried to sleep. But the faces of the dead boys haunted him, and in a fitful but troubled sleep, he dreamt of young boys that circled his camp, laughing cruelly as they prepared their vengeance.

❧

The Altair Mountains were black, but the desert at their feet was red. Red rocks and red sand. Even the sparse grasses were coated with red dust.

Huang Fa and the monk led his mare into a small fortress with adobe walls at a trading village called Arumchee on the border of the Taklamakan Desert.

For two days, Huang Fa had not been able to sleep. At night he dreamt of vengeful spirits circling in the grass, and by day he felt dazed and exhausted.

Every soul embodies both the yin and yang, he told himself. Each is balanced between darkness and light. I gave into the darkness for a moment, and now I must seek balance again.

The thought soothed him. Still, it felt comforting to hear the crow of chickens and to see silk garments hanging upon bushes outside of the adobe huts, and to smell fresh beans and chicken cooking in the houses. It felt even better to be inside the strong walls of a fortress, even if those walls were as red as the desert.

Here Huang Fa went to report the killings. Slaying raiders wasn't a simple matter, even if it was just a pair of young horse thieves. This had been a righteous kill, and everyone needed to know that—otherwise there could be reprisals.

Huang Fa wasn't worried for himself. He was just passing through. Six weeks from now, he'd be home, safe in his cabin on the lake. He'd have a fine horse for his stables and a dowry to give Yan's father.

But the traders and settlers here had to live among the barbarians. Mostly, the settlers were jade carvers who worked the stone gathered near Black Mountain, but every year there were more and more caravans heading for Persia and Greece. The caravanserais paid good bribes and hefty tolls to the barbarians for safe passage; these people needed to know that the barbarian raiders had failed to keep their bargain—and so paid with their lives.

Huang Fa reported to the garrison commander, a wealthy fellow named Chong Deming who wore a wide golden belt of office over armor made from layers of red silk. He sat on a stool outside a weathered manor house while sipping porridge from a red ceramic bowl. He had white hair and a beard so long that he must have thought himself the equal to one of the Emperor's counselors.

A barbarian woman in bright blue silks squatted on the ground next to him, as if she was his wife. Huang Fa humbly kowtowed, joining his fists together and bowing solemnly, and then approached and bore his news upon further invitation.

Alarm grew evident on the commander's face on hearing Huang Fa's news.

"You killed two barbarian boys?" Chong Deming asked, his penetrating gaze spearing Huang Fa. "Which tribe?"

Huang Fa shrugged. He had come across so many barbarians the past few months that he no longer knew or cared what tribe they came from.

"What did they look like?"

"They were merely youths," Huang Fa answered frankly. "They wore bright pants of purple, and had their teeth all filed down like fangs. Their faces were tattooed with the symbol of the Holy Tree. One had this hunting spear," he said, holding up a javelin with a dark-green jade tip, "and the other had a bow made from the horn of an aurochs."

Chong Deming pulled at his beard thoughtfully. "Oroqin barbarians," he said. "As I thought. Normally they are peaceful people, eating sheep and goats from their flocks, and hunting for wild asses in the mountains. But their animals have been hit hard by a plague of anthrax, and so the barbarians have been starving for the past few seasons.

"Some of their men tried to rob a caravan last spring. The caravan guards made quick work of these unskilled barbarians, and my men hunted those that escaped. We tracked them for five days, and caught them in their yurts in the mountains. We hunted them from chariots and finished off the men with our long-handled halberds. But we spared the women and children. We did not have the heart . . . "

The old general fell silent, and Huang Fa looked to the monk for his reaction. The young man shook his bald head sadly and asked the general, "Did your compassion gain them nothing?"

The general mourned, "I'd hoped that they would find their way back into the mountains, that their own people would feed them. But I fear that they are doomed." He looked to Huang Fa. "Did these two young men have any distinguishing features?"

"One was a runty kid that squinted, with bowed legs. The other was clean and handsome. He wore a necklace made of jade and bear's teeth."

At that, Chong Deming's face fell, and he peered down into his bowl of morning porridge thoughtfully. Steam curled up from it. At long last, he blew over the wide lip of the clay bowl, but did not sip from it. "That would be Battarsaikhan's son, Chuluun." His voice became soft, frightened. "You've heard of Battarsaikhan?"

The name stirred at the back of Huang Fa's brain, like a rat in its burrow. "I think . . . "

"It means . . . 'hero who wins without battle.' He is a hunchback, a powerful sorcerer who kills with magic rather than the ax or bow. He is the most dangerous man in all these mountains. His oldest sons died in our attack at White Ox River last summer. . . . "

"Gah," the monk muttered. The news was terrible.

"Battarsaikhan was in the mountains then, training the boy that you killed,"

Chong Deming said. His voice came hoarse, bitter with sorrow. "Now, the sorcerer has no children left. Couldn't you have let those boys live? They were just trying to feed their starving tribe. You could have just taken your horse. . . . "

Huang Fa stared at the old commander wordlessly, shame thick in his throat. "I did not know of their need. I did not want them coming for me again. You, as a general, know that only a fool spares an enemy."

"Then because you were afraid of retribution, I fear that you shall suffer retribution," Chong Deming said. "If I were you, I'd run from here as fast as I could. The last caravan of the season passed the fortress only two days ago. There was a wizard traveling with it. He might be able to protect you. You can catch them if you hurry—but you should leave now. Battarsaikhan will be reeling from rage, and his spells can reach far. . . . "

"I am sorry," Huang Fa said. "I . . . " he got an idea. The traders paid tolls every year, and among the barbarians, it was said that the life of a man was worth little. "Can we send a gift to this sorcerer? A peace-offering?"

"Do you think anything in the world will be enough to assuage his wrath?" the monk asked.

There was little in Huang Fa's saddlebags that might be worth the life of an only son. The silver was a soft metal, of less value than bronze to the barbarians. The spices . . . were questionable. Huang Fa answered, "I have a dragon's tooth that was dug from out of the stone in Persia. It is worth the price of many horses."

He went to his saddle packs and pulled out the tooth—eight inches long, serrated, and curved like a dagger. Huang Fa had seen the giant dragon skull encased in stone that it had been pulled from. It had been polished by its previous owner, so that the ancient bone glowed like amber.

"Perhaps," Chong Deming said thoughtfully, "it will please. Perhaps to a sorcerer it will be worth enough."

For four days, Huang Fa traveled with the monk and led his mare, skirting the grasslands at the edge of the desert, chasing the wizard's caravan. Here there had once been wild asses, giant wild bulls, and red deer in abundance, and cheetahs to hunt them. But over the past twenty years the rising number of caravans had driven many herds away, and the plague of anthrax had killed most other animals. Some said that the caravans themselves spread the disease. It was well known that one could catch it from handling the skins of animals that had died from the plague.

Now, the red plains seemed barren, almost lifeless. In two days Huang Fa saw only a few wild ostriches and a couple of giant elephants that the emperor's men sometimes harnessed and trained for war. Such beasts were difficult for the barbarians to hunt, he knew. The swift ostriches were a temptation, forever running just out of the bow's range. The elephants, masters of the plains, were four times the weight of the smaller Indus elephants, and had rust-colored tusks that could grow to over twelve feet in length. The bull elephants sometimes became mad and attacked even caravans.

For Huang to travel past such a herd in a caravan was a bold deed. To creep past them with only a monk at his side, pulling his mare on a rope, was terrifying. Yet to his surprise, the larger bulls only sniffed the air with their trunks and flapped their ears in agitation. They did not stomp the grass or throw hay in the air. They did not charge.

Still, the young men kept a respectful distance, and traveled as long as they could. Such was Huang Fa's urgency to find the caravan, to get home to Yan, that he did not want to camp until well after dark.

The monk spoke little as they traveled. He plodded along, staring ahead evenly, whispering poems that he composed in his head.

Huang Fa was bumbling along, eyes growing heavy, imagining what it would be like to take Yan into his arms at last when he dreamed of the feral children.

There were dozens of them, circling a campfire in a large cavern. They were thin creatures with protruding bellies and skin clinging tightly over their ribs. Their bare backs had been tattooed with images of snake-headed lizards. Their gaunt faces were just flesh-colored bones, and their teeth had all been filed.

There were children of all ages in the group, from toddlers to the ages of ten or eleven. They were practically naked, all bare flesh.

Now, a couple of the nearest turned, peered at him hungrily, and jostled their neighbors. They too turned to search for him, but many of the children seemed unable to spot him, as if he were far away.

Suddenly, in the midst of the bonfire, a sorcerer appeared, as if bursting up from the flames. He wore a mask of red jade, a demon's face, and he wore a cloak made of tiger hide. He danced among the flames, hopping among the coals without apparent harm. He carried a huge rattle made from a giant cobra's skull in his right hand, and held the dragon's tooth in his left. He sang as he danced, his voice rising and falling in the quavering manner of one who grieves.

The children around the fire chanted words that Huang Fa could not quite understand. They pounded their right fists into their left hands, and one by one it seemed that all of the children became more aware of him. They began turning and peering at him with greater eagerness. Huang Fa spotted saliva dripping down the chin of one starving girl toddler, drooling down from a mouth full of fangs.

Suddenly the sorcerer snarled a curse, almost spitting his words, and hurled the dragon tooth through the darkness. Huang Fa jerked, as one sometimes will in his sleep, as he tried to dodge. The fang slapped Huang Fa in the chest.

His eyes sprang open.

He stood, heart pounding in fear at the terrible dream. *It is just my guilt that haunts me*, he reassured himself. *Someday I will forget it.*

The sun cast immeasurable shadows. He glanced behind and saw it sailing over the edge of the world, hanging beneath some clouds like a red, staring eye.

"Ai!" he whispered to the Taoist monk, still wrestling his fear. "I had a terrible dream."

"Tell me what you saw, and perhaps I can divine the meaning," the monk suggested.

It had been so vivid, Huang Fa could still feel where the dragon's tooth had hit him. He reached down to touch the spot—and found the dragon's tooth lodged in the hair of his sheepskin vest.

The monk gaped at the tooth.

Huang Fa peered all around the plains, to see if someone could have thrown it, but all that he could see was rippling fields of grass.

That's when he knew. The sorcerer had thrown the tooth at him—a distance of more than three hundred li.

"It does not take a divine scholar," the monk said, "to know that sorcerer has rejected your apology."

Darkness came, and with it came the howling of wolves and the cries of hunting cats in the desert. Huang Fa and the monk loped up a hill, and far in the distance, miles away, they spotted the bright-colored silk pavilions of the caravan. The pavilions, made in the peaked Arab style, had lamps and campfires lit within, and each glowed a different color like radiant gems in the desert in shades of ruby and tourmaline, diamond and sapphire. The pavilions beckoned, but Huang Fa's legs felt like lead. "A march of a single night would bring us to the wizard's caravan."

"I cannot go on," the monk begged, panting. "The stars are strangely dark tonight." He leaned over and grabbed his knees, trying to catch his breath.

It was true. There was a cloudy haze across the heavens, obscuring the River of Stars. Huang Fa had a star chart, painted upon a silken map, that could help guide a man across the desert at night, but on a night like this it would be no use. "We should camp," the monk suggested. "A man who races headlong in the night is sure to fall in a hole."

Huang Fa considered lighting a knot of grass and using it as a torch, but felt reluctant to do so. It might attract unwanted eyes. He glanced behind him, with an uncanny certainty that he was being watched.

In his dream that night the feral children stalked him.

He dreamt first that the moon was out, as bright as a mirror of beaten silver, and by its light he saw a strange creature—grand and majestic. It was an elk, he thought, or something like an elk. Its hair was as pale as cotton and it stood taller than two men; its antlers had many tines and were so broad that a man could have lain between them. At first he thought that there were cobwebs between the tines, but then he realized that it was a thickening of the horn, unlike any that he had seen upon an elk before.

The creature mesmerized him. Never had he seen such a regal animal, so full of power and strength.

Then he heard a rustling behind, and realized that something was creeping toward him through deep grass. He whirled and glimpsed pale bodies, naked children sneaking on all fours, like wolves on the trail of a wounded ibex. He was not sure if they were after him or the majestic elk.

In his dream, he knotted a clump of dry grass and struck a flint with his knife, igniting it. He raised his makeshift torch in the cold air, hoping that it would frighten the feral children away, but they only growled low in their throats, crawling ever closer. Their eyes glowed strangely in the night, the color of blood sapphires, and they were close enough so that he could see their teeth filed down to fangs and the glint of their green jade daggers in their hands.

Some were nearly men in size, others mere toddlers.

In that dream, the monk was not beside him, and Huang Fa called out in terror, "Where are you, my friend?"

Lost in the distance, the monk called back, "I have chosen to take the Way. You should have, too."

Dawn came with muddled results. Huang Fa awoke, with the monk shaking him insistently. "Something is wrong," he whispered. Huang Fa sensed it before he even opened his eyes. The air felt stifled, dead, and for a moment he just lay in his blankets, imagining that dawn was hours off.

"The sun is up," the monk warned, "but it is a day unlike any I have ever seen. A storm comes."

Huang Fa squinted. The whole world had gone red, from heaven above to the earth beneath. On the horizon was a red cloud, a wall of filth, filling the air, rising incredibly high, taller than thunderheads. The sun could not pierce through it, and so it seemed more like night than morning. Indeed, the sun was less than a sooty smudge, and the grim light that filtered through was the color of a poor ruby.

"My friend," Huang Fa shouted, leaping to his feet, "the Yellow Wind is coming!"

"Yellow Wind?" the monk asked.

"Yes, a dust storm out of the Gobi! One blew over our village when I was but a child, but it will be worse here! Quick, grab our blankets. I will get the horse. We must find shelter!"

The fine mare was tied to a small tree, peering east with her ears slanted forward, eyes dull with terror and fatigue. Her right knee was bent forward, as if her hoof was sore. She wheezed, and muscles in her shoulder spasmed. She lost her balance and stumbled a bit.

Resting a palm on her snout, Huang Fa found that she was feverish. She did not respond to his touch. She did not lean in for affection or shy away nervously. It was as if he didn't exist, as if he were a ghost.

She coughed lightly, trying to clear phlegm from her lungs, and then just stood, wheezing.

"Don't touch her," the monk warned. "She has anthrax. I have seen it before."

Huang Fa peered at the coming storm. He'd never heard of one so immense. It came like the night, a grim shade. The dust rose higher than the tallest cloud, blotting out the sun. The storm did not ride on a great gust of wind. Indeed, the wind felt sullen, still, almost dead. The storm only crept toward them.

"Cover your nose," Huang Fa said. "The dust will clog your throat. When it hits, don't dare to stop moving. If you lie down, the dust might bury you."

The monk, a thin young man, looked terrified.

"Can we run from it?" the monk asked. "It moves slowly."

"We cannot run faster than the storm," Huang Fa said. "Even if we could, it would catch us when we tired. The only shelter is ahead of us—at the caravan."

The monk peered back down the trail, glanced at a mound of rocks not five hundred yards off. It might provide some shelter from the coming wind, but not much.

"Let us hurry, then," the monk urged.

Huang Fa patted his horse, quickly untied her.

"Leave her," the monk whispered. "She will only slow us, and she does not have long to live. Besides, if we reach the caravan, she might sicken the other animals."

"I can't leave her," Huang Fa said. She was his future. The silver might be a dowry, but the mare was worth far more. "She might get better. Even anthrax does not always kill."

The monk shrugged, leaving the decision to him.

Huang Fa pulled at the mare's rope, but she would not follow. He wrapped an arm around her neck. "Come, Bojing," he whispered, "please . . . "

The mare stood, ears leaning forward. She knew what he wanted. She staggered a step, but then just stood.

"It is a curse," Huang Fa wailed, wringing his hands.

The monk tried to calm him. "Sometimes a storm is just a storm," he said. "Sometimes a sickness is just a sickness. I think, these things are beyond the powers of even a famed sorcerer like Battarsaikhan."

Huang Fa hung his head, thinking furiously. He remembered the dragon's tooth. The sorcerer had thrown it hundreds of li.

Huang Fa covered his head with a straw hat from his pack, wrapped a rag across his face, then strode toward the storm.

"Try to remember where we saw the lights of the caravan last," the monk suggested. "We should make straight for it."

Huang Fa gazed toward the horizon but could not be sure of the direction. He followed the monk. Grimly, the curtain of red dust rolled toward them until it swallowed them whole.

All through the morning, Huang Fa and the monk pushed through the dust storm. The gritty dust stung Huang Fa's eyes, and he kept them narrowed to slits. Even then, his eyes soon streamed from tears.

The dust filled his sinuses, until sludge ran from his nose, and when he tried to breathe from his mouth, mud clogged his throat and left him gasping. He'd never imagined such a hell.

The dust was incredibly fine, and it coated everything, gritting up his skin, filling every orifice.

It was all that he could do to keep plodding, placing one foot in front of another. Time and again, the monk would reach back and grab Huang Fa, who was trying to pull the mare. She grew more headstrong as her sickness worsened.

The only thing that kept Huang Fa moving was the thought of Yan at the end of his trail.

The tracks of the caravan would normally have been easy to follow, but dust was rapidly settling over everything, creating a red carpet that filled hoof prints. Dust infiltrated his lungs, so that they felt heavy, as if he carried stones in them.

They had not gone far into the cloud when the mare simply stopped.

"What's wrong?" the monk called. Huang Fa looked but could not see the monk, until the fellow suddenly materialized out of the dust not ten feet ahead.

"Bojing!" Huang Fa cried.

The monk tugged at the rope and cursed, but it did no good. Bojing merely stood, coughing and wheezing. Huang Fa leaned his head against her chest, to listen to her lungs, and Bojing seemed to take that as a sign. She dropped to her front knees, and then lay down to die.

Huang Fa did not want to leave her in such misery. He put his coat over her face, hoping that it would keep the dust from her lungs. Then he knelt beside her for several long minutes, just stroking her.

"Leave her," the monk begged. "Don't touch her. The anthrax might spread to you!"

"I can't leave her," Huang Fa shouted.

He realized now that it was hopeless. He only wanted to comfort the precious beast as it died. "I'm sorry, my princess," Huang Fa whispered again and again as he stroked her gritty hide.

Between the dusty air and the anthrax, she died within an hour.

When she was gone, Huang Fa removed her saddle packs, filled with what was left of his treasure, and stumbled on.

He closed his eyes against the storm and let the monk guide him.

The world seemed darker, and when Huang Fa looked up, he wondered if he had lost track of time, for it seemed that night was falling. Then he realized his mistake: he'd stood at the edge of the storm and marveled at how terrible it was, but standing upon the brink of it was nothing compared to what he saw now: the wind that had seemed gentle, subdued, was beginning to gust stronger, and as it did, the dust belted them in waves. The haze that had hidden the sun an hour earlier now thickened and threatened to blot it out entirely.

Surely I am cursed, Huang Fa thought. I wanted so badly to save my mare. Now the sorcerer has ripped her from my grasp. Battarsaikhan is fierce indeed!

So he staggered forward blindly, led by the monk, whose ability to negotiate through the storm felt nothing less than mystical. Huang Fa could not breathe, could not get air into his lungs for all the dust, and began to fear that despite his best efforts, he would suffocate in the storm.

Coughing, his face hidden beneath his robes, at last in a perpetual gloom he dropped to his knees to crawl, holding on to the cuff of the monk's robe. At last his hand bumped something that yielded, and realized that they had found a tent.

The monk knelt and untied some fastenings, and they lunged into a pavilion where several merchants in their finest wares—in multicolored silks as bright as songbirds and butterflies—sat on cushions around a single golden lantern, drinking tea. Even in here the air was thick with dust. A courtly scholar in dark blue robes peered at Huang Fa knowingly and announced, "And here, good sirs, are the visitors that I promised: one man who is holy, and another who is damned."

The silk merchants gaped at Huang Fa and the monk in astonishment.

"Incredible!" one of them cried. "In the midst of a killer storm!" another shouted. Two of the men actually clapped in delight at such a spectacle.

That night, as wind prowled outside the pavilion like a demon spirit and dust filtered through the air in a dense fog, Huang Fa peered through gritty eyes at the wizard, a eunuch with a face that was somehow regal despite the fact that he had no beard.

"You should not have given Battarsaikhan the dragon's tooth," the wizard warned after he had heard Huang Fa's tale. It had been hours since he'd entered the pavilion, but only now was he able to breathe well enough to plead for help. The day was dying, the sun descending into a bland orange haze, and the silk merchants lay about in a strange lethargy, weary of breathing, so that only the wizard, Huang Fa, and the monk were up. "If a sorcerer has something that you have touched and owned," the wizard continued, "it can give him power over you."

"I only hoped to gain his forgiveness, Master Wong," Huang Fa apologized.

"There shall be none," the wizard intoned. He peered down into his lap.

"Is there nothing we can do?" the monk begged. "How will the sorcerer attack?"

"I am an expert in divination," Master Wong replied. "I am not an expert in all sorceries, but I have traveled the Earth, and I know something of these barbarians. He will send an animal spirit to possess Huang Fa, one that will fill him with animal desires and lead him to ruin."

"What kind of spirit?" the monk asked.

The wizard shook his head. "I cannot be sure. A fox spirit would fill him with lust, a wolf with a thirst for blood. A boar will turn him into a glutton. An ape spirit would make him act like a fool, but we are far from the land of apes. It will be . . . an animal close to the sorcerer."

Master Wong clapped his hands and asked a young boy, his assistant, to bring his "special trunk." The boy hurried to another pavilion, and returned moments later. Master Wong had Huang Fa lie down; he took a bottle of henna dye and a calligraphy brush and began to write spells of warding upon Huang Fa's face. As he worked, he explained, "Animal spirits cannot take control of you unless you welcome them in. You can fight them. You *must* fight them. The spells that I am writing will help. The spirits will seek to enter through an orifice—your nostrils or mouth are the weakest points, and so I will surround them with spells."

"You told the others that I was damned," Huang Fa said. "How did you know?"

Master Wong hesitated in his brush stroke. "I cast the yarrow stalks this morning and formed a trigram, then read from the *I-Ching*."

Huang Fa was skeptical at this. The *I-Ching*, or *Book of Changes*, suggested that all of life is in a flux. Every person's situation was always about to change, and by casting the yarrow stalks, one could then consult the book and learn direction for the future. But it was not as simple as that. In part, one had to rely upon the abilities of the wizard who did the divination. One had to trust his insights.

"So you learned that I was damned from the *I-Ching*?"

"I have felt your coming for days," replied Master Wong. " 'A stranger is coming,' the yarrow stalks foretold, 'one with blood on his hands and a curse on his soul. He has an enemy more powerful than this storm.' "

"You divined all of this?"

The wizard nodded solemnly, then set down his brush and folded his hands. "I could learn little more—except for the hour or your coming."

"Is there any hope for me?"

Master Wong frowned. "This Battarsaikhan has powers that go far beyond mine. He sent this storm to slow you down—or kill you, and that is no small feat. Yet this I also know: the human heart has a magic of its own, as powerful as any spell. Perhaps if we understood his powers better. . . . "

Huang Fa's heart hammered, filling him with hope. "Is there a surer form of divination than the *I-Ching*?"

Master Wong leaned over Huang Fa and gave an inscrutable expression, as if he might be annoyed. "You are a skeptic? You don't trust me? I do my own readings twice a day. I would not have survived for a hundred and twelve years without them! If the stalks tell me to eat an apricot today, I eat it. If they tell me to stay out of the rain—"

The monk's mouth dropped in surprise. "You are a hundred and twelve years old?"

The wizard did not look a day over fifty. He kept a straight face for a moment, and burst out laughing at his own jest. "If you want a surer form of divination," he suggested to Huang Fa, "we can consult the turtle's oracle bones."

This was a form of divination that Huang Fa could trust. The turtle was the most blessed creature under heaven. Because of this, the gods had granted the turtle long life and great wisdom, and it held a special place close to the gods as one of the four holy animals. Indeed, Huang Fa sometimes prayed to turtles, for they could act as intermediaries to the gods.

To consult oracle bones, the wizard merely carved a question into the shell of a turtle that had been ritually sacrificed. Then he would drill small holes in the shell, insert a stick of incense into each hole, and light the incense. When the stick burned down, the heat would weaken the shell, causing it to crack. If the bone cracked inward, toward the center of the shell, then the answer to the question was "yes." If it cracked toward the outer part of the shell, then the answer was "no."

This form of divination limited the wizard to asking yes-or-no questions. That was its weakness. But the virtue of this method was that heaven left no ambiguity in the answer.

"Suggest a question," Master Wong offered, "and I will consult the oracle bones tonight."

Huang Fa blew his nose. The air was so dusty that the mucus came out black. He felt dirty down to his lungs, in every pore of his skin, to the very core of his soul.

Huang Fa formed his question for the gods: "Can I escape the Sorcerer Battarsaikhan's curse?"

The wind shrieked outside the tent, drumming at the silk and tugging at the pegs and stays. Inside the pavilion, all was dark and strangely cold. The only light came from eight sticks of incense that rose from holes in the turtle shell. The sweet scent of jasmine curled up from the cherry coals, so that the dusty room bore a cloying air.

Huang Fa lay in a troubled dream, shaking from chills. He dreamt of children crawling stealthily through the storm, faces bared to the wind. They dragged something large and bulky behind them as they crawled, something with hair, though the dim light defeated Huang Fa's vision.

It is the mare's head, Huang Fa thought unreasonably, and whimpered in horror.

But the children came on—toddlers with knives in their hands, and young girls in nothing but loin clothes. There were fierce boys with sharpened teeth and eyes that shone with their own inner light, as if stars might burst from them.

They reached the door flap to the pavilion, and crept inside. Huang Fa felt vaguely detached as they neared his bed, dragging their hairy burden, even though he expected them to plunge their daggers into his flesh.

"I meant no harm," he apologized. "I did not know your need."

The feral children gave no answer.

A chill swept over him, as if an icy wind blew up from the caverns of hell and rippled up his spine. His muscles felt as rubbery as dead eels.

Now half a dozen children stood above the hairy thing. By the light from the incense, Huang Fa could see an animal hide rolled up and tied into a bundle.

It is the hide from my horse, he thought. *They will put it upon me so that I catch the anthrax.*

He felt torn between the desire to run or fight, or simply to lie still and accept whatever fate the feral children deemed fit.

Three children uncut the strings that bound the hide and rolled it out, almost celebrating with excitement. Even in the dim light Huang Fa could see that it was not the hide of his fine red mare. This skin was as white as satin, the hair upon it almost as thick as wool.

Four waifs spread the great hide over him with great ceremony, and Huang Fa breathed the luxurious scent of a well-tanned hide. The fur upon it was like heaven, like a banked fire that warmed him through and through.

The children turned to leave; Huang Fa suddenly roused to a sense of danger. His eyes flew open and he stilled his breathing to listen for the sound of stealthy motion.

The room was dark, the dead air heavy with dust. Outside, the storm had quieted. Nothing moved in the pavilion. The only sound was the soft snoring of a trader on the far side of the tent, hidden beneath a sheepskin.

Droplets of sweat stood out on Huang Fa's forehead and made his shirt cling to his chest. Briefly he worried that he had caught anthrax, but then realized that he had been lost in a fever dream and that his fever had broken.

For days he had been sick with worry, and now he felt suddenly released. He leaned up on one elbow, peered around the room. There were no feral children here.

He touched the blanket upon him, a fine animal hide unlike any that he could recall seeing. The fur was thick, luxurious, and the animal was huge.

Perhaps it is a white yak, he wondered, and then realized that someone must have discerned just how chilly the night had become and laid the hide over him. His fever had turned a kindness into a nightmare.

Huang Fa pulled the hide over his head and wished that could lie beneath it forever, smell the clean scent of the leather, fall into the embrace of its everlasting warmth.

At dawn, Huang Fa woke to the scent of tea brewing while sunlight streamed through the tent. Someone had gone outside and was using the branch from a bush to sweep dust from the walls of the pavilion.

"Good news," the monk said. "The storm blew out last night, and the bad air is clearing. The sun came up as red as a phoenix this morning, but all is well."

The silk merchants were up and bustling about, in their colorful silks, packing kegs of precious oils and spices outside while Master Wong merely sat drinking his tea, his face looking drawn and hard.

Huang Fa got up and stretched, pulling the white hide up to him. He then looked upon a small trunk to where the turtle shell lay. The brown lines upon its curved back looked like cracks in the mud after a river dries. The stubs of eight incense sticks poked up from it.

Huang Fa felt good, full of light and hope. He nodded to the shell and begged the wizard, "Have you checked the oracle bones?"

Master Wong gazed at him for a long moment, his face stoic. He finally nodded a bit, and said evenly. "You cannot escape your fate. I'm sorry. We cannot always escape the consequences of our errors, no matter how bitterly we regret our deeds."

At that moment, Huang Fa wakened to a strange sensation. His face felt numb, and he noted that the skin itched on his forehead. He reached up and touched the side of his head—and felt a distinct nub protruding sharply up, stretching the skin taut.

"What?" he asked, fear lurching in his stomach. He noted something odd about his hand, and saw that a fine soft fur had begun to grow out of it, as white as the hide that he'd slept beneath.

Huang Fa screamed in wordless terror, and leapt out from under the hide.

"The animal spirit has entered you," the wizard said apologetically. "Battarsaikhan's spell is more powerful than I could have dreamed. It is not just your *nature* that will change."

Huang Fa leapt away from his bed, shoving the great white hide away. He peered at the luxurious fur.

"In the land of the Kazakhs," Master Wong explained, "the animal that wore that skin is called a 'giant deer,' and its meat is treasured as the sweetest of all venison. Its hide is as pure as the driven snow in the mountains where it lives, and its wide antlers are valued by all, but it is so rare that some believe it to be only a myth. Here near the Altai Mountains, a few still survive, but even in our tales it is hardly more than a myth—the Xie Chai. Though it has two horns, some insist that it is a type of unicorn."

Huang Fa tried to climb out of bed and obeyed a strange compulsion to stand on all fours. He felt a sudden excruciating pain in his ankles as bones twisted. He knew the name of the Xie Chai, of course. It was said that the unicorn could smell good and evil and was attracted by the scent of righteous men while it punished the evil. The Buddhists said that it often carried the book of law in its antlers.

"Haaaawlp!" Huang Fa cried, but the words twisted in his mouth, and only an animal's mewling cry escaped his lips.

"This is your fate, the fate that Battarsaikhan, the peaceful sorcerer, has placed upon you," the wizard said sadly: "You shall roam the land upon four hooves, and be doomed to paw beneath the snow for lichens and grass at the feet of the Altai Mountains. You shall never know the love of a woman, for you are among the last of your kind.

"You shall be hunted for all the days of your life, by both barbarians and by true men, and by wolves and snow leopards in the mountains, and by cheetahs on the plains. There is no escape for you, oh man with a gentle soul, nowhere that you may hide. I fear that you will not last the winter, for most of all you shall be hunted by the feral children, from whose mouths you have taken their livelihood, and it is the will of the sorcerer that you shall be found.

"At the very last, you shall feed the feral children with your own flesh."

An image of Yan flashed before Huang Fa. He saw her at the foot of a screen, painting an image of a phoenix upon black silk. She looked up toward the sunlight streaming in through a window.

Huang Fa lunged toward the flap of the tent and lurched through it into the dusty air. His animal instincts made him yearn for freedom, to run under the open sky, and he clattered the last few steps upon hooves that slipped upon the silk beneath him; his growing antlers caught in the flaps of the tent and threatened to break his neck before he tore free. The sky outside was filled with dust and had a surreal glow to it, as red as if lit by the Sun God's fires.

Yan, he thought.

Huang Fa snorted and whirled, his feet kicking up dust, and peered into the tall grass near camp. There he saw tiny figures—the sprawling bodies of half-starved children, hiding in the grass, teeth filed sharper than daggers.

He turned and bounded away, his tail raised high like a flag of warning, his hooves exploding with power as he ascended into the air, dipped to the earth, and then soared upward again.

In late winter, Yan woke one night. The lunar New Year had just begun, and it was the night of the lantern festival. A great red lantern hung from the rafters on her porch, giving a little light that streamed through her window.

She'd dreamt of Huang Fa again, and the excitement of the holidays was dulled by a sense of loss. He had never come home. She feared that he was trapped in the snowy mountains, or that he had died while crossing the desert.

Yet tonight her heart told him that he still lived, and she imagined that he had come to her bed.

She inhaled deeply, trying to catch the scent of him. She tried to remember the light in his eyes, his broad handsome smile, but the memory had faded.

Yan untangled herself from the sheets of her bed, from the arms of her little sister whom she feared might waken and beg for breakfast. She went to the door. The red lantern hung above her head, burning gaily in the night.

She gazed out across the wooden bridge in front of her house, toward the bamboo grove whose leaves rustled in a light wind.

A beast stood there—huge and white. It was so large that at first she thought that it was a horse. Then she saw that it dwarfed even a stallion. Its broad antlers were like those of an enormous elk, yet webbing stretched between the tines, as if to catch the light of the full moon.

It tiptoed toward her, into the circle of light by the door, and she knew it for what it was—a Xie Chai unicorn.

It extended its snout, as if to catch her scent, and she put forth her hand for it, hoping that it might enjoy the allure of the rosewater perfume that she wore. Such animals could discern a man's heart. It would tell her if she was good or evil.

She longed to be good, but she knew that her love for Huang Fa was too great.

The unicorn stepped near, and she was astonished at how huge it was. She saw its eyes, shining in the light of the lantern, all filled with some unimaginable desire.

Suddenly she caught its scent, the musky scent of a young man that often haunted her dreams. She knew that scent intimately, knew the young man's clean limbs and sweet breath.

"Huang Fa?" she wondered aloud. The beast looked startled. The muscles in its shoulders bunched, as if it would dart away.

She knew him, knew what had happened. Huang Fa had turned into this magical beast, and yearning for her, he had come to her at last.

But how had this happened?

Inside the house, her little sister woke in the night. "Yan?" she cried. "Yan, I'm hungry!"

In that instant the unicorn grew afraid. There was no more coherent thought in its head, only nameless animal fear that now took over.

The proud beast whirled and bounded, leaping through the stream.

"Huang Fa!" Yan called, rushing to the edge of the porch.

A low fog covered the ground, and the unicorn bounded through it, as if leaping upon clouds, until it disappeared into the plum orchard, lost under a silver moon.

VYLAR KAFTAN writes speculative fiction of all genres, including science fiction, fantasy, horror, and slipstream. Her work has appeared in *Lightspeed Magazine, GigaNotoSaurus, Realms of Fantasy, Strange Horizons, Clarkesworld, Cosmos, Escape Pod, Beneath Ceaseless Skies, Sybil's Garage,* and in the World Fantasy Award-winning anthology *Paper Cities.* She lives with her husband Shannon in northern California. Learn more at vylarkaftan.net.

The practice of suspension is horrifying to some and beautiful to others. "Suspending" the human body by having hooks placed through the skin is unquestionably one of the more extreme forms of body modification in practice today. People do this for purposes of spirituality or art, and for private reasons all their own.

For the Native American Mandan nation, at the core of the practice was personal sacrifice. The deliberate agony of suspension was just the beginning of what a young man was expected to offer up to the spirits of his tribe.

In both the modern and traditional contexts, the suspendee is never forced. The spirit must be willing.

In our next story, Kaftan brings us a short tale of suspension and sacrifice, as a young woman endures the unimaginable, making us ask ourselves: What would we be willing to endure if the stakes were high enough?

THE ORANGE-TREE SACRIFICE
VYLAR KAFTAN

The naked peasant girl swung from rusted hooks in the throne room's center. Her hands and feet were bound with leather straps, which laced the hooks together like a bodice. Blood trickled from her scarred back. She was just alive enough for the pain to crush her thoughts.

Lords from the eleven kingdoms sat in the eleven iron thrones. They chewed turkey legs and spat gristle on the floor. Bones piled beneath the girl, stained with meat and blood and chunks of flesh. They were foreign sorcerers, these bare-chested lords with gold-ringed noses and iron-studded cheekbones. Sharpened stakes pierced their chests—one for each stolen century. Someone stirred the brazier, thickening the acrid smoke. The room was hot as a bonfire.

"Is she dead yet?" asked the lord of the wasted grassland.

"Not yet. She must submit to the magic," replied the lord of the bloodied sea.

"But she chose this path, no?"

They fell silent. The girl sagged, skin glistening with sweat and turkey fat. She had chosen this, truly, but no one could ask her. She drifted silently through haze and pain. Each hook burned like wildfire. Smoke seeped into her wounds, blackening her blood with magic. Her drippings thickened to tar, oozed off her body, and clotted on the turkey bones.

"Soon her heart will harden," said the lord of the rotted jungle. "They never last more than a song once they blacken."

"I wish she'd get on with it," said the lord of the caustic crater, smoothing his gray-streaked beard. "My back is killing me."

He reached up and pushed her. Hooks tore her flesh. She moaned, spilling black blood to the ground. Wings of pain sprung from her back as dark magic filled her veins. She couldn't take it. Couldn't survive. But she'd sworn her vow, unknown to these demon-men. The fruit still tingled her lips, the sweet tangy citrus of the Goddess these men thought dead. The orange-tree guardian knew where she was.

The lord pushed her again like a loose chandelier. Lightning-pain shot from torso to fingertips, and she nearly passed out. *Stay conscious.* She had to stay conscious. Until the magic reached her center—the place where she pulsed with life.

"We should do this more often," said the lord of the salted fields. "I don't like the aches I get at this age. Don't we have other peasants? They breed like swine."

"They need to come willingly," said the lord of the poisoned island. "If they don't, it won't work."

"Tighten the laces," ordered the lord of the glittering cesspool. "Make her scream."

She knew that the magic didn't need that. They just wanted to hurt her. She bit her tongue as they racked her. Flesh tore from her back. Black blood seeped toward her heart. The orange-tree Goddess had warned her of this—said she would die like the land these sorcerers now ruled. She remembered the Goddess's breezy hands stroking her hair. Back in the orange-tree grove, the choice had seemed easier.

But now agony seared like juice in her wounds. It wasn't pain happening *to* her, it was *her* happening to the pain, her tortured body wildly throwing her soul into the abyss. She sank below herself. She was screaming. Dying.

The lords gasped in delight. "It's starting!" cried the lord of the stagnant river. "I feel it!"

The tar spread into her core, seeking her heart. But her heart was missing. In its place lay the Goddess's orange, the flavor of life which would drive these demons from her land.

The orange burst. Its peel scattered like ashes. Eleven orange segments flew from her body and drove wedges through the sorcerers' hearts. Screams echoed through the throne room—the sounds no longer hers.

O my Goddess. Now I can die.

The girl fell from the hooks, her body broken. An orange tree sprung from where she landed, bursting from seed to sapling. The tree grew until its roots rocked the throne room, tore the walls down, stretched to the heavens and drove through the earth. Oranges blossomed from every branch. The girl's soul entered the tree, shy as a child, to meet her Goddess. The orange-tree guardian kissed the girl's soul, breathed her a new body, and sent her forth.

On a farm near what had been the eleventh kingdom, a woman birthed a baby girl who smelled of oranges.

DESIRINA BOSKOVICH has published fiction in *Realms of Fantasy, Fantasy Magazine,* and *Clarkesworld,* and in the anthology *Last Drink Bird Head.* She is a graduate of the Clarion Science Fiction and Fantasy Writers' Workshop, and when not writing fiction, she works as a freelance copywriter and creative consultant. She lives in Brooklyn, where she claims to pet cats, drink coffee, and enjoy other stereotypical things. Learn more at desirina.com.

Fantasy literature is full of characters from the real world exploring wondrous dreamlike landscapes—the Pevensie children in *The Lion, the Witch, and the Wardrobe,* Alice in *Alice's Adventures in Wonderland* and *Through the Looking Glass,* and Dorothy in *The Wonderful Wizard of Oz,* to name just a few. Often the challenge the characters face in the fantasy world mirrors those they face in the real world, and the courage to confront an evil wizard is the same courage they need to face the school bully. A fantasy world allows characters to face their problems from a new angle, and therefore discover within themselves new resources they never knew they had.

A fantasy world serves much the same function for writers as well, allowing them to use the prism of the imagination to face issues that would otherwise be too painful to think about, or to comment on political or social issues with more subtlety and less stridency than might be possible with a head-on approach. Our next story is about this interplay between a fantasy world and the real one, and about the important role that fantasy serves for both readers and writers when dealing with difficult subjects.

Love Is the Spell That Casts Out Fear
Desirina Boskovich

Long ago, far away, in another time, and another place.

In this world, there lives a wizard.

She is old, but not that old.

She is young, but not that young.

The wizard lives alone in a tiny house at the forest's edge. To the north are the tangled woods, home to unlikely zoological and botanical specimens the wizard has spent several lifetimes cataloging; she plans to spend several more. To the south lies the city: Perta Perdida, the City of Lost Girls.

The girls of Perta Perdida call the wizard Hanna D'Forrest, when they think of her at all. She's charged with their protection. Whether this responsibility is one for which she volunteered, or one forced upon her, they no longer remember. Neither does she. Time moves differently here, languid as a summer stream. A place of refuge, this city was built to elude change. If they could trap this world like a leaf in amber, they would. But in the absence of that kind of magic, they settle for slowed clocks. They cling to their world as tightly as they can.

Still, occasionally time gets tangled, and change slips through the loops in the knots. Dangers force their way in through the cracks.

A wizard's job is to untangle time, to retie the ropes. And to fight the danger they're facing now.

The wizard came from the forest. She was abandoned there as a child, lost by parents too poor either in funds or spirit to give her the care she deserved. She had been too naive to carry bread or pebbles. Hungry, cold, and stark naked, she wandered until she found the witch's hut. The witch was an outcast from the city, but an outcast by choice. There are no women the city turns away, only women who find they can no longer stay.

Cunning yet kind, the witch took a good look at this lost girl, and then took her in. She made the girl tea, brewed from dandelion leaves and dried birch and the dehydrated leaves of stinging nettles. She gave her a dress, the gray cloth scratchy to the skin, woven from the rough wool of her pet goat. She fed the girl hot stew, seasoned with herbs that grew in the shadows and had many names.

Like all children, the girl had been taught to fear witches. She had also been taught to trust and obey her parents. Having learned the folly of the second lesson, she had no trouble discarding the first.

She slept on the hearth. Tended the garden. Harvested herbs and learned their names. Petted and sheared the goat, then carded and spun and wove its wool. Hunted the rabbits and wild boars and fall stags, and cured their meat for winter.

In turn, the witch taught the girl all the spells and petty magic she knew. She did not mind when the girl danced bare in the moonlight, or streaked naked through the woods, or swam nude in the river, flashing like a fish.

In time, the girl's power surpassed that of the witch. The witch was growing old, and to tell the truth, she had always been somewhat plain. But the girl was beautiful, and she grew more beautiful every day. Being a woman, her beauty and her power were inextricably linked. She could have chosen to ignore the connection, of course; she could have sought deeper learning in dusty books and ancient spells. She might even have turned her wand on herself, assuming whatever shape she liked; possibly one less risky.

Yet the dusty books had been transcribed by old men, and the ancient spells were first uttered by old men. Even the wand had been pioneered by a *young* man, who'd needed a tangible object with which to focus and thus wield his power.

The girl needed none of this. The raw energy of her feminine strength was power enough.

The witch understood this. She was not resentful. She did not envy the girl her beauty, nor did she envy her power. She knew these gifts were volatile and untameable. Possibly even extremely dangerous.

She also knew that, despite everything, there's still something to be said for dusty books and ancient spells. So when her garden-variety mutterings and petty incantations no longer held the girl's awe, she called on an old friend who lived in a tower in another land. The books were sent. The girl studied these, too.

Time moved slowly in the forest, especially in winter.

The girl learned to assume the shapes of various animals. When she leapt like a deer or swam like a fish, she *was* a deer, she *was* a fish. She brooded like an owl. She flew high as a crow. She frolicked like a squirrel. She hid and waited with the patience of a snake.

Inspired by tales of the past, she came to imagine the future.

She longed to see the world.

So she did. She traveled far and wide, and grew in beauty and power, and had.

many adventures, all beyond the scope of this tale, until she was no longer just a girl, but a wizard. Though, of course, even as a wizard, she was still just a girl.

She came to Perta Perdida, and met its princess. She was invited to serve in its court. Yet she knew in her heart that she was still a wild creature, and though she would always be tied to this jeweled city, she could not live there. So she made her home at the edge of Perta Perdida, in the wild liminals where deeper magic remained possible, fueled by the tension between city and forest, structure and chaos.

And the years passed, like silver drops falling from a leaking tap.

In the world we call the real world, Hannah is seventeen years old. She's not a wizard; she is a musician. She knows that music holds magic, that songs can be like spells.

In the safety of her bedroom, she plays the electric keyboard and practices the drums. She begged her mother for those drums for months and months. Her mother still disapproves. The drums are pushing a dangerous line. Percussion can lead to rock music, and rock music is the devil's soundtrack.

At church youth group meetings and school worship sessions, Hannah plays and sings the familiar songs that everyone knows. They are simple, but powerful. In the language of spells they are the tools of beginners, easy to master and simple to recite, yet still surprising in their strength. Hannah plays and sings them with all her soul; she loses herself in that music.

Though she doesn't know it, the depth of that emotion is visible to everyone. Her love shines on her face. Her desire radiates from her voice. Her friends feel more, and when they raise their hands to the Lord, the movement comes from a sense of inspiration rather than duty. They can't tell if it's her spirituality they find beautiful, or her beauty they find spiritual. It doesn't matter.

Whatever it was, it attracted Peter, the youth minister. He put her on stage when she was just 14. He helped her find her voice.

She composes her own songs too, faltering through false notes. Those songs are pleas and prayers set to music. Passion and frustration inflect each note she plays and drip from each word she sings. Carefully she guards against the intrusion of rock music, and suppresses the relentless attacks of the demons of despair and rage.

Hannah lives in a ranch-style house in a middle class suburb. She lives with her mother and father, and her sister, who is thirteen years old. Hannah's mother is a homemaker. Hannah's father is a certified public accountant. Hannah's sister is named Frances, Franny for short. Though Hannah loves her sister very much, she's the first to admit that Franny can be extremely annoying: stubborn, self-involved, somewhat babyish. Sometimes they scrap like cats and dogs, out of the earshot of their mother, who would tell them that quarreling isn't Christlike. Blessed are the peacemakers, after all. Maybe that's true, but did Christ ever contend with a clingy younger sibling sneaking into his bedroom to "borrow" his clothing, read his diary or unearth contraband?

(Hannah's contraband: three rock music CDs, a black eyeliner pencil, and a story about a wizard.)

The wizard Hanna D'Forrest's world is shattered one morning in late spring. This is the day the first girl appears at the edge of the forest: naked and hungry, drained of will. She's forgotten her name.

The wizard cares for the girl as the witch cared for her. She nurses the girl back to strength and health, but she can't help the girl find her memories.

Then another girl stumbles from the forest in the same pathetic condition.

The wizard cares for her, too. When the girls are strong enough, she brings them to the nearest farmhouse, where they will be safe until their sisters come looking for them.

She needs to be alone. She has work to do.

Once home, she goes to her mirror.

What is this mirror, this wizard's tool?

The mirror sees the past. It sees the future. It sees cities and worlds far beyond. All of them are somehow contained in the wizard. The mirror sees her, too. She cannot stare into it without learning something she does not want to know. She cannot stare into it without revealing something she does not want to show.

It is not an easy tool to use.

She keeps it wrapped in fold after fold of cloth, nestled in a chest, locked in a closet. She sleeps with the key around her neck.

Now, she approaches the mirror with dread, knowing a threat is gathering strength and that she must use her mirror to understand this danger's shape.

She gathers her courage. Though the mirror is always dangerous, it's doubly dangerous to those who are afraid.

Your weapon is only your weapon if you're strong enough to hold it.

She banishes her fear . . .

. . . and faces the mirror.

And the mirror shows her a dark creature, penetrating their boundaries, forcing itself into their world, whether by accident, choice, or fate. The dark creature cannot be seen; it exists only through the havoc it creates.

Using the same malicious agility by which it found its way into their world, it flows through windows and beneath the cracks of doors. It comes to girls as they sleep and gives them nightmares. It leads them like sleepwalkers into the forest, and then it leaves them stranded.

An incubus.

Troubled, the wizard Hanna D'Forrest travels to the palace to tell the princess what she's seen.

How long has it been since she last walked the streets of Perta Perdida? Time means nothing in fairy tales; continually evolving, the city feels new to her each time.

The streets are paved in gold, lined by trees like turquoise cotton candy. Mechanical butterflies cruise overhead, carrying laughing riders. She's ridden a butterfly before—stroked its iridescent wings, worked its mechanical gears. She's seen the city from dizzying heights.

Today, she is content to walk, revisiting her city and her sisters.

She watches them as they walk in twos and threes, pausing at shop windows. The glass fronts display scones and tarts, buttons and boots, polished lamps and brass keys. Girls run barefoot through the fountain, dresses clinging to their knees.

She climbs toward the city center. Colorful houses with tiled roofs sprinkle the hillside like candy. Gardens hang from windows and flowers bloom around the doors.

She reaches the palace grounds, passing beneath a bay of spiders weaving tensile webs like copper wire. Metallic tendrils caress her as she passes, simply wanting to know her. She walks a wide-open lane, lined with fragrant orange trees. Robots guard the way, their eyes enigmatic emerald, their fingers grasping ancient keys; they let her pass.

Finally she comes to the heart of the palace, where the princess lives.

The princess wears her hair free and wild, circled only by a silver band. Her skin is smooth as milk chocolate, her smile as sweet. Her bare arms are muscular, circled with metal bracelets; her simple dress swirls to the floor. She is barefoot.

The princess and the wizard take one another in, accepting what has changed and savoring what has not.

"You know why I'm here," says the wizard.

"Yes. I know."

The wizard describes the chaos she saw in the mirror: the attacks of the incubus and the summer of suffering.

The princess asks her questions, contemplates the consequences.

Finally she says: "My warriors can do nothing against a threat like this one. It is up to you."

"Yes. I know," she says. She knows enough to be afraid.

❧

The creaking bus is filled with the smells of exhaust and Doritos, and the fruity-floral scents of teenage girls. Hannah sits by the window and watches the miles as the sun rises over the mountains. CD player in her lap, headphones in her ears: she's as faraway as she can make herself.

They're heading to a daylong Bible retreat.

Hannah's sister Franny sits across the aisle with her best friend Krista. Their furtive conversation is drowned by the rumbling of the bus and the aural onslaught of Hannah's private music. They bend their heads together, whispering and giggling.

Peter sits four seats up, talking with two guys across the aisle.

He became their youth minister four years ago. He'd been twenty-five then, idealistic and charismatic. Hannah's mother campaigned hard to get him the position. When he had it, she invited him to dinner. She baked her delicious chicken potpie, and they all listened as Peter told them stories about the year he'd spent volunteering in Guatemala. His eyes shone as he described building a house for a poor family, or playing ball in the dirt street with a bunch of rowdy boys.

He told them about his plans for youth group. He wanted to shake things up. "More energy," he said. "More passion for Christ! We've got to get these kids' attention." He wanted more hands-on service activities, more dynamic sermons, more music.

"Hannah sings, you know," her mother said. "And plays the keyboard."

"Fantastic," Peter said. "I'm putting together a worship team. Wanna come try out?"

Of course she said yes.

That night, Hannah lay awake thinking about him. He was the way she imagined Jesus: handsome and kind. When he told stories, you wanted to listen. When he looked at you, you couldn't look anywhere else.

That was before the demons came. (Despair. Rage. Guilt and Shame. The perfect quartet.)

Peter swings out of his seat. He walks down the aisle of the bus, pausing at each seat to say hello. He talks to Krista and Franny for a long time, leaning to catch their words over the noise of the bus. She watches them watch him. She watches *him* watch *them*. Their faces are full of adoration.

He doesn't speak to her, just flashes her a smile she still can't read.

And the creaking bus forces its way forward.

What's the value of seeing the future if you don't know how to change it? You can brace for the wave, but you can't calm the sea. Helplessly, the wizard peers into her mirror, searching for knowledge to illuminate her path; she pores over her books, looking for anything that will help defeat the incubus.

And while she searches, the city devolves into a waking nightmare. Perta Perdida is a world linked not by geography but by desire, mapped onto far-flung hidden spaces, governed by laws of the soul and not the mind. It falls victim to enemies that are equally fragmented, and thus untouchable. The city is everywhere and nowhere, fleeting and timeless; the threat they face is the same way.

The incubus, irrational and lacking in substance, drifts through windows and beneath doors. Girl after girl falls victim to its night time whispering, cajoled in the darkness of deep sleep to places beyond consciousness, islands without a name, castles ruled by fear. Sleepwalking, they wander into the forest's wilds, the shadowy in-between where the spirit dwells, safe from the prying sunlight. Girl after girl, wrenched from home, lost to herself, stranded in the badlands of her own mind.

Afraid to fall asleep, the girls set watches through the summer nights. With lamplight and candlelight they sit vigil through sultry July, counting the hours 'til morning. They walk through the days pale as ghosts. Things fall apart: the bakeries are empty, the soup kitchens abandoned, the fountains dry. Even the butterflies are grounded, as the technicians lose their focus. The seamstress shops are closed, the tailors too blurry-eyed to see tiny stitches.

There are desperate orgies. Girls drink all the sweet sangria they can hold, then dance half-clothed among the magnolias and orange blossoms until they collapse at dawn. If these are the last days, they want to enjoy them to the fullest.

Still, there are disappearances.

The Bible retreat ends with a sermon. Like every sermon to kids Hannah's age, this one is about purity. The minister talks about purity in body, purity in mind. He talks about pledging the flesh to God. He talks about reclaiming lost virginity; without that loophole, the whole thing would be too harsh. He talks and talks.

After the sermon, while the woman at the organ endlessly loops the same emotive chords, the minister invites anyone who feels moved to come to the front and pledge themselves to God. It doesn't matter if you're understanding for the first time that you're a sinner in need of grace, or realizing that you've strayed from your path and need that grace once more. God doesn't care. God's always there.

But he doesn't say anything about God's opinion of a teenage girl sitting behind a keyboard and playing a duet alone with her youth minister, losing herself first in the music and then in his piercing eyes, so that when he reaches out to touch her chin, she finds herself paralyzed, and as his lips touch hers, she's lost in euphoric betrayal, swimming in the shallows of a secret that she already knows is too deep for her to navigate, that becomes deeper with each illicit meeting, until she's drowning in it with no anchors, and as the girl loses interest in her meals and becomes increasingly withdrawn, with dark circles under her eyes, spending more and more time in her room picking her way through weighty songs, well, she's a teenager, what do you expect?

One by one the kids streak down the aisles and kneel at the edge of the stage, and the minister prays for them, calling down God's forgiveness and blessing.

Hannah's been down that road before—or down that aisle, to be more precise. God's forgiveness might be endless, but she won't accept it until the day comes when she can forgive herself. In the meantime, no matter how many times they promise absolution, she's staying in her seat.

When the tears streak down her cheeks, the girl beside her clutches Hannah's elbow and then puts her arms around her. "Go on up," she whispers. "It's okay. I'll come with you."

Hannah just shakes her head.

She dreams of the day she can run. She's thinking of a women's college; she likes the pictures, girls nestled under an oak tree on the quad, or meeting for class in the library.

She doesn't particularly care which women's college, as long as it's far, far away.

The days crawl by, and slowly the wizard Hanna D'Forrest learns more about the spirit. Her books hold drawings of a creature that preys on young girls by night and morphs into a stag by day. She hears reports from girls who've seen such a stag, bounding toward the forest in the first light of dawn.

If it assumes a physical form, she can defeat it.

But how to draw the creature to her?

She knows a way, but it isn't easy.

After her travels across the world, she retains only a few treasured possessions from her childhood days—items that once belonged to the witch. There are the books, of course; they existed for centuries before they fell into her hands, and she hopes they'll exist for centuries more. There is a small stone carving of a cat, which she has always liked and never understood. There is also a vial of perfume so intensely precious that it contains only three drops.

The witch refused to tell Hanna what was in the vial. She would only caution her against its use. The witch herself inherited the vial from a sorceress—she would never describe the events that led to this gift—but she had never used it, never sniffed it, never even opened it. The vial contained dark magic, deep and dangerous. The witch knew it was beyond her capacity to control.

Your power is only your power if you know its limits.

Later, under tutelage from great wizards, magicians and sorceresses, Hanna learned about the vial's contents. Now she understands that this perfume holds the same power that gives her magic its force: feminine sexuality. It is feral. It is treacherous. It is extremely unstable.

The incubus is dark energy. So is she. (If she can find the courage to tap that power. If she can find the resolve to do what must be done.)

That night, the wizard trembles in her sleep.

She dreams of lands she has never seen, lovers she has never tasted, spells she will never utter. She sees shining seas, glittering towers, assembly lines and forest floors. She smells frying noodles, hot metal, marina waters and sweet honeysuckle. She hears chiming bells, raucous construction, rock and roll.

She dreams of the world she's afraid to explore and the one she's afraid to give up.

She is old, but not that old.

She is young, but not that young.

She has never been so afraid.

That Friday evening Hannah finds him after youth group.

"I need to talk to you," she says.

Peter doesn't say anything, just takes her elbow and leads her to his office.

He leaves the door ajar.

"What's on your mind?" he asks. His face is concerned. His eyes are fixed on hers.

Now she's lost for words.

Finally she says: "What you did was wrong."

It isn't the way she planned to start, but it's the most succinct way of expressing everything she'd planned to say.

He looks at her and says nothing.

She tries again. "I was *thirteen*."

He stands, walks past her, closes the door. He sits again. He continues to watch her. Finally she sees an expression she can read: shame.

"I *trusted* you," she says. "We *all* trusted you."

She doesn't tell him about the heartbreak she felt when he stopped touching her, the loneliness when he no longer picked her up for extra practice sessions.

That's her own shame to bear.

"You stand up there every week and talk about purity and chastity. If true love waits, then why couldn't you?"

She begins to cry. She'd hoped she wouldn't; she wanted to be strong. But she's contained these words for so long that she can no longer hold anything else.

He hands her a tissue box. She pulls out one tissue for her nose, a second for her eyes. When she can see again, she realizes that he has tears in his eyes, too.

She feels terrible.

"Hannah, listen to me," Peter says. "I am so, so sorry. You are right. What we did was wrong. You are a precious gift from God and you've always been precious to me. Not a day goes by that I don't regret my actions. I pray for forgiveness all the time."

He moves from his chair and kneels in front of her. He takes her hands in his. "Hannah, please understand. I am terribly, terribly ashamed. But I know that God's forgiveness is limitless. And I also know that God wants me to keep doing my work here. I'm reaching kids and saving souls all the time. That's God's plan for me. It would be terrible if something got in the way of that. Do you understand?"

"Yes," Hannah says. "I understand."

"Sometimes I feel overwhelmed by guilt and I think that maybe I'm the wrong man for the job, but then I realize that's just the devil whispering to me, trying to make me weaker. God wants me here."

Hannah blows her nose again.

"I'm sorry, Hannah," Peter says. "Please forgive me."

"I can't," she says. Wiping her eyes, she gets up, opens the door.

"Hannah!" he says. "Stop."

She doesn't stop.

She climbs in the van, where Franny is waiting with their dad. "What took you so long?" Franny asks.

"I was talking to Peter."

"Are you crying?"

"I'm okay, Franny."

"You look like you were crying."

"Drop it, Fran."

That night, Hannah can't sleep. She lies awake as the clock ticks past eleven, then twelve. She grapples with the same old problem she's been wrestling with for years.

She slips out of bed. Turns on the lamp. Opens her Bible to that dog-eared passage she marked five months ago:

"If you abide in My word, you are My disciples indeed.
You shall know the truth, and the truth shall make you free."

The truth is hard. The truth is shameful. The truth will turn her parents against her, alienate her friends, tear apart her community and leave her ostracized. The game was rigged against her from the beginning; she's sinned, too.

The truth will destroy her life.

For five months she's known what to do, but she's been too afraid to do it.

Now she slips out of her bedroom, down the hall, and into Franny's room. Fran is asleep, hair across the pillow, lips parted, blankets kicked aside. Hannah cuddles up next to Fran without waking her.

She wonders what imaginary worlds Fran visits in her mind, if they're as rich and colorful as Hannah's own. Perhaps she'll never know. Sisters can be like that—inscrutable. But maybe she can make the real world a little safer for her. To protect Fran's adolescence, she's got to let go of her own.

Hannah is afraid, but she has an incantation for that:

"There is no fear in love. Perfect love casts out fear."

Strong magic.

Powerful magic.

She recites the words until she falls asleep.

The wizard Hanna D'Forrest sets her things in order. She polishes the mirror and dusts the books. She weeds her garden. She sweeps the floor of her cottage and drinks a cup of tea. These things give her courage and comfort.

Evening shadows slant longer and night falls. She braids her hair. She opens the window. She says the prayers she knows, which are really spells in disguise: because what is magic, but desire wedded to language? Her language is careful, her desire is strong.

She uncorks the vial.

Being a wizard, she knows when she's in the presence of power—and this is it. The perfume will draw the beast to her tonight, but it may also draw other dangerous creatures and lost monsters, lurking in this world or the next. She's doing her best to save Perta Perdida, but she could just as easily bring a host of hauntings down upon their heads.

When you dabble in dark magic, you run that risk.

She dabs one drop onto her left wrist. She dabs another onto her right. She dabs one onto the collarbone above her heart.

She's setting a trap, with herself as bait.

She lies in bed and waits, watching the barest trickles of summer breeze manifest in the gauzy curtains as they tilt towards the window and then away.

The rest of Perta Perdida sleeps safely that night, as the spirit rambles restlessly, searching for the source of that teasing scent.

When it comes, she's ready. She feels the weight of it descend on her like fog in the forest, a blanket of damp emptiness, a gaping void that longs to be full but can only invade, swallowing soul like a leaking sieve. She utters the words that will bind it to her until morning: a spell for star-crossed lovers, a spell for cloud-free starlight, with some improvements of her own design.

Through the arduous night she grapples and dances with that cold entity. She embraces the abyss, struggling to retain the strength of her own identity with the strongest magic she knows. She makes love to the spirit. She seduces the insatiable force. She comes to understand it with frigid certainty, though it threatens everything she knows.

When the first rays of dawn bleed into the dark sky, the power of the binding spell begins to fade. The shadow slips through the window and becomes the stag, finding refuge in beastly form. And shadowlike in her stealth, the wizard slips through the window and becomes a deer.

She follows the stag into the forest, leaping as it leaps, running as it runs.

She speaks to it in the language they both know.

She sings to it, the ancient songs.

She teaches it poems and prayers.

The forest knows no morning; the branches block out golden rays of light, making twilight eternal.

She runs, bidding it follow, and so it comes. They run with supernatural strength through the long dim day, miles falling between them and the city. They run as if they've never done anything else and will never do anything else again. Deeper into the forest she leads the spirit astray, losing it the way she was once lost herself.

And as the hours pass, she loses herself again in the joy of kinetic energy, the swift motion of hooves, the grace of nimble leaps. She's never spent so much time out of her own body. As she leaves the city far behind, she leaves herself behind, too. There are minutes where she thinks of herself as nothing but that body in motion.

They run until they come to the other edge of the forest. On this side is a highway that lies in another world, the world we call the real world.

A world where the only magic is the magic of metaphor.

A world where love is the spell that casts out fear.

A world where a deer is just a deer.

In this world, the deer that was once a wizard leaps fleet-footed across the highway, into the safety of the thicket on the other side.

PETER S. BEAGLE is the author of the beloved classic *The Last Unicorn*. His first novel, published when he was just nineteen, was the critically-acclaimed *A Fine and Private Place*. Other major novel-length works include *The Innkeeper's Song*, *The Folk of the Air*, and *Tamsin*. Beagle is also a prolific author of short fiction, most of which has been gathered in the collections *The Rhinoceros Who Quoted Nietzsche and Other Odd Acquaintances*, *The Line Between*, *We Never Talk About My Brother*, and *Mirror Kingdoms*. For his work, he has won many awards, including the Hugo, Nebula, Mythopoeic, and Locus awards.

According to legend, when young Romulus began building the city of Rome, his twin brother Remus mocked the effort by leaping over the walls. Romulus was so enraged that he slew Remus, and swore that the same fate would befall anyone who dared pass over the walls of Rome.

Sibling rivalry isn't always this brutal, but it's usually pretty close. We weren't all raised by wolves, but you'd never know it from watching the way some siblings go at each other. In his recent book *Bro-Jitsu: The Martial Art of Sibling Smackdown*, author Daniel H. Wilson raises this sort of hazing to an art form, cataloguing 126 techniques for achieving family domination, from ear flips and tripping to wedgies and wet-towel snaps.

Jealousy over simple things—like popularity or grades or how much mom loves you—can lead to some pretty bitter feelings, so just imagine what sort of jealousy might be provoked by discovering that your sibling got the wizard gene and you didn't. Of course, no matter how much siblings may squabble, you can be sure of one thing—nothing unites them like someone from outside the family coming around and picking a fight.

El Regalo
Peter S. Beagle

"You can't kill him," Mr. Luke said. "Your mother wouldn't like it." After some consideration, he added, "I'd be rather annoyed myself."

"But wait," Angie said, in the dramatic tones of a television commercial for some miraculous mop. "There's more. I didn't tell you about the brandied cupcakes—"

"Yes, you did."

"And about him telling Jennifer Williams what I got her for her birthday, and she pitched a fit, because she had two of them already—"

"He meant well," her father said cautiously. "I'm pretty sure."

"And then when he finked to Mom about me and Orlando Cruz, and we weren't doing *anything*—"

"Nevertheless. No killing."

Angie brushed sweaty mouse-brown hair off her forehead and regrouped. "Can I at least maim him a little? Trust me, he's earned it."

"I don't doubt you," Mr. Luke agreed. "But you're fifteen, and Marvyn's eight. Eight and a half. You're bigger than he is, so beating him up isn't fair. When you're . . . oh, say, twenty-three, and he's sixteen and a half—okay, you can try it then. Not until."

Angie's wordless grunt might or might not have been assent. She started out of the room, but her father called her back, holding out his right hand. "Pinky-swear, kid." Angie eyed him warily, but hooked her little finger around his without hesitation, which was a mistake. "You did that much too easily," her father said, frowning. "Swear by Buffy."

"What? You can't swear by a television show!"

"Where is that written? Repeat after me—'I swear by *Buffy the Vampire Slayer*—' "

"You really *don't* trust me!"

"'I swear by *Buffy the Vampire Slayer* that I will keep my hands off my baby brother—' "

"My baby brother, the monster! He's gotten worse since he started sticking that *Y* in his name—"

" '—and I will stop calling him Ex-Lax—' "

"Come on, I only do that when he makes me really mad—"

" '—until he shall have attained the age of sixteen years and six months, after which time—' "

"After which time I get to pound him into marmalade. Deal. I can wait." She grinned; then turned self-conscious, making a performance of pulling down her upper lip to cover the shiny new braces. At the door, she looked over her shoulder and said lightly, "You are way too smart to be a father."

From behind his book, Mr. Luke answered, "I've often thought so myself." Then he added, "It's a Korean thing. We're all like that. You're lucky your mother isn't Korean, or you wouldn't have a secret to your name."

Angie spent the rest of the evening in her room, doing homework on the phone with Melissa Feldman, her best friend. Finished, feeling virtuously entitled to some low-fat chocolate reward, she wandered down the hall toward the kitchen, passing her brother's room on the way. Looking in—not because of any special interest, but because Marvyn invariably hung around her own doorway, gazing in aimless fascination at whatever she was doing, until shooed away—she saw him on the floor, playing with Milady, the gray, ancient family cat. Nothing unusual about that: Marvyn and Milady had been an item since he was old enough to realize that the cat wasn't something to eat. What halted Angie as though she had walked into a wall was that they were playing Monopoly, and that Milady appeared to be winning.

Angie leaned in the doorway, entranced and alarmed at the same time. Marvyn had to throw the dice for both Milady and himself, and the old cat was too riddled with arthritis to handle the pastel Monopoly money easily. But she waited her turn, and moved her piece—she had the silver top hat—very carefully, as though considering possible options. And she already had a hotel on Park Place.

Marvyn jumped up and slammed the door as soon as he noticed his sister watching the game, and Angie went on to liberate a larger-than-planned remnant of sorbet. Somewhere near the bottom of the container she finally managed to stuff what she'd just glimpsed deep in the part of her mind she called her "forgettery." As she'd once said to her friend Melissa, "There's such a thing as too much information, and it is not going to get me. I am never going to know more than I want to know about stuff. Look at the President."

For the next week or so Marvyn made a point of staying out of Angie's way, which was all by itself enough to put her mildly on edge. If she knew one thing about her brother, it was that the time to worry was when you didn't see him. All the same, on the surface things were peaceful enough, and continued so until the evening when Marvyn went dancing with the garbage.

The next day being pickup day, Mrs. Luke had handed him two big green plastic bags of trash for the rolling bins down the driveway. Marvyn had made enough of a fuss about the task that Angie stayed by the open front window to make sure that he didn't simply drop the bags in the grass, and vanish into one of his mysterious hideouts. Mrs. Luke was back in the living room with the news on, but Angie was still at the window when Marvyn looked around quickly, mumbled a few words she couldn't catch, and then did a thing with his left hand, so fast she saw no more than a blurry twitch. And the two garbage bags went dancing.

Angie's buckling knees dropped her to the couch under the window, though she never noticed it. Marvyn let go of the bags altogether, and they rocked alongside him—backwards, forwards, sideways, in perfect timing, with perfect steps, turning with him as though he were the star and they his backup singers. To Angie's astonishment, he was snapping his fingers and moonwalking, as she had never imagined he could do—and the bags were pushing out green arms and legs as the three of them danced down the driveway. When they reached the cans, Marvyn's partners promptly went limp and were nothing but plastic garbage bags again. Marvyn plopped them in, dusted his hands, and turned to walk back to the house.

When he saw Angie watching, neither of them spoke. Angie beckoned. They met at the door and stared at each other. Angie said only, "My room."

Marvyn dragged in behind her, looking everywhere and nowhere at once, and definitely not at his sister. Angie sat down on the bed and studied him: chubby and messy-looking, with an unmanageable sprawl of rusty-brown hair and an eyepatch meant to tame a wandering left eye. She said, "Talk to me."

"About what?" Marvyn had a deep, foggy voice for eight and a half—Mr. Luke always insisted that it had changed before Marvyn was born. "I didn't break your CD case."

"Yes, you did," Angie said. "But forget that. Let's talk about garbage bags. Let's talk about Monopoly."

Marvyn was utterly businesslike about lies: in a crisis he always told the truth, until he thought of something better. He said, "I'm warning you right now, you won't believe me."

"I never do. Make it a good one."

"Okay," Marvyn said. "I'm a witch."

When Angie could speak, she said the first thing that came into her head, which embarrassed her forever after. "You can't be a witch. You're a wizard, or a warlock or something." Like we're having a sane conversation, she thought.

Marvyn shook his head so hard that his eyepatch almost came loose. "Uh-uh! That's all books and movies and stuff. You're a man witch or you're a woman witch, that's it. I'm a man witch."

"You'll be a dead witch if you don't quit shitting me," Angie told him. But her brother knew he had her, and he grinned like a pirate (at home he often tied a bandanna around his head, and he was constantly after Mrs. Luke to buy him a parrot). He said, "You can ask Lidia. She was the one who knew."

Lidia del Carmen de Madero y Gomez had been the Lukes' housekeeper since well before Angie's birth. She was from Ciego de Avila in Cuba, and claimed to have changed Fidel Castro's diapers as a girl working for his family. For all her years—no one seemed to know her age; certainly not the Lukes—Lidia's eyes remained as clear as a child's, and Angie had on occasion nearly wept with envy of her beautiful wrinkled deep-dark skin. For her part, Lidia got on well with Angie, spoke Spanish with her mother, and was teaching Mr. Luke to cook Cuban food. But Marvyn had been hers since his infancy, beyond question or interference. They went to Spanish-language movies on Saturdays, and shopped together in the Bowen Street *barrio*.

"The one who knew," Angie said. "Knew what? Is Lidia a witch too?"

Marvyn's look suggested that he was wondering where their parents had actually found their daughter. "No, of course she's not a witch. She's a *santera*."

Angie stared. She knew as much about *Santeria* as anyone growing up in a big city with a growing population of Africans and South Americans—which wasn't much. Newspaper articles and television specials had informed her that *santeros* sacrificed chickens and goats and did . . . things with the blood. She tried to imagine Marvyn with a chicken, doing things, and couldn't. Not even Marvyn.

"So Lidia got you into it?" she finally asked. "Now you're a *santero* too?"

"Nah, I'm a witch, I told you." Marvyn's disgusted impatience was approaching critical mass.

Angie said, "Wicca? You're into the Goddess thing? There's a girl in my home room, Devlin Margulies, and she's a Wiccan, and that's all she talks about. Sabbats and esbats, and drawing down the moon, and the rest of it. She's got skin like a cheese-grater."

Marvyn blinked at her. "What's a Wiccan?" He sprawled suddenly on her bed, grabbing Milady as she hobbled in and pooting loudly on her furry stomach. "I already knew I could sort of mess with things—you remember the rubber duck, and that time at the baseball game?" Angie remembered. Especially the rubber duck. "Anyway, Lidia took me to meet this real old lady, in the farmers' market, she's even older than her, her name's Yemaya, something like that, she smokes this funny little pipe all the time. Anyway, she took hold of me, my face, and she looked in my eyes, and then she closed her eyes, and she just sat like that for so long!" He giggled. "I thought she'd fallen asleep, and I started to pull away, but Lidia wouldn't let me. So she sat like that, and she sat, and then she opened her eyes and she told me I was a witch, a *brujo*. And Lidia bought me a two-scoop ice-cream cone. Coffee and chocolate, with M&Ms."

"You won't have a tooth in your head by the time you're twelve." Angie didn't know what to say, what questions to ask. "So that's it? The old lady, she gives you witch lessons or something?"

"Nah—I told you, she's a big *santera*, that's different. I only saw her that one time. She kept telling Lidia that I had *el regalo*—I think that means the gift, she said that a lot—and I should keep practicing. Like you with the clarinet."

Angie winced. Her hands were small and stubby-fingered, and music slipped through them like rain. Her parents, sympathizing, had offered to cancel the clarinet lessons, but Angie refused. As she confessed to her friend Melissa, she had no skill at accepting defeat.

Now she asked, "So how do you practice? Boogieing with garbage bags?"

Marvyn shook his head. "That's getting old—so's playing board games with Milady. I was thinking maybe I could make the dishes wash themselves, like in *Beauty and the Beast*. I bet I could do that."

"You could enchant my homework," Angie suggested. "My algebra, for starters."

Her brother snorted. "Hey, I'm just a kid, I've got my limits! I mean, your homework?"

"Right," Angie said. "Right. Look, what about laying a major spell on Tim Hubley, the next time he's over here with Melissa? Like making his feet go flat so he can't play basketball—that's the only reason she likes him, anyway. Or—" her voice became slower and more hesitant "—what about getting Jake Petrakis to fall madly, wildly, totally in love with me? That'd be . . . funny."

Marvyn was occupied with Milady. "Girl stuff, who cares about all that? I want to be so good at soccer everybody'll want to be on my team—I want fat Josh Wilson to have patches over both eyes, so he'll leave me alone. I want Mom to order thin-crust pepperoni pizza every night, and I want Dad to—"

"No spells on Mom and Dad, not ever!" Angie was on her feet, leaning menacingly over him. "You got that, Ex-Lax? You mess with them even once, believe me, you'd better be one hella witch to keep me from strangling you. Understood?"

Marvyn nodded. Angie said, "Okay, I tell you what. How about practicing on Aunt Caroline when she comes next weekend?"

Marvyn's pudgy pirate face lit up at the suggestion. Aunt Caroline was their mother's older sister, celebrated in the Luke family for knowing everything about everything. A pleasant, perfectly decent person, her perpetual air of placid expertise would have turned a saint into a serial killer. Name a country, and Aunt Caroline had spent enough time there to know more about the place than a native; bring up a newspaper story, and without fail Aunt Caroline could tell you something about it that hadn't been in the paper; catch a cold, and Aunt Caroline could recite the maiden name of the top medical researcher in rhinoviruses' mother. (Mr. Luke said often that Aunt Caroline's motto was, "Say something, and I'll bet you're wrong.")

"Nothing dangerous," Angie commanded, "nothing scary. And nothing embarrassing or anything."

Marvyn looked sulky. "It's not going to be any fun that way."

"If it's too gross, they'll know you did it," his sister pointed out. "I would." Marvyn, who loved secrets and hidden identities, yielded.

During the week before Aunt Caroline's arrival, Marvyn kept so quietly to himself that Mrs. Luke worried about his health. Angie kept as close an eye on him as possible, but couldn't be at all sure what he might be planning—no more than he, she suspected. Once she caught him changing the TV channels without the remote; and once, left alone in the kitchen to peel potatoes and carrots for a stew, he had the peeler do it while he read the Sunday funnies. The apparent smallness of his ambitions relieved Angie's vague unease, lulling her into complacency about the big family dinner that was traditional on the first night of a visit from Aunt Caroline.

Aunt Caroline was, among other things, the sort of woman incapable of going anywhere without attempting to buy it. Her own house was jammed to the attic with sightseer souvenirs from all over the world: children's toys from Slovenia, sculptures from Afghanistan, napkin rings from Kenya shaped like lions and giraffes, legions of brass bangles, boxes and statues of gods from India, and so many Russian *matryoshka* dolls fitting inside each other that she gave them away as stocking-stuffers every Christmas. She never came to the table at the Lukes without bringing some new acquisition for approval; so dinner with Aunt Caroline, in Mr. Luke's words, was always Show and Tell time.

Her most recent hegira had brought her back to West Africa for the third or fourth time, and provided her with the most evil-looking doll Angie had ever seen. Standing beside Aunt Caroline's plate, it was about two feet high, with bat ears, too many fingers, and eyes like bright green marbles streaked with scarlet threads. Aunt Caroline explained rapturously that it was a fertility doll unique to a single Benin tribe, which Angie found impossible to credit. "No way!" she announced loudly. "Not for one minute am I even thinking about having babies with that thing staring at me! It doesn't even look pregnant, the way they do. No way in the world!"

Aunt Caroline had already had two of Mr. Luke's margaritas, and was working on a third. She replied with some heat that not all fertility figures came equipped with cannonball breasts, globular bellies and callipygous rumps—"Some of them are remarkably slender, even by Western standards!" Aunt Caroline herself, by anyone's standards, was built along the general lines of a chopstick.

Angie was drawing breath for a response when she heard her father say something in Korean behind her, and then her mother's soft gasp, "Caroline." But Aunt Caroline was busy explaining to her niece that she knew absolutely nothing about fertility. Mrs. Luke said, considerably louder, "Caroline, shut up, your doll!"

Aunt Caroline said, "What, what?" and then turned, along with Angie. They both screamed.

The doll was growing all the things Aunt Caroline had been insisting it didn't need to qualify as a fertility figure. It was carved from ebony, or from something even harder, but it was pushing out breasts and belly and hips much as Marvyn's two garbage bags had suddenly developed arms and legs. Even its expression had changed, from hungry slyness to a downright silly grin, as though it were about to kiss someone, anyone. It took a few shaky steps forward on the table and put its foot in the salsa. ·

Then the babies started coming.

They came pattering down on the dinner table, fast and hard, like wooden rain, one after another, after another, after another . . . perfect little copies, miniatures, of the madly smiling doll-thing, plopping out of it—*just like Milady used to drop kittens in my lap*, Angie thought absurdly. One of them fell into her plate, and one bounced into the soup, and a couple rolled into Mr. Luke's lap, making him knock his chair over trying to get out of the way. Mrs. Luke was trying to grab them all up at once, which wasn't possible, and Aunt Caroline sat where she was and shrieked. And the doll kept grinning and having babies.

Marvyn was standing against the wall, looking both as terrified as Aunt Caroline and as stupidly pleased as the doll-thing. Angie caught his eye and made a fierce signal, *enough, quit, turn it off*, but either her brother was having too good a time, or else had no idea how to undo whatever spell he had raised. One of the miniatures hit her in the head, and she had a vision of her whole family being drowned in wooden doll-babies, everyone gurgling and reaching up pathetically toward the surface before they all went under for the third time. Another baby caromed off the soup tureen into her left ear, one sharp ebony fingertip drawing blood.

It stopped, finally—Angie never learned how Marvyn regained control—and things almost quieted down, except for Aunt Caroline. The fertility doll got the look of glazed joy off its face and went back to being a skinny, ugly, duty-free airport souvenir, while the doll-babies seemed to melt away exactly as though they had been made of ice instead of wood. Angie was quick enough to see one of them actually dissolving into nothingness directly in front of Aunt Caroline, who at this point stopped screaming and began hiccupping and beating the table with her palms. Mr. Luke pounded her on the back, and Angie volunteered to practice her Heimlich maneuver, but was overruled. Aunt Caroline went to bed early.

Later, in Marvyn's room, he kept his own bed between himself and Angie, indignantly demanding, "What? You said not scary—what's scary about a doll having babies? I thought it was cute."

"Cute," Angie said. "Uh-huh." She was wondering, in a distant sort of way, how much prison time she might get if she actually murdered her brother. *Ten years? Five, with good behavior and a lot of psychiatrists? I could manage it.* "And what did I tell you about not embarrassing Aunt Caroline?"

"How did I embarrass her?" Marvyn's visible eye was wide with outraged innocence. "She shouldn't drink so much, that's her problem. She embarrassed me."

"They're going to figure it out, you know," Angie warned him. "Maybe not Aunt Caroline, but Mom for sure. She's a witch herself that way. Your cover is blown, buddy."

But to her own astonishment, not a word was ever said about the episode, the next day or any other—not by her observant mother, not by her dryly perceptive father, nor even by Aunt Caroline, who might reasonably have been expected at least to comment at breakfast. A baffled Angie remarked to Milady, drowsing on her pillow, "I guess if a thing's weird enough, somehow nobody saw it." This explanation didn't satisfy her, not by a long shot, but lacking anything better she was stuck with it. The old cat blinked in squeezy-eyed agreement, wriggled herself into a more comfortable position, and fell asleep still purring.

Angie kept Marvyn more closely under her eye after that than she had done since he was quite small, and first showing a penchant for playing in traffic. Whether this observation was the cause or not, he did remain more or less on his best behavior, barring the time he turned the air in the bicycle tires of a boy who had stolen his superhero comic book to cement. There was also the affair of the enchanted soccer ball, which kept rolling back to him as though it couldn't bear to be with anyone else. And Angie learned to be extremely careful when making herself a sandwich, because if she lost track of her brother for too long, the sandwich was liable to acquire an extra ingredient. Paprika was one, Tabasco another; and Scotch Bonnet peppers were a special favorite. But there were others less hot and even more objectionable. As she snarled to a sympathetic Melissa Feldman, who had two brothers of her own, "They ought to be able to jail kids just for being eight and a half."

Then there was the matter of Marvyn's attitude toward Angie's attitude about Jake Petrakis.

Jake Petrakis was a year ahead of Angie at school. He was half-Greek and half-Irish, and his blue eyes and thick poppy-colored hair contrasted so richly with his olive skin that she had not been able to look directly at him since the fourth grade. He was on the swim team, and he was the president of the Chess Club, and he went with Ashleigh Sutton, queen of the junior class, rechristened "Ghastly Ashleigh" by the loyal Melissa. But he spoke kindly and cheerfully to Angie without fail, always saying *Hey, Angie*, and *How's it going, Angie?* and *See you in the fall, Angie, have a good summer*. She clutched such things to herself, every one of them, and at the same time could not bear them.

Marvyn was as merciless as a mosquito when it came to Jake Petrakis. He made swooning, kissing noises whenever he spied Angie looking at Jake's picture in her yearbook, and drove her wild by holding invented conversations between them, just loudly enough for her to hear. His increasing ability at witchcraft meant that scented, decorated, and misspelled love notes were likely to flutter down onto her bed at any moment, as were long-stemmed roses, imitation jewelry (Marvyn had limited experience and poor taste), and small, smudgy photos of Jake and Ashleigh together. Mr. Luke had to invoke Angie's oath more than once, and to sweeten it with a promise of a new bicycle if Marvyn made it through the year undamaged. Angie held out for a mountain bike, and her father sighed. "That was always a myth, about the gypsies stealing children," he said, rather wistfully. "It was surely the other way around. Deal."

Yet there were intermittent peaceful moments between Marvyn and Angie, several occurring in Marvyn's room. It was a far tidier place than Angie's room, for all the clothes on the floor and battered board game boxes sticking out from under the bed. Marvyn had mounted *National Geographic* foldout maps all around the walls, lining them up so perfectly that the creases were invisible; and on one special wall were prints and photos of a lot of people with strange staring eyes. Angie recognized Rasputin, and knew a few of the other names—Aleister Crowley, for one, and a man in Renaissance dress called Dr. John Dee. There were two women, as well: the young witch Willow, from *Buffy the Vampire Slayer*, and a daguerreotype of a black woman wearing a kind of turban folded into points. No Harry Potter, however. Marvyn had never taken to Harry Potter.

There was also, one day after school, a very young kitten wobbling among the books littering Marvyn's bed. A surprised Angie picked it up and held it over her face, feeling its purring between her hands. It was a dark, dusty gray, rather like Milady—indeed, Angie had never seen another cat of that exact color. She nuzzled its tummy happily, asking it, "Who are you, huh? Who could you ever be?"

Marvyn was feeding his angelfish, and didn't look up. He said, "She's Milady."

Angie dropped the kitten on the bed. Marvyn said, "I mean, she's Milady when she was young. I went back and got her."

When he did turn around, he was grinning the maddening pirate grin Angie could never stand, savoring her shock. It took her a minute to find words, and more time to make them come out. She said, "You went back. You went back in time?"

"It was easy," Marvyn said. "Forward's *hard*—I don't think I could ever get really forward. Maybe Dr. Dee could do it." He picked up the kitten and handed her back to his sister. It was Milady, down to the crooked left ear and the funny short tail with the darker bit on the end. He said, "She was hurting all the time, she was so old. I thought, if she could—you know—start over, before she got the arthritis . . . "

He didn't finish. Angie said slowly, "So where's Milady? The other one? I mean, if you brought this one . . . I mean, how can they be in the same world?"

"They can't," Marvyn said. "The old Milady's gone."

Angie's throat closed up. Her eyes filled, and so did her nose, and she had to blow it before she could speak again. Looking at the kitten, she knew it was Milady, and made herself think about how good it would be to have her once again bouncing around the house, no longer limping grotesquely and meowing with the pain. But she had loved the old cat all her life, and never known her as a kitten, and when the new Milady started to climb into her lap, Angie pushed her away.

"All right," she said to Marvyn. "All right. How did you get . . . back, or whatever?"

Marvyn shrugged and went back to his fish. "No big deal. You just have to concentrate the right way."

Angie bounced a plastic Wiffle ball off the back of his neck, and he turned around, annoyed. "Leave me alone! Okay, you want to know—there's a spell, words you have to say over and over and over, until you're sick of them, and there's herbs in it too. You have to light them, and hang over them, and you shut your eyes and keep breathing them in and saying the words—"

"I knew I'd been smelling something weird in your room lately. I thought you were sneaking takeout curry to bed with you again."

"And then you open your eyes, and there you are," Marvyn said. "I told you, no big deal."

"There you are where? How do you know where you'll come out? When you'll come out? Click your heels together three times and say there's no place like home?"

"No, dork, you just *know*." And that was all Angie could get out of him—not, as she came to realize, because he wouldn't tell her, but because he couldn't. Witch or no witch, he was still a small boy, with almost no real idea of what he was doing. He was winging it all, playing it all by ear.

Arguing with Marvyn always gave her a headache, and her history home-work—the rise of the English merchant class—was starting to look good in comparison. She went back to her own bedroom and read two whole chapters, and when the kitten Milady came stumbling and squeaking in, Angie let her sleep on the desk. "What the hell," she told it, "it's not your fault."

That evening, when Mr. and Mrs. Luke got home, Angie told them that Milady had died peacefully of illness and old age while they were at work, and was now buried in the back garden. (Marvyn had wanted to make it a horrible hit-and-run accident, complete with a black SUV and half-glimpsed license plate starting with the letter Q, but Angie vetoed this.) Marvyn's contribution to her solemn explanation was to explain that he had seen the new kitten in a petshop window, "and she just looked so much like Milady, and I used my whole allowance, and I'll take care of her, I promise!" Their mother, not being a true cat person, accepted the story easily enough, but Angie was never sure about Mr. Luke. She found him too often sitting with the kitten on his lap, the two of them staring solemnly at each other.

But she saw very little evidence of Marvyn fooling any further with time. Nor, for that matter, was he showing the interest she would have expected in turning himself into the world's best second-grade soccer player, ratcheting up his test scores high enough to be in college by the age of eleven, or simply getting even with people (since Marvyn forgot nothing and had a hit list going back to day-care). She could almost always tell when he'd been making his bed by magic, or making the window plants grow too fast, but he seemed content to remain on that level. Angie let it go.

Once she did catch him crawling on the ceiling, like Spider-Man, but she yelled at him and he fell on the bed and threw up. And there was, of course, the time—two times, actually—when, with Mrs. Luke away, Marvyn organized all the shoes in her closet into a chorus line, and had them tapping and kicking together like the Rockettes. It was fun for Angie to watch, but she made him stop because they were her mother's shoes. What if her clothes joined in? The notion was more than she wanted to deal with.

As it was, there was already plenty to deal with just then. Besides her schoolwork, there was band practice, and Melissa's problems with her boyfriend; not to mention the endless hours spent at the dentist, correcting a slight overbite. Melissa insisted that it made her look sexy, but the suggestion had the wrong effect on Angie's mother. In any case, as far as Angie could see, all Marvyn was doing was playing with a new box of toys, like an elaborate electric train layout, or a top-of-the-line Erector set. She was even able to imagine him getting bored with magic itself after a while. Marvyn had a low threshold for boredom.

Angie was in the orchestra, as well as the band, because of a chronic shortage of woodwinds, but she liked the marching band better. You were out of doors, performing at parades and football games, part of the joyful noise, and it was always more exciting than standing up in a dark, hushed auditorium playing for people you could hardly see. "Besides," as she confided to her mother, "in marching band nobody really notices how you sound. They just want you to keep in step."

On a bright spring afternoon, rehearsing "The Washington Post March" with the full band, Angie's clarinet abruptly went mad. No "licorice stick" now, but a stick of rapturous dynamite, it took off on flights of rowdy improvisation, doing outrageous somersaults, backflips, and cartwheels with the melody—things that Angie knew she could never have conceived of, even if her skill had been equal to the inspiration. Her bandmates, up and down the line, were turning to stare at her, and she wanted urgently to wail, "Hey, I'm not the one, it's my stupid brother, you know I can't play like that." But the music kept spilling out, excessive, absurd, unstoppable—unlike the march, which finally lurched to a disorderly halt. Angie had never been so embarrassed in her life.

Mr. Bishow, the bandmaster, came bumbling through the milling musicians to tell her, "Angie, that was fantastic—that was dazzling! I never knew you had such spirit, such freedom, such wit in your music!" He patted her—hugged her even, quickly and cautiously—then stepped back almost immediately and said, "Don't ever do it again."

"Like I'd have a choice," Angie mumbled, but Mr. Bishow was already shepherding the band back into formation for "Semper Fidelis" *and* "High Society," which Angie fumbled her way through as always, two bars behind the rest of the woodwinds. She was slouching disconsolately off the field when Jake Petrakis, his dark-gold hair still glinting damply from swimming practice, ran over to her to say, "Hey, Angie, cool," then punched her on the shoulder, as he would have done another boy, and dashed off again to meet one of his relay-team partners. And Angie went on home, and waited for Marvyn behind the door of his room.

She seized him by the hair the moment he walked in, and he squalled, "All right, let go, all right! I thought you'd like it!"

"Like it?" Angie shook him, hard. "*Like* it? You evil little ogre, you almost got me kicked out of the band! What else are you lining up for me that you think I'll *like*?"

"Nothing, I swear!" But he was giggling even while she was shaking him. "Okay, I was going to make you so beautiful, even Mom and Dad wouldn't recognize you, but I quit on that. Too much work." Angie grabbed for his hair again, but Marvyn ducked. "So what I thought, maybe I really could get Jake what's-his-face to go crazy about you. There's all kinds of spells and things for that—"

"Don't you dare," Angie said. She repeated the warning calmly and quietly. "Don't. You. Dare."

Marvyn was still giggling. "Nah, I didn't think you'd go for it. Would have been fun, though." Suddenly he was all earnestness, staring up at his sister out of one visible eye, strangely serious, even with his nose running. He said, "It is fun, Angie. It's the most fun I've ever had."

"Yeah, I'll bet," she said grimly. "Just leave me out of it from now on, if you've got any plans for the third grade." She stalked into the kitchen, looking for apple juice.

Marvyn tagged after her, chattering nervously about school, soccer games, the Milady-kitten's rapid growth, and a possible romance in his angelfish tank. "I'm sorry about the band thing, I won't do it again. I just thought it'd be nice if you could play really well, just one time. Did you like the music part, anyway?"

Angie did not trust herself to answer him. She was reaching for the apple juice bottle when the top flew off by itself, bouncing straight up at her face. As she flinched back, a glass came skidding down the counter toward her. She grabbed it before it crashed into the refrigerator, then turned and screamed at Marvyn, "Damn it, Ex-Lax, you quit that! You're going to hurt somebody, trying to do every damn thing by magic!"

"You said the D-word twice!" Marvyn shouted back at her. "I'm telling Mom!" But he made no move to leave the kitchen, and after a moment a small, grubby tear came sliding down from under the eyepatch. "I'm not using magic for everything! I just use it for the boring stuff, mostly. Like the garbage, and vacuuming up, and like putting my clothes away. And Milady's litter box, when it's my turn. That kind of stuff, okay?"

Angie studied him, marveling as always at his capacity for looking heart-wrenchingly innocent. She said, "No point to it when I'm cleaning her box, right? Never mind—just stay out of my way, I've got a French midterm tomorrow." She poured the apple juice, put it back, snatched a raisin cookie and headed for her room. But she paused in the doorway, for no reason she could ever name, except perhaps the way Marvyn had moved to follow her and then stopped himself. "What? Wipe your nose, it's gross. What's the matter now?"

"Nothing," Marvyn mumbled. He wiped his nose on his sleeve, which didn't help. He said, "Only I get scared, Angie. It's scary, doing the stuff I can do."

"What scary? Scary how? A minute ago it was more fun than you've ever had in your life."

"It is!" He moved closer, strangely hesitant: neither witch, nor pirate nor seraph, but an anxious, burdened small boy. "Only sometimes it's like too much fun. Sometimes, right in the middle, I think maybe I should stop, but I can't. Like one time, I was by myself, and I was just fooling around . . . and I sort of made this *thing*, which was really interesting, only it came out funny and then I couldn't unmake it for the longest time, and I was scared Mom and Dad would come home—"

Angie, grimly weighing her past French grades in her mind, reached back for another raisin cookie. "I told you before, you're going to get yourself into real trouble doing crazy stuff like that. Just quit, before something happens by magic that you can't fix by magic. You want advice, I just gave you advice. See you around."

Marvyn wandered forlornly after her to the door of her room. When she turned to close it, he mumbled, "I wish I were as old as you. So I'd know what to do."

"Ha," Angie said, and shut the door.

Whereupon, heedless of French irregular verbs, she sat down at her desk and began writing a letter to Jake Petrakis.

Neither then nor even much later was Angie ever able to explain to anyone why she had written that letter at precisely that time. Because he had slapped her shoulder and told her she—or at least her music—was cool? Because she had seen him, that same afternoon, totally tangled up with Ghastly Ashleigh in a shadowy corner of the library stacks? Because of Marvyn's relentless teasing? Or simply because she was fifteen years old, and it was time for her to write such a letter to someone? Whatever the cause, she wrote what she wrote, and then she folded it up and put it away in her desk drawer.

Then she took it out, and put it back in, and then she finally put it into her backpack. And there the letter stayed for nearly three months, well past midterms, finals, and football, until the fateful Friday night when Angie was out with Melissa, walking and window-shopping in downtown Avicenna, placidly drifting in and out of every coffeeshop along Parnell Street. She told Melissa about the letter then, and Melissa promptly went into a fit of the giggles, which turned into hiccups and required another cappuccino to pacify them. When she could speak coherently, she said, "You ought to send it to him. You've got to send it to him."

Angie was outraged, at first. "No way! I wrote it for me, not for a test or a class, and damn sure not for Jake Petrakis. What kind of a dipshit do you think I am?"

Melissa grinned at her out of mocking green eyes. "The kind of dipshit who's got that letter in your backpack right now, and I bet it's in an envelope with an address and a stamp on it."

"It doesn't have a stamp! And the envelope's just to protect it! I just like having it with me, that's all—"

"And the address?"

"Just for practice, okay? But I didn't sign it, and there's no return address, so that shows you!"

"Right." Melissa nodded. "Right. That definitely shows me."

"Drop it," Angie told her, and Melissa dropped it then. But it was a Friday night, and both of them were allowed to stay out late, as long as they were together, and Avicenna has a lot of coffeeshops. Enough lattes and cappuccinos, with double shots of espresso, brought them to a state of cheerfully jittery abandon in which everything in the world was supremely, ridiculously funny. Melissa never left the subject of Angie's letter alone for very long—"Come on, what's the worst that could happen? Him reading it and maybe figuring out you wrote it? Listen, the really worst thing would be you being an old, old lady still wishing you'd told Jake Petrakis how you felt when you were young. And now he's married, and he's a grandfather, and probably dead, for all you know—"

"Quit it!" But Angie was giggling almost as much as Melissa now, and somehow they were walking down quiet Lovisi Street, past the gas station and the boarded-up health-food store, to find the darkened Petrakis house and tiptoe up the steps to the porch. Facing the front door, Angie dithered for a moment, but Melissa said, "An old lady, in a home, for God's sake, and he'll never know," and Angie took a quick breath and pushed the letter under the door. They ran all the way back to Parnell Street, laughing so wildly that they could barely breathe . . . .

. . . and Angie woke up in the morning whispering *omigod, omigod, omigod*, over and over, even before she was fully awake. She lay in bed for a good hour, praying silently and desperately that the night before had been some crazy, awful dream, and that when she dug into her backpack the letter would still be there. But she knew dreadfully better, and she never bothered to look for it on her frantic way to the telephone. Melissa said soothingly, "Well, at least you didn't sign the thing. There's that, anyway."

"I sort of lied about that," Angie said. Her friend did not answer. Angie said, "Please, you have to come with me. Please."

"Get over there," Melissa said finally. "Go, now—I'll meet you."

Living closer, Angie reached the Petrakis house first, but had no intention of ringing the bell until Melissa got there. She was pacing back and forth on the porch, cursing herself, banging her fists against her legs, and wondering whether she could go to live with her father's sister Peggy in Grand Rapids, when the woman next door called over to tell her that the Petrakises were all out of town at a family gathering. "Left yesterday afternoon. Asked me to keep an eye on the place, cause they won't be back till sometime Sunday night. That's how come I'm kind of watching out." She smiled warningly at Angie before she went back indoors.

The very large dog standing behind her stayed outside. He looked about the size of a Winnebago, and plainly had already made up his mind about Angie. She said, "Nice doggie," and he growled. When she tried out "Hey, sweet thing," which was what her father said to all animals, the dog showed his front teeth, and the hair stood up around his shoulders, and he lay down to keep an eye on things himself. Angie said sadly, "I'm usually really good with dogs."

When Melissa arrived, she said, "Well, you shoved it under the door, so it can't be that far inside. Maybe if we got something like a stick or a wire clotheshanger to hook it back with." But whenever they looked toward the neighboring house, they saw a curtain swaying, and finally they walked away, trying to decide what else to do. But there was nothing; and after a while Angie's throat was too swollen with not crying for her to talk without pain. She walked Melissa back to the bus stop, and they hugged goodbye as though they might never meet again.

Melissa said, "You know, my mother says nothing's ever as bad as you thought it was going to be. I mean, it can't be, because nothing beats all the horrible stuff you can imagine. So maybe . . . you know . . . " but she broke down before she could finish. She hugged Angie again and went home.

Alone in her own house, Angie sat quite still in the kitchen and went on not crying. Her entire face hurt with it, and her eyes felt unbearably heavy. Her mind was not moving at all, and she was vaguely grateful for that. She sat there until Marvyn walked in from playing basketball with his friends. Shorter than everyone else, he generally got stepped on a lot, and always came home scraped and bruised. Angie had rather expected him to try making himself taller, or able to jump higher, but he hadn't done anything of the sort so far. He looked at her now, bounced and shot an invisible basketball, and asked quietly, "What's the matter?"

It may have been the unexpected froggy gentleness of his voice, or simply the sudden fact of his having asked the question at all. Whatever the reason, Angie abruptly burst into furious tears, the rage directed entirely at herself, both for writing the letter to Jake Petrakis in the first place, and for crying about it now. She gestured to Marvyn to go away, but—amazing her further—he stood stolidly waiting for her to grow quiet. When at last she did, he repeated the question. "Angie. What's wrong?"

Angie told him. She was about to add a disclaimer—"You laugh even once, Ex-Lax—" when she realized that it wouldn't be necessary. Marvyn was scratching his head, scrunching up his brow until the eyepatch danced; then abruptly jamming both hands in his pockets and tilting his head back: the poster boy for careless insouciance. He said, almost absently, "I could get it back."

"Oh, right." Angie did not even look up. "Right."

"I could so!" Marvyn was instantly his normal self again: so much for casualness and dispassion. "There's all kinds of things I could do."

Angie dampened a paper towel and tried to do something with her hot, tear-streaked face. "Name two."

"Okay, I will! You remember which mailbox you put it in?"

"Under the door," Angie mumbled. "I put it under the door."

Marvyn snickered then. *"Aww*, like a Valentine." Angie hadn't the energy to hit him, but she made a grab at him anyway, for appearance's sake. "Well, I could make it walk right back out the door, that's one way. Or I bet I could just open the door, if nobody's home. Easiest trick in the world, for us witches."

"They're gone till Sunday night," Angie said. "But there's this lady next door, she's watching the place like a hawk. And even when she's not, she's got this immense dog. I don't care if you're the hottest witch in the world, you do not want to mess with this werewolf."

Marvyn, who—as Angie knew—was wary of big dogs, went back to scratching his head. "Too easy, anyway. No fun, forget it." He sat down next to her, completely absorbed in the problem. "How about I . . . no, that's kid stuff, anybody could do it. But there's a spell . . . I could make the letter self-destruct, right there in the house, like in that old TV show. It'd just be a little fluffy pile of ashes—they'd vacuum it up and never know. How about that?" Before Angie could express an opinion, he was already shaking his head. "Still too easy. A baby spell, for beginners. I hate those."

"Easy is good," Angie told him earnestly. "I like easy. And you *are* a beginner."

Marvyn was immediately outraged, his normal bass-baritone rumble going up to a wounded squeak. "I am not! No way in the world I'm a beginner!" He was up and stamping his feet, as he had not done since he was two. "I tell you what—just for that, I'm going to get your letter back for you, but I'm not going to tell you how. You'll see, that's all. You just wait and see."

He was stalking away toward his room when Angie called after him, with the first glimmer both of hope and of humor that she had felt in approximately a century, "All right, you're a big bad witch king. What do you want?"

Marvyn turned and stared, uncomprehending.

Angie said, "Nothing for nothing, that's my bro. So let's hear it—what's your price for saving my life?"

If Marvyn's voice had gone up any higher, only bats could have heard it. "I'm rescuing you, and you think I want something for it? Julius Christmas!" which was the only swearword he was ever allowed to get away with. "You don't have anything I want, anyway. Except maybe . . . "

He let the thought hang in space, uncompleted. Angie said, "Except maybe what?"

Marvyn swung on the doorframe one-handed, grinning his pirate grin at her. "I hate you calling me Ex-Lax. You know I hate it, and you keep doing it."

"Okay, I won't do it anymore, ever again. I promise."

"Mmm. Not good enough." The grin had grown distinctly evil. "I think you ought to call me O Mighty One for two weeks."

"What?" Now Angie was on her feet, misery briefly forgotten. "Give it up, Ex-Lax—two weeks? No chance!" They glared at each other in silence for a long moment before she finally said, "A week. Don't push it. One week, no more. And not in front of people!"

"Ten days." Marvyn folded his arms. "Starting right now." Angie went on glowering. Marvyn said, "You want that letter?"

"Yes."

Marvyn waited.

"Yes, O Mighty One." Triumphant, Marvyn held out his hand and Angie slapped it. She said, "When?"

"Tonight. No, tomorrow—going to the movies with Sunil and his family tonight. Tomorrow." He wandered off, and Angie took her first deep breath in what felt like a year and a half. She wished she could tell Melissa that things were going to be all right, but she didn't dare; so she spent the day trying to appear normal—just the usual Angie, aimlessly content on a Saturday afternoon. When Marvyn came home from the movies, he spent the rest of the evening reading *Hellboy* comics in his room, with the Milady-kitten on his stomach. He was still doing it when Angie gave up peeking in at him and went to bed.

But he was gone on Sunday morning. Angie knew it the moment she woke up.

She had no idea where he could be, or why. She had rather expected him to work whatever spell he settled on in his bedroom, under the stern gaze of his wizard mentors. But he wasn't there, and he didn't come to breakfast. Angie told their mother that they'd been up late watching television together, and that she should probably let Marvyn sleep in. And when Mrs. Luke grew worried after breakfast, Angie went to his room herself, returning with word that Marvyn was working intensely on a project for his art class, and wasn't feeling sociable. Normally she would never have gotten away with it, but her parents were on their way to brunch and a concert, leaving her with the usual instructions to feed and water the cat, use the twenty on the cabinet for something moderately healthy, and to check on Marvyn "now and then," which actually meant frequently. ("The day we don't tell you that," Mr. Luke said once, when she objected to the regular duty, "will be the very day the kid steals a kayak and heads for Tahiti." Angie found it hard to argue the point.)

Alone in the empty house—more alone than she felt she had ever been—Angie turned constantly in circles, wandering from room to room with no least notion of what to do. As the hours passed and her brother failed to return, she found herself calling out to him aloud. "Marvyn? Marvyn, I swear, if you're doing this to drive me crazy . . . O Mighty One, where are you? You get back here, never mind the damn letter, just get back!" She stopped doing this after a time, because the cracks and tremors in her voice embarrassed her, and made her even more afraid.

Strangely, she seemed to feel him in the house all that time. She kept whirling to look over her shoulder, thinking that he might be sneaking up on her to scare her, a favorite game since his infancy. But he was never there.

Somewhere around noon the doorbell rang, and Angie tripped over herself scrambling to answer it, even though she had no hope—almost no hope—of its being Marvyn. But it was Lidia at the door—Angie had forgotten that she usually came to clean on Sunday afternoons. She stood there, old and smiling, and Angie hugged her wildly and wailed, "Lidia, Lidia, *socorro*, help me, *ayúdame*, Lidia." She had learned Spanish from the housekeeper when she was too little to know she was learning it.

Lidia put her hands on Angie's shoulders. She put her back a little and looked into her face, saying, "*Chuchi, dime qué pasa contigo?*" She had called Angie *Chuchi* since childhood, never explaining the origin or meaning of the word.

"It's Marvyn," Angie whispered. "It's Marvyn." She started to explain about the letter, and Marvyn's promise, but Lidia only nodded and asked no questions. She said firmly, "*El Viejo puede ayudar.*"

Too frantic to pay attention to gender, Angie took her to mean Yemaya, the old woman in the farmer's market who had told Marvyn that he was a *brujo*. She said, "You mean *la santera*," but Lidia shook her head hard. "No, no, *El Viejo*. You go out there, you ask to see *El Viejo*. *Solamente El Viejo*. *Los otros no pueden ayudarte.*"

The others can't help you. Only the old man. Angie asked where she could find *El Viejo*, and Lidia directed her to a *Santeria* shop on Bowen Street. She drew a crude map, made sure Angie had money with her, kissed her on the cheek and made a blessing sign on her forehead. "*Cuidado, Chuchi*," she said with a kind of cheerful solemnity, and Angie was out and running for the Gonzales Avenue bus, the same one she took to school. This time she stayed on a good deal farther.

The shop had no sign, and no street number, and it was so small that Angie kept walking past it for some while. Her attention was finally caught by the objects in the one dim window, and on the shelves to right and left. There was an astonishing variety of incense, and of candles encased in glass with pictures of black saints, as well as boxes marked Fast Money Ritual Kit, and bottles of Elegua Floor Wash, whose label read "Keeps Trouble From Crossing Your Threshold." When Angie entered, the musky scent of the place made her feel dizzy and heavy and out of herself, as she always felt when she had a cold coming on. She heard a rooster crowing, somewhere in back.

She didn't see the old woman until her chair creaked slightly, because she was sitting in a corner, halfway hidden by long hanging garments like church choir robes, but with symbols and patterns on them that Angie had never seen before. The woman was very old, much older even than Lidia, and she had an absurdly small pipe in her toothless mouth. Angie said, "Yemaya?" The old woman looked at her with eyes like dead planets.

Angie's Spanish dried up completely, followed almost immediately by her English. She said, "My brother . . . my little brother . . . I'm supposed to ask for *El Viejo*. The old one, *viejo santero?* Lidia said." She ran out of words in either language at that point. A puff of smoke crawled from the little pipe, but the old woman made no other response.

Then, behind her, she heard a curtain being pulled aside. A hoarse, slow voice said, "*Quieres El Viejo?* Me."

Angie turned and saw him, coming toward her out of a long hallway whose end she could not see. He moved deliberately, and it seemed to take him forever to reach her, as though he were returning from another world. He was black, dressed all in black, and he wore dark glasses, even in the dark, tiny shop. His hair was so white that it hurt her eyes when she stared. He said, "Your brother."

"Yes," Angie said. "Yes. He's doing magic for me—he's getting something I need—and I don't know where he is, but I know he's in trouble, and I want him back!" She did not cry or break down—Marvyn would never be able to say that she cried over him—but it was a near thing.

El Viejo pushed the dark glasses up on his forehead, and Angie saw that he was younger than she had first thought—certainly younger than Lidia—and that there were thick white half-circles under his eyes. She never knew whether they were somehow natural, or the result of heavy makeup; what she did see was that they made his eyes look bigger and brighter—all pupil, nothing more. They should have made him look at least slightly comical, like a reverse-image raccoon, but they didn't.

"I know you brother," *El Viejo* said. Angie fought to hold herself still as he came closer, smiling at her with the tips of his teeth. "A *brujito*—little, little witch, we know. Mama and me, we been watching." He nodded toward the old woman in the chair, who hadn't moved an inch or said a word since Angie's arrival. Angie smelled a damp, musty aroma, like potatoes going bad.

"Tell me where he is. Lidia said you could help." Close to, she could see blue highlights in *El Viejo*'s skin, and a kind of V-shaped scar on each cheek. He was wearing a narrow black tie, which she had not noticed at first; for some reason, the vision of him tying it in the morning, in front of a mirror, was more chilling to her than anything else about him. He grinned fully at her now, showing teeth that she had expected to be yellow and stinking, but which were all white and square and a little too large. He said, "*Tu hermano está perdido*. Lost in Thursday."

"Thursday?" It took her a dazed moment to comprehend, and longer to get the words out. "Oh, God, he went back! Like with Milady—he went back to before I . . . when the letter was still in my backpack. The little showoff—he said forward was hard, coming forward—he wanted to show me he could do it. And he got stuck. Idiot, idiot, idiot!" *El Viejo* chuckled softly, nodding, saying nothing.

"You have to go find him, get him out of there, right now—I've got money." She began digging frantically in her coat pockets.

"No, no money." *El Viejo* waved her offering aside, studying her out of eyes the color of almost-ripened plums. The white markings under them looked real; the eyes didn't. He said, "I take you. We find you brother together."

Angie's legs were trembling so much that they hurt. She wanted to assent, but it was simply not possible. "No. I can't. I can't. You go back there and get him."

El Viejo laughed then: an enormous, astonishing Santa Claus *ho-ho-HO*, so rich and reassuring that it made Angie smile even as he was snatching her up and stuffing her under one arm. By the time she had recovered from her bewilderment enough to start kicking and fighting, he was walking away with her down the long hall he had come out of a moment before. Angie screamed until her voice splintered in her throat, but she could not hear herself: from the moment *El Viejo* stepped back into the darkness of the hallway, all sound had ended. She could hear neither his footsteps nor his laughter—though she could feel him laughing against her—and certainly not her own panicky racket. They could be in outer space. They could be anywhere.

Dazed and disoriented as she was, the hallway seemed to go soundlessly on and on, until wherever they truly were, it could never have been the tiny *Santeria* shop she had entered only—when?—minutes before. It was a cold place, smelling like an old basement; and for all its darkness, Angie had a sense of things happening far too fast on all sides, just out of range of her smothered vision. She could distinguish none of them clearly, but there was a sparkle to them all the same.

And then she was in Marvyn's room.

And it was unquestionably Marvyn's room: there were the bearded and beaded occultists on the walls; there were the flannel winter sheets that he slept on all year because they had pictures of the New York Mets ballplayers; there was the complete set of *Star Trek* action figures that Angie had given him at Christmas, posed just so on his bookcase. And there, sitting on the edge of his bed, was Marvyn, looking lonelier than anyone Angie had ever seen in her life.

He didn't move or look up until *El Viejo* abruptly dumped her down in front of him and stood back, grinning like a beartrap. Then he jumped to his feet, burst into tears and started frenziedly climbing her, snuffling, "Angie, Angie, Angie," all the way up. Angie held him, trying somehow to preserve her neck and hair and back all at once, while mumbling, "It's all right, it's okay, I'm here. It's okay, Marvyn."

Behind her, *El Viejo* chuckled, "Crybaby witch—little, little *brujito* crybaby." Angie hefted her blubbering baby brother like a shopping bag, holding him on her hip as she had done when he was little, and turned to face the old man. She said, "Thank you. You can take us home now."

El Viejo smiled—not a grin this time, but a long, slow shutmouth smile like a paper cut. He said, "Maybe we let *him* do it, yes?" and then he turned and walked away and was gone, as though he had simply slipped between the molecules of the air. Angie stood with Marvyn in her arms, trying to peel him off like a Band-Aid, while he clung to her with his chin digging hard into the top of her head. She finally managed to dump him down on the bed and stood over him, demanding, "What happened? What were you thinking?" Marvyn was still crying too hard to answer her. Angie said, "You just had to do it this way, didn't you? No silly little beginner spells—you're playing with the big guys now, right, O Mighty One? So what happened? How come you couldn't get back?"

"I don't know!" Marvyn's face was red and puffy with tears, and the tears kept coming while Angie tried to straighten his eyepatch. It was impossible for him to get much out without breaking down again, but he kept wailing, "I don't know what went wrong! I did everything you're supposed to, but I couldn't make it work! I don't know . . . maybe I forgot . . . " He could not finish.

"Herbs," Angie said, as gently and calmly as she could. "You left your magic herbs back—" she had been going to say "back home," but she stopped, because they *were* back home, sitting on Marvyn's bed in Marvyn's room, and the confusion was too much for her to deal with just then. She said, "Just tell me. You left the stupid herbs."

Marvyn shook his head until the tears flew, protesting, "No, I didn't, I didn't— look!" He pointed to a handful of grubby dried weeds scattered on the bed—Lidia would have thrown them out in a minute. Marvyn gulped and wiped his nose and tried to stop crying. He said, "They're really hard to find, maybe they're not fresh anymore, I don't know—they've always looked like that. But now they don't work," and he was wailing afresh. Angie told him that Dr. John Dee and Willow would both have been ashamed of him, but it didn't help.

But she also sat with him and put her arm around him, and smoothed his messy hair, and said, "Come on, let's think this out. Maybe it's the herbs losing their juice, maybe it's something else. You did everything the way you did the other time, with Milady?"

"I thought I did." Marvyn's voice was small and shy, not his usual deep croak.

"But I don't know anymore, Angie—the more I think about it, the more I don't know. It's all messed up, I can't remember anything now."

"Okay," Angie said. "Okay. So how about we just run through it all again? We'll do it together. You try everything you do remember about—you know—moving around in time, and I'll copy you. I'll do whatever you say."

Marvyn wiped his nose again and nodded. They sat down cross-legged on the floor, and Marvyn produced the grimy book of paper matches that he always carried with him, in case of firecrackers. Following his directions Angie placed all the crumbly herbs into Milady's dish, and her brother lit them. Or tried to: they didn't blaze up, but smoked and smoldered and smelled like old dust, setting both Angie and Marvyn sneezing almost immediately. Angie coughed and asked, "Did that happen the other time?" Marvyn did not answer.

There was a moment when she thought the charm might actually be going to work. The room around them grew blurry—slightly blurry, granted—and Angie heard indistinct faraway sounds that might have been themselves hurtling forward to sheltering Sunday. But when the fumes of Marvyn's herbs cleared away, they were still sitting in Thursday—they both knew it without saying a word. Angie said, "Okay, so much for that. What about all that special concentration you were telling me about? You think maybe your mind wandered? You pronounce any spells the wrong way? Think, Marvyn!"

"I am thinking! I told you forward was hard!" Marvyn looked ready to start crying again, but he didn't. He said slowly, "Something's wrong, but it's not me. I don't think it's me. Something's *pushing* . . . " He brightened suddenly. "Maybe we should hold hands or something. Because of there being two of us this time. We could try that."

So they tried the spell that way, and then they tried working it inside a pentagram they made with masking tape on the floor, as Angie had seen such things done on *Buffy the Vampire Slayer*, even though Marvyn said that didn't really mean anything, and they tried the herbs again, in a special order that Marvyn thought he remembered. They even tried it with Angie saying the spell, after Marvyn had coached her, just on the chance that his voice itself might have been throwing off the pitch or the pronunciation. Nothing helped.

Marvyn gave up before Angie did. Suddenly, while she was trying the spell over herself, one more time—some of the words seemed to heat up in her mouth as she spoke them—he collapsed into a wretched ball of desolation on the floor, moaning over and over, "We're finished, it's finished, we'll never get out of Thursday!" Angie understood that he was only a terrified little boy, but she was frightened too, and it would have relieved her to slap him and scream at him. Instead, she tried as best she could to reassure him, saying, "He'll come back for us. He has to."

Her brother sat up, knuckles to his eyes. "No, he doesn't have to! Don't you understand? He knows I'm a witch like him, and he's just going to leave me here, out of his way. I'm sorry, Angie, I'm really sorry!" Angie had almost never heard that word from Marvyn, and never twice in the same sentence.

"Later for all that," she said. "I was just wondering—do you think we could get Mom and Dad's attention when they get home? You think they'd realize what's happened to us?"

Marvyn shook his head. "You haven't seen me all the time I've been gone. I saw you, and I screamed and hollered and everything, but you never knew. They won't either. We're not really in our house—we're just here. We'll always be here."

Angie meant to laugh confidently, to give them both courage, but it came out more of a hiccupy snort. "Oh, no. No way. There is no way I'm spending the rest of my life trapped in your stupid bedroom. We're going to try this useless mess one more time, and then . . . then I'll do something else." Marvyn seemed about to ask her what else she could try, but he checked himself, which was good.

They attempted the spell more than one more time. They tried it in every style they could think of except standing on their heads and reciting the words backward, and they might just as well have done that, for all the effect it had. Whether Marvyn's herbs had truly lost all potency, or whether Marvyn had simply forgotten some vital phrase, they could not even recapture the fragile awareness of something almost happening that they had both felt on the first trial. Again and again they opened their eyes to last Thursday.

"Okay," Angie said at last. She stood up, to stretch cramped legs, and began to wander around the room, twisting a couple of the useless herbs between her fingers. "Okay," she said again, coming to a halt midway between the bedroom door and the window, facing Marvyn's small bureau. A leg of his red Dr. Seuss pajamas was hanging out of one of the drawers.

"Okay," she said a third time. "Let's go home."

Marvyn had fallen into a kind of fetal position, sitting up but with his arms tight around his knees and his head down hard on them. He did not look up at her words. Angie raised her voice. "Let's go, Marvyn. That hallway—tunnel-thing, whatever it is—it comes out right about where I'm standing. That's where *El Viejo* brought me, and that's the way he left when he . . . left. That's the way back to Sunday."

"It doesn't matter," Marvyn whimpered. "*El Viejo* . . . he's him! He's *him!*"

Angie promptly lost what little remained of her patience. She stalked over to Marvyn and shook him to his feet, dragging him to a spot in the air as though she were pointing out a painting in a gallery. "And you're Marvyn Luke, and you're the big bad new witch in town! You said it yourself—if you weren't, he'd never have bothered sticking you away here. Not even nine, and you can eat his lunch, and he knows it! Straighten your patch and take us home, bro." She nudged him playfully. "Oh, forgive me—I meant to say, O Mighty One."

"You don't have to call me that anymore." Marvyn's legs could barely hold him up, and he sagged against her, a dead weight of despair. "I can't, Angie. I can't get us home. I'm sorry . . . ."

The good thing—and Angie knew it then—would have been to turn and comfort him: to take his cold, wet face between her hands and tell him that all would yet be well, that they would soon be eating popcorn with far too much butter on it in his real room in their real house. But she was near her own limit, and pretending calm courage for his sake was prodding her, in spite of herself, closer to the edge. Without looking at Marvyn, she snapped, "Well, I'm not about to die in last Thursday! I'm walking out of here the same way he did, and you can come with me or not, that's up to you. But I'll tell you one thing, Ex-Lax—I won't be looking back."

And she stepped forward, walking briskly toward the dangling Dr. Seuss pajamas . . .

. . . and into a thick, sweet-smelling grayness that instantly filled her eyes and mouth, her nose and her ears, disorienting her so completely that she flailed her arms madly, all sense of direction lost, with no idea of which way she might be headed; drowning in syrup like a trapped bee or butterfly. Once she thought she heard Marvyn's voice, and called out for him—"I'm here, I'm here!" But she did not hear him again.

Then, between one lunge for air and another, the grayness was gone, leaving not so much as a dampness on her skin, nor even a sickly aftertaste of sugar in her mouth. She was back in the time-tunnel, as she had come to think of it, recognizing the uniquely dank odor: a little like the ashes of a long-dead fire, and a little like what she imagined moonlight might smell like, if it had a smell. The image was an ironic one, for she could see no more than she had when *El Viejo* was lugging her the other way under his arm. She could not even distinguish the ground under her feet; she knew only that it felt more like slippery stone than anything else, and she was careful to keep her footing as she plodded steadily forward.

The darkness was absolute—strange solace, in a way, since she could imagine Marvyn walking close behind her, even though he never answered her, no matter how often or how frantically she called his name. She moved along slowly, forcing her way through the clinging murk, vaguely conscious, as before, of a distant, flickering sense of sound and motion on every side of her. If there were walls to the time-tunnel, she could not touch them; if it had a roof, no air currents betrayed it; if there were any living creature in it besides herself, she felt no sign. And if time actually passed there, Angie could never have said. She moved along, her eyes closed, her mind empty, except for the formless fear that she was not moving at all, but merely raising and setting down her feet in the same place, endlessly. She wondered if she was hungry.

Not until she opened her eyes in a different darkness to the crowing of a rooster and a familiar heavy aroma did she realize that she was walking down the hallway leading from the *Santeria* shop to . . . wherever she had really been—and where Marvyn still must be, for he plainly had not followed her. She promptly turned and started back toward last Thursday, but halted at the deep, slightly grating chuckle behind her. She did not turn again, but stood very still.

El Viejo walked a slow full circle around her before he faced her, grinning down at her like the man in the moon. The dark glasses were off, and the twin scars on his cheeks were blazing up as though they had been slashed into him a moment before. He said, "I know. Before even I see you, I know."

Angie hit him in the stomach as hard as she could. It was like punching a frozen slab of beef, and she gasped in pain, instantly certain that she had broken her hand. But she hit him again, and again, screaming at the top of her voice, "Bring my brother back! If you don't bring him right back here, right now, I'll kill you! I will!"

El Viejo caught her hands, surprisingly gently, still laughing to himself. "Little girl, listen, listen now. *Niñita*, nobody else—nobody—ever do what you do. You understand? Nobody but me ever walk that road back from where I leave you, understand?" The big white half-circles under his eyes were stretching and curling like live things.

Angie pulled away from him with all her strength, as she had hit him. She said, "No. That's Marvyn. Marvyn's the witch, the *brujo*—don't go telling people it's me. Marvyn's the one with the power."

"Him?" Angie had never heard such monumental scorn packed into one syllable. *El Viejo* said, "Your brother nothing, nobody, we no bother with him. Forget him—you the one got the *regalo*, you just don't know." The big white teeth filled her vision; she saw nothing else. "I show you—me, *El Viejo*. I show you what you are."

It was beyond praise, beyond flattery. For all her dread and dislike of *El Viejo*, to have someone of his wicked wisdom tell her that she was like him in some awful, splendid way made Angie shiver in her heart. She wanted to turn away more than she had ever wanted anything—even Jake Petrakis—but the long walk home to Sunday was easier than breaking the clench of the white-haired man's malevolent presence would have been. Having often felt (and almost as often dismissed the notion) that Marvyn was special in the family by virtue of being the baby, and a boy—and now a potent witch—she let herself revel in the thought that the real gift was hers, not his, and that if she chose she had only to stretch out her hand to have her command settle home in it. It was at once the most frightening and the most purely, completely gratifying feeling she had ever known.

But it was not tempting. Angie knew the difference.

"Forget it," she said. "Forget it, buster. You've got nothing to show me."

El Viejo did not answer her. The old, old eyes that were all pupil continued slipping over her like hands, and Angie went on glaring back with the brown eyes she despaired of because they could never be as deep-set and deep green as her mother's eyes. They stood so—for how long, she never knew—until *El Viejo* turned and opened his mouth as though to speak to the silent old lady whose own stone eyes seemed not to have blinked since Angie had first entered the *Santeria* shop, a childhood ago. Whatever he meant to say, he never got the words out, because Marvyn came back then.

He came down the dark hall from a long way off, as *El Viejo* had done the first time she saw him—as she herself had trudged forever, only moments ago. But Marvyn had come a further journey: Angie could see that beyond doubt in the way he stumbled along, looking like a shadow casting a person. He was struggling to carry something in his arms, but she could not make out what it was. As long as she watched him approaching, he seemed hardly to draw any nearer.

Whatever he held looked too heavy for a small boy: it threatened constantly to slip from his hands, and he kept shifting it from one shoulder to the other, and back again. Before Angie could see it clearly, *El Viejo* screamed, and she knew on the instant that she would never hear a more terrible sound in her life. He might have been being skinned alive, or having his soul torn out of his body—she never even tried to tell herself what it was like, because there were no words. Nor did she tell anyone that she fell down at the sound, fell flat down on her hands and knees, and rocked and whimpered until the scream stopped. It went on for a long time.

When it finally stopped, *El Viejo* was gone, and Marvyn was standing beside her with a baby in his arms. It was black and immediately endearing, with big, bright, strikingly watchful eyes. Angie looked into them once, and looked quickly away.

Marvyn looked worn and exhausted. His eyepatch was gone, and the left eye that Angie had not seen for months was as bloodshot as though he had just come off a three-day drunk—though she noticed that it was not wandering at all. He said in a small, dazed voice, "I had to go back a really long way, Angie. Really long."

Angie wanted to hold him, but she was afraid of the baby. Marvyn looked toward the old woman in the corner and sighed; then hitched up his burden one more time and clumped over to her. He said, "Ma'am, I think this is yours?" Adults always commented on Marvyn's excellent manners.

The old woman moved then, for the first time. She moved like a wave, Angie thought: a wave seen from a cliff or an airplane, crawling along so slowly that it seemed impossible for it ever to break, ever to reach the shore. But the sea was in that motion, all of it caught up in that one wave; and when she set down her pipe, took the baby from Marvyn and smiled, that was the wave too. She looked down at the baby, and said one word, which Angie did not catch. Then Angie had her brother by the arm, and they were out of the shop. Marvyn never looked back, but Angie did, in time to see the old woman baring blue gums in soundless laughter.

All the way home in a taxi, Angie prayed silently that her parents hadn't returned yet. Lidia was waiting, and together they whisked Marvyn into bed without any serious protest. Lidia washed his face with a rough cloth, and then slapped him and shouted at him in Spanish—Angie learned a few words she couldn't wait to use—and then she kissed him and left, and Angie brought him a pitcher of orange juice and a whole plate of gingersnaps, and sat on the bed and said, "What happened?"

Marvyn was already working on the cookies as though he hadn't eaten in days—which, in a sense, was quite true. He asked, with his mouth full, "What's *malcriado* mean?"

"What? Oh. Like badly raised, badly brought up—troublemaking kid. About the only thing Lidia didn't call you. Why?"

"Well, that's what that lady called . . . him. The baby."

"Right," Angie said. "Leave me a couple of those, and tell me how he got to be a baby. You did like with Milady?"

"Uh-huh. Only I had to go way, way, way back, like I told you." Marvyn's voice took on the faraway sound it had had in the *Santeria* shop. "Angie, he's so old."

Angie said nothing. Marvyn said in a whisper, "I couldn't follow you, Angie. I was scared."

"Forget it," she answered. She had meant to be soothing, but the words burst out of her. "If you just hadn't had to show off, if you'd gotten that letter back some simple, ordinary way—" Her entire chest froze solid at the word. "The letter! We forgot all about my stupid letter!" She leaned forward and snatched the plate of cookies away from Marvyn. "Did you forget? You forgot, didn't you?" She was shaking as had not happened even when *El Viejo* had hold of her. "Oh, God, after all that!"

But Marvyn was smiling for the first time in a very long while. "Calm down, be cool—I've got it here." He dug her letter to Jake Petrakis—more than a little grimy by now—out of his back pocket and held it out to Angie. "There. Don't say I never did nuttin' for you." It was a favorite phrase of his, gleaned from a television show, and most often employed when he had fed Milady, washed his breakfast dish, or folded his clothes. "Take it, open it up," he said now. "Make sure it's the right one."

"I don't need to," Angie protested irritably. "It's my letter—believe me, I know it when I see it." But she opened the envelope anyway and withdrew a single folded sheet of paper, which she glanced at . . . then *stared* at, in absolute disbelief.

She handed the sheet to Marvyn. It was empty on both sides.

"Well, you did your job all right," she said, mildly enough, to her stunned, slack-jawed brother. "No question about that. I'm just trying to figure out why we had to go through this whole incredible hooha for a blank sheet of paper."

Marvyn actually shrank away from her in the bed.

"I didn't do it, Angie! I swear!" Marvyn scrambled to his feet, standing up on the bed with his hands raised, as though to ward her off in case she attacked him. "I just grabbed it out of your backpack—I never even looked at it."

"And what, I wrote the whole thing in grapefruit juice, so nobody could read it unless you held it over a lamp or something? Come on, it doesn't matter now. Get your feet off your damn pillow and sit down."

Marvyn obeyed warily, crouching rather than sitting next to her on the edge of the bed. They were silent together for a little while before he said, "You did that. With the letter. You wanted it not written so much, it just *wasn't*. That's what happened."

"Oh, right," she said. "Me being the dynamite witch around here. I told you, it doesn't matter"

"It matters." She had grown so unused to seeing a two-eyed Marvyn that his expression seemed more than doubly earnest to her just then. He said, quite quietly, "You are the dynamite witch, Angie. He was after you, not me."

This time she did not answer him. Marvyn said, "I was the bait. I do garbage bags and clarinets—okay, and I make ugly dolls walk around. What's he care about that? But he knew you'd come after me, so he held me there—back there in Thursday—until he could grab you. Only he didn't figure you could walk all the way home on your own, without any spells or anything. I know that's how it happened, Angie! That's how I know you're the real witch."

"No," she said, raising her voice now. "No, I was just pissed-off, that's different. Never underestimate the power of a pissed-off woman, O Mighty One. But you . . . you went all the way back, on *your* own, and you grabbed *him*. You're going to be *way* stronger and better than he is, and he knows it. He just figured he'd get rid of the competition early on, while he had the chance. Not a generous guy, *El Viejo*."

Marvyn's chubby face turned gray. "But I'm *not* like him! I don't want to be like him!" Both eyes suddenly filled with tears, and he clung to his sister as he had not done since his return. "It was horrible, Angie, it was so horrible. You were gone, and I was all alone, and I didn't know what to do, only I had to do *something*. And I remembered Milady, and I figured if he wasn't letting me come forward I'd go the other way, and I was so scared and mad I just walked and walked and walked in the dark, until I . . . " He was crying so hard that Angie could hardly make the words out. "I don't want to be a witch anymore, Angie, I don't *want* to! And I don't want *you* being a witch either . . . "

Angie held him and rocked him, as she had loved doing when he was three or four years old, and the cookies got scattered all over the bed. "It's all right," she told him, with one ear listening for their parents' car pulling into the garage. "*Shh, shh*, it's all right, it's over, we're safe, it's okay, *shh*. It's okay, we're not going to be witches, neither one of us." She laid him down and pulled the covers back over him. "You go to sleep now."

Marvyn looked up at her, and then at the wizards' wall beyond her shoulder. "I might take some of those down," he mumbled. "Maybe put some soccer players up for a while. The Brazilian team's really good." He was just beginning to doze off in her arms, when suddenly he sat up again and said, "Angie? The baby?"

"What about the baby? I thought he made a beautiful baby, *El Viejo*. Mad as hell, but lovable."

"It was bigger when we left," Marvyn said. Angie stared at him. "I looked back at it in that lady's lap, and it was already bigger than when I was carrying it. He's starting over, Angie, like Milady."

"Better him than me," Angie said. "I hope he gets a kid brother this time, he's got it coming." She heard the car, and then the sound of a key in the lock. She said, "Go to sleep, don't worry about it. After what we've been through, we can handle anything. The two of us. And without witchcraft. Whichever one of us it is—no witch stuff."

Marvyn smiled drowsily. "Unless we really, *really* need it." Angie held out her hand and they slapped palms in formal agreement. She looked down at her fingers and said, "*Ick!* Blow your *nose!*"

But Marvyn was asleep.

Ursula K. Le Guin is the author of innumerable SF and fantasy classics, such as *The Left Hand of Darkness*, *The Lathe of Heaven*, *The Dispossessed*, and *A Wizard of Earthsea* (and the others in *The Earthsea Cycle*). She has been named a Grand Master by the Science Fiction Writers of America, and is the winner of five Hugos, six Nebulas, two World Fantasy Awards, and twenty Locus Awards. She's also a winner of the Newbery Medal, The National Book Award, the PEN/Malamud Award, and was named a Living Legend by the Library of Congress.

There are few fictional realms as well-loved and respected as Ursula K. Le Guin's Earthsea. It is a place of islands and water, wizards and words, and for more than thirty years, it has been a remarkable influence on the writers and readers of fantastic fiction.

While the books set in the Earthsea universe are most famous—*A Wizard of Earthsea*, the first Earthsea novel, was originally published in 1968 and remains in print to this day—the world was first introduced in our next story. It is the tale of Festin the wizard, an introverted lover of nature confronted by the dark greed of an evil sorcerer for whom one life is not enough.

As Festin struggles to escape from what he believes is eternal captivity, his powers as a wizard are challenged, and a hungry darkness revealed. As evil settles over his homeland, Festin must find a way to save not only himself, but the place he loves.

Here is a classic story of one man's courageous fight against evil—and the power we hold when we sacrifice everything for love.

The Word of Unbinding
Ursula K. Le Guin

Where was he? The floor was hard and slimy, the air black and stinking, and that was all there was. Except a headache. Lying flat on the clammy floor Festin moaned, and then said, "Staff!" When his alderwood wizard's staff did not come to his hand, he knew he was in peril. He sat up, and not having his staff with which to make a proper light, he struck a spark between finger and thumb, muttering a certain Word. A blue will o' the wisp sprang from the spark and rolled feebly through the air, sputtering. "Up," said Festin, and the fireball wobbled upward till it lit a vaulted trapdoor very high above, so high that Festin projecting into the fireball momentarily saw his own face forty feet below as a pale dot in the darkness. The light struck no reflections in the damp walls; they had been woven out of night, by magic. He rejoined himself and said, "Out." The ball expired. Festin sat in the dark, cracking his knuckles.

He must have been overspelled from behind, by surprise; for the last memory he had was of walking through his own woods at evening talking with the trees. Lately, in these lone years in the middle of his life, he had been burdened with a sense of waste, of unspent strength; so, needing to learn patience, he had left the villages and gone to converse with trees, especially oaks, chestnuts, and the grey alders whose roots are in profound communication with running water. It had been six months since he had spoken to a human being. He had been busy with essentials, casting no spells and bothering no one. So who had spellbound him and shut him in this reeking well? "Who?" he demanded of the walls, and slowly a name gathered on them and ran down to him like a thick black drop sweated out from pores of stone and spores of fungus: "Voll."

For a moment Festin was in a cold sweat himself.

He had heard first long ago of Voll the Fell, who was said to be more than wizard yet less than man; who passed from island to island of the Outer Reach, undoing the works of the Ancients, enslaving men, cutting forests and spoiling fields, and sealing in underground tombs any wizard or Mage who tried to combat him.

Refugees from ruined islands told always the same tale, that he came at evening on a dark wind over the sea. His slaves followed in ships; these they had seen. But none of them had ever seen Voll. . . . There were many men and creatures of evil will among the Islands, and Festin, a young warlock intent on his training, had not paid much heed to these tales of Voll the Fell. "I can protect this island," he had thought, knowing his untried power, and had returned to his oaks and alders, the sound of wind in their leaves, the rhythm of growth in their round trunks and limbs and twigs, the taste of sunlight on leaves or dark groundwater around roots.—Where were they now, the trees, his old companions? Had Voll destroyed the forest?

Awake at last and up on his feet, Festin made two broad motions with rigid hands, shouting aloud a Name that would burst all locks and break open any man-made door. But these walls impregnated with night and the name of their builder did not heed, did not hear. The name re-echoed back, clapping in Festin's ears so that he fell on his knees, hiding his head in his arms till the echoes died away in the vaults above him. Then, still shaken by the backfire, he sat brooding.

They were right; Voll was strong. Here on his own ground, within this spell-built dungeon, his magic would withstand any direct attack; and Festin's strength was halved by the loss of his staff. But not even his captor could take from him his powers, relative only to himself, of Projecting and Transforming. So, after rubbing his now doubly aching head, he transformed. Quietly his body melted away into a cloud of fine mist.

Lazy, trailing, the mist rose off the floor, drifting up along the slimy walls until it found, where vault met wall, a hairline crack. Through this, droplet by droplet, it seeped. It was almost all through the crack when a hot wind, hot as a furnace-blast, struck at it, scattering the mist-drops, drying them. Hurriedly the mist sucked itself back into the vault, spiralled to the floor, took on Festin's own form and lay there panting. Transformation is an emotional strain to introverted warlocks of Festin's sort; when to that strain is added the shock of facing unhuman death in one's assumed shape, the experience becomes horrible. Festin lay for a while merely breathing. He was also angry with himself. It had been a pretty simpleminded notion to escape as a mist, after all. Every fool knew that trick. Volt had probably just left a hot wind waiting. Festin gathered himself into a small black bat, flew up to the ceiling, retransformed into a thin stream of plain air, and seeped through the crack.

This time he got clear out and was blowing softly down the hall in which he found himself towards a window, when a sharp sense of peril made him pull together, snapping himself into the first small, coherent shape that came to mind—a gold ring. It was just as well. The hurricane of arctic air that would have dispersed his air-form in unrecallable chaos merely chilled his ring-form slightly. As the storm passed he lay on the marble pavement, wondering which form might get out the window quickest.

Too late, he began to roll away. An enormous blank-faced troll strode cataclysmically across the floor, stopped, caught the quick-rolling ring and picked it up in a huge limestone-like hand. The troll strode to the trapdoor, lifted it by an iron handle and a muttered charm, and dropped Festin down into the darkness. He fell straight for forty feet and landed on the stone floor—clink.

Resuming his true form he sat up, ruefully rubbing a bruised elbow. Enough of this transformation on an empty stomach. He longed bitterly for his staff, with which he could have summoned up any amount of dinner. Without it, though he could change his own form and exert certain spells and powers, he could not transform or summon to him any material thing—neither lightning nor a lamb chop.

"Patience," Festin told himself, and when he had got his breath he dissolved his body into the infinite delicacy of volatile oils, becoming the aroma of a frying lamb chop. He drifted once more through the crack. The waiting troll sniffed suspiciously, but already Festin had regrouped himself into a falcon, winging straight for the window. The troll lunged after him, missed by yards, and bellowed in a vast stony voice, "The hawk, get the hawk!" Swooping over the enchanted castle towards his forest that lay dark to westward, sunlight and sea-glare dazzling his eyes, Festin rode the wind like an arrow. But a quicker arrow found him. Crying out, he fell. Sun and sea and towers spun around him and went out.

He woke again on the dank floor of the dungeon, hands and hair and lips wet with his own blood. The arrow had struck his pinion as a falcon, his shoulder as a man. Lying still, he mumbled a spell to close the wound. Presently he was able to sit up, and recollect a longer, deeper spell of healing. But he had lost a good deal of blood, and with it, power. A chill had settled in the marrow of his bones which even the healing-spell could not warm. There was darkness in his eyes, even when he struck a will o' the wisp and lit the reeking air: the same dark mist he had seen, as he flew, overhanging his forest and the little towns of his land.

It was up to him to protect that land.

He could not attempt direct escape again. He was too weak and tired. Trusting his power too much, he had lost his strength. Now whatever shape he took would share his weakness, and be trapped.

Shivering with cold, he crouched there, letting the fireball sputter out with a last whiff of methane—marsh gas. The smell brought to his mind's eye the marshes stretching from the forest wall down to the sea, his beloved marshes where no men came, where in fall the swans flew long and level, where between still pools and reed-islands the quick, silent, seaward streamlets ran. Oh, to be a fish in one of those streams; or better yet to be farther upstream, near the springs, in the forest in the shadow of the trees, in the clear brown backwater under an alder's roots, resting hidden . . .

This was a great magic. Festin had no more performed it than has any man who in exile or danger longs for the earth and waters of his home, seeing and yearning over the doorsill of his house, the table where he has eaten, the branches outside the window of the room where he has slept. Only in dreams do any but the great Mages realize this magic of going home. But Festin, with the cold creeping out from his marrow into nerves and veins, stood up between the black walls, gathered his will together till it shone like a candle in the darkness of his flesh, and began to work the great and silent magic.

The walls were gone. He was in the earth, rocks and veins of granite for bones, groundwater for blood, the roots of things for nerves. Like a blind worm he moved through the earth westward, slowly, darkness before and behind. Then all at once coolness flowed along his back and belly, a buoyant, unresisting, inexhaustible caress. With his sides he tasted the water, felt current-flow; and with lidless eyes he saw before him the deep brown pool between the great buttress-roots of an alder. He darted forward, silvery, into shadow. He had got free. He was home.

The water ran timelessly from its clear spring. He lay on the sand of the pool's bottom letting running water, stronger than any spell of healing, soothe his wound and with its coolness wash away the bleaker cold that had entered him. But as he rested he felt and heard a shaking and trampling in the earth. Who walked now in his forest? Too weary to try to change form, he hid his gleaming trout-body under the arch of the alder root, and waited.

Huge grey fingers groped in the water, roiling the sand. In the dimness above water vague faces, blank eyes loomed and vanished, reappeared. Nets and hands groped, missed, missed again, then caught and lifted him writhing up into the air. He struggled to take back his own shape and could not; his own spell of homecoming bound him. He writhed in the net, gasping in the dry, bright, terrible air, drowning. The agony went on, and he knew nothing beyond it.

After a long time and little by little he became aware that he was in his human form again; some sharp, sour liquid was being forced down his throat. Time lapsed again, and he found himself sprawled face down on the dank floor of the vault. He was back in the power of his enemy. And, though he could breathe again, he was not very far from death.

The chill was all through him now; and the trolls, Voll's servants, must have crushed the fragile trout-body, for when he moved, his ribcage and one forearm stabbed with pain. Broken and without strength, he lay at the bottom of the well of night. There was no power in him to change shape; there was no way out, but one.

Lying there motionless, almost but not quite beyond the reach of pain, Festin thought: Why has he not killed me? Why does he keep me here alive?

Why has he never been seen? With what eyes can he be seen, on what ground does he walk?

He fears me, though I have no strength left.

They say that all the wizards and men of power whom he has defeated live on sealed in tombs like this, live on year after year trying to get free. . . .

But if one chose not to live?

So Festin made his choice. His last thought was, If I am wrong, men will think I was a coward. But he did not linger on this thought. Turning his head a little to the side he closed his eyes, took a last deep breath, and whispered the word of unbinding, which is only spoken once.

This was not transformation. He was not changed. His body, the long legs and arms, the clever hands, the eyes that had liked to look on trees and streams, lay unchanged, only still, perfectly still and full of cold. But the walls were gone. The vaults built by magic were gone, and the rooms and towers; and the forest, and the sea, and the sky of evening. They were all gone, and Festin went slowly down the far slope of the hill of being, under new stars.

In life he had had great power; so here he did not forget. Like a candle flame he moved in the darkness of the wider land. And remembering he called out his enemy's name: "Voll!"

Called, unable to withstand, Voll came towards him, a thick pale shape in the starlight. Festin approached, and the other cowered and screamed as if burnt. Festin followed when he fled, followed him close. A long way they went, over dry lava-flows from the great extinct volcanoes rearing their cones against the unnamed stars, across the spurs of silent hills, through valleys of short black grass, past towns or down their unlit streets between houses through whose windows no face looked. The stars hung in the sky; none set, none rose. There was no change here. No day would come. But they went on, Festin always driving the other before him, till they reached a place where once a river had run, very long ago: a river from the living lands. In the dry streambed, among boulders, a dead body lay: that of an old man, naked, flat eyes staring at the stars that are innocent of death.

"Enter it," Festin said. The Voll-shadow whimpered, but Festin came closer. Voll cowered away, stooped, and entered in the open mouth of his own dead body.

At once the corpse vanished. Unmarked, stainless, the dry boulders gleamed in starlight. Festin stood still a while, then slowly sat down among the great rocks to rest. To rest, not sleep; for he must keep guard here until Voll's body, sent back to its grave, had turned to dust, all evil power gone, scattered by the wind and washed seaward by the rain. He must keep watch over this place where once death had found *a* way back into the other land. Patient now, infinitely patient, Festin waited among the rocks where no river would ever run again, in the heart of the country which has no seacoast. The stars stood still above him; and as he watched them, slowly, very slowly he began to forget the voice of streams and the sound of rain on the leaves of the forests of life.

JOHN R. FULTZ is the author of several short stories which have appeared in the magazines *Black Gate*, *Weird Tales*, *Space & Time*, and in my own *Lightspeed*. His work has also appeared in the anthology *Cthulhu's Reign*, and he is the author of the epic fantasy comic *Primordia*. He currently lives in California's Bay Area, where he teaches high school English Literature. Learn more at johnrfultz.wordpress.com.

Fultz says that this next story was inspired by a lifetime exploring used and new bookstores, searching for the next great book. And truly, what else besides a good book can so thoroughly transport us to new worlds and distant realities? What else can shine the light of knowledge so brightly inside our own hearts?

For Jeremy March, a trip to a used bookstore turns into a journey beyond our own reality and into a vibrant world. The leather-bound volumes he discovers suggest that this magical universe is the true reality, hidden behind a veil of illusion. This true reality is a realm of green sunshine, beautiful women, and mysteries beyond the ken of the modern world. But the truth he learns about himself just might be more wild than the universe he is reading to life.

This short story may be fiction, but it's drawn from Fultz's real-life wisdom. As he says, musing over the role of books in his life: "We don't find the books we're truly meant to read, THEY FIND US."

And if that's not magic, what is?

THE THIRTEEN TEXTS OF ARTHYRIA
JOHN R. FULTZ

The first book called to him from a row of shelves smothered in gray dust.

Alone and friendless, he stumbled upon the little bookstore among a row of claustrophobic back-alley shops. It had been a month since his move, and he was still discovering the city's secrets, the obscure treasures it could offer. Quaint restaurants serving local fare; tiny theatres showing brilliant old films; and cluttered shops like this one, filled with antiques and baroque artifacts. *The Bearded Sage* read the sign above the door in Old English script. He smiled at the sign's artwork: a skull and quill lying atop a pile of moldering books.

There is something in here for me, he thought as he turned the brass doorknob. A little bell rang when he stepped across the threshold; it was beginning to rain in the street behind him. Inside were books and more books, stacked on tables, lining rows of shelves, heaped in piles on the floor. The pleasant odor of old paper filled his nostrils.

A whiff of dust made him cough a bit as he entered. An old lady sat behind the counter, Chinese or Filipino. She wore horn-rimmed glasses and slept with her head reclined against the wall. A stick of incense burned across the back of a tiny stone dragon near the cash register, emitting the sweet aroma of jasmine to mix with the perfume of ancient books.

He walked the cluttered aisles, staring at the spines of wrinkled paperbacks, vertical lines of text in his peripheral vision . . . called onward by the book. He knew it was here, somewhere among these thousands of realities bound by ink and paper. His eyes drank the contents of the shelves, his breathing slow and even. This was the way he moved through any bookstore, corporate chains or obscure nooks of basement treasures.

How do you always find so many great books? his wife had asked him, back when they were still married. *You always give me something good to read.*

I don't find them, he had told her. *They find me.*

She didn't believe that, as she discounted so many things he told her, but it was true.

His hand reached toward a shelf of heavy volumes near the back of the store.

They were all leather-bound editions, a disorganized blend of fiction and non-fiction, encyclopedia and anatomical treatises, first editions and bound runs of forgotten periodicals, books in many languages—some of which he could not recognize. Running along the shelf's edge, his fingers stopped at a black spine engraved with cracked golden letters. He grabbed it gently and pulled it from its tight niche, accounting for its heaviness. With both hands he brought it down to eye level. Blowing the dust off the cover allowed him to read the title:

The One True World
Volume I: Transcending the Illusions of Modernity and Reason

There was no author listed, and no cover illustration . . . only faded black leather and its gold leaf inscription. On the spine was a Roman numeral "I" but he saw no accompanying volumes, just the singular tome.

It was the reason he was drawn to this place.

He opened it to the first page. His "acid test" for books: If he read the first few paragraphs and the author impressed him with style, content, imagery, or any combination of these, he would buy it. There was no use struggling through a dull text waiting for it to improve . . . if an author failed to show some excellence on the very first page, he would likely never show it at all.

After reading the first three sentences, he closed the book, marched to the counter, and woke the old lady by tapping on a little bell.

"I'll take this one," he said. His hands trembled as he drew thirty-four dollars out of his wallet and paid her. His gut churned the way it had when he'd first met Joanne . . . the thrill of discovery, the sense of standing on the edge of something wonderful and strange. *Love* . . . or something close to it.

"Great shop. How long have you been in business?" he asked the lady.

"Been here . . . *for-evah!*" said the old lady. She smiled at him with crooked teeth.

He laughed. "I'm Jeremy March," he told her, though he had no idea why.

She nodded, as if confirming his statement, and waved goodbye. "Please come again, Mr. March."

The tiny bell rang again as he left the shop. He tucked the book under his coat and walked into the pouring rain. Somehow, he walked directly back to his parking spot without even thinking about it. By the time he reached his apartment and laid the book on his bedside table, thunder and lightning had conquered the night.

Perfect night to read a good book.

Alone in his bedroom, his feet tucked beneath the warm covers, he began to read about the One True World.

഍

The first thing you must understand is that the One True World is not a figment of your imagination, and it does not lie in some faraway dimension. To help you understand the relationship between the True World and the False, you must envision the True World lying beneath the False, as a man can lay hidden beneath a blanket, or a woman's true face can be hidden by an exquisite mask.

The Illusion that hides the True World from the eyes of living men is called the Modern World. It is a dense weave of illusory strands called facts, together composing the Grand Veil of Reason.

The True Philosopher, through dedication and study, comes to realize that Reason is a lie because it is Passion that fuels the universe; that Modernity is a falsehood because the Ancient World has never gone away. It only transforms and evolves, and is never any less Ancient. By meditating on the nature of the One True World, one may cause it to manifest, as Truth always overcomes Illusion, even if buried for eons.

In order to master these principles, to tear aside the dense fabric of Illusion and completely understand the One True World, you must not only read this text in its entirety, but also its succeeding volumes.

Of which there are twelve.

He woke the next day to emerald sunlight shining through the bedroom window. Blinking, he recalled a dream where the sun was not green, but orange, or an intense yellow-white. Or *was* it a dream? The sun was green—of course—it always had been. He shook the dream from his mind and headed for the bathroom. He'd stayed up most of the night reading the book, finishing it just before dawn. He'd never read a book that before.

Visions of the One True World danced through the steam in his bathroom mirror as he shaved . . . forest kingdoms and cloud cities . . . mountains full of roaming giants . . . winged ships soaring like eagles . . . knights in silver mail stalking the battlements of jade castles . . . griffins and manticores and herds of pegasi bearing maidens across an alien sea. He shook himself free of this trance, stumbled to the kitchen, and grabbed a diet soda.

He dressed in a T-shirt and jeans and walked outside, staring up at the ball of emerald flame. The day was warm, but not too hot. He pulled car keys from his pocket. There was no time for breakfast. The second book was calling out to him. There was a used book shop in a city some ninety miles north.

There he would find what he needed.

His next glimpse of the One True World.

ॐ

Books & Candles was a corner shop in the city's most Bohemian district. The proprietors were an old hippie couple in their mid sixties. The husband gave a peace sign greeting from behind a pair of John Lennon glasses. Jeremy nodded and walked toward the rows of bookshelves massed together on the left side of the store. On the other side stood a massive collection of handmade candles in all shapes and sizes, almost a shrine, a temple of tiny, dancing flames.

His eyes scanned the shelves, moving up and down, searching. Like walking toward a room where music was playing, and as he came closer to the doorway the melody grew louder.

He moved aside a cardboard box of mildewed paperbacks to reveal a low shelf, and he saw the book. It was identical to the first volume: Bound in black leather with gold leaf etching on spine and cover. He pulled it from the shelf with a symphony blaring between his ears, and stood with its comfortable weight in his hands.

The One True World

Volume II: The Kingdoms of Arthyria, and the Greater Cities

Despite their benign appearance, the hippie couple could tell he wanted the book badly. He had to pay over two-hundred dollars; luckily they accepted his credit card. Forgetting where his car was parked, he walked along the street to a fleabag hotel used mainly by the homeless. He couldn't wait; he had to read the book *now*. The day was warm and most of the usual boarders were out roaming the streets. He paid for a cot and lay himself down to read.

Hours later, when the sun set, the city's disaffected came wandering in to sip at their brown-bagged bottles and play gin rummy on battered folding tables. He never even noticed. His attention was claimed by the book and—just like the first volume—he could not stop reading until he finished every page.

He devoured the words like a famished vagrant at a royal feast.

The rightful name of the One True World is Arthyria. Twenty-one kingdoms there are in total, nine being the Greater Realms and twelve called the Lesser. Three mighty oceans gird the One True World, each taking its color from the emerald flames of the sun, and each with its own mysteries, island cultures, and hidden depths.

Among the nine Greater Realms thirty-three Great Cities thrive, each dating back to the Age of Walking Gods. Some of them have been destroyed many times over, yet always were rebuilt by faithful progeny.

The mightiest and most ancient of the Great Cities are seven in number. These are: Vandrylla (City of the Sword), Zorung (City of Stargazers), Aurealis (City of Wine and Song), Oorg (City of the Questing Mind), Ashingol (City of the Godborn), Zellim Kah (City of Sorcerers), and Yongaya (City of the Squirming Toad).

Among all the Great Cities, there is only one *where no living man may tread. Even to speak the name of that Dreaded Place is punishable by death in all kingdoms Greater and Lesser.*

Therefore, the name of the Shunned City will not be set down on these pages.

In his dreams, he was still married. He dreamed of Joanne the way she used to be: smiling, full of energy, her hair long and black as jet. The picnic at Albatross Lake was the usual setting for these kinds of dreams. A weird yellow sun blazed in an azure sky, and the wind danced in her hair. They drank a bottle of wine and watched the ducks play across the water before storm clouds rolled in to hide the sun. They lay under a big tree and made love while the rain poured down and leaves sighed over their heads.

I've never been this happy, he told her that day. He was only twenty-five, she was a year younger, and they were living proof that opposites attract. He never knew why someone like her had fallen for an eternal dreamer. He was more concerned with writing the perfect song than making a living. She worked at a bank for the entire three years they were married; he worked at a used record store and taught guitar lessons. The first year was bliss, the second a struggle, and the third a constant battle.

You're such a dreamer, she used to say. As if there was something *wrong* with that. A few months into the marriage he realized that as long as she made more money than him, he would be a failure in her eyes. That started his suit-and-tie phase, when he hung up his guitar for a mind-numbing corporate job. He did it all for her. She cut her hair short and seemed happy again for a while . . . but he became more and more miserable. Sterilized rows of cubicles comprised his prison . . . and prison was a place without hope.

You're such a dreamer. She told him this again in the dream, unaware of the irony, and her wedding dress turned to ashes when he kissed her.

She stood on a strand of cold gray beach, and he watched her recede as some kind of watercraft carried him away. Eventually she was just a little doll-sized thing, surrounded by other dolls on the beach. He turned to look at the boat, but it was empty. He stood alone on the deck, and a terrible wind caught the sail and drove him farther from shore.

Looking back, he called her name, but he'd drifted too far out on the lonesome tide. He dove into the icy water, determined to get back to shore, to get back to *her*, to get their love back. It was his only hope. There was nobody but her. There never had been, never would be.

But when the cold waters closed over his head, he remembered that he couldn't swim. He sank like a stone, salty brine rushing into his lungs.

He woke up gasping for breath among tall stalks of lavender grass. The sun burned high in the lime sky. There was no sign of the cheap boarding house, or the homeless men whose refuge he shared. He lay in a field, alone. He stood and faced the soaring black walls of Aurealis.

Ramparts of basalt encircled the city. They curved several miles to the west, toward the bay where a thousand ships sat at anchor. This was the great port-city, famed far and wide for its excellent wines and superb singers. He walked toward the shore where the proud galleons lingered. He dreaded the open water, but he knew the next book lay beyond the emerald sea. It called to him, as surely as Spring calls forth a sleeping blossom.

By meditating on the nature of the One True World, one may cause it to manifest . . .

Following a road to the southern gate, he made his way through a crowd of robed pilgrims, armored watchmen, cart-pulling farmers, and simple peasants. Clusters of jade domes and towers gleamed in the distance, surrounded by a vast network of wooden buildings where the common folk worked and lived. The sounds of Aurealis were music and commerce: Bards and poets performed on street corners. The smells of the city were horse, sweat, woodsmoke, and a plethora of spices.

Palanquin chairs borne by servants carried the wealthy through the streets. The rich of Aurealis dressed themselves for spectacle. Their robes were satin and silk, studded with patterned jewels to signify the emblems of their houses. Their heads were towering ovals of pastel hair sculpted with strands of pearls and golden wire. Rings sparkled on the fingers of male and female; both sexes painted their faces in shades of amber, ochre, and crimson. Squads of guards in silver ringmail flanked the palanquins, curved broadswords across their backs. The crests of their iron helms were serpents, falcons, or tigers.

As he moved aside to let a nobleman's entourage pass, Jeremy noticed his own clothing. It was like none worn by the folk of Aurealis. A black woolen tunic covered his chest and arms, tied with a thin belt of silver links. His breeches were some dark purple fabric, supple yet thick as leather, and his tall boots were the same material. A crimson cloak was secured at his neck by a ram's head amulet forged of silver, or white gold. His clothes smelled of horseflesh and dirt. Instinctively he reached for his wallet and found instead a woolen purse hanging from his belt. He poured the clanking contents into his hand: Eight silver coins with the ram's head on one side and a shining tower on the other.

Somehow he knew these coins were *drins*, also called rams, and they were minted in some distant city. He could not recall its name.

He smelled saltwater above the swirling odors of Aurealis. It was a long walk to the quays where the galleons were taking on cargo. Their sails were all the colors of the rainbow, but he recognized none of the emblems flying there. He looked past the crowded bay and the swarm of trading vessels, toward the distant horizon. The sun hung low in the sky now, and the ocean gleamed like a vast green mirror.

Tarros.

The name surfaced in his mind as if rising from the green sea. It was the name of the island kingdom where he would find the next book.

After much inquiry, he discovered a blue-sailed galleon bearing a white sea shell, the standard of the Island Queen. Brown-skinned sailors loaded bales of fabric and casks of Aurealan wine, and it was easy to find the captain and inquire about passage.

"Have you money, Philosopher?" asked the sweaty captain. He was round of body and face, with thick lips and dark curly hair. A necklace of oyster shells hung round his neck.

"I have eight silver rams," said Jeremy.

The Tarrosian smiled, teeth gleaming like pearls. "Aye, that'll serve."

He dumped the coins into the captain's palm and stared out at the waves.

"We sail by moonlight, when the sea is calm and cool," said the captain.

Stars blinked to life in the fading sky. The moon rose over the horizon, a jade disc reflected in the dark waves.

He followed the captain—who introduced himself as Zomrah the Seasoned—up the gangplank. Suddenly he remembered the second volume, and the flophouse where he'd fallen asleep after reading it. He had no idea where the book was . . . did he leave it in the field? Was it somewhere in the city? Or had it disappeared completely? He wanted to run back across the city, back into the open field and see if it lay there among the violet grass.

No, he told himself. *I've read it.*

His path lay forward, across the green waves.

The closer to the island kingdom he came, the more he remembered of himself. By the time the wooded shores of Tarros came in sight, he knew why the captain had called him "philosopher," and why he wore the silver ram's head on his breast. He recalled his boyhood in the white towers of Oorg, City of the Questing Mind, the endless libraries that were the city's temples, and a thousand days spent in contemplation. Much of it still lay under a fog of non-memory, obscured by lingering visions of high school, college, and other lies. Yet after five days on the open ocean, he was certain that he was a trained philosopher from the white city, and that he always had been. On the sixth day out, he remembered his true name.

I am Jeremach of Oorg.

"I am Jeremach of Oorg!" he shouted across the waves. The Tarrosian sailors largely ignored his outburst, but their narrow eyes glanced his way when they thought he wasn't looking. Most likely they expected eccentric behavior from a man who spent his life pondering the meaning of existence.

But that's not all of it, he knew. *There's more . . . much more. Oorg feels like a memory of what I used to be . . . not what I am.* He knew that he was more than a simple child of Oorg, versed in the eight-hundred avenues of thought, savant of the fifty-nine philosophies. Perhaps the answer lay in the next volume of *The One True World*.

The rest of his memory lay somewhere within those pages.

After fourteen days of calm seas and healthy winds, the galley dropped anchor in Myroa, the port city of Tarros. It was a pale imitation of Aurealis, a humble collection of mud-walled dwellings, domed temples, and atop its tallest hill the modest palace of the Tarrosian Queen. A single tower rose between four spiked domes, the entire affair built of rose-colored marble veined with purple. The city was full of colorful birds, and the people were simple laborers for the most part, dressed in white shifts and pantaloons. Most of the men and women went bare-chested, though all wore the sea-shell necklaces that were the sign of their country and queen. The breath of the salty wind was sweetened by the tang of ripe fruit trees.

Zomrah the Seasoned was a trader captain in service to the queen's viceroy, so he had access to the palace. The viceroy was an old, leathery man with silvery robes and a ridiculous shell-shaped hat on his gray head. Or perhaps it was an actual shell. He examined Zomrah's bill of lading in a plush anteroom and gave the captain a bag of gold. When Zomrah introduced him the viceroy looked him over as if examining a new piece of freight. Eventually the old man nodded and motioned for the philosopher to follow him.

Jeremach followed him through winding corridors. Some were open-air walkways hemmed with rows of trellises thick with red and white orchids. Tapestries along the palace walls showed scenes of underwater peril, with trident-bearing heroes battling krakens, sharks, and leviathans. Somewhere, a high voice sang a lovely song that brought the ocean depths to mind.

The Queen of Tarros received Jeremach on the high balcony of her rosy tower. A tall chair had been placed in the sunlight where she could observe the island spreading to the west and north, and leagues of open sea to the east and south. Three brawny Tarrosians stood at attention, her personal guard armed with trident and sword, naked but for white loincloths and sea-shell amulets.

The queen rose from her chair, and he gasped. Her loveliness was stunning. The narrow chin and sapphire eyes were familiar, and her hair was dyed to the hue of fresh seaweed. It fell below her slim waist, shells of a dozen colors woven among its braids. Her dress was a diaphanous gown, almost colorless, and her brown body was perfect as a jewel.

She greeted him with a warm hug. "You look well, Philosopher. Much *younger* than when last you visited." She smiled.

Jeremach bowed, remembering the proper etiquette for such a situation. *I've been here before. She knows me.*

"Great Queen, your realm is the soul of beauty, and you are its heart," he said.

"Ever the flatterer," she said. She raised a tiny hand to his cheek and cupped it, staring at him as if amazed by his features.

"You've come for your books," she said, taking him by the hand. Her touch was delicate, yet simmering. "I've kept them safe for you."

Yes. There is more than one volume here.

Jeremach nodded. "Your Majesty is wise . . . "

"Please," she said, leading him into the tower. "Call me by my name, as you used to do. You have not forgotten it?"

He searched the murky depths of his memory.

"*Celestia*," he said. "Sweet Celestia."

She led him up spiral stairs into a library. Twenty arched windows looked out upon the sea, and hundreds of books lined a shelved wall. He walked without direction to a specific shelf, and his hands reached (as they had done twice before) directly for the third book. Two more volumes sat beside it. He lay all three of them on a marble table and examined their golden inscriptions.

Volume III: The People and Their Faiths
Volume IV: The Lineages of the Great Kings and the Bloodlines of the Great Houses
Volume V: The Societies of the Pseudomen and the Cloud Kingdoms

"You see?" the queen said. "They are safe and whole. I have kept your faith."

He nodded, aching to open the third volume and read. But first he had to know. "Thank you," he said. "But how did you come to possess these texts?"

She looked at him quizzically, amused by the question. "You *gave* them to me when I was only a little girl. I always knew you would return for them, as you promised. I wish you'd have come while Father was still alive. He was very fond of you. We lost him four years ago."

He recalled a broad-chested man with a thick green beard and a crown of golden shells. In his mind, the King of Tarros laughed, and a little girl sat on his knee.

King Celestior. My friend. She is his daughter, once my student, and now the Queen of Tarros. How many years has it been?

He kissed the queen's cheek, and she left him to his books. Hours later, her servants brought him seafood stew, Aurealan wine in pearly cups, and a box of fresh candles. He read throughout the long night, while the warm salt air swept in from the sea, and the jade moon crept from window to window.

For days he sat in the chamber and read. Finally, they found him collapsed over the books, snoring, a white beard growing from his chin. They carried him to a proper bed, and he slept, dreaming of a distant world that was a lie, and yet also true in so many ways.

"You're walking out on me?" she said, eyes brimming with tears.

"You walked out on *me*," he told her.

She said nothing.

"Joanne . . . sweetheart . . . you know I'll always love you. But this isn't working. We . . . don't belong together."

"How can you be so *sure*?" she cried.

"Because if we did . . . you would have never climbed into bed with Alan."

Her sadness turned to anger, as it often did. "I told you! I never meant for it to happen."

"Yeah, you told me," he said. "But you did it. You *did* it, right? Three times . . . that I know of."

She grabbed him, wrapped her arms around his neck. Squeezed. "You can't just leave me behind," she said.

Now he was crying too. "I'm done with this," he said.

"No," she whimpered. "We can still fix it."

"How?"

She stood back from him, brushing a dark strand of hair from her forehead. Her eyes were dark, too. Black pearls.

"We'll get counseling," she pleaded. "We'll figure out what went wrong and we'll make sure it never happens again."

He turned away, lay his forehead against the mantle.

"You cheated too," she said, almost a whisper.

After you did. He didn't say it out loud. Maybe she was right. Maybe there still was hope.

He had never loved anyone but her.

Never.

They stood with their arms wrapped around each other for a little while.

"I'll always love you," he said. "No matter what happens."

The people of Arthyria differ greatly in custom, dress, and culture, and wars are not unknown. Each kingdom has its share of inhuman denizens, humanoid races who live in proximity or complete integration with the human populace. These are the Pseudomen, and they have played a great role in many a war as mercenary troops adding to the ranks of whatever city-state they call home. There is generally little prejudice against the Pseudomen, although the Yellow Priests of Naravhen call them "impure" and have banned them from the Yellow Temples.

There are five Great Religions in practice across the triple continents of Arthyria, faiths that have survived the upheaval of ages and come down to us through the fractured corridors of time intact. The cults and sects of lesser deities are without number, but all of the Five Faiths worship some variation of the One Thousand Gods.

Some faiths, such as the Order of the Loyal Heart, are inclusive, claiming that all gods be revered. Others are singular belief systems, focused on only one god drawn from the ranks of the One Thousand. Through these commonalities of faith we see the development of the Tongue, a lingua franca that unites most of Arthyria with its thirty-seven dialects.

Here mention must be made of the Cloud Kingdoms, whose gods are unknown, whose language is incomprehensible to Arthyrians, and whose true nature and purpose has remained a mystery throughout the ages.

When he woke he was closer to being himself, and the people of Tarros were restored. He walked through the palace in search of Celestia, marveling at the beauty of those he had forgotten. Their glistening skins were shades of turquoise, their long fingers and toes webbed, tipped with mother-of-pearl talons. They wore very little clothing, only the same white loincloths he'd seen yesterday. Webbed, spiny crests ran up their backs, across the tops of narrow skulls, terminating on their tall foreheads. Their eyes were black orbs, their lips far thicker than any human's, and only the females grew any hair: long emerald tresses woven with pearls and shells.

They were amphibious Pseudomen, a marine race that had evolved to live on land. The island kingdom was a small portion of their vast empire, most of which lay deep beneath the waves. Some claimed they ruled the entire ocean, but Jeremach knew better. There were other, less civilized societies below the sea.

Now that he had read three more volumes, Arthyria was one step closer to being whole. So was he. Vastly important things lay just on the edge of his awareness. He must know them . . . everything depended on it.

He found Celestia in her gardens, surrounded by a coterie of amphibious subjects. They lounged around a great pool of seawater fed by undersea caverns.

"Jeremach . . . you look more like yourself today," said the queen, beckoning him with a webbed hand.

"I should say the same to you, Majesty," he replied. He saw himself now in the surface of the pool. His garb had changed little, but he looked older. At least forty, he guessed, but his hair and thick beard were as white as a codger's. *How old am I really?* he wondered. *Will I continue aging as the world keeps reverting to its true state?*

"I trust you found what you were looking for in those dreadful books?" she asked. She offered him a padded bench beside her own high seat. Tiny Tarrosian children splashed in the pool, playing subaquatic games and surfacing in bubbles of laughter.

"I did," he said. "I found the truth. Or *more* of it, at least."

"It is good to see you again, Old Tutor," she said, smiling with her marine lips. Her eyes gleamed at him, onyx orbs brimming with affection.

"You were always my favorite pupil," he told her honestly.

"How long will you stay with us?"

"Not long, I fear. I hear a call that cannot be denied. Tell me, did your father sign a treaty with the Kingdom of Aelda when you were still a child?"

"Yes . . . " Celestia raised her twin orbs to the sky. "The Treaty of Sea and Sky, signed in 7412, Year of the Ray. It was you who taught me that date."

"And your father received a gift from the Sovereign of Aelda . . . do you still have it?"

Clouds of jade cotton moved across the heavens. The next book called to him from somewhere high above the world.

She led him below the palace into a maze of caverns created by seawater in some elder age, and three guards accompanied them bearing torches. When they found the great door of obsidian that sealed the treasure vault, she opened it with a coral key. Inside lay a massive pile of gold and silver coins, centuries of tribute from the realms of Arthyria, fantastic suits of armor carved from coral and bone, spears and shields of gold and iron, jewels in all the colors of the prism, and objects of painful beauty to which he could not even put a name.

Celestia walked about the gleaming hoard until she found a horn of brass, gold, and jet. It might have been the horn of some mighty antelope, the way it twisted and curved. Yet Jeremach knew that it was forged somewhere no land animal could reach. She presented it to him with an air of satisfaction. She was still the student eager to please her tutor. He kissed her cheek and tucked the horn into his belt.

"Something else," she said. Wrapping her hand about a golden hilt, she drew forth from the piled riches a long, straight sword. The blade gleamed like silver, and the hilt was set with a blue jewel carved to the likeness of a shell. Jeremach remembered this blade hanging on the broad belt of King Celestios. Even a peace-loving king had to fight a few wars in his time.

"Take this," said the queen.

Jeremach shook his head. "No, Majesty," he protested. "This was . . . "

"My father's sword," she said. "But he is dead, and he would have wanted you to have it." She drew close to him, and whispered in his ear. Her voice was the sound of the ocean in the depths of a sea shell. "I know something of what you are trying to do. As do others. You may *need* this."

Jeremach sighed and bowed. To reject her gift would be to insult her. He took the blade and kissed the hilt. She smiled at him, the tiny gills on her neck pulsing. She found a jeweled scabbard to sheathe the weapon, and he buckled it about his waist alongside the silver belt of the philosopher.

A philosopher who carries a sword, he thought. *How absurd.*

Yet, was he a philosopher still? What further changes lay in store for him when the last of the One True World was revealed?

He feasted with the queen and her court that night, getting rather drunk on Aurealan wine and stuffed full of clams, crabs, and oysters. By the time he stumbled up to his bed in the high tower, he was nearly senseless. He took off his belts, propped the sword in its scabbard against the bed post, and passed out.

It wasn't pain that woke him, but rather the terrible lack of air. He saw a green-blue haze, and wondered if Tarros had sank beneath the waves and he was drowning. The pain at his throat was his second sensation, dulled as it was by the great quantities of wine in his belly.

A shadow crouched above him, the toes of leather boots on either side of his face, and a thin strand of wire was cutting through the flesh under his chin, pulling terribly on his beard. It was the beard's thickness that prevented a quick death, giving him a few seconds to wake and realize he was being strangled.

He gasped for air, his fingers clawing at nothing, his legs wracked by spasms. Any second now the wire would cut through his throat—probably before he suffocated. The strangler tightened its iron grip on the wire, and Jeremach's body flailed. He could not even scream for help. They would find him here, dead in the queen's guest chamber, with no idea who killed him.

What will happen when I'm gone? he wondered.

Then, he knew of a certainty, some bit of memory racing back into his head; his face turned purple and his lungs seized up. If he did not finish reading the thirteen volumes, the One True World would fade back into the world of Modernity and Illusion.

If he died, Arthyria died with him.

His grasping fingers found the hilt of Celestior's sword. He wrapped them about the grip and yanked the sheathed blade up to crack against the strangler's skull. The stranglehold lessened, but he could not remove the sword from its scabbard, so it was no killing blow. Twice more he bludgeoned the strangler with the sword, wielding it like a metal club wrapped in leather.

On the third blow, the strangler toppled off the bed, and Jeremach sucked in air like a dying fish. He scrambled onto the floor and tried to unsheathe the sword. A dark figure rose across the mattress, hooded and cloaked in shades of midnight. It stepped toward him, face hidden in the shadows of the hood. An iron dagger appeared in its gloved fist, the blade corroded by rust. A single cut from that decayed iron would bring a poisonous death.

He scrambled for air and found his back against the wall. A frog-like croaking came from his throat. He fumbled at the scabbard. Why wouldn't the damn sword come clear?

The assassin placed the rusted blade against his throat.

"*You cheated too*," said a cold voice from inside the hood.

No, that's not . . . that's not what I heard.

Three golden prongs burst from the assassin's stomach. A Tarrosian guard stood behind the attacker, his trident impaling it.

Jeremach finally tore the sword free of the scabbard. He rolled onto his side as the skewered assassin drove its dagger into the stone wall, ignoring the trident jutting from its back.

The guard pulled his trident free for another jab, but Jeremach was on his feet now, both hands wrapped about the sword's hilt, swinging it in a silver arc. The hooded head flew from the assassin's body and rolled across the floor to lie at the foot of the bed.

The headless body stood for a moment, holding the rusted dagger. Then it collapsed with a sound like snapping wood, and became only a mound of bones and mildewed black cloth.

He stared at the face on the severed head. A woman with long hair dark as her robes. He blinked, coughed, and he would have screamed in terror, but could not.

Joanne . . .

He said her name through purple lips, his voice a rasping moan.

She stared up at him: weeping, bleeding, bodiless.

"You can't do this," she said, and black blood trickled from her lips. "You can't throw it all away. *You're destroying our world*. You're destroying the Past. How do you know *this* is the True World and not the False?"

He had no words; he fell to his knees and stared at her face. His heart ached more terribly than his throat.

"You said . . . you'd always love me," she wept. "But you're throwing it all away. How can you be *sure?*"

Her tongue, and then the rest of her face, withered into dust.

He stared into the blank sockets of a grinning skull.

Before the sun kissed the ocean, he left the palace and went alone to the beach. As the first green light seeped into the sky, he blew on the horn of brass, gold, and jet. One long, loud note that rang across the waves and into the clouds of morning.

The island kingdom came to life behind him, and he stared across the waves. Soon he saw a speck of gold gleaming between the clouds. It grew larger, sinking toward the ocean, until it came clearly into view: A slim sky galleon bearing cloud-white sails. It floated toward the island like a great, soaring bird. Some distance from the shore it touched keel to water soundlessly. By the time it reached the sandy embankment, it looked no stranger than any other sea-going vessel. The figurehead on its pointed bow was a beautiful winged woman.

Someone let down a rope ladder, and Jeremach climbed it, dropping himself onto the deck. The sky galleon's crew were stone men, living statues of pale marble. They said nothing, but nodded politely when he showed them the horn of brass, gold, and jet. Then the stone captain took it from him, crushed it in his massive fist, and dropped its remains into the sea.

The sails caught a gust of wind, and the ship rose from the sea toward the clouds. The island of Tarros was a tiny expanse of forest surrounded by endless green waves; now it was a mote, now completely gone. Continents of cloud passed by on either side of the galleon. Higher and higher it rose, until all of Arthyria was lost below a layer of cumulus. The green sun blazed brightly in the upper realm.

Now the city of Aelda came into view: a sparkling crystal metropolis perched upon an island of white cloud. The spiral towers and needle-like pinnacles were like nothing in the world below. But a sense of vague familiarity flavored Jeremach's awe.

The rest of the books are here, he remembered.

All but one.

The Winged Folk had no voices, and their bodies were translucent. They moved with all the grace of swans, gliding through the sky on feathery appendages grown from their lean backs. Their beauty was incredible, so much that none could be classified as singly male or female. Their bodies were the sexless perfection of inhumanity. The highest order of all the Pseudomen, the people of the Cloud Kingdoms were also the most mysterious.

A flock of them glided by as the sky galleon docked alongside a crystal tower. They stared at the visitor with eyes of liquid gold. They neither waved nor questioned his presence. He had sounded the horn. Otherwise, he would not be here.

The galleon's crew of marble men followed him into a corridor of diamond and took their places in carved niches along the walls. Now they were only statues again. Someday, someone in Arthyria would blow another horn of brass, gold, and jet; and the statues would live again to man the golden ship. Jeremach left the stone men to their silent niches.

The scent of the Cloud Realms made his head swim as he walked toward the books. Up here lingered the aromas of unborn rain, naked sunlight, and the fragrance of unsoiled clouds. The diamond walls rang with musical tones, sweet enough to mesmerize the untutored into immobility. But Jeremach heard only the call of his books.

He found them right where he had left them so long ago, in a domed chamber supported by seven pillars of glassy quartz. The tomes lay upon a round table of crystalline substance, and they looked as incongruous here as the tall philosopher's chair he had placed before the table.

He sat in the chair, sighed, and ran his fingers over the faces of the seven books.

Volume VI: The Knights of Arthyria and the Secret Orders of Starlight
Volume VII: Wizards of the First Age
Volume VIII: Wizards of the Second Age and The Forces Unleashed
Volume IX: Wizards of the Third and Fourth Ages, and the Death of Othaa
Volume X: The Doom of the Forty-Two Gods
Volume XI: The Great Beasts of Arthyria and the Things From Beyond
Volume XII: The Fifth Cataclysm and the Preservation of Ancient Knowledge

Don't think about Joanne, he told himself.

But her words haunted him.

You're throwing it all away.

How do you know this is the True World?

He opened the sixth volume, breathing in the smell of ancient papyrus and ink.

It's my choice.

I choose Arthyria.

He read.

In the year 7478, the Wizard Jeremach returned to the Shunned City.

Legions of the living dead rose from its ruined halls to assail him, but he dismissed them with a wave of his hand, turning them all to pale dust. He walked among the crumbled stones of the First Empire, frigid winds tearing at his long white beard.

As he neared the palace of the Dead King, a horde of black-winged devils descended screeching from the broken towers. These he smote with a flashing silver blade bearing the sign of Tarros. As the last of the fiends died at his feet, the wizard sheathed his weapon. He walked on, toward the Shattered Palace.

Before the Dead King's gates a band of ghosts questioned Jeremach, but he gave them riddles that would haunt them well into the afterworld. He spoke a single word, and the gates of blackened iron collapsed inward. He entered the utter darkness of the castle and walked until he found the Dead King sitting on a pile of gilded skulls, the heads of all those he had conquered in battle over the course of seven thousand years.

A red flame glowed in a pit before the Dead King's mailed feet, and he looked upon Jeremach. Similar flames glowed in the hollow pits of his eyes. His flesh had rotted away millennia ago, but his bones refused to die, or to give up his hard-won empire. In the last five thousand years, none but Jeremach had entered these gates and lived to speak of it.

The Dead King took up his great black sword, but Jeremach laughed at him.

"You know that I've not come to battle you," said the wizard.

The Dead King sighed, grave dust spilling from between his teeth. With fleshless fingers he lifted an ancient book from the floor of his hall. He offered it to Jeremach.

The wizard wiped away a coating of dust and saw the book's title.

The One True World
Volume XIII: The Curse of the Dead King and the Undying Empire

Jeremach did not need to read it, for he knew its contents with a touch.

The Dead King spoke in a voice of grinding bones. "You have won," he said.

"Yes," said Jeremach. "Though you cheated, sending an assassin after me. How desperate."

"I might claim you cheated with these books of yours," said the skull-king, "But in war all sins are forgiven."

"Still, I did win," said the wizard. "I proved that Truth will always overcome Illusion. That a False reality—no matter how tempting—cannot stand against that which is Real. I escaped your trap."

The Dead King nodded, and a crown of rusted iron tumbled from his skull. "For the first time in history, I have been defeated," he growled.

Was that relief *in his ancient voice?*

"Now . . . will you keep your promise, Stubborn King?" asked Jeremach. "Will you quit the world of the living and let this long curse come to an end? Will you let men reclaim these lands that you have held for millennia?"

The Dead King nodded again, and now his skull tumbled from his shoulders. His bones fell to dust, and a cold wind blew his remains across the hall. The moaning of a million ghosts filled the sky. In the distant cities of Oorg, Aurealis, Vandrylla, and Zorung, the living woke from nightmares and covered their ears.

Jeremach left the ruins of the Shunned City as they crumbled behind him. He carried the black book under his arm. As he walked, the moldering slabs of the city turned to dust, following their king into oblivion, and the frozen earth of that realm began to thaw in the sunlight. After long ages, Spring had finally come.

By the time Jeremach crossed the horizon, there was no trace of the haunted kingdom left anywhere beneath the emerald sky.

MARION ZIMMER BRADLEY was the author of the best-selling classic Arthurian novel *The Mists of Avalon*, the long-running *Darkover* series, and many other novels. Her short fiction has appeared in magazines such as *Amazing Stories, The Magazine of Fantasy & Science Fiction, Fantastic, If,* and in numerous anthologies. She was also editor of the acclaimed and influential *Sword and Sorceress* anthology series and *Marion Zimmer Bradley's Fantasy Magazine.* She was a winner of the Locus Award and the recipient of the World Fantasy Lifetime Achievement Award. She died in 1999.

Our next story originally appeared in the first installment of the *Thieves' World* shared world anthology series. The series, which invited different fantasy authors to write stories set in the rough-and-tumble backwater of Sanctuary, achieved immense popularity but eventually succumbed to mischievous feuding among the various authors, who dreamt up ever more elaborate and sadistic fates for each other's characters, causing the whole project to spin out of control.

Marion Zimmer Bradley later took her sorcerer Lythande (pronounced "lee-thond"), first introduced in this tale, and produced a book-length collection of stories about the character, titled *Lythande.* Lythande is an adept of the Blue Star, and such wizards are bound by some of the most interesting rules of magic ever presented in a fantasy story. Each adept must choose a secret to be the source of his power—the greater the secret, the greater the power. But if that secret is discovered by a fellow adept, the rival can steal all of that wizard's magic. It's a brilliant conceit that fits perfectly with the cloak-and-dagger milieu of Sanctuary, a city roiling with dark prophecies, bitter rivalry, and life-or-death intrigue.

THE SECRET OF THE BLUE STAR
MARION ZIMMER BRADLEY

On a night in Sanctuary, when the streets bore a false glamour in the silver glow of a full moon, so that every ruin seemed an enchanted tower and every dark street and square an island of mystery, the mercenary-magician Lythande sallied forth to seek adventure.

Lythande had but recently returned—if the mysterious comings and goings of a magician can be called by so prosaic a name—from guarding a caravan across the Grey Wastes to Twand. Somewhere in the wastes, a gaggle of desert rats—two-legged rats with poisoned steel teeth—had set upon the caravan, not knowing it was guarded by magic, and had found themselves fighting skeletons that bowled and fought with eyes of flame; and at their center a tall magician with a blue star between blazing eyes, a star that shot lightnings of a cold and paralyzing flame. So the desert rats ran, and never stopped running until they reached Aurvesh, and the tales they told did Lythande no harm except in the ears of the pious.

And so there was gold in the pockets of the long, dark magician's robe, or perhaps concealed in whatever dwelling sheltered Lythande. For at the end, the caravan master had been almost more afraid of Lythande than he was of the bandits, a situation that added to the generosity with which he rewarded the magician. According to custom, Lythande neither smiled nor frowned, but remarked, days later, to Myrtis, the proprietor of the Aphrodisia House in the Street of Red Lanterns, that sorcery, while a useful skill and filled with many aesthetic delights for the contemplation of the philosopher, in itself put no beans on the table.

A curious remark, that, Myrtis pondered, putting away the ounce of gold Lythande had bestowed upon her in consideration of a secret which lay many years behind them both. Curious that Lythande should speak of beans on the table, when no one but herself had ever seen a bite of food or a drop of drink pass the magician's lips since the blue star had adorned that high and narrow brow. Nor had any woman in the quarter even been able to boast that a great magician had paid for her favors, or been able to imagine how such a magician behaved in that situation when all men were alike reduced to flesh and blood.

Perhaps Myrtis could have told if she would; some other girls thought so, when, as sometimes happened, Lythande came to the Aphrodisia House and was closeted long with its owner; even, on rare intervals, for an entire night. It was said, of Lythande, that the Aphrodisia House itself had been the magician's gift to Myrtis, after a famous adventure still whispered in the bazaar, involving an evil wizard, two horse traders, a caravan master, and a few assorted toughs who had prided themselves upon never giving gold for any woman and thought it funny to cheat an honest working woman. None of them had ever showed their faces—what was left of them—in Sanctuary again, and Myrtis boasted that she need never again sweat to earn her living, and never again entertain a man, but would claim her madam's privilege of a solitary bed.

And then, too, the girls thought, a magician of Lythande's stature could have claimed the most beautiful women from Sanctuary to the mountains beyond Ilsig; not courtesans alone, but princesses and noblewomen and priestesses would have been for Lythande's taking. Myrtis had doubtless been beautiful in her youth, and certainly she boasted enough of the princes and wizards and travelers who had paid great sums for her love. She was beautiful still (and of course there were those who said that Lythande did not pay her, but that, on the contrary, Myrtis paid the magician great sums to maintain her aging beauty with strong magic) but her hair had gone grey and she no longer troubled to dye it with henna or goldenwash from Tyrisis-beyond-the-sea.

But if Myrtis were not the woman who knew how Lythande behaved in that most elemental of situations, then there was no woman in Sanctuary who could say. Rumor said also that Lythande called up female demons from the Gray Wastes, to couple in lechery, and certainly Lythande was neither the first nor the last magician of whom that could be said.

But on this night Lythande sought neither food nor drink nor the delights of amorous entertainment; although Lythande was a great frequenter of taverns, no man had ever yet seen drop of ale or mead or fire-drink pass the barrier of the magician's lips. Lythande walked along the far edge of the bazaar, skirting the old rim of the Governor's Palace, keeping to the shadows in defiance of footpads and cutpurses. She possessed a love for shadows which made the folk of the city say that Lythande could appear and disappear into thin air.

Tall and thin, Lythande, above the height of a tall man, lean to emaciation, with the blue-star-shaped tattoo of the magician-adept above thin, arching eyebrows; wearing a long, hooded robe which melted into the shadows. Clean-shaven, the face of Lythande, or beardless—none had come close enough, in living memory, to say whether this was the whim of an effeminate or the hairlessness of a freak. The hair beneath the hood was as long and luxuriant as a woman's, but greying, as no woman in this city of harlots would have allowed it to do.

Striding quickly along a shadowed wall, Lythande stepped through an open door, over which the sandal of Thufir, god of pilgrims, had been nailed up for luck; but the footsteps were so soft, and the hooded robe blended so well into the shadows, that eyewitnesses would later swear, truthfully, that they had seen Lythande appear from the air, protected by sorceries, or by a cloak of invisibility.

Around the hearth fire, a group of men were banging their mugs together noisily to the sound of a rowdy drinking song, strummed on a worn and tinny lute—Lythande knew it belonged to the tavernkeeper, and could be borrowed— by a young man, dressed in fragments of foppish finery, torn and slashed by the chances of the road. He was sitting lazily, with one knee crossed over the other; and when the rowdy song died away, the young man drifted into another, a quiet love song from another time and another country. Lythande had known the song, more years ago than bore remembering, and in those days Lythande the magician had borne another name and had known little of sorcery. When the song died, Lythande had stepped from the shadows, visible, and the firelight glinted on the blue star, mocking at the center of the high forehead.

There was a little muttering in the tavern, but they were not unaccustomed to Lythande's invisible comings and goings. The young man raised eyes which were surprisingly blue beneath the black hair elaborately curled above his brow. He was slender and agile, and Lythande marked the rapier at his side, which looked well handled, and the amulet, in the form of a coiled snake, at his throat. The young man said, "Who are you, who has the habit of coming and going into thin air like that?"

"One who compliments your skill at song." Lythande flung a coin to the tapster's bay. "Will you drink?'

"A minstrel never refuses such an invitation. Singing is dry work." But when the drink was brought, he said, "Not drinking with me, then?"

"No man has ever seen Lythande eat or drink," muttered one of the men in the circle round them.

"Why, then, I hold that unfriendly," cried the young minstrel. "A friendly drink between comrades shared is one thing; but I am no servant to sing for pay or to drink except as a friendly gesture!"

Lythande shrugged, and the blue star above the high brow began to glimmer and give forth blue light. The onlookers slowly edged backward, for when a wizard who wore the blue star was angered, bystanders did well to be out of the way. The minstrel set down the lute, so it would be well out of range if he must leap to his feet. Lythande knew, by the excruciating slowness of his movements and great care, that he had already shared a good many drinks with chance-met comrades. But the minstrel's hand did not go to his sword hilt but instead closed like a fist over the amulet in the form of a snake.

"You are like no man I have ever met before," he observed mildly, and Lythande, feeling inside the little ripple, nerve-long, that told a magician he was in the presence of spellcasting, hazarded quickly that the amulet was one of those which would not protect its master unless the wearer first stated a set number of truths—usually three or five—about the owner's attacker or foe. Wary, but amused, Lythande said, "A true word. Nor am I like any man you will ever meet, live you never so long, minstrel."

The minstrel saw, beyond the angry blue glare of the star, a curl of friendly mockery in Lythande's mouth. He said, letting the amulet go, "And I wish you no ill; and you wish me none, and those are true sayings too, wizard, hey? And there's an end of that. But although perhaps you are like to no other, you are not the only wizard I have seen in Sanctuary who bears a blue star about his forehead."

Now the blue star blazed rage, but not for the minstrel. They both knew it. The crowd around them had all mysteriously discovered that they had business elsewhere. The minstrel looked at the empty benches.

"I must go elsewhere to sing for my supper, it seems."

"I meant you no offense when I refused to share a drink," said Lythande. "A magician's vow is not as lightly overset as a lute. Yet I may guest-gift you with dinner and drink in plenty without loss of dignity, and in return ask a service of a friend, may I not?"

"Such is the custom of my country. Cappen Varra thanks you, magician."

"Tapster! Your best dinner for my guest, and all he can drink tonight!"

"For such liberal guesting I'll not haggle about the service," Cappen Varra said, and set to the smoking dishes brought before him. As he ate, Lythande drew from the folds of his robe a small pouch containing a quantity of sweet-smelling herbs, rolled them into a blue-grey leaf, and touched his ring to spark the roll alight. He drew on the smoke, which drifted up sweet and greyish.

"As for the service, it is nothing so great; tell me all you know of this other wizard who wears the blue star. I know of none other of my order south of Azehur, and I would be certain you did not see me, nor my wraith."

Cappen Varra sucked at a marrowbone and wiped his fingers fastidiously on the tray-cloth beneath the meats. He bit into a ginger-fruit before replying.

"Not you, wizard, nor your fetch or doppelgänger; this one had shoulders brawnier by half, and he wore no sword, but two daggers cross-girt astride his hips. His beard was black; and his left hand missing three fingers."

"Iles of the Thousand Eyes! Rabben the Half-handed, here in Sanctuary! Where did you see him, minstrel?"

"I saw him crossing the bazaar; but he bought nothing that I saw. And I saw

him in the Street of Red Lanterns, talking to a woman. What service am I to do
for you, magician?"

"You have done it." Lythande gave silver to the tavernkeeper—so much that
the surly man bade Shalpa's cloak cover him as he went—and laid another coin,
gold this time, beside the borrowed lute.

"Redeem your harp; that one will do your voice no boon." But when the minstrel
raised his head in thanks, the magician had gone unseen into the shadows.

Pocketing the gold, the minstrel asked, "How did he know that? And how did
he go out?"

"Shalpa the swift alone knows," the tapster said. "Flew out by the smoke hole
in the chimney for all I ken! That one needs not the night-dark cloak of Shalpa to
cover him, for he has one of his own. He paid for your drinks, good sir, what will
you have?" And Cappen Varra proceeded to get very drunk, that being the wisest
thing to do when entangled unawares in the private affairs of a wizard.

Outside in the street, Lythande paused to consider. Rabben the Half-handed
was no friend; yet there was no reason his presence in Sanctuary must deal with
Lythande, or personal revenge. If it were business concerned with the Order of
the Blue Star, if Lythande must lend Rabben aid, or if the Half-handed had been
sent to summon all the members of the order, the star they both wore would have
given warning.

Yet it would do no harm to make certain. Walking swiftly, the magician had
reached a line of old stables behind the Governor's Palace. There silence and
secrecy for magic. Lythande stepped into one of the little side alleys, drawing
up the magician's cloak until no light remained, slowly withdrawing farther
and farther into the silence until nothing remained anywhere in the world—
anywhere in the universe but the light of the blue star ever glowing in front.
Lythande remembered how it had been set there, and at what cost—the price an
adept paid for power.

The blue glow gathered, fulminated in many-colored patterns, pulsing and
glowing, until Lythande stood within the light; and there, in the Place That Is
Not, seated upon a throne carved apparently from sapphire, was the Master of
the Star.

"Greetings to you, fellow star, star-born, shyryu." The terms of endearment
could mean fellow, companion, brother, sister, beloved, equal, pilgrim; its literal
meaning was sharer of starlight. "What brings you into the Pilgrim Place this
night from afar?"

"The need for knowledge, star-sharer. Have you sent one to seek me out in
Sanctuary?"

"Not so, shyryu. All is well in the Temple of the Star-sharers; you have not yet been summoned; the hour is not yet come."

For every Adept of the Blue Star knows; it is one of the prices of power. At the world's end, when all the doings of mankind and mortals are done, the last to bill under the assault of Chaos will be the Temple of the Star; and then, in the Place That Is Not, the Master of the Star will summon all of the Pilgrim Adepts from the farthest corners of the world, to fight with all their magic against Chaos; but until that day, they have such freedom as will best strengthen their powers. The Master of the Star repeated, reassuringly, "The hour has not come. You are free to walk as you will in the world."

The blue glow faded, and Lythande stood shivering. So Rabben had not been sent in that final summoning. Yet the end and Chaos might well be at hand for Lythande before the hour appointed, if Rabben the Half-handed had his way.

It was a fair test of strength, ordained by our masters. Rabbet, should bear me no ill will . . .

Rabben's presence in Sanctuary need not have to do with Lythande. He might be here upon his lawful occasions—if anything of Rabben's could be said to be lawful; for it was only upon the last day of all that the Pilgrim Adepts were pledged to fight upon the side of Law against Chaos. And Rabben had not chosen to do so before then.

Caution would be needed, and yet Lythande knew that Rabben was near. . . .

South and east of the Governor's Palace, there is a little triangular park, across from the Avenue of Temples. By day the graveled walks and turns of shrubbery are given over to predicants and priests who find not enough worship or offerings for their liking; by night the place is the haunt of women who worship no goddess except She of the filled purse and the empty womb. And for both reasons the place is called, in irony, the Promise of Heaven; in Sanctuary, as elsewhere, it is well known that those who promise do not always perform.

Lythande, who frequented neither women nor priests as a usual thing, did not often walk here. The park seemed deserted; the evil winds had begun to blow, whipping bushes and shrubbery into the shapes of strange beasts performing unnatural acts; and moaning weirdly around the walls and eaves of the temples across the street, the wind that was said in Sanctuary to be the moaning of Azyuna in Vashanka's bed. Lythande moved swiftly, skirting the darkness of the paths. And then a woman's scream rent the air.

From the shadows Lythande could see the frail form of a young girl in a torn and ragged dress; she was barefoot and her ear was bleeding where one jeweled earring had been torn from the lobe. She was struggling in the iron grip of a huge burly black-bearded man, and the first thing Lythande saw was the hand gripped around the girl's thin, bony wrist, dragging her; two fingers missing and the other cut away to the first joint. Only then—when it was no longer needed—did Lythande see the blue star between the black bristling brows, the cat-yellow eyes of Rabben the Half-handed!

Lythande knew him of old, from the Temple of the Star. Even then Rabben had been a vicious man, his lecheries notorious. Why, Lythande wondered, had the Masters not demanded that he renounce them as the price of his power? Lythande's lips tightened in a mirthless grimace; so notorious had been Rabben's lecheries that if he renounced them, everyone would know the Secret of his Power.

For the powers of an Adept of the Blue Star depended upon a secret. As in the old legend of the giant who kept his heart in a secret place outside his body, and with it his immortality, so the Adept of the Blue Star poured all his psychic force into a single Secret; and the one who discovered the Secret would acquire all of that adept's power. So Rabben's Secret must be something else . . . . Lythande did not speculate on it.

The girl cried out pitifully as Rabben jerked at her wrist; as the burly magician's star began to glow, she thrust her free hand over her eyes to shield them from it. Without fully intending to intervene, Lythande stepped from the shadows, and the rich voice that had made the prentice magicians in the outer court of the Blue Star call Lythande "minstrel" rather than "magician" rang out:

"By Shipri the All-Mother, release that woman!"

Rabben whirled. "By the nine-hundred-and-ninety-ninth eye of Ils! Lythande!"

"Are there not enough women in the Street of Red Lanterns, that you must mishandle girl-children in the Street of Temples?" For Lythande could see how young she was, the thin arms and childish legs and ankles, the breasts not yet full-formed beneath the dirty, torn tunic.

Rabben turned on Lythande and sneered, "You were always squeamish, *shyryu*. No woman walks here unless she is for sale. Do you want her for yourself? Have you tired of your fat madam in the Aphrodisia House?"

"You will not take her name into your mouth, *shyryu*!"

"So tender for the honor of a harlot?"

Lythande ignored that. "Let that girl go, or stand to my challenge."

Rabben's star shot lightnings; he shoved the girl to one side. She fell nerveless to the pavement and lay without moving. "She'll stay there until we've done. Did you think she could run away while we fought? Come to think of it, I never did see you with a woman, Lythande—is that your Secret, Lythande, that you've no use for women?"

Lythande maintained an impassive face; but whatever came, Rabben must not be allowed to pursue *that* line. "You may couple like an animal in the streets of Sanctuary, Rabben, but I do not. Will you yield her up, or fight?"

"Perhaps I should yield her to you; this is unheard of, that Lythande should fight in the streets over a woman! You see, I know your habits well, Lythande!"

Damnation of Vashanka! Now indeed I shall have to fight for the girl!

Lythande's rapier snicked from its scabbard and thrust at Rabben as if of its own will.

"Ha! Do you think Rabben fights street brawls with the sword like any mercenary?" Lythande's sword tip exploded in the blue starglow, and became a shimmering snake, twisting back on itself to climb past the hilt, fangs dripping venom as it sought to coil around Lythande's fist. Lythande's own star blazed. The sword was metal again but twisted and useless, in the shape of the snake it had been, coiling back toward the scabbard. Enraged, Lythande jerked free of the twisted metal, sent a spitting rain of fire in Rabben's direction. Quickly the huge adept covered himself in fog, and the fire-spray extinguished itself. Somewhere outside consciousness Lythande was aware of a crowd gathering; not twice in a lifetime did two Adepts of the Blue Star battle by sorcery in the streets of Sanctuary. The blaze of the stars, blazing from each magician's brow, raged lightnings in the square.

On a howling wind came little torches ravening, that flickered and whipped at Lythande; they touched the tall form of the magician and vanished. Then a wild whirlwind sent trees lashing, leaves swirling bare from branches, and battered Rabben to his knees. Lythande was bored; this must be finished quickly. Not one of the goggling onlookers in the crowd knew afterward what had been done, but Rabben bent, slowly, slowly, forced inch by inch down and down, to his knees, to all fours, prone, pressing and grinding his face farther and farther into the dust, rocking back and forth, pressing harder and harder into the sand . . .

Lythande turned and lifted the girl. She stared in disbelief at the burly sorcerer grinding his black beard frantically into the dirt.

"What did you—"

"Never mind—let's get out of here. The spell will not hold him long, and when he wakes from it he will be angry." Neutral mockery edged Lythande's voice, and the girl could see it, too, Rabben with beard and eyes and blue star covered with the dirt and dust—

She scurried along in the wake of the magician's robe; when they were well away from the Promise of Heaven, Lythande halted, so abruptly that the girl stumbled.

"Who are you, girl?"

"My name is Bercy. And yours?"

"A magician's name is not lightly given. In Sanctuary they call me Lythande." Looking down at the girl, the magician noted, with a pang, that beneath the dirt and dishevelment she was very beautiful and very young.

"You can go, Bercy. He will not touch you again; I have bested him fairly upon challenge."

She flung herself onto Lythande's shoulder, clinging. "Don't send me away!" she begged, clutching, eyes filled with adoration. Lythande scowled.

Predictable, of course. Bercy believed, and who in Sanctuary would have disbelieved, that the duel had been fought for the girl as prize, and she was ready to give herself to the winner. Lythande made a gesture of protest.

"No—"

The girl narrowed her eyes in pity. "Is it then with you as Rabben said— that your secret is that you have been deprived of manhood?" But beyond the pity was a delicious flicker of amusement—what a tidbit of gossip! A juicy bit for the Streets of Women.

"Silence." Lythande's glance was imperative. "Come."

She followed, along the twisting streets that led into the Street of Red Lanterns. Lythande strode with confidence, now, past the House of Mermaids, where, it was said, delights as exotic as the name promised were to be found; past the House of Whips, shunned by all except those who refused to go else- where; and at last, beneath the face of the Green Lady as she was worshiped far away and beyond Ranke, the Aphrodisia House.

Bercy looked around, eyes wide, at the pillared lobby, the brilliance of a hundred lanterns, the exquisitely dressed women lounging on cushions till they were summoned. They were finely dressed and bejeweled—Myrtis knew her trade, and how to present her wares—and Lythande guessed that the ragged Bercy's glance was one of envy; she had probably sold herself in the bazaar for a few coppers or for a loaf of bread, since she was old enough. Yet somehow, like flowers covering a dungheap, she had kept exquisite fresh beauty, all gold and white, flow- erlike. Even ragged and half-starved, she touched Lythande's heart.

"Bercy, have you eaten today?"

"No, master."

Lythande summoned the huge eunuch Jiro, whose business it was to conduct the favored customers to the chambers of their chosen women, and throw out the drunks and abusive customers into the street. He came, huge-bellied, naked except for a skimpy loincloth and a dozen rings in his ear—he had once had a lover who was an earring-seller and had used him to display her wares.

"How may we serve the magician Lythande?"

The women on the couches and cushions were twittering at one another in surprise and dismay, and Lythande could almost hear their thoughts:

None of as has been able to attract or *seduce the great magician, and this ragged street wench has caught his eyes?* And, being women, Lythande knew, they could see the unclouded beauty that shone through the girl's rags.

"Is Madame Myrtis available, Jiro?"

"She's sleeping, O great wizard, but for you she's given orders she's to be waked at any hour. Is this"—no one alive can be quite so supercilious as the chief eunuch of a fashionable brothel—"*yours*, Lythande, or a gift for my madame?"

"Both, perhaps. Give her something to eat and find her a place to spend the night."

"And a bath, magician? She has fleas enough to louse a floorful of cushions!"

"A bath, certainly, and a bath woman with scents and oils," Lythande said, "and something in the nature of a whole garment."

"Leave it to me," said Jim expansively, and Bercy looked at Lythande in dread, but went when the magician gestured to her to go. As Jiro took her away, Lythande saw Myrtis standing in the doorway; a heavy woman, no longer young, but with the frozen beauty of a spell. Through the perfect spelled framers, her eyes were warm and welcoming as she smiled at Lythande.

"My dear, I had not expected to see you here. Is that yours?" She moved her head toward the door through which Jiro had conducted the frightened Bercy. "She'll probably run away, you know, once you take your eyes off her."

"I wish I thought so, Myrtis. But no such luck, I fear."

"You had batter tell me the whole story," Myrtis said, and listened to Lythande's brief, succinct account of the affair.

"And if you laugh, Myrtis, I take back my spell and leave your grey hairs and wrinkles open to the mockery of everyone in Sanctuary!"

But Myrtis had known Lythande too long to take that threat very seriously. "So the maiden you rescued is all maddened with desire for the love of Lythande!" She chuckled. "It is like an old ballad, indeed!"

"But what am I to do, Myrtis? By the paps of Shipri the All-Mother, this is a dilemma!"

"Take her into your confidence and tell her why your love cannot be hers," Myrtis said.

Lythande frowned. "You hold my Secret, since I had no choice; you knew me before I was made magician, or bore the blue star—"

"And before I was a harlot," Myrtis agreed.

"But if I make this girl feel like a fool for loving me, she will hate me as much as she loves; and I cannot confide in anyone I cannot trust with my life and my power. All I have is yours, Myrtis, because of that past we shared. And that includes my power, if you ever should need it. But I cannot entrust it to this girl."

"Still she owes you something, for delivering her out of the hands of Rabben."

Lythande said, "I will think about it; and now make haste to bring me food, for I am hungry and athirst." Taken to a private room, Lythande ate and drank, served by Myrtis's own hands. And Myrtis said, "I could never have sworn your vow—to eat and drink in the sight of no man!"

"If you sought the power of a magician, you would keep it well enough," said Lythande. "I am seldom tempted now to break it; I fear only lest I break it unawares; I cannot drink in a tavern lest among the women there might be some one of those strange men who find diversion in putting on the garments of a female; even here I will not eat or drink among your women, for that reason. All power depends on the vows and the secret."

"Then I cannot aid you," Myths said, "but you are not bound to speak truth to her; tell her you have vowed to live without women."

"I may do that," Lythande said, and finished the food, scowling.

Later Bercy was brought in, wide-eyed, enthralled by her fine gown and her freshly washed hair, that softly curled about her pink-and-white face. The sweet scent of bath oils and perfumes hung about her.

"The girls here wear such pretty clothes, and one of them told me they could eat twice a day if they wished! Am I pretty enough, do you think, that Madame Myrtis would have me here?"

"If that is what you wish. You are more than beautiful."

Bercy said boldly, "I would rather belong to *you,* magician," and flung herself again on Lythande, her hands clutching and clinging, dragging the lean face down to hers. Lythande, who rarely touched anything living, held her gently, trying not to reveal consternation.

"Bercy, child, this is only a fancy. It will pass."

"No," she wept. "I love you, I want only you!"

And then, unmistakably, along the magician's nerves, Lythande felt that little ripple, that warning thrill of tension which said: *spellcasting is in use.* Not against Lythande. That could have been countered. But somewhere within the room.

Here, in the Aphrodisia House? Myrtis, Lythande knew, could be trusted with life, reputation, fortune, the magical power of the Blue Star itself; she had been tested before this. Had she altered enough to turn betrayer, it would have been apparent in her aura when Lythande came near.

That left only the girl, who was clinging and whimpering, "I will die if you do not love me! I will die! Tell me it is not true, Lythande, that you are unable to love! Tell me it is an evil lie that magicians are emasculated, incapable of loving women. . . . "

"That is certainly an evil he," Lythande agreed gravely. "I give you my solemn assurance that I have never been emasculated." But Lythande's nerves tingled as the words were spoken. A magician might lie, and most of them did. Lythande would lie as readily as any other, in a good cause. But the law of the Blue Star was this: when questioned directly on a matter bearing directly on the Secret, the Adept might not tell a direct lie. And Bercy, unknowing, was only one question away from the fatal one hiding the Secret.

With a mighty effort, Lythande's magic wrenched at the very fabric of Time itself; the girl stood motionless, aware of no lapse, as Lythande stepped away far enough to read her aura. And yes, there within the traces of that vibrating field was the shadow of the Blue Star. Rabben's; overpowering her will.

Rabben. Rabben the Half-handed, who had set his will on the girl, who had staged and contrived the whole thing, including the encounter where the girl had needed rescue; put the girl under a spell to attract and bespell Lythande.

The law of the Blue Star forbade one Adept of the Star to kill another; for all would be needed to fight side by side, on the last day, against Chaos. Yet if one adept could prise forth the secret of another's power . . . then the powerless one was not needed against Chaos and could be killed.

What could be done now? Kill the girl? Rabben would take that, too, as an answer; Bercy had been so bespelled as to be irresistible to any man; if Lythande sent her away untouched, Rabben would know that Lythande's Secret lay in that area and would never rest in his attempts to uncover it. For if Lythande was untouched by this sex spell to make Bercy irresistible, then Lythande was a eunuch, or a homosexual, or . . . sweating, Lythande dared not even think beyond that. The Secret was safe only if never questioned. It would not be read in the aura; but one simple question, and all was ended.

I should kill her, Lythande thought. *For now I am fighting not for my magic alone, but for my Secret and for my life. For surely with my power gone, Rabben would lose no time in making an end of me, in revenge for the loss of half a hand.*

The girl was still motionless, entranced. How easily she could be killed! Then Lythande recalled an old fairy tale, which might he used to save the Secret of the Star.

The light flickered as Time returned to the chamber. Bercy was still clinging and weeping, unaware of the lapse; Lythande had resolved what to do, and the girl felt Lythande's arms enfolding her, and the magician's kiss on her welcoming mouth.

"You must love me or I shall die!" Bercy wept.

Lythande said, "You shall be mine." The soft neutral voice was very gentle. "But even a magician is vulnerable in love, and I must protect myself. A place shall be made ready for us without light or sound save for what I provide with my magic; and you must swear that you will not seek to see or to touch me except by that magical light. Will you swear it by the All-Mother, Bercy? For if you swear this, I shall love you as no woman has ever been loved before."

Trembling, she whispered, "I swear." And Lythande's heart went out in pity, for Rabben had used her ruthlessly; so that she burned alive with her unslaked and bewitched love for the magician, that she was all caught up in her passion for Lythande. Painfully, Lythande thought: *If she had only loved me, without the spell; then I could have loved.*

Would that I could trust her with my Secret! But she is only Rabben's tool; her love for me is his doing, and none of her own *will . . . and not real . . .* And so everything which would pass between them now must be only a drama staged for Rabben.

"I shall make all ready for you with my magic."

Lythande went and confided to Myrtis what was needed; the woman began to laugh, but a single glance at Lythande's bleak face stopped her cold. She had known Lythande since long before the Blue Star was set between those eyes; and she kept the Secret for love of Lythande. It wrung her heart to see one she loved in the grip of such suffering. So she said, "All will be prepared. Shall I give her a drug in her wine to weaken her will, that you may the more readily throw a glamour upon her?"

Lythande's voice held a terrible bitterness. "Rabben has done that already for us, when he put a spell upon her to love me."

"You would have it otherwise?" Myrtis asked, hesitating.

"All the gods of Sanctuary—they laugh at me! All-Mother, help me! But I would have it otherwise; I could love her, if she were nor Rabben's tool."

When all was prepared, Lythande entered the darkened room. There was no light but the light of the Blue Star. The girl lay on a bed, stretching up her arms to the magician with exalted abandon.

"Come to me, come to me, my love!"

"Soon," said Lythande, sitting beside her, stroking her hair with a tenderness even Myrtis would never have guessed. "I will sing to you a love song of my people, far away."

She writhed in erotic ecstasy. "All you do is good to me, my love, my magician!"

Lythande felt the blankness of utter despair. She was beautiful, and she was in love. She lay in a bed spread for the two of them, and they were separated by the breadth of the world. The magician could not endure it.

Lythande sang, in that rich and beautiful voice, a voice lovelier than any spell:

> Half the night is spent; and the crown of moonlight
> Fades, and now the crown of the stars is paling;
> Yields the sky reluctant to coming morning;
> Still I lie lonely.
> I will love you as no woman has ever been loved.

Lythande could see tears on Bercy's cheeks.

Between the girl on the bed, and the motionless form of the magician, as the magician's robe fell heavily to the floor, a wraith-form grew, the very wraith and fetch, at first, of Lythande, tall and lean, with blazing eyes and a star between its brows and a body white and unscarred; the form of the magician, but this one triumphant in virility, advancing on the motionless woman, waiting. Her mind fluttered away in arousal, was caught, captured, bespelled. Lythande let her see the image for a moment; she could not see the true Lythande behind; then, as her eyes closed in ecstatic awareness of the touch, Lythande smoothed light fingers over her closed eyes.

"See—what I bid you to see!"

"Hear—what I bid you hear!"

"Feel—only what I bid you feel, Bercy!"

And now she was wholly under the spell of the wraith. Unmoving, stony-eyed, Lythande watched as her lips closed on emptiness and she kissed invisible lips; and moment by moment Lythande knew what touched her, what caressed her. Rapt and ravished by illusion, that brought her again and again to the heights of ecstasy, till she cried out in abandonment. Only to Lythande that cry was bitter; for she cried out not to Lythande but to the man-wraith who possessed her.

At last she lay all but unconscious, satiated; and Lythande watched in agony. When she opened her eyes again, Lythande was looking down at her, sorrowfully.

Bercy stretched up languid arms. "Truly, my beloved, you have loved me as no woman has ever been loved before."

For the first and last time, Lythande bent over her and pressed her lips in a long, infinitely tender kiss. "Sleep, my darling." And as she sank into ecstatic, exhausted sleep, Lythande wept.

Long before she woke, Lythande stood, girt for travel, in the little room belonging to Myrtis. "The spell will hold. She will make all haste to carry her tale to Rabben—the tale of Lythande, the incomparable lover! Of Lythande, of untiring virility, who can love a maiden into exhaustion!" The rich voice of Lythande was harsh with bitterness.

"And long before you return to Sanctuary, once freed of the spell, she will have forgotten you in many other lovers," Myrtis agreed. "It is better and safer that it should be so."

"True." But Lythande's voice broke. "Take care of her, Myrtis. Be kind to her."

I swear it, Lythande."

"If only she could have loved *me*"—*the* magician broke and sobbed again for a moment; Myrtis looked away, wrung with pain, knowing not what comfort to offer.

"If only she could have loved me as I am, freed of Rabben's spell! Loved me without pretense! But I feared I could not master the spell Rabben had put on her . . . nor trust her not to betray me, knowing . . . "

Myrtis put her plump arms around Lythande, tenderly.

"Do you regret?"

The question was ambiguous. It might have meant: *Do you regret that* you *did not kill the girl?* Or even: *Do you regret your oath and the secret* you *must bear to the last day?* Lythande chose to answer the last.

"Regret? How can I regret? One day I shall fight against Chaos with all of my order; even at the side of Rabben, if he lives unmurdered as long as that. And that alone must justify my existence and my Secret. But now I must leave Sanctuary, and who knows when the chances of the world will bring me this way again? Kiss me farewell, my sister."

Myrtis stood on tiptoe. Her lips met the lips of the magician.

"Until we meet again, Lythande. May She attend and guard you forever. Farewell, my beloved, my sister."

Then the magician Lythande girded on her sword, and went silently and by unseen ways out of the city of Sanctuary, just as the dawn was breaking. And on her forehead the glow of the Blue Star was dimmed by the rising sun. Never once did she look back.

ACKNOWLEDGMENTS

Many thanks to the following:

Sean Wallace at Prime Books for publishing this anthology, and his continuing support of my editorial career.

Gordon Van Gelder, who taught me the mysterious and magical Way of the Editor.

My former agent Jenny Rappaport, for helping me launch my anthology career. (Enjoy retirement!) And to my new agent, Joe Monti, for picking up where Jenny left off.

David Barr Kirtley and Wendy N. Wagner for their assistance wrangling the header notes. All the clever things in the header notes are all their work. Anything lame you came across is mine.

Rebecca McNulty, for her various and valuable interning assistance—reading, scanning, transcribing, proofing, doing most of the work but getting none of the credit as all good interns do.

My mom, for the usual reasons.

All of the other kindly folks who assisted me in some way during the editorial process: Christie Yant, Grady Hendrix, Moshe Siegel, Stacey Friedberg, Becky Sasala, Rebekah White, and to everyone else who helped out in some way that I neglected to mention (and to you folks, I apologize!). Thanks too to the folks who made reprint recommendations in my online recommendations database.

The NYC Geek Posse—consisting of Robert Bland, Desirina Boskovich, Christopher M. Cevasco, Douglas E. Cohen, Jordan Hamessley, Andrea Kail, and Matt London, (plus Dave Kirtley, who I mentioned above, and the NYCGP Auxiliary)—for giving me an excuse to come out of my editorial cave once in a while.

The readers and reviewers who loved my other anthologies, making it possible for me to do more.

And last, but certainly not least: a big thanks to all of the authors who appear in this anthology.

Acknowledgment is made for permission to publish the following:

"El Regalo" by Peter S. Beagle. © 2006 Peter S. Beagle. Originally published in The Line Between (Tachyon Publications, 2006). Reprinted by permission of the Avicenna Development Corporation.

"Love is the Spell That Casts Out Fear" by Desirina Boskovich. © 2010 by Desirina Boskovich.

"The Secret of the Blue Star" by Marion Zimmer Bradley. © 1979 by Marion Zimmer Bradley. Originally published in *Thieves' World,* ed. Robert Lynn Asprin (Ace, 1979). Reprinted by permission of the Marion Zimmer Bradley Literary Works Trust.

"Jamaica" by Orson Scott Card. © 2007 by Orson Scott Card. Originally published in *Wizards, Inc.,* eds. Martin H. Greenberg & Loren L. Coleman (DAW, 2007). Reprinted by permission of the author.

"Cerile and the Journeyer" by Adam-Troy Castro. © 1995 by Adam-Troy Castro. Originally published in *100 Wicked Little Witches,* eds. Stefan R. Dziemianowicz, Robert H. Weinberg & Martin H. Greenberg (Sterling, 1995). Reprinted by permission of the author.

"The Trader" by Cinda Williams Chima. © 2010 by Cinda Williams Chima.

"John Uskglass and the Cumbrian Charcoal Burner" by Susanna Clarke. © 2006 Susanna Clarke. Originally published in *The Ladies of Grace Adieu and Other Stories* (Bloomsbury, 2006). Reprinted by permission of the author.

"Feeding the Feral Children" by David Farland. © 2010 by David Farland.

"The Tiger by Its Tail" by C.C. Finlay. © 2010 by C.C. Finlay.

"The Sorcerer Minus" by Jeffrey Ford. © 2010 by Jeffrey Ford.

"The Thirteen Texts of Arthyria" by John R. Fultz. © 2010 by John R. Fultz.

"How to Sell the Ponti Bridge" by Neil Gaiman. © 1985 by Neil Gaiman. Originally published in *Imagine #24,* March 1985. Reprinted by permission of the author.

"Street Wizard" by Simon R. Green. © 2010 by Simon R. Green.

"Endgame" by Lev Grossman. © 2010 by Lev Grossman. Originally published on *Borders.com.* Reprinted by permission of the author.

"The Ereshkigal Working" by Jonathan L. Howard. © 2010 by Jonathan L. Howard.

"The Orange-Tree Sacrifice" by Vylar Kaftan. © 2010 by Vylar Kaftan.

"Card Sharp" by Rajan Khanna. © 2010 by Rajan Khanna.

"Family Tree" by David Barr Kirtley. © 2010 by David Barr Kirtley.

"The Word of Unbinding" by Ursula K. Le Guin. © 1964, 1992 by Ursula K. Le Guin. First appeared in *Fantastic*, January 1964; from *The Wind's Twelve Quarters* (Harper & Rowe, 1975); reprinted by permission of the author and the author's agents, the Virginia Kidd Agency, Inc.

"Too Fatal a Poison" by Krista Hoeppner Leahy. © 2010 by Krista Hoeppner Leahy.

"Counting the Shapes" by Yoon Ha Lee. © 2001 by Yoon Ha Lee. Originally published in *The Magazine of Fantasy & Science Fiction*, June 2001. Reprinted by permission of the author.

"The Wizards of Perfil" by Kelly Link. © 2006 by Kelly Link. Originally published in *Firebirds Rising: An Anthology of Original Science Fiction and Fantasy*, ed. Sharyn November (Firebird, 2006). Reprinted by permission of the author.

"In the Lost Lands" by George R. R. Martin. © 1982 by George R. R. Martin. Originally published in *Amazons II*, ed. by Jessica Amanda Salmonson (Daw 1982). Reprinted by permission of the author.

"The Go-Slow" by Nnedi Okorafor. © 2010 by Nnedi Okorafor.

"Mommy Issues of the Dead" by T.A. Pratt. © 2010 by T.A. Pratt.

"Winter Solstice" by Mike Resnick. © 1991 by Mike Resnick. Originally published in *The Magazine of Fantasy & Science Fiction*, October/November, 1991. Reprinted by permission of the author.

"Wizard's Apprentice" by Delia Sherman. © 2009 by Delia Sherman. Originally published in *Troll's Eye View: A Book of Villainous Fairy Tale*, eds. Ellen Datlow & Terri Windling (Viking, 2009). Reprinted by permission of the author.

"The Sorcerer's Apprentice" by Robert Silverberg. © 2004 by Agberg, Ltd. Originally published in *Flights: Extreme Visions of Fantasy*, ed. Al Sarrantonio (ROC 2004). Reprinted by permission of the author.

"One-Click Banishment" by Jeremiah Tolbert. © 2010 by Jeremiah Tolbert.

"So Deep That the Bottom Could Not Be Seen" by Genevieve Valentine. © 2010 by Genevieve Valentine.

"The Secret of Calling Rabbits" by Wendy Wagner. © 2010 by Wendy Wagner.

"The Magician and the Maid and Other Stories" by Christie Yant. © 2010 by Christie Yant.

ABOUT THE EDITOR

John Joseph Adams (www.johnjosephadams.com) is the best-selling editor of many anthologies, including *Wastelands, The Living Dead* (a World Fantasy Award finalist), *The Living Dead 2, Seeds of Change, By Blood We Live, Federations,* and *The Improbable Adventures of Sherlock Holmes.* Barnes & Noble.com named him "the reigning king of the anthology world," and his books have been named to numerous best of the year lists. Future projects include *The Mad Scientist's Guide to World Domination, Brave New Worlds,* and *The Book of Cthulhu.*

John is also the fiction editor of the online science fiction magazine *Lightspeed* (www.lightspeedmagazine.com). Prior to taking on that role, he worked for nearly nine years in the editorial department at *The Magazine of Fantasy & Science Fiction.*

John is currently the co-host of *The Geek's Guide to the Galaxy* podcast and has published hundreds of interviews and other pieces of non-fiction. He lives in New Jersey.